THE
MASTER
OF
Verona

THE
MASTER
OF
VERONA

DAVID BLIXT

ST. MARTIN'S PRESS ✠ NEW YORK

This is a work of fiction. All of the characters, organizations, and events portrayed in this novel are either products of the author's imagination or are used fictitiously.

English language excerpts of *L'Inferno* that appear in the novel are from, or adapted from, *The Inferno* by Dante Alighieri, translated by Robert Hollander and Jean Hollander (Doubleday, 2000).

www.stmartins.com

Design by Susan Walsh

Map designs by Jackie Aher

Library of Congress Cataloging-in-Publication Data

Blixt, David.
    The master of Verona / David Blixt.—1st ed.
        p. cm.
    ISBN-13: 978-0-312-36144-0
    ISBN-10: 0-312-36144-0
    1. Dante Alighieri, 1265–1321—Fiction. 2. Italy—History—1268–1492—Fiction. 3. Verona (Italy)—Fiction. 4. Shakespeare, William, 1564–1616—Fiction. 5. Conspiracies—Fiction. I. Title.

PS3602.L59M37 2007
813'.6—dc22

                                                                                    2007012057

First Edition: July 2007

10   9   8   7   6   5   4   3   2   1

For Jan—

*"I shall live in thy heart,
die in thy lap,
and be buried in thy eyes. . . ."*

CONTENTS

DRAMATIS PERSONAE

✦ a characters recorded by history ✧ a character from Shakespeare

Della Scala Familia of Verona

✦ FRANCESCO "CANGRANDE" DELLA SCALA—youngest son of Alberto I, sole ruler of Verona and Imperial Vicar of the Trevisian Mark (Vicenza, Padua, Verona, and Treviso)

✦ GIOVANNA DA SVEVIA (*IN* DELLA SCALA)—illegitimate descendant of Emperor Frederick II; wife of Cangrande

✦ FRANCESCHINO "CECCHINO" DELLA SCALA—nephew of Cangrande

✦ FEDERIGO DELLA SCALA—Cangrande's cousin

✦ ALBERTO DELLA SCALA II (b. 1306)—Cangrande's nephew, brother of Mastino II

✦✧ MASTINO DELLA SCALA II (b. 1308)—Cangrande's nephew, brother of Alberto II

✦✧ FRANCESCO "CESCO" (b. 1314)—adopted son of Katerina Nogarola

Nogarola Familia of Vicenza

✦ ANTONIO NOGAROLA II—elder son of Antonio I, firmly Scaliger in sympathies

✦ BAILARDINO NOGAROLA—younger son of Antonio I; husband of Cangrande's sister, Katerina

+ KATERINA DELLA SCALA (*in* Nogarola)—daughter of Alberto della Scala
  I; wife of Bailardino
+ BAILARDETTO "DETTO" NOGAROLA (b. 1315)—son of Bailardino and
  Katerina

Alaghieri Familia of Florence

+ DURANTE "DANTE" ALAGHIERI—Florentine poet, exiled from his
  home in 1302
+ GEMMA DONATI—wife of Dante, living in Florence
+ PIETRO ALAGHIERI—Dante's eldest living son; joined his father in exile
  in 1312
+ JACOPO "POCO" ALAGHIERI—Dante's younger living son; joined his
  father in exile in 1314
+ ANTONIA "IMPERIA" ALAGHIERI—Dante's only surviving daughter

Carrara Familia of Padua

+ GIACOMO "IL GRANDE" DA CARRARA—Paduan lord, uncle of
  Marsilio, great-uncle of Gianozza della Bella
+ MARSILIO DA CARRARA (b. 1294)—knight, nephew of Paduan leader
  Giacomo ("Il Grande"); cousin of Gianozza
✧ GIANOZZA DELLA BELLA (b. 1300)—distant relative of the Carrara
  family, raised in Battaglia, south of Padua

Montecchio Familia of Verona

GARGANO MONTECCHIO (b. 1265)—father of Mariotto and Aurelia
✧ ROMEO MARIOTTO "MARI" MONTECCHIO (b. 1298)—son and heir of
  Gargano
AURELIA MONTECCHIO (b. 1301)—daughter of Gargano

Capecelatro Familia of Capua

LUDOVICO CAPECELATRO—head of a merchant family from Capua; father of Luigi and Antonio

❖ LUIGI CAPECELATRO (b. 1294)—eldest son of Ludovico, father of Theobaldo

ANTONIO "ANTHONY" CAPECELATRO (b. 1297)—second son of Ludovico

❖ THEOBALDO CAPELLETTI (b. 1315)—son of Luigi

SUPPORTING CHARACTERS

The Veronese and Their Allies

ZILIBERTO DEL ANGELO— Cangrande's Master of the Hunt

✦ PASSERINO BONACCOLSI—Podestà of Mantua, close ally of Cangrande

✦ FERDINANDO BONAVENTURA—cousin of the Bonaventura heir, Petruchio

✦ PETRUCHIO BONAVENTURA—Veronese nobleman looking for a wife

THEODORO OF CADIZ—Moorish slave of the astrologer Ignazzio da Palermo

✦ GUGLIELMO DA CASTELBARCO—Veronese noble, Cangrande's armorer

✦ UGUCCIONE DELLA FAGGIUOLA—ruler of Lucca, former patron of Dante; friend of Cangrande

AVENTINO FRACASTORO—personal physician to Cangrande

BISHOP FRANCIS—Franciscan who replaces Bishop Guelco in 1315

✦ MANOELLO GIUDEO—Cangrande's Master of Revels

BISHOP GUELCO—bishop of Verona

TULLIO D'ISOLA—Grand Butler to Cangrande

BENVENITO LENOTI—fiancé of Aurelia Montecchio

✦ BROTHER LORENZO—young Franciscan monk with family in France

✦ NICOLO DA LOZZO—Paduan-born knight who changed sides to fight for Cangrande

GIUSEPPE MORSICATO—doctor to the Nogarola family in Vicenza, knight

IGNAZZIO DA PALERMO—personal astrologer to the Scaligeri

MASSIMILIANO DA VILLAFRANCA—constable of Cangrande's palace

Verona's Enemies

+ ALBERTINO MUSSATO—Paduan historian-poet

+ PONZINO DE' PONZONi—Cremonese-born knight; elected Podestà of Padua in 1314

VANNI "ASDENTE" SCORIGIANI—Paduan knight who lost part of his face in battle with Cangrande

+ VINCIGUERRA, COUNT OF SAN BONIFACIO—last of an exiled Veronese family, veteran of the war with Cangrande

+ FRANCESCO DANDOLO—Venetian ambassador and nobleman

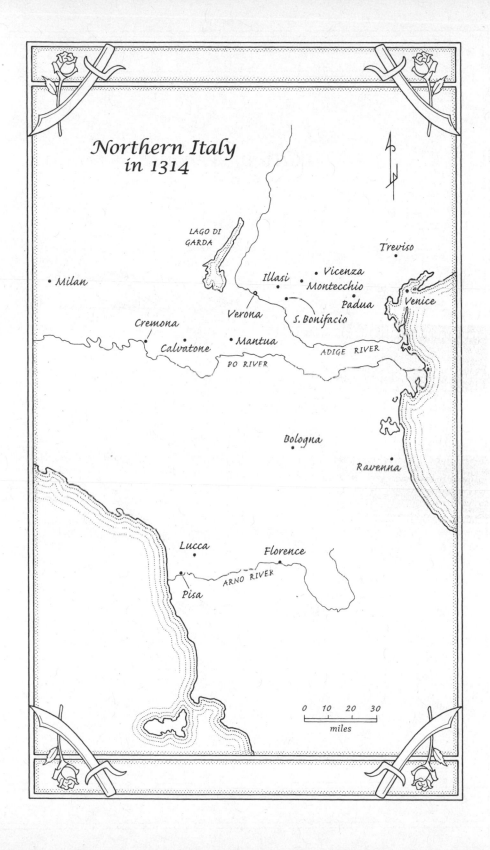

Northern Italy
in 1314

LAGO DI
GARDA

• Milan

Illasi   • Vicenza
• Treviso

Montecchio
• Padua   • Venice
Verona   S. Bonifacio

Cremona
Calvatone   • Mantua   ADIGE RIVER
PO RIVER

Bologna

Ravenna

Lucca   Florence
ARNO RIVER
Pisa

0   10   20   30
miles

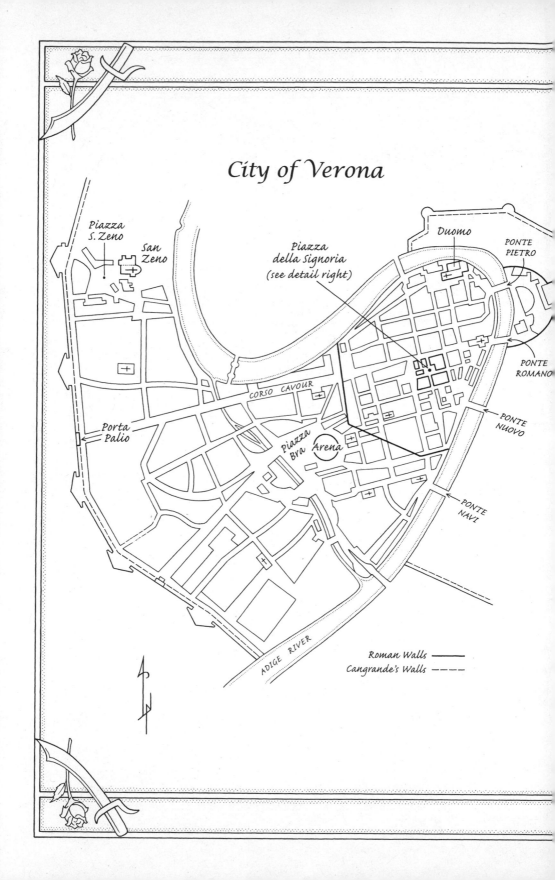

City of Verona

Piazza S. Zeno

San Zeno

Piazza della Signoria (see detail right)

Duomo

PONTE PIETRO

PONTE ROMANO

PONTE NUOVO

PONTE NAVI

CORSO CAVOUR

Porta Palio

Piazza Bra

Arena

ADIGE RIVER

Roman Walls ———
Cangrande's Walls ------

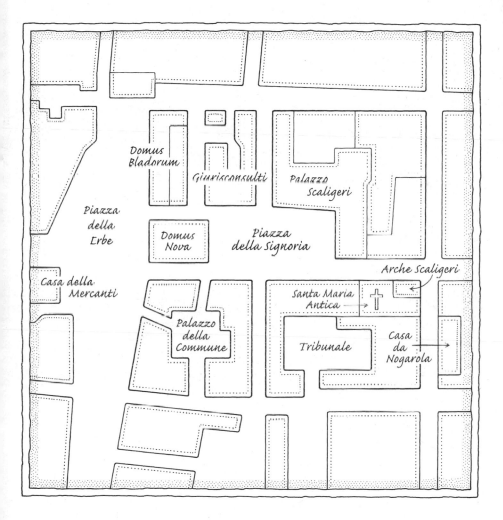

Domus
Bladorum

Giurisconsulti

Palazzo
Scaligeri

Piazza
della
Erbe

Domus
Nova

Piazza
della Signoria

Arche Scaligeri

Casa della
Mercanti

Santa Maria
Antica

Palazzo
della
Commune

Tribunale

Casa
da
Nogarola

Piazza della Signoria

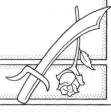

"A te convien tenere altro viaggio,'
rispuose, poi che lagrimar mi vide,
'se vuo' campar d'esto loco selvaggio:

ché questa bestia, per la qual tu gride,
non lascia altrui passar per la sua via,
ma tanto lo 'mpedisce che l'uccide;

e ha natura sì malvagia e ria,
che mai non empie la bramosa voglia,
e dopo 'l pasto ha pi à liu fame che pria.

Molti son li animali a cui s'ammoglia,
e più saranno ancora, infin che l'veltro
verrà, che la farà morir con doglia.'

"It is another path you must follow,"
he answered, when he saw me weeping,
"If you would flee this wild and savage place:

For that beast that moves you to cry out
Lets no man pass her way,
But so besets him that she slays him.

Her nature is so vicious and malign
Her greedy appitite is never sated—
After feeding she is hungrier that ever.

Many are the creatures she mates with,
and there will yet be more, until the Greyhound
shall come who'll make her die in pain."

—Dante, *L'Inferno*, Canto I, 91–102,

PROLOGUE

Padua

16 SEPTEMBER 1314

Ciolo's nerves jangled like spurs as he looked about. During the whole ride they hadn't seen a soul. Not on the road, not in the fields. No one at all.

"What does it mean?" asked Girolamo.

"I don't know," said Ciolo.

"Is Padua under siege?"

"I don't know. Let's keep going."

"How will we get in?"

"Keep riding."

"But—"

"Think of golden florins."

"I've never been to Florence!"

"Shut up!" hissed Ciolo.

Empty fields gave way to empty suburbs. Some of the spaced-out hovels and shacks of the laborers were burnt out, but more were intact, even new. Ciolo saw fresh-cut timber struts and new bricks—marks of an old siege, not a new one. If there were a present siege the hovels would all be still-smoking hulks and by now he should have heard the sounds of hundreds of men muttering and cheering and singing, the stamp of impatient horses, the crack and whine of the siege machines, the smell of fire and filth. Ciolo's nose twitched.

But the only smells were the common night scents. The only sounds were crickets and the occasional goose or dog. There were no tents or firebrands, no bristling spears. The city wasn't under siege. So where the devil was everyone?

Ciolo's skin went cold with a horrible notion. A pest. A pest had come and even now the Paduans were hiding in their homes scratching at scabs and vomiting blood. He glanced at Girolamo but kept his mouth shut. He thought of the money, then put his dirty hand over his mouth to keep out the bad air and rode slowly on.

They approached the bridge to the city's north gate. The Ponte Molino was an old Roman bridge, the length of fourteen horses, whose triple arches spanned the Bacchiglione River. The center arch was supported by two massive stone columns rising from the rippling river. Nearby water mills creaked and groaned.

The bridge ended right at the lip of the fortified gate. Ciolo squinted hard. No bodies piled up outside the gate. A good sign. With no one in sight, Ciolo nudged his horse onto the bridge and began to cross it. Girolamo followed.

Halfway across the bridge Ciolo could make out that the gates into the city were open, but dark. Ciolo paused, looking ahead.

Girolamo said, "I've got a bad feeling about this job."

Suddenly a flame showed high on the tower above them. A torch. Two more joined it. At the same moment Ciolo heard a human noise. Thousands of voices cheering. Men, women, children. Bells pealed and musicians played. All the people were inside the city walls, watching for sunset and the lighting of torches.

Ciolo sagged in his saddle and mopped his brow. "See, it's nothing. A celebr—"

Then he heard a noise like thunder and his relief shattered. An army of horses was pouring out of the gate right in front of them. Plumed helmets and shining breastplates reflected light from the brands held high as countless Paduan knights emerged from the city, riding furiously across the Ponte Molino.

Riding right at Ciolo and Girolamo.

In panic Ciolo threw himself from his saddle, abandoned his horse, and ran, arms pumping, to the edge of the bridge and jumped. He hit the water feet-first, plunging below the surface. The sound of hooves vanished as the river swallowed him. He didn't know how to swim. He lunged in the water, using his arms and legs as if he were running, flailing toward the bridge. Something hit him hard in the shoulder and he grabbed onto it as best he could. He couldn't see at all but his fingers recognized the feel of stone.

Whatever it was he grasped it and pulled himself along it. It was slimy and slippery, hard to hold. He dug in with his fingernails. His lungs were beginning to burn. Then his hand emerged from the water and he pushed his head up and through and sucked down sweet air.

Ciolo was holding onto one of the arches of the Roman bridge. Above him he heard the continued cascade of mounted soldiers. Idiots. Wherever their enemy was, it wasn't here. Why charge, then—in darkness, when a horse was likely to trip and fall? Ciolo had nearly been killed in a night charge once. The horse in front snapped a leg, killing not only its rider but the two riders behind him.

He could still hear the cheering in the city, and he knew that he had almost been killed for the sake of a parade. A show of honor, of skill. Fools. Sputtering and shivering, Ciolo mouthed a string of curses against whoever had come up with the notion of chivalry.

Hand over hand he dragged himself to the edge of the support. He was lucky that the Bacchiglione wasn't flowing hard, and luckier that what current there was had been dulled by the mills. Otherwise he would have been swept clean away. For the first time he wondered what had happened to Girolamo. But it was useless to call. If he'd survived, he'd meet Ciolo at the house.

It took Ciolo ten minutes to reach the river's edge. Though the riverbank was solid, there was no way to reach the high gate from below. The only way was from the bridge. Ciolo took a breath and began to scale the cracked stone walls carefully. His wet fingers made it difficult. Muttering and cursing he pulled himself onto a carving of some old god just below the lip of the bridge. There he stayed, waiting for the horsemen to get past. He squirmed until he found a position that freed his arms so he could wrap them around himself. He was cold, teeth chattering. Damn all Paduans and their stupid *patavinitas*.

Then he heard the last horseman pass, with the citizens chasing after, cheering their fool lungs out. He twisted and pulled himself up onto the bridge proper. No one stopped to help him. In fact, he was almost knocked over again by the press of the people. God, did he hate Paduans.

He was swept along with the mob, wept with joy and pride. He tried to cheer through his chattering teeth. But the crowd was warming him up, and he was pleased when he realized how easy it would be to get into the city now. Knowing his own horse had probably bolted, he didn't bother to look for it. He just played the part of happy citizen watching his army go off to glory.

The thrill of the moment passed for the Paduans and slowly they began to return to their homes. Recrossing the Ponte Molino, Ciolo made jokes, slapped backs, joining in the laughter at his obvious misfortune. Halfway along the bridge he found the body of Girolamo. Ciolo recognized him from his vest, since his face had been crushed. Ciolo bent down quickly, but it was no use. He'd already been robbed.

Ciolo entered the city with a smile on his face and joined a group of men entering a tavern. He'd been to Padua three or four times before. He'd even once been defended on some petty theft charge by the famous Bellario. So Ciolo was able to fake the accent. He held himself to one bottle of wine, but he sang with gusto and thumped the table for as long as it took for his clothes to dry. Then he told his new best friends that there was a wench waiting and took his leave. He had a job to get on with.

A life to end.

✦ ✧ ✦

In another quarter of an hour he found the house, right where it was supposed to be. There was the hanging garden. There was the juniper bush. The house was frescoed with a pagan god holding a staff with two snakes on it. The god was between two barred windows and above two massive lead rings for tethering horses. Just as described.

The front of the house had torches burning, and Ciolo passed through the flickering light, walking drunkenly in case anyone was watching. He'd been told there was no possible entrance from the ground, so he didn't waste time looking for one. Instead, he circled the block until he came to a three-story wall outside a dyeyard. The wall's covering plaster had worn away at the street level, showing the mix of round stones and proper bricks that made the wall. It was dark in this street, the light from the stars the only illumination. Still playing the drunkard, he stood in the open, loosened the points on his hose, and relieved himself against the wall. Using his free hand to lean against the wall, his fingers quested. No one passed, not even a cat. Readjusting his points he rubbed his hands together and, having found the promised finger-holds, he began his ascent.

Along the top were curved spikes to keep intruders out of the dyeyard. But Ciolo didn't want in. He wanted passage. Reaching up one hand he carefully wrapped his fingers around the inch-thick base of the spike. He didn't put much pressure on it at first. It might be sharpened along its whole length, not just at the curve. But in this too his instructions were accurate. The flat edges of the spike were dull. Ciolo gripped the spike harder, praying it would bear his whole weight. It did. He swung his free hand up to grasp the next spike. Then the next. Hand over hand he passed down the row of spikes, around the shadowed corner between two houses.

By now his breath was coming hard, his hands and shoulders aching sourly. But he only had another half length of the wall to travel. He started on it, then froze as a noise came from the house behind him. Did they have dogs? Or, worse, geese? Pressing himself against the high wall, feeling his sweaty fingers slipping, he wished for a cloud to hide the stars and plunge him into deeper shadow. Ciolo listened.

It was a child. A child's cry in the night. Unattended, it went uncomforted.

Ciolo glanced over his shoulder. It came from the house he was aiming for. In a perfect world he could have waited for the child to sleep again. But his hands were losing their strength. He continued quickly down the final length of the wall, mouthing foul pleas not to slip. The next move was tricky—he had to twist around until he was hanging with his back against the high wall and leap to a window across the four-foot divide. He doubled up his grip with his one hand, then twisted around and threw up his free hand. It brushed past one bar but firmly found the next. Now he was facing his target, an arched window. It was open, the wooden door swung wide. He knew the longer he waited the worse his nerves would get. Ciolo curled his feet up to press against the wall at his back, released the bars, and pushed off hard.

His ribs banged against the windowsill. He hit his chin as he began to slip. Flinging his arms wide, he pressed his elbows against the inside walls. His feet scrambling, he pulled himself awkwardly over the lip and into the house.

Crouching low beside the window, Ciolo found himself in a long hall, narrow, with a pair of doors on each side. He squinted until he was sure all the doors were closed. He felt like his breathing was making more noise than a bellows. But no alarums. No cries but the child's, which were subsiding. If someone came now he would be useless, his arms were shaking so fiercely. He flexed and stretched, each second gaining him another breath, each breath easing his beating heart. His eyes began to play tricks on him in the dark. He imagined that the doors were all open, and twice he swore he saw movement. But each time he was wrong. Or hoped he was.

After two or three minutes of watching from the shadowy corner by the window, Ciolo was as ready as he was going to be. His right hand dropped to his left hip. Gripping the leather-wrapped hilt, he withdrew a dagger nine inches long.

Keeping well out of the faint light coming in the window, he made his way down the hall. The house plan Ciolo had memorized indicated he had not far to go. Down this hall, a right turn into a grand room, and up a single flight to a double door. Simple.

The hallway was tiled and clear of rushes. Ciolo placed first one foot, then another, so much on his toes that his boot heels hardly brushed the floor. He came to the pair of doors facing each other. Both were closed. Holding his breath, he picked up the pace past them. Nothing leapt out at him. He sighed a little and instantly cursed himself for the slight noise.

The second pair of doors were also closed. Again, everything was proceeding as planned. He forced himself to stop and listen. One flight up the infant was still making noise, but the rest of the house was still.

Fortune favors the bold, thought Ciolo. He crept around the corner, feeling along the wall for the beginning of the stairs. Tripping would be bad.

Most stairs creaked, but Ciolo kept his weight to the far outsides of each step, where the wood was unlikely to bend. At the top of the stair there was another window, facing north. He could see the sliver of the moon, and it could see him. He crouched down, his back to the wall, and looked for the double doors.

There they were. The light from the partial moon just brushed their bottom edges. Staying out of the light, Ciolo pressed himself up to one side of the doors. Inside he could hear the child. It was neither wailing nor giggling. More of a string of burbling noises. Ciolo thought the room must be small because he could hear an echo, as if the child's own voice was answering itself.

Ciolo waited, listening to the room beyond the doors. Was there a nurse waiting with the baby? Surely not. Or else she was dead to the world. And soon would be more so. Ciolo smiled and trained his eyes on the moonlight. He prayed to a merciful God to send a cloud, then on second thought redirected the entreaty to the Fiend.

Whoever heard his prayer, it was answered almost at once. The light crept away. Once it was dim, Ciolo moved swiftly. Lifting his knife, he grasped the handle of the nearest door to the child's room and pulled.

Blackness within. Ciolo stood to one side of the doorway, pausing for his eyes to adjust to the more complete darkness. Still the child burbled. Ciolo squinted at the corner the noise was coming from and thought he saw an outline. Ciolo reversed his dagger from point up to point down—a stabbing grip. Then he stepped fully into the gap, one hand on the door frame to guide him into the room.

There was a movement in the corner. A sharp cracking noise made Ciolo wince. Instantly the breath exploded from his body. Confused, he found himself sprawled several feet back down the hallway. Something had hit him in the chest, hit him hard enough to stun him. His free hand came up and found a thin line of wood protruding from his breastbone. His fingers brushed the fletched end absently. He whimpered, afraid to pull on the arrow's shaft.

A hinge creaked as the second door opened. Light appeared as a shuttered lantern was unveiled. The light approached, growing brighter. To Ciolo's dazed eyes, it seemed to be borne in the hands of an angel. He blinked away the shapes that were creeping into his vision. She was still there, standing above him now. An angel all in white. The color of mourning.

"Not dead, then?" asked a voice. "Good."

"Holy Madonna . . . ," he sputtered, the blood on his lips leaving the taste of metal on his tongue.

"Shhh." The angel set aside both the candle and the instrument of his demise, a small trigger-bow. Her arm must have been hurt firing it, for she used her off hand to take the blade from his unresisting grasp.

Behind her was another shape, a young girl clutching a baby. The baby Ciolo had come to murder. He didn't know if it was a boy or girl, it was too young to tell and he'd never asked. He wanted to ask now, but breathing was trouble enough. Still his mouth tried to work at the words.

The woman shook her head. With a lilting accent Ciolo found beautiful, she said, "Say nothing except the name of the man who paid you."

"I—I don't . . ."

"Not a good answer, love."

"But—Madonna forgive me, but—it was a woman."

The angel nodded but didn't smile. Ciolo wanted her to smile. He was dying. He wanted absolution—something. "Angel, forgive me."

"Ask forgiveness of God, man—not of me."

His own knife flashed left to right in her pale hand. He made the effort to close his eyes so as not to see his life's blood spill to the floor. With a choked whimper, Ciolo lay still.

I

THE ARENA

ONE

"Giotto's O."

In the middle of a dream in which no one would let him sleep, it seemed to Pietro that the words were deliberately meant to annoy him. Almost unwillingly he dreamed of a rock, a paintbrush touching the rock, forming a perfect circle.

The painter used red. It looked like blood.

"Pietro, I'm speaking to you."

Pietro sat up straight in the rattling coach. "Pardon, Father."

"Mmm. It's these blasted carriages. Too many comforts these days. Wouldn't have fallen asleep in a saddle."

It was dark with the curtains drawn, but Pietro easily imagined his father's long face grimacing. Fighting the urge to yawn, Pietro said, "I wasn't asleep. I was thinking. What were you saying?"

"I was referencing Giotto's mythic O."

"Oh. Why?"

"Why? What is nobler than thinking of perfection? More than that, it is a metaphor. We end where we begin." A considering pause. Shifting, Pietro felt his brother's head on his shoulder. Irritation rippled through him. *Oh, Poco's allowed to sleep, but not me. Father needs an audience.*

Expecting his father to try out some new flowery phrase, he was astonished to hear the old man say, "Yes, we end where we begin. I hope it's true. Perhaps then I will go home one day."

Pietro leaned forward, happily letting Jacopo's head fall in the process. "Father—of course you will! Now that it's published, now that any idiot can see, they'll have to call you home. If nothing else, their pride won't let anyone else claim you."

The poet laughed sourly. "You know little about pride, boy. It's their pride that keeps me in exile."

Us, thought Pietro. *Keeps us in exile.*

Pietro felt a rustling beside him, and suddenly there was light. Jacopo was groggily pulling back one of the curtains. Pietro tried to feel ashamed at his satisfaction for having woken his brother up.

"The stars are out," said Jacopo, peering out of the window.

"Every night at this time," said Pietro's father. Now Pietro could see the hooked nose over his father's bristly black beard. The poet's eyes were deeply sunken, as if hiding from illumination. It was partly this feature that had earned Dante Alaghieri his fiendish reputation. Partly.

The light that came into the cramped carriage wasn't from the sky but from the brands held aloft by their escort. No one traveled by night without armed men. The lord of Verona had dispatched a large contingent to protect his latest guest.

Verona. Pietro had never been, though his father had. The youth said, "Giotto's *O*—you were thinking about Verona, weren't you?" Dante nodded, stroking his beard. "What's it like?" Beside Pietro, Jacopo turned away from the stars to listen.

Pietro saw his father smile, an unusual event that utterly transformed his face. Suddenly he was young once more. "Ah. The rising star of Italy. The city of forty-eight towers. Home of the Greyhound. My first refuge." A pause, then the word *refugio* was repeated, savored, saved for future use. "Yes, I came there when I gave up on the rest of the exiles. Such plans. Such fools. I stayed in Verona for more than a year, you know. I saw the Palio run twice. Bartolomeo was Capitano then—a good man, honest, but almost terminally cheerful. In fact, it *was* fatal, now I think of it. When his brother Alboino took over the captainship, I made up my mind to leave. The boy was a weasel, not a hound. Besides, there was that unfortunate business with the Capelletti and Montecchi."

Pietro wanted to ask what business, but Jacopo got in first, leaning forward eagerly to ask, "What about the new lord of Verona? What about the Greyhound?"

Dante just shook his head. "Words fail me."

Which probably means, thought Pietro, *he doesn't really know. He's heard the stories, but a man can change in a dozen years.*

"But he is at war?" insisted Jacopo.

Dante nodded. "With Padua, over the city of Vicenza. Before he died, the Emperor gave Cangrande the title of Vicar of the Trevisian Mark, which technically means he is the overlord of Verona, Vicenza, Padua, and Treviso. Of course, the Trevisians and Paduans disagreed. But Vicenza is ruled by Cangrande's friend and brother-in-law, Bailardino Nogarola, who had no trouble swearing allegiance to his wife's brother."

"So how is the war about Vicenza?" asked Pietro.

"Vicenza used to be controlled by Padua until they threw off the yoke and joined Verona. Two years ago Padua decided it wanted Vicenza back." Pietro's father shook his head. "I wonder if they realize how badly they erred. They gave Cangrande an excuse for war, a just cause, and they might lose more than Vicenza in the bargain."

"What about the Trevisians, the Venetians?"

"The Trevisians are biding their time, hoping Padua wears down Cangrande's armies. The Venetians? Well, they're an odd lot. Protected in their lagoon, neither fish nor fowl, Guelph nor Ghibelline, they don't care much about their neighbor's politics unless it affects their trade. But if Cangrande wins his rights, he'll have their trade in a stranglehold. Then they'll intervene. Though, after Ferrara, I imagine the Venetians won't desire land anytime soon," he added, laughing.

"Maybe we'll see a battle!" Jacopo was fourteen and didn't care about politics. Ever since Poco had joined them in Lucca, Pietro had been treated to a litany of dreams involving membership in some mercenary condottiere until Poco was proven so brave he was knighted by whatever king or lord was handy. Then, Jacopo always said, came the money, leisure, comfort.

Pietro wanted to want such a life. It seemed like the right kind of existence, leading to the right kind of death. Women, wealth, maybe a heroic scar or two. And comfort? That was a dream he and his siblings had held in the way only a once wealthy, now ruined family can. Dante's exile from Florence had beggared his children, and his wife had only kept their house by using her dowry.

But Pietro couldn't imagine himself as a soldier. At seventeen he'd hardly been in a friendly scuffle, let alone a battle. He'd had a lesson in Paris, one quick tutorial that basically told him which end of the sword was for stabbing. The only other combat moves he knew he'd copied from fightbooks.

As the second son he'd been intended for a monastic life. Books, prayers, and perhaps gardening. Some politics. Lots of money. That was the life Pietro was brought up for, and he'd never really questioned it. But two years ago, Pietro's older brother Giovanni had died while with their father in Paris. Suddenly Pietro was elevated to heir and summoned to join his father. Since then they had traveled over the Alps back into Italy, down to Pisa and Lucca. A stone's throw from Florence. No wonder his father was thinking about their home.

If asked, Pietro would have said he was a disappointment to his father. He hadn't the wit to be a poet, and he was a poor manager for his father. Pietro thought that his little sister would be a better traveling companion for the great Dante. She had the mind for it. Pietro's sole consolation was that Poco, by his very presence, made Pietro look good.

Like now, as Jacopo pressed their father further. "The Greyhound. What's he really called?"

"Cangrande della Scala," said Dante. "The youngest of the three sons, the only one still living. Sharp, tall, well-spoken. No. That won't do. I said, words don't do him justice. He has a . . . a streak of immortality inside him, inside his mind. If he continues unchecked, he will make Verona the new Caput Mundi. But ask me no more about him. You will see." When Jacopo opened his mouth, Dante held up a hand. "Wait. And. See." He pulled the curtain shut, blocking the stars and plunging them once more into darkness.

They rode on through the night. Awake now, Pietro listened to the easy chatting of the soldiers outside. They talked of nothing important. Horses, wenches, gambling, in the main. Soon Pietro heard his father's breathing become regular. A minute later the coach was filled with snores as Poco joined in.

Pietro couldn't sleep now, though, if he tried. So instead he carefully peeled back a section of curtain and watched the miles pass by. Dante always insisted on riding facing forward, so Pietro could only see the road behind them, illuminated in bizarre twisted patches by the torches of their escort. A wind was fretting the oak trees and juniper bushes that lined the road. He could smell the fresh breeze. A storm, maybe. Not tonight. Maybe not even tomorrow. But a storm.

In a little while the trees thinned out, replaced by farms, mills, and minor hamlets. There was a jolt of the wheels, and suddenly they were rattling over a stone road, not a dirt one. The clop of each hoofbeat hung crisply in the night air. Pietro was again glad of their escort. Too many things happened to foolish nighttime travelers.

One of the men spied Pietro and cantered his mare closer to the carriage. "We're coming up on the city. Won't be long now."

Pietro thanked him and kept watching. Verona. They were Ghibelline, which meant that they supported the Emperor, who was dead, rather than the pope, also dead. Verona had a famous race called the Palio. They exported, well, everything. Any goods from Venice that weren't going out by ship had to pass through either Florence or Verona. Florence led only to the port at Ostia, but Verona was the key to Austria and Germany, and thus on to France and England. It lay at the foot of the Brenncro Pass, the only quick and sure route through the Alps.

All of a sudden the suburbs were upon them, the disposable homes, shops, and warehouses of those not wealthy enough to buy property inside the city walls. But already it smelled like a city. Pietro found it strange that the smell of urine and feces was a familiar comfort, but he'd lived in cities all his life. Florence, Paris, Pisa.

The carriage slowed to a walk, then stopped. Pietro's father roused. "What's happening?"

"I think we're outside the city gates, Father."

"Excellent, excellent," said the poet sleepily. "I was so consumed with composing the encounter with Cato—I told you about Cato? Good—I lost all track of our travels. Open the curtains. And wake your brother!"

Their escort had been hailed by the guard at the gate. The escort now shouted out the names of the passengers—one name, really, followed by "and his sons!" The city's guards acknowledged the claim and came forward to confirm the number of passengers in the carriage. And, Pietro saw, to gawk a little at his father.

"It is you, then?" asked one.

"I thought you'd have Virgil with you," said the other. Pietro hoped he was joking.

Dante said, "You didn't recognize him? He's the coach driver." One guard actually looked, then laughed in an abashed way. The poet passed a few more words with the guards, and one of them made a comment that he thought witty until Dante sighed. "Yes, yes. Hellfire singed my beard black. My sons are tired. May we enter?"

They were delayed while word was sent ahead and the gate was opened. Then the coach resumed its course, passing into the dark archway that led into the city. When Dante recognized a church or a house, he named it.

All at once Dante smacked his hands together and cried, "Look! Look!"

Pietro and Poco twisted around to see where he was pointing. Out of the darkness Pietro could make out an arch. Then another, and another. Arches above arches. Then the torches revealed enough of the structure for Pietro to guess what it was. The only thing it could be.

"The Arena!" Poco laughed. "The Roman Arena!"

"It's still in use," said Dante. "Now that they've evicted the squatters and cleaned it out so they can use it for sport again. And theatre," he added sourly.

Quickly they were past it, but Pietro kept picturing it in his mind's eye until the coach pulled to a stop. The driver called down, "The full stop!" and laughed. Everybody was itching to show off his wit to the exiled master poet.

A footman opened the door to the coach, and Pietro, hearing a sound, poked his head out. Word of their arrival must have spread faster than fire. There was a crowd of men, women, and children, growing larger every second. After two years of walking from place to place, of leaving their hats on posts in each new city they came to until someone lifted them, thus offering lodging and food, Pietro still wasn't used to his father's newfound fame.

Pietro stepped out of the coach, first making sure his hat was at the proper angle—he liked his hat, a present from the lord of Lucca and his only expensive garment. But even in his fancy hat with the long feather, he heard the crowd's sigh of disappointment. He didn't take it personally. Instead, he turned to hold out his arm to his father.

Dante's long fingers took the youthful arm, putting more pressure than he showed onto his son's flesh. His foot touched the stones of the square and the crowd took a single step back, pressing the rearmost hard against the walls.

"Fool carriages," muttered Dante. "Never get cramped like this on a horse."

Jacopo had popped out of the other side. Now he came around the back of the carriage, an idiot grin on his face. With a word to the porters to stow their baggage, they followed a beckoning steward.

Awed the crowd parted for them. They were gathered to glimpse Dante, an event Pietro guessed they'd tell their friends of while making the sign to ward off evil. The old man *was* evil, but not in that way.

Following the steward's lamp, they passed under an archway with a massive curved bone dangling from it. "La Costa," said Dante. "I had forgotten. That bone is the remains of an ancient monster that the city rose up and killed in olden times. It marks the line between the Piazza delle Erbe to the Piazza della Signoria." The marketplace, the civic center.

The alleyway opened out into a wide piazza enclosed all about by buildings both new and old. The whole square was done up in cloth of gold and silken banners that shimmered in the torchlight. Below this finery were Verona's best and brightest. Dressed in fine gonnellas or the more modern— and revealing—doublets, the wealthy nobles and upper crust watched now as Dante Alaghieri joined their ranks.

The buildings, ornaments, and men were all impressive, but Pietro's eyes were drawn to a central pillar flying a banner. A leap of torchlight caught the flapping flag, revealing an embroidered five-runged ladder. On the topmost rung perched an eagle, its imperial beak bearing a laurel wreath. At the ladder's base was shown a snarling hound.

Il Veltro. The Greyhound.

Then the crowd before Pietro's father parted to reveal a man standing at the center of the square, looking like a god on earth: massively tall, yet thin as a corded whip, his clothes were of expensive simplicity—a light-colored linen shirt with a wide collar that came to two triangular points far below his neck, under a farsetto, a doublet of burgundy leather. Instead of the common leather ties, it bore six metal clasps down the front. His hose, too, were dark, a wine red close to black. Tall boots reached his knee, the soft leather rolled back to create a wide double band about his calf. He wore no hat but was crowned with a mane of chestnut hair with streaks of blond that, catching echoes of the brands, danced like fire.

Yet it was his eyes that struck Pietro most. Bluer than the sky, sharper than a hawk's—unearthly. At their corners laughter lurked like angels at the dawn of the world.

Cangrande della Scala stood surrounded by minions and fellow nobles to greet the greatest poor man in all the world. A man's whose only wealth was language.

Dante released Pietro's arm and, drawing himself up, walked with dignity to the center of the square. He took off his hat with the lappets and, just as he had done a hundred times during his exile, placed it at the base of the plinth at the center of the square. From Dante they might have expected speeches. But Pietro's father had a keen sense of drama.

Pietro watched with the rest as Cangrande stooped for the limp, old-fashioned cap. As he rose, Pietro caught his first glimpse of Cangrande's famous smile, the *allegria,* as the lord of Verona twirled the hat between his fingers.

"Well met, poet."

"Well come, at least," said Dante. "If not well met."

Cangrande threw back his head and roared with laughter. He waved a hand and music erupted from some corner of the square. Under its cover Dante spoke, and Pietro was close enough to hear. "It is good to see you, my lord." The poet directed his gaze to the ornate decorations. "You shouldn't have."

"I must confess, it was luck. Our garlands are for tomorrow's happy wedlock. But they are far better suited to grace your coming."

"Silver-tongued still," replied Pietro's father. "Who is to marry?"

"My nephew, Cecchino." Cangrande gestured to a not-so-sober blond fellow, raising his voice as he did. "Tonight he takes his last hunt as a bachelor!"

Dante also pitched his voice to carry. "Hunt for what, lord?"

"For the hart, of course!" The crowd broke with laughter. Pietro wondered if they were indeed hunting deer, or girls. But his eyes found a handsome young man, dark of hair, well dressed, who carried a small hawk. So, deer. Pietro was both relieved and disappointed. He was seventeen.

Dante turned to face his sons. "Pietro. Jacopo." Jacopo tried to flatten down his hair. Pietro stepped eagerly forward to be introduced, ready to make his best bow.

But his father forestalled him with a gesture. "See to the bags."

With that, the poet turned in step with Cangrande and departed.

TWO

Vicenza

17 SEPTEMBER 1314

The Count of San Bonifacio sat on horseback atop a hill overlooking the walls of San Pietro, a suburb of Vicenza. Beneath the metal protecting his arms, the muscles were thick from years of slinging a sword. The beefy hands inside the gauntlets were callused from fire and leather. The stout legs were well used to the combined weight of plate and chain armor. A large man, he sweat freely and now mopped his forehead with a cloth. His aged visage was round and cheerful, a face belonging to a merry friar or a troubadour with a fondness for German beer. It seemed sorely out of place atop the body of a knight-soldier.

Beside him was the Podestà of Padua, Ponzino de' Ponzoni. Not only an unfortunate victim of alliteration, but a poor man's general. At the moment the Podestà was visibly sickened by the destruction of his honor. Ponzoni said, "Is there nothing we can do?"

The Count shook his head, daubing his face with a handkerchief. "Nothing until they've spent themselves. If we try to stop them now, we'll get a spear in the back and be robbed of our armor."

The day had not gone well for the Podestà of Padua. So auspiciously begun, it had turned into a waking nightmare. *Too intellectual,* judged the Count. *Too devoted to the damn Chivalric Code.*

But then, Ponzino was a disappointment in every regard. He'd wasted the summer campaigning months, insisting upon avoiding confrontation, concentrating instead on razing the enemy's lands. Against a different foe it might have worked, but Ponzoni hadn't comprehended the vast resources at his opponent's fingertips. In the last four years the enemy had taken prime land to the north, south, and west. All that remained was the east. Since Padua was the key to the east, the city elders had forced Ponzino to attack, raid—do something!

Not that the fate of Padua concerned the Count of San Bonifacio. He couldn't have cared less about Paduans or their thrice-damned *patavinitas,* the exclusively Paduan code of honor that seemed to rule every waking moment in their benighted city. The Count was a foreigner, a guest, an advisor, an observer. Unwelcome, but necessary.

This invasion of Vicenza—his idea—was supposed to be the answer, Padua's salvation. It had started well. The army had made the ride to the city unobserved. Silencing the guards at Quartesolo, they had skulked the four miles from there to the target. Like most city-states, Vicenza was a series of walled rings, with more walls between, like the spokes on a wheel. The outermost circles were the suburbs. Here dwelt the poorer classes, and here the less essential commodities were stored. The next set of walls enclosed the city itself.

The strategy was to infiltrate the outer suburb called San Pietro. The Count himself led the foray, cutting down the guards in the tower and opening the gates. Revealing himself to the peasants, he had been cheered. He wondered if they genuinely adored him or if they were simply in fear for their lives. Not that it mattered. He had taken San Pietro, the key to Vicenza.

To that point, everything had gone according to plan. The presence of the Count of San Bonifacio had precluded the need to slaughter the innocents, something the Podestà quailed at. Ponzino had led his army through the suburb toward the next ring of walls, only to discover himself surrounded by flame.

That had been the first crack in Ponzino's armor. Though, in fairness, even the Count admitted the fire was surprising. Who would have thought Nogarola would be willing to risk the loss of the whole city to fire rather than cede to Padua? Fire was one of the threats most feared in any metropolis, especially one more than half made of wood.

Fire was a setback, but not fatal to their plans. If handled properly. But it took Ponzino too long to gather his wits. He had wandered fecklessly, failing to call the Paduan leaders together and form a new strategy. It was the Count who convinced him to order the army to pull back just outside the city wall, leaving a breach in it to renew the attack when the fires died.

The army disobeyed. After four years of meaningless battles and a shortage of food, they were loath to relinquish the foothold they had gained in Vicenza. When the order to withdraw was given, the men revolted. They began to torch the parts of the suburb not yet ablaze. They plundered, robbing the inhabitants. The Count had been with Ponzino when they'd come across a dozen of their own citizens—not even foreign auxiliaries!—sacking a convent and violating the nuns there. Together they had put the rapists to the sword, but what could be done about the rest? The Podestà rode glumly out through the city gates and waited for his men's rage and bloodlust to die down, his hopes for glory crumbling around his ears.

The Count of San Bonifacio could not have cared less for the plight of the citizenry—after all, they had supported the Pup. What he deplored was the wasted time. The San Bonifaci family had been fighting the Scaligeri since before Mastino the First came to power. As a young man the Count himself had fought against that first Scaliger leader of Verona. He remembered the dark brown hair and sharp features. He also remembered the Mastiff's eyes—light green with the dark ring about them. They had been otherworldly, as if the man had trekked through all the fields of Hell and seen all the unthinkable horrors there. The Count remembered well and blessed the day his father, working through Paduan tools, had had the bastard killed.

Recalling the fierce joy Mastino showed on the battlefield, he shivered. Almost four decades later he could hear the bastard's laugh. It was a trait Mastino's nephew shared, causing the Count to worry now. If they took too long in breaching the inner walls, word would reach the Scaliger. He would come, and that could be disastrous. Of all the Pup's traits in battle, the worst was his unpredictability.

Vanni Scorigiani appeared, the man known as Asdente or the Toothless Master. The previous year at Illasi he'd earned his nickname by taking a sword in the mouth and living to boast about it. A mere look from the scowling, twisted face could make a hardened knight blench.

Now he was grinning, completely unfazed by the carnage inside the suburb. "Well, that's a mess, isn't it?" Vanni's twisted grin looked like the rictus of a corpse. Blood soaked his left arm up to the elbow. "I do so love Dutch soldiers!" he chuckled.

"And they love you," replied the Count ironically, passing Asdente a wineskin.

"Can't you stop them?" asked the Podestà desperately.

Asdente chuckled while he drank and patted Ponzino familiarly on the arm. "Don't worry. They're good boys. In another hour they'll be tired and ashamed and back here for orders. Then we'll take that damn gate." He gave a snort of disgusted respect. "Have to admit, firing the houses—didn't think Nogarola had it in him."

"He learned from the Pup," said the Count.

"*He* never plunders," said Ponzino.

San Bonifacio was silently scornful. Ponzoni didn't seem to realize that plunder was the reason most men-at-arms went to war. There was little talk of the "just cause" among the common foot soldiers, or even among the knights. A soldier signed on with a troop for wealth and to vent his spleen on the world.

Asdente said, "It's just pragmatism. Nogarola has to fight. He's fixed himself too firmly to Cangrande's star to do anything but!"

Ponzino cuffed a bead of sweat from his face, surreptitiously blinking back the dampness in his eyes. "Do you think the citizens will ever forgive us? After they welcomed us in the way they did, to be so betrayed?"

Vanni looked at the Podestà in shock. "Who cares?"

The Count changed the subject. "Do you think a rider got off?"

Asdente nodded happily. "We saw one heading west just as the fires were starting." He washed out his mouth from the wineskin and spat, a difficult exercise without front teeth. Sometimes, as now, he forgot, and grinned abashedly as crimson spittle ran down his chin. "A child. Some of my boys tried to catch him, but I called them off."

"Why?" demanded the Podestà, aghast. "The longer Cangrande is unaware, the better our chances of success!"

Vanni Scorigiani looked at the ground, feigning embarassment. "Aw, well, sir—you don't know the Greyhound as I do. No doubt he's brave, but he's reckless. Foolhardy. Thinks he's indestructible. He'll likely set out rapidly and poorly prepared." His face twisted even further, intent added to injury. "We'll make mincemeat out of him."

Ponzino goggled at Vanni, whose tone was unmistakable. If Cangrande arrived, they wouldn't take him prisoner, as the rules of chivalry dictated. They would kill him outright. Murder? How much honor was he going to lose this day?

The Count saw the struggle in the young general. "It's the sensible course," he said.

The Podestà wiped his brow again and said, "Vanni, get down there and calm this mob. I want the women protected, and the men-at-arms rounded up and ready for the siege."

"I'll try," said Asdente. The Count of San Bonifacio had no doubt he would. It was an excellent excuse to crack a few skulls. "But this kind of rage has to burn itself out."

"Do it now or I'll feed you to the Greyhound myself."

Vanni smirked. "Now, that's downright unchivalrous." He spurred off.

Together the Count and the Podestà turned their mounts back to watch the rape and slaughter of San Pietro. The first hint of clouds began moving in from the east. Vinciguerra sniffed the air. Tomorrow it would rain, perhaps the next day.

Ponzino is doubtless wishing for rain this very second, thought the Count in disgust. *It would hide his tears.*

Verona

"Alighieri! Hola! Alighieri!"

Weaving in and out of the midday crowd, Pietro turned at the hail and was at once knocked to the ground. He felt the trod of feet and a buffet of absent blows before a hand caught him by the shoulder. "Alighieri!"

"Alaghieri." Dazed, Pietro staggered to his feet, brushing dirt and filth from his best doublet.

"Are you all right?" He was turned about to behold a face no older than his own, with hair jet black and eyes as blue as sparrow's eggs. The doublet bordered on frippery, but the hose, boots, and hat were of the finest quality. He was closely shaved, showing off a mouth a trifle too pretty.

"Fine," said Pietro shortly, aware that his best doublet was his best no longer. The teen looked familiar. But the previous night had been chaotic. With all his father's luggage to bestow and his brother running about pointing out the windows, Pietro hadn't caught half the names thrown at him. Embarrassment mounting, he tried to remember . . .

"Montecchio," supplied the comely youth. "Mariotto Montecchio."

"You had the baby hawk."

Montecchio's smile was dazzling. "Yes! I'm training it so I can hunt with the Capitano. Maybe you can join us next time?"

Giving up on the doublet, Pietro nodded eagerly. "I'd like that." He had missed the revelry last night, consigned to unpacking. The Alaghieri paterfamilias had, of course, participated, riding forth with the nobility on the midnight hunt. All night long Pietro and his brother had groused, and this morning he felt the pangs even worse, for everyone was talking of the sport.

Not that Pietro really enjoyed hunting. Like soldiering, it was more that he wished he were the kind of man who enjoyed it. It seemed to be something he should love.

Montecchio looked him up and down, checked the length of his arms. "We'll get you a sparrow hawk. It'll match the feather in your—" Mariotto's brows knit together as he glanced at Pietro's head. "Where's your hat?"

Pietro ran a hand up and discovered his head was bare. Looking about, he spied his fine plumed hat a few feet away, wilted and trampled.

Montecchio leapt forward to snatch it out from under the trod of boots and sandals. "I am so sorry," he said gravely. He looked genuinely pained as he held it in his hand. Mariotto took attire seriously.

Pietro did his best to smile as he took the limp cloth with its broken feather out of Montecchio's hands. "It doesn't matter. It wasn't a very nice cap."

It had been a very nice cap. A trifle, surely, but Pietro was allowed few trifles. His father had an austere code that applied to all things, including dress. Pietro had barely managed to win the right to wear the doublet and hose, which his father viewed as extravagant and showy. The hat had been a gift from the great Pisan lord Uguccione della Faggiuola, who knew all about young men and their vanity. Pietro had convinced his father that refusing the gift would have been an insult. "I only wear the hat out of respect for your patron, Father," he'd said. Somehow the old cynic had bought it. Now it was crushed and covered with dirt.

"I'll replace it," declared Mariotto instantly.

"You don't—"

Mariotto insisted. "It's your first day here! No, we're going to the best haberdasher in the city. Follow me!"

Not to agree would have been churlish. The late morning sun warmed Pietro's back as he ducked and weaved through the myriad enticements of the Piazza delle Erbe, trying to keep up. (*The finest whips and crops!*) Men of all shapes and sizes jostled with each other as buyers and sellers called out their wares to pilgrims, palmers, Jews, even the occasional heathen Moor. (*Fish! The fruit of the sea, the Capitano's favorite!*) Pietro's eyes encountered millers, fishmongers, barbers, and smiths, all crying their wares from tented stalls or storefronts. (*Love potions! Dump the man you have and get the one you deserve!*) There were many small nooks, but Pietro didn't have the time to even glance into one before Mariotto was off in another direction. (*Skins, well cured! Don't let the heat fool you! Winter's coming! Stay warm!*)

It was loud! Anvils chimed in their workshops, and the cries of exotic animals on display added to the din. Monkeys hopped around in cages, hawks screamed, hounds barked, all underscored by guitars, lutes, flutes, viols, rebecs, tambourines, and the voices of the troubadors. It was Nimrod's Tower come to life, cacophonous pandemonium. A seller of headstones was immediately replaced by a purveyor of sweet pasties who held his samples in the air, enticingly aromatic. Legally a vendor couldn't physically accost a traveler, but that only increased the assault on the other senses, and the huge signs that hung over the stalls were worse than grabbing hands. Each proclaimed the trade of the stall owner, even as the owner shouted insults at the vendor across the way. Above the signs, in row after row of low balconies, men capered and shouted to friends below, watching the course of various arguments and fistfights and making loud bets with each other as to the outcome.

Mariotto easily navigated the shops and stalls, using shortcuts through alleys and leaping over barrels that blocked their path. Pietro followed him down a sidestreet perfumed with mulled wines and spiced meats. Trying to keep up, Pietro continued to make the proper protestations. "Actually, I was on an errand for my father."

Mariotto grinned. "Something devilish?"

Pietro laughed because he was expected to. "I have to order him some new sandals."

Mariotto turned to walk backward as he asked, "What happened to his old ones? Burned in the hellfire?"

"No," said Pietro. "My brother."

Montecchio nodded wisely, as though the answer made sense. "We'll head to the river and circle around to Cobbler Lane on the way back to the palace—you cannot deny me the opportunity to replace your cap. It would stain my family's honor to let this injustice go unanswered." Pietro's guide laughed as he whirled off into the crowds. Pietro followed.

Behind them came the sound of the human tongue in disjointed harmony. Each traveler spoke his or her native language, rendering the air thick with a war of French, English, Flemish, Greek, and more. Interlaced in the tumult were the harsh guttural sounds of German. Veronese speech owed at least as much to German as it did to Italian, and the local dialect was redolent with its accents.

Over the noise Pietro said, "Why are *you* out this morning? Weren't you in the wedding party?"

"Yes! I did my best, but I couldn't talk him out of it! Cecchino, poor fool—just a couple years older than us and already tied down to a wife! But until the feast there's nothing but servants racing about the palace and women cooing about how lovely it all was. I had to escape."

A roar of approval from the men around them caused them to raise their eyes to the highest balconies of the building nearby. Several young women had emerged and draped themselves over the railings, their garments falling revealingly open. One girl waved at Pietro and flashed something pink from beneath her bodice. Pietro blushed and waved shyly back.

Mariotto said, "I could arrange an introduction."

I shouldn't be shocked, thought Pietro. *This is the market plaza, after all.* Aloud he said, "In Florence they're forced to wear tiny bells."

"You don't say."

"Yes. There's an old joke about churches and prostitutes—the bells call a man to repent what the bells call a man to do."

Montecchio never stopped talking as he led a merry chase down the long street. Figuring that Pietro would soon be sent to hunt for tools linked to his father's profession, Mariotto made sure to point out where to find the best wax for sealing, the best cut quills.

Then they reached milliner row, close to an ancient tufa wall, a stark contrast to the rose marble and red brick all around them. These were the old walls, built by the Romans or their forebears—no one knew for certain. The first true inhabitants of Verona were lost to memory. Regardless, the walls existed, enclosing the oldest and richest part of the city—though what good they would be if attacked, Pietro wasn't sure.

Twenty minutes later Pietro was once more appropriately, if ostentatiously, hatted. He had settled on a puffed-out burgundy affair sporting a thin green feather just above the left ear—the Ghibelline ear. Feeling rakish, he followed Mariotto to a string of cobblers where he ordered sandals to be ready for the poet the following day.

The sun was directly overhead, the bridal dinner nigh. Mariotto unfettered his infectious grin. "We'd better get back. My father asked me to be amusing for Monsignore Alighieri's children."

"Alaghieri."

"That's what I said." He clapped a hand on Pietro's shoulder. "To tell you the truth, I was dreading it. Thank you for being nothing like what I imagined the son of a poet to be."

Again Pietro smiled because he was supposed to. Inside his skin he shuddered. *That's the question, isn't it? What is the son of a poet—of any great man—if not less than? Inferior. Useless.*

To cheer himself up, Pietro looked for a way to repay Mariotto's kindness. Being lost and alone in a new city was nothing new, but having a friend was. When they were five minutes from the palace, traversing the Piazza delle Erbe once more, he spotted the perfect gift. "Wait here," he said, dashing off through the crowd. A few moments later he reappeared.

"For you, signore," said Pietro with an elaborate bow, twisting his new hat between his fingers in a flourish. With his free hand he offered a pair of fine corded leather straps. From one end of each hung a solid silver *vervel* for engraving the owner's name.

Montecchio's eyes lit up. "Jesses!" Reaching out, he checked. "Really, Alighieri, it's too much." Now it was Montecchio's protests that were feeble.

Pietro was helpless to stop his embarrassingly lopsided smile. "Your hawk should be as well dressed as you are."

Mariotto admired the small token. "Tomorrow we'll go riding along the Adige and see if the fellow will fly at all."

Pietro nodded. *If Father will let me.* Out loud he said, "I'd like that."

A bell began to ring to the south, then another to the east. Mariotto's eyes grew wide. "We're late!"

THREE

The Benedictine bells were just finishing the call to Prime when the two panting teens raced up the inner stairs of the great Scaliger palace in Verona. Attaining the top, they skidded to a halt at a demure distance from the open double doors. Listening, they heard arguing and laughter echoing down the hall to them. They grinned at each other in relief. They were not too late.

An understeward came bustling forward. "Master Montecchio, welcome. Your father and brother are already within." He glanced at the other young man, with an inquiring inclination of his head.

"This is my friend, Pietro Alighieri," said Montecchio.

"Alaghieri," said Pietro automatically.

"Right, sorry. Pietro Alaghieri. He's the son of—"

"Of course," said the steward, unable to entirely hide the sign against evil he made behind his back. "Your esteemed father is also within. If you will both doff your boots, I have slippers waiting by the door. You are the last to arrive."

This statement renewed their panic. Hastily they removed their boots in favor of soft-soled, pointy-toed slippers.

Montecchio said, "I've always heard your name as Al-ee-gary. What's this Al-ah-gary business?"

Pietro shrugged. "It's my father biting his thumb. Alighieri is the Florentine pronunciation. Since the banishment, he's insisted on the older pronunciation—Alaghieri, after our ancestor, Alaghiero di Cacciaguida."

Mariotto nodded as if he were truly interested. "And your brother came with you?"

Pietro grunted as he struggled with his right boot. "Jacopo."

"What's he like?"

Familial pride battled honesty. He settled on saying, "He's fourteen."

"Ah. No brothers here, just a sister. She's all right, if a little quiet. Aurelia."

"Mariotto and Aurelia?"

"Actually, Romeo and Aurelia. My mother named us—or so my father tells me. I never knew her. She chose Romeo as my baptismal name, but he wanted to honor his father, so I am Romeo Mariotto Montecchio. Call me Romeo and I'll murder you." He finished fitting his own slippers on and stood up tall. "Ready to face the lion's den?"

If it were a lion I wouldn't be so terrified. "How do we explain being late?"

Mariotto clapped Pietro on the shoulder and together they made for the grand hall. "Some things you just have to take a deep breath and live through."

Just before they reached the door, Pietro halted. There was a fresco on the wall by the door, one of a set of five. Each depicted a man on horseback, behind whom flew the banner of the five-runged ladder. The five men showed a great deal of resemblance, but it was at the last, closest to the door, that Pietro gazed.

"Our lord," said Mariotto.

Pietro peered at the glazed paintwork. If you didn't know the man, the fresco might have been deemed flattery. Mounted on a great destrier, mace in one hand, sword in the other, head free of his hound-shaped helmet, Cangrande was fiercely beautiful. The face was full of dark joy. Above his head, alongside the banner of the ladder, flew a personal banner with a greyhound racing across an azure field. The artist had added some dark spots to the banner, signifying the blood spilt in battle by this magnificent cavaliere.

But it was the actual paint that had Pietro's interest. "This is excellent work."

"It surely is," nodded Montecchio, looking close. "The neck of the stallion is just right, and also the length of the mane . . . Oh—sorry. My family breeds horses. These were painted by Giotto di Bondone." Pietro startled Mariotto with an abrupt laugh. "You've heard of him?"

"Better," said Pietro. "I know him. He's a friend of my father's. Sort of. We visited him often in Lucca." Pietro opened his mouth, then shut it, visibly resisting temptation. Knowing he was missing something, Mariotto made an open gesture with his hands. "What?"

Pietro shook his head, then said, "Have you ever seen Giotto's children?

They're as sweet as can be, really nice. But they're repulsive. Girls as well as the boys. Ugly as sin. Well, we're eating supper in their house one night when Father asks how a man who paints such beautiful frescoes could make such ugly children."

"Oh dear God! What did Giotto say?"

Pietro did his best imitation of the cheery painter. " 'My dear fellow, I do all my painting by daylight.' "

Smothering their laughter, they entered the salon.

✦ ◇ ✦

Somewhere near Torre di Confine a lone rider reined in before an inn. He was young and frantic-looking, leaping from his sweat-streaked horse and calling for a fresh one. A stable boy emerged from beside the inn, a hunk of cheese in his hand. At the same moment the inn's proprietor, a burly man with one arm, sauntered out the door. The stable boy looked on, bored, as his master gave first the youth then his horse an appraising look.

"No," he said over his shoulder. "No horse for him. To judge by this one, he'll kill it."

The breathless rider was by his side clutching his arm before he had fully turned. Gasping, the boy gave his news. At the same moment he spilled his purse at the innkeeper's feet.

Whether it was the news or the gold, the innkeeper changed his tune at once. The boy was brought some stout ale while the best horse was saddled. The boy shivered the whole time, looking as though he were about to weep. He was certain he'd barely escaped with his life, and he was equally sure that each moment of delay brought a whole army in his wake.

In ten minutes he was on the road again, a fresh wineskin hanging from his belt, digging his heels harder and harder into the new horse, leaving the innkeeper to call his neighbors together to decide if they should flee.

✦ ◇ ✦

Sunlight spilled in through billowing curtains to frame the lord of Verona and his honored guests in the arched loggia. The open side of the long covered balcony faced east, providing a magnificent view of the Adige River.

It was not, however, the view one first noticed upon entering. Cangrande della Scala would stand out in any gathering. His chestnut hair was sun-bleached a dark gold and hung to frame his muscular jaw. Well over six feet tall, practically a giant, he possessed enormous energy: even in repose his movements were crisp and economical. *As much hawk as hound,* thought Pietro, seeing both kinds of animals scattered among the crowd. A fraction of Cangrande's hawk collection was here, at ease on wooden stands that bore the marks of their pounces. Several guests were attempting to feed the blind-folded birds without losing fingers.

At the Capitano's feet were a pair of wolfhounds. Huge, with long narrow faces, they looked the most feral of creatures until Cangrande reached out a hand, whereupon they became puppies, craving attention from their master.

One dog lay before them in the position of dominance. This was a fine, wiry greyhound with the characteristic long face and curved teeth. Can-grande tossed him a little something, and he fetched it back quick as a wink. As he settled in again to gnaw at it at his master's feet, Pietro saw his back-cloth was embroidered with the silver ladder and imperial eagle—the della Scala family crest. Under the cloth the beast's fur was long and slightly mat-ted, showing it was one of the tougher breed of that dog known as the *veltro*—a term that was also synonymous with *bastard.* For those who called Cangrande "Il Veltro," there was always that extra, amusing, connotation.

Seated in the place of honor to the Capitano's left was Pietro's father. Born Durante Alighieri di Fiorenza, he was now known to the cultured world as the poet Dante. A head and a half shorter than the young lord of Verona, he suffered mightily in comparison. His movements were jerky and incomplete, his breathing audible. His frame was mostly hidden beneath a gonnella, the comfortable long gown favored by scholars, and his head was covered by the hooded cappuccio. Both garments were of black and scarlet, expensively dour colors. Like Pietro, Dante possessed a patrician face with an aquiline nose and large eyes. His jaw was large too, and the lower lip protruded a bit past the upper. But unlike his brown-haired son, his hair and beard were thick, black, and shiny.

As Mariotto and Pietro stood in the doorway of the loggia, servants rushed over to wash their hands. Watching them approach, Pietro saw the need for the slippers. The palace floor was not covered in the usual straw rushes, but bare marble. Great care was taken to keep mud and filth outside. *The dogs must drive the servants insane,* Pietro thought.

As the servants tended to them, Mariotto whispered, "There, in the deep green, that's Passerino Bonaccolsi, Podestà of Mantua—it's said he's Cangrande's best friend, but there's politics there, so you never know. Next to him, in the fur, that's Guglielmo da Castelbarco-Stick-in-the-Mud. He recently became the armorer for our army, and makes a nice bit of money from it. The one playing with the bread knife is Federigo della Scala—a remote cousin. He's a little quiet, but he defended the city brilliantly this summer. And there, standing just behind the Capitano, is Nicolo da Lozzo, but Cangrande calls him Nico. He's young, only a little older than the Capitano, and he's the army's second-in-command. The post was given to him as a reward for deserting Padua, and he's doing very well with it . . ." Mariotto continued naming all the powerful men gathered in this room. Pietro took in each one with interest, though he doubted he'd remember many names. Bonaccolsi he'd heard of, and da Lozzo. For the rest, some of the surnames were familiar. Those denied the regal daybeds either stood or sat on cushioned boxes and stools.

Mariotto paused, looking at a broad-shouldered man with long hair braided at the back of his head. The deep blue of the ribbon that held the braid distracted the eye from the traces of silver and white that were mixed with the black and deep brown. Pointing to him, Mariotto said, "I don't know who that is."

Pietro said, "That's Uguccione della Faggiuola, my father's current patron. He brought us here to renew father's introduction to the Scaliger—though I think he wants to use us to impress Cangrande. He needs an ally in the north."

Looking wise, Mariotto nodded. "Ah."

"He also bought me my old hat."

Mariotto grinned. Uguccione looked up and gave Dante's son a cheerful nod. Pietro was in the midst of waving back when a prickling sensation crept up his spine. Eyes traveling a few feet beyond the Pisan lord, he saw his father's gaze fixed upon him. A muscle below the poet's left eye twitched as he took in the new hat. Pietro felt his blood drain to his knees.

Pietro strained to filter out the several conversations along the loggia to hear what his father and Cangrande were discussing. They were debating with a young abbot, a bishop whose aged gonnella swept the floor, and a midget with a wide nose and dark skin. This last was dressed extravagantly, with bells on his cuffs in an outlandish parody of style.

"Clement is dead," said the elder clergyman. "The Church should move to reclaim the papacy from Philip!"

"What does the nationality of your pope matter?" asked the garish midget, tone innocuous.

Pietro's father and the old man both responded with varying degrees of heat, yet their sentiment was the same. Dante just expressed it better. "My dear misguided juggler—through converting the noble pagans of ancient Roma to Christianity, God chose Italy to be the seat right royal of his faith. Rome is the true home of the papacy, and the office belongs to an Italian! You are a Jew. Compare the exile of the papacy in France to the Babylonian Captivity, and you will perhaps grasp the significance."

"Italy is a myth," said the motley fool. "An intellectual's conceit. A philosopher's fancy. Or a poet's."

"A dream of truth is no fancy, fool."

"Yet the last Italian pope was no friend to you, poet."

"True, fool, but a French pope is friend to no one."

Mariotto tugged Pietro's sleeve, and together they drifted toward the raucous sounds of those nearer their own age. The bridegroom was at their center, answering war questions put to him by a large, well-muscled fellow with a thatch of unruly sand-colored hair. But the majority of the groom's friends were only interested in plying him with liquid courage and eliciting love poetry from him. "Ah, Constanza!" he sighed, earning a chorus of catcalls. Pietro and Mariotto joined in.

"I should be so lucky," groused a man in his twenties, muscular and broad-shouldered, handsomely bearded. Absentmindedly tricking with a scrap of rope, he smiled even as he complained, "I'll never get married!"

The groom cried, "Of course you won't, Bonaventura! You've managed to get on the wrong side of every father in Verona!"

"I know it!" growled the grouser, hunching forward, the rope suddenly lifeless.

Someone else joined in. "Ever since your father—God rest his blessed soul—kicked off, you've been on a rampage! Wine, women, and song!

"Not too many songs, I think," said the groom. "Mainly wine and women."

"Don't forget his hundred falcons!"

Bonaventura said, "If I don't marry soon, I won't have any money left!"

The groom said, "Well, you better start looking outside Verona's walls."

"There's a world outside Verona's walls?"

"You better hope so. If not, you'll die a bachelor." The groom's eyes were taking on the sly look drunks get. "Maybe we'll win this war with Padua soon. Then you can go there and steal a wealthy Paduan heiress."

The rope began to dance again as Bonaventura grew thoughtful. "A Paduan heiress . . ."

"Oh, yeah, the women there have the biggest . . ." The groom sighed. "But I'm married now! Ah, Costanza!" The jeers began anew.

A hand descended on Mariotto's shoulder. "Son. A moment." Lord Montecchio spoke softly to his son in a manner that young Alaghieri knew all too well. Pietro decided perhaps he ought to join his father's conversation. Just to be safe.

As he shuffled through the circle of adults, he could hear the abbot speaking vehemently. He had evidently departed from the topic of the papacy, for the object of the abbot's ire was now Dante himself.

"There cannot be more than one Heaven! Even the pagan heretic Aristotle affirms that this cannot be so. The very first lines of his ninth chapter on the heavens states it irrefutably."

"Thank you." The poet's lagubrious lips formed a sinister, lopsided smile. Dante Alaghieri did not suffer fools gladly. "You have just made my point. There cannot be more than one Heaven, you say. But you then refer to the plurality—the heavens. How are we to reconcile this?"

The abbot, who bore a vague resemblance to the Scaliger, sputtered. "A figure of speech—the heavens refer to the skies, not the greater Heaven above!"

The little man with the bells spoke. "I am surprised, lord Abbot, that you are so public with your confessions."

"What?"

The little man flipped over to stand on his head. "Reading the Greek is heresy, and punishable by death. You must have friends in high places." The abbot blushed. "But I will join you on the pyre, for I too have read his works—worse, I've read The Destruction. As I recall, dear Abbot, Aristotle had a numerical fixation not unlike our infernal friend's here. But whereas monsignore," he nodded to Dante, "obsesses in *noveni,* the Greek was more economical. Did he not say there were three 'heavens'?"

"Bait someone else, jester," replied the abbot. "He was acknowledging the common uses of the word. Aristotle then goes on to insist that there is only one Heaven, for nothing can exist outside of Heaven."

Cangrande sat forward, perfect teeth flashing in a grin. "Now I'm ashamed I haven't read Aristotle. Does that mean we are now in Heaven? Doesn't seem we have much to look forward to." The low ripple of amusement in the crowd was mostly genuine. The Scaliger leaned forward, running a hand over the shoulders of a hound. His eyes narrowed. "I am interested, though, in the idea of three in one. Was it an early prophecy of the Trinity? Should we count Aristotle among the Prophets?"

The abbot snorted. "No doubt Monsignor Alighieri would agree. He certainly made a saint of that pagan scribbler Virgil. So many pagan poets and philosophers got fine treatment, while good churchmen were lambasted. But you missed one, Alighieri! I didn't notice the Greek philosopher Zeno in your journey through Hell."

The aquiline lips curled beneath the black beard. "That doesn't mean he isn't there. There are so many souls, I did not have time to name them all. If there is anyone you are particularly curious about, I'll inquire on my next visit."

The crowd erupted. Only Pietro knew how hard Dante had to work to maintain his composure. Embedded in his many fine qualities was a discomfort in crowds. Over the years he'd learned to mask it with an acerbic wit.

Above the noise the abbot leveled an accusing finger. "You, sir, are a pagan, posing as a Christian."

"Better that than an ass posing as a lamb of God." Beneath a fresh spate of laughter, Dante's head turned and his eyes fixed on Pietro. *Oh no,* thought Pietro. Recusing himself, Dante crooked a beckoning finger. "My lords, this is my elder son. Pietro, remind our host, what were the three types of heaven Aristotle named?"

Pietro wanted to hide himself in the fluttering drapes. *So here it is,* he thought, *the punishment for being late. And for the hat. First the abbot is put down for calling Virgil a scribbler. Now it's my turn.* He spied his little brother's large grin in the crowd. *Shut up, twerp.* Endeavoring to recall his lessons, he took a breath. "The first he uses is closest to what we mean by Heaven. It is the seat of all that is divine."

"Correct. And the second?"

"Next, he uses heaven to encompass the stars, the moon, and the sun. The heavens of astrology."

Pietro hoped his father would expound and expand, but all he was rewarded with was a curt nod. "And the third?"

"The third . . . it's . . . well, ah—"

"Yes?"

Pietro took a chance. "It's—it's everything. The whole universe. It's the totality of the world, everything in and around us. Just as all the pagan gods were only aspects of Jupiter, or Zeus, so all living beings are—are aspects of heaven."

Dante gazed at his son. "Crudely put. But not inaccurate."

Thank God Antonia isn't here. Pietro's sister would have quoted it, exactly. *In Greek.*

Cangrande's voice was rich and deep. "Sounds like Bolognese rhetoric. The body, the body, the body is all. So, Abbot, it seems Heaven is all around us. Is that your argument? Are we indeed inside Heaven without our knowing it?"

Before the abbot could answer, the fool in silk raised his head. "I don't know about your faith—I try not to learn more than I have to of the divine carpenter—but mine says that man was created outside Heaven. And that Lucifer was cast out of Heaven for warring against Jehovah. How can you be cast out of the infinite?"

"Theology!" sneered the abbot. "We need no God logic here, however fashionable. What is, is!"

Dante said, "The fool raises an interesting question. Aristotle was, of course, discussing more the nature of physics than that of astrology. But we have strayed. I did not say that there was more than one Heaven. I said that the heavens were written, and must be read. I apologize for my use of the word *heavens.* I should have said *the stars.*"

The abbot stamped his foot. "I object to the idea that the—that Heaven is a *book!* No doubt you think it is written in the vernacular as well?" Pietro's father had written *L'Inferno* in the tongue the churchmen called *vulgare,* eschewing the Latin of the scholars. He maintained that *vulgare* was what the Romans had spoken a thousand years before, while the Church Latin was far removed from the common speech of all Italians, past and present. Ironically enough, he'd used Latin when writing his treatise praising the common tongue.

In place of defending *vulgare,* Dante said, "The Book of Heaven is written in a universal language, for it is our universe. It is the language spoken by all the world before the Tower of Babel. When God created the planets and stars, he gave us a map of our fate. By reading the stars, we create ourselves. It takes a willful act upon the part of the reader to interpret that fate. You would know that if you were a true pastor."

Before the abbot could reply, Cangrande leaned forward, radiating intensity. "You're saying that how a man interprets the stars affects how his life will run?"

"Yes."

Nearby, the bishop shook his head. "That seems to mean there is a fixed path to man's journey. That is predestination, and clearly contrary to church doctrine." At his elbow the abbot stamped a foot for emphasis.

Dante smiled. "Imagine you are reading a book—any book. The author has written a lovely poem, with a picture clear in his mind. He describes a cloud-laden sky. When you read over his words, an entirely different picture comes to your mind's eye. Where for him the skies are full of puffy white clouds, you imagine them to be grey and full of evil portents. You are not wrong, the picture is your own. It is not, however, what the author intended. The act of reading changes both the poem and the reader.

"Thus it is with the stars. Astrology is a science as much about man as about the celestial spheres. It is not enough to observe them. They must be interpreted actively. On those interpretations rest our fates, individual and collective."

Cangrande's interest was palpable. "So, the Lord has given us the song of each life, but it is up to us to sing it well?"

One bored man shifted his legs and said, "It's a shame, then, O great Capitano, that your own singing makes your dogs run and hide."

"Truth from Passerino!" cried someone else.

Cangrande was the first to laugh, and the loudest, but his eyes remained on Dante. "Well, poet?"

An audition. Or a challenge. Or acknowledgment of a test already passed? "It is well put, my lord. It takes an act of will on both the part of the Divine Author and the humble mortal reader to create a destiny. God has made his will known—but are we intelligent enough to read it in his stars?"

The abbot was about to continue the argument, but the Capitano had evidently heard enough. Canting his head to one side, he addressed his fool. "This talk of poetry has put me in the mind to hear some. Come, rascal, entertain us briefly before we dine."

Pietro had met the short clown the night before. Emanuele di Salamone dei Sifoni, better known as Manoello Giudeo—Manuel the Jew—cynic, bawd, and Master of Revels for my lord Cangrande's court. He bowed, a comical sight in itself. From somewhere a rebec and bow appeared. A sprightly jig filled the hall. This was not a poem of lofty aims. The Jewish fool hopped in step, causing the bells on his sleeves to ring in time with the music. When he sang it was in the coarsest Veronese dialect:

Indeed a crown
Verona wears,
This trumpet blown
This deed declares!

Warhorse and charger,
Fighting man, banner,
Cuirass and sword,
All a-charging!

Hear the tramp, tramp,
Foot soldiers stamp.
Tramp tramp tramp tramp tramp!
Hear how they go!

As he bellowed, he mimicked the soldiers he sang of, and the palisade echoed with roars of approval. He then threw his hips forward and his shoulders back, imitating Cangrande's stride. The Capitano's chest heaved and his eyes watered. Even the grizzled bishop tapped his toe on the marble floor in time with the rhythm. The greyhound by the Capitano's feet watched the bishop's toe, ready to pounce.

The falcons caw caw
The hounds grr grr
The greyhounds grr rr rr
So they can have their sport!

Enjoying the song as much as anyone, Pietro looked about to share it with his new friend. Mariotto was standing close to the elder Montecchi. His body language indicated he was put out.

Here are great sports
For all and for few
And I've seen a joust
Played with fiery swords!

Clapping hands encouraged Emanuele to move in wider and wider circles through the crowd as he rushed about imitating the butting of rams. Dante, politely sitting and gazing out the window, flinched as the jester dashed by.

Pietro slipped away from his father's side to join Mariotto. Sotto voce, he asked, "What's wrong?"

"I'm in trouble. I was supposed to greet the son of another visiting noble as well as you." He shook his head. "Seems like a—"

Detecting a snobbery that, in truth, didn't surprise him, Pietro said, "Like a what?"

"See for yourself. He's over there." He pointed to the burly youth who had been engaged in the war discussion with the bridegroom. The fellow was obviously enjoying the improvised song, stomping his feet and clapping loudly.

> *For love is in the hall*
> *Of the Lord of the stair*
> *Where even without wings*
> *I seemed to fly!*

"He's from Capua," whispered Mariotto. "His father is thinking about relocating the family business here."

"His family's in business? I thought—"

"Yes, I know. They are noble. But it's a nobility that cost them."

"Ah." Mariotto didn't have to say more. The greatest blight on the nobility was the sale of noble titles by kings, popes, and emperors. When a noble died without heir, the local ruler was able to take the defunct title and the land attached and sell it for a profit to any wealthy, ambitious member of the merchant class. They often lived as nobles before nobility was granted them. These *gente nuova* dressed in noble fashion, kept house, ate, read, traveled exactly as the nobility did. A disgrace to be sure, but a growing practice nonetheless.

There was another side, of course. Though the nobility was loath to admit it, the influx of new blood into their ranks often helped maintain their thinning numbers. Many who were noble today came from ignoble origins—such as the della Scalas. No one was ever crass enough to point that out, though.

"I'm to show him around the city," said Mariotto.

"You ought to charge a fee." The attempt at levity fell on young Montecchio's ears with all the aplomb of a wounded duck. "What if I joined you?"

Mariotto looked up. "Would you? Would your father let you?"

"It might take some doing, but I think I can arrange it." Pietro grimaced. "We might have to bring my little brother with us."

Mariotto brightened. "My thanks, nevertheless . . ."

The noise rose to a deafening pitch, drowning out Montecchio's words. The Master of Revels was bringing his song to a crashing end.

> *And this is the lord*
> *With great valor,*
> *Whose grand honor*
> *Is spread on earth and sea!*

Cangrande didn't wait for the accompanying music to stop. He jumped to his feet and embraced the diminutive genius, kissing him on both cheeks. Then he turned to Dante, still unmoved by the revels around him. Eyes twinkling, the Capitano said, "I am astonished that this man who plays the fool has gained the favor of all, while you who are called wise can't do the same."

Dante Alaghieri looked up at the lord of Verona, face devoid of expression. "You should not be astonished that fools find joy in other fools."

At which Cangrande fell in beside the poet and laughed until he cried.

✦ ◇ ✦

The lone rider had tears streaming from his eyes when he was stopped by the guards at Verona's Ponte Pietro, the gate leading east. "Where's the fire, lad?" asked the captain of the guard.

"I know him," said the sergeant-at-arms. "Muzio. He's a page to Lord Nogarola's brother."

Realizing this might be something serious, the captain of the guard's tone grew more brusque. "What's happened?"

The boy couldn't speak. He reached for a wineskin at his hip, but a soldier got to him first with a flask of spirits. The boy coughed, then croaked out his news. "Vicenza. It's burning!"

FOUR

The good humor on the loggia gave way to hunger as the smells drifting from the dining hall—wine, spiced meat, melting cheese, warm bread and olive oil—started men salivating.

Pietro was singing a ribald chorus with the groom's friends, hoping his father wasn't listening, when he noticed a woman in the great doorway. She was older than he might have thought, but lovely, done up in the new fashion, with her dark hair in wavy curls framing her oval face. Dressed in hanging panels of brocaded gold and burgundy, she glided into the room. Giovanna of Antioch, great-granddaughter of Emperor Frederick, sister of Cecchino's mother, and wife to the Capitano of Verona.

Removing himself from the cluster of men, Cangrande strode over to her, the wiry greyhound dogging his heels. She went up on her toes and spoke in his ear.

At the corners of the doorway beyond her, two children appeared. Pietro nudged Mariotto and whispered, "I thought Cangrande didn't have an heir."

"Not by his wife, anyway," replied Mariotto dourly. Realizing he'd spoken aloud, he colored. "I apologize. Those are his brother's sons, Alberto and Mastino."

From Mariotto's indicating nods, Pietro learned that Alberto was the larger of the pair. He was a pleasant-looking child, about eight or nine years old. Indeed, he seemed embarrassed to be where he knew he shouldn't. The youngest man in the room was probably Pietro's brother at fourteen years, almost a man, also a guest. Alberto knew the world of adults was still outside his sphere.

Just behind him, prodding him onward, young Mastino looked to be about six. Undoubtedly a della Scala, his face bore all the easy magnificence that graced his uncle. Yet in watching him, Pietro saw a little devil at work. Mastino pressed his brother on into the room. When Alberto wasn't scolded, little Mastino strode boldly past his pliable older brother. He stood on his heels, hands on hips, looking around the room as if he owned it. He was a genuinely gorgeous child.

Cangrande bowed to his wife, stepping back as she addressed his guests. "Gentlemen, lords, and honored guests! The wedding feast is prepared!" A cheer. "I regret to say, though, that my husband has shamed me. Shamed me, his loving wife, by offering his nephew a feast that far outstrips the one for our own nuptials all those years ago. He has done me shame by offering to you what he never gave to me. So you must all assist him by making sure there is no evidence left!" Laughter, more appreciative cheers.

Cangrande draped an arm around his wife's shoulders. "Someone, assist the groom to his seat at the head of the table. He seems to have found the courage he needs to face his wedding night—if only he can remember what to do!" With an accompanying roar the group broke apart and prepared to move into the feasting hall below.

A hand slapped Pietro's shoulder. "Nice job of wriggling."

Pietro didn't bother to turn. "You're just jealous, Poco. You couldn't have done it." As a boy, Pietro had had such trouble with his brother Jacopo's name that he'd reversed the sounds, turning it into Poco. As Jacopo grew older, the nickname became an appropriate joke. The boy was short for his age. He'd also inherited their father's protruding lower lip, which set his young face in a perpetual pout.

"Who needs Aristotle?" asked Poco.

"Anyone with sense," came the voice that made them both stiffen. Dante's fingers clipped his younger son a light flick on the ear. "Pietro, who is your new friend?" Pietro told him. The poet looked surprised and uttered a mysterious, "Interesting." Before Pietro could say anything, though, Dante said, "Come along, Jacopo. Pietro, I'll see you downstairs."

Cowed, Poco trailed closely behind as Dante made for the exit. The bridegroom was being physically carried out the same doors by three friends while a fourth friend plied him with bread and water. Little Mastino and Alberto followed, poking the groom in the ribs to see if they could make him vomit.

Mariotto and Pietro hung back from the crowd of guests wandering out to their various suites to change for the meal. It would be at the least another half hour before they were all seated and able to eat, and Pietro recognized it as the perfect time for Mariotto to approach the young Capuan he was obliged to befriend.

The fellow was staring out the arched palisade at a rider galloping into the courtyard below. The Capuan's doublet and hose were very fine but showed a reckless neglect around the elbows and knees. His muscles looked as slack as a sackful of horsefeed. Hearing footsteps on the marble behind him he turned, face haughty. "I'll be there in a minute." He must have thought they were servants.

"Ah, good day," said Pietro. "I'm, ah, my name is Pietro—"

"He's Pietro Alaghieri of Florence," said Mariotto, making sure to pronounce it correctly. "He's the son of the great poet Dante. I'm Mariotto Montecchio."

"Veronese?"

"Just like the best horses, I was born and bred right here."

After a brief pause, the sandy-haired stranger realized he had not reciprocated the introduction. "I'm Antony—Antonio Capecelatro, second son of Ludovico Capecelatro of Capua."

Mariotto nodded. "We were wondering if you'd care to explore the city with us."

Antony frowned. "I thought you said you lived here?"

"I do," said Mariotto.

"Don't you know it already, then?"

For the first time Mariotto was flustered. "Well, yes—I do. But Alaghieri here is new to Verona. So are you. I thought we might go out after dinner and explore the city together. Maybe we can find some contests or games to take part in."

"Games?" said Antony, livening up. "Are there games here?"

"All the time, when the Capitano is in residence. Didn't you hear—he commanded games for tomorrow."

The Capuan was skeptical. "All princes do that—and they're always pitiful!"

Mariotto smiled knowingly. "You haven't seen Cangrande's games. He held a Corte Bandita three years ago, and eight men died. Three more lost an eye apiece." His own eyes gleamed. "There are cat-battings and bear-baitings. And there's the Palio every year. That's known as the toughest race in Italy."

The Capuan was intrigued. "Inventive, is he?"

"You have no idea," said Mariotto. "Now, do you want to come with us tonight—or would you rather wait here with the old men and the women?"

Antony clapped Mariotto on the shoulder. "I should throw you over the balcony for that, pipsqueak."

Eyes beaming, Mariotto said, "Try it! Look, we can find our supper in the city, and perhaps meet some women. Tomorrow there'll be knife fights and wrestling matches on the bridge—maybe even a goose-pull!"

To a mental list of Mariotto's attributes, Pietro added fickle. He felt himself being relegated to the role of tagalong. He said, "Maybe we can have a swimming race in the Adige." Swimming was one arena Pietro excelled in.

Antony reached out a hand to grip Pietro's shoulder. Though not taller than either youth, his bulk and wide peasant hands made him seem gigantic. "I will follow you two to the end of the earth, if it means not another minute of poetry—no offense, Alaghieri."

"None taken," said Pietro, moving out of range of Antony's grasp and surreptitiously rubbing life back into his arm.

One of the huge falcons let loose a cry. The birds were all still on their perches, waiting for the Master of the Hunt to return them to the aviary. They were fidgety, having been disturbed by the noisy dance.

"Do you want to see my bird?" asked Mariotto. He raced over to the far end of the loggia where a young sparrow hawk, just growing to maturity, was sitting. "Dilios!" The red hawk twisted its blindfolded head toward its master's voice. Montecchio reached out a hand to lift the creature from the stand. He unhooked the tether on its leg and transferred the hawk to his own arm. "He's still small enough that I can hold him without protection," he said, indicating his arm. It bore only one sheath of leather from the light-colored farsetto. Had the bird been grown, it could have easily pierced Mariotto's arm with its pounces. "Here, Dilios. There's a good boy."

"Dilios?" said Antony, puzzled. "What kind of name is that?"

"It's Greek." Mariotto produced the new jesses Pietro had bought him.

"The only survivor of Thermopylae," supplied Pietro.

Antony look a little embarrassed. He said, "I'm a dunce about literature." Mariotto and Pietro shared an amused look.

Montecchio had just begun placing the new jesses on Dilios's leg when a door slammed, causing all the hawks and falcons in the hall to cry out. The

three youths turned to see Cangrande della Scala stalking into the empty palisade, a parchment in his hand. His air of languid amusement was gone. In its
place was the crisp, clipped stride of the general.

Trailing behind the Capitano was a dust-covered messenger, no more than
thirteen years old, breathless and exhausted. No one came to wash his hands
or stop his shoes leaving tracks across the marble. Behind them capered
Jupiter, the Scaliger's greyhound, tail stiff, head low.

Something was happening. With a quick look among them, the trio of
youths quickly slipped behind the nearest curtain. Mariotto used the loop
that hung from Dilios's blindfold to clamp his beak closed. From their hiding
place at the far end of hall, they watched and listened.

"This happened this morning?" The Capitano's eyes scanned the few
written lines again and again, ripping every ounce of meaning from them.

"Just—before dawn," gasped the rider. "Ant—Ant—"

The Scaliger looked up. "When you can! Don't waste my time!" The
youth cowed, Cangrande's tone softened. "Get your breath back, then tell.
You did well getting this past the enemy. A minute more won't break us." The
parchment was glanced at once more. A wry grin came to the thin lips.
"Good for you, Ponzoni. I didn't think you had it in you."

Cangrande turned his full attention to the messenger. "I'm going to put
some questions to you. You will answer with nods. Understand?"

The young rider started to speak, then caught himself and nodded.

"Vicenza's suburb is taken?"

Nod.

"They put up a fight?"

Shake.

"They went willingly?"

A hesitant, almost fearful, nod. There was no change in the face that questioned him.

"Antonio Nogarola is in charge in the city?"

Nod.

"Bailardino must still be in the north."

It wasn't a question, but the young messenger nodded anyway.

"Has he fortified the inner city wall?"

A nod, but there was some hesitation.

"He was just ordering it when you left."

A vigorous nod, then the lad opened his mouth. His breath had returned. "Not only the walls—Ser Nogarola ordered the houses in San Pietro fired to deprive the enemy of cover."

"Excellent!" Cangrande clapped a hand on the messenger's shoulder. "You've done well. One more question—was there any sign of the Count of San Bonifacio?"

"They say he led the assault into the suburb."

Cangrande swore, then patted the boy on the shoulder. "What is your name, youngster?"

"Muzio, lord."

"Muzio, you've completed your charge. You may now have any bed in the palace. Just repeat what you told me to my master-at-arms below. Ask for Nico da Lozzo. Tell him I said to muster as many men as he can and ride to Vicenza." His eyes flickered to a wineskin hanging from the lad's belt. "Is it full?" Without being asked the boy unslung it from his belt and handed it to the Capitano. "My thanks," said Cangrande, gripping the skin in one hand while the other made a fist to gently prod the boy's shoulder. "Now go, tell Nico what you know. And tell him I've gone already."

Full of new energy, the boy made to run off when the great man touched his shoulder again. "One last question. Is the wife of Bailardino Nogarola well?"

"She was when I saw her, lord. She was helping Signore Nogarola give the orders."

"Of course she was. Go now, lad."

The sound of the boy's footsteps echoed among the empty loggia. For a moment the great man stood alone. He lifted the wineskin to his lips and drank off the contents in a single pull, then tossed the empty bladder aside.

In a flurry of movement, the Scaliger approached one of the perches. His hands moved among several of the birds waiting there. They made noise as he released the tether from one of them. It was the same merlin he had petted earlier. With a light step, the blindfolded bird was on his shoulder.

To the seemingly empty hall he said, "If you're coming, try to keep up."

Then Cangrande disappeared behind the billowing curtains of the nearest arch of the loggia. Seconds later Jupiter began to whimper. The three hidden watchers emerged a second later. Save for the greyhound and the falcons, they were quite alone.

Glancing around, Antony said, "Where the hell . . . ?"

"Was he talking to us?" wondered Mariotto.

"He didn't know we were here," said Antony with certainty.

Pietro ran to the arch Cangrande had disappeared behind. The lord of Verona was gone. The only thing here was the greyhound, straining against the railing to the balcony. Looking at the cobbled street one level below Pietro said, "He jumped."

"What?" Mariotto and Antony joined him, arriving just in time to see a golden-headed blur race out from the stables below them, heading east down a private street. Not bothering with stairs, Cangrande had found a horse and started out for Vicenza.

Pietro shared blank looks with Mariotto and Antony. In unison, Mariotto and Antony imitated Cangrande, leaping off the balcony to the stables below, Mariotto still bearing the bird on his arm.

Pietro thought they were both crazy. But already he had swung his own legs over the rail and dropped hard to the cobbled street. In moments he was joining them in their search for horses.

Above them the greyhound raced for the door, down the stairs to the stable, determined not to be left behind.

FIVE

Outside Verona

On a borrowed—*stolen!*—horse, Pietro tried to keep up with Mariotto and Antony as they tore after the Capitano. Already he was out of sight. Blessedly they'd taken the time to saddle their horses, something Cangrande hadn't bothered with.

It was not hard to trace the path he had taken. He'd barreled through streets, dodging or jumping all obstructions, shouting out curt warnings. Shaken citizens were just recovering as three more horses dashed past, two of their riders whooping and hollering. All assumed it was another of the Capitano's games—a hunt through the streets, with a live rider as the prey. Stranger things had happened.

Even though they followed the path he made for them, somehow the three riders were unable to catch up to the lord of Verona. When they reached the Roman bridge on the bank of the Adige, they were stymied by a caravan of millet-bearing mules. But before they had passed a dozen words with the on-lookers, the dog Jupiter dashed past them, heading north toward a smaller bridge atop the Adige's oxbow embrace of the city. Mariotto watched the greyhound go and cried, "He's making for the Ponte di Pietro!" Wheeling their horses around, they followed in the dog's wake.

The stone and wood bridge was not as sturdy as the Roman one, and thus was less crowded. Passing under the open gate they left the city, hoping against hope to catch up to the madman leading them on.

Pietro could already feel the stiff leather saddle biting into him. The stirrups hurt his slippered feet. It had been almost a year since he had ridden this hard, in sport, not war. Not that Capecelatro acknowledged the difference. He shouted as though this were nothing but a great adventure, and Pietro could tell that Mariotto was infected with the Capuan's joy.

Pietro wished he could feel it, too, but his misgivings held him in check. *What is the Scaliger thinking? He can't take on the whole Paduan army single-handed!*

He won't be single-handed if we can catch him, insisted the devil's advocate in his head.

And what can we do? he retorted. *We don't even have knives! Stupid wedding etiquette!*

Still, he didn't turn back. Seventeen years old, he'd been raised on stories of the battle of Campaldino, where a certain young cavalryman named Durante from the undistinguished house of Alighieri had fought with distinction. Poet, lawyer, politician, and soldier. So much to live up to. Pietro spurred on.

The hound Jupiter, trailing behind the horses, tongue dangling, again dashed ahead and barked. Seconds later Cangrande came into view. He glanced back but didn't slow down, counting on the boys to catch up to him. He didn't stop until they reached a bridge just south of San Martino. A man was bathing on the near bank of the Fibbio. He leapt from the water and, throwing a grubby cloak over his nakedness, ran to collect his toll. Cangrande looked back with an abashed grin. "Anyone have any money?"

Pietro reached into his meager purse and paid the hermit for their passage.

"Well," said Cangrande. "Come on!"

Soon they left the road, angling north through patches of wood and hills. "Wait!" cried Antony. "Where are we going?"

Cangrande was already pulling ahead, leaving the three boys riding together. Mariotto said, "If he keeps going he'll pass the castle at Illasi. He took it last year, rebuilt it, and filled it with loyal men. We'll probably change horses there and gather troops. To get there we have to ford the Illasi River."

"Lead the way!" roared Antony.

Taking his place in the rear, Pietro winced as the saddle jumped under him.

✦   ✧   ✦

They heard the river before ever they saw it. Two hours had passed since the mad leap from the balcony, and they were riding through a wild orchard.

Their horses' hoofbeats knocked loose cherries from the branches. Sweat poured down the animals' bodies. Pietro couldn't feel anything other than the chill sweat on his face, and he was sure he'd never walk again. Or unclench his hands. Or relax his jaw. He was having a devilish time just keeping himself in line behind Antony and Mariotto. They were both excellent riders, the one well taught and used to the saddle, the other a born sportsman. And the unsaddled Cangrande was outstripping them all. Pietro felt stupid and sluggish.

They had to stop outside the gate of the castle at Illasi while Cangrande proved who he was, then they were in a courtyard scarred and blackened by old siege fires. Servants were sent running to and fro, horses were saddled, knights donned armor.

"What about us?" asked Antony loud enough for Cangrande to hear him, but the great man was busy in conference with the garrison commander.

"I'll get fresh horses," said Mariotto and ran off.

"I'll steal some swords," said Antony.

"I'll . . ." Pietro couldn't think of anything to do, so he examined the hurrying soldiers. Thirty or so. Versus the full-armed might of Padua. The madness hadn't ended. It was still impossible.

His father's voice said, *You could stay here. No one would think less of you.*

Except you, thought Pietro.

Antony returned with swords and helms. "They don't have spare armor," he said. "Just pourpoints." Pietro found himself fitted with the Eastern-style armor whose popularity had grown in the West since the Crusades. Composed of layers of cloth, rags, or tow, it was quilted to a foundation of canvas or leather, then covered in linen or silk. Usually an undergarment in battle, a secondary layer of protection.

Pietro's helmet was a simple practice helmet of plain steel, little more than a bucket with a cross cut for eyes. It didn't fit well, leaving four inches between the dome and his scalp. The sword was a decent three-foot-long bastard, the technical term for a hand-and-a-half grip. Plenty of burrs but serviceable. Pietro strapped a leather baldric across his chest and fitted the sword home on his left hip.

As opposed to Pietro, the Capuan wore on his head a coif of mail. A single band of thick metal encompassed his head. Below and above that band, chain links clinked and clattered together. The links went under his chin and hooked in front of his left ear.

From a building Cangrande emerged hopping on one foot, pulling on a stolen boot. Pietro thought that was a good idea but had no idea where in the castle to lay hands on some, or whom to ask.

From a page the Scaliger took a helmet, old-fashioned in design, a silver-plated dome with closing cheek pieces pocked with fifty holes for breathing, the holes too small for any weapon to catch.

Mariotto arrived with fresh horses. Pietro eyed his, a fine dusty gelding.

"These are beautiful horses," observed Antony as he mounted.

Mariotto preened. "They come from my family stables. Half of the Capitano's horses come from Montecchi stock."

"I'll have to come and have a look," said Antony. "See what the hell you feed these monsters."

Cangrande leapt into the stirrups of a fine stallion and waved to his band of men. He flashed a fine set of teeth at the three young men and said, "Keep up!" With characteristic abandon, the Scaliger spurred out through the gate. Jupiter appeared from a corner of the yard and dashed off after his master, and the boys joined the rush of soldiers out the gates after the Greyhound.

The Greyhound. The title was certainly apt. How could anyone see the man and not believe he was the prophesized savior of Italy? Pietro's father, at least, had no doubt. *And there shall come in Italy Il Veltro* . . . Dante had taken the ancient prophecy and given it form in the very first canto of his *Commedia*. Having now met the Capitano, Pietro would have followed Cangrande into the Pit of Cocytus.

The riders found a steady rhythm across the hilly land at the foot of the Alps. There were cherry trees on this side of the Illasi River too. A wrong twist of the reins, and both rider and horse would come to an ignominious end. The leading horses brought cherries crashing down from the branches, pelting the riders at the back of the formation.

The ride overland was slowed twice by muddy streams. Cangrande's horse didn't slacken pace until actually in the water. The garrison knights were not as confident. They slowed at each sign of water and walked their heavily armored mounts across. Cangrande didn't wait for them. Once out of the water, he and Jupiter tore off again at a breakneck pace, followed directly by the trio of youths. Soon the garrison was just a distant rumble behind them.

Cresting a low ridge after the second water crossing, Pietro pulled closer to Cangrande's horse and heard something startling. The Scaliger was singing, matching the rhythm to the stride of his horse:

Here lions are,
Here leopards fare,
And great rams,
I saw, butt one and all!

And for a laugh,
That echoes far,
Ha ha ha ha!
Until you want to die!

He noticed Pietro staring incredulously and laughed. "Come on, you must know it by now!" He began again in his deep baritone, and Pietro tried to remember the words. He picked it up the second time through, and they sang together.

Sentirai poi li giach
Che fan guei padach—
Giach, giach, giach, gaich, gaich—
Quando gli odo andare!

This wasn't war they were riding to. It was a joust, a lark, a joyful day of sport. Pietro sang out loud and long in his best church voice. Antony joined in, and when they ran out of lyrics they created new ones.

They were passing a vineyard during a lull and Mariotto shouted, "It's close to here!"

"Vicenza?" asked Pietro hopefully.

"No! My family's castle! Montecchio! It's off that way! Through the haunted wood!" He gestured to a thick forest off to the right.

"Haunted?"

Montecchio put his finger to his nose with a knowing look. Pietro laughed warily. "If we live, you'll have to show it me!"

"If? I'll have you by for supper tonight after we whip their hides raw! Then we can face the ghosts!"

Antony cheered, "That's the way!"

Pietro smiled and turned in time to duck a low-hanging branch. "I can't see a damned thing," he muttered, his voice reverberating around his helmeted head like a lone psalm in a church.

✦ ◇ ✦

Cangrande was slowing, his horse tramping along a line of juniper bushes. They were still a good four miles from the city proper, but smoke was visible. Pietro glanced back—the knights of the Illasi garrison were probably two miles back. Ahead were the closed northern gates, far from the invested suburb of San Pietro. A handful of men stood atop the outer ring of walls. He remembered thinking just this morning that the Roman walls of Verona were obsolete, but if an army penetrated a city's outer walls, it would be just those walls that the citizens would rally behind. The walls of any city were fortifica tion against beasts and lunatics as well as armies and weather. But now Vicenza's walls were holding out friend and foe alike.

The trio pulled up when Cangrande did. Jupiter stopped too, panting. The Capitano removed his silver helm to better view the scene. "How now? How now? What have we here?"

Pietro squinted, looking for whatever it was that the Capitano thought he saw.

"It's clear," said Antony brightly.

"Indeed it is," replied Cangrande.

"Shouldn't we go on, then?" asked the Capuan.

The Scaliger waved a hand at the open field below them. "I was thinking we should have a picnic."

Mariotto snickered. Antony looked put out. Pulling his horse around to face them, Cangrande turned his back on the city he'd ridden all afternoon to rescue. He swung one leg up and rested it on the neck of his sweating beast, careful of the spur.

"A picnic?" asked Antony.

"Well, we missed the wedding dinner. Things are always escaping me. I should have brought some wine from Illasi for us to share. Or at least some sausage. You'd like that, wouldn't you, Jupiter? Yes! Sausage!" The hound barked twice in assent.

The trio didn't quite know what to make of the Scaliger's demeanor. Pietro watched the great lord of Verona lift his face to scan the sky. "What are you looking for, lord?"

"Velox."

"Velox?"

"Fortis Velox—the merlin. He's been trailing us, but I don't see him now.

At least I have Jupiter. I can use him to instruct Ponzino and Asdente how to hunt foxes."

Pietro couldn't make heads or tails of this conversation. It was Mariotto who knew a cue when he heard one. "Foxes?"

"Yes, foxes. But I thought they already knew." He sighed.

Antony was smiling. "How do you hunt foxes?"

The Capitano took on the air of a patient teacher. "There are two ways. You can beat the bushes, and chase it when it emerges. Or you can lay a trap for it and let it come to you."

Now Pietro was smiling as well. "What kind of trap?"

"Why, a nice plump chicken, of course. With three big feathers." He held three fingers over his head, imitating the three flags hanging limply on the walls of the city behind him. "We are the foxes, my boys. Here is our chicken. And look—the guard dog is away! What could be better?" A finger went up in the air. "But the fox is a clever little devil. He sees no guard dog, no fence, no impediment at all between him and his plump, juicy chicken. What does this make him think?"

"Too good to be true," said Pietro.

"Just so." The Scaliger turned to look over his shoulder at the open slopes between themselves and the city. "A hunter must choose his bait carefully. In this case, our Paduan friends have been a little too cautious. I doubt they honestly expected to see me here today. And they know I'm worried that the population of Vicenza might change sides if faced with a long siege. It's common knowledge that I am not at the height of my popularity inside the city."

"What does that matter?" asked Antony. "You're their vicar."

"The only authority I have here," said Cangrande tranquilly, "was given to me by Emperor Heinrich, and what good is the favor of a dead man? So, Ponzino de' Ponzoni, from all evidence a decent though uninspired soldier, knows that I am worried about the safety of the Vicentine garrison. In the throes of that fear, I might do something foolish, like riding out alone and unarmed to the defense of an invested city."

"My lord," observed Antonio, "that's what you did."

"Ridiculous. I had you three. So I arrive, and what do I see?"

Again Pietro looked toward the city gates. There was a stone bridge, pre-Roman by its decrepit appearance. It crossed a deep dip in the land that had probably once been used as a moat but had since dried up. Around the bridge there was nothing but green grassy slopes slowly changing color as the season dictated. Not even a bird stirred. "Nothing."

"Exactly! Not a thing! An open field for me to ride across and devour the chicken. How wonderful!" Cangrande pulled a comic frown. "Only I am a little disturbed. I was forced to recite my Gallic Wars, my Vegetius, even my Homer. I know the importance of surrounding an invested city. It prevents reinforcements from strengthening the will of those unfortunates besieged. It's the basic principle that Caesar used so brilliantly at Alesia. Now, if I have read these works, I know that my worthy opponent the Podestà of Padua has read them as well. I wonder how he could have forgotten so basic a lesson? But he must have! For I see no troops! The henhouse is open and ripe for pillaging." He gestured to the open expanse of land between them and the gates.

Pietro nodded. "Where are they?"

"Under the bridge," answered Cangrande, "and possibly in the ravine farther north. If he had any brains, he'd have put a thin line of men in the open. Then I might have raced for the far gates in the hope of outrunning the guards. At that moment the hidden soldiers could have leapt out and slaughtered me." He sighed in evident disappointment. "Upon reflection, I would wager it was Vanni who set it up. One thing is for certain, though: Bonifacio knows nothing about this. That's excellent news. It means they're poorly organized, and not making use of the wiser heads among them." He grinned at the trio as they drank in his every word. "Someday I'll meet an equal, and then you'll see some fireworks, boys." Then, mock-mournfully, he added, "But so far, it hasn't happened."

"So what do we do?" asked Antony. "Just sit here?"

"I think we can make it," opined Mariotto. "We know where they are. With luck, we can be past them and to the gates before they ride out from their bridge."

Cangrande shook his head, "Though I always like to have it, I never expect luck to side with me. Too often luck is a fickle bitch. And though you're right, we might make it past them, they could still raise an alarum, and I don't want Asdente and the Count to know I'm here. Yet."

Antony practically spat. "So we do nothing?"

"We remind Asdente of a fact he seems to have forgotten."

"And that is?"

The Capitano's blue eyes twinkled. "I am not the fox in this drama. I am the hound."

"The Great Hound," supplied Mariotto.

"The Greyhound," said Pietro.

The Scaliger's blue eyes fixed on Pietro coldly. Flustered, young Alaghieri braced himself for a rebuke. Before it was delivered, however, Cangrande cocked an ear. "How now? What's this noise?" Behind them, the Illasi garrison was arriving. "Not bad time for horses so heavily laden. Now, I'm going to have a word with my commander and then, because you've been so patient, I'll take you with me on a little constitutional."

He cantered away, leaving Pietro wondering what he'd said. For the first time in their brief acquaintance, the Greyhound had seemed genuinely angry. The chill from those blue eyes still clung to Pietro's skin. *I called him the Greyhound. But isn't that his title?* The Greyhound was on all his banners. Pietro's own father had referred to him as such over and over again. Why, then, had his eyes blazed at the mention of it?

Whatever it was, Mariotto had missed it. "Constitutional?"

Antony rubbed his huge hands together. "I'll say this—he isn't boring!"

Pietro looked out at where Cangrande had said the enemy would be waiting in ambush. At first he saw only the vague multicolored shapes that danced inside his eyes. He blinked them away and tried again. For several seconds he saw nothing at all. Then a shadow under the bridge shifted. Pietro didn't think it was a trick of the light. The Capitano had been prescient. There were mounted knights under the bridge, waiting.

He was so focused on the spot under the bridge that he didn't notice Cangrande's return, and he jumped when he heard a voice say, "Shall we take their bait, signores?" Without waiting for a reply the Scaliger spurred ahead out of the treeline and down the hill. Antony and Mariotto followed on either side, and Pietro quickly fell in with the others.

"Slow and easy," murmured Cangrande. They obeyed, cantering down the slope four abreast, their horses grateful for the relaxed pace. They rode at an easy gait, Cangrande feigning an interest in their surroundings—the hills above, the fields around. Their leader was a consummate actor, and their meandering progress belied the thudding of the young men's blood.

If I die today, thought Pietro, *will my father write the tale? Will he make us brave or foolish?* He tried to put words together as his father would, but the only words that came to him were from *L'Inferno*. He found himself speaking them aloud:

> *Just so do I recall the troops*
> *afraid to leave Caprona with safe-conduct,*
> *Finding themselves among so many enemies.*

Twisting in the saddle to face him, Cangrande spoke Virgil's lines from another canto:

> *And he, as one who understood:*
> *"Here you must banish all distrust,*
> *here all cowardice must be slain.*
> *We have come to where I said*
> *You would see the miserable sinners*
> *Who have lost the good of the intellect."*

Pietro flushed. He hadn't thought he'd spoken loud enough to be heard. "I think my father meant to scorn those who forgo intellect, not praise them."

Cangrande shrugged. "This afternoon he insisted that everything is open to interpretation. Sometimes the intellect must succumb to valor."

"I doubt he'd agree."

"He's a poet. He's forgotten what it feels like to live through deeds!"

Antony snorted. "Poets!"

"Give them their due," said Cangrande. "Without them no one would know of our deeds—and why else do we fight and die but to live on in eternal fame?"

"What else is there to do?" asked Mariotto. "Farm? Raise sheep?"

"There's always women!" cried Cangrande.

"Forgive me, lord," said Mariotto, "but no one was ever famous for loving—at least, no one I'd want to be."

"Hear hear," said Antony.

"Ah, but the best wars are always over a woman!" said Cangrande fondly. "Think of Troy! Helen, she must have been a prize worth winning!"

Antony said, "Think of Abelard! For his love he lost his balls!"

The ensuing laughter carried them down the crest. The enemy had been waiting all day in hope of this moment. The Scaliger, anticipating their impatience, was rewarded. When the four riders were only halfway across the open field, the Paduans crashed from their hiding places under the bridge, emitting shouts of victory.

Cangrande wheeled his horse about and gave it his spurs. "Run!"

Expecting some wonderful attack from the Scaliger, Pietro was stunned. *Run?* Paduan knights bearing down on him, fear crept into his throat and turned his bowels to liquid. He yanked the reins in his left hand and kicked his horse. For one terrifying moment it balked, shaking the muscles on its neck with anger. Pietro kicked again. Finally the horse obeyed, turning to run after the Scaliger, now a good twenty yards away.

It was an uphill race they couldn't win. The slope was rocky, and Pietro's tired horse was having trouble keeping its legs. The horses in pursuit were fresh and the men driving them eager.

Cangrande turned in his saddle, looking back at the approaching soldiers. Pietro saw a hungry smile inside the open cheek pieces of Cangrande's helmet and understanding struck him.

Up the hill, the Illasi garrison stepped out of the treeline to face an entirely unprepared enemy. Now their slower progress was justified. Fully armed and armored, Cangrande's men swung their shields into place and raised their weapons. Some had axes, maces, morning stars, or spears. Most had long swords.

The Paduans saw the garrison and checked. They had numbers, but terrain and the element of surprise were all with the Veronese. They pulled at their reins, turned their horses' heads. But they knew, they had to know, they were trapped.

Still riding uphill, Pietro was passed by the score of Cangrande's men angling full-tilt down into the ambushers, themselves ambushed in return. Some Paduans fought, some tried to flee. It made no difference in the end.

Pietro watched as the Capitano's men ruthlessly chased each of the Paduans down and killed them. It was the first time Pietro had seen so much death, and he made sure he did not turn away. Eerily, Cangrande's men made no noise. The Paduans screamed and shouted, but the Veronese soldiers did their best to do their work in silence. Only the scrape of metal and the thump of hooves marked their passing.

Then the silence was complete. No Paduan had been spared. *That's odd,* thought Pietro with a shiver. *The Scaliger is famous for his clemency.* Reining in beside the Capitano, he asked about this.

Cangrande shrugged. "I couldn't let them live," he said simply. Pietro thought he heard a touch of regret. "If I had, they would have warned Asdente and the Count. I'm in no position to take prisoners, and without an army at my back I need all the advantage surprise can give me."

Which, thought Pietro, *explains the order to kill in silence.*

Cangrande swung his horse back toward the invested city. "Now let's walk these tired horses where they can rest. We have work to do."

✦　◇　✦

At an easy trot Cangrande and his three companions rode up to the gate of Vicenza. It opened, and in minutes Cangrande was standing on the steps to the main palace in conference with Antonio Nogarola, a gruff man of medium height and rotten teeth. They were related by marriage and tragedy, these two families, the Nogarolese having tacked themselves firmly to the tail of the ascendant della Scala star. Quickly Nogarola apprised the Scaliger of recent events. Pietro, eavesdropping shamelessly, thought he heard a reference to a cat and a mention of fishing rods. Then clearly he heard Cangrande ask, "Is she safe?"

In response Nogarola pointed to the windows of the palace above them. "Within, giving orders to the servants. It was her idea to fire the houses in San Pietro."

"Of course it was." Cangrande's voice was bemused. Pietro lost the next words as they turned to look up into the palace. Whatever Nogarola said, Cangrande merely shook his head in reply.

Apropos of nothing, Pietro realized where else he had heard the name Vicenza before. Back in school in Florence, he'd been examined beside the son of a famous Pisan called Vincentio. Probably meant he hailed from Vicenza originally.

Pietro's ears pricked up as Cangrande and Nogarola turned back toward him.

". . . knows I'm here she'll do something foolish."

"Such as?" inquired Nogarola.

"Such as putting on breeches and a helmet and hiding among the knights.

No, let her remain ignorant of my presence until after the battle. Is there any sign of our friendly saint?"

"The Count?" Nogarola spat at the ground. "He's out there. Waved his flag and San Pietro fell over itself welcoming him. You'd think the San Bonifaci would be tired of opposing you. They keep losing."

Nogarola's eyes scanned Cangrande's unlikely companions. He knew Mariotto, of course. Cangrande introduced Antony then pointed to Pietro. "Lord Nogarola, Pietro Alaghieri."

"Alighieri—any relation to the poet?"

Before Pietro could reply, Cangrande said firmly, "Pietro appears to be his own man." A fresh set of horses arrived girded for war. "Come. Time to live forever in glory." Nogarola unclasped the scarlet general's cape from his shoulders and handed it to Cangrande.

An old woman emerged from a nearby doorway. She was visibly drunk, and she stumbled into the street. Cangrande veered, scooped her into his arms, and plucked the wineskin from her fingers. "Mother, *con permisso.*" He quaffed it in one pull, then tossed woman and wineskin to a startled soldier. Bowing, he and Nogarola stalked off to give orders.

Pietro remained where he was, struck dumb by what Cangrande had said. It was a wholly new thought, arriving breathless and filling shoulders, diaphragm, knees. Pietro had been taught from birth that his duty in life was to reflect well upon his father. For all his years, he had endeavored to become the ideal son. That he had succeeded never occurred to him. He constantly saw himself as a failure to both his father and his name.

Seven words from Cangrande and a tangle in Pietro's liver was torn loose. In that moment Pietro Alaghieri began the process of emerging from his father's shadow. It was lost upon him that, in so doing, he passed into one even more dreadful.

SIX

San Pietro

The evening sky was a glorious red as Count Vinciguerra of San Bonifacio viewed the shambles of the Paduan plan.

The slaughter of the suburbanites had ended. That was the good news. The bad news was that the day was wasted, and with it all momentum and surprise. The citizens within the main gates were now girded for a siege. It was up to the Count to give them one. Ponzoni was useless. He couldn't get past the idea that the sacking should never have happened. Why couldn't the little pimple see that the only way to justify it was to take the city? A goal that the Count despaired of reaching with every hour that passed.

It should have been so easy—they had more than enough men to storm the walls of the inner city and savage the guard. But the Paduan men-at-arms had dispersed, all semblance of discipline vanished. The glorious army of justice was now drinking and sleeping in the gardens surrounding the outer wall, using their armor for shade.

Worse than the attack not moving forward, their army was vulnerable. No guards had been posted anywhere in San Pietro. Few of the nobles even wore their weapons, choosing instead to partake of the lesser knights' pleasures. A sea of excess stretched before the Count. It occurred to him that perhaps Asdente's brutal methods were required here. God knew nothing else worked. But weak-stomached Ponzino couldn't bring himself to become that sort of man—a man without honor. It was a damned nuisance that the army was saddled with a general who owned a conscience.

Vinciguerra da San Bonifacio approached the one Paduan commander he felt had the authority to wrench them free of this mess. Giacomo da Carrara was standing with Albertino Mussato, historian and poet. For all the reported antipathy between those two families, they seemed amicable enough at the moment. A good move on Carrara's part. It was never wise to get on the wrong side of a writer.

But then Carrara was one to watch. This unflappable, unreadable man was on the rise. Three years before, there had been five noble families who stood united against the Pup. Murder and death removed two the next year, da Camino departed to assume the lordship of nearby Treviso, and Nico da Lozzo had defected. This left Carrara, or "Il Grande," as he was known, standing alone in the field. It was he who had calmed Padua after the great internal upheavals of the past year. The Count had tried to read his mind over the past three months but could discern nothing beyond a profound patience.

Now the Count didn't bother to bow but simply burst into their conversation. "It's time to intervene," he said, "before the whole day is lost."

Carrara nodded. "Albertino was just saying something similar—though he used more words." Mussato snorted.

The Count addressed Carrara. "We've got to get Ponzino out of sight and tell everyone the orders he's issued."

"He's issued orders?" asked Mussato.

Carrara smiled. "I think Count Vinciguerra means that with him out of sight, no one can say he didn't issue them."

Mussato cocked his head and asked, "Are we sure the Dog isn't here already?"

"Our spies say that not only is he home for his nephew's wedding, but his puppet, Bailardino Nogarola, has gone to beg some help from Germany. The only one left to command is Nogarola's brother."

"And the Dog's blaspheming bitch of a sister," spat the poet.

The Count shouldered the poet out of his way and stood in front of Carrara. "You're the one he'll listen to."

Another voice entered the fray. "And if we get him to hide in his tent, who will be issuing these orders?" Standing beside his uncle, Marsilio da Carrara was darkly handsome. He stared at San Bonifacio, suspicion etched into his sour young face.

"Marsilio." The elder Carrara's tone carried a warning note. "He's right."

"He's Veronese! He's one of the Greyhound's men!"

Giacomo barked out his nephew's name again, harshly, but the Count didn't require anyone to fight his battles for him. Not his personal ones, at any rate. "I am Veronese," said the Count equably. "There is no title I bear more proudly. My ancestors were grinding yours into dust in the days of the first Roman Republic. What I am not, *boy,* is the servant of some jumped-up usurper. The Count of San Bonifacio is no one's minion. I am the scion of a great line. Call me a Scaligeri sympathizer again, and you'll be the last of your father's line."

The boy's uncle edged his horse in close. His face was grim. "We are all gathered here to put down Cangrande, nephew. We are allies in that cause. Now stop wasting time. We have work to do."

Bonifacio lifted his helmet and placed it firmly on his head. It had been his father's helmet, and his grandfather's. Ironically, like Cangrande's, it was of the old style, peaked and plumeless. The face guard didn't lower into place but closed like a gate on both sides. Wearing it, Vinciguerra looked like a cathedral, a wide form capped by a scarred silver steeple. He deliberately closed the cheek pieces, cutting off Marsilio's stare. "Let's go."

✦   ◇   ✦

With the connivance of the elder Carrara, they finally convinced Ponzino to return to his command tent, there to weep for his lost honor. They emerged, the Count and Il Grande, giving orders that they claimed originated with the Podestà. At last the necessary work was begun—the gates in the outer wall were undergoing destruction, and guards had been set around the perimeter of the camp, if not in the suburb itself.

The Count collected what few men he could to continue the demolition of the gate south of San Pietro. He had decided it would be easier to destroy the gate itself rather than carve a hole in the stone walls. It would take fewer men. Lord knew, there were few enough willing to work.

The Count had found no time to sleep. He felt sluggish, dim-witted—twice he found himself listing right in the saddle while watching the dismantling of the great wooden and metal gates. Years ago a sword stroke had broken Bonifacio's leg. It had mended crooked, and on foot he was not sufficiently mobile. In the saddle, though, he was as capable as a twenty-year-old, which was all that mattered.

Except now it was beginning to show. He never used to get so tired. Despairing of staying upright, he dismounted to lift an axe himself. It was not the gesture of unity and cooperation that it appeared. It was to give him something to *do,* in the hope that action would keep him awake.

He swung the giant axe into the wood near the lower hinge of the inner gate. More men were hacking at the outer set of gates on the other side of the stone archway. As he finished his next swing he paused to wipe sweat from his brow. It was hot. The clouds he had spotted four hours before were still far to the east and provided no relief. He'd retrieved his plate armor from his tent, but had no desire to wear it. The solid breastplate and gorget lay within reach, as did his helmet, no doubt hot enough to burn naked flesh. He still wore the trousers with the wide metal bands to protect his legs, for they were harder to get on and off. It made his legs clatter slightly with each stroke of the axe, and his bad leg ached under all the weight.

Beside him stood young Carrara, alternating strokes with him. The Count chose to find Marsilio's distrust amusing.

"We should post guards in the city," declared Marsilio angrily.

"Truth!" replied the Count, swinging with added vigor.

"We're too exposed here." Marsilio timed his stroke a little too close, nearly grazing the Count's axehead.

"Mmm!" The Count swung so hard he had difficulty freeing the blade.

Marsilio smugly checked his blow. "There's no one between us and the gate on the inner wall."

"If you're worried about the lack of guards, why don't you and your uncle go and keep a watch on the inner gates?"

"Why don't you?" the youth shot back.

The Count lifted his axe and swung. "I'm busy—trying to win this town for you."

Fuming, Marsilio dropped his axe and walked over to his uncle. They spoke, and evidently Il Grande agreed. Together they mounted and rode north into the smoldering suburb, vanishing in a cloud of black soot and smoke. *Good riddance,* thought the Count, resting the axehead on the cobblestones and closing his eyes. His thoughts turned, as they invariably did, to the Pup. Cane Grande. A name given when he was still a child. It wasn't until later that the people translated his nickname into the title he now used—the Greyhound, mythic savior of Italy.

What kind of man was this Greyhound, really? The Count thought he knew. An arrogant, impulsive, sport-loving, bloodthirsty son of a murderer, for all his shows of clemency and frugality. He claimed he cared nothing for money, yet he kept three hundred hawks for his pleasure, dressed in the finest clothes, ate and drank well. Rumor had it he was none too faithful to his wife, either. His bastards littered Lombardy, though the delightful rumors said they were all girls.

How did that sort of man lead his troops against all adversity? More important, why did they follow? What quality did he own? Was it bravery? Vinciguerra da San Bonifacio owned as much as the next man. What was it?

The sound of voices lifted in song made him turn his head. Around a corner of the smoking suburb appeared Vanni Scorigiani leading a group of about sixty men, all carrying plunder—candelabra, sacks of silver, even an overstuffed seat with carvings of curled claws at the feet. No doubt these men, most of them from a condottiere of Flemings, had been handpicked to do Vanni "Asdente" Scorigiani's plundering for him.

Upon spying the Count, Vanni called, "Ho! Ho ho!" The Toothless Master was drunk. He attempted to dance a quick step on the cobblestones but hit his head on a blackened wooden sign hanging above him. He cursed, drew his sword, and unleashed a flurry of drunken blows on the offending slab of wood. The Flemish soldiers gleefully urged him on.

Ill luck chose that moment for the Podestà to ride up. Having emerged from his tent against advice, he'd ridden with Albertino Mussato to see how the demolition was coming. When he saw Asdente, something in the man snapped—he looked like he was about to have a fit. "Scorigiani! What the hell do you think you're doing, man? Are you incompetent as well as cruel?"

"Sir?" puzzled Asdente.

At last the Podestà had found a target for his frustrations. "You're drunk, man! Have you no shame? Here are men, gentlemen, men of high birth, doing the work of common laborers, while you drink and carouse with your pet mercenaries! What kind of man are you? Certainly no gentleman! You don't deserve your knighthood! This whole day has been a fiasco because of behavior like yours! We could own the city now if it weren't for the base impulses of your men! Well, what have you got to say for yourself?"

Asdente was sober enough to take offense. The Count watched as Vanni considered using his sword to rid them all of this jumped-up Cremonese who was so obsessed with *dignity* and *honor* that he couldn't lead his men. Of course, if Vanni did kill the Podestà, he'd be executed for murder. There were too many witnesses who could testify that it wasn't a proper duel. Mussato, a historian with a flair for the dramatic, was watching with interest. Ponzino didn't even have a sword. There was no way for Vanni to kill the weak-livered bastard and get away with it.

Weighing the scales of intervention, the Count decided it would be worth Vanni's death if this enterprise could be led by a practical, competent man. Giacomo da Carrara would take charge, and though Il Grande had his honor, it never got in the way of hard decisions. So when Asdente moved forward with blood in his eye, the Count did not move.

From somewhere nearby they heard the sound of hoofbeats. Two horses were pounding the stones toward them. Beneath that sound, a little farther away, there came thunder. The Count looked up at the sky. *No, the clouds haven't moved.* Yet the thunder continued, rumbling closer to them.

The Count was so tired, it took several long moments before he recognized the sound for what it was—the echoes of a mounted force galloping down paved city streets.

Vanni recognized it sooner. Besotted, honorless man he may have been, but he'd been a soldier all his life. Blind with drink, he ran to a nearby water trough and plunged his head in. Emerging, he quickly ordered his Flemings to abandon the trophies and draw their weapons. Trouble was approaching through the roiling cloud of smoke that enveloped the suburb.

Seconds later Marsilio and his uncle Giacomo burst out of the cloud bank, scarlet faces matching their family's scarlet crest. "They're coming!" both men shouted. There wasn't time for anything more.

San Bonifacio raced for his horse, tethered just inside the wall to the left of the arch. As he ran he reached out a hand and plucked up his breastplate from where it lay, scalding his fingers on the hot metal. All his senses were alert, his weariness banished in a rush of blood. Despite the horrid feeling of being unprepared, a strange gladness billowed up inside him. There couldn't be many attackers, only what the garrison could muster. *Two hundred men, perhaps three.* The Vicentines would ride out and attack, kill maybe as many Paduans. It was just the spur the Paduans needed. Anger at being taken unawares and a thirst for revenge would carry them through these attackers right on to the city gates. Those gates would fall and Vicenza would belong to Padua.

The Count's only task now was to stay alive long enough to see it. He was just turning his horse, armor dangling from his fingertips, when something emerged from the smoke. Expecting a horse, he was amazed to see a dog—a wiry black greyhound with its teeth bared and jaws snapping. Tears streamed down its face from the smoke, making it appear even more awful.

Then came the horse. At first only the legs were visible from out of the swirling black cloud, then a head emerged, a wide horse's head hidden by the leather and metal headpiece. The Count recognized the device between the eyes, below the single spike, as the Nogarola eagle.

The next stride of the horse brought into view a giant in a billowing scarlet cloak. A silver helmet was fixed on his head, plumeless and fierce. He bore no shield, but wielded a huge mace with studded spikes. He was not the short, broad Antonio Nogarola. This knight was high as a mountain, towering over the beast he rode. Probably the family champion, if they had one. Who else would be using their armor and horses?

Whoever he was, he was frightening to behold. The Count saw him make the sign of the cross on his forehead, then stand in his stirrups to keen a loud war cry. Behind him, bursting out of the foul smoke, more armed horsemen emerged. The wind shifted, and the smoke funneled up, revealing a wall of men.

Count Vincinguerra da San Bonifacio turned his horse and rode for his life. Ahead of him the Podestà was doing the same. San Bonifacio kicked his heels to force his big horse across the bridge. On either side of him rode a Carrara, and just ahead to his right the Podestà and Mussato. Suddenly the historian's horse pitched forward. Mussato's mount had stuck its foot in a hole in the planks and fallen, snapping its leg. Now man and beast were a barrier across the Count's path. Vinciguerra was unable to do anything but ride on. He heard a scream from beneath him. *Poor luck, poet.*

✦ ◇ ✦

Back at the gate, Vanni Asdente led his men afoot into the flank of the attacking party. Under his direction four horses went down on the right side of the Vicentines' column. The Vicentines stopped, turned, and began the process of decimating the drunken Flemings. In spite of the howling and spitting Asdente, the sixty Flemings lost their nerve and edged under the stone arch to run across the bridge, only to be cut down as they presented their backs to the mounted soldiers. Asdente disappeared among his own fleeing men.

The main body of galloping Vicentine horsemen continued on under the stone arch and over the bridge to bring destruction to the army that outnumbered them more than fifty times. Ahead of them, the Count followed Ponzoni and the two Carrarese to where the Paduan army disported itself in the gardens and hills beyond the moat.

San Bonifacio rode along the front lines of the soldiers now mustering. All were struggling to their feet and reaching for weapons. It was as he had hoped—threat was stirring them to action. Satisfied, he pulled up his reins, halting in the center of the line. He still held his breastplate, the family crest blazoned across it, but his grandfather's helmet was lost on the bridge. No matter. If this worked right, he'd have it back in a very few minutes.

He looked toward the city. The Vicentine force had checked just this side of the bridge, watching the twenty remaining Flemings run for safety. The tall Nogarola champion shifted in his saddle as he waited, his back to the banks of the moat. The Vicentines lined up behind him. The Count watched with grim pleasure as the Vicentine champion took in the numbers he faced. He couldn't possibly ignore the vast hoard of men arrayed against him. Even disorganized as the Paduans obviously were, the odds were impossible. He would count it a moral victory and order his men back. The moment he turned, San Bonifacio would lead a charge and destroy this force, then press on to the center of the city and victory.

The champion did not turn back. With the hound prowling about at his horse's legs, he stood in his stirrups and tore the helmet from his head. Light from the western sun set the hair ablaze. Dangerously handsome, the face was clear to all. Even those who had never seen him knew who he was—Cangrande della Scala, the Greyhound, in all his glory.

Vinciguerra da San Bonifacio felt the Pup's damned smile settle on him. *The bastard's baiting me, daring me! The fool! Doesn't he realize how badly he's outnumbered?*

As if in answer, Cangrande gestured upwards with his mace. There was a massive cheer from a thousand throats. More voices by far than just the Vicenzan knights. The sound was deafening even at this distance. Around the Count men stepped back and horses shied. But who was cheering?

"Dear Christ!" Beside the Count, Ponzino was aghast. "Look! Look! Oh, has he no honor?!"

The Count glanced up and swallowed his heart. All along the walls of San Pietro, those same walls he had scaled that morning, hundreds of helmets glinted in the light of the setting sun. Enough of them bore the outlines of bows to show that they were archers. But they did not hold crossbows. They held bows of yew.

Somehow, beyond all possibility, the Scaliger's army had come. Worse, he had armed his soldiers—against dictate of emperors, kings, knights, and church—with longbows. A violation of every code of chivalry, it was political suicide. It was also deadly.

Instead of indugling in outrage, the Count was doing the math. Those weapons could drive an arrow three times the distance of any crossbow. It wasn't an army the Greyhound had brought. It was death, in the form of a hail of arrows.

Below the rows of archers, the Scaliger howled a wordless cry that froze the blood. Ponzino actually shivered at the sound. For a moment he believed it was the dog that had made the noise, so feral it was. The Count saw Cangrande throw his helmet aside in a show of contempt. Still standing in the stirrups, he lifted his reins in his left hand and kicked his horse into a gallop. The spiked mace in his right hand was poised and ready to crush his enemies. Behind him, against all reason, his followers charged, screaming for blood.

In that moment San Bonifacio understood. It was not courage, nor reason, nor a grasp of tactics. It was not honor nor chivalry. It was a streak of madness that defied reason, thought, life. It was a kind of immortality, perhaps the only kind a man owns. For this heartbeat of time the Greyhound was more than human. He was the Angel of Death, descended from the heavens to reap a fearful harvest.

Ponzino was horrified. "They can't possibly . . ."

The Count said, "They already have. Run!"

All around them men in every state of readiness—sober, drunk, valiant, cowardly—fell back before that charge. They'd witnessed their daring leaders run to them for protection, and had felt unsure. They'd watched the Flemings, darlings of the fierce Asdente, run as if the devil nipped their heels. They'd seen men armed with bows along the walls. Now this giant, this impossibly fearless, murderous man, rode at them like Mars on the field of war.

The Paduans broke. The massive army began disintegrating into clusters of terrified men. In their desperate flight they shed their booty, their weapons, their provisions, and their armor. Into ditches or into the Bacchiglione it all went as the men scrambled back to preserve their lives.

The Count of San Bonifacio didn't hesitate. Tossing his family armor aside, he turned his horse about, kicking hard. Grabbing the reins of the Podestà's horse, he dragged the stunned commander with him. Ponzino ripped every seal of office from his body, wanting no sign to mark him as Cangrande's enemy. For the first time that day, the Paduan commander did not think of his honor. He thought only of his life.

SEVEN

The gait of the warhorse felt unusual under Pietro. He had never ridden a fully barded animal, and the weight of the horse's armor took some getting used to. The sound of his horse's hooves on the stones was odd. Glancing at the closest destrier, he saw sharp nail heads protruding from the horseshoes. Pietro felt a shiver and made sure he was firmly settled in the saddle.

Pietro had no idea where the archers had come from. He was only certain that they had saved his life. What was he doing? Cangrande had charged, and Pietro had instinctively followed. Now he was in the field, flanked by friends, riding into glory. He was out of his mind with terror and pride.

Cangrande was in the lead, and some impetuous Paduans, probably hoping to make names for themselves, had reversed their course of flight and set themselves to slay the enemy prince. Seeing the five horsemen riding toward him, Cangrande made a whoop of joy and spurred harder.

"Come on! Ride! Ride!" cried Montecchio. Pietro tried to speed up, but because he lacked spurs his horse failed to respond. Pietro kicked again, but the pointed slippers offered no purchase in the stirrups, and the kicking hurt his heels worse than the horse.

The rider in the best position held the lance, riding a few paces behind the leader. Cangrande would probably survive that first blow only to be spitted on the sharpened point of this one's lance.

Cangrande edged his horse slightly to his right, even with the lancer. His helmet gone, his eyes made contact with the grinning face across from him. He smiled back, briefly showing them his perfect teeth. Then he pursed his lips and blew. Seeing this, the Paduans thought their prey was making an obscene face at them and gritted their teeth.

Cangrande bent lower, kicking free his stirrup and dropping his right boot to the dirt. Then he hitched that leg up onto the horse's back, knee crooked out and forward, right heel under his own rump. *Like a daredevil at a fair,* Pietro thought, *or an acrobat.* Cangrande cocked his head as if listening to music. The first sword would be on him in three more strides. Two. One . . .

Oh my God!

The merlin struck. Called by a whistle from its master, it swooped out of the sky past its master's left shoulder. For a moment the huge golden-headed bird seemed to hang in the air before the startled Paduans. Then it was upon them. The wicked pounces raked the head of the leading horse. The steed was armored, so the talons did little damage. But the rider forgot his weapon as his arms went up automatically to protect his face.

When the merlin attacked, Cangrande moved. With a convulsive pull on the bridle he yanked the horse's head back and right. Well trained, it reared. But Cangrande kept pulling, and the combination of his strength and the heavy armor conspired to bring the horse down. With a burst of air expelled and legs flailing the animal fell on its right side—directly in the path of the attacking horses.

It was too late for the Paduans to stop. Through the screams of both men and mounts Pietro heard the snaps as the horses on the left broke their front legs. They pitched forward, throwing their riders headfirst into the ground. One rider was held in the saddle by his stirrups, and his neck was broken as his own horse toppled end over end. The other rider was thrown clear, landing in an ignominious heap of broken bones.

Had the Scaliger not waited to the very last moment, the two approaching horses would have leapt the living hurdle with ease. As it was, he left it almost too late. Using the hitched leg under him he barely had time to propel himself sideways off the falling beast. He rolled shoulder over shoulder clear of the massacre.

The three remaining attackers rode past, hardly understanding what had happened. Before they could come to grips, the Vicentines were upon them and they were cut to pieces. Pietro stunned one Paduan with the flat of his blade, setting him up to be killed by Antony.

Cangrande, meantime, was on foot, facing down an oncoming rider. He gripped his mace with one hand on either end and blocked the downward blow. He twisted and jabbed back with the head of the mace in a move Pietro recognized from one of his old fightbooks. It was called the murder stroke, and had Cangrande been holding a sword the man would have been sliced open. Instead, the mace pulped his ribs. Cangrande hauled the man's carcass out of the saddle, mounted, and spurred the battle on.

"Dear Christ," breathed Pietro. "He is the Greyhound."

✦ ◇ ✦

Behind the charge, under the arch of the Porte San Pietro, a trampled pile of bodies shifted. Some were dead, some were dying. All but one bled. In the midst of the carnage Asdente feigned injury, biding his time. When his men had been cut down in their flight he had used their fallen bodies to protect himself. Now he lay among them, on the city side of the bridge, watching the backs of the Veronese as they rode into the fleeing Paduans. He watched, waiting for his chance. His withered, scarred, and twisted face was slack in a picture of death, but his eyes were vivid, his mind hard at work. Impossibly, Cangrande had slipped past the ambush at the north gates. *But he won't escape now.*

Asdente required a horse. *There.* An obliging latecomer to the fray approached, oblivious to the bodies of dead Flemings whose condottierre would never be paid. Asdente had lost his sword in the scrum, but there was an obliging morning star in a nearby dead man's hand. Covertly he grasped it. It had a good, long chain attaching the spiked ball to the wooden handle.

Timing was important, and the Toothless Master knew his senses were blunted with drink. He needed a trick. He slowly reached his left hand out and grasped a part of his plunder, a fine linen tablecloth now covered in blood.

The rider was almost under the arch. Asdente leapt up and threw the cloth, which snagged on the man's helmet, momentarily blinding him. In that moment Asdente hit him full in the chest with the heavy spiked ball. The rider hit the ground with a wet smack. The Paduan swung the ball again, and again, pulping the man's helmet and head. The linen covered the knight's dented face like a shroud, glued by gore.

The Toothless Master grinned. "That's one." Stepping into the dead man's stirrups, Asdente raised the square shield of the fallen rider. It would be his passport—no one would look too closely at a man bearing a Vicentine shield.

He could escape easily now. But escape was not his plan. He galloped over the bridge, his horse leaping over the prone figures of men and beasts that littered it. He carried the dripping morning star low on his right side, ready to bring it down in a deadly arc over his head to smash a skull—the skull of a Dog.

✦ ◇ ✦

Numbers no longer mattered. The eighty cavalieri spread themselves out to chase the fleeing Paduans. The Vicentines had what all soldiers on horseback throughout history longed for most—a scattered army on open ground.

Mariotto and Antony rode together, following Antonio Nogarola in pursuit of at least a hundred men running down the road to Quartesolo. Some turned to fight. Most fled. Mariotto considered it ungentlemanly to hack into a man whose back was turned. Instead he used the flat of his sword to club them down. Antony used his stolen mace caked with Flemish blood to crack shoulders and skulls. Most would live, though if their bones would ever knit from those blows Mariotto wouldn't care to say.

Ahead two Paduans were attempting to rally their men-at-arms to stand and fight. They both wore red farsettos under their armor with some sort of family device over their plate mail. They rode their horses around, attempting to corral the men-at-arms running south and force them to face the oncoming Vicentines. They were having little success, but there was danger in such an action. If one man's reckless courage could cause a panicked flight, so too could two men restore order to their army and reverse the fortunes of the day.

Recognizing the danger the men posed, Nogarola led a charge, raking his spurs down the flanks of his steed, raising streaks of blood. "Onward, for victory!" he shouted, only to be silenced as the younger of the two mounted nobles lifted a crossbow from his saddle, took aim, and fired. Nogarola spun right to left in his saddle as the force of the bolt knocked him sideways off his horse.

Nogarola's fall was witnessed by several of his fellow Vicentines. Though some resented Cangrande, they had nothing but respect for the house of Nogarola. When their leader was felled from his horse no less than fourteen men stopped their horses to surround his senseless body on the ground, among them young Montecchio. Because his helmet cut off his peripheral vision, Mariotto did not see Marsilio da Carrara finish loading a second bolt in his crossbow.

On Mariotto's far side, Capecelatro's mail coif allowed him better range of vision. He saw the crossbow out of the corner of his eye. Just as the bolt was released from its catch, Antony cried, "Mari!" and launched himself sideways out of his saddle. Landing clumsily, he banged his ribs on the side of Montecchio's horse. With his left arm he dragged Mariotto out of his saddle, clear of the path of the bolt just as it ripped through the air overhead. They were falling, and both felt the air stirred by the movement of the legs of Montecchio's horse.

They landed badly, rolling over each other, desperately trying to stay clear of the spiked hooves by their ears. A buffet of blows and churned earth was their universe for the next several seconds. One hard knock sent both end over end, then they came to a rest, Mariotto half underneath Antony, miraculously unscathed.

"What the devil are you about?" shouted Mariotto, trying to be heard over the noise around them. He struggled to get his helmet off then slapped at Antony, trying to get out from underneath him. "Idiot! We could have been killed!" Capecelatro was silent. Mariotto realized the Capuan was unconscious, knocked senseless in the fall. Montecchio tried to get purchase under his left shoulder. *What do I do? I can't leave him here . . .*

He was still deciding on a course of action when the sun above him went out. He looked up to see what had caused the sudden shadow. A Paduan on horseback, backlit by the sun, raised a spear to run them both through together.

Heaving with every muscle he owned, Mariotto rolled the limp Capuan off to the right, then threw himself left. The spear dug into the earth where they had lain. Cheated of blood, it came easily away again for another blow.

Mariotto scrambled up desperately. Under the pourpoint he wore only a cloth shirt, his finest, donned for the wedding this morning. He realized he would die in his best shirt. The thought did not please him. "Come on!" he shouted, stepping farther away from the unconscious Capuan. By making himself the target he could keep Antony safe.

The spear came again, plunging toward Mariotto's breast, and the youth twisted away just in time. He tried to grasp the shaft but pulled back at once. It was barbed. His fingers dripped blood.

As the Paduan noble drew back for another thrust, Mariotto's hands searched for a weapon. There was nothing on his person, only little leather straps tucked into his belt—

The other jess! His fingers yanked it free from where it hung just as the faceless Paduan delivered the deathblow. Mariotto twisted sideways again. The barbed tip caught his armor and ripped it wide, making a deep gash across the muscles of his chest. Even as he cried out he looped the ring of the jess over one of the jutting barbs on the length of the spear. With the long end of the leather strap wrapped around his bleeding knuckles, Mariotto yanked the spear out of his enemy's grip.

Weapon gone, the Paduan turned toward the bridge and fled, only to be caught short by a Vicentine on horseback who, to Mariotto's satisfaction, removed the man's head from his shoulders.

Mariotto moved to Antony's side and stood with the spear poised, ready to defend his unconscious friend against all comers.

✦ ✧ ✦

Asdente rode through the rear echelons of the Veronese and Vicentine defenders. He held his stolen shield high, hoping no one looked too closely at the color of his surcoat. He cast around, looking this way and that.

Some poor Paduan stumbled across his path. Keeping in his character of an angry Vicentine, the Toothless Master swung his weapon in an upward stroke. The horrible spiked metal ball hit, and a cloud of pink mist hit the air. The fool's chin came right off, landing on the ground behind him. The man flailed, but Vanni was too busy to do him the favor of killing him. He had just spied what he was looking for, a dark gold head where the fighting was heaviest. His prey's back was turned invitingly.

He veered his horse and set it at an easy canter, to all appearances off to help his lord, weapon held at the ready.

✦ ✧ ✦

Following in the Scaliger's wake, Pietro hacked and slashed with his longsword. He tried to remember his one lesson from years ago. The voice of the instructor rose up from memory, shouting, "Thrust, don't hack! A point always beats an edge!" But when your enemy was running with his back to you, a swing was as good as a stab. Working to control his blade while staying in his saddle, Pietro was too busy now to be terrified. His greatest fear was of losing his weapon. It seemed far too big for his hands.

What astonished him was how fast everything seemed to move. He'd seen the fightbooks with their orderly woodcut prints of stately knights doing slow, measured battle. In the field it was completely different, and the learning curve was deadly. But before him was the best teacher a man could wish for. Even as he chopped at the men around him, Pietro was aware of the easy martial moves of the Capitano's mace—the arcing swings that killed, then looped around for the next victim. Pietro tried his best to emulate the moves.

Some Paduans were turning now, knowing that they couldn't outrun death. Pietro saw an axe rising and quickly hauled his blade up to meet it. He caught the axehead on the upstroke, yanking the weapon from the Paduan's grip. Pietro hurtled past the man, who flung himself to the ground in terror. Already there was another threat looming on Pietro's right, a man with a spear, but the Capitano was there first. A golden-headed wheel of destruction, the Scaliger bared his teeth in a terrible grimace as he pulled back on the reins. The horse under him checked as Cangrande leaned back in the saddle, dodging a spear thrust that would have caught him under the chin. His left leg flicked out of its stirrup. Snaking out, he wrapped it around the spear, pinning the shaft neatly between the saddle's wooden front and the groove of his left knee. The silver spur at his heel flicked out, slicing into the soldier's arm. The weapon involuntarily released from his grip, the Paduan fled.

But four more Paduans moved in to kill the Scaliger and take his horse. Still leaning back, Cangrande used the mace to fend off an attack on his right side. Sitting up, his left hand grasped the haft of the trapped spear, spinning it over his head to slice through a man's cheek, then reversing the weapon to hammer the butt end into an exposed throat. Jupiter took down another man, pinning him to the ground and snapping at his face. The greyhound's teeth were covered in blood.

Pietro had pulled up on his reins at the same time as Cangrande, thinking to move to the Scaliger's aid. Now he just watched in amazement as the Veronese lord dispatched his assailants. "Good God . . ." Pietro realized he'd let his sword hang at his side, his mouth open. If a Paduan had come across him, he'd have died a stupid death then and there. But the enemy were all ahead of him, fleeing toward Quartesolo and the bridge over the Tessina to safety.

Just to be sure there were no Paduans at his back, he wheeled his horse about. The field behind him was littered with the dead and wounded and surrendered, but there were no armed men on foot. Pietro was about pick up the chase again when he noticed a single rider galloping toward them. He carried a Vicentine shield, the castle tower and the winged lion quite visible on the red and white background. But there was something wrong. Pietro was hard pressed to put a name to it.

The rider wasn't looking at the Paduans running toward the river—his eyes were fixed on Cangrande's back! There was the faintest glimpse of triumph across the snarling wrecked face.

Pietro shouted, "Cangrande!"

The shout turned the Scaliger, but too late. The bastard had already launched his attack, a heavy swing with a morning star, the ball and chain at the peak of its arc. Cangrande's head was bare, his helmet tossed aside in defiant contempt.

The fingers on the Capitano's right hand relaxed, discarding the mace. The spear came up across the head of his horse, the free hand gripping the spear's lower haft. Thus braced in both hands, the wooden pole whipped up over Cangrande's head. He leaned back over the *secondo arcione,* arching his spine painfully, holding the spear away from him, a bar over his body.

The hurtling chain bit into the spear's haft and the metal ball curled underneath and around it, passing the Scaliger's face by inches. The chain wrapped itself harmlessly around and around the wooden pole, leaving the spiked ball hanging impotently.

Cangrande yanked forward and pulled the handle from Asdente's grasp. In a continuation of the same move the spear was reversed and thrust backward. The butt connected with the Paduan's groin. Asdente gasped, doubling over in his saddle and letting the morning star fall to the dirt.

"Be grateful, Vanni," said Cangrande. "I could have used the sharp end."

"Go—to Hell," gasped the Paduan.

"You should really stick to making shoes," observed the Scaliger. Pietro laughed—it was yet another literary allusion—but Asdente looked blank. Cangrande sighed. "For Christ's sake, man, read a poem!" He cracked Asdente's skull with the spear's end, and the Paduan's limp body toppled out of his saddle to land in an ungainly heap on the trampled earth. For good measure, Jupiter bit him on the upper thigh.

The Capitano dropped to the ground and retrieved the morning star. Weighing it in his hands, he flashed a bright grin at Pietro. "Sneaky bastard."

"Yes, lord," agreed Pietro.

Cangrande climbed back into his saddle. "Pietro, my darling boy, you just came between me and death. That renders something as formal as 'lord' a trifle ridiculous, don't you think? Come up with another title. And I'll think of one for you."

Pietro heard the hinted promise of distinction. "Thank you, lord," he said, and immediately flushed.

Cangrande was already spurring after the fleeing Paduans. "*Giach giach giach giach!* Come on!" The Scaliger touched his spurs and his mount raced forward.

Pietro tried to follow, but his spurless heels did nothing to convince his horse to move. Pietro hissed at it, hit its sides with his fists, shook the reins—nothing. *I guess I'm stuck,* he thought.

He glanced around him, looking for danger. If his horse wouldn't move he was a sitting target. The battle was carrying on past him, and try as he might he couldn't get the beast to budge.

Suddenly the horse reared violently. It let loose with a frightened whinny. Whatever spooked it, a noise, a wasp, a sudden blinding reflection off someone's armor, all Pietro knew was the lurch beneath him as his horse went up on its hind legs and pawed the air.

With a fierce thud the front hooves returned to earth. Pietro rocked back, his jaw snapping shut inside his helmet. He fought to sit upright again as the horse gallopped madly toward the battle. "Whoa! Whoa!"

✦   ◇   ✦

At the bridge of Quartesolo the fighting had grown desperate. The bridge was the Paduan path to freedom, and the killing field between it and San Pietro was utter chaos.

It was at the bridge that the score of men gathered by the Carrarese held their ground. This tight cluster of defenders had begun to notice how few the Scaliger's forces really were. They could turn the fight around with a hard push—as long as the archers on the walls did not open fire. Several men glanced up, wondering why they had not been hit with a hailstorm of arrows. Perhaps the archers didn't want to hit their own men? That made them all the more eager to engage in close fighting.

The Paduan ring naturally earned the attention of all the unengaged Vicentines. They pressed forward, only to have their horses speared and to fall under a trample of hooves. The bodies of the mounts provided a wall for the Paduans that the next wave of attackers had to navigate, exposing themselves as they did to their enemies' blades.

"Hold them!" shouted Marsilio, echoing his uncle a few feet away. He was again loading his crossbow and scanning the field to find quarry. His uncle disapproved of the weapon, as it was not strictly within the knight's code. But Cangrande had used bowmen, and Marsilio was feeling rightously vengeful.

There! Cangrande was in sight, held up in helping some Vicentines deal with a smaller group of men who had turned to fight. It was a tricky shot— sighting down the length of the weapon, Marsilio waited for a clear line of fire. He tracked the riding figure, squinted, braced himself, and triggered the release.

Suddenly a knight in a plain helmet and gambeson darted into his vision, blocking Cangrande from view. Had the bolt hit its target? Marsilio couldn't tell. All he could see was the madman riding recklessly for the Paduan line. His horse was a giant destrier, unlike any that they had speared, and armored, making it unlikely they could bring this one down. The beast could tear a hole in the Paduan resistance, opening a gap that the other Vicentines would exploit.

"Stop him!" cried Il Grande, seeing the same danger.

Such a monster might not even feel anything less than a mortal blow. Marsilio began reloading his crossbow. He couldn't stop the horse, but the rider was easy pickings. His practiced hands racheted the new bolt into place as his angry eyes looked for a clear shot.

✦　◇　✦

Pietro was frantically trying to get his horse under control. It ran willy-nilly, carrying the bone-jolted teen along for the ride. Worse, he could see where it was blindly charging—straight into a tight band of Paduans bristling with spears and halberds and swords. "Come on, boy!" he cried as he yanked on the reins again. Anywhere but there! Perhaps if he'd worn spurs he could have made the beast veer, but reins alone were no good. The most he achieved were slight variations in the horse's angle.

Looking up into that fearsome band of men by the bridge, Pietro saw a dark-haired young knight on horseback just behind the front line of Paduans.

Then Pietro caught sight of the wooden cross and a long curved piece of metal at its head. A crossbow! The comely Paduan brought it up level with his target, squinting along the bolt for the center of the Scaliger's chest.

Pietro had no breath left to shout a warning. Instead, he steered his horse directly into the path of the arrow's flight. He saw the bolt release, a faded grey line tracing through the air at him. Fearful of the impending missile but unable to veer off, he closed his eyes. *Dear Christ, please . . . !*

Bows had long been prohibited by the law of men and the rule of the Church, called cowardly by knights and unholy by priests. The closest to a compromise that fighting men had made was employing the crossbow in the place of the bow of yew. Slower to load, heavier, the crossbow also had a power that could take a fully armored knight out of his saddle and leave his body seemingly hanging in midair as his life spilt out of him.

The bolt did not carry Pietro out of his seat. The moment passed. He felt the horse beneath him, the air around him, but nothing else.

I'm alive. Oh, dear God, I'm—

As the horse's hooves met the earth, Pietro dragged air into his lungs and screamed. His eyes opened wide, tears at the corners. He looked down and saw his wound. The bolt had entered his right thigh just above the knee, continuing on through the meat and out the other side. The power of the bolt at this close range had carried the metal head straight through the leather beneath him and into the metal covering the horse's ribs.

The horse plowed on, every hoof-fall shooting lightning through Pietro's leg. Each step moved the powerful horseflesh, in turn tugging and jerking Pietro's leg, now horribly pinned to it. The youth slipped right in the saddle to alleviate the pull, but it did no good. Blood seeped from both sides of the wound as Pietro's life force mixed with his mount's.

Through a blurred veil of sweat and pain, he saw the Paduan reloading. "No," breathed Pietro, ducking low and hanging on. His thoughts were incoherent, but through it all he knew he had to keep riding.

✦ ◆ ✦

In the ring of resisting soldiers, Il Grande glanced at his nephew. "If they break, ride like hell." He glanced at the lone rider bearing down on them. "He's brave."

Marsilio had no comment about the rider's bravery, busy looking for a clear shot, but the coward had ducked behind the horse's armored head. It was no longer about stopping the horse. The rider had cost him his chance at Cangrande, and Carrara was determined to kill the bastard before they were forced to turn and flee. "Come on, show your face!"

The destrier clambered up over the bodies of horses and men, its hooves tearing a purchase through the flesh, plunging forward into a wall of spears. One of those spears penetrated the heavy armor, but it was not nearly enough to check the beast's charge. It lowered its head, and the single unicorn spike gored the first two men in the wall.

The lowered head exposed the rider. "At last!" crowed Marsilio. He pulled the trigger.

✦   ◆   ✦

Pietro was barely able to see inside his helmet, but he felt the impact of something bouncing hard off it. The blow snapped his head back and canted him right in the saddle, toward his bad leg. Entirely limp again, Pietro wasn't able to put his weight on his right stirrup, and so began to fall. Through the narrow slit of the helmet, everything was confusion. He thought he saw a sword's blade coming at him, but already he was past it as his steed barreled on. Something ripped in his leg, and he screamed. All he knew for sure was that he was falling. Releasing his sword, he threw his arms wide to find something to catch onto. Cries were all around him, but as his fingers gripped something metal there was a startled shout. For a moment he was suspended in the air, hanging between his saddle and whatever he'd grabbed hold of. Then he toppled to the earth, the bulk of what he had hold of falling with him to land heavily beside him.

Gasping, eyes filling with tears, Pietro struggled out of a helmet that fit him more snugly than before. On the ground beside him lay the dark youth, holding a broken crossbow. Since he was wearing armor, the fall had been much more damaging for him. *Good,* thought Pietro. He reached for the fellow's belt and removed a dagger. There had to be men all around him—he expected a sword to split his head in two at any moment. Twisting about, he slashed with the knife at—empty air?

The gap in the Paduan line had broken the men. The men-at-arms turned tail and ran. Seconds later, Vicentine horses thundered past Pietro to round up and kill the last of them.

The only Paduan who didn't run appeared to be someone with authority. He remained on horseback, his hands raised in the universal gesture of submission. "I surrender!" he shouted, his eyes on the young archer lying unmoving at Pietro's side.

Pietro stared around blankly, then thought of his helmet. Examining it, he saw something protruding from just below the crest. Picking it up, he discovered a crossbow bolt running all the way through the steel, end to end. He remembered his head rocking back and realized that the bolt must have penetrated above his scalp, in the gap just above his head. A shiver of insane laughter ran through him.

Pietro heard a sound beside him. The young Paduan groaned and sat up, only to feel the pressure of Pietro's blade against his Adam's apple. The Paduan blinked, taking in the youth kneeling next to him with a look of contempt.

Pietro was just grateful to be alive. With a strange half-smile he said, "I guess you're my prisoner."

✦ ✧ ✦

Cangrande halted the pursuit at Quartesolo. He set his forces to rounding up the Paduans, a chore that would take days. Men had scrambled in every direction, throwing themselves down into ditches on either side of the road. Some had jumped into the flowing waters of the rivers that intersected at Quartesolo, whether they could swim or not. Many of them floundered in the muddy waters, weighted down by armor and weapons they struggled furiously to shed. Cangrande's men, who just moments before had been their destroyers, now became their saviors. They stripped themselves of their own armor and dove in to rescue the Paduans.

There was no more fighting. It had never been a battle, it had been a rout. Now the rout was over.

Under a tree on a hill to the south of Quartesolo, Cangrande dismounted his blood-spattered horse. Walking around to the front of the animal, he unbuckled the *testiera* that covered its head, let the piece fall to the earth, and began to stroke the long nose absently. Jupiter dropped and lay at his feet, exhausted.

Cangrande did not glance back at the city that was now indisputably his. He gazed south, beyond the men who ran to safety. The south and east, where lands were lush and green. There were rivers and vineyards, mills, ranches, farms. Harvest was three weeks away. This was some of the richest land in the world, fought over and died for throughout history. This was the Trevisian Mark.

Cangrande della Scala, titular Vicar of the Trevisian Mark, looked down on the half of the Mark that he did not rule. If anyone could have seen his face in that moment, they would not have been able to decide if his eyes bore responsibility—or delight.

He was twenty-three years old.

EIGHT

Though the battle seemed to last hours, it was over in less than twenty minutes. Of actual bloodshed there had been little, as armed engagements went. The dead numbered only seven Paduan nobles and fifty-seven foot soldiers. With the exception of the Carrarese, all the mounted knights had fled the field. Of the remaining foot soldiers, many were wounded. But the real surprise came from the number captured. Over a thousand men-at-arms had surrendered themselves to a band of eighty men.

A modern Caesar, Cangrande was famous for his clemency toward captured foes, and this day he was true to form. Returning to the northern edge of Quartesolo, he welcomed captured Paduan nobles as old friends. The poet Albertino Mussato had been discovered in the moat bearing no fewer than eleven wounds, the worst being a cracked skull and a broken leg. His wrist, too, hung at an ugly angle. It was a miracle he'd survived. Trampled by his own side, he'd flung himself headlong into the foul water. Addressing him, Cangrande commended his valor. In great pain, lying on a makeshift stretcher, the poet-historian was as gracious as the situation allowed.

Sitting awkwardly and wrapping his leg using strips torn from a dead man's shirt, Pietro observed this exchange. He had already presented his prisoners to the Scaliger. Cangrande had used his belt to cinch Pietro's leg just above his wound. Fortunately the broken wooden shaft protruding through both sides of his thigh prevented too much bleeding, but it hurt like the devil. Sure that the Paduans were in good hands, Pietro hauled himself onto a stray horse and went to find his friends, carrying his skewered helmet with him. Behind him Cangrande was particularly flamboyant in his praise of the two Carraras. "That was a feat without equal, attempting to stop an army in full retreat."

Il Grande inclined his head. "It was quite a feat to put fear into the hearts of over ten thousand men."

"Still, you two deserved to win, purely for heart!"

Marsilio snarled. "That won't stop that little shit from collecting my ransom, will it?"

Cangrande gazed back at him, amused. "You'd rather Pietro had killed you?"

"Is that his name?"

"Pietro Alaghieri, of Florence, recently arrived from Paris, via Pisa and Lucca."

"To our detriment," observed Il Grande. "Dante's son?"

"Yes."

"As I told my nephew, a brave lad."

Marsilio opened his mouth, but his uncle stepped on his foot. Instead of the intended insult, the youth found himself saying, "Your army isn't here, is it?"

"Sadly, no. My army, by this time, is just exiting the gates of Verona."

"So you won by luck."

"I suppose so," replied the Scaliger brightly.

"Not by brilliant generalship," pressed the Paduan.

"No," said Cangrande with a grin.

"Never underestimate the power of luck," said Il Grande.

Cangrande smiled at the young Carrara. "Of course, when you know the extent of my trickery, you will be furious."

"What's that?" But he was already talking to the Capitano's back. Someone had run up to Cangrande carrying a large breastplate decorated with azure. He whispered softly in the Capitano's ear. Cangrande examined the armor, chuckled once, then looked at Il Grande. "You know to whom this belongs."

"I do."

"A shame he's fled my hospitality."

"His loss, I'm sure."

"You're too kind." Cangrande handed the armor back to the soldier and issued instructions. "Take three men and return to where you found this, then trace the most direct path to Padua from there. If you haven't found him in an hour, turn back. Don't go past Camisano. Go." The man bowed and went.

Cangrande began walking, a new expression of delight on his lips. That look promised that the Count of San Bonifacio's life was going to be more difficult for his flight, not less.

The Scaliger left the Carrarese in the hands of some knights whose instructions as to their comfort were explicit and made his way to where Antonio Nogarola had fallen. Nogarola was awake, screaming bloody murder at the men who insisted he return to the city.

"I'm fine, damn you!" he cried, staunching the flow of blood from his shoulder with a sleeve torn from a dead man. He kicked at one of his servants who had come to the battlefield to tend the wounded. "Go help someone else, I don't need you! I'll be in when I'm good and ready!"

"You always were a baby when you were sick." Cangrande stooped over Nogarola's shoulder and lifted the bloody cloth away from the wound. "It's not good. Can you move the arm?"

Nogarola grunted. "Some."

Cangrande replaced the cloth around the crossbow bolt. "I'll handle the mopping up. You go back and have that looked at." After a friendly pat on the older man's good arm, he was off.

With anyone else, Nogarola would have protested vehemently. Instead he meekly stood upright and followed his servants into the city.

✦   ✧   ✦

Not far off, Pietro discovered his friends. Antony was sitting upright with his head in his hands, while Mariotto was semiprone on his back, using his elbows to prop himself up.

"Christ," cried Mariotto when he saw Pietro's leg.

"It's not so bad," said Pietro.

"He wins," said Antony, with an envious look.

Pietro's leg collapsed beneath him when he dismounted, but he managed not to cry out. He knelt awkwardly beside Antony and Mariotto. Holding up the helmet with the crossbow bolt sticking out both ends, Pietro said, "Look at this!"

Antony had to laugh. "What are you, a target?"

They let him tell his story. He tried not to embellish it, but still they found it hard to believe he'd lived through the charge. When he was done they related their own adventures, each interupting the other frequently.

Antony was saying, "So the same one who took a shot at your head let one fly at Mari here—"

"There was no crossbow aimed at me," interrupted Mariotto. "You're just a clumsy oaf in the saddle and can't own up to it!"

"Oh, there was a crossbow, all right!" shot back Antony. "What there wasn't was some mysterious spear-wielding horseman!"

"How did I get this?" asked Mariotto, sitting up and pointing to his wound. He winced at once and settled back on his elbows.

"How should I know?" roared Antony. "Maybe you got caught on a this-tle, oh delicate flower!" They made rude gestures at each other, then Antony continued. "You're right about one thing, though. I fell. I didn't leap to save you. If I'd had my way, that bolt would have split your head like a melon!" He raised his voice on the last word, then rolled his eyes backward and groaned, head ringing. Pietro and Mariotto were overcome by a fit of giggling. Antony shot them a sour look that made them laugh all the harder.

The pain across his chest stifling his breath, Mariotto looked down and asked, "Do you think I'll have a scar?"

"Probably," observed Pietro.

"Good," said Mariotto happily.

The Scaliger approached the trio, with Jupiter still panting from the long day's chase. Seeing wounds that were not particularly grave, the Capitano said, "And what happened here?"

Antonio looked up, the corners of his mouth twisting. Mariotto tried to sit up, but Pietro reached out a hand to hold him back. Both of them spoke at the same time, while Pietro bit his grinning lip.

"I saved his life—"

"—and now he's—"

"The ingrate, he says—"

"There was this crossbow—"

"I'm sure I'll hear all about it," said Cangrande gravely. "Will you live?" Both nodded. "Good. Now you can start thinking of something to say to your fathers. Unless you had their permission to join my army?"

Antony stared at him wide-eyed. Mariotto looked as if he had swallowed a toad. Pietro felt a weight in his stomach. The Capitano looked at them all, then gestured to Pietro. "Are you going back to the city to have your leg looked at?"

Pietro hadn't thought about it, but decided it was a good idea. "Yes, lord."

The Scaliger nodded. Looking slightly discomfited, he said, "I need some-one to deliver a message for me, and I need to know it will be done expedi-tiously, as well as with a modicum of tact. Are you up for it?" Pietro started to reply, but the Scaliger held up a hand. "Don't be hasty. This errand will be more dangerous than anything you have tried today." Cangrande took a deep breath. "I need you to find Donna Katerina Nogarola and tell her I will see her shortly. Until then, if she pleases, she will see to the wounded." It sounded simple enough until Pietro noticed Mariotto's surprised look. "She was last seen in the palazzo where we armed, but by now she might be along the walls of San Pietro, or even here in the field. If she's here, no doubt she'll find me herself," he finished in almost a mutter.

Pietro clambered awkwardly into the saddle of his fourth borrowed horse. "I'll do it, lord." *Who is this woman, that she makes Cangrande so un-comfortable?*

Cangrande bobbed his head in thanks and moved off, the matter immedi-ately forgotten as he focused on the next task in the battle's aftermath.

Pietro faced Mariotto. "Who is she?" Antony drew close to hear.

Still lying prone on the earth, Mariotto looked up with an idiot grin. "Bailardino's wife, Donna Katerina. If you wait a moment, we'll go with you. You might want some strong friends at your back. She can be outspoken."

"Outspoken? How?"

Mariotto struggled to his feet. "She's notorious for arguing with the Capi-tano in public, and winning more often than not. That's why he doesn't want to face her—she's going to flog him sideways for not talking to her before the battle."

As he remounted, Pietro recalled the snippets of conversation he'd over-heard on the steps of the palazzo. Something about a woman donning men's attire.

Antony was incredulous. "She argues with him? In public? Who is she?"

Mariotto's light blue eyes twinkled as he settled into a saddle. "His sister."

✦ ◇ ✦

The first stars were appearing in the sky as the proudly wounded trio reen-tered the city of Vicenza amid thunderous cheering. Hundreds of citizens swarmed around them like wasps, then buzzed past them out through the gates. Gazing at them, Pietro was astonished. He turned to Antony, who was looking on in slack-jawed amazement.

"So that's how he did it," muttered Mariotto in awe.

The citizens streaming past him bore improvised helms and arms, some looking quite ridiculous with old pots and pans on their noggins and fishing rods or long walking sticks strung with catgut in their hands. The women, children, and elderly of the proud city of Vicenza, the "archers," were thrilled with their role in the battle. They had routed the Paduan invaders and could tell this story for generations to come. Now they ran out to assist in rounding up the prisoners, dragging hounds to aid in chasing down the fugitives. Hungry for revenge, the citizens hooted and hollered, along with their animals, promising to show much less respect for the captured soldiers than Cangrande had.

Looking at the improvised bows and helms, Pietro released an appreciative breath. An old woman stopped to ask if they were hurt. *"Va bene,"* he replied, shaking his head. She kissed his foot and ran off to help in the chase.

"Is that your girlfriend?" asked Mariotto, shouting to be heard.

"Another Helen!" observed Antony loudly.

"Shut up." Pietro was busy trying to remember everything his father had ever told him about the Scaligeri line. The images from Giotto's frescos in the Scaliger palace rose before his mind's eye. Bartolomeo had been the first son of old Alberto della Scala. There followed the middle brother, cunning Alboino, who had died three years before. And finally a boy baptized Francesco della Scala, known from age three as Cangrande. But had anyone ever mentioned girl-children in the family?

"Mari!" Pietro was already addressing his friend in the familiar. His father would have been appalled.

"Ho!"

"She—his sister—she's married to Bailardino Nogarola, correct?"

"Yes!" shouted Mariotto.

"How now? How now?" called Antony from Pietro's other side. His tone was an exact replica of the Scaliger's.

"Would you stop that?" growled Mariotto.

"Stop what?" asked Antony with innocence.

Mariotto sighed in mock exasperation, then addressed Pietro. "The Capitano's sister. She's Bailardino's wife."

Antony was confused. "You already said that!"

Pietro broke in. "But Bailardino raised Cangrande, didn't he? Is she much older?"

Mariotto's wound had him sitting stiffly upright. "She certainly doesn't look it!"

Pietro decided that was about all the information he would get. They were now surrounded by citizens with another chore in mind—the salvation of their homes. The denizens of San Pietro were now madly fighting the fires that had been set to their buildings. Water could not arrive soon enough from the wells, and precious time was lost arguing whose house should be saved first. The three young riders skirted the crowds as best they could.

✦ ❖ ✦

Forty minutes after the cessation of hostilities, they arrived back at the Plaza Municipale. Where Pietro alighted there were several pages, easily distinguished from the general crowd by their dirty yellow tunics. They had been busy during this day of siege, running messages through smoke-filled streets, their faces lined with grime and soot. One dashed forward to take charge of their mounts.

"Thank you," said Pietro through gritted teeth as he put weight on his wounded leg. His mind was rapidly being consumed with the idea of a bed. But first he had to find this lady and give her the Capitano's message. He held the boy's gaze. "Is Donna Nogarola within?" He spoke loudly, for here too the noise of the populace was near deafening. "I have a message from the Capitano!"

From the shadows behind a rose-marble pillar a woman appeared. Tall and graceful, she wore a deep-blue gown of heavy brocade. The floral pattern in the material was fine and delicate, but the gown lacked the hanging panels down the back that style dictated. Its length, too, was shorter than was common, only just brushing the stone steps beneath her, rather than trailing after her. Her stride was confident and long, and Pietro decided from her manner that the alterations to her dress were for function rather than fashion. At her neck and wrists were none of the hanging ornaments Pietro had often seen adorning the ladies of the countless courts his father had visited. Her hands, he noticed as she waved away the page, were ringless beyond the heavy gold band on her third finger. Hanging at her waist, affixed to her sparsely jeweled girdle, was a ring of many keys that clattered softly. If a woman's position in society was evinced by the number of keys she wore, this lady was someone of great distinction. Her head was covered in a breezy, translucent veil that was pulled well back from her face with a band of the same brocade as her dress. Under it, her hair was tightly coiled at the back of her head. Thus her face was framed in blue, with only a cresent of chestnut above her brow.

It was a face different from Cangrande's—her nose was smaller and her cheeks were more angular. Her flashing blue eyes, however, removed all doubt.

Katerina della Scala *in* Nogarola halted a scant three feet from Pietro. By this time Antony and Mariotto were standing at his side. All three bowed—or tried. Each for his own reason had difficulty executing the move. The effort made Pietro wince, as all his weight was on his right leg. Mariotto's legs worked fine, but his upper body was stiff, and Antony grimaced as he lowered his aching head and spread his arms wide.

Amused, she said, "No, please. There is no need to wound yourselves further." The chatelaine's cadence was a near-perfect echo of the Scaliger's. "If you wish to do me honor, give me the message you bear."

Embarrassed, Pietro could not help noting her appeal. Montecchio couldn't be blamed for not guessing the lady's age. She must have been at least in her teens at the time of her marriage twenty years ago, but she looked no older than her warrior brother. *What beautiful wrists.*

"Donna," he said correctly, "the Capitano says he will see you shortly. He is busy clearing the field and seeing to the captives. He asks if you would undertake the succor of the wounded."

It was subtle, her reaction. The face changed not a whit, but Pietro noticed the delicate hands at her sides relax. "He is well, then."

It was not a question but Pietro saw fit to reply. "He is, Donna," he said, then cast about for more words. "The Paduan army is scattered, and he is victorious."

"Of course he is." Her tone carried a mild disapproval. She looked the trio over. Pietro's leg was bloody to the ankle, and the gash across Mariotto's chest seeped crimson to his waist. Mari was trying to cover it in the name of modesty. With a brisk gesture—so like him!—she beckoned several waiting attendants to her side. "He is unhurt, so he sends three wounded knights on his errands while he struts the field like the peacock he is." She waved their protests to silence. "No, please. You have heard his orders. I am to succor the wounded. I would be more than glad to begin here and now." With the aid of the attendants, the three youths were escorted within the palazzo, Donna Nogarola leading their way. "As we progress, you could perhaps honor me with your names."

The flustering of the three youths was suddenly complete. They literally fell over themselves apologizing for their lack of manners and hastily introduced themselves. "Mariotto, how delightful to meet you again—though I suppose the circumstances are a trifle unfortunate. You should come visit us with your father. You know he dines here often. Capecelatro—I'm afraid—ah, from Capua. Do you know Signore Gostanzo? He represents my husband's interests there. Indeed, you must meet. Alaghieri—son of? Of course. I have read your father's work. Did you help with the research?"

"Research, lady?" Pietro realized she shared her brother's sense of humor.

As the wounded young men were helped up a sweeping staircase, the chatelaine said, "I hope you all have the sense to stay here tonight. Even the immortal chevaliers of legend took time to let their wounds heal properly."

At the top of the stairs they encountered a group of Paduan nobles under a light guard. Antony pointed. "Mari! Look!" Pietro and Mariotto traced the line of the Capuan's finger to a well-built young man with dark hair and crimson pourpoint.

Mariotto shouted, "It's him!"

"Who?" asked Pietro, knowing full well who it was, but not understanding how Mariotto knew him.

"He's the one who shot at Mari!" declared Antony loudly, voice echoing in the palace confines.

"He shot Antonio Nogarola!" exclaimed Mariotto.

"He shot me," said Pietro, an odd satisfaction flitting through him. "He's the one I captured. He's my prisoner."

The small group of Paduans had stopped in response to the noise. The dark-haired young man turned to look at his accusers. "Ah. Nogarola, is it? Good. I like to know the names of the men I kill."

"You missed, turd!" shouted Antony.

"Fut. I won't next time. And Alaghieri—that's a name I won't forget."

"You can't," Montecchio sneered. "You're going to be sending him money for the rest of your life."

"However short that may be," added Antony.

"Don't pay him any mind," said Pietro dismissively. "He's a coward who uses a coward's weapon."

The young Paduan broke free of the group he stood with to approach Pietro. No one stopped him, though several guards gripped the swords in their scabbards. Pietro swallowed his pain to stand upright, so that when the dark-haired youth arrived, they were nose to nose.

"A coward's weapon?" hissed the Paduan. "I'll tell you who's a coward— your blessed Capitano, who hides behind fake bows and old men and women instead of fighting like a man."

"I didn't see him hiding," said Pietro, feeling his blood coursing through his veins. "That's more your style—cowering behind a woman's weapon. You were going to run after you fired that bolt, weren't you?"

"I'm here, aren't I?"

"Only because I took you down. More's the pity that you didn't go down fighting like a real knight."

The Paduan looked fierce. "My name is Marsilio da Carrara. You and me Alaghieri. Whenever you like, wherever you like, however you like."

Pietro felt the heat rising in him, and before he was aware he was saying, "Sorry, not interested. I won't be one of your Paduan *bardassi.*" Apparently Pietro had inherited his father's gift for insults. Marsilio flushed and lifted a fist. Pietro tensed.

Suddenly Marsilio screamed. Pietro was so startled he glanced at his own fist to be sure he hadn't actually hit him. It took him a moment to realize that the lady had put a restraining hand on Marsilio's arm—though why that should make him cry out, he couldn't tell. Then he saw the blood seeping from a gash in his arm, hidden until now.

"Oh, I'm sorry, young man," said Katerina della Scala in her most pleasant voice. "I didn't see your wound. That must hurt you. We'll have a doctor come around to look at it for you."

"I can manage," muttered the Paduan through a clenched jaw. He looked at Pietro. "Next time, Alaghieri, you won't have a woman's skirts to hide under."

"Next time," replied Pietro hotly, "she won't be here to save you."

"Wait in line, Pietro," cried Mariotto, shouldering forward. "He's mine first."

"Over my dead body," said Antony, also pressing toward the Paduan. "I owe him a clout on the head."

"Children, children!" smirked Marsilio. "There's enough man in me to face you all." He made an elaborate bow to Donna Katerina. "Madonna mia, it is an honor to be under your roof. I hope I can feel the hospitality I've heard you extend to all your male guests."

Katerina smiled warmly. "Young man, your tongue would have to be a good deal more talented than that for me to extend that hospitality."

Startled in mid bow and aware of the muffled laughter at his expense, Marsilio scowled. "*Putanna,*" he whispered. The lady's only response was to nod politely. Yet somehow when he turned he managed to get his feet tangled up, one on the other. He landed on his wounded arm and let out a shriek. Bleeding on the rushes, he had to be carried off in the wake of the other prisoners.

Katerina looked to Mariotto. "Did I hear you say my brother-in-law was wounded?"

"Yes," he answered. "Shot by that little—"

"Yes, yes. He made it quite clear what he is." She whispered instructions to a maid standing close by, who then scampered off. Pietro inferred her chore. She was to discover where the elder Nogarola's wounds were being dressed and by whom. Pietro pitied the short lord. If his wounds were not sufficiently grave, he would never hear the end of not seeking Katerina's aid.

The trio were escorted through a large receiving chamber into a private suite and told to recline on three fine daybeds. Their protests of soiling them came to nothing. "My maid Livia has a brother who is an upholsterer," said Donna Katerina, "I have been looking for a reason to employ him—at my brother's expense, of course."

The surgeon arrived, introduced by the lady as Ser Dottore Morsicato. He was long-armed and bald with a forked beard that curled up at the tips. Around his neck was the ubiquitous symbol of the medicine man: the *jordan,* or urine glass. Modern diagnostic theory was the balance of the four humors—phlegm, blood, bile, and urine. The *jordan* was designed to collect any and all of these, but the one most often used for diagnosis was "yellow bile"—hence the unsavory nickname of the glass. The doctor would collect his sample, then compare its color with a chart that listed twenty or more distinctive shades, each with a short list of illnesses attached.

Today, however, it was not the urine glass but the surgeon's saw that was required. "Good God," cried Morsicato sourly, examining the wounds, "I was brought here for this? There are men really hurt out there!" He dealt with Antony's head first, pronouncing him fit as long as he did not sleep for another twelve hours. "Strange things have been known to happen if a man

sleeps after a blow to the head. Sometimes he doesn't awake again at all."
Antony kept to his feet after that, pacing while the doctor dressed Mariotto's
wound. It was rather superficial and was medicined with a salve the surgeon
described only as "coming from Greece." He advised changing the dressing
that he wrapped about the youth's torso as often as three times a day.

With the two simpler wounds now behind him, the surgeon began to examine Pietro's leg. The lady tactfully withdrew as Pietro's ruined hose were
cut away and the process of removing the broken shaft of the crossbow bolt
began.

Morsicato had long experience with battle wounds—indeed, most of his
knowledge had been earned on one field of Mars or another—and thus knew
the best way to remove such a shaft. The problem was that, in all Pietro's activity after receiving the wound, the broken shaft in his thigh had shifted
slightly right to left. The doctor turned toward Mariotto and Antony. "I may
need your help to hold him."

With fire, with boiling water, with strong hands and several different-sized
blades, the surgeon went to work. To his credit, Pietro resisted crying aloud
for a very long time. He spent long moments comparing his plight to the souls
in torment in his father's work. He tried to joke about it, saying, "The Male-
branche's claws can't be as bad as this."

"Shhh," said Morsicato.

"Now, upside-down, with hot pokers at your feet, now that's painful . . ."

"Lie still," whispered Antony, holding his shoulders.

"No, I'm just saying that—damn—Hell can't be as bad as all that . . ."

"It's almost over," said Mariotto, hoping he wasn't lying.

Morsicato pulled one end as gently as he could, tapping the other end
with a hammer. Pietro howled at last, fighting to move his limbs.

"Hold him!" shouted Morsicato.

But, blessedly, Pietro had fainted.

NINE

The room was eerily dim when Pietro awoke. The curtains were drawn and the shutters closed, and the rows of candelabra that lined the far walls had all been extinguished. But a central brazier still glowed, warming the room and casting creeping shadows of infernal light into the rafters.

Sweating and gasping for breath in the close room, Pietro winced as he shifted his joints. He wiped the damp from his brow and blinked several times. Lying on a daybed, his lower body was covered with a steaming flannel—Florentine, he noted. Gingerly, fearfully, he reached out a hand to lift the coverlet.

Both legs were present. Breath hissed out between his clenched teeth. He had feared that the surgeon would just give up and amputate. But no, his leg was still attached, wrapped tightly in linen bandaging with a swaddled hot brick beneath it. No wonder he was drenched in sweat.

Across the dim room came a noise. It was the rustle of cloth over the rush-strewn floor. A figure approached, tall and regal. Donna Katerina halted a few feet away from him. In the warmth of the room she had released her hair. It was not sun-bleached like her brother's but a magnificently rich chestnut color, and it fell to the top of her thighs, draping across her back and swaying with every movement. With that luscious hair as a frame, and her face lit from below by the warm glow of the coals, she was no longer severe—she was breathtakingly beautiful.

Pietro recalled the banter before the battle when his friends had mocked the idea of going to war for a woman. In this moment it wasn't impossible to imagine.

Realizing he was holding his breath, he blew it out and inhaled quickly, swallowing a gust of brazier smoke that made him choke.

"Are you all right?" she asked, settling onto a stool beside him.

"Thirsty—" he choked.

A cup appeared, and though the water was warm he gulped it down greedily. "Thank you, lady."

"Shhh. Lie back."

He obeyed, settling back onto the daybed, propped up by a pillow he had been biting down on an hour before. From a bucket she produced a cloth, which she wrung out, then placed gently on his forehead. It felt wonderfully cool. Suddenly he was aware of just how much he was sweating. Worse, he was acutely aware of his nakedness under the flannel. He lay there, willing himself not to move as she mopped the sweat from his face and neck. It was, in the darkness, a very intimate act.

When his father had been nine years old, the poet had met a woman like no other. Donna Beatrice Portinari had inspired Dante to devote himself to her, a devotion that long outlasted the lady's life. Though he'd married elsewhere, in his mind, in his soul, Dante Alaghieri had given himself to the image and idea of a woman who was above and beyond all women—divine.

Father—I understand.

A stirring across the room caused the lady to pause. She replaced the cloth in the bucket and glided across the room, away from him. He took the opportunity to pull the flannel a little higher. The sweat was gathering at his back, making the daybed damp. He shifted again, this time rolling slightly to his left. He'd closed his eyes, so they took several moments to adjust to the light from the brazier when he opened them again. Strange shapes swam into and out of his vision. He'd had a fever as a child. This was very like fever, but far more relaxing.

Morsicato had spoken of this during the operation, trying to distract his patient. "The room will have to be kept warm to simulate the fever, and perhaps we can convince the body that a prolonged fever isn't necessary. Hopefully we'll purge the evil humors and restore balance to the gasses that've been lost."

"Signor Alaghieri?"

He hadn't heard her come back. "Yes, Domina?" He felt the thumping of his heart in his throat, the coarseness of the flannel across his legs.

"I thought you might still be awake." She resumed her seat, the keys jangling gently as they fell into the folds of her lap. "Do you know where you are?"

"Yes, Domina." His voice seemed very hoarse. He closed his eyes again.

"Good. Signore Montecchio has accompanied Signore Capecelatro on a walk through the city in an effort to keep him moving. Ser Morsicato has gone on to tend other patients, leaving you to aid me in fulfilling my brother's orders." Again Pietro heard the touch of disdain in her voice. The lady's hand resumed its chore, stopping only to refresh the damp cloth. "Signor, do you mind speaking?"

"Not at all, Domina." Pietro tried to sit upright, only to be restrained by a gentle hand.

"You must rest. I should not be speaking with you at all. But I find that the time goes by more quickly in conversation. Don't you agree?"

"Yes, Donna."

"You are recently arrived from Paris, no? Do you mind if we converse in French? I get to practice less often than I would like."

"As you wish," replied Pietro, switching to that tongue. If the lady wished to speak or listen was still to be determined, but either way Pietro was eager to aid her. He shifted again, trying to remove himself from the dampest part of the daybed while not dislodging the flannel. He found a more comfortable position—reclining rather than lying on the pillows—from here he could meet her eyes and remain at rest.

"You are uneasy," she observed, leaning slightly forward. "Is it the wound?"

The scent of her—*lavender,* he thought—filled Pietro's senses like a balm. "*Non, madame.*" It was true. At that moment, the wound was the farthest thing from Pietro's thoughts. For the rest of his life he would smell lavender and think of her, leaning over him, her gown's neckline opening . . . He hastened to change the topic. "Who else is here?"

She sat upright, half turning to glance over her shoulder. "My brother-in-law. He, too, had to have a bolt removed from his body—but he was attempting to do the surgery himself. He had the notion that I would be angry with him for some reason. Can you imagine that? A grown man, a knight, avoiding me?" Somehow French seemed to suit her mood, carrying both amusement and scorn.

"It is beyond all comprehension."

"Quite. I had to send several of my pages to fetch him here. As soon as Morsicato was finished with your wound, he began on Lord Nogarola's. There is some doubt as to the condition of his shoulder, but evidently he will live to face my wrath. Do you fear my wrath, Monsieur Alaghieri?"

"I should fear doing anything to displease you, Donna."

The soft mirthful ripple was more breath than voice. "I see. Diplomacy is a lost art, monsieur. You ought to lend it your skills. It would no doubt undergo a renaissance."

"Oui, Madame Nogarola."

"Pietro," she said, switching back to their native tongue, "I have been informed that you have, beyond all reason, risked yourself to save my brother's life. And that you rode into a band of armed men alone and unaided, thus winning the engagement for our city. When we are in company, you may refer to me as donna or domina. In private, my name is Katerina."

Pietro looked into the eyes of this woman twice his age and knew she could never be his. He also knew it didn't matter.

"Yes, Donna."

✦　◇　✦

The conversation continued in fits and starts, pausing as Donna Nogarola checked her brother-in-law or sent servants for fresh linens and water. After each brief interval, she returned to Pietro's bedside to ask more questions. He tried to describe her brother's actions, but she was more interested in Pietro. He found himself being asked about his life—growing up in Florence; the exile of his father; the brilliant, ambitious little sister; the youthful deaths of two little brothers followed by the death of his older brother Giovanni, which catapulted Pietro to the role of heir. He talked of the journey two years before to join Dante in Paris, after being separated from his father for ten years. He described their return to Italy in the wake of the Emperor Heinrich, and their eventual settling in Lucca.

When he reached their arrival in Verona the night before, the lady leaned back, her eyes narrowed. "So you had never met my brother before today?"

"Yesterday," he corrected as if it made a difference.

"Ah. Yet you rode, unhesitating, to his rescue?"

Pietro shook his head. "He didn't require rescue, Donna. We probably only got in his way."

She waved his protestation away. "Nonsense. He would be dead this minute, and the city entirely in the grip of the Paduans, if not for you three. You must be very skilled."

Pietro grunted. "At being a pincushion."

"No self-pity," said the lady firmly. "Francesco is blessed to have such inspired knights to remove his neck from the noose he made for himself." Pietro pointed out that none of them had been knighted. The lady said, "Not yet, at any rate. That, at least, is something he can rectify."

"Yes, I can," came a deep voice from the doorway. "And will."

Pietro sat up, but the lady did not even incline her head. "You took your time."

"I stopped to pick you flowers, Donna, but there was a frost when I entered your hall and they all withered away." The Scaliger approached as he spoke. Hooking a bench with his foot and dragging it to rest beside Pietro's daybed, he seated himself opposite his sister's perch. "How fares my guardian angel?"

"I'm fine, lord."

"He will live," supplied Donna Katerina. "No doubt he will follow you again someday, so you can attempt once more to cure him of that failing."

"I do what I can. No doubt Pietro will throw himself in the path of a hail of arrows next time and complete my chastisement." His posture bespoke a tension that he had not evidenced in battle. "It is fascinating to see you so— *motherly*, Donna. Perhaps the lady wishes to rectify a past error?"

"I tender my mercies on those I find deserving of them," said the lady. "And I am like Pietro. I loyally follow orders."

That riposte went ignored. "The room is quite warm, in spite of your chilling presence. I assume that it is Ser Dottore's advice?"

"Indeed, we must try to burn from these men the fever of their devotion to a false idol. We can only hope that they will regain their senses."

Cangrande glanced around the chamber. "Is that Antonio?"

"You noticed?" The lady's voice carried a mild surprise. "Indeed. He, too, turned pincushion for your cause. He was foolish enough to try to remove the pin himself. I cannot imagine why. Perhaps he heard a folk legend that inspired him."

"No doubt," said the Scaliger crisply.

Pietro couldn't believe his ears. The Capitano was losing his temper.

Katerina gazed down at Pietro. "There is a tale of a knight who was wounded thrice by his enemies and left overnight to die of bleeding and exposure."

"Perhaps Pietro has already heard the tale," interrupted Cangrande.

His sister ignored him. "As it goes, the knight removed the shaft of a crossbow and dressed his other wounds in the pelt of a wolf that had tried to dine on him. The next day he found the camp of the two attackers and gave them wounds identical to those he had borne, then left them together to fend for themselves." Finally, her eyes rose level with the Capitano's. "They did die, did they not, Francesco?"

"They did, Donna, but not from their wounds. They died because there was a frost that night and no friendly wolf came along to give them his warm fur."

She held her brother's eyes without flinching, "Then it seems that you are fortunate in your friends. They are always there to rescue you."

"I need no rescuing, Donna, when I am not in your presence."

The lady rose from the short stool. "Then I shall relieve you of that need by removing myself." The chatelaine handed him the damp cloth. Pietro noted that they were careful not to let their hands touch. "Signor Alaghieri, if you will excuse me."

At the door she turned. "Please do not leave quite yet. I have news." With those words, she departed.

There was an almost imperceptible sagging in the great man, a release of air held tightly in his lungs. He returned his gaze to Pietro. "Are you well?"

"Yes, lord."

"Good." He gave no explanation of the interchange with his sister.

Pietro, as the lady had herself noted, was adept at diplomacy. "Do you have word of the army?"

"Which? Ours or the Paduan?"

"Both."

"Ours will be here sometime in the morning—about ten hours from now, I would guess. No doubt ragged and ill-organized, but it will be here. By then I expect the bulk of the Paduan army will have reached home and started the fortifying process."

"Oh." Pietro was fighting the desire to ask the next question.

The Capitano saw the look and knew what it was. "Is there something on your mind?" he asked, all innocence.

"No, lord."

"You're wondering why I'm not riding headlong toward Padua and taking them unawares." Pietro nodded. "I tried that already this summer—you weren't here."

The Scaliger allowed Pietro to sit upright. "I heard about it."

"Good. So last month I had the whole Veronese army and I couldn't take the city. There is nothing to make me think I could take it with less than a hundred men, no matter how invincible they feel. The Paduans are very secure within their series of rivers and walls, and they've got those damned priests, della Torre and Mussato, who can breathe backbone into a willow. So without my army, why bother?"

The words sounded hopeless, yet Pietro sensed something in the Scaliger's tone. "So we don't go to Padua?"

In reply, Cangrande changed the subject. "I didn't see their general, did you?"

Pietro thought. He had seen many nobles, over a hundred, but no one with the deportment of the leader of this army. "He escaped?"

"I hope so. I know another friend of ours has. Though we fished his armor from the river, the slippery Count Vinciguerra of San Bonifacio has eluded us. Vinciguerra means 'In War I Win,' doesn't it? I might just make him change it. Fishmonger, maybe."

"Is that why we aren't going to Padua?" asked Pietro, trying to find the connection. "Because he escaped?"

"Oh, we're going." Cangrande's voice was level. "I just want to give their army a head start."

"But they'll be warned, they'll man the walls . . ."

In the red light from the glowing coals nearby, the Capitano's face was demonically delighted. "Have you ever seen a broken army come home? Yes, Padua will have more men—but they'll be frightened men, fatigued men, disillusioned and panicked men. They were sure they'd win today—dear God, how could they lose? Did you see the size of their army? No, this time I'll let the Paduan army do my work for me. The sight of all their men running for their lives, led by San Bonifacio in his shirt and hose—that may break the Paduans more thoroughly than I broke their army." The Scaliger laid a gentle hand on Pietro's shoulder. "Now, rest. Morsicato is the best at what he does—I'd hire him in a trice if he'd ever leave Katerina. Let yourself sweat out the reaction to your wound and by tomorrow you should be able to move around a little."

"But, lord, I—"

"I promise, Pietro, that when we are ready to undertake the journey to Padua, I will inform you. You won't be left behind. But only if you rest now. Close your eyes. I have nowhere to be for some time. I will stay here until you are asleep."

He helped Pietro settle himself comfortably on the daybed, changing the sweat-soaked flannel for another, fresh with steam. He paused to check the dressing on Nogarola's shoulder, then returned to Pietro and sat on the stool vacated by Donna Katerina. Taking up the cloth again, he laid it across Pietro's forehead. The wounded youth closed his eyes and allowed himself to relax. The heat of the room, the coolness of his brow, the soft smell of burning wood and spices in the brazier, all mingled into a drowsy miasma that consumed him.

+ ◇ +

Pietro dreamed, a series of images his unconscious mind could make nothing of. Though the setting was familiar, he didn't recognize the key figure, a shadowy fellow with long curling hair and a curved sword. Waking with a start, he found Cangrande's eyes upon him.

"You were talking in your sleep," said Cangrande. "Do you remember anything?"

"No, lord," said Pietro. His head was in a fog.

"Here, drink this." The Scaliger lifted the cup of wine with its mixture of poppy juice and hemp seeds that Morsicato had prescribed. As Pietro slipped back into the comforting mists, he wondered absently what he'd been saying.

Pietro dreamed again, but this time the visions were less obscure. He was lying on a bed, eyes closed, listening again to the voices of the two beautiful siblings. This time man and woman did not spar. Their voices were kept soft, their tones clear and concise.

"News, you said?"

"A woman has been to see me. She serves the Signora de Amabilio."

"Ah."

"Indeed. It seems the signora's husband was killed falling from a horse last April."

The voice was grave. "I take it she has a request."

"Sanctuary, if you take the city."

"Tell her it is granted." In the dream the Veronese lord rose to leave.

"It is not that simple." A brief pause. "The signora has recently given birth."

A silence, then the brother resumed his seat. He sighed. "A boy."

"Yes."

"Have you taken any steps?"

"I've sent for Ignazzio."

"And the Moor." As it wasn't a question, the lady did not respond. "She cannot be allowed to keep him."

"No. For all our sakes, but especially for the child's. There has already been an attempt."

"Has there? Who else knows?" There was a long stillness between them, broken by the words, "I must take him in."

"Yes, you must."

"If he lives."

"He will live."

"This will hurt my wife, of course."

"Better this pain now than the pain of her heir losing his station."

"If she has an heir."

"There are other children, are there not?"

The brother's voice was almost amused. "You are unusually delicate. Yes, there are. Two, at least. But girls."

"Well, then. Hide this one among the others. What is one more?"

"Interesting that she sent to you, not me."

"She knows the prophecy as well as we do."

"I see I have no choice. Will you help?"

For a heartbeat there was no sound in the room but the crackling of the fire in the blackened brazier.

"Thank you, Francesco. Of course I will."

"Don't thank me," he said bitterly. "I am only a tool of Fate."

Then an opiate-aided sleep reclaimed Pietro. He dreamed of a greyhound pursued by a pack of hyenas. Pietro twisted as in his dream the greyhound was brought down at the base of a collossal theatre, an ancient arena, staining the steps with blood.

II

THE HORSE *Palio*

TEN

Cities in Italy were reflections of local geology, each one owning a distinctive character based on local stone. Verona was made mostly of rose marble and brick, Padua banded marble and cold stone. In Siena one found a burnt red color everywhere. Bologna was terra cotta, and Assisi was the color of fresh salmon. Venice, with no local geology, was constructed from all of them, at great expense.

Self-proclaimed fountainhead of freedom, the city of Florence was composed of brown stones and clay tiles, lending it a no-nonsense air. Unlike many other city-states, Florence was not a cult of personality but a city of ideas. "The mother of all liberty" covered 1,556 acres enclosed by three sets of walls and was filled with nearly 300,000 people.

Straddling the River Arno, the birthplace of Dante Alaghieri was enjoying a breeze from the north. Clouds slid across the sky, growing ever darker. But the break in the heat was welcome on this, a market day like any other, as the thick crowds clogged the streets, stopping at the tents that lined the wide walkways. Citizens bantered and bartered with members of the various guilds in order to find the best use for their precious florins.

The coin of Florence was one of the most stable currencies in the world, perhaps because it did no homage to king, pope, or emperor, but to the city itself. One side bore the city's symbol, the lily. The other depicted John the Baptist, the city's patron saint. Thus the florin survived unaltered during sieges, riots, or coups, passing from hand to hand and making Florence's economy grow astronomically.

One shop owner was not attempting to strangle a final florin from a customer. His name was Mosso, and he was one of the great booksellers. His was not a mere tent but a fine wooden stall covered in awnings, erected each morning and deconstructed each night, at some cost. His precious wares needed the best protection from the elements. A few of the books were cheap prints of woodcuts, but the majority were hand-printed tomes, painstakingly copied by master scribes. All were of immense value—an edition of the Bible sold for a small fortune, so that only the richest men had copies. Which was fitting, as they were the only ones with the Latin to understand it.

The reason Mosso was not vying with customers stood before him. An unlikely representative for the unlikeliest of best-selling poets. Not knowing how to begin, the bookseller tried small talk.

"A cloudy day." After a pause, Mosso further observed, "I hear they're being drowned up north."

The author's representative wasn't interested in the weather. "How are sales?"

"It's going well—better than well, splendid. I'll be sold out in another week."

"I told you."

Mosso held up a hand. "Yes . . ."

"I told you to order more," insisted the representative.

The bookstall owner bit back his initial response. What one would usually tell a prickly proxy—to take a running jump in the Arno—did not apply here. Instead he forced himself again to agree. "Yes, you did, didn't you."

Pointing to an expensive book bound in engraved metal, the representative asked, "Is this the new edition of Paolino Pieri?"

"His *Cronica,* yes," said Mosso fastidiously. He pushed by the clerk who handled sales and slid to the end of the stall the representative had wandered to. The bookseller had to ask for more copies. They both knew it. The demand was incredible—a hundred copies gone in a day! His whole stock was almost gone, and worse, illicit copies were undoubtedly being made at this moment. He had to get more.

Yet it galled him, so he tried to talk around his problem. "What I can't figure out is why everyone wants it, when all he does is insult the city."

"He does quite a bit more than that." The *Cronica* was laid aside and a leather-bound copy of *Gesta Florentinorum* was unlocked instead.

"All that stuff about Fiesole—that's aimed at us."

"I'm surprised you noticed."

Bristling, the bookseller brought indignation into his voice. "Talking about the plant that springs out of their shit—begging your pardon—and turning into a nest of malice, a—what was it? A—"

" 'A city full of envy.' Canto Six." The representative's eyes studied the calligraphy of the fine Latin letters, an art that had been rediscovered by Brunetto Latini, just twenty years in his grave. Unfortunately he was burning in Hell among the sinners against nature and its goodness, according to the only authority that mattered.

"Yes!" cried Mosso. "Full of envy? For what, him? His writing? He's got talent, but too much hubris by far!"

Dante's representative didn't look up from the hand-painted letters, but the eyes had stopped scanning. "Hubris?"

Mosso realized his error. "I didn't mean . . ."

Slam! The *Gesta Florentinorum* dropped to the countertop. Mosso nearly screamed as he scooped it up. "For God's sake!" The thing was worth a small fortune, and he'd had to pay up front.

Dante's representative was unrepentant. "If you find it so intolerable, then you shouldn't be required to sell it. I'll give the contract to the Covoni. Return whatever copies you have left and I'll reimburse you three-quarters." The representative turned to leave, pushing past the buyers who now hurried to get their copies before they vanished.

Mosso was out from behind his stall as swift as quicksilver. "Whoa, whoa there, little miss. I didn't mean to insult you or your—"

"You're blocking my way," observed Dante's representative, her eyes level with Mosso's breastbone.

"Don't go to the Covoni. They'll take a month getting organized and by then the demand will have died down."

"Will it?" The voice was icy.

"I mean, it may have—I mean, no—probably not, but—" Mosso grasped at anything he could think of to retain this contract. "Their books aren't in order! Everyone knows that the author never sees the full amount agreed to—copies go missing and are sold under the table while they claim the loss—"

"Better that than a man who insults the book in front of prospective buyers. Please step aside."

Mosso looked about at the throng of people here in the street, all here to buy this very book, all listening with glee to the scene he was creating. He couldn't lose this contract! Grabbing the girl by her shoulders he pulled her into the lee of his stall. "Listen, little girl—we have a binding contract, you and I! I am the sole supplier for this quarter, and if you try to break it I'll have you in court!"

There was a light misting in the young lady's eyes, no doubt fright from being so roughly handled. But her expression became, if anything, more resolved. "Do. In the meantime release me or I'll have you up on charges for assault!"

The bookseller was trembling more than the girl as he let go and stepped back. "Please—my wife—she'll murder me if I lose this contract."

Dante's representative gazed at him, mouth thin. Finally she said, "You will triple your order, and another ten percent of the profit returns to the author." She waited for his nod of agreement, which he bobbed uncertainly at first, then more rapidly, before informing him that a clerk would be by later today with the new contract to sign.

Mosso sagged in relief. "I'm really very sorry." She stared pointedly at him until he moved aside and allowed her to pass into the street. He moved and she resumed her brisk pace, Mosso calling after her, "Those bits about the Sienese were really very funny . . ." He watched as she disappeared in the crowded street. He'd begun this battle to keep his pride and had ended up losing a fair chunk of gold. But it was difficult to acknowledge that his head for business was not as good as that of a thirteen-year-old girl.

Mosso glanced at the youth manning his stall and snarled, "What are you looking at? Get back to work!" Then, resuming his place behind the counter, he began to call his wares. "The *Inferno*! Dante's *Inferno*! Get it here, and here only! The only seller in this quarter, and the best price anywhere! Read the greatest epic since Homer! More daring than the *Odyssey*, more exciting than the *Aeneid*! Go to Hell with Dante, Florence's lost son . . ."

✦ ✧ ✦

Around the corner from Mosso's shop, Antonia Alaghieri leaned against a wall, breathing hard. That she had succeeded in the negotiation only made it more frightening. Her mother would certainly disapprove—*unladylike* would be the word. Brushing her mouse-brown hair from her face (for she was too young to hide her hair in public), Antonia daubed her eyes. Taking a few deep breaths, she stepped out into the lane and continued on her way.

The clouds in the sky were heavy as she strolled through the crowd. Antonia paused at the edge of the Ponte Vecchio, near the Martocus. The statue was the remains of the ancient god of war who had been the patron of Florence long before John the Baptist was born. As she always did, she looked to the enraged and broken marble face and whispered, "Forgive them. Please, forgive them, and bring him home."

Canto Thirteen declared that, because the city had turned its back on Mars, he would plague them with strife forever. It was through that strife that the Great Injustice had entered Antonia's life.

"Bring him home." In her mind's eye she conjured up the cover of the Pisan publication—the one bearing a stamp of an engraving of her father's face. It was as close as she could come to picturing his face, for she had never laid eyes on him, having been a babe in arms when the great poet was forced to leave Florence forever. Exiled.

Yet not knowing his face wasn't the loss it might have been. She knew his writings and, through them, him. Poems, epistles, canziones—and especially his letters. Early in his exile Dante had corresponded perfunctorily with his wife, not even acknowledging Antonia until, at the tender age of nine, she enclosed a note in one of her mother's replies. The note commented on a poem Dante had sent to be delivered to his copyist in Florence. Antonia had read it and secretly corrected a reference in it before it went to the copyist—he had referred to the wrong Caesar when citing Catullus, saying that the Roman poet had lived in the days of Augustus. It was clearly a mistake, for Catullus was famous for his wicked satires of Caius Julius Caesar.

Antonia made the correction, then wrote directly to her father to apologize for tampering with his work. The letter that arrived three months later—addressed to her!—was curt:

> The correction was, it seems, justified, for the mistake was not mine but your brother Giovanni's, whose understanding of dictation is more lacking than his grasp of hygiene. For the sake of the poem, I am grateful, but you must understand how wary I remain of any tampering with my words. Never do it again. Your loving father, et cetera.

This letter, a few scant lines from a man who was known to fill pages with irrelevant gossip, became Antonia's most prized possession. She wanted to reply immediately, but was wise enough to refrain until she had another literary subject to address.

She hadn't long to wait. A fortnight later, Cecco Angiolieri stole lines from an early work of Dante's to use in his own new poem. Antonia wrote to inform her father, who was furious and wrote a scathing diatribe regarding Angiolieri's talent and wit, to be published in Florence. This he addressed not to his wife, Gemma, but to Antonia. From that day forward his daughter was his connection to his Florentine publishers.

Over time his letters grew a little longer, and by the time she was ten, he treated her as equal to his many other correspondents. "I do miss her," he wrote early in 1312, just after the death of Giovanni and on the eve of Antonia's eleventh birthday. He was referring not to Antonia's mother but to the woman who had possessed his soul from the time he was seven—Beatrice Portinari.

> *The bringer of blessings has been dead more than two decades, longer than I can fathom having lived. Though she survives in my mind and in my words—much of which was written to be read by her—with each passing day it grows harder to remember her face. I suppose I grow old. My eyes have begun to fail me. But to have my innermost eye blinded by time, that is a cruel fate. I know she is a cherished soul in Heaven, but my earth is poorer for the lack of her. Only when I write to her can I feel her presence. And of late I cannot take up my pen to write to her, for I feel she is truly dead.*

Antonia's response was simple. It read:

> *In the future, you may address me as Beatrice.*

The change this brought to the poet's correspondence was as night to day. From a single sheet, his letters grew to ten or twelve pages on average. From four times a year they appeared almost every fortnight. At the same time all letters to Gemma ceased completely. "Tell their mother that my sons are well," he would often append, the only mention he would make of his wife. No longer curt, there remained discussion of poetry, but suddenly much more. Dante shared every daily event, every idea, everything he thought his beloved Beatrice might wish to know. His letters became long and rambling. Sometimes he seemed to forget which Beatrice he was writing to; but Antonia accepted that. She was fulfilling a function in her father's life. His writing flourished, and she found great joy thinking she might have contributed in some way.

Her present contributions were mundane rather than artistic. But necessary nonetheless. With a last superstitious nod to Mars, Antonia resumed her walk past the food shops of the Ponte Vecchio. She saw a new sign, freshly hung. A silversmith? On the Ponte Vecchio, where fruit, nuts, and grain were sold? Antonia deemed it foolish and moved on.

Over the Arno River she walked to an interview that promised to be at least as unpleasant as the one with Mosso. But it was their own fault, they hadn't listened! Not when she told them how popular *L'Inferno* had been in Rome and Verona and Venice and Pisa and even the small bits Dante had shown people in Paris; not when she told them that it would be twice as popular here, in the poet's birthplace, regardless of his political status; and not when she told them that they stood to make a killing if only they ordered enough copies to satisfy demand—a demand that would shame both *La Roman de la Rose* and all those silly Arthurian romances.

They hadn't listened, fearing instead the wrath of the Arti, the guilds, who had been part of Dante's exile. It was now clear that *L'Inferno* was something more than a mere novella, and now the whole city paid the price. Florence, one of the most literate cities in the world, suddenly feared being left out of a cultural phenomenon. *It serves them right,* thought Dante's daughter tartly. Since the order of exile had also beggared her family, she saw it as only justice that the whole city of Florence should pay them back tenfold.

Climbing the slight uphill grade to the road, she passed the house whose rooms she had let months ago. Inside scribes hunched day and night over vellum, cramped fingers scratching away. She decided to step inside and pass an hour. She was still a little shaken. And besides, it looked like rain.

Vicenza, Nogarola Palace

Over a hundred miles north of Florence the skies wept fiercely, pouring down in sheets that reduced sight to less than the width of a man's hand from his face. Torches illuminated nothing more than their brackets. Reports came of oxen and horses lost in mudslides.

Pietro sat with his leg propped up high on cushions, looking out over the balustrade of the covered loggia above a central atrium. The rain created a shimmering wall just beyond the lip of the roof, through which the other side of the building was made quite invisible. He could just discern the shape of a fountain below with three female figures pouring their water into the basin. Intently, he watched rainwater dancing in the overflowing fountain. He played with the laces of his doublet. He recited bits of poetry. He tried in vain to ignore the maggots wrapped into his leg's wound.

Maggots. Nothing in all Dante's traversing of Hell was so—disgusting. *Maggots.* Literally eating him. Morsicato, the Nogarolas' physician, had sworn that they were the best way to fight infection, that they only ate dead meat, not living flesh. So they were wrapped under the bandages, right in there with his puckered wound. *Maggots.* Pietro couldn't help imagining the soggy little white things gnawing away at him—*what if they move away from the knee? What if they move up . . . ?*

Cavalcanti. You were thinking of Cavalcanti. "Bilta di donna e di saccente core e cavalieri armati che sien genti . . ."

But poetry was no refuge from his imagination. Pietro had woken this morning from dreams of gigantic worms feeding on his blood and tears to find his little brother newly arrived and poking under the folds of the bandages for a glimpse of the little devils at work.

Of course Poco's curious. His brother is a walking feast for worms.

As if to illustrate the point, one of Morsicato's apprentices approached bearing a tray. "Master Alaghieri, if I may?"

"Of course." Pietro fought to keep his bile down. He'd already vomited twice today. It was one of the reasons he'd moved into the open air.

The apprentice physician knelt beside Pietro's outstretched leg, removed the blanket and lifted the long shirt, then began gently unwrapping the injury. "Rain shows no sign of letting up," he said.

"No," said Pietro, who was desperate not to watch the procedure of adding or subtracting maggots to the wound. "But it's good to be outside regardless. After two days of sweating, I'm glad to be outside."

"The army would disagree," said Morsicato's man. "I was out in their tents this morning looking after—well, nothing really, minor ailments." (*Venereal ailments,* thought Pietro.) "Anyway, they're all huddled in tents, wrapped in straw and murdering time by using pigs' knuckles for dice."

"How are they holding up?"

"They're anxious, I think. Wondering why we're not moving. They're full of rumors."

Pietro actually looked at the man. "What rumors?"

"Oh, some say having his victory snatched away by rain has driven him mad. That he's slain all of us in the palace and torn out hunks of his hair and dashed his brains out against the walls. Others say he's kept to the private chapel of the Nogarolas, begging the Lord to clear the skies. A few said he's found a new mistress to keep him occupied until the rains pass." The fellow gave a grim chuckle. "That, at least, would explain his delaying the attack."

Suddenly he looked guiltily up. "I mean—I didn't . . ."

Pietro pressed his lips together. But the man was only echoing what was in the mind of every man in Vicenza. When Cangrande's army had arrived a day after the battle, the Capitano had immediately dispatched a century directly back to Verona with most of the prisoners. Fourteen hundred in all, there were far too many to shackle, so Cangrande had their ankles bound in single file for the march. That done, everyone waited to hear him give the order to march for Padua.

That order never came. Instead Cangrande had called five of his most trusted councilors together, given them orders, and retired to his sister's palace. And now it was too late. For two days the rain had not stopped, swelling the natural defenses of Padua, turning the roads to muck, destroying any chance of taking the city and ending the war.

If he hadn't delayed, they might have been victorious. But to say so aloud was treason.

Pietro took a breath, thinking of what a man of his position should say. "I know it's difficult, but you have to trust our lords. Especially this lord."

"Of course, sir." The fellow bowed his head and continued gently examining Pietro's leg. An awkward pause lasted until Pietro said, "How is Lord Nogarola's arm?" Pietro hadn't seen the aging knight in the last day.

The man kept his head down, shaking it slightly. "Recovering from the surgery."

Pietro tensed. Surgery meant that Antonio Nogarola's broken arm had begun to fester. He was going to lose the arm. Pietro looked at his own leg, silently urging the little maggots on in their horrible work.

Squirming, he found himself wishing for the one person who could take his mind off his wound. He hadn't seen her since the early morning. Nonchalantly he said, "So is Donna Katerina with him?"

"No, sir. She is with her brother. They have been closeted all day with his closest advisors."

"I'm still new to Verona. What can you tell me about the Scaliger and his family?"

The apprentice gave him a quick glance, then said, "Well, sir, their father was the great Alberto della Scala. He had three sons by his wife. Two have died. Bartolomeo and Alboino. And there were two daughters, Donna Katerina and her sister Costanza, who was the eldest."

"Is she still alive?"

"Oh no," said the apprentice, lifting a fat maggot from the wound and staring at it. Pietro turned away. "She died around the same time as her second husband, Lord Passerino Bonaccolsi's brother."

Pietro had his eyes closed again, but he thought that the rewrapping had begun. "Passerino Bonaccolsi—he's the Mantuan lord. Someone told me he's Cangrande's best friend."

"They're close, but I'd have to say the Scaliger is closer to my master, Donna Katerina's husband. But then my master helped to raise him. The day he married Katerina he accepted her little brother as a squire . . ."

Pietro listened to the pieces of della Scala family gossip and tried to puzzle out Katerina's age. If Katerina was just married when she took her brother in, she was at least twelve years her brother's senior. That put her somewhere between her thirty-fifth and fortieth year, as close as he could guess. Twice his own age.

The apprentice was still praising the lord of Vicenza, and Pietro felt the need to change to topic. "You said that they're with advisors. Who?"

The fellow thought hard to list all the famous names. "Their cousin Federigo. The Mantuan lord Passerino Bonaccolsi. Lords Montecchio and Castelbarco, of course. And the Paduan Nicolo da Lozzo. Bishop Guelco. Oh, and the new man in Verona, Cap-something."

"Capecelatro," supplied Pietro, intrigued that Antony's father, so new and of an ignoble background, was being included. A cynical voice wondered how wealthy he really was.

"That's right. Oh, and your father! I'm sorry, he should have been first."

Pietro laughed. "You're forgiven. My father isn't known for his diplomacy."

The apprentice chuckled dutifully and leaned back. "There, sir. Is that comfortable?"

Pietro said it was, lying through his teeth. He knew he couldn't actually be feeling the maggots wriggling, yet he had to force himself to lie still. "Who else?"

Morsicato's apprentice made a face. "I heard that they've invited the two captured Paduans, Giacomo 'Il Grande' da Carrara and his nephew."

"That ass," growled Pietro involuntarily.

The apprentice said nothing to that, but added, "And a Venetian ambassador called Dandolo."

That made Pietro sit up. "A Venetian? What's he doing here? Is Verona going to war with Venice?"

"I have no idea, sir," said the fellow quickly, holding up his hands. "Please sit back. I've said all I know. Except . . ."

"Yes?"

"I don't want to speak out of turn." Pietro gave him an urging look. "Well, it's just that—I was passing the door not long ago and it sounded like—"

"Like what?"

"Like they were playing at dice."

"Dice?"

"That's what it sounded like. And Katerina was ordering more wine for them all."

Pietro digested this for a moment, then had to laugh. The fate of three cities, perhaps more, decided over dice.

The apprentice was gathering up his instruments and poultices, placing them on his tray. Pietro said, "When is her husband due back?"

"In two days, perhaps three."

If I were wed to Katerina I would never leave her side, thought Pietro. "Well, thank you for looking after me. And for the news."

The fellow tugged his forelock. "My honor, sir. There's much talk of your bravery. Your father speaks of it to everyone."

Pietro blinked at that. Before he could muster a proper response, the apprentice was gone to other duties.

Brave? Pietro's father hadn't used that word to him. The poet had been tight-lipped in public, only to launch into a caustic diatribe the moment they were alone. What had he said? Not brave, Pietro was sure of it. *Stupid,* yes. *Foolhardy,* certainly. *Thoughtless heedless jolt-head determined to land in an untimely grave,* that was still ringing in his ears. *But brave?*

He wondered if Katerina thought he was brave. He wondered about Katerina a lot. He found himself acutely resenting the shadowy figure of her absent husband. Insanely, he was also jealous of her relationship with her brother. However acrimonious, the connection was obvious. In the lady's disdainful treatment of her brother he saw a depth of feeling he had never witnessed before.

Thinking of Katerina had allowed him a blessed moment of forgetfulness. But an itching in his leg—*in* his leg!—reminded him, and he shifted it closer to the brazier that was pleasantly toasting his right side. *Maybe I can smoke them out.* He'd come out here hoping to drift into sleep. But the gnawing at his flesh, imagined or real, kept him awake.

To distract himself he continued piecing together the mosaic of Cangrande's family. There was Cangrande's uncle, the first Scaliger ruler of Verona, called Mastino. Then his father, Alberto, his three brothers, and two sisters. Pietro remembered his own father talking of Bartolomeo warmly, and disdainfully of Alboino. And with open hostility toward the late Abbot of San Zeno, father of the current one. A bastard of Alberto's, wasn't he? *I wonder if there are any other by-blows out there, any bastards with the Scaligeri blood. Mariotto hinted that way.*

There was a thought there, something nagging at his memory . . . a conversation between brother and sister—but he couldn't grasp it. With a sigh he sat back, closing his eyes and focusing on the rain, feeling the heat of the brazier gently warming him . . .

A hand shook Pietro awake. He opened his bleary eyes and found the Scaliger himself kneeling at his side. "Do I bother you? Were you dreaming?"

"Just dozing," said Pietro, shaking his head clear.

"Mmm. These days when I dream, I dream of rain." Cangrande crossed to the other side of the brazier where a cushioned chair had been placed. "I hope you don't mind if I make use of your brazier. Supper will be served soon." Cangrande reclined in the chair, fingers steepled at his lips, eyes on the rain.

"Are the conferences over?"

"Yes. Everything is settled."

Pietro was dying of curiosity, but he bit his tongue. They sat together for a time, staring into the shimmering wall of water that pounded the cobblestones beyond the lip of the roof. The sound was hypnotic, as was the shivering light from the brazier reflecting off the rain. Pietro's eyes grew heavy-lidded again.

"Do you think your father is right?"

Pietro had to rouse himself, shifting to sit upright. "About what, lord?"

"About the stars." The Veronese lord shifted in his seat so that he leaned toward the rain. It brought his face into view on the far side of the smoking brazier.

"I, ah—I don't know what you mean, lord," was Pietro's feeble response.

Cangrande rose and clapped Pietro's shoulder. "Come. We'll discuss it at supper."

Confused, Pietro felt himself lifted upright. "Me? At supper, lord?"

"Yes, you, at supper. It's a small party—your father, the Venetian envoy, Il Grande and his nephew, the poet Mussato, Asdente, and myself. With you, we'll make eight. We need another to make up your father's magic number, but who? Not Guelco—I've foisted him off on Mariotto's father, with the impressive figure of Signore Capecelatro as his second. And your two friends are off exploring the Montecchi stables, I believe, so they're out of reach. Poor Nogarola is back in surgery. I know—I'll invite Passerino to join us, that will be nine. The Nine Worthies. Your father will approve."

ELEVEN

It took time for Pietro to navigate the halls, and the others were already gathered when he and Cangrande arrived. The Scaliger greeted them genially, as if half their number were not sworn enemies, with feathers on the right side of their caps and red roses pinned to their gowns. "Please, sit! This is an informal gathering. Now that we are no longer wrangling we can enjoy each other's company."

"Just tell Asdente to keep his dice to himself," declared Passerino Bonaccolsi genially. "I've lost a month's rents to him."

Vanni gave his ghastly grin. "Fine. We'll use yours."

Cangrande named everyone at the table to Pietro, ending with the only man Pietro didn't already know. "This is Francesco Dandolo, Venetian ambassador and co-owner of two of my names. He is a *Cane,* too. Isn't that right, Dandolo?"

The Venetian made a deep bow to Pietro, ignoring what was obviously some kind of jab. "Honored to meet you, sir. I hear you acquitted yourself well in your first battle."

"That he did," said Cangrande before Pietro could answer. "And from a man once destined for the church! If things had gone apace, he might have been able to intervene for you with the pope!"

The Venetian saw Pietro's puzzlement and sighed, saying, "I was entrusted with the task of removing the excommunication Pope Clement laid on the Serenissima, our noble city."

"That floats on a bog," remarked Cangrande. "And this noble man, to do honor to his home . . ."

"Come," interrupted Il Grande, "the meal waits."

Cangrande was not averse to letting his story go, having already made the Venetian visibly uncomfortable. To his credit, Dandolo regained his composure as he settled at the far end of the table.

Pietro found himself at the table's middle. Close on his right sat Il Grande, and directly across the table sat Giacomo's nephew. That one refused to speak or even look up, which suited Pietro fine.

On Pietro's other side Albertino Mussato had been given a wide leeway for his splints. The historian-poet bore a broken leg, a broken arm, and a fierce knob on the top of his head. Down the boards, Asdente sat bolt upright in a straight-backed chair, a fresh bandage wrapped about his head like a turban.

Pietro's father and Mussato were acquainted, having both attended the crowning of the last Holy Roman Emperor in Milan. As they sat, Dante asked after Mussato's head wound.

Albertino grimaced. "It's hard to say if it's addled my brains or not. I'm able to write, but someone else will have to read it to see if it makes any sense."

"I'll read it happily," offered Cangrande, taking his place at the head of the table. On his right sat Il Grande, on his left the Mantuan lord Passerino Bonaccolsi. Cangrande looked past the latter to Il Grande's nephew. "Marsilio, the wine stands by you." Young Carrara grudgingly passed the wine.

"You may not enjoy my new piece," warned Mussato. "It's a screed against you."

The brilliant smile leapt forth. "Really? Will it be good?"

"Oh, it will be excellent. But, my dear Dante, I have yet to congratulate you—*L'Inferno* is the finest epic since Homer."

"Well, Virgil, at least," corrected Dante. He had been placed across from Mussato, no doubt to let the two men converse on their craft. As the company settled itself, there was some technical talk between the poets regarding canticles and cantos, publishers and copyists. Mussato was grandiose in his praise, though Pietro thought he was forcing it a little. Il Grande busily chatted with Cangrande, but Passerino Bonaccolsi turned to add his praise to the *Inferno*. "Wonderful—though I do take umbrage over your treatment of dear sweet Manto. We Mantuans keep Virgil near to our hearts, and to hear him excise her son Ocnus entirely from the birth of our city—well, I wouldn't come visit for a while, is all I can say."

This, thought Pietro, *from a man whose own father is treated harshly in the story. More upset because Father removed the magic from the founding of Mantua.*

Dante answered blandly, invoking God's gifts, not his own. Mussato said, "Don't you mean 'the gods'? That's what your beloved Virgil says, with the words you put in his mouth."

Dante said, "My poor mentor never knew Christ's glory, since he died before the birth of our Savior. He refers to the divine in the only terms he would have known. But just because they were so unfortunate as to not know the true Divinity does not mean they were incapable of glimpses of truth."

Mussato glanced at the Scaliger. "That's true of a lot of people today."

Asdente said, "We had a fellow on campaign who could read—he was probably killed yesterday, come to think of it. Each night, to scare the younger soldiers, he'd read aloud from your poem. I really enjoyed seeing them shit themselves from fright. 'That's what you'll get,' I told them, 'for impiousness and fornication!' Kept them out of my hair for months." The Toothless Master cackled.

"Indeed," said Mussato, "your use of *contrapasso* is brilliant. Bertran de Born, carrying his own head! A marvel! I mean to steal it to use against the Greyhound there. For God's sake, someone, pass the wine. My head's killing me."

As the wine was passed again Dante leaned his forearms on the table. "Tell me, what form will your screed take? Epic?"

Passerino Bonaccolsi said, "For Cangrande? I'd be surprised if you could fill three stanzas with his life story. Look at him! Still a stripling! If he were a fish, I'd throw him back!"

"A damned lucky stripling," snorted Asdente into his wine goblet. The metal bowl made his voice reverberate. "He always gets what he wants."

"Now, now, Vanni," grinned Cangrande, "I don't always get what I want. If I did, then you'd be Veronese, and my sworn man to the death. Padua couldn't stand without you."

Asdente chuckled. "Padua could stand against anything in the world— except you, Pup!"

Cangrande beamed. "Pup! Now there's a title I haven't heard for a while! And how does the great Count of San Bonifacio?"

"Not so well, I imagine," said Il Grande. "After this, he'll have to admit that his Pup has grown into a proper hound."

"With teeth for tearing," added Mussato. "I'm lucky my right hand can still scratch a few lines."

"Which brings us back to my question," said Dante patiently. "What form?"

"I'm writing a play," said Mussato happily. "Seneca would be proud."

"A play in Seneca's style?" cried Dante. "Fascinating."

"God," implored Asdente. "Here I thought we had a good conversation going—death, treason, murder, war. But no! Poetry! It always comes back to poetry. Pah!" He spat as if he were eager to be rid the word.

Dante ignored him. "So this is to be a dark tragedy?"

"A tragedy for the people of Verona, as dark as my mind can make it."

"And I'm the villain of the piece?" asked Cangrande proudly.

"Oh, no, no! I'm setting it back in the days of Ezzelino da Romano, when he was ripping up the countryside like you are now. The play will show what happens when a tyrant is let to rule over us. Your name will not be mentioned."

Disappointed, the Scaliger nevertheless raised his glass to Mussato. "When it is finished, you must send me a copy. I'll fund the first production."

"Figures," growled Asdente. "Everybody knows you enjoy hanging around with actors and other parasites."

"And you, my sweet Asdente, and you."

Amid the jeering and laughter the first course arrived, and for a short time everyone was occupied with plates of armored turnips, a dish of ash-baked turnips covered in spices, cheese and butter. Pietro was grateful for the activity. He was extremely uncomfortable in this august company, and well aware that the only person near his own age and rank was staring murder at him from across the table.

Il Grande swallowed and pointed his knife at Dante. "Tell me, Maestro Alaghieri. You were once a devout Guelph."

"How devout can a White Guelph be?" interjected Marsilio.

Ignoring his nephew, Il Grande continued. "Now you live at a staunchly Ghibelline court and are a supporter of the Emperor. I admit that being an exile would sour me against my home, and I can certainly understand how a bad pope can make one jaded about the Church—but do you really, truly believe that the Emperor should not be subject to the papacy?"

"I do."

"Oh God," muttered Asdente, rolling his eyes at his neighbor Dandolo. "Here we go."

"It's what this war is about!" cried Marsilio da Carrara.

"It's not," growled Asdente. "It's about land and taxes, like everything else."

"I think you underestimate men," said the Venetian Dandolo. "For some it is as you say. But to many men this issue matters."

Cangrande pointed an accusing finger. "Says the man whose country takes no position. You are certainly a politic politician, Dog Dandolo."

"But he's correct," said Il Grande, leaning back and regarding Dante. "It matters to men like me. So how, Maestro, do you get around the biblical argument? Genesis says two lights, a greater and a lesser, one for day and the other for night. Science tells us that one is reflected light, so if the pope's light is the sun, and the emperor's light is the moon, the emperor must derive his power from the pope."

Dante smiled thinly under his beard and swallowed. "That is indeed the *common* argument. But broaden your horizons. God, infallible, created man as a dual creature—one part divine, one part earthly. The pope's dominion is over the divine, the soul, the spirit—but he has no authority over the temporal part of us. That is the emperor's domain."

"But isn't the flesh subject to the soul?"

"Not necessarily. What is true is that flesh is corrupt—we wither and we die—while the spirit remains incorruptible. The two are separate by their natures, ergo God has set us two goals: *Beatitudenem huis vitae et beatitudenem vitae eterne*. I believe the emperor's authority *must* be derived directly from God Himself, as he is charged with maintaining order and peace during this testing time of humanity—for it is while we wear this weak flesh that we can prove our true devotion. If anything, the emperor's charge is the more important, because the one essential for man and the reason to reach their full potential is lasting peace. Only when the whole world is governed by one man whose power comes directly from God above can humanity have the calm it requires to return to its state before the Fall."

Marsilio da Carrara sneered. "And from which demon did you hear this nonsense?" The other faces around the table grew stiff, including his uncle's.

"Nonsense?" interjected Pietro. "I'd like to hear you do better defending the corruption of the Church!"

"I don't talk," sneered Marsilio. "My voice is in my sword."

"A shame that isn't true," retorted Pietro. "If you were half the swordsman you are a braggart—"

"My lord," said Dante, turning toward Cangrande and waving a hand in front of his face, "I think we require another brazier. There are a couple of gnats buzzing around in here that need smoking out."

"No, there's enough hot blood in the room already," said Il Grande, shooting his nephew a dark glare. Marsilio sank back and glowered. Pietro held his eyes, trying to look hard-bitten.

Asdente watched the two of them with pleasure. "Ah, youth. The young make the best soldiers. They have so much energy!"

"I think it's because every little thing matters," said Passerino Bonaccolsi, pushing back a plate and licking his fingers. "A molehill becomes a mountain."

Il Grande smiled. "It is fortunate then that we Paduans are not governed by a single youth. I wonder that Verona can cope."

Cangrande grinned. "Ah, young though I am, my wisdom is Solomon's because my light is not reflected. It is my own."

A second course arrived—an almond fricatella, which consisted of crushed almonds strained through milk and rosewater, then added to ground chicken breast, meal, egg whites, and sugar. Most of the table fell to with gusto. Pietro and Marsilio continued to glare at each other.

Cangrande resumed civilized discourse, saying, "I would like to renew a debate we were having while you gentlemen"—here he indicated the Paduans—"were storming the walls of San Pietro. We were discussing the role the stars play in our lives."

Predictably Dante spoke first. "The significant phrase here is 'Ratio stellarum, significatio stellarum.' Pietro?"

Pietro cleared his throat and spoke to Marsilio, as if explaining to a child. "Ratio stellarum, significatio stellarum—the order of motion versus the significance of that motion. Ratio—the stars circle above the world in an ordered pattern. Significatio—that pattern has a purpose . . ."

"There's a leap of faith," muttered Asdente.

"It's rude to interrupt, Vanni," chided Cangrande, but Pietro was grinning—the sneering Marsilio had turned away.

"Asdente does have a point, though," observed the Venetian Dandolo. "Is it wise to assume that there is a purpose to the stars? Why that only? Why not the motion of the clouds, or the flight of an owl?"

Il Grande shook his head. "That's paganism."

Dandolo chuckled. "I suppose it is."

"Is it?" asked Mussato. "Or would we be wise to look for God's will in all His creation?"

Cangrande's grin created creases on each side of his mouth. "Dear Lord, do Dandolo and I have something in common? Tell me it's not so. Still, as excommunicants we would, I suppose. I know it's hard to believe, but I once believed I was a good Christian. As I get older, I worry. I often get caught up in this—what did Abelard call it?"

"Theology," supplied Mussato.

"Yes. 'God logic.' And am regularly chastised for it by clergy near and far."

Passerino Bonaccolsi thumped the table with his fist and pointed. "Perhaps by the time you can shave you will have already worried yourself gray, hound!"

The Mantuan roared at his own joke. Cangrande sighed, then continued. "Monsignor Carrara, have you noticed that no matter how often they are derided, some ideas can never be extinguished? The ancients believed in the power of the stars. So do we. Ours are even named for the old Roman gods, and they have much the same power. They live in the sky, choosing life or death for the mortals who are merely pawns to their amusement. Some refer to the true God the same way."

Pietro said, "You are no one's pawn, lord. You just proved it." There were murmurs of assent from the Veronese.

"Did I?" The Scaliger waved a hand at the ceiling upon which rain pelted down. "Look outside and tell me what I achieved."

"You can't blame yourself for the rain," said Asdente. "Luck, nothing more. Good for us, bad for you."

Cangrande shook his head. "Luck, or fate? Ask the stars, Vanni! Perhaps it is God's desire for Padua to remain independant. Perhaps I will never . . ." His voice trailed off, silence lingering in the wake of his words.

"What is this?" asked Dandolo abruptly from the far end of the table. "The great Greyhound doubting himself?"

When Cangrande did not reply, Mussato cleared his throat and said, "The Church tells us the science of astrology is God's plan made manifest."

Il Grande shook his head. "What if the stars are not the celestial book of Fate? What if the ancients were correct? What if the stars are active participants in our lives?"

"They are," said Dante. All eyes turned to him. "It is not paganism. The stars do exert influence over us. They make plants grow and wither. They create imbalances in the mind. Venus arouses the loins, Mars the sword."

Cangrande stirred. "I am told Mars was in the House of Aries when I was born. Does that mean I was destined to be a soldier? What if I had denied that fate? What if I had said no?"

Asdente said ungrudgingly, "You are the best soldier in Italy."

"Thank you for that, Vanni. But I had a good teacher." The Capitano slapped his hands together. "Even that! Was Bailardino put in my path by the heavens to create my destiny? What if I had said no? *Could* I have said no?"

Puzzled, Asdente said, "Why would you have wanted to?"

The Scaliger was earnest. "Because then we would know that we have a choice in our own lives."

All the men at the table sat quietly for some time, chewing upon their meals and their thoughts. At last Francesco Dandolo spoke, his voice a dreamy whisper "Have you ever been to sea? I find the best example of the power of the stars is at sea. At sea, the stars are both the guide and the enemy. They give the sailor a map to his destination while at the same time they stir the seas he sails on. They show the path, at the same time creating obstacles to that path."

Cangrande's eyes narrowed as he listened. "They show the prize, then strip it away."

Hoping to avert the Scaliger's dark thoughts, Pietro turned to Dandolo. "The stars don't always make the seas rough, do they? Couldn't they create a smooth course just as easily? Why must they be the enemy?"

The Capitano's head swiveled. "Quite right. Why must they?"

But Il Grande chose to follow an earlier thought. "Still, the choice is theirs. The stars choose which men to aid, which to oppose. What does it say about the men they befriend? Are those men more capable, or less?" His eyes met Cangrande's. "Which did they do for you, lord Capitano?"

"I don't know," replied the Scaliger. "Some men would say they favor me."

"But what do *you* say?"

Cangrande pursed his lips. "Can a man ever know the Lord's will?"

"It would be arrogance to try," observed Mussato. "His will is a mystery. Man's fate is up to God alone."

"But that denies free will," countered Dante, "a concept that the Church does allow for. A man takes active participation in deciding his own fate. Or else what's the point of living?"

Mussato leaned as far forward as his injuries allowed him. "Ah, but what if he chooses a different interpretation of that fate than God intended? A man meant to be a soldier becomes a farmer. Will the stars oppose him? Will God?"

"What do you say, Pietro?"

The Scaliger had seen the change in Pietro's expression. But Pietro was too embarrassed to share his thought. "I—I don't know. I do know that my father has a very strict view on astrology."

The Scaliger threw Dante a sly glance. "I know. Soothsayers get tossed into the infernal ring reserved for fraud."

"There is a specific distinction," corrected Dante. "A soothsayer is not an astrologer, but a reader of entrails. That is superstistion. Astrology is a science, one I adhere to. But, like priests, there are good and bad astrologers. The only astrologers I condemn are the ones who try to alter the will of Heaven, or else try to curry favor by creating prophecies out of whole cloth."

"Poor Manto!" cried Passerino. "Dante, throw us a bone!"

"I did—hers."

There was some little hilarity at this remark, but Cangrande was not deterred. He clapped his hands together and divided the air in front of him. "Where is the line, poet? As someone who finds himself accused of being a figure from a prophecy, it concerns me deeply. What separates the active interpretation you advocate from the willful disobedience you deplore—or, should I say, He deplores?"

Dante wore his best enigmatic expression. "I suppose it comes down to the will of the Lord."

The Scaliger's mocking grin grew wide as he shook his head in disgust. "As always, poet, you wax eloquent on broad themes but on specifics remain cryptic."

Dante spread his hands. "Of course, my lord. What else are poets for?"

The subject was left alone and the supper went on, course after course. Conversation wandered into easier topics, no less hotly debated. There were discussions of battle tactics, of women, of politics, of wine. The meal ended with a delicious apple fricatella and a vigorous debate over the fate of the Knights Templar, finally stamped out earlier in the year. Jacques de Molay, Grand Master of the Knights Templar, had been burned at the stake for heresy. Before falling to the flames he proclaimed his innocence and declared that God would be his avenger. He called down a curse upon the French king and his issue down to the thirteenth generation. His last words were a summons for both King Philip and Pope Clement to meet him at the seat of God's judgment before the year was out.

The whole affair was forgotten until Clement dropped dead less than a month later. Pietro remembered the frantic editing, the numerous messages sent to all the hired copyists, as Dante added a prophecy of the pope's death to the nineteenth canto.

The men seated about the Capitano's supper discussed with great relish the prospects for the demise of the French monarch. Though all were skeptical of the Templars, not a one held a doubt as to the cause of their ultimate destruction—the greed of Philippe le Bel, the French king.

Pietro listened, trying to absorb the thoughts of these great men. The whole evening had amazed him. Not just the debates, but the camaraderie of the men. Asdente had tried to split Cangrande's skull not three days past, but here the Scaliger treated him like a beloved cousin. Il Grande was courteous and friendly and seemed to truly enjoy Cangrande's company. Mussato had visibly relaxed, relishing the evening as much as his injuries allowed. Even the sullen Marsilio had perked up when the talk had shifted to battles won and lost.

The only exception was the Venetian. Cangrande needled Dandolo at every opportunity. Cheerfully, playfully, with a veneer of civility. But mercilessly.

Eventually the meal broke up. Marsilio da Carrara was the first to rise, perfunctorily asking his uncle's permission to retire. He didn't glance back as he left the hall. Asdente and Passerino headed back to the salon for a game of dice. Dandolo and Il Grande helped Mussato to his feet, from whence a bevy of servants conveyed him to his "cell," as Cangrande jokingly put it. No prison ever had the luxuries the Paduans were presently enjoying. The Capitano believed in killing his enemies with kindness.

Cangrande was still talking to various servants when Dante approached his son. "How are you feeling, boy?"

"Fine, sir," replied Pietro, trying not to picture what was going on under the bandage on his leg.

"Good," said Dante gruffly. "Then I'm going to bed." He glanced up at his son's bare head. "The new hat?"

"Lost on the road," said Pietro.

"Mmm." With a pleased smile Dante departed.

Finished instructing the servants, Cangrande turned to Pietro. "Staying up? Then let us return to your perch on the porch."

Back under the portico, a fresh brazier beside them, Cangrande said, "You were fairly quiet tonight, Pietro."

"I didn't have much to add."

"Take it from one who knows, lying is a bad habit to fall into. You had plenty to say. And not just to Marsilio," he added wickedly.

Pietro felt his face grow warm. "I was the youngest there—"

"Marsilio only has a couple of years on you, and you're infinitely better mannered. So, what was it you were thinking?"

"It—it's about—when you all were discussing the stars," said Pietro hesitantly. "You asked where the line was, between interpretation and willful disobedience. Perhaps—" He stopped short. His words did not seem adequate to express the idea in his head. But the Scaliger was waiting. "Maybe it's a little of both. A man may not deny what the heavens have in store for him—as a sailor cannot control the waves—but he can choose what he does when the waves hit."

Cangrande seized the thought. "You mean that, though the stars may give him a map, it is up to him to follow it."

"Something like that," nodded Pietro. "But more than a map. Fate throws an obstacle in our way. We decide how to deal with it. That's our free will. We cannot fight Fate, but we can choose our reaction to it."

He ground to a halt, realizing how stupid he sounded. He watched as Cangrande kindly turned his words over and over, as though they were worth considering. When the Scaliger spoke, his tone was musing. "A man may be master of his actions, but not his stars."

"It was just a thought, lord," added Pietro hastily.

The Scaliger looked up from his contemplation. "And a fine one, Signor Alaghieri! I wish you had spoken it at supper. That sentiment far outstrips anything said by the warriors, diplomats, and poets tonight. You are wise beyond your years."

"This surprises you?" mocked a feminine voice from behind them. Pietro twisted around to see.

"Ah, Donna Katerina." A glimpse of his sister was all he needed for his glib demeanor to return. "No doubt he is wise, but for the desire to see me yet living."

"Age may well temper that desire," said the lady. Again her hair was down, held back by a single band of black.

Pietro managed to stand awkwardly. He was graced with a brief nod before Donna Nogarola again fixed her eyes on her brother. "If you are done wallowing, I have news."

"It is arranged?"

"It is. Do you wish me to go?"

"Have you tramping about in this weather, catching your death from the chill?" replied Cangrande with mock horror. "That would never do. Bailardino would never forgive me."

"Then I owe my health to your fond feelings for my husband?"

"He raised me. I am the man I am today because of him."

"Perhaps I should thank him with a gift each year on your birthday. What should I choose?"

"A knife?"

His perfect smile was returned in kind. "My dear brother, you read my thoughts. But the knife that kills my husband would have to be sharpened on both ends, so it would cut out my heart as well."

As before, Pietro had trouble following the exchange. Their discourse was like an onion, each layer revealing another. It was impossible for an outsider to know what lay at the core. Something ugly, that was certain.

Katerina sighed. "So I am not to ride out tonight. Whatever would I do without your regard for me?"

"You shall never have to know, my sweet, for of all people, you have my fondest regard."

"So, whom do you propose sending on so formidable an evening?"

"No one."

A frown passed over the lady's face. "Have you changed your mind?"

"Not at all. I do not propose sending anyone. I shall undertake the voyage myself."

The lady's disapproval was manifest. "You will be missed."

"I will be drunk, if anyone asks. Or perhaps I have taken myself to pray in the chapel. Or at an orgy—in the chapel. I leave it to your imagination."

"My imagination often falls short of your reality. Nevertheless, I will play the spider and spin a web of lies for you. You should not go alone."

"Should, could, would, dear sister. I will have it my own way."

"Not if I say otherwise."

"Even then."

Their gazes locked, neither giving ground.

He didn't know where Cangrande planned to journey, nor why Donna

Katerina wanted to undertake the trip herself. All he knew was he wanted to be helpful to them. Almost before he realized it he was saying, "I'll go with you, lord."

Both Scaligeri turned. Pietro felt a frisson of unease as their eyes examined him. Still, he pressed on. "I'm well enough, and I've been going mad lying still all the time. I want to *do* something."

Brother and sister exchanged a look. Cangrande spoke first. "I would be glad of the company. With that said, I don't want you to worsen your injury or fall ill from a drenching. I have a long ride ahead of me. We wouldn't be back before morning. If at all," he added ominously.

"I would be honored to aid you in any way, my lord."

"You didn't answer my question, Pietro," he said.

"Perhaps you should ask one, then." Katerina was severe. She stepped forward and laid a light hand on Pietro's sleeve. He could smell a hint of spiced malmsey on her breath, mixed with the wonderful lavender. Her proximity was enough to make Pietro forget the chill rain. "What we want to know is if you're well enough. Are you?"

"Yes, lady."

"This errand will be a secret, though its outcome will not. These events must always remain beneath the rose, as it were."

"Or *herkos odonton*," said Cangrande. "As the Greeks say, within the hedge of your teeth."

Katerina examined her brother with dismay. "Show-off. But I find the image of Cupid bribing some fool's silence for a rose somehow endearing."

"And appropriate, if I am to play Cupid. But Pietro is no fool."

"No, he is not." Katerina faced him. "May we trust you with this secret, Pietro?"

A secret mission! thought Pietro. *It's dangerous—dangerous enough to have the Scaliger asking about Fate and the stars. This is what he's been waiting for! He's wrong, I am a fool—I doubted him!*

Cangrande mistook Pietro's silence for embarrassment and interceded for him. "Sister, you are unworthy. Trust cannot be promised. It either is or isn't. Twice now Signore Alaghieri has acted to my benefit. That is proof enough."

"I stand chastised." The lady removed her hand from Pietro's sleeve. "In any case, it is not *my* secret, is it?"

If it was a thrust, Cangrande did not parry. Pietro was beginning to notice how often her taunts—if that was truly what they were—went ignored. Instead Cangrande said, "What was it you came up with, Pietro? A man may control his actions, but not his stars."

"Actually, it was you who—"

"Tonight we shall test how fixed fate is. We shall see if the ordained comes to pass." A steely look hardened the ocean-blue eyes. "If my fate is indeed written, then the stars will see that my actions are still worthy of the Greyhound."

It was the first time Pietro had ever heard that particular title pass the Capitano's lips. Of all the names the Scaliger owned, the Greyhound was perhaps his most revered. It was unsettling, therefore, to hear him utter it with such loathing.

TWELVE

Pietro cracked the door to his father's room. Both Dante and Poco were asleep. Pietro crept as best he could to a trunk in the corner, wincing at every creak in the floor. He imagined the picture he made, a limping thief with a crutch, and grimaced. Opening the trunk was so noisy he gave up on secrecy and went for speed.

Sure enough, Poco sat up in bed and said, "Pietro? What are you doing?"

"Looking for breeches." To prove his point he held up the trousers in the dim brazier light.

Disgust played over Poco's face. "Why?"

"I'm going riding," said Pietro. Telling Poco the truth was the best way to make him disbelieve it.

"Is this about your stupid leg?"

"Shut up."

"Did you ask Father if you could wear his breeches?"

"No, Poco," said Pietro. "But if you want to wake him, I'll wait."

Poco gave Pietro the fig and rolled over. Pietro left the room bearing the breeches in hand. He stopped off in a shadowed hall and struggled into the unfamiliar apparel. Looking down, he was pleased to see they hid his wound entirely. Boots back in place, he picked up his crutch and followed the directions Katerina had given him. On the ground floor there was a panel covered by a tapestry of a pastoral scene. Opening the panel Pietro discovered a staircase spiraling down. With a hand on the wall to steady himself, he hobbled down to the bottom. It smelled dank and musty here, and Pietro had to bat at his nose to keep himself from sneezing. He was in a narrow tunnel that sloped upward. Thankfully Cangrande had left a lighted candle behind him, so Pietro didn't have to navigate it in total darkness.

In three minutes he was at the tunnel's end. A solid wall stood before him. He felt for the catch, found it after several tries, and opened a sliding wooden panel. Immediately he smelled the wet straw of a stable. He slipped through the panel and closed it behind him.

The place was deserted except for Cangrande and two saddled horses. Both horses were remarkably dark-colored. As he heard Pietro's step disturbing the straw, the Scaliger turned. "That was quick. Any trouble?"

"No sir."

"Good. I hope you don't mind, I've chosen your horse for you." While the Capitano's horse was a huge ebony beast, Pietro's was a rust-brown palfrey, a short-legged, long-bodied horse that had a gentle amble for a gait. Pietro ran a hand over its neck. The muscles under his dark coat rippled. It was a fine-looking young thing, obviously just broken to the saddle.

The choice of this horse was more solicitous than Pietro had expected. Palfreys weren't always as fast as other horses, but the smooth ride they afforded made them suitable mounts for the wounded or aged, who also might have difficulty mounting a taller horse.

The Capitano had laid two extra cloaks across the necks of both horses. The cloaks on Cangrande's horse covered the broadsword strapped tightly to his saddle. The hereditary sword of the della Scala clan wasn't a fancy or attractive weapon—it bore no jewels or ornate carvings, the wooden grip was long enough only for one hand. Bound with thin iron wire, the grip ran between a gilt steel pommel and cross guard with a decorated triangle of metal at the tang for protection from rain. Overall the weapon measured about twice the length of the Scaliger's forearm. A deep groove ran down in the center of either side of the double-edged blade. It shone as he lifted it from its scabbard and fitted it in the sheath on the saddle.

Pietro lifted the cloak on his mount and found a good one-handed sword and a long, thick dagger. "Should we have shields? Or helmets?"

"No, but put this on," said Cangrande, handing Pietro a quilted gambeson. "Real armor would slow us down as well as give us away. We want to look like unfortunate travelers." As Pietro laced the gambeson vest in place, Cangrande produced two huge sagum cloaks, scarves, and a pair of wide-brimmed hats to keep them dry.

"Now, don't be offended, Pietro," said the Scaliger, "but I'm tying a lead from my horse to yours. The last thing we need is to lose each other in this tempest, and where we're going calling out would be—unadvisable." Curious and excited, Pietro said it was fine with him. "May I also suggest, in deference to your injury, that you ride like an Arab. Or half an Arab. Put your left foot in the stirrup, but tuck your right knee around the saddlehorn. Here, allow me to get you situated. Good, now cover your injury with the cloaks. Excellent. Hopefully that will stay dry. Does it hurt?" It did, but Pietro couldn't bring himself to say so.

Cangrande had just finished helping Pietro to mount when a voice from the door said, "You both look quite menacing. Perhaps you should try your hands at highway robbery while you're out." In her arms she carried wineskins and a bundle of what smelled like meat. The fact that she brought it herself did more to impress upon Pietro the secrecy of the evening than anything so far.

Handing the food to her brother, Katerina said, "No fasting tonight, if you please, Francesco. You need strength."

"We'll see," was the reply. "Certainly Pietro may eat."

She shook her head. "You're too obstinate to be related to me. Here." From the folds of her skirts she lifted a long, thin metal object the width of her hand. "Don't forget an offering."

Cangrande opened the object at two hinged corners. Pietro leaned forward and saw a gilded triptych with a saint on both outside panels, flanking the Virgin and child in the centerpiece.

Cangrande squinted at the religious icon. "San Giovanni I can make out," he said. "But who is the other?"

"Zeno, of course." It took Pietro a moment to remember that San Zeno was the patron saint of Verona.

Cangrande was turning the icon over. "When did you have this made?"

"Years ago, for just this occasion."

"It's a nice touch." Cangrande placed the icon in a leather satchel hanging from his saddle. He mounted.

Katerina laid a hand on the horse's neck. "Be civil. Reassure."

Cangrande leaned down from the saddle and, lifting her head covering, placed a kiss on her forehead. She stepped back and pulled wide the stable door. The noise from the rain was deafening. Cangrande pulled his cloak tighter about him and kicked his heels. Unperturbed by rain, Cangrande's black horse set out into the shuddering night.

Pietro wanted to wish the lady farewell, but the lead from the Capitano's horse was tightening, so he kicked. His horse responded at once. Passing Katerina, Pietro smiled from under his hat. Donna Katerina smiled in return. It made his heart pound so hard that at first he didn't notice the rain that pelted his hat as he was engulfed in darkness.

They exited Vicenza to the east through a series of narrow gates. The Scaliger produced a ring of keys at each. Pietro couldn't be sure in the rain, but he thought these gates were unguarded. Probably because they were too small for an army or even an armored horse. Pietro had to lie flat on his horse's neck as Cangrande led the horses through on foot. Passing under each wall there was a blessed slackening of rain, and Pietro was able to hear Cangrande's cheerful humming.

Once they were out of the city they turned. The trees around them bent low under the wind. Pietro imagined they were heading south, but there was no way to tell. He kept his eyes on the treacherous road beneath him. The water had turned the dirt to mud and the mud to a sloshy river that sucked at the palfrey's hooves.

Suddenly they stopped. Pietro thought he saw Cangrande dismount again and dash forward. Was it danger? It couldn't be, not this close to Vicenza! Still, Pietro's hand slipped under the cloak and gripped the hilt of his sword. His heart hammered until he saw the Scaliger return, a lighter shadow in the shadowed night. He passed his own mount and stopped beside Pietro, who leaned down to hear what Cangrande was saying. "We're at Quartesolo. Had to make sure the bridges aren't washed out. The river's leaping up, but they're solid so far. Brace yourself." Pietro thought he saw a flash of a grin.

Cangrande remounted and started them across the first bridge. The lead tightened and Pietro followed. The horse's shoes had just contacted the stone of the bridge when a huge wave came crashing up over Pietro, drenching him sideways. It was followed by another, and another. Pietro hugged his palfrey, leaning down to keep from being washed from his saddle.

Then they were over the first bridge and onto the second. Pietro wondered how many bridges connected the suburb of Quartesolo across the swelling river. The sagum cloak was well waterproofed, but already Pietro's arms were soaked to the skin. His left boot was soggy in the stirrup. Only his aching right leg, under two layers of cloak and his father's breeches, was dry.

The thunder cracked mightily overhead as they left Quartesolo behind. They weren't still on the main road. The smell of damp earth and raw wind was thick in his nose. Lesser branches flipped end over end through the air, the twigs pelting him. It was as if the mortal world was being scoured raw.

Lightning began to strike, the dry vapor pent up in the clouds above the rain catching fire and exploding down toward the earth, ripping the fabric of night. The horses were uneasy, but less so than Pietro. The flashes of illumination made the riders visible for miles.

Pietro felt his hat pelted by something harder than rain. He held out a hand and felt the sting of hail in his palm. A bad omen, a poor night to be traveling.

He had quickly lost all sense of time. With its crashing rain, wind, and now hail, the night seemed endless. Sometimes Cangrande stopped to check the road ahead. Pietro was grateful for these breaks, not just for the chance to stretch his muscles but because they managed brief snatches of conversation, the thunderous downpour eliminating any chance of being overheard.

It was at one of these stops, when Cangrande came to tell him the road ahead was particularly sodden and they would be turning off to a side track, that Pietro finally asked the important question. "Lord, where exactly are we going?"

Cangrande leaned close and said, "Exactly? We're entering the land of La Lupa." Then he returned to his horse, leading the way across to an uphill track.

La Lupa. The She-Wolf. What does that mean? Riding doggedly behind Cangrande, bits of the ancient prophecy came back to Pietro. The Greyhound was supposed to kill the She-Wolf before Italy's great golden age could begin. But what could any of that have to do with this journey? Was Cangrande chasing his destiny, or—

There was a crack, a horrible rending sound. An attack? Pietro checked the reins and reached for his sword. He was looking this way and that, unable to see a thing. Cangrande shouted "Pietro! Move!" At the same moment Cangrande yanked on the lead. Pietro kicked with his left heel and the palfrey darted forward just as a rotten tree collapsed across the road where Pietro had been. It took down another tree across the road, throwing clumps of earth up into the air to rain down on them.

Cangrande was tugging urgently on the lead. Pietro was shaking and needed a moment to collect himself. Then he heard what the Scaliger was hearing—voices! Someone calling out to help a poor traveler who had shouted. *Who does that?* thought Pietro perversely. *Who helps strangers these days?* There must be an inn or a church not far off the road. Cangrande's shout had saved Pietro and imperiled them both. Pietro kicked his left heel again and followed Cangrande as they rode away as fast as the rain would allow. For the next hour Pietro could swear he heard hoofbeats close behind them, racing as fast as his heart.

✦   ◇   ✦

At last, after carefully climbing a slope that begged to slip out from under them, Cangrande halted with an air of finality. Pietro looked around but couldn't see more than a couple feet in any direction. There was no light at all. He tried to figure out the distance they had covered. In this slow going it couldn't be more than ten or twelve miles. The fact that Cangrande had led them so unerringly in the complete darkness was yet another in a string of feats that made Pietro believe the Capitano was something more than human.

Slowly Cangrande edged them forward, and Pietro sensed rather than saw a structure of some kind. Possibly a hut or small house. Cangrande dismounted, and this time Pietro did the same. He stood for a moment, stretching out his muscles and arching his back.

A sudden bolt of lightning illuminated the sky. It was too quick to take anything in, but Pietro closed his eyes and could see the afterimage of the building. At the top of its walls Pietro could swear he'd seen a jutting timber post. Were they going to a barn, a stable?

Cangrande led his horse to a tree a dozen yards from the building. He used a low branch as a makeshift hitching post, and Pietro copied him. As he was tying the reins, Cangrande leaned close and said, "Bring the sword."

Pietro drew the knife first and tucked it in his belt. Then he unsheathed the sword and paused. What to do about his crutch? Were they going into trouble? He had to assume they were, but if he fell he would be no help. He quickly decided to leave the crutch. Holding the sword low on his right side, he limped after Cangrande toward the unlit structure.

There was no door, just a stone frame. Cangrande paused under the lintel and stood there, listening, looking like a hound catching a scent. Pietro strained to hear something beyond the rain. *Is there someone in there? Is it an ambush?*

Ears pricked to the slightest sound, his heart thudding in his ears, Pietro turned to guard the Scaliger's back. A rasping noise brought him spinning around, sword ready to strike. Cangrande was kneeling and striking a flint on the stone lintel, covering it close with his hand. In moments he had lit a taper. He lifted a candle from a nook near the door. Careful to shield it from the wind, he placed the lit candle back in its sconce. The illumination it cast was poor, as if the weather outside had commanded the air to obstruct light's passage. But in the hazy light Pietro discovered that the building was a small chapel, with benches set up in rows. At the far end was an altar with a massive carved stone cross suspended above it.

Cangrande was across the small chapel in four strides and kneeling before the altar, using the haft of his sword for a cross as he prayed. Finished, he stood and shook himself as a dog would, throwing water everywhere. Then he turned and grinned. "Pietro, you're soaking. Don't you want to come in and get dry?"

Pietro didn't need telling twice. Genuflecting in the aisle he followed Cangrande's example and spread his cloak on a bench to dry. He then gratefully settled himself on a bench a couple rows in, away from the wind that sent the rain spitting through the doorway. Cangrande had brought his two spare cloaks with him indoors, now hanging them up to dry on a peg by the door. Pietro felt foolish—he'd left his atop his mount. *At least I remembered the sword.*

· Cangrande found another candle in a sconce and lit it off the one he'd brought, then rejoined Pietro in the pews by the door. Setting the leather satchel with its icon close to hand, he slapped his thigh and said, "Well well, here we are. I hope the Lord will forgive us our trespass, and our presumption of being armed. These are dangerous times. How is the wound?"

"Glad of the rest," said Pietro honestly, struggling to find a comfortable postion for his leg.

The Scaliger laid his broadsword beside him and opened the neck of a wineskin. He passed it across and Pietro gulped down a healthy draught. It was followed by a sweetmeat wrapped in a greasy cloth. The treat was sticky and oozed juices out through the pasty exterior, but it was still almost warm. The Capitano ate his slowly, interspersing bites with pulls at the wineskin.

Pietro was hungry, but his nerves kept him from eating. If he was right about the distance and direction traveled, they had to be somewhere in Paduan territory. Padua was less than twenty miles from Vicenza. Still shaking from cold and fear, Pietro rubbed his hands and tried to wrap his mind around what they were doing. Was this another of Cangrande's insane plans, one of those things only he could bring off? Had the agreement with Il

Grande included a secret negotiation with someone? But no, then Cangrande would have brought someone else, someone like Passerino Bonaccolsi. This seemed—personal, somehow.

Not knowing how to phrase it, Pietro simply asked, "My lord—are we invading Padua?"

"Just the two of us, yes." The Scaliger looked up from his treat, grinning and wiping his mouth with the wrapping cloth. "It's a little late to be asking, don't you think?"

Pietro reddened. "I was just—"

"Everything to do with Padua has been decided in council over the past three days. It is not what I had in mind, but it is the best I can hope to do." He popped the end of his sweetmeat into his mouth and pointed to its mate in Pietro's hand. "Are you going to eat that? No? Here, I'll split it with you. The short version is this: Padua will officially recognize my claim to Vicenza, and relinquish all rights thereto. Both the Vicentines and the Paduans will retain any land that was theirs before the conflict began. All prisoners on both sides will be released." He gazed sorrowfully at Pietro. "That means, I'm afraid, you'll get no ransom for Marsilio. I'm sorry. But I'll make it up to you."

Licking his sticky fingers, Pietro shrugged off the loss—it was a fortune gone, but he'd hardly had time to think about it. It galled him a little bit to think that Marsilio da Carrara would be able to crow about keeping his fortune. Both Mari and Antony would be livid, and indignant on Pietro's behalf. That was a comforting thought—he had made friends for life in those two. Far more valuable than Carrara's gold.

But Pietro balked at what this meant for Cangrande. Between the recent battle and other skirmishes, the Capitano had more than two thousand Paduan captives, a least a hundred of whom could have been ransomed at a high price. If he was forcing his men to give up a fortune, he was losing several more himself. He said, "What prisoners do the Paduans have?"

"Though they hold no Veronese of note, they do have many Vicentines. Remember, I wasn't fighting this war in the name of Verona. I was asked by the people of Vicenza to be their champion against the Paduans, and the Emperor named me their Imperial Vicar before he died. This has been mostly a defensive war, in a *cause juste*. That is what I have on my side. The law. The right. Justice.

"I haven't been fighting only the Paduans, either. Bologna, Ferrara, and

Treviso have all sent food, money, soldiers. They are worried, you see. If Padua falls, they think they'll be next. And behind them all are the Venetians. Venice doesn't want Verona's influence expanded any further. As long as all the inland city-states are warring, Venice has everything its own way." The Capitano's voice grew steely. "I won't allow that, if I can help it."

"You sound as if you're planning a war against Venice."

That drew a low chuckle that almost sounded admiring. "War with Venice is unwinnable. The Serenissima, that most serene city, is unique in the world, I believe—a city without walls. Why bother building walls when you've got the water to protect you? They have no land assets, a recent lesson hard learned from Ferrara. They have no real armies but their fleets. For land war they just hire mercenaries or, even more practical, get someone else to do their dirty work while they reap the profit. Think of the Fourth Crusade. Because profit is their aim, not land, and trade is their sword. They can do more with an abacus and a scale than any army." Cangrande got a sly look. "But if I were to plan a war with Venice, I know how I'd do it."

"How?"

"I'd hurt them where they'd feel it. I would block their merchants, levy fines and dues on their traders. Pope Clement showed me how. I would erode their trade."

"You'd side with Genoa?" said Pietro.

"No no! The Genoese deal with gold in one hand and a knife in the other. No, Pietro, this is my real plan. Once I have showed the world what I can do in war, I will awe them by what I can make of peace. I shall use your father's words as an example. His notion of empire. The only way mankind can prosper is through peace, and peace can only occur under a single ruler empowered by God to make war. That's probably the best definition of a strong government—one that's willing to go to war to maintain the peace."

"If that's true, why not make a treaty with the Paduans two years ago?"

"I cannot appear weak. Nor could I betray my oath to the Vicentines."

Pietro shifted, bringing his leg up to rest on the bench in front of him. "So you wouldn't've taken Padua?"

The blue eyes narrowed. "I didn't say that. As Vicar of the Trevisian Mark, I am supposed to have ultimate control, under the Emperor, over both Padua and Treviso. But since the throne in Germany is vacant, I have no one to appeal to. I hear they're holding elections next month, but there are no frontrunners for the throne. It'll be a mess." He grinned happily.

"So it would aid you," said Pietro, "if they would settle on an emperor."

"At this moment, I am pleased with things the way they stand. True, there's no emperor to help me, but by the same token, there's no emperor to hold me back, either."

"What does all this mean for Padua?"

Cangrande rubbed his hard hands together. "Eventually I have to take both Padua and Treviso. I know it, and so do they. I have the authority already, but only paper authority. Until they're mine I cannot step into the larger Arena. This damned rain means there will be peace—for now. I'll agree to it because it makes me look magnanimous and just. They'll agree to it because it buys them time." The *allegria* returned. "And because they have to. I just smashed the largest army they've ever had with fewer than a hundred men. Do you know, Pietro, how certain they were they'd win? In the tents and wagons they left behind we found goblets and dishes of gold, silver, beds with exquisite coverings and soft pillows, baskets and barrels filled with sweet delicacies. You'd be forgiven for thinking they were on their way to my nephew's wedding and not a war!"

Drawn into the great man's confidences, Pietro was paying close attention. However, it was difficult not to wriggle each time he felt his leg itch. Unwilling to shift his legs yet again, he contented himself with fidgeting his hands, running them across a few inches of the splintering bench, back and forth, hoping the feel of the texture could distract him. It didn't seem to annoy the Scaliger, who now stood and walked to the open doorframe.

"In any case," said Cangrande, staring out into the rain, "if the Paduan *Anziani* don't make peace, Dandolo will tell the Venetians to withdraw their money. Panicked and worried, they'll find their citizens in revolution again, the third time in a year. No, I expect that in a fortnight I will be sending my representatives to Venice to sign a treaty."

"Why Venice?"

"They have the power to enforce the terms and are officially neutral. Whatever their private inclinations."

"So why did you—" Pietro stopped himself.

"Why did I set out to make Dandolo the butt of the evening? Because he's one of the coming men in Venice. Because Venice and I are at loggerheads. If I take Padua and Treviso, I control their waterways. They are still reeling from their tussle with the Pope over Ferrara—the excommunication of the whole city hurt their trade badly. If not for Dandolo, they would be hurting still. I kept him humble because he had pulled off a great feat of diplomacy. Though the rumor is that the Pope made him crawl under the table and wear a dog's collar."

"So that's why you called him '*cane.*'"

"Yes, the Dog. But still we need him, or someone like him. And this peace will be a feather in his cap, advance his candidacy to become the next Doge."

"Who suggested it?"

"Everybody. Once the rain started, taking Padua became impossible. Their natural defenses were swelling, my men were tired by the race to Vicenza. It had to be peace." The Scaliger leaned his back against the stone frame of the door and continued gazing out at the falling rain. "But the terms were proposed by Giacomo da Carrara. He came to us yesterday with the whole thing laid out. He knew granting me Vicenza was the concession I needed. We spent the rest of the day working out the details."

Pietro leaned forward. "How can he make terms? He's not the Podestà."

"He's a smart fellow, our Il Grande. He'll go far. There's no central authority in Padua. I think he means to change that."

"How?"

"By making himself indispensable. Like Dandolo, he's the coming man. Il Grande is now the architect of a peace that will save his city from the deadly Scaligeri. I imagine within five years he'll be fully in control of Padua."

"So you're putting in power the man charged to defeat you."

"In a way, yes."

"I got the impression the two of you were becoming friendly."

"We get on famously. I like him very much. His nephew, too."

Pietro chose not to remark on Marsilio. "But if you want to rule the Trevisian Mark, you'll have to take Padua eventually."

"Even if I didn't plan on making my title a reality, I'd take Padua. I have to. It is a point of honor."

"In spite of the treaty?"

"Oh no. When I attack Padua I'll be sure to have a *cause juste*. As in this war, I'll find some legal pretext to take them down."

"But you'll be going up against Il Grande."

"Yes."

"Whom you like."

"Yes."

"What will you do then?"

"I will grind him into the dust."

There was nothing to say to that. Pietro sat, feeling the gusts of wind that blew into the church through the unbarred doorway. "Lord," he said softly. "If we're not here to invade the city, why are we here?"

"I promised you a picnic!" responded Cangrande, gesturing grandly at the remnants of their meal. "Besides, this is a beautiful church. Look at the craftsmanship! I don't doubt that when you and I are long forgotten, this house of God will still be standing."

A fierce gust of wind thrust into the church, blowing out the candle by the open door. Drops of rain struck Pietro's face, stinging like nettles. He breathed in the wet night air and waited until the Scaliger had relit the candle before picking up the conversation again. "Lord, you didn't answer my question."

Cangrande stood half in the door, only one side of his face illuminated by the candle. "You're like one of my mastiffs, Pietro. Once you catch the scent, you don't let go." A moment passed. "We are here to beard the She-Wolf in her den."

"You said that before."

"You know the legend?"

"Pieces of it."

Face half in shadow, the Scaliger began to recite:

> To Italy there will come the Greyhound.
> The Leopard and the Lion, who feast on our Fear,
> He will vanquish with cunning and strength.
> The She-Wolf, who triumphs in our Fragility,
> He will chase through all the great Cities
> And slay Her in Her Lair, and thus to Hell.
> He will unite the land with Wit, Wisdom, and Courage,
> And bring to Italy, the home of men,
> A Power unknown since before the Fall of Man.

Cangrande shifted out of the doorway and into the room. The candle was behind him now, and he became a dark shape lit only at the edges. "That's the part that everybody knows. There is a coda, however."

He will evanesce at the zenith of his glory.
By the setting of three suns after his Greatest Deed,
Death shall claim him.
Fame eternal shall be his, not for his Life, but his Death.

The Scaliger paused, then said, "I don't know about you, Pietro Alaghieri. But for my single self, I'd rather I was remembered for my life, not my death." Walking nearer, he lowered himself onto a bench. "Your father claims I am the Greyhound predicted. He believes I am the man who will unite this Italy and restore the unity of pope and emperor."

"You are," agreed Pietro.

Cangrande's hand slammed down on the bench again and again. "I. Am. Not! Pietro, I'm not. An astrologer made a chart for me when I was born. I have seen it. I even called in the great astrologer Benentendi to confirm it. I am not this mythic Greyhound."

"But—your device, the banner—"

"It is the same dog my father used. The Scaligeri hound was created for Mastino. And I am, after all, Cane Grande." He flashed a brief, heartless version of his famous smile. "But I am not *Il Veltro.* I do not use the title. I have no right to it. When I ride into battle, it is to fight for my city and my honor. I will fight for God, if he asks." His voice became hard. "But I will not be the tool of Fate."

A silence passed, and thunder rumbled overhead. In a quiet voice Pietro said, "Why are—you hardly know me."

Cangrande's true grin returned. "Can't you tell? I want you to stay. I'm a good judge of character, Pietro, and you seem like a handy man to have around. So I'm seducing you—first, I give you political confidances, then personal ones." He sipped some wine. "Your father has expressed a desire to settle in one place. Have you thought about what you're going to do once he does?"

Pietro took in a breath. "I have no idea. I was meant for the Church, but now that I'm the heir I have to find another career. I don't know what."

Cangrande's lips turned up at the corners. "I'm sure we can come up with something. In the meantime, you can do something for me."

"Anything, lord."

"I want you to convince your father I'm not what he thinks I am."

Pietro shook his head. "He'll have you walking on water in the next volume."

"Perhaps not, then." After an awkward moment, he continued quietly. "Pietro, I know what I am. A man with gifts, though no better than most—quite a bit worse than the best I have known. But how can a man live life as a myth? I tell you this—if I thought that I was truly the chosen champion of the heavens, I would fight it." His voice possessed a feverish quality. "Just to see her fail, I would fight it with all my might."

Her? Pietro had an idea whom Cangrande meant. He chose not to comment. Instead, he was about to remark that they had hardly touched the wine when he heard a horse let out a short grunt. Their mounts were tied yards from the church. In the time they had been waiting, he'd not heard them once. This horse seemed closer—just outside the door.

The Scaliger's hand edged closer to his sword, proving he had heard it too. He gestured to Pietro to stay still, then stood, sword low by his side.

Someone appeared in the weak illumination of the doorframe. Covered in a hooded cloak, the figure was a full head shorter than Pietro, hunched over a bundle carried gingerly and close. There was something in the way the figure moved that reminded Pietro, inexplicably, of a Pietà.

"Donna Maria," said the Capitano, standing and leaving his sword behind. "You did not have to come yourself."

"Then we're both surprised. I certainly didn't expect you to come." The voice under the folds of the cloak carried a strange lilt to it. Nor could Pietro place the dialect. There were hints of Paduan, but something more polished beneath. Nor did Italian seem to be her first tongue, though she was perfectly used to it.

Cangrande crossed to her, lifting one of the spare cloaks from off its peg as he passed. Seeing Pietro, the lady held up a forestalling hand. "You are not alone."

"I thought a witness might be useful. If ever you should need him, his name is Pietro Alaghieri." Pietro stood awkwardly and bowed. "You may trust him."

"Do you? I should tell you I am expected elsewhere."

Cangrande bowed. "Then we will not keep you."

Reluctantly she allowed herself to be guided past Pietro to the altar, far from door and rain. The Capitano lifted the drenched cloak off of her and, tossing it aside, covered her in the folds of the dry one. By the weak candlelight Pietro glimpsed dark hair coiled tightly against the lady's head. Woven into the braids were many pearls. She didn't glance up, but Pietro sensed no fear in her. Something else was behind her furtiveness. Her head was bent over the thing she bore in her arms. She carried it like—

Like a baby.

It was. She was carrying a child. Now that he listened, Pietro could hear it murmuring. A baby? What was going on?

Cangrande and the woman rested themselves close to the altar, a decent space separating them. They spoke for only a few minutes, the Scaliger doing most of the talking. Once or twice he put a question to the woman and she answered. All the time she looked at the child in her arms.

Pietro was unable to hear their hushed words, nor was he meant to. Trying not to look like he was eavesdropping, Pietro continued to fidget, running his hands over the bench under him. His fingers encountered a thing protruding from the wood. Absently he began prying at whatever it was. The wood was old and after a few seconds the object came away in his hand. Examining it by feel alone, it felt like a disc, large, round, and flat.

Surreptitiously he lifted it to the light, keeping it low by his side. On one side there was an impression of a laurel wreath with the word *PAX* over it. Turning it over in his fingers he saw a helmet with wings, but it took some scraping with his nails to uncover the word at the top.

MERCVRIO.

Lightning struck a mile away, illuminating the church with bizarre shadows behind their heads. The accompanying thunder rolled overhead. The baby began to cry. Pietro looked up, unconsciously tucking the coin into his purse. The lady made a shushing noise and whispered to the child as she removed the satchel holding it from around her neck. She seemed to be favoring one arm, as if injured. Hugging the child to her breast, she crooned some soft words meant for the infant alone. She kissed the bundled babe, then passed it over to Cangrande's waiting embrace.

The Scaliger had to raise his voice to be heard over the still-rolling thunder. "Has he received baptism?"

"He has."

"And christening?"

"He has. His name is—"

"I know what his name was. He will have to go through it again."

"Fine." Standing, the lady produced a sealed letter. "All you need is here."

The Capitano tucked the letter away inside his doublet. Abruptly the lady turned and strode the length of the chapel, passing Pietro. She lifted her soaked hooded cloak from where it lay, dropping the thick dry one the Scaliger had given her.

From the altar Cangrande said, "What will you do?"

She paused by the door. As she turned her head Pietro thought he could just make out the color of her eyes as the candlelight flickered across them. They were a shade so dark as to almost be black. "I? I shall disappear. But I will be watching."

"If you ever need . . ."

She almost laughed. "I shall not come to you."

"He will be well guarded. Always, Maria. You have my word."

The lady's hand swept over her face in a violent motion. There was a swirling of the layers of her skirts, then she was gone.

Pietro stared at the darkness where she had stood. *This can't be it,* thought Pietro. *Tell me this wasn't our secret mission.* For now he recalled a piece of the conversation he had heard between Cangrande and Katerina and leapt to the obvious conclusion. *A by-blow! A bastard!* The battle, his wounds, Mari and Antony's daring, Nogarola's lost arm, so many dead, all for this? This daring and dangerous midnight invasion of Padua, through a storm that could still murder them on the return, not to take the city, but to collect the Scaliger's illegitimate son!

All this talk of just cause, of Fate, bad luck, the stars, his grand plans, all sacrificed on this altar of pride or—what? Blood? The need for a son, even one from the wrong side of the sheets? Pietro was aghast. *How could he?*

Back near the altar, Cangrande was preparing to leave. Unable to hide his incredulity, Pietro said, "This is why you didn't invade Padua?"

The Scaliger stood beneath the large stone cross, the wriggling bundle in his arms. "Shhh." Looking down into the face hidden in the folds of the bundle, Cangrande's visage was shadowed from the light. "Yes."

Pietro could hardly draw breath. He managed one word in a horrified whisper. "Why?"

"This was more important. Come and see."

Pietro stood and limped over to the altar. Cangrande lifted the covering completely from the child's face, and Pietro looked down at the fine cheekbones, the fair hair, the perfect chin. There could be no doubt. This child was a Scaligeri.

Cangrande shifted the bundle into the candlelight, allowing them both to see the boy's open eyes. Though he was fussily opening and closing his mouth like a baby bird, he stared back wide and unafraid, his eyes two orbs of brilliant, startling green.

"I am sacrificing nothing, Pietro. I am doing only what is necessary. Trust me."

Smothering his disbelief, Pietro bowed his head. "I do, lord."

"Thank you." Cangrande turned the child toward him, staring into those vivid eyes. He let out a long breath. *"O sanguis meus."*

There are some moments in the lives of men that impress themselves on the witnesses, coming back in dreams, both sleeping and waking. In years to come, the details of the battle at Vicenza would be half remembered, half imagined in exaggerated glory. But this moment, the Scaligeri lord standing beneath the old stone cross in a dank and humble church and looking into the child's eyes—this moment would haunt Pietro the rest of his nights.

"What is his name?"

For the first time since viewing the child, the Scaliger pursed his lips in a thin smile. "He will be called Francesco."

THIRTEEN

Three months after the Paduan defeat at Vicenza saw the conflict's effect reaching many places. In Venice, Ambassador Dandolo returned and made his report to the new Council of Ten, relating many trade secrets he had bought while staying in Vicenza. He expressed his concern that, should Verona ever renew hostilities and win, the Serenissima would be in jeopardy. He was heeded, and at his advice steps were taken against the day Cangrande should grow too powerful.

In Padua, Il Grande had a parade thrown in his honor. It was generally agreed that his skilled diplomacy had saved the city. At the same time, his nephew Marsilio was being talked about as the flower of Paduan honor, and his tales of Verona's latest bastard kept his friends enthralled.

It was not the end of the war but the bastard that had people talking. The official story was that the Scaliger's sister, the beautiful and lively Katerina Nogarola, had simply adopted a child. One day she was another barren wife, the next she was the foster mother of a boy not six months old.

The lady's husband had returned home to find a baby in his wife's arms. He had taken it well enough and was said to be fond of the infant in an avuncular way—which, if the rumors were true, was precisely the relationship. The gossips denied that it was his own bastard adopted by his wife. Why? Because the night before the child appeared, the Greyhound had vanished entirely from the palace. The next morning his servants had found his discarded clothes, soaked completely through.

Many people delighted in the news, and most of these were friendly with Verona. Cangrande's enemies sighed in bemusement, reconciling themselves that yet another Scaligeri was being bred to torment them. Their only comfort was in thinking what the Scaliger's wife was saying about it.

But at the end of November, with a suddenness that unnerved everyone in Europe, one event removed all other news from prominence. News had come from the royal court in France. The curse of Jacques de Molay, the last of the Knights Templar, had come true. King Philip the Fair—ruler of France, maker and breaker of popes, scourge of Paris—was dead.

As Dante's sons packed for the move to Verona, the poet received a letter from his friend Enguerrand of the locality of Coucy in Picardy. The facts as Enguerrand related them were quite in the realm of the supernatural. King Philip had suffered no accidents or injuries to his person since falling from his horse some weeks earlier. A man in his prime, he suddenly dropped to his knees on a bright November day. He began to foam about the mouth, his eyes rolling back in his head. Then he pitched forward and screamed. Still screaming, he was taken to bed, and there he stayed until he left the mortal world. De Coucy related to Dante that the king was unable to utter words, though many were the final phrases attributed to him. Enguerrand closed his letter by writing:

> *It will be a matter of future history whether or not Jacques de Molay's curse upon the King's line down to the thirteenth generation comes true. Though I feel in my bones it will.*

The ripples this stone cast in the international pond were wild and unpredictable. King Philip had been brother-in-law to the heiress of the Latin Empire of Constantinople. He had been connected by blood and commerce to the kings of Naples and Hungary. The kings of England and Minorca had been his vassals. After the English defeat last summer at Bannockburn, Philip had allied himself with the new Scottish king, called the Bruce. In fact, his political alliances had reached as far as the mystic Orient. In spite of this, or perhaps because of it, the moment his death became known, men everywhere looked for ways to profit from it.

In Italy, the *cause celebre* was the return of the pope to Rome. It was the topic of the Christmas sermon in Florence, delivered by the visiting Cardinal Deacon Giacomo Gaetani Stefaneschi, who purchased Grace by spending a great deal of his sermon praising the life of Pope Celestine V. His Latin was scholarly and beautiful to hear.

Dante's daughter Antonia knelt, her eyes closed in what was supposed to be prayer for an end to the Avignon papacy. But her thoughts were fixed on a package that had arrived yesterday. It had come from Pisa, from her father.

The moment it had arrived she had whipped off the covering, expecting a packet of letters. Instead she had discovered a small wooden box with yellow leather tacked in place by fine brass studs. The box was sealed both in wax and twine. The seal was impressed with her father's ring.

Rushing off to find a knife, she had returned to find her mother waiting, the box stowed on a high shelf. "You shall wait until Christmas morning," her mother had said.

Perverse. Unfair. But Antonia hadn't argued, knowing it would only give her mother an excuse to further delay the unwrapping. So she knelt now between her mother and her aunt, pretending to listen to the sermon, wondering what was in the package. To her right, Gemma di Manetto Donati *in* Alighieri knelt stiffly, back perfectly straight, head properly bowed. It would have taken a keen eye to see the pinch she gave her daughter as the girl began to sag back onto her heels. Antonia bolted upright and fought the impulse to rub her bottom. She was aware of the eyes on her.

It was natural, now that her father was both famous and rich, that she should have suitors. But it annoyed her. Where had they been when her family was poor, beggared, hardly able to survive? Now that *Dante* and *genius* were being uttered in the same breath, fathers with eligible sons were beginning to call at the house. So far she had managed to frighten them away by embarrassing them. As her mother frequently pointed out, the fact that she was involved in the publishing business was a mark against her as far as marriage was concerned. Her intelligence was another. So when suitors called, she made sure to discuss her negotiations with Mosso, to quote Homer or Virgil, or recite a history lesson on the man's family that was never to his advantage. Their discomfort led to rapid departures and a certainty that no amount of gold was worth the bride that came with it.

Her learning came from her free time in a house of books. Most girls lamented not being men, but Antonia would not have changed her state for the world. Boys didn't have free time. Men of noble birth had to split their attentions between learning, riding, hawking, swordplay, war tactics, and a hundred other pursuits. Even her brother Pietro, who before being cata-pulted to the position of eldest living son had always had his head in a book or scroll, had as a youth undergone a few hours of the most basic training in arms. Whereas Antonia's time was focused solely on learning. It was either that or weaving, and her weaving was atrocious.

Still, there was one class of boys who did not have those active pursuits, who read as much as she. Those second and third sons of the nobility who en-tered into the church had no need to learn arms. Antonia imagined their lives filled with only study and prayer. It was the life for which Pietro had been in-tended, before Giovanni's death. Now it seemed a warrior's life was in store for him, something no one had ever foreseen. Antonia was alone in thinking it was his loss.

Of course, Jacopo should have taken Pietro's place in studying for the Church, but no one had been foolish enough to suggest it. He wasn't suited to such a life.

No, thought Antonia, *it's up to me to heed God's call.*

It was not unusual that at the tender age of thirteen she thought idyllically of a religious life. Fearing the marriage act, it was the perfect alternative. In the cloister she foresaw no chores, no duties save to love God and read. She longed for such a life. Antonia's hope was that, left to his own devices, her fa-ther would leave her unwed. But her mother—stern, rigid, unforgiving Gemma—wanted her betrothed. For the good of the family, of course. Gemma imagined an alliance with a rich count. With her father's star rising once more, she was growing in attractiveness. Time was running out.

The only salvation was the long-dreamed-of summons. Her father might send for her. *But it will have to be soon, Father, soon! Else Mother will have me married off to some idiot who* doesn't *read!* It was the worst insult Antonia could conjure. Not reading meant a man lacked imagination, culture, intel-lectual curiosity. There was no nobler pursuit in this world than the written word, for it was her father's chosen profession.

She rose and followed her mother to the altar for Communion. Christmas always made wine sweeter and bread less dry. Then, with final words from Bishop Venturino thanking their visiting cardinal deacon for officiating, the crowd dispersed.

Aunt Gaetana patted Antonia on the head and softly said to Gemma, "Sis-ter, will I see you at Francescino's for dinner?"

"No, sister," said Gemma. "I regret to say we have plans. Tell your brother we wish him a happy Christmas."

Gaetana smiled and shook her head. Antonia's mother never associated with her husband's family. The shock of the exile and the ensuing poverty had made her overly vigilant in regard to her social perception. Her family had been at odds with her husband. Her family's side had won, so while she did not repudiate Dante's half brother and sister, she was never seen with them outside of church.

"Antonia," whispered her mother, "there are some friends we must greet. Behave yourself."

The *or else* was implicit. Wishing Aunt Gaetana well, Antonia emerged into the piazza outside just as a gust of wind dislodged some snowmelt, peppering the lingering parishioners with wet. Some cursed, some laughed. Unsure of her mother's mood, Antonia wrapped herself tighter in her wool shawl and followed Gemma into the crowd. Antonia was not tall by any standard save one—her mother. Gemma was a tiny woman, birdlike, with hair dyed black and teased into curls. Her short legs never covered much ground, and on this of all mornings Antonia had to take care not to outpace her.

"*Buongiorno,* Signora Scrovegni! I hope you are feeling better? Splendid. Signora Boundelmonte! Are you on your feet so soon?" Gemma was wearing her public face. In these busy public streets she was the long-suffering wife of that foolish poet Dante—so patient, so loyal. Impoverished by his exile, forced to live off her relations, only recently returned to her proper sphere. "Monna Giandonati! You look like a ray of sunshine!"

Antonia was swept into embrace after embrace as the entire Donati clan descended upon her mother, kissing cheeks and exclaiming. Gemma was the daughter of Manetto and Maria Donati, a name that carried great clout in Florence. Antonia never quite understood her mother's great affection for the Donati family. It was Gemma's late cousin Corso who had been responsible for Dante's exile. But family was complicated. Corso's brother Forese had been Dante's close friend and the namesake for Gemma's own brother. Indeed, Corso's father-in-law was the poet's current host, the Pisan ruler Uguccione della Faggiuola.

Both mother and daughter kissed their relations, who had sat nearer the front of the church and thus been allowed to exit earlier. Some cousin exclaimed, "We saw you two tucked away like thieves at the back. That will never do! You must come up and sit by us! Why, just yesterday Nanna Compagni was quoting poetry at me and I was able to wipe her eye by saying 'That's nothing! I'm related to Dante Alighieri!' What do you think she said? She gasped and began asking me all about your husband."

Another said, "Oh yes, we really must have him recalled! It's a shame that such a genius isn't able to perform for us in person. He does performances, doesn't he?"

Feeling her face screwing up to make a tart reply, Antonia quickly turned away and ran straight into her uncle Forese, who was saying, "Yes, I've read it twice! Even memorized the good bits. Though I disagree with my name-sake. I quite like the bosoms one sees in the city. On a soggy morning like this the women make sure to paint their nipples! Though I'm glad my niece is too young for such displays," he added, sending an inappropriate wink Antonia's way.

"Oh Uncle," she said. "Watch out or I'll have my father putting words in your mouth."

"He's welcome to, sweetie, just as soon as I'm dead!" Forese laughed and turned his back on her.

"I can't wait," muttered Antonia.

Her uncle continued to speak. "It's a shame her brother is fighting on the wrong side. Word is he fought bravely up in Vicenza. Got a wound, did my nephew, a good wound to show from it. I hear it's disfiguring, just horrible. I'm so proud. Would never have thought it of him."

Antonia wouldn't have thought it of Pietro either. She couldn't imagine her bookish brother even riding a horse, let alone wielding a sword. He had written once since September, hardly mentioning the battle and completely omitting his own part in it. Maybe there was news of Pietro in the package at home . . .

She was drifting, her mother might notice. Turning back she found herself facing a portly man in his mid-forties, not of her family. He was grinning down at her, and she couldn't help smiling back as she curtsied. "Good morning, Signore Villani. Are you returned? How does Christmas find you?"

Giovanni Villani bowed. "I am indeed returned from Flanders once more, the bearer of secrets of trade, innuendo political, and gossip grave. As for Christmas," with his back leg still bent he gave a furtive look to each side, "it finds me hiding from the Peruzzi, as usual. The youngest keeps hounding me to put money into some mad venture or other. This time it's an artist, I think. But how does Christmas find you, my formidable foe?"

Antonia looked slyly up at the portly dark fellow. "I don't know what you—"

"Oh, you know full well. The parchment, girl, the parchment! Here I am trying to write an account of the world without the parchment to write upon. You've bought it all up for your father's infamous *Inferno*! If you were older, or a man, or far less clever, I would set my hounds on you." He grinned.

Antonia said, "I don't think your complaint is with me. You should talk to the Villoresi parfumerie."

"Fiends! Despoilers! If men took time to bathe, they wouldn't need these fancy perfumes, and our poor parchment would be left alone." Perfume makers often burned parchment to create their pleasing aromas. "Damned biblioclasts! I tell you, there is nothing so vile as the destruction of a book."

"I quite agree."

"Then, please, stop destroying the book inside my head. I must have parchment! Oh, but I like writing on parchment! Each time you turn a page it rumbles like thunder. My words are so portentous—that's portentous, dear, not pretentious—it seems appropriate. Like Jove. Alas, without it I'm forced to use paper. Eeugh!" Villani shivered, throwing out his arms as if ridding himself of an insect. "Hemp. Boiled underwear. The pieces of animals even the minolo won't eat. I swear, my fingers shrivel away at the merest touch. I'll catch a plague from paper, I'm sure of it."

"Nothing of the kind," said Gemma, having concluded her conversation to descend upon her daughter's. "My husband spent years composing on paper. Or in the leaner years in chalk upon the walls. There is nothing disreputable about paper, not in these enlightened times. Paper is the new standard. Antonia, don't you agree?"

Antonia didn't but said she did. Villani looked scandalized. "But, madam, writing is a sacred act! Do we not call Christ, he who was born on this day, *Logos*? He is the word! Did not San Giovanni eat the book the angel gave him? Was it not sweet like honey in his mouth? Could such a book be written on *paper*?"

Antonia couldn't help herself. "Signore Villani, you forget. When it reached his stomach it was bitter."

"Did it transubstantiate, then? Parchment in the mouth, paper in the belly? I will ask the cardinal. But, ladies, are you alone this morning? May I see you home?"

Gemma smiled and declined the offer. "Gagliardo di Amerigo and his son have offered to accompany us, along with my cousin Cianfa. We have kept them waiting too long. Send my regards to your wife, Signore Villani!"

The portly fellow swept his hat off in a bow, then turned and let out a kind of yelp. "Ah, Peruzzi, my dear fellow, where have you been hiding?"

Antonia was still smiling when her mother reintroduced her to the wealthy Amerigo father and son. She curtsied before them, and the father said, "I've never seen you looking so fine, my dear. It can't be the weather, so it must be you! Boy!" He tapped his son hard on the head. "The lady is looking fine, isn't she?"

"Is she? Oh, she is! Yes, you are!" Amerigo's son made a hasty leg to her, then said, "Sorry, I was listening to your cousin. He's just back from—where in Greece?"

"Anatolia," said an unfamiliar man. Was he her cousin? "Bursa, to be precise. I was there trading. Travel is fine, but it's good to be home, even if there are homely cousins to escort." He had already examined Antonia with a bored gaze. "Come, shall we go? I have plans for the evening."

They began to navigate the streets, quite a chore these days, as most were torn apart and under reconstruction. It was part of a city plan to straighten out the curved streets so that the city would look to God like a wheel, with spokes coming from a central hub, thus conveying to the Almighty a sense of good government.

Hopping over gaps in the cobblestones or crossing plank bridges, Antonia found herself not needing to employ her bag of tricks to dissuade her mother's latest choice of suitors. Young Amerigo was paying her no attention, agog over her cousin Cianfa's doings in the Christian city of Bursa, and neither the pesterings of Gemma nor the pointed comments of the elder Amerigo could regain his attention. Thus Antonia reached home without having either abased herself or displeased her mother. Having already decided she disliked cousin Cianfa, she found herself uncomfortably thankful for his company. Perhaps he could call every time a new suitor arrived. Though she suspected she would have to pay him for his trouble.

Bidding their companions farewell, Gemma and Antonia entered the house Durante Alighieri had been born in. Over the door was painted the family crest, half green, half black, with a silver bar across the center. Simple, elegant—and, according to Gemma, undistinguished. They entered by the addition on the side of the house, the second door for callers added the year Dante had joined the Arti of Physicians and Apothecaries. He hadn't had any interest in such pursuits, but in Florence one had to belong to a guild in order to take part in public life. His membership, combined with the marriage his father had arranged for him, had allowed him the political career that had ruined his name.

Like the city, the Alighieri home was undergoing a spate of new construction. The family name now rehabilitated, Gemma was adding room after room to the original four-story tower until its interior rivaled anything in this quarter. The exterior would still lack a stable, so horses would continue to be hitched to the rings hanging from the stone wall out front. It wasn't part of Gemma's design to appear to live in luxury. From the outside it would remain a humble home, one more cross to bear.

The door had hardly closed when Gemma began a diatribe against fickle young suitors, though she quickly changed her aim to cousin Cianfa. "Just back after all the trouble he gave his family—they had to pay through the nose not to have him exiled, did you know, yet your father is still banished. Is that fair? I don't think so! And Cianfa's still the same—oh, thank you, Gazo." As the steward helped them remove their coverings, Gemma gave him instructions for their Christmas meal. The domestic set obediently off, leaving Antonia standing by her mother in the high-ceilinged entryway.

Though Antonia remained absolutely still, excitement shone in her eyes. Gemma heaved a sigh. "Go ahead, open it. But tell me if anything else has happened to Pietro."

At once Antonia transformed from obedient daughter to exuberant child. She ran across the rushes, skidding to a halt beneath the box on the shelf. She was just decorous enough not to scale the doorframe. Instead, she found a stool, clambered up, pulled the package down, and sped to the large sitting room upstairs.

Wood was already smoldering in the brick pit in the middle of the room, and holiday cinnamon and cloves smoked and snapped in the fire. It was otherwise blessedly quiet. Between the streets and the construction of the new duomo, the Republic of Florence was a daily cacophony, but on Christmas day the workers were at home and the city was at peace.

Antonia used a poker to slit the twine that held the box. She was careful of the seal, keeping the impression of Dante's ring that resembled a coin of blue wax. The coin bore the Alaghieri family crest with the letters *D.A.* across it. She had a collection of these wax coins, and this one she set far from the fire so it wouldn't melt. Then she pushed back the lid of the box.

The first thing she saw was a fur. Lifting it out she saw it was not an expensive fur, but inexpertly cut from an animal who had seen some hard living. Beneath the fur lay two little sealed bundles of paper. One bore Pietro's seal, the other her father's. Which to read first? Her instinct was to savor her father's by reading it second. But by rights she should read his first, being the word of the paterfamilias. Such things mattered.

No, she decided. *It's Christmas. I will take both letters slowly.*

She broke the seal and twine binding Pietro's letter and unfolded the pages. It was thankfully longer than usual. She resented her brother's customary brevity. Pietro was often able to tell her facts about their travels that her father had left out, but without enough detail to satisfy her. For a long time after he had gone to join Dante in Paris, Antonia had been insanely jealous. But now she recognized her father's need for someone like Pietro. Acutely aware of her own role in Dante's life, it never occurred to her that her brother might not recognize, or appreciate, his own.

Still, Pietro was a better correspondent than Jacopo, who had not written at all. She settled in to read:

9 December 1314 Anno Domini

Mia Sorellina,

Greetings from Lucca, on the eve of our departure. We're packing our rooms here. Why, you ask? Well, remember when I wrote in October (or didn't you get that letter?) that the lord of Verona had made an offer to become Father's patron? It was a handsome offer, too. Housing, a hefty income, and the promise of readings and publications, all in return for the poet's visible presence at court.

As you might imagine, it was the "visible presence" that tripped up Father. He's not one for public displays, he tends to get moody and let his tongue run away with him. While at the same time he loves being the center of attention, which means he can't just sit in a corner and laugh with the rest of us.

But after weighing the choices, Father made the decision at last and we're leaving soon for the Scaliger's court. Father claims he's doing it so Cangrande will make me a knight, but I think it's because he admires Cangrande as much as I do. Martial yet cultured, witty and decisive. I know all good Florentines revile him, but really he's quite amazing. He certainly took time to be kind to me, he and his sister both.

Anyway, we're leaving Lucca none too soon. The natives are grumbling. I think they've finally interpreted Father's lines about Pisa— though I honestly don't know how they could have missed them. I keep expecting to wake up in the middle of the night and find our rooms on fire. So all in all, it's a good thing to be leaving.

Our host Uguccione took the news of our departure hard. It may be that he is disappointed to lose his poet-in-residence. Now that Father is gaining international fame, I think Uguccione planned to tout his patronage to the skies. It might have helped smooth his rough edges. Even his own people call him a power-hungry and avaricious tyrant. I think he wants to be known as a patron of the arts. I'm amused that a man who hates to read and can barely write his own name takes such pride in "owning" a poet, as he put it.

At least he's pleased in Father's choice of new domiciles. Verona is more to his liking than Polenta. Oh yes, Guido Novello has been urging us to settle down in his court. But Lord Faggiuola says that Novello is a fop who likes paintings and poetry more than warfare—an accurate description, I think, but there could be nothing more insulting as far as our Pisan host is concerned. On the other hand, Uguccione speaks of Cangrande in the most lavish terms. He says if he ever leaves Pisan employ, he will take up residence in Verona.

(That might be sooner than we all think, by the way. As I mentioned, the locals here in Lucca don't have a favorable opinion of our host. His most recent troubles have something to do with bankers and England, I didn't really understand it all.)

Uguccione is correct, of course, about Cangrande. He's like a lamp, I swear. He lights up any room he enters. I've never met a man so very alive!

Thank you for the scarf. It is chilly in Verona this time of year—at least, I hear it is. I haven't been in the north since the end of October. But it was already growing quite cold. I was discussing the temperature with the Donna Nogarola's physician, Giuseppe Morsicato—I mentioned him before, I think. He's the one who treated my wound in Vicenza. He says he's made a study of temperatures in the past, and he is of the opinion that the world is growing colder. He says in Roman times the winter was shorter, and there was nowhere near the amount of snow we get now. If he's correct, I wonder what it means? Father is sure there is religious significance. No doubt he is correct, but neither of us can fathom what that significance is. If the world is growing colder, does that mean that humankind is moving towards heaven, or are we drawing nearer to the fiendish realm? He is leaning toward the latter, seeing as how the center of the Nine Rings is filled with ice. I would like to hear your thoughts.

The letter paused, then resumed in a slightly different ink.

Our bags are packed and we are about to embark to our new home in the old Scaligeri mansion. It's the home the family lived in before they ruled the city and Mastino built their great palace. I saw it several times back in October, after the battle. It is a grand home, like a Memory Place made real. The Capitano has harnessed the remains of a Roman bath in the cellar—apparently their Piazza della Signoria is built over the remains of Verona's old Roman forum. I have yet to visit these baths— somehow I am untrusting of a cellar filled with water. But Father visited them often during our last stay. It's all quite a change from the years of sleeping in barns or woodsheds with students and other vagabonds. I've decided that it's better to have money than not.

I don't have to tell you how excited Poco is about Verona—by the way, the fur is his Christmas gift to you. He's very proud, he caught and skinned it himself. "I'll send it to Imperia," he said—you've never told me why he calls you that. (Am I the only member of the family that doesn't have a nickname for you?) Anyway, the fur is from him. Hideous, isn't it? But I know you'll do something to make it bearable. Poco caught it during the hunt on our last day in Verona. Embarrassingly, it was held in my honor. As a token of his esteem, Cangrande presented me with the best of a litter of pups sired by his favorite hound, Jupiter. I've named him Mercurio.

Mari and Antony came to Lucca for a visit last week. As we were walking through the streets here, we noticed a group of older women nearby. They'd stopped in a small cluster and were pointing at me and whispering. Antony and Mari started making some dirty jokes and I told them it wasn't what they imagined—the women thought I was my father. Mari said that was ridiculous, noting I don't look anything like him—the nose a little, and the high forehead. "But he wears a beard!" he told me.

Since it's been so long you might not know it but Mari's right— Father has taken to wearing a long beard these last few years. He shaves it off whenever he has his portrait painted so he can look more like Virgil or Cicero—Roman, you know. He wants to be remembered as their heir, and since they were clean-shaven when they were painted, he is too. So, because I look more like his portrait than he does, people stare.

"They're mistaking you for him?" asked Antony. I told them to go over and ask. They did, looking over their shoulders at me like I was mad. After just a minute of conversation Mari and Antony burst out laughing. Grinning from ear to ear they returned and repeated their conversation with the old ladies. "Do you see that man giving us his shadow?" one of the old biddies had said. "He's the one that goes to Hell and back again, and brings back stories of friends below." Antony had asked how they knew it was me. They said that my fine hat marked me as the devil's own.

It was all funnier then, I guess. But it made me think. This will always be the way for us—known for our father, not for ourselves. They do say greatness skips a generation.

I cannot think of anything else to write. Tell mother not to worry about me. My wound is healing. I thank you both for all your prayers on my behalf. They seem to have worked.

Another change in ink, then:

A delay has caused us to remain a little longer in Lucca. Father has had some sort of inspiration and refuses to budge until the fit has passed. I'll admit to you if you promise not to pass it along, I'm very upset. I was looking forward to Christmas in Verona. I miss Mari and Antony. Their coming for a visit only showed me what fast friends they have become in my absence. They've been racing all over the countryside around Mari's estate, exploring and hunting.

I'll admit I'm jealous. The only people I've ever known were family, teachers, or Father's contemporaries. And now I feel like I'm missing my chance to have close friends of my own age. The two of them have become joined at the hip, and I'll be the tagalong, the third wheel on a chariot.

Listen to me whine like a mamet. It looks like we'll be setting out for

*Verona after the Roman New Year. So when you write back—and be sure
to write back—send the letters there.*

*Give my love to mother, and give both Gazo and Laura my best
wishes. Have a wonderful Christmas.*

Tuo fratello maggiore,
Pietro Alaghieri

Well—a strange letter! And from Pietro, no less. His thoughts were never
that fragmented. It was far more like her father to jump from topic to topic—
Dante enjoyed the freedom of letter-writing, as opposed to crafting poetry,
two very separate endeavors in his mind. Pietro always knew what he was going to write long before he put quill to paper.

Jacopo was still an idiot, she saw with amusement. Pietro was right, the fur
was truly horrible.

Pietro hardly mentioned his wound. Antonia's mother had made a great
show at church of lighting candles and praying for the health of her oldest living child. Antonia's prayers had been less obtrusive but no less ardent. Obviously from his letter he was up and around again. As for his—what was it,
self-pity?—Antonia had no time for it. He was with their father, he was a
hero, he could lump his sorrows.

Setting Pietro's letter aside she lovingly broke the seal on her father's letter. It was a long one, she saw happily. She began to read.

Cara Beatrice,

*I write you, my sweet, on the fifth day after the calends of December,
a day before the ides, from Lucca, where my sons and I are spending the
final moments of this momentous year. It has seen the death of a corrupt
order of knights, whose curse has brought down both king and pope. It
has seen the throne of the great empire of Charlemagne grow cold, with
the last election divided and the fate of both claimants uncertain. It has
seen the idea I had nearly fifteen years ago, the true life's work of a poor
Italian poet, one-third done.*

*It has also seen my oldest living son become a man. I must tell you,
your last letter was insightful beyond your years. You appreciate that,
having taken part in battle myself, I know the thrill of holding a sword,
and the terror of the thousand deaths you die before you meet the foe. My*

son is braver than you know. That, however, is a topic I shall leave for the end of this missive, because I know you, my love, and you will be blinded with tears.

Our former host, Uguccione della Faggiuola, is distraught at our imminent departure. I fear we are abandoning him at a time of crisis. He has just suffered a terrible omen. His prized tame eagle has suddenly died. As the creature was in murderously perfect health just days before, many people are suspecting foul play (there is no pun in that, I tell you honestly—I abhor them! But, having written thus far, I am loath to begin again on fresh paper—too expensive). There is even a rumor that I had a hand in the giant bird's death. But then, the citizens of Lucca have never recovered from the rumor—most amusing—that I am a sorcerer! They claim I have the Sight—the ability to see far-off lands, and even the future, like some cheap oracular hooligan. Because on the page I consort with demons, travel to unearthly planes, and speak to the long dead, it is thought I must also belong to the dark orders that the Templars were accused of forming.

I take it as quite the compliment, I must say. For hundreds of years it has been thought that Virgil was a magician. He was said to have possessed a horse of bronze that, by its very existence, prevented all the horses of Naples from becoming swaybacked; a bronzed fly that, as long as it rested on his doorsill, kept the city free of flies; and an enchanted storeroom that would keep meat for six weeks without spoiling. It was said too that he had made a statue of a bowman with bow drawn and ready. As long as the arrow in the statue's grip was kept pointed at Vesuvius it would not erupt. It would be interesting to learn, therefore, the position of that statue in AD 79, would it not?

It was related to me by a local priest that my master, the noble Virgil, built the Castel dell'Ovo upon an egg. The castle will stand until the egg is broken. It was when I heard that tale I knew my sojourn in pretty Lucca must end.

That, and I can no longer bear living so close to the fetid city, the cancer of Italy, which houses but one pearl—you yourself. Since my return from France I have lived too close to the country of my birth, and the stench of that befouled place burns my nostrils. The single product of Florence that goes uncorrupted is my Beatrice.

Returning to the subject of magic, I have stated publicly my abhorrence of these rumors that persist about my person. I have done this both *in love of all that is true and in hatred of all that is false. I am, after all, a loyal servant of God above. Yet it amazes me how superstitions persist in the minds of men. Pliny the Elder tells us that men in his day who bit the wood of a tree struck by lightning would not suffer from the toothache. He wrote those words before the explosion of the volcano after the arrow was shifted. Yet this practice continues to this day! What creatures are men that they believe such things? Someday I will make a study of this phenomenon, to expose the roots of this idiocy.*

Yet there is magic in this world—no one knows this better than I! Except, perhaps, Philip the Fair. But since he is no longer of this world, he offers no competition.

Speaking as I am of curses, one may be brewing in my new home. I wrote to you of Cangrande's little bastard—il veltro di Il Veltro, as it were. The child adopted by Donna Katerina Nogarola. Well, a witch's hex lies over him like the sword of Damocles.

You gasp. You choke. You rear back in horror at the thought. Where did this curse originate, you ask? From the Scaliger's wife, I say. The blood tie to the Emperor Frederick has been diminished over two generations, yet one can detect in Giovanna da Svevia's eye the gleam of the fire of that fiendish emperor. Whereas Frederick fought only against three popes, his distant offspring must compete with a hundred mistresses all fighting for the Scaliger's favor. Of course, she is much older than he. She has turned a blind eye to the tomcatting of her canine husband—until now, that is. With the evidence of Cangrande's philandering being flaunted before her eyes—by her own sister-in-law!— Giovanna has declared a silent war. And not against her husband. Like a jealous she-wolf, she has her teeth firmly locked into the back of Katerina's neck and is tearing mightily. It began with the invitations to Verona's Christmas feast, which I hear were mysteriously lost on the way to Vicenza. Then the new crib Katerina had commissioned was unexpectedly sold to another family at quite a loss to the maker—unless you count the payment he received from the Scaliger's wife. There are more, culminating in death by paper cuts. Thus far Katerina has ventured no response. The whole court is waiting breathlessly for this feud to break into the open. If it does, my money is on the Scaliger's sister. She is a fascinating lady, as your brother has troubled himself to inform me no less than five times now.

On a side note about natural children—I regret taking delight in the demise of another man, but you know how satisfied I was by the death of the Scaliger's natural brother, Giuseppe, the despicable abbot of San Zeno. Cangrande's father made this unnaturally natural child an abbot while he had one foot in the grave. He must not have been thinking clearly so close to the end, for never was there a more avaricious and spiteful man to hold the office of Benedictine abbot. But—I can scarcely credit it—his son is worse! I had an encounter with him on our first day in Verona, and he's another Ciolo degli Abbati, talented only in sponging what he can from the state and the church. Worse for Verona, the decent if ineffectual Bishop Guelco has been called to Rome indefinitely.

The good news, though, is that the Franciscans have sent a new and better man to lead their order in Verona, who brings with him a group of new initiates. Already the Scaliger is talking of moving most of the major services during the Palio away from the basilica of San Zeno and into the Duomo of Santa Maria Marticolare. This promises to put the collective noses of the Benedictines in Verona quite out of joint. They are already enraged that the Franciscans have the Scaliger's ear in religious matters. Now the disciples of San Francesco seem to be winning the political war. Perhaps it is all in the name—Cangrande's baptismal name is Francesco. I can already hear the abbot ranting.

That is unfair, though. My new patron is an enlightened man and is creating a garden of culture and learning in Verona, a new Caput Mundi. It is fitting that he listens to Francis's disciples more than Benedick's. He is a modern man, struck in a modern mold.

In women's news, I was invited, but sadly could not attend, the long-delayed wedding of Verde della Scala—sister to the odious Mastino and the oblivious Alberto—to Rizardo del Camino, the twin of the wedding of Cecchino della Scala to Rizardo's sister that was so rudely interrupted back in September. Since there is now a treaty in place and peace looms at every corner, the wedding went forward at last. I must say, these attempts at strengthening political ties by marrying off one's young children is growing ever more cynical. I despair that my new patron shall have any good of either of these matches—del Camino will take the dowered lands and do as he pleases. Wait and see.

If I am reduced to writing of uninspired weddings, I have clearly prevaricated and procrastinated long enough. Cara mia, it is time you heard

*the worst. But I do not know how to phrase the words—I, who am said
to have the power to control men's souls with my thoughts, cannot find it
within me to soften the bluntest of cudgels—my son Pietro will never
run again. The magnificent doctor of the Nogarola palace, a famous
knight named Morsicato, working together with the Scaliger's own
physician, Aventino Fracastoro, was able to save my child's leg, it is true.
But he has a third leg now, the polished crutch that balances his movements. Pietro walks as slowly as I—I with my curved spine, bowed by
the act of writing. And he has taken to wearing breeches, not hose, to
hide the injury from view. Alas, nothing can hide the crutch and the horrible slowness of his gait.*

*He has not spoken to me of this cross he now carries. For all the world
he has nothing but a smile. Yet that smile carries a wound of its own, one
that I cannot imagine how to heal. He has now tasted a knight's life, and
finding it to his liking, discovers it suddenly denied him. It is a level of
Hell I never envisioned. He is my son, yet he belongs among the Nine
Worthies. I am consumed with admiration for him, both for his deeds
and for his cheer in the face of misfortune. But I do not know how to help
him, poor lad.*

*I have written to my friends at the University of Bologna—I imagine
he'd be uncomfortable studying in Padua. I don't know if that is the answer. I am a man whose life is the written word, but is he? I can't send
him away, the choice must be his, but how I wish to help him!*

*Can you advise me, Beatrice? How can I tell my son there is more
for him in life than the cavaliere's sword? How can I heal the wound in
his smile?*

Distinti,
Dante A.

Antonia was indeed weeping when she finished her father's letter. Pietro—
a cripple! And never a word of it in his own letter. How dreadful, how brave!

She tried to imagine her brother through her father's eyes. Dante had
nominated him to stand with Hector, Alexander, Julius Caesar, Joshua,
David, Judas Maccabeus, Arthur, Charlemagne, Godfrey Bouillon—the Nine
Worthies. Instantly Pietro was transformed in her mind. No longer the plod-
ding, pedantic boy she had known as a child, he now stood in her inner eye

clad in golden armor, with Roman eagle-banner in one hand the longsword of
Charlemagne in the other. She imposed upon that frame the crutch, and he
was transformed again into a noble sufferer. His wounds were glorious. Her
brother was now a brother to Christ.

From that lofty perch it took a few moments more for her thoughts to return to earth. But soon her mind started onto its accustomed trail. *If Pietro's
going off to university, who will take care of Father now? Not Poco!*

There was only one answer. *I have to go. I have to join them in Verona.* Finding her bottle of ink and a fresh sheet of paper, she began to write her reply.

Shortly thereafter Gemma Donati came looking for her only daughter.
"Antonia? Franco and his brood will be joining us after all, so . . ."

But the girl wasn't in the study, having left the house to find a rider to bear
her message to her father. Unknowing, Gemma picked up the two letters her
daughter had left out. At first she was amused by the contents, then startled.
"Oh, Durante . . ."

She wept until she heard her daughter in the entryway below, arriving just
as Gemma's brother-in-law rode up with his family. Daubing her eyes,
Gemma rose and placed the letters just where Antonia had left them. She
knew what her daughter would ask, and was tired of refusing. Gemma's attempts to find her daughter a husband were a desperate ploy to tie the girl to
Florence, so that at least one of her children would remain with her. But she
knew the power of her husband's way with words, made only stronger in Antonia by his absence. Realizing it was to be her last Christmas feast with her
only remaining child, she descended the stairs with a slow, heavy gait.

The Suburbs of Padua

The same moment Antonia was leaving church, the Count of San Bonifacio was entering one. It was not a grand Paduan church but a mean humble
one outside the city walls. Unknown to him, it was the same one Cangrande
had used as a rendezvous months before. On this holy day, it had only two occupants. One, a frightened-looking priest, stood at the door. The other knelt
in prayer by the altar. Nodding to the man of God, the Count crossed himself
and sat down. He was resigned to the long wait. If he could enlist this penitent's aid, his cause might yet be won. He had the key to this man's spiritual
vault, and it had been the Pup who had given it him.

After hours of painful kneeling on the stone floor, the figure rose. And rose. And rose. He was as tall as he was thin, a grotesque figure made more so by deliberate starvation. He crossed himself before turning about. "You didn't come here to pray," he said at once. "Your presence here is profane." His voice was deep and rich, odd to hear from such a strange figure.

"Merely secular," said the Count.

"I told you no," said the penitent.

"And I respected that," said the Count. "But things have changed."

"Your defeat means nothing to me." The man wore a medallion with an odd cross surrounded by pearls. Some pearls were missing.

"No reason it should. Still, you live so far from the city I wondered if you'd heard."

"Heard what?"

"Cangrande has taken in a son—a bastard son—and named him his heir."

The skeletal penitent remained entirely still, yet a change came over the chapel. Suddenly it was cold, as if a pall had swallowed the sun.

"A bastard heir?"

Seeing the fire in the penitent's eyes, the Count knew that at last he had found the lever to drive the man into action. He checked his smirk and carefully began setting his plan in motion.

Venice

The Count's was not the only wheel set turning because of the child. Late Christmas night, a ship was admitted past the bar and through the Lido, an unusual event after dark. It dropped anchor in a misty port of the Castello. Within ten minutes, two cloaked figures were stepping from the arriving ship into a sky-blue gondola. The leading cloaked figure was short with the shoulders of a scribe. His shadow was built more like a mason or a soldier, tall and broad. As they settled into the bottom of the tiny gondola, its black-hatted oarsman pushed off and started angling them toward the Rio di Greci— Greek Street, a causeway of water entering the Castello directly opposite the small island of San Giorgio Maggiore.

They passed under the first bridge of the Greci in silence but for the slapping of the waters against the gondola's sides. Here and there, music or snippets of conversation floated by. At the second bridge, they were forced to stop. A deep-red and gold gondola had gotten turned, a mishap common with inexperienced polers. The figures in the immobile gondola were masked and showed signs of drink. Some helpful fellows on the bridge had gotten sticks to aid in the turning, and now the unfortunate gondola was straightening out.

In the front of the sky-blue gondola, the smaller man asked, "Can't we get by them?"

The oarsman touched the wide brim of his hat and obediently shoved hard to angle them past the stalled gondola. Through no fault of his, the two bumped. There was a jeer from the masked men in the red-gold gondola, then another from the bridge.

Suddenly figures were leaping onto the sky-blue gondola from all directions. In an orchestrated move, the four men from the red-gold gondola threw off their cloaks, revealing shining weapons as they scrambled over. Their masks were firmly in place. Two more men vaulted the short stone balustrade of the bridge to land lightly, knives ready. They had donned *bauta* masks as well, thus disguising their features entirely.

The oarsman of the sky-blue gondola dove into the freezing waters to preserve his life. Clearly the accident had been a sham. Whoever his passengers were, someone was out to murder them. This was the kind of ambush that left no survivors, and the oarsman valued his skin.

Back in his boat, the smaller man let out a yelp of surprise as he was forced to lie down by his companion, who rose to his full height. From under the taller man's cloak an arc of steel sliced the air, making the attackers jump and hiss in frustration.

The ambushers fought hard, but their numbers dwindled in the face of the tall man's falchion, a curved sword that ended in a wicked point. Having lost half their number and the element of surprise, one shouted, "The devil with this!" He dove into the water. His remaining companions hesitated, swore, then followed.

The driverless gondola drifted to the next bridge, the blue on its sides now flecked with crimson drops. Four men lay in its bottom. Two were screaming, one was whimpering, and one was entirely still. The final figure stared at the carnage as his upright companion wiped the massive blade clean.

Poles appeared and knocked the craft roughly to a stone and tile jetty. Wounded in leg and wrist, the larger man ignored his injuries as he helped his companion find footing on the stone steps. Some citizens reached for the little man, pulling him along into their ranks and comforting him while eagerly asking what the fracas had been about.

"I have no idea," the little man told them.

Thinking his brave companion might have a better answer, they made to pull him along as well. But as the man sheathed his curved German blade, his wrist became visible between the glove and the sleeve. One Venetian saw the man's skin and recoiled. "He's a damned blackamoor!"

There were hisses of distaste and disgust. Instantly the tide changed and people began to wonder whose side was in the right, the survivors' or the ambushers'.

"Call the constable!" someone cried. "Take him to the gaol!"

"The devil with that! He killed a Venetian! Let's string him up!"

"Right! The gallows, not the gaol!"

"What about this one?" demanded someone of the littler fellow, who promptly found his hood pulled back until the knot under his chin choked him. The violence subsided when they saw a pale face growing paler by the second.

The mob on the jetty grew, more torches heralding the new arrivals. There was talk of tarring the black man. The little man rubbed his throat and tried to protest, but the crowd paid no attention. Through it all the larger man stood with perfect stillness, his gloved hands in plain view. His whole body was tensed, yet his breathing was eerily steady. Blood continued to trickle down his leg, pooling in his boot.

Rubbing his throat, the little man tried to intervene. "My name is Ignazzio da Palermo, and this man is my servant!"

"Man!" scoffed someone. "Monster, more like." Emboldened by the large man's stillness, he stepped out of the crowd and reached up to yank off the concealing hood and scarf. His fingers had just closed on them when he uttered a choked sob and fell to his knees, clutching his throat. The crowd tensed, knives and clubs at the ready, but the large man's hands were still empty.

The crowd's eyes were not on his hands. The bold Venetian had dislodged the muffling hood and scarf. The man's skin was dusky black, not ebony, marking him as Spanish. He was clearly a Moor.

Someone gasped as the light hit the Moor's neck. Criss-crossing it were lines of white and pink, raised above the level of his natural skin. The bands were linear, created by some manmade implement. Running the entire circle of his neck, a single blistered scar made a horrible kind of collar about the Moor's throat. In some places it was bubbled, in others it was worn. It was a very old burn scar, and it made the man who had survived it even more fearsome.

The aggressive Venetian retreated into the crowd, gasping and sputtering as his eyes streamed, obviously calling for vengeance but unable to make the words come out clear.

The Moor placed a hand on the hilt of his falchion and said, "We have done no harm. Let my master pass." His voice rasped as if the words were scraped by a rusty spoon from somewhere deep within.

The little man called Ignazzio crossed to the Moor's side. "Theodoro and I are stopping in Venice for the night only on our way to Vicenza. We have been the victims of a crime. We demand an audience with the authorities at once. Disperse and bother your wives, not us!"

The crowd was muttering again. Then, as if on cue, came the stomp and clink of official boots. The crowd parted for the two dozen men-at-arms. The man who led them was easily one of Venice's most recognized faces. Francesco Dandolo was a hero in the Serenissima and still young enough to have great days ahead.

The choking man had recovered enough to step in front of the approaching Dandolo. "Ambassador, this—creature just assaulted me! He—"

Dandolo pushed past him to give Ignazzio and the Moor a deeply respectful bow. "Ser Ignazzio, we have been waiting on you at the Doge's palace this last half hour. Then I heard of an altercation along your route. I hope you are not hurt."

"Theodoro is," said Ignazzio angrily. "We were attacked in our gondola—an ambush by professionals, no less—and now these fools are waylaying us!"

Dandolo gave the scene an appraising glance. Turning to the captain of the men-at-arms, he pointed into the bloody gondola and said, "Take the living to the gaol at once. Use whatever means necessary, but find out who put them up to it." He turned sharply and pointed to the aggressive Venetian still rubbing his throat. "Take him as well. Don't kill him but thrash him soundly." The man gasped, his watering eyes now wide with horror. Dandolo turned back to Ignazzio. "Unless his offense warrants worse?"

"No," said Ignazzio grimly. "He was abusive, but Venice has given us worse welcomes."

"Very well. Take them away." Dandolo looked at the Moor, busy replacing his scarf and hood. "Does your man need a doctor?"

Ignazzio turned to the Moor, who shook his head. "No, thank you."

"Then, please," said Dandolo, bowing again, "allow me to escort you to the Doge personally. He is eager to consult with you."

Ignazzio followed Dandolo without sparing the crowd a single glance. The large Moor followed a few paces behind. The mob took a collective step back. Some may have been discontented, but all were unified in their wonder. Who were these men to be treated so solicitously by Dandolo and the Doge?

One found his courage. Stepping out, he called to Dandolo's receding back, "Ambassador, who is this man? Where is he from?"

Over his shoulder Dandolo said, "Disperse, citizens, before you're unlucky enough to find out!"

FOURTEEN

Verona

Dawn was hours off and the night air was sharp, the remnants of the last snowfall hardening underfoot. The noise in the streets defied anyone to sleep, and Pietro didn't try. He lay in bed beside his brother, imagining the day to come.

When he had first heard of the city of Verona, before he had ever heard the name Cangrande or the Greyhound, Pietro had heard tell of this day. The day of the Palio. Arriving in Verona five weeks ago in the bitter January frost, he noticed at once that it was all anyone talked of. The betting was fierce, the speculation wild. Mariotto couldn't shut up about it. He had Antony and Pietro on the edge of their seats with excitement.

His return to Verona had happily thrown Pietro in with his two friends again. Since it was a poor season for hunting, Pietro's bad leg didn't hamper them as they settled into a raucous routine of storytelling, mock duels with wooly clubs, and surreptitious drinking. As they navigated the streets they earned the nickname "The Triumvirs" from a proud and welcoming city. The Triumphant Trio that had helped Cangrande rescue Vicenza. Antony had even paid to have a song written, and Pietro laughed whenever he heard it. It was terrible.

Through it all, Mari kept talking about the Palio. Dating back to Roman times, it marked the city's great victory over a monster whose bone still hung in the alleyway called Via dei Sagari. Held the first Sunday of Lent, the revelry

served to take the citizens' minds off their fasting and the sumptuary conces-
sions. Traditionally celebrated with parades and dancing, feasting and drinking, all manner of spectacle could be seen—pig wrestling, knife fighting,
bear-baiting, duels, magicians, oracles, jugglers, gymnasts, fire-eaters.

Best of all was the Palio, the famous races of Verona. The first Palio, at
midday, would be run on horseback though the western streets. Wild and
reckless, it was only a prologue to the midnight race through the city's eastern
streets across the Adige and back. The route, hand-picked by the Capitano,
was tricky by the light of the stars. Many of the participants fell to grisly injury and even death. The citizens not participating came every year to cheer
as the competitors ran, not merely barefoot, but entirely naked.

Antony declared his intent to run. Mari, a native, was going to race for the
first time this year. They hadn't been able to think about anything else for
weeks. Pietro, who wasn't racing, teased them both by making bets on one or
another of them, settling on both of them to come in second place.

The celebration came early this year, February Sixteenth, right upon the
heels of the New Year's games. Verona was one of the few cities that still celebrated the Roman New Year, January First. The rest of Europe chose to celebrate Easter as the start of the year—that being, they said, the month God
created the earth. The Turks and Greeks were even stranger, choosing September as the month to begin their calendar. Thus while most of the world
was still in the year 1314, Verona had already turned the page to 1315.

Inside the city walls, the streets were all but impassable. Spectators, gam-
blers, merchants, peasants, petitioners—all had traveled for days to vie for
what lodging they could find. The decent rooms were already rented out to
triple or quadruple capacity. Pietro knew how lucky he was to be housed with
his father and brother in the *Domus Bladorum,* the former home of the della
Scala family. Many visitors, even noble ones, were forced to sleep on dirty
floors, or in stables, where the beds were somewhat more comfortable. But
fully half the people in the city were not sleeping. Other attractions called—
treats and spectacles and mythical beasts, lights and sounds and smells.

At some point each visitor stood in the Piazza della Signoria, hopeful for a
sign of the Capitano at work or play. Even viewed from without, the Scaligeri
palaces were full of life. Cangrande's staff was well used to working through
the night when the Capitano was in residence—there was always an event to
be planned, arriving or departing guests to be catered to, or the detritus of
feasts or minor festivals to be cleared away. To provide these services, the

Scaliger employed a bevy of men and women. All had their own duties and fiefs within the household. Having watched them prepare for today, though, Pietro had truly pitied them.

Shivering now in his bed, he listened to the catcalls outside, the cheerful jeering of borrowers and lenders. Money would be being spent lavishly today. Not on clothes or food or wine or music, but on alms and charity. Many of Verona's lesser citizens would be put themselves hopelessly in debt, yet consider it money well spent. Pietro himself had been given a modest sum by his father to donate to San Zeno, along with a remark about "ostentatious piety."

A polite tapping on the door of his family's suite made Pietro sit up. He had to be sure not to jostle his brother. Before retiring, they'd dragged the frame of their bed closer to the huge brazier that warmed the chamber. They could have more easily moved the brazier, but the metal dish was placed to warm their father. To tamper with it would have risked a fate worse than freezing.

Curled at the brazier's foot was the pup Mercurio, a gift from Cangrande. The young lean head was up, tail slapping the cold tiles. Hanging from the collar around his neck was the inspiration for the dog's name. It was the old Roman coin Pietro had stumbled across during his midnight adventure with the Scaliger.

The tapping on the door was persistent. The dog rose with an answering growl. Pietro shot a hand from under the covers and gripped Mercurio's collar. Where was his father's manservant?

As if in answer, Pietro heard the door being unbarred. There was whispering between Dante's steward and whomever it was. Then the slow, measured steps of the poet, grumbling as he went to satisfy his curiosity. Pietro lay back in bed and pretended to sleep.

There was more discussion, then Dante's footsteps again but much faster. Suddenly Pietro felt his father's hand on his shoulder. "Pietro. Pietro!"

Rolling over, Pietro asked, "What's wrong?" Along with his father, light was coming into the room. Pietro blinked dumbly. There were five men coming in, all bearing lanterns. Dante was standing beside the bed, a thick blanket pulled over his nightshirt and sleeping robe. The comatose Jacopo continued to snore.

"They're from *il patrono*," said Dante.

Sure enough, the lead figure wore a medallion with the seal of the ladder. Pietro recognized Cangrande's Grand Butler, Tullio d'Isola.

Mercurio was up and scampering back and forth between Dante and the visitor. D'Isola presented a sealed roll of parchment to the poet, then reached down a hand to pat the greyhound. Having a good rapport with hounds was an important part of Tullio's office.

"I can't see as well as I used to," replied Dante, taking the scroll and passing it to his son. "Could you assist me, please?"

That aroused Pietro's suspicions. Dante would never normally admit his eye trouble in front of anyone, especially servants. No, there was some other reason for making his son read the scroll. He took the rolled sheet and broke the seal. By lantern light he read:

> *On this day February 9 in the Year of Our Lord 1315*
> *the Eldest Living Son of the Noble House of Alaghieri*
> *Baptized in the name of Christ's Apostle Peter,*
> *will before the whole Assembled Nobility of the Ancient Country of Verona*
> *be made a Cavaliere under the Authority of the Great Lord of that City,*
> *the Imperial Vicar, Can Francesco della Scala.*

"What does it say?" asked the father, who already knew.

"I—I'm to be knighted! Today!" Eyes wide, he looked up, first at his beaming father, then at the Grand Butler. He'd had hopes, of course, but as the days grew closer to the festival it had seemed he was to be passed over. He'd reconciled himself to the disappointment, which was perhaps why he protested, "But—it's too late! There have to be days of fasting—confession, prayer!"

Dante smiled. "It *is* Lent. You've been praying and fasting already. I imagine you'll be allowed to confess this morning before the festivities begin."

Pietro rose, reaching out to grasp the cane that had over the past five months become an extension of his being. He thanked the Grand Butler, and Tullio said several kind words in return before stepping back before a veritable parade of servants bearing gifts.

Jacopo awakened when the first chest crashed home at the foot of their bed. He sat up in a groggy haze as it was opened to reveal a complete suit of armor and all the small arms appropriate to knighthood. Pietro paid particular attention to the sword, a single-handed, double-edged blade that was almost the twin to the Scaliger's own. "From his own smith," the Butler informed Pietro.

Next came the chest of clothes that would be Pietro's uniform for the day. Jacopo gasped at the suit of purple and silver before realizing there was no matching suit for him. "You mean I'm not being knighted too?" Nearly four years Pietro's junior, he again started the refrain he had been singing ever since October: "Why didn't you take me with you? You hate me!" He ran from the room. Dante and Mercurio both sniffed, united in their disdain.

Cangrande's gifts were more than generous. In addition to the armor and clothes there were two cloaks lined with fur, one of rabbit and one of wolf. There was also a trunk full of the utility needs of a knight, from grinding-stones right down to socks and candle wax. All expensive, all for him.

Trapped at one side of the last trunk, wrapped in linen, was a small bundle. Pietro lifted it gingerly. Unwrapping it, he found a book. He angled the embroidered leather cover to the light. It was the *Book of Sidrach*, hand-copied in beautiful Latin script. Pietro lifted the cover to peer inside. In the frontispiece there was an inscription:

A Man may control his Actions, if not his Stars. —Cg.

"Wise words," said Dante, leaning over his shoulder. "A private message?"

"Just a conversation we once had," said Pietro, closing the cover. The book was a popular tome of universal knowledge, from court etiquette to deadly poisons. His father had often decried such collections, but Pietro was sure they would both read it cover to cover. Dante would of course claim he was looking for mistakes.

Looking at this incredible largesse, these kind gifts, Pietro felt a wave of bitterness sweep over him. Not because he wasn't grateful, but because the main gift, the arms and armor, were filled with irony now. The armor would never get used. The weapons would hang in a place of honor. Unused. Unblooded.

Pietro sighed. Using his cane to tap the lid of the nearest trunk closed, he looked up at Cangrande's Grand Butler and said, "Thank Lord della Scala for me, but—"

"Sir?" said the Grand Butler. "The Capitano has sent something more. A letter, and a gift." Handing over a sealed note, he then walked to the windows that opened out onto the Piazza della Signoria. Pietro watched as the double shutters were unbarred and pulled wide. It was dark, but there were torches flickering just beneath the window. The Grand Butler nodded him forward.

Pietro hobbled over toward the window. His leg hurt worst in the mornings, stiff and weak at the same time. He had taken to soaking it in hot water or wrapping it in warm cloths. He had even started visiting the baths in the cellar, soaking for hours in the warm waters beneath the mansion. He'd created a whole regimen of care based on observations given him by the doctor Morsicato.

Morsicato and his maggots had saved Pietro's leg. If not for the days of discomfort with them gnawing at his decaying flesh, he would have been another amputee walking about on a wooden stump. For this, he was infinitely grateful. He was still a whole man.

But above his knee the muscle had shrunk, pulled in on itself. Morsicato speculated that, with time, he might get around without a cane or crutch. But never without a limp, and never without pain.

Still, he was not as badly off as his father kept telling people. He could walk. He could even run, after a fashion. A skipping sort of gait he'd discovered chasing Mercurio around a table. It was more a run-hop that involved a hip twist in midstride, but it propelled him forward fast enough to catch his puppy, a major feat no one had witnessed. Nor had they seen him almost bite through his lip at the pain.

But the fact remained that Pietro would never take part in another battle. There was no use for a soldier who couldn't stand, couldn't put weight on his leading leg. Which made everything the Scaliger was giving him just so much he couldn't accept.

Grasping the window's edge for support, Pietro leaned out. The torches below were held by two grooms and reflected off the snow in the piazza. In the reflected light, Pietro saw two animals. The first beast made him smile. It was the rust-colored palfrey he had ridden on the night he and Cangrande had snuck across the Paduan border.

But the second animal took Pietro's breath away. Much larger than his palfrey and black as the night itself. Heavily muscled, it was standing rigidly still, forbidding and dangerous. A destrier.

A thrill ran through Pietro. *Dear God! A destrier! A warhorse!* The true symbol of a knight.

A breeze ruffled the note in his hand. Sliding his forefinger past the wax seal, he read it by the light of the lanterns. It was a promissory note, declaring that Ser Pietro Alaghieri would receive a silver Veronese solidus a day in perpetuity. He did the math. That meant that every twenty days he would possess

the equivalent of a pound of pure silver! His eyes opened wide as he looked
up at the Grand Butler, smiling serenely back at him.

"In confidence I will tell you, Ser Alaghieri, the Capitano made no other
such gifts." He nodded at the note. "I can also pass on to you a message from
his own lips. He offers you a commission in his army as banneret whenever
you wish."

"I—I . . ." Pietro couldn't find words. *A banneret!* The banneret was a
man who led a whole squadron of knights. Was the Scaliger serious?

The Butler leaned out the window and gave orders for the horses to be
taken to the Scaliger's own stables until such time that the young lord would
find suitable arrangements for them. He then closed the shutters and said,
"You have the Scaliger's permission to use his private chapel for your confession. The priest is waiting." Then, smiling, he bowed himself out.

Pietro's mind was spinning. For a moment he allowed himself to be carried away in the thought—Pietro Alaghieri, leader of men, knight of the Mastiff, world-renowned soldier and swordsman.

"You cannot accept, of course," said his father, bringing Pietro's wild
imaginings crashing down.

"What? Why not?"

"Oh, you will take the knighthood. It would be insulting to our host to refuse it, or these gifts. But you will not accept any money, nor will you take up
the commission to lead men. Don't look at me that way, boy. You know I'm
right."

Pietro began to protest, then realized his father wasn't being cruel. He was
being honest. The commission was being offered out of charity. Out of pity.
Pietro couldn't accept. Honor forbade it. "Yes, you're right."

"Now, now," said Dante with an uncharacteristic unease. He rapped his
son on the head with his knuckles, then mussed his hair. "You're being
knighted today, son. I'm—well, I'm proud, is what I am. Yes, I'm proud of
you." Pietro looked up, startled, and Dante hurried on. "So go make confession, then get back here and get dressed in this ridiculous frippery. You'll
want to make sure the hat fits perfectly, I imagine."

Pietro laughed and nodded. Dressing quickly in his own clothes, he left
his proud father in the *Domus Bladorum* and stepped out into the crowded
Piazza della Signoria, the puppy trotting along on a leash ahead of him. Not
able to see in front of him through the mass of people, Pietro used the land-
mark towers of the square to navigate. He no longer needed Mariotto to

name the buildings for him. There was the Palazzo del Ragione with its tower, the *Domus Nova,* the Palazzo dei Giurisconsulti, and other smaller buildings angling for a space between the palace Cangrande's uncle had built and the one the Scaliger's father had ordered, just recently finished, on the southeast corner of the square. Called the Tribunale, Cangrande had brought in the famous Micheli to finish it, and it outstripped the palaces the architect had designed in Mantua and Treviso.

Beside the Tribunale was Pietro's destination. The church of Santa Maria Antica. Built around the year 1000, it owned a distinctive Veronese facing, consisting of alternating bands of brick and stone. The church tower was surmounted by a fine square belfry, dimpled with mullioned windows and topped by a roof of conical brown tiles. In the corners of the tiles, barely illuminated by the stars overhead, snow clung fiercely. This was the Scaliger's private chapel, and where the family buried their dead.

Pietro stumped toward the chapel, Mercurio leading. Pietro's new fashion of wearing breeches that tied below the knee (to hide the puckered scar easily visible through hose) had the added benefit of being quite warm. Which was fortunate on this night. He could see his breath, and his crutch kept slipping on the ice, jerking him off balance. He hoped that his heavy cloak hid his clumsiness. He certainly needed it in the chill air.

In the crowded square, everyone was trying to stay warm. One figure in particular caught Pietro's eye. At first his height made Pietro think it was the Scaliger, but this fellow was twice as broad as Cangrande, with shoulders as massive as blocks of marble. Whoever he was, he must have really been feeling the cold. Under the heavy drapes of his cloak, hood, and scarf, none of his skin was exposed to the open air. He was loitering not far from the church, and Pietro had to skirt around him to reach his destination.

Pietro was about to enter when he heard Mercurio huff out a breath. Suddenly the hound was straining on his leash, pulling Pietro past the door into the small churchyard. The animal stopped to sniff at a large rose-marble box. An open-air crypt. It was one of four sarcophagi standing along the outside of the church, the oldest perhaps only thirty or forty years old, the newest less than five.

Mercurio was snuffing around at the nearest with an excited air. Pietro tugged the leash to stop the pup from disturbing the dead, but the animal leapt up with his paws, knocking snow off the marble slab. Pietro put a hand inside the dog's collar and yanked him back, yet even as he did he couldn't help reading the words now uncovered by snow:

LEONARDINO MASTINO DELLA SCALA D. 1277——CIVIS VERONAE.

So this is the enigmatic first lord of Verona? Mastino della Scala the First. It was not a grand epitaph, but Pietro found himself moved by the simplicity.

Moved, but cold. "Come on," he said to the dog, who obediently followed Pietro back to the entrance to the church. Passing under the stone lintel of the church, Pietro pushed open the wooden door of the small western entrance. He hooked the dog's collar to a chain near the door and hastened to remove his hat and gloves. Stepping into the aisle, he knelt in genuflection to the altar, dipping his fingers into the font beside him to make the sign of the cross. He then turned to his right, where the confessional booth stood. Finding it empty of both penitent and absolver, Pietro looked around the deserted church. It was bright and cheery, even in this dark night, the alternating cream and red raising the eyes up and up to the magnificent cross cut in the ceiling. Having been in one church or another almost every day of his life, Pietro had never seen a chapel so—cozy.

Pietro was gazing upward when a rumbling voice echoed around the room. "By God! It's one of the Triumvirs of Vicenza!"

Startled, Pietro looked to the end of the apse. He colored and bowed. "Lord Nogarola."

Bailardino Nogarola strode forward. Upon arrival in January, Pietro had been introduced to Cangrande's brother-in-law, then visiting from Vicenza. Flaxen-haired, barrel-chested, with a bristling beard, he was nothing like what Pietro imagined Katerina's husband to be.

"Damned cold, isn't it?" demanded Bailardino, stamping his beefy feet and slapping his own shoulders bracingly. "But the Palio will take the snap out of it! Isn't that right?"

"I don't know, lord," said Pietro. "I've never seen it."

"You'll do more than see it, lad! Today you experience one of the wonders of the modern world! You may have to go become a hermit afterward, because nothing else can compare. Except, of course, next year's race!" Bailardino glanced at Pietro's crutch. "I wish I had one of those. Women love war wounds. Look at my brother. With two arms he couldn't find a lass to give him the time of day. One-armed, he's swimming in tail. I expect it's the same with you, right, lad? You've got a dozen mistresses all clambering over each other to stroke your wound. And the adjacent demesnes, eh?" Bailardino shook with laughter.

"No, lord." Pietro was smiling in spite of himself. Bailardino's cheer was infectious. Which made it all the more staggering that Katerina was married to him, or that Cangrande liked him so well. They were cool people, and Bailardino was an inferno of back-slapping camaraderie. But Pietro had never yet seen Katerina and her husband together. Perhaps they were different with each other.

Bailardino had come from a curtain that hung in front of an alcove that held the church's tiny baptismal font. Now the Scaliger emerged, his head uncovered. For a moment he looked grim, then he caught sight of Pietro and exclaimed, "Ser Alaghieri! I take it that you've heard. God bless and keep you on this, your day. Has Bail been harassing you badly?"

"Only telling him how to make the most of this, his day."

"Don't listen to him," said Cangrande. "Age has touched him."

Pietro didn't know what to say so he bowed, his crutch clacking on the cobblestones as he used it for balance. Mercurio trotted forward to be petted, and Cangrande reached absently down to scratch at the pup's muzzle. The Scaliger was dressed for the festival in a burgundy farsetto under a fine robe embroidered with red and white pastoral patterns. The only ornaments on Cangrande's clothes were tiny silver rosebuds along the fringes of each piece. Similar rosebuds adorned the folded cuffs of his boots. Bailardino's clothes were flashier, but also more comfortable—a doublet that laced down the front and an over-robe made of heavy black bear fur.

Still playing with the dog, Cangrande said, "You don't have to bow to me in here, Pietro. Only to God."

Bailardino shook his head. "He did the same to me. You'd think he wasn't the darling of every lass in the land!"

Rising, Pietro said, "No, that's Mariotto."

Cangrande laughed, but Bailardino pressed his point. "No, goddammit, really, I tell you, a wound is guaranteed sex! Pull up your breeches to show a girl that knee, and she'll pull them off you to see the rest."

Pietro flushed, smiling hugely. It was simply impossible not to like Bailardino.

"Bail," chided the Capitano. "We *are* in a church."

Bailardino was unrepentant. "The Lord appreciates sex. Wouldn't've made it so fun if he didn't."

Cangrande sighed. "Pietro, Tullio's been to see you?"

"Just now, lord," Pietro confirmed. "Thank you."

"I'm sorry it's so long in coming."

"It's wonderful, lord," said Pietro wholeheartedly.

"You've come for confession, I imagine."

"What, is he supposed to confess to you?" asked Bailardino.

"Yes, lord," answered Pietro.

"Good. I cannot have a potential leader of men not conform to all the rules of knighthood. Many wink at them," he nudged Bailardino in the ribs, "and some of us fail, but we all must try."

Pietro took a breath. "Lord, I'm very grateful for the charity you've bestowed on me." Cangrande frowned and Pietro hurried on. "But I cannot accept the commission. Or the promissory note." *There!* He'd gotten it out.

Cangrande's face was grim. "Why, may one ask?"

"Because I can never fulfill the terms of the commission, and therefore I would be taking money under false pretenses."

Scaliger and Nogarola shared an amused glance. "Nonsense, Pietro. The money is not extravagant. It comes from my own purse, not the coffers of the state. So there are no pretenses, false or otherwise. Consider it payment for services already rendered. A solidus a day is a small price to pay for my life."

"Too much, by half," muttered Bailardino. "I wouldn't part with a florin for it."

"If you refuse," continued the Capitano, eyes twinkling, "I will be greatly offended. You'll be telling me my life is worth nothing. Besides, how else are you going to pay for the upkeep of your horses?"

"They are beautiful," Pietro admitted.

"The warhorse is a direct descendant of my own. When I'm not riding him, I have him covering some of Montecchio's mares. Now, as to the commission—in that, too, I am quite serious. It isn't the free ride you may think. A banneret is a leader of men, but those men must be his own. He pays them, he commands them, he takes responsibility for their behavior. You are welcome in any army I ever command, as soldier or civilian. But to be a banneret you must raise your own force, train it, and command it."

Pietro gestured helplessly to his crutch. "Lord—how can I? I'm . . ."

Bailardino clucked his tongue. "Are you sure you want him, Francesco?

He's seems a little thick." He turned to Pietro and laid a hand on his shoulder. "A knight is a *mounted* soldier, son. He does very little fighting on foot. In fact, only an idiot jumps off his horse." He dug his elbow into his brother-in-law's ribs.

Cangrande clasped his hands to plead to the cross on the far wall. "Dear Lord, what good is it to give me power when I cannot use it to smite those who ridicule me?" Then he smiled at Pietro. "But Bail's not wrong. There is nothing preventing you from being a great soldier, Pietro. Unless," he added, "you think it's not in your stars?"

"Don't answer him, Pietro," came a familiar, cool voice. "He doesn't believe in the stars."

Pietro hadn't heard that voice in months, not since he'd left the palace at Vicenza. She had been too busy with her new charge, and far too unwelcome in Verona these last months. Turning, he saw Donna Katerina emerge from the curtains enclosing the baptismal font. Clasped in her arms was the child—Cangrande's bastard heir. The infant had grown in the months since Pietro had seen him last, limbs long and thin. Now his eyes were wide, his mouth working silently, and his was body damp.

A low huff came from the door. Turning, Pietro saw Mercurio's ears curiously flattened, his tail wagging intensely.

A Franciscan priest was now crossing the threshold of the baptistery. Feeling monumentally stupid, Pietro finally made the connection between the alcove, the water, the priest, and the baby.

Pietro started to bow to the lady, but the baby reached out a hand and grabbed his nose. Pietro yelped. Though the adults chuckled, the baby himself seemed disinterested as he let loose a long yawn.

"From the mouths of babes." Cangrande beckoned his chaplain forward. Indicating Pietro, he said, "This lad needs to receive confession and be dressed in time for the first entertainment of the day." He slapped Pietro on the shoulder. "One of a knight's merits must be punctuality!"

Pietro made way for them as the family exited via the metal-studded double doors of the south exit. The hound moved to follow, straining at his tether.

The priest stepped toward the confessional. "Come, young man. It's a busy day."

"And an early one," observed Pietro.

The priest, a weary-looking fellow with a knowing eye, nodded. "Well, as the lord of today's festival, the Capitano had to be shrived. Though why the christening had to be today, I have no idea." His tone was disapproving. "The child—well, you won't guess what name the Capitano gave him."

"Francesco."

"Oh, you knew? I can't say I approve. The Capitano has never formally acknowledged any of his natural children before."

That caught Pietro's attention. "Did he now?"

The priest considered. "No-o-o," he said, drawing out the sound. "But his own sister is raising a child he has given his name? It seems to me that he might be planning—if, God forbid, Donna Giovanna remains barren . . ." His voice trailed off. "Well, God works in mysterious ways. Come."

As Pietro stepped into the penitent's seat, his thoughts were on the boy. Francesco. But Pietro alone knew that wasn't the name he'd received at his first baptism. His mother had given him a different name, a name the Capitano saw fit to erase from memory.

Another thought occurred to him. The custom was that the ceremony of baptism would drive the evil spirits from a child, making him cry as they departed. This child hadn't cried. Did that mean the demons had already departed at his first baptism? Or did they still lurk within?

FIFTEEN

The walk to the Arena was an ordeal. After confession, Pietro had struggled back to the room, trying twice to run, falling both times. Poco, under strict instructions from their father, was now extravagant in his compliments. "Really, no one deserves it more. It's the least he can do, and it's really about time! It's not like he's been busy. I wonder what took him so long—"

"Shut up, Poco." Pietro hurried over to his uniform for the ceremony and dressed rapidly.

Poco examined his brother's new farsetto with great interest. "The Capitano knows his fabrics." Lifting a fine pair of knee breeches, he added, "And he's considerate—he knows about your aversion to hose. And that hat! Look at that feather! It's perfect. Daring but not foppish."

Dante was beginning to laugh. Pietro said, "Seriously, Poco, I mean it, shut up."

But his little brother was on a roll. The purple of the doublet was a subject of particular eloquence. "This is a Tyrian dye—you know, the sign of senators and emperors. It's not the purple of violets, but more a plum color. Do you know where they get it? From the ink sacks of a Mediterranean mussel. It takes hundreds of shells to obtain just a pound of it. First you have to crack the shell, then pull out the tiny sack, which contains only a few drops."

From across the room Dante said, "And how, pray, do you know so much about dyes?"

"When we were in Lucca, I—knew someone involved in the art."

The patriarch's left eyebrow arched. "Oh? And you didn't introduce me, why?"

Jacopo shrugged, kicked the bed with his toe. "You wouldn't've liked—I mean, this person wasn't very—"

"She wasn't very what?" asked the father gravely.

"Did I say it was a girl?"

"No, but evasion is as good as an oath. I swear, Jacopo, if you've—"

"Father," said Pietro, "the Capitano is waiting."

Dante's jaw moved from side to side under his beard. But the poet decided to let it go for the moment. With a mutter about Poco being blown by eternal winds, he wrapped a scarf about his face. At fourteen, Jacopo was already close to being notorious, and Pietro was vaguely jealous of his little brother.

They departed the *Domus Bladorum* in the predawn light, Mercurio pacing dutifully by Pietro's legs. As they passed by the arch with the highly decorated monster's bone, a newly established phenomenon occurred. The occupants of the Piazza delle Erbe spied Pietro, and a murmur began to ripple through the crowd. Applause started close by, not for the poet, but for Pietro. Bailardino hadn't been lying—everyone loved a battle wound. Nothing gave more proof of devotion to a just cause and to God.

Strangely, this reverence of injury had grown into a passion for disfigurement. The worse the wound, the greater the knight's daring and endurance. Pietro himself thought this a little backward. A skilled knight avoided injuries, as Cangrande had. But while the common people revered their Capitano as something akin to a warrior angel, popular lore had embarrassingly turned Pietro into an earthy romantic hero. His wound was just right, not being hard on the eye, only evidenced in his limp.

"Stay awake, boy," muttered Dante, as Pietro bumped into someone. "You're not as spry as you used to be."

"Mi dispiache," muttered Pietro, as he struggled with his crutch. It was all he could do to look self-sufficient enough to fend off the well-wishers pressing forward to carry him to the Arena. Even more disturbing, several young ladies were making eyes at him. Mercurio growled at them.

They continued through the throng all the way up to the Porta Borsari. Once past the old Roman arch, Pietro suggested that they turn up a small side street. "It'll be less crowded."

His brother looked put out, but Dante was grinning. "So. For once it is you being harassed in the streets, not I. A pleasant change." Incredibly, the wryness of the old master's grin indicated pride.

Not that father is old. He just acts it. The poet was stooped from years of reading and writing, but that did not indicate age, as Pietro knew full well. Thirty-five at the turn of the century, the years since Dante had found himself "midway though the journey of our life" had been darker than the wood he'd written of. Denied fire and water, his property confiscated, forced to borrow his wife's dowry to survive, he was declared *hostis* to his friends and family—a family whittled down from a healthy six children to three. Alighiero, the brother nearest Pietro's age, had died at twelve when a pestilence swept through the city. The same plague had claimed the baby of the family, little Elisio, aged eight. Dante had never even seen his youngest child, who was born three months after the exile was imposed.

The most deeply felt loss was Dante's eldest son, Giovanni. A few years older than Pietro, he'd had the duties and rights of the firstborn. Just nine when the poet was exiled, Giovanni had joined his father traveling through northern Italy for his next nine years. Then, as Dante prepared to visit the University of Paris, Giovanni was drowned in a river mishap. The city of Florence refused Dante the right to return and bury his son. So Dante's firstborn now lay in a tomb in Pisa, courtesy of Uguccione da Faggiuola.

That tragedy had altered Pietro's life. Nearly sixteen, Dante's second-born son had been summoned to follow his ever-wandering father to Paris in his brother's stead. His two remaining siblings, Poco and Antonia, had remained in Gemma's care, with Dante's brother Franco as guardian. But last year, when Florence's city leaders started making noise, about executing all male heirs of exiles, Gemma had quickly sent her remaining son off to join his father. Dante hadn't exactly been pleased—he'd rather have had Antonia than Poco. And now it appeared she was coming, if her last letter was any indication. The whole family together at last.

It might have been the exile that had aged Dante, but Pietro fancied it was the poem itself. An auspicious fifty years old this June, at the end of each day the poet looked far older. Though sleep was a great restorative, each stroke of the quill removed a day of his life. Today was an unaccustomed respite, a pleasure-filled day, yet Pietro could sense the resentment in his father. As his patron's client, he was obligated to show himself in public. But it meant a writing day lost, a terrible price.

Pietro was so lost in these thoughts that he was startled to look up and see a wide area, like a Greek agora or a Roman forum, filled with thousands of massed bodies pressed against their neighbors for warmth, blocking out the chilling air. The Piazza Bra. The sun was peeking between the city towers and the first race was still some five hours away, but already the rowdies, having begun their celebrations hours, nay, days early, were being trounced by men in Scaliger livery.

Pietro stopped in his tracks. In front of him, rising like a magnificent island in a sea of men, was the Roman Arena. He had only glimpsed it in the autumn, and since his return he had been pretty well confined to the streets around the palace.

Though dressed in brick, the body of the Arena was made of cement mixed with river pebbles and tile fragments. Supporting the body were arches—huge, square blocks of rose-marble, creating in each space an arch four times taller than a man, wide enough for five men to walk abreast with room to spare. Pietro counted twenty arches before it began to curve out of sight. It was titanic, colossal, far greater than he'd ever imagined.

"The one in Rome dwarfs it," murmured the voice at his elbow.

"I don't believe it," said Pietro, awed. Finally he understood his father's obsession with the Arena, which had been the poet's model for Hell.

Dante pointed to the top of the Arena, indicating a set of removed arches that rose higher than the rest. "See that? It is the remains of an outer wall that collapsed in an earthquake long ago."

Pietro tried to imagine the arches running all the way around, but had trouble adding anything to the massive structure. He drew in a second awed breath.

Dante nodded. "Literally inspiring, I see. Come. The Scaliger waits."

Several civic caretakers bearing the badge of Verona were cleaning new graffitti off the lower walls. A trickle of water seeped between the stones of the Arena. It mixed with dirt, claylike and red, that must have been left over from some event. The red dirt turned to mud, making it appear that the stones themselves were bleeding. Just like the dream. A river of blood flowing out of Hell, between the stones, and out into the mortal world.

✦ ◇ ✦

The Alaghieri party emerged from the corridors beneath the Arena, arriving at the balcony reserved for the Capitano's personal guests. They were guided to the second row on the left-hand side. Not bad seats, though more for being seen than for seeing.

Opposite them on a twin balcony sat many of the city elders and local nobles. Craning his neck this way and that, Pietro looked for Antony and Mari. He hoped they were on this side. He hadn't seen them in days.

Cangrande himself had not yet arrived. Pietro got Mercurio settled in at his feet. As they waited in the biting air, Dante fidgeted with his cap and scarf. Poco was twisting in his seat and winking at older girls in rows behind them. Seated between them, Pietro was still looking around for people he knew when the horns began to sound.

Down in the Arena's pit, fifty mounted knights appeared from the arches and rode headlong at each other as if to clash at the Arena's center. Suddenly all wheeled, merging into a tight formation for a series of mounted maneuvers that had the crowd on its feet. Drawing up into dual battle-lines, the knights stilled their mounts and drew longswords. The scraping of fifty blades departing their sheaths echoed around the great bowl. Slowly the lines advanced toward each other until the steel tips of the swords touched.

A hush fell over the crowd. Pacing slowly under the canopy of swords was young Mastino in the role of the Herald of Verona. He carried before him the ceremonial bow to launch the Bolt of the People, an honor long held by the Scaligeri. In his youth, Cangrande had walked in this place. Mastino's older brother had been the Herald for the past three years. Now it was Mastino's turn. The bow in his grip was symbolic of the weapon that had slain the legendary monster in La Costa.

Reaching the open air beyond the swords, he lifted the bow. He took no particular aim but loosed his bolt high into the air. People watched the shaft hurtle into space, wondering upon whose unfortunate head the bolt would fall. When they glanced back down, the men-at-arms had melted away to the far walls of the Arena, and Mastino had vanished. In his place, mounted on his magnificent warhorse, was Cangrande. He wore his finest armor, his famous houndshead helm resting in his lap. In his left arm he held the two scrolls that symbolized his sovereignty over the merchants. In his right hand he held a ceremonial sword. On his head was the laurel wreath, denoting his victory over the Paduans.

The audience surged forward, calling and cheering, stamping their boots and shouting his name. Cangrande stepped lightly from his saddle to kneel on the ground. The crowd stilled somewhat as the same priest who had heard Pietro's confession a couple hours before recited a loud, short invocation to the Virgin Mary and her son. The moment the prayer ceased to echo around the Arena, Cangrande rose to his full height and threw a balled fist into the air. "Let the festivities commence!" The crowd went wild and Cangrande withdrew, making way for the actors.

At the center of the Arena floor, a stage was marked out, and the rising sun coincided neatly with the start of the first entertainment. Far from the usual miracle or mystery plays, what erupted onstage was a bawdy romp by Aristophanes in which the women of Athens stormed the Acropolis, demanding that the Greek men stop warring or else live lives of involuntary chastity.

"Hardly appropriate to Lent," observed Dante.

"Unless one viewed the denial of sex as a religious concession," said Pietro. That drew a laugh from Poco. "I hear Cangrande asked for something light and silly."

Dante sniffed. "This qualifies. Tcha! They're ruining the text."

On the stage were about twenty men, most dressed as women (acting was a degenerate profession, and in those parts of the world where women were allowed onstage, the word *actress* was synonymous with *whore*). Some of the "girls" sported long beards, much to the elaborate dismay of the "men" on the makeshift stage. They spoke loudly, but the crowd paid little attention to the dialogue as they pointed at the actors' enormous false bosoms.

There was a bustling on the balcony as Cangrande arrived and took his place at the center beside his wife. He'd shed his parade armor for the grave clothing Pietro had seen that morning. At once the performers started to play up to the Scaliger, blowing him kisses and offering protestations of their affection. The Master of Verona readily returned the proffered love, and the crowd whooped with glee—everyone knew how much Cangrande loved actors.

One member of the company ran to stand below the Scaliger, a huge bouquet of flowers in his hand, and began to climb the balcony with cries of love. The Capitano made a big show of coyly refusing, but swayed in tune with the love song of the afflicted actor. Finally he took the flowers from his would-be paramour.

"Give us a kiss, lovey?" asked the "girl."

Lifting a flagon from beneath his seat, the Capitano poured the contents over "her" head. The actor sputtered, smacked his lips, and cried, "A good year!" The crowd cheered. Cangrande tossed the fellow a coin and demurely handed the flowers to his wife. The show went on.

Pietro glanced sidelong at his father. "Fun stuff!"

Dante shook his head. "Poor Aristophanes. If anyone should take such liberties with my work, I should rise from the dead and castrate them."

Pietro murmured, "That's real *contrapasso.*" To which his father had to chuckle.

The Capitano's wife appeared unappreciative of his antics. Or perhaps it was her neighbors that bothered her. To Giovanna's right was Cangrande's sister Katerina, with only Bailardino separating them. Katerina behaved as if there were nothing the matter whatsoever. She was gay and lively, thoroughly enjoying the antics of the jugglers.

At least there was no sign of the boy. Already the people had glommed onto this child as Cangrande's successor. If the Scaliger had no legitimate son, this child, they said, would be the natural heir. The term "natural" was thought to be a nice double entendre.

As Pietro watched, Giovanna carefully avoided Katerina's eyes as their husbands chatted across her. Instead the first lady of Verona conversed with Passerino Bonaccolsi, the Mantuan lord whose late brother had been married to Cangrande's eldest sister, Constanza. Too much to remember, thought Pietro.

The rest of the Capitano's family was in evidence. In the front row just past Donna Katerina sat Cecchino, the groom of Pietro's first day in Verona. He held his wife's hand and smirked. Rumor said she was already with child.

Past them sat the two little nephews of the Scaliger, Alberto and Mastino. Alberto was watching the goings on in the pit with avid interest. Mastino, on the other hand, listened intently to the adult conversations around him. A fortnight in the Scaligeri household had not increased Pietro's liking for the child. His first impression had been correct. Mastino ran about causing all sorts of trouble, leaving the blame to rest squarely on the shoulders of his older brother, the kind and oblivious Alberto. No matter how often Alberto was chastised for his brother's deeds, he came lumbering back to fall into the trap anew. The servants, in amused sympathy, had taken to calling the older boy Alblivious.

Pietro scanned the rest of the faces around him. By now he knew the Scaliger's intimates well enough. Directly in front of Pietro sat Nicolo da Lozzo and Guglielmo da Castelbarco, both of whom wore their wartime gorgets to the festivities, following the latest of French style. As Pietro returned their nods, his father coughed and muttered, "Dandies."

On the other side of the balcony, far from Pietro, Marsilio and Giacomo da Carrara sat in the front row. No doubt it was an invitation of politics, but the uncle appeared to be enjoying himself. Marsilio looked as handsome and mean-spirited as ever. Pietro recalled the lost fortune of his ransom with a little bitterness—he had grown up poor, and money was nothing to be lost without regret.

Turning in his seat and looking over heads, Pietro finally spied Mariotto. The Montecchi clan were seated a row behind the Paduans, a position Mari must have hated. Pietro's friend was wearing the purple and silver, though the feather in his hat was from a swan, pure white. While Pietro knew he cut a fine figure in his new clothes, withered leg and all, he couldn't hold a candle to Mariotto. The fellow couldn't be unhandsome if he tried.

Sitting to Mari's left was his sister Aurelia. Both obviously came from the same stock—dark hair, long face, big expressive eyes. But Aurelia was sadly lacking the overt beauty owned by her brother. She sat upright, looking down on the Arena floor with a smile on her open face.

On Mariotto's far side the Montecchi patriarch was chatting with a large, ruddy-faced man with thick broken veins across his face. Unlike Monsignor Montecchio, who was dressed in sumptuous but understated clothes, this man wore a wild compilation of layers, brocade, lace, and fur all fighting for dominance. The cacophony of colors and textures fought to swallow the man, but to his credit they failed. He was impressive for his girth and the gleam of intensity in his eyes—eyes that looked strangely familiar. The man threw back his head in a loud laugh, and Pietro thought, *It's Antony, twenty or thirty years down the road.* This observation was borne out when a sandy blond head capped with purple leaned into view to converse excitedly with Mariotto.

Antony noticed Pietro looking at them. He waved and said something to Mari, who turned and winked. Pietro waved in return, pointing to his cap. Mariotto pointed to his own and grinned.

When Antony leaned back, Pietro caught a glimpse of another Capecelatro. This tight-lipped figure had to be Antony's older brother. He did not wear the purple his sibling did, and Pietro wondered how jealous he must be to be forced to watch as his little brother was knighted by the lord of their new home.

Next to the Capecelatro heir sat a veiled woman who was at least eight months' pregnant. Pietro assumed this was Antony's sister-in-law. So the Capecelatro family was about to produce another generation. The woman pulled back her veils for a breath of unfiltered air, and Pietro was shocked at how fair she was. Her skin was so pale it was almost translucent. She seemed not to have eyebrows at all, her hair was so light. She was everything a classical beauty should be, yet her face was pinched and uncomfortable.

The balcony contained other faces. The unwelcome Abbot of San Zeno, along with the Scaliger's personal priest and the new Franciscan bishop, appropriately called Francis. Seated between the abbot and the bishop was a Dominican abbot, who tried to bridge the gap between the two men.

Behind them was a young fellow in a Franciscan cowl, doing service to his master as a page would to a knight. The young monk was in the spring of his orders, his tonsure new and carefully tended. His eyes were light grey, the color of a cloudy sky, his hair a raw black. He had a long, solid chin and was quite comely. Pietro wondered why such a handsome man would take the cloth so young in life—though clerical celibacy was the base of a hundred jokes. *There was a priest who lived with six girls . . .*

Dante was staring at his son. "What are you smiling at?"

"The play, Father," said Pietro quickly.

An arched eyebrow. "The play is over."

"Oh."

Jugglers came next, followed by acrobats and trick riders. As the sun mounted, so did the anticipation. The first Palio would take place just after noon, just after the ceremony of knighthood. Other than himself, Mari, and Antony, Pietro counted twelve more men in the purple and silver scattered though the nearby crowd, shifting excitedly in their seats.

Pietro realized he'd missed an announcement from the heralds. Worried that he might miss the knighting ceremony, he turned to his brother. "What did they say?"

Jacopo was waving to some girl, her father staring angrily over her shoulder. "The next performer is the oracle."

"An oracle?"

"It's tradition," affirmed Nico da Lozzo, looking back from the front row. "It's the most delicious of the warm-up acts. The oracle always predicts doom and destruction, with just a hint of hope."

"It's disgusting," said Dante sternly. "The art of prognostication is not for entertainment."

"What other use is there?" asked Nico lightly. "You can't live your life according to prophecy. Look at the prophets of history—always vague. No matter what happens, they can claim the credit for it. But it's great for stirring up a dull crowd! Set them up for you new cavalieres to knock down. Make the crowd gasp and pray to avert some doom, then reveal the new knights, the only ones who can save them." Looking up past Pietro, Nico's eyes fell on the abbots and the new Franciscan bishop. "Of course, the Church has to put its seal of approval on the enterprise long in advance."

"You mean," said Pietro slowly, "that what the oracle says is decided ahead of time?"

"Of course! You can't let her make it up on the spot! What if she predicts a plague, or a poor harvest? No, it's usually war or the death of Verona's enemies. Oh, look! Here she comes!"

The quality of the crowd's noise changed as the oracle shuffled out. She was a tiny thing. In defiance of the chilled air she wore no robe, no fur, only a shapeless gown of black. Her body was so thin as to be shapeless too—no hips, no breasts, nothing to disturb the line of the gown. Her arms hung loosely at her sides, thin and almost nonexistent. Pietro would have mistaken her for a boy if Nico hadn't already indicated her gender.

The complete lack of form to the body or the clothes only brought more strongly to the fore the oracle's most striking feature—her hair. Long and so black in the light it was almost blue, it reached all the way to her ankles. Entirely without curl, it shimmered in the February sun.

She stopped beneath the Scaliger's balcony. Without raising her head she bowed to the lord of Verona. The Scaliger rose and bowed in return. He remained standing high above her as she lifted her head past him to the sky, eyes shut in concentration. Her body swayed, head dipping left, then down to her chest. She repeated this move three times before the swaying stopped. A sudden shudder made the crowd gasp.

The grey eyes opened to stare at the Scaliger. Slowly, in a soft voice that carried throughout the Arena, the oracle addressed Verona's lord:

"Can Francesco della Scala! Verona will reach its greatest heights under your rule! Your fame will be great while you live. Though forgotten in two generations by the world outside our walls, it shall never cease to be spoken in the city of your birth. You are the flower of Verona's pride."

A murmur of approval ran through the crowd.

"Only once will you fail in battle, and that day shall be far from your last in the field. Only once will you fail in friendship, though that will be a far greater stain on your name than the defeat in war. You shall survive both of these to be the victor of all that is your right."

On the balcony, Il Grande raised an eyebrow at that last phrase.

"Yet while you live the seeds will be sown for the destruction of this fair city."

This was more like it! Doom and gloom! A thrilled crowd pressed forward to hear more.

"It will not be wars that destroy this fair city, but hates! Yet the hates will be born of love. Three great loves shall bring Verona low. They will also seal its fame. Two of these loves will be consummated in marriage. One will not. The love that is denied will shape the man to come. It will be his duty to save Verona. He will destroy it instead. His is a twisted path. The stars are against him, yet in spite of all, they love him. He will renew lost arts, and will be the great unsung hero of both Verona and mankind. The heavens weep for him."

The murmurs were rising, and the question was repeated from lip to lip. None raised their voice, but they all urged Cangrande to ask what was on everyone's mind.

He did. "Who?"

"Look to your cousins," was the reply.

Cangrande's wife frowned. So did Katerina. Bailardino looked puzzled. The crowd cast quick glances at Mastino and Alberto. Glances, too, were sent toward young Cecchino and his pregnant bride of five months. All of these were "cousins," but only in the broader sense, for Cangrande owned no true cousins, children of his father's brother.

The Scaliger stared at the oracle with an expression as fixed as the low stone wall his fingers were gripping. "Tell us more!"

"Two of these great loves will occur within your lifetime. One will be born this very year, one within a year of your death. The last—the last will come in its own time. All three loves will be united in the last, and though it will diminish the city in power, it will raise it in fame. Verona will always be remembered for love."

The eyes closed. The head drooped. The long hair swept over the face, obscuring it from view.

The Capitano did not wait. He took a purse from his belt and threw it down into the pit. It clattered at the oracle's feet. The crowd roared to life and

immediately the voices began to chatter. Hadn't she said their city would be famous? And the Capitano would win everything he dreamed of! Terrific stuff!

But what about the darkness? People whispered, nudging their neighbors,
looking at the children on the balcony near the Scaliger. Which of them
would be that unsung hero of Verona? Certainly not that Alberto. He had
none of his grandfather's daring or piety. And that Cecchino was a wastrel.
But there, looking down on the oracle as she was led away, there was little
Mastino. Gossip said he was a wild one—hadn't she said a twisted path? Oh,
he was the one to watch.

Pietro saw the realization pass over the six-year-old as he felt the eyes bent
upon him. The boy straightened, basking in the attention. Pietro could see
his pleasure and, beneath it, a hunger for more.

Da Lozzo had said that the oracle's words were written ahead of time—
she was supposed to have been another part of the pageant, like the actors
and the jugglers. But something in the air told Pietro she had departed from
her script.

Poco nudged him. "What's wrong with your dog?"

Pietro glanced down to Mercurio. Until now he'd been in a fine mood,
lapping Pietro's hand happily. Suddenly the greyhound was shaking, traces of
froth and drool around his mouth. His eyes, angled up to the open sky, were
strangely opaque.

"Mercurio? Hey, boy," said Pietro, his voice urgent. He rubbed Mercurio's ear. "What's the matter?"

Eyes blinking, the hound turned its head and laid his chin on Pietro's right
thigh. Mercurio always arranged himself on Pietro's wounded side, the better
to protect it. Pietro used both hands to lift the dog's face and nuzzle it with
his own. "You all right, boy?"

A plucking at his sleeve. The Capitano's Grand Butler saying, "It is time,
my lord."

Lord? Dear God, he means me! Pietro turned to his father. "Could you
keep an eye on Mercurio?"

Dante nodded, reaching out a hand to brush the Mercurio's snout, a game
the poet and the hound had developed. The dog ducked and swiveled his
head over the extended hand, waiting for Dante's second try. Dante glanced
at Pietro. "Go on. We're fine."

Rising, Pietro leaned on his crutch and hobbled after the rest of the prospective knights as they passed under the seats on their way down to the Arena floor. It was good to be out of the chilled air for the moment. The braziers on the balcony had helped, but the cold air threatened to freeze the blood in a man's veins.

Or perhaps it was the oracle's eyes.

SIXTEEN

As Pietro followed the steward's lead, Antony and Mari fell in beside him. "Let's get this over with," said Antony, rubbing his hands together and blowing on them. "I want to get to the race."

Mariotto hit his friend on the arm. "Just like you, 'Tonio, to think of the greatest day of your life as nothing but the race. We're to be knighted!"

Antony said, "You're running, aren't you, Pietro?"

Pietro almost answered in the negative. Then he remembered Bailardino's comment about riding. He couldn't compete in the midnight footrace, but that didn't stop him from riding his new palfrey in the noon stampede. He nodded. "I think I will!"

"Good!" Antony clapped a hand on Pietro's back, hard. "Mari and I have a bet on who will win."

"There's no chance you'll win, oaf, unless you fall off your horse onto me again," replied Mariotto.

"Would you listen to him? I save his life—"

"You fell! You said so yourself!"

"I saved your life!"

"I saved yours!"

"Pfah! You should have that Morsicato look at your head, pretty boy. Phantom knights with spears!"

"Phantom crossbows is more like it—"

"Girls, girls," laughed Pietro. "You're both pretty."

There was more good-natured scuffling as they walked down a ramp and under the outer ring of the Arena's lower level. All around them were remnants of past times: grooves in the marble floor worn by centuries of traffic; the rough sockets in the walls where, after Rome's fall, citizens suspended timbers to create homes out of the Arena walls; and here and there a touch of the original paint still lingered, reminding everyone that the Roman Empire had been a garish place.

"Say," said Mari suddenly, "look what Antony and I have!" He drew a long silver dagger from its sheath at his back. "Show him yours, you big lout! Or have you lost it already?"

"I have mine right here," retorted Antony, tossing his dagger up by Mariotto's head.

Mari's gloved hand plucked the blade from the air. "Nice."

"Daggers?" Pietro wondered why he didn't get a silver dagger in his box of weapons. Or had he overlooked it?

"Something Mari and I had made," said Capecelatro. "We got one for you, too. A gift." He handed over a third matching weapon.

Mari held out the ones in his hands. "Look, on one side it says 'The Triumvirate,' and on the other a name engraved on it." Sure enough, Pietro saw *Mari* etched with acid into the finely wrought silver of one, *Tonio* in the other. The one in his hand read *Pietro*.

He looked up into their expectant faces. "I don't know what to say!"

"Say you can juggle!" Antony and Mari started tossing their knives back and forth with practiced ease, causing people around them to duck and curse. Pietro tossed his up into the mix and nearly sliced his free hand open as he caught the one that flicked back at him.

"We were thinking of working up an act for the next festival," said Mariotto. "You should join up—we'd be famous!"

"Yes, the three-fingered trio," laughed Pietro, ducking. "Watch out!"

"Did you listen to that oracle?" asked Antony, catching a knife and waving it back and forth mystically as he crossed his eyes and began to moan. "Loooovvve! All of you will die for loooooove! Where do they get this nonsense?"

Mariotto snickered. "Wait a minute—she didn't say it was the love of a man for a woman. Perhaps it will be love of battle that will destroy the city!"

"Or of poetry," growled Antony.

"Or of wine," observed Pietro.

"Well, then, I'm safe," sighed Antony happily. "I prefer beer."

Mariotto snorted. "You would! You're probably really a German. The whole Capua story is a lie."

"That's right," nodded Antony. "Spying for the Empire, here to report on who's fit for battle. I've told them that of the whole Montecchi clan, only Monsignore Gargano Montecchio is fit for duty."

They were trailing the crowd of new knights around the outer ring of the Arena, below the vaulted arches that held the seats. Mari said, "I have a pretty fierce aunt in a convent in Treviso. Perhaps your father would fancy her," he added to Pietro. "Her name is Beatrice."

"Ouch! One is enough, thank you." He explained that his sister would soon be joining them in Verona. "The old man calls her Beatrice."

"Maybe your father and Mari's will arrange a match," muttered Antony.

Pietro was shocked. "What?"

"Don't mind him," chuckled Mariotto breezily. "He's only cross because he meets his bride today."

"Don't remind me!" shouted Antony.

"Bride?" said Pietro, eyes wide.

Mariotto glanced down at the dagger in his hand. "Hey, 'Tonio—you've got mine."

"And I'm going to keep it," muttered Antony, slicing the air. "If you bring her up again, I'll give it back to you up to the hilt!"

Grin widening Pietro repeated, "Bride?"

"Yes, yes!" proclaimed the Capuan hotly. "My father's arranged a marriage for me. I meet her today."

Mariotto was positively joyful. "There will even be a formal betrothal on Wednesday. And a solemn supper, and a clasping of hands, and a —"

"And a dead Montecchio for dessert," growled Antony.

They reached the exterior of the Arena and circled around to where their horses waited, the giant destriers. Their saddles were all equipped with swords and bucklers. Apparently they were to ride out in full glory.

As he was being helped into his saddle Pietro said, "So who is she? Some old widow?" The look that earned him was deadly.

"She's Paduan," Mariotto told him brightly.

"No!" said Pietro incredulously.

"Not only a Paduan," beamed Mari as he mounted. "She's a Carrara!"

That took a little of the joy out of Pietro's smile. "What?"

"Yes, yes, she's that bastard's cousin," moaned Antony. "My father went to the Capitano and they decided it would be a fine way to signal the peace. Cangrande has no relatives of marriageable age, so he agreed to present me to the Carrarese."

"That's—quite a match," said Pietro. He didn't know much about Antony's family, but such a union was certainly above their station. It was a signal honor the Capitano was bestowing on the Capecelatro family. *Just how much money does Antony's father have?*

Antony bristled. "Oh, she's not too good for me," he said with sour perceptiveness. "Don't worry your snobbish little head off."

Pietro frowned. "I didn't say—"

"No, you didn't! No one does. But I see it in your eyes. You too, Mari!" He swung a fist that barely missed Mariotto. "Everyone wonders why we left Capua, how we made our money. How does anyone make it? Just because we came to ours lately, we get snubbed! We run *commendi* now! We just provide capital! How did your ancestors get their wealth, Montecchio? Hmm? Are you so proud of the horse thieves in your family stable?"

It was a coarse and boorish thing to say, worse because it was true. For all their lands and respectability today, the Montecchi fortune had been founded by a branch of the family famous for stealing horses. Even the family motto, *Montibus in claris semper vivida fides,* had derived from that practice. *Faith is always vigorous in the clear mountains*—it would be if you were praying to avoid capture, riding your stolen horses to your hiding place.

Around them the other soon-to-be-knights shifted, either turning away or watching with eagerness. Mariotto's voice was level. "Take that back."

Antony was uncowed. "Make me."

Mariotto was about to launch a punch at Antonio's head when Pietro walked his horse between them, holding up his crutch. "Umm—I don't think this is how knights are supposed to behave."

Mari looked murderous. "We're supposed to uphold our honor."

"Then think of the dishonor your family will suffer if you don't get knighted today. Antony, if you're mad at anyone, be mad at me. But apologize to Mariotto so we can get on with this." Already the other prospective knights were being summoned to the tunnel that led to the Arena floor.

Antony looked sullen. "I'm sorry, Mari."

Mariotto waited a beat before answering. "I should have let you get skewered."

"I should have let you get shot."

"You fell."

"So I did."

"I'm going to kill you in the Palio, you know."

"You'll die trying."

Mariotto raised one of the small silver daggers they had been playing with. "Don't forget, I've got a dagger with your name on it."

"So do I," Capecelatro said, lifting his own knife. And just like that, it was over.

"Hey, you two," said Pietro, "remember that my name's on one of these knives. Don't get any ideas."

"Pietro, you really need to stop worrying," said Mari, as they fell in behind the line of young cavalieres at the tunnel's mouth.

"Yeah." Antony grinned. "You could start going prematurely grey."

"At least it won't be from my wife nagging me."

"A hit!" cried Mari.

Antony laughed as they rested in the shadow of the tunnel. "Keeps me from a life in church, though. Did you see that poor sod waiting on Guelco and the abbot?"

Pietro recalled the young monk with the new tonsure. "I did, in fact. I'm surprised he isn't married."

"Probably likes the boys," said Antony, scandalizing his friends. "But, thank God, I've avoided the cloisters. Now I only have to weather a wife!"

"It won't be too bad, Antony," observed Mariotto.

"How do you know?"

"I don't. I was just trying to make you feel better."

"Why don't you ask your daddy to make you a match," suggested Antony sweetly. "Then we can both put our heads into the noose together."

"Not me," said Mariotto, puffing out his chest. "Footloose and fancy-free. When I marry, I want to have lived a little."

"Oh, thank you!" snarled Antony, rolling his eyes back in his head.

"Shhhh!" Pietro pointed. The steward was signaling that it was time to ride out into the Arena. He began to give them their instructions. The three young men in back shifted on their horses and straightened their farsettos as they listened.

"Pietro," whispered Antony urgently. "Seriously, dine near our table tonight. I don't want to meet her alone. Mari will be there."

"I will," Pietro whispered back.

Then they were riding out to huge applause under the noonday sun.

All fifteen looked exquisite in their identical uniforms. The only difference among them was that no two bore the same feather in their cap. Here there was a peacock plume, there the pinfeather from a duck.

Entering from the west, directly opposite the Scaliger's balcony, they rode around the pit twice, then made for the center where they dismounted and knelt. A struggle for Pietro.

With solemn voice Cangrande read off the names of the chosen. When he came to the names of the Triumvirs he had to stop, so deafening was the applause. Then the Capitano called everyone into prayer, after which he gave all of them the charge of the Code of knighthood. He listed first the three ideals—Justice, Right, Piety—and then the four houses—the house of the Church, the house of the Widow, the house of the Orphan, and the house of the Oppressed—they must defend as cavalieri.

Bishop Francis came forward. Reaching the edge of the balcony, the holy man recited the ten commandments of chivalry:

> *Thou shalt believe all that the Church teaches, and shalt observe all its directions.*
> *Thou shalt defend the Church.*
> *Thou shalt respect all weaknesses, and shalt constitute thyself the defender of them.*
> *Thou shalt love the country in the which thou wast born.*
> *Thou shalt not recoil before thine enemy.*
> *Thou shalt make war against the Infidel without cessation, and without mercy.*
> *Thou shalt perform scrupulously thy feudal duties, if they be not contrary to the laws of God.*
> *Thou shalt never lie, and shall remain faithful to thy pledged word.*
> *Thou shalt be generous, and give largess to everyone.*
> *Thou shalt be everywhere and always the champion of the Right and the Good against Injustice and Evil.*

"Now," commanded the bishop, "I call upon each of you in turn to proclaim two of the tenets in the Code of knighthood. Ser Bellinzona, you may begin."

Oh God. No one had told Pietro about this! *Let's see. There are thirty-six tenets in the Code. Which should I choose?* His choices mattered a great deal, for they would characterize his life as a knight from this day forward.

On the far end the man named Bellinzona raised his head and proclaimed "Live for freedom, justice, and all that is good! Never attack from behind!" There was applause.

The next declared: "Administer Justice! Die with Valor and Honor!"

Bastard took three! Dying with Valor and Dying with Honor are separate! Pietro resisted the urge to administer a little justice of his own.

"Destroy evil in all of its forms! Respect women!"

Two more good ones gone. Pietro was almost at the end of the line, with only Mariotto and Antony coming after him. Though he could repeat tenets used by other knights, it would be frowned upon. He had to find two of his own—but which two were obscure enough that no one in front of him would take them? He hardly wanted his life as a knight to be defined as "Avoid torture" or "Exhibit manners."

"Never attack an unarmed foe! Fight with Honor!"

Obvious. I knew they'd be snapped up right away.

"Always keep one's word of Honor! Avoid cheating!"

I can't believe someone used the cheating line. He must be more panicked than I am.

"Exhibit self-control! Fight for the ideals of Capitano, country, and chivalry!"

Clever, swapping out king for Capitano.

"Exhibit Courage in word and deed! Be polite and attentive!"

There's a rather noncombative oath. Pietro listened as the list went on from knight to knight down the line toward him. Since many of the tenets overlapped, there were many references to Honor, Courage, Freedom, and Justice. One fellow, clearly desperate, used the torture line, which got a loud jeer from the crowd.

Pietro was planning on two that he thought were rather obscure—*Always maintain one's principles* and *Avenge the wronged.* He was lucky to have thought of those two, because he couldn't remember any others that were left.

Just as he was running over the words again in his mind, he heard the knight two places down from him proclaim them both! *Oh fut!* He had to find two more, but he hadn't been listening. *Which ones have been used?*

The knight beside him proclaimed, "Live to serve God, Capitano, and country and all they hold dear!" It was clever, the way he pushed two tenets into one fine sentiment.

It was Pietro's turn. He took a breath, raised his head, and let loose with the first two that came to mind.

"Live a life that is worthy of respect and honor! Protect the innocent!"

Cheers, not jeers. He sighed and lowered his chin as Mariotto looked up.

"Never abandon a friend, ally, or noble cause! Avoid deception!" More cheering, even though avoiding deception was awfully close to avoiding cheating.

Antony's head didn't move as he whispered, "Had to take the friendship one, didn't you?" He lifted his own head as Mari, grinning, dropped his. The big Capuan exclaimed, "Never use a weapon or stratagem on an opponent not equal to the attack! Respect authority!"

Mari snickered. "Respect authority?"

"Shut up, witless," hissed Antony. "I didn't mean you."

"Be quiet, the pair of you!" Pietro was pressing his lips tight together. "Cangrande's talking again!"

The Scaliger was gesturing for silence. When the applause ended he put on a grave face. "There is more to being a knight than skill at arms and wit. To become a knight is to take upon you the responsibility of being God's sword of justice here on earth. A knight does not enrich himself. He does not, as many today do, seek fame," here the Scaliger couldn't help smiling slightly, "or dress in the finest apparel." His angel's eyes returned to their most serious. "A knight rights wrongs. A knight protects the innocent. A knight listens to the words of the Lord. Do you understand this?"

"We do," proclaimed the assembled youths.

"Then take the communion I offer you, and be one with the Lord!"

As Cangrande finished speaking the charge his father had given him many years ago, several priests and monks appeared. Pietro heard the chiming of the bells—it was exactly noon on the first Sunday of Lent. The prayers the priests spoke as they gave the fifteen of them communion also gave absolution to the citizens for not attending church on this holy day, using the creation of the knights as a special dispensation.

Pietro took the bread and drank the wine, thinking not of God but of how he could possibly endure kneeling any longer. His right leg was trembling, and he could feel sweat dappling his forehead in spite of the chilling cold. He was just thinking, *Ceremony be hanged, I'm going to sit down,* when he saw it was over. The Scaliger was signaling them to rise. Pietro wobbled slightly as he did.

"I bestow on each and every one of you the highest honor Verona can bestow—I proclaim you Cavalieri del Mastino!"

The new Knights of the Mastiff, Verona's private order of chivalry, stood basking in cheers. Antonio raised his hands above his head in sign of victory. Mariotto blew kisses and waved, flashing his brilliant smile. Other new knights danced and cavorted around the inside of the Arena.

Pietro was grinning, tears in his eyes. He had seen, up on the balcony, his reserved father stand and shout with the rest. The poet's hand went up to his eye, as if to wipe away a tear. That put the seal on the proudest day of Pietro's life.

But it wasn't over. Outside the Arena there was cheering as well. For now that the ceremony of knighthood was over, the Palio could begin.

✦ ✧ ✦

Sitting in a shaded corner in a tavern along the route of the Palio, two men conferred. One, a remarkable figure, attempted to disguise himself from prying eyes by keeping well out of the light. The other, more average, was dressed in clothes a bit too fine for the usual patron of such an establishment. Between them sat a hunk of cheese and some spirits, so far untouched.

The shadowed man stopped listening long enough to say, "That's a poor jest."

"It's no jest."

"The Scaligeri palace." The voice dripped with sarcasm.

"Right under the Greyhound's nose, yes."

"You're mad. I've been in Vicenza this last month and more, I've seen how he's watched. Day and night. In fact," the speaker leaned forward, a dangerous glint in his eye, "I overheard their instructions from the lady herself. She said there had already been an attempt. What haven't I been told?"

The average-looking man frowned in what might have been genuine puzzlement. "What attempt?"

"She didn't say much, but it happened in Padua. I swear, if I've been lied to . . ."

"I know nothing about Padua. Look, friend, I only bear the message. So either listen or walk." He waited, scrabbling off a corner from the block of cheese on the table. "Want some? No? Fine. Then let's get to it. They're running the horse race as we speak. Tonight is the footrace, yes? While that's going on, there's going to be a horde of people in the palace—there always is. You are to wait until the race is over and the winner is being feted. Then you make your move."

"The boy will be there?"

"I have it on the best authority that he will."

"And how, pray tell, am I supposed to get in, much less get out? With a child, no less."

A diagram was slid across the scarred table. "Alberto della Scala was a cautious man. What the people giveth, the people taketh away. And he learned a lot from the death of his brother. Always have an escape route, that was the lesson." A finger landed on a cross in the diagram. "There is a passage here, leading both to the feasting hall on the ground floor, and up to Cangrande's salon above it. It opens onto the street, here at the side, see? It's carefully painted in fresco, the seams are invisible unless you know to look."

"And this secret side door, it will be open?"

"It will."

"Who is going to open it for me?"

"You don't need to know that. Just be there before the second race starts. While the Scaliger is distracting everyone by starting the race, you can slip in. No one will see you."

A hand darted out to grasp the planner's wrist. "Tell me why I should trust you. It may be well worn, but your accent—"

"—is not your concern. Nor the name of my employer. Your needs are aligned with ours for this fraction of time. Do not expect to see me ever again. Remove your hand and go."

Their eyes held, and slowly physical contact was ended. The diagram was tucked away and the men parted, one eager to disappear into the crowd outside, the other content to watch him go.

A nearby door opened and another man sidled up to the bench and sat. "He seems a pleasant type. Can he do it?"

"We'll see. He's certainly determined enough." They each quaffed a drink. "What about that other piece of business?"

"Done and done. The future is behind her now."

"Good." They finished their spirits and stood, leaving the tavern to watch the race before returning to the palace for an evening that promised even greater excitement.

SEVENTEEN

Even with the capable Tullio d'Isola organizing affairs, it was closer to one than to twelve before all the prospective contestants were mounted and ready on the Arena floor. Flasks passed from hand to hand to keep off the cold, jokes were told, surreptitious sabotage attempted on saddles and reins. But now, at last, all awaited the Scaliger's command to begin.

Pietro had traded his destrier for his palfrey. Warhorses were forbidden entry—a beast bred and trained to trample, bite, and kick would give unfair advantage. Thinking he'd have to dash to the Scaliger stables to fetch it, Pietro was surprised by a squire racing forward trailing the thin brown horse already saddled, new spurs dangling. They were knight's spurs, recognizable by their length. Since a mounted soldier rode tall, legs locked, the long necks allowed the rowels to reach the horse's flanks. He fitted them on as the squire led his destrier away. "Hey! What's his name?!" But the squire was already gone.

Pietro shifted the caparison under him. A knight's horse was often covered with a large cloth with the ornamental designs corresponding to the knight's heraldic patterns. It served as a form of identification in battle and on parade. There were several fancy devices in the press. Others were bare under the saddle. Pietro's borrowed caparison bore the Scaligeri ladder. Pietro wondered what he could add to the boring old Alaghieri family crest to spice it up some. Perhaps a sword.

Other young men had forgone the ceremony and the blessing to fetch their own horses from nearby stables. Stallions, mares, and palfreys all came trotting into the center of the Arena, both the start and finish line. Young and old alike, the men on the Arena floor were breathless with excitement.

On the balcony Cangrande watched the preparations with real longing in his eyes. He had been the victor of every Palio, horse and foot, from age thirteen until his brother's illness. The only consolation was that now it fell to him to design the route. The course was different each year. Servants had been out during the morning hours frantically hanging banners at street corners. Those at the forefront of the race would have to have their wits about them or else they would find themselves off the track, disqualified or hopelessly left behind.

On the Arena floor, Pietro mounted, whispering names in his palfrey's ear. "Zeus? Apollo?" The beast hardly noticed him. "Frederick? Peppin?" Nothing.

Familiar faces emerged from the mob. Nico da Lozzo was there, trying to strike up a conversation with Antony's dour elder brother. *Good luck with that,* thought Pietro. The fellow hadn't even congratulated his brother on being knighted. Pietro stopped feeling bad for forgetting his name.

A dark-haired knight on horseback rode in, dressed in a starched white farsetto and brilliant red hose—the colors of Padua. Under the white doublet he wore a tunic closed at the throat that was as red as his hose. The fellow's only concession to the cold was a black woolen scarf wrapped around his throat, its ends jammed into the collar of the white leather doublet. The crowd oohed as he came into view, and others riders moved aside to make a path.

The horse under the rider was not a palfrey. Few men could afford the upkeep of more than two or three horses, and most of a knight's money went towards the upkeep of his destrier, followed by his riding horse. But this horse was a courser. A strong, lean horse made for racing, this one probably had "hot" blood in its veins, bred from Arabian or Turkish stock. There were five or six coursers in the Arena, but none so magnificent.

Astride this magnificent piece of horseflesh sat Marsilio da Carrara, bolt upright. Beneath the saddle, the caparison was starched a stainless, expensive white. With his blinding hues, Carrara stood out white as snow against the furs and the cloaks around him.

"Showy son of a . . ." muttered Mariotto.

"Hope that thing bolts right out from under him," spat Antony.

Pietro felt Carrara's eyes sweep over to him and forced himself to ignore the Paduan's noxious presence. "Caesar? Augustus. Nero!" Not a twitch.

Nearly fifty men had chosen to participate. Tullio arranged the riders in front of the eastern balcony in five rows. Each row held ten men except for the last, which held eight. Some riders were youths hoping to make a name for themselves. Others were men well into their forties who had participated in the Palio every year since coming of age, determined to do so until they won or died. Every man clutched his reins and breathed in the harsh winter air. Pietro was grateful that, unlike the footrace tonight, this race was run fully clothed.

"Brutus? Cassius? Hades. Pluto. Mars?"

Pietro saw Cangrande beckon Dante up to join him in the front row of watchers. Women were no longer in evidence, though young Mastino and Alberto remained, poised at the edge of their seats. Pietro was secretly crestfallen. He'd desired Katerina to see him ride. Perhaps she would have waved.

Dante whispered something to the Capitano, who instantly burst out laughing. At his side Bailardino howled. He beckoned Monsignore Montecchio and Monsignore Capecelatro forward, demanding the poet to repeat his joke. Capecelatro looked offended but recovered himself quickly and chuckled. Lord Montecchio smiled wanly, then his eyes furrowed in thought. Bailardino was still clutching his sides. Dante sighed complacently.

Oh, God, thought Pietro. *What did he say now?*

The mirthful Cangrande stood and spread his arms wide. "Riders! On this Holy Day you are racing not for money or fame, but for the honor of your city! To win, you must all use your heads as well as your horses! And remember, those you ride against are your fellows, your friends! This is sport, not war! Do not mistake the two!" There were several grim chuckles among the more experienced riders.

Pietro, wondering what his father's jest had been, patted his horse. "Cicero? Socrates? Ptolemy?" He was stuck in a classical rut. He tried other legends. "Merlin? Lancelot. Galahad."

Above, Cangrande continued in his public voice: "You will exit the western gates of the Arena and turn right! After that, the track is marked by crimson flags!"

Crimson! Of the many differently colored flags lining the streets, they fixed that color in their minds. "Follow the flags, wherever they may lead, and you will be brought back here." The riders shifted, anxious to start, and the Scaliger held up a forestalling hand. "There is a twist this year. I have decided to lengthen the routes of both the horse race and the footrace. With the footrace that was easy enough. But for the horse Palio, I created a double route. You must ride the track twice, thus doubling the distance from four to eight miles. It has been the trend of the past few years that the fastest horse wins. A quick steed will no longer assure victory. You must rest your horses, husband their strength for the second half of the race." Cangrande's blue eyes twinkled. "I have also a few surprises for you. To be sure you truly enjoy them, you will pass through them twice!"

There was a little nervous chatter as the riders quickly rethought their strategies. In this, Pietro was far ahead of them. He had no prepared strategy for winning. He was just going to ride hard and see what happened. In some ways, the double lap would be an advantage for him. Wrong turns made could be avoided on the second time around the track. "Aries. Ganymede. Bucephalous." He'd returned to the classics. Still no name roused a response from the horse. "Not Phaeton, I hope."

The Scaliger gestured to his Grand Butler. Under the command of the steward, the forty-eight men turned about, facing away from the Capitano's balcony. Now they were all aimed for the west end, with the row of eight riders in the front. Pietro saw Mari and Antony close to the center of the second line from the front. It was a risky position. They would either get out the gate quickly or else be trapped in the crush.

Pietro had lined up closest to the Capitano, so now he was on the far right of the rear line. His first challenge would be getting his horse through the arch as fifty other horses vied with him to squeeze through an opening that was only wide enough for six.

"Venus—no, sorry, you're not a Venus, are you, boy? Cupid. Vulcan. Hermes?" The palfrey shook his head in irritation. Pietro patted the mane, eyes on the crimson flag in Tullio d'Isola's hand.

A cheer as the crimson cloth became a downward blur. Human and animal voices shrieked together as spurs drove home. All five lines lurched forward. The Palio was under way!

The palfrey was well trained. At the barest touch of Pietro's spurs it bounded forward. "Go go go!" Already the front line of riders was entering the arch of the tunnel. Among the furs and cloaks of these could be seen the bright white of Marsilio's doublet. The Paduan almost fell out of his courser's saddle, righting himself just in time for the stone archway to miss his head. Then he was lost in shadow. Pietro couldn't help thinking, *A shame he wasn't trampled.*

But Pietro had no time for his dislikes. He'd decided there was no chance of making his way through the center of the pack. He raced up along the outside, passing the fourth and then the third line. That was as far as he could go without risking being forced headlong into a stone wall. He jerked the reins left, trying to cut in, and the horse obediently veered into the throng. This angered a half-dozen riders. Obscenities in Latin, Italian, German, and French followed him. Most of these were in the form of personal insults: "*Figlio di buona donna!*" "*Tete de merde!*" "*Unde ars in tine naso!*" "*Culibonio!*" "*Pezzo di merda!*" "*Fellator!*" and so on. One bashed his horse's hind into Pietro. It could have been disastrous, but the palfrey was game for a rough ride. So was Pietro. He released the reins from the grip of his left hand, looping them over a wrist so he wouldn't lose them. He shocked his reserved father up on the balcony by thrusting a protruding thumb between the first and second fingers of his closed fist. This was the *fico,* the fig, a very insulting gesture indeed.

His assailant saw the fig, grinned, and slammed into Pietro again, making him clutch at the saddle to recover himself. Pietro pulled left again, then felt something painful brush his left leg. Pietro turned his head and saw a glimpse of gold. The bastard was kicking out with his spurs. There was a trickle of blood just above Pietro's boot. Wondering why everyone went after his legs, Pietro kicked out with his heel. His spur caught and he pulled back hard. The man yelped. *Too bad, friend,* thought Pietro. *I didn't start it.*

"*Porco dio!*" With that joyful curse, the man beside him used his reins as a whip, flinging the leather straps at Pietro's eyes. Ducking, Pietro looked ahead. The wall was coming up quickly. He pulled hard to the left and again his palfrey responded just in time. He felt a rush of air as his scalp passed the marble slab. Darkness engulfed him, and he joined the crush in the tunnel.

Just ahead of him, Pietro's friend jerked his horse sideways. This was dangerous. He could career into the tunnel wall and fall to be trampled to death. Pietro pulled back on his reins. An opening formed just to the fellow's left, and Pietro steered his horse into it, effectively swapping places. The reins flicked again toward his face and Pietro leaned left, where his body brushed another rider.

The light was growing. The western arch to the tunnel was only a few feet away. The reins came again, snapping in the air above Pietro's head. He ducked, reached up, and grasped his competitor's reins in his right hand. He yanked backward and down. His assailant's horse resisted and the rearing horse slammed its rider into the arched tunnel ceiling. The man took the blow on his shoulder and cursed, shouting, "Twenty florins to the man who unhorses that rider!"

Emerging into daylight Pietro angled his horse right and hoped no one took the offer too seriously. Everyone was too busy trying to take the lead. Ahead Pietro could see the figure of Marsilio, kicking out with spurs and reins, but much more viciously than the horseplay in the tunnel.

"Cunnus," growled Pietro in a low voice.

The horse raised his head.

"Cunnus?"

Racing full tilt to the north now, the palfrey let out a short grunt.

"Of course," said Pietro, scandalized. But the name seemed to work. "Come on, Cunnus! Let's go!"

It was a wild chase, and a surprisingly straight one. The track led north, shifting briefly west along the Corso Mastino until they came to another junction. A crimson flag was easily visible fluttering in the breeze from a second-story balcony. It turned them north again. For what seemed an eternity they rode along the riverbank. To their left were houses and apartments belonging to the lower and middle classes. On their right was the curving Adige just beginning its S-bend at the top of the city. The air off the river was crisp and biting.

Pietro was among the second tier of riders. There were a few fists, but these were random and largely without malice. Ahead, those riders who hadn't had to fight their way through the tunnel led by a good four lengths. But the pioneers were hampered by having to look everywhere for the little red flags. Among the leaders were Mariotto and Antony, riding neck and neck. As Pietro watched, Marsilio bolted past them, vying for first place with two other knights. One more knight was close behind the small knot of horsemen. These six ran close, eyeing each other with suspicion while they scanned the horizon for the next flutter of crimson. Marsilio's beautiful courser took long graceful strides, eating up great distances with each step. If the course had been a straight one, the Paduan would have won easily.

Along the banks of the Adige, obstacles abounded. Barrels everywhere, fishing equipment discarded hither and yon. The path was half paved and half mud. The horsemen had to dodge around short piers and ramps. It made for quite a course. To their left, on low rooftops, and their right, in boats, common citizens cheered. These were the best seats for the race, certainly better than the Arena.

Pietro began to feel warm under his heavy fur-trimmed cloak. Sweat pooled at the base of his spine, soaking his new shirt. He recognized what

Carrara had known at the start. While standing about without cover in the cold chilled the bones, the race would be less tiring if one wasn't sweating under the weight of furs and weaves. Pietro did waste a moment thinking of his fine new rabbit-fur shoulder-cloak, but then he reached up a hand and released the catch.

Looking about, he saw many different colored flags—blue and gold and white and black. But no crimson. Pietro was just beginning to think the race would take them out of the city when the six riders in the lead turned west. A few seconds later Pietro saw the crimson flag hung on a sconce on the side of a tallow shop. He made the turn, only to see the leaders turning again. The next flag indicated north.

He followed. To his right loomed the church of San Zeno. The track of the race ran right past its front steps, with the engraved metal doors below the massive circular window. From the basilica of Verona's patron, the race turned south for several city blocks, then west down the Strade di San Bernardino. For the first time, passage became difficult. The two long straightaways had closed most of the gaps between the riders. Now, hedged in by the new stone wall on their right, the racers jockeyed for position, anticipating the next turn. Riding close to Pietro was Antony's older brother—irrelevantly, his name bubbled up—Luigi! Luigi's eyes were focused like daggers on his younger brother's back.

Pietro was penned in against the wall by other riders. Just ahead was one of the city gates, called the Porta San Sisto, but rechristened by the inhabitants of the quarter in honor of this very event. The Porta Palio was a wide affair, with five stone arches leading out to the western suburbs. Pietro saw the griffin on the top, and then a flutter of red across the square caught his eye. It was a flag, marking a hard left turn back toward the city center.

But the riders ahead of him hadn't seen it! Mari, Antony, and the other leaders had thundered blithely on. Carrara had missed the flag by less than two feet. Pietro could take the lead.

His problem was that, hedged in by the riders to his left, there was no way he could make it across to the gap between buildings without coming to a complete halt and letting the others race by—a tactic that would draw attention. *Maybe I can pretend my horse threw a shoe . . .*

But just then another racer spied it and shouted. Nico da Lozzo, Luigi Capecelatro, Pietro's friend from the tunnel—all saw it and cheered, delighted to suddenly advance to the lead. As one the forty-one riders turned their horses left, east down the Strade di Porta Palio, a route that would lead them back to the Corso Mastino.

Pietro was about to jerk his horse's reins left after the others when he happened to glance ahead. Mariotto and Antony and the rest of the former front-runners were still pushing hard as ever, not realizing they had missed the turn. Hadn't they heard the cheer?

Squinting, Pietro saw what they had seen already—far ahead, just as the city walls curved inward, there was a flutter of red. Another flag? How could that be? How could they turn here and at the next block as well?

Pietro had to make a choice. His little voice told him to be suspicious of the nearer flag. Swallowing hard, he ignored it. Instead, he followed the six in the lead. As he kept on south, he tried to put a finger on what it was that bothered him.

He caught sight of Marsilio's bright white farsetto over the matching caparison of the horse. The colors jogged his memory. The Paduan had ridden within a handspan of the false flag. Another image flashed into Alaghieri's mind—Marsilio almost falling out of his seat at the beginning of the race. It had seemed an accident, but what if it hadn't been? Why else would he. . . .

The starter's flag. Carrara had lifted it from where the Grand Butler had thrown it down. That same flag now had forty-one men racing in the wrong direction.

Crafty Carrara. He's eliminated most of the competition. It was a good ploy. If he hadn't been hedged, Pietro would have made the turn without hesitation. Now only he and the six ahead of him stood a chance of winning. By the time the others realized they had taken a wrong turn, they'd be well into the eastern portion of the city, beyond hope of finding the trail again.

Pietro urged his horse on. With the field open around him, he was able to close much of the gap between himself and the riders in the lead.

✦　◇　✦

Mariotto and Antony were pushing each other joyfully, cursing and playing. At the start of the race, both had been grimly set on winning. But as they had passed San Zeno, Antony had been unable to resist reaching across and tugging Mari's saddle horn up into his friend's crotch. Mari's response was to grab an apple from an outstretched hand in the crowd, bite, and spit the chunks of it at Antony. These antics kept either one from pulling into a decisive lead. But they weren't even halfway through the course—this was the time for fun!

Mari pulled out his knife and flipped it into the air. Antony grabbed it and, unsheathing his own, tossed both back. A juggling match began, shimmering arcs of silver slicing the frosty air between them. The trick for the thrower was to flip in such a way that the other had to grab it by the blade. For the recipient, it was important to catch the blade without slicing through the glove.

"Be careful!" shouted Mari. "You might need that hand on your wedding night!"

"Shows what you know!" cried Antony, snatching a blade from the air with three fingers. "You don't use your hands! Unless that's all you have!"

Mari gave Antony the fig.

✦　◇　✦

Marsilio da Carrara was farther back, spurring furiously on. He'd fallen back to drop the false flag and was now racing to catch up to Montecchio and Capecelatro. Carrara had much to prove.

The luxury of his imprisonment had made it all the more humiliating. They had been well fed, wined and dined until all hours as if they were visiting royalty and not captives. Their rooms in the Vicentine palace had been sumptuous. Uncle Giacomo took it as a sign of respect. Marsilio had not seen it that way. It was disdainful—they should have been tortured, starved. That was Marsilio's own inclination toward "guests" of Padua. Yet the Scaliger held nothing but contempt for them, and he showed it by pampering them.

The rain had been a tonic to Marsilio's soul. His homeland was safe from the ravages of the Veronese bastard. It was his shame that Nature, and not man, had been Padua's savior. And when his uncle had suggested meeting with the Scaliger to settle terms for peace, Marsilio had balked. If Il Grande had been any less persuasive or powerful a man, Marsilio would have voiced his outrage in public. As it was, he argued for hours in the privacy of their rooms. Uncle Giacomo had stressed the political advantage of arranging this peace now. Padua would see them as saviors, and their family would rise to preeminence. Marsilio had countered bitterly that there was no need for peace, that with the rains blocking the roads and swelling Padua's defenses, their homeland could reform their army. Vicenza could still be theirs. Il

Grande had actually laughed at his nephew. "Vicenza will never be ours, boy. Not after this defeat. Perhaps someday the Vicentines will be under Paduan rule, but not in our lifetimes. Besides," he'd added cruelly, "if we don't agree, we'll have to ruin ourselves by paying our ransom to Alaghieri. Unless you have a fortune stashed away somewhere?"

When the short traitor da Lozzo had opened the doors to escort them to the farcical meeting, Marsilio played his part. He'd watched as his uncle discussed terms with the Scaligeri minions over a game of dice—dice! And the result proved his uncle correct. Giacomo Il Grande was now the favored name on every lip, a sure bet for Podestà. Marsilio's own name was highly praised as well, receiving reflected glory for his uncle's deeds. It was somehow worse. His uncle was allowing him to reap the benefits of the peacemaking, though he himself had opposed it. It told Marsilio that he could never attain political heights on his own.

And now they were here, in this vaunted cesspool for some irreligious festival. Told his *duty* was to show the new amity. Marsilio had resisted coming, even to the point of faking a fever, until he remembered the famous Palio. A chance to show these trumped-up, Frenchified, German-loving, boot-licking, quasi-Italians what they lacked.

Now his path was blocked by the shenanigans of these two—the pretty stripling he'd tried to skewer and the oaf that had saved him. Carrara had not forgotten them, nor the shame of the mocking he'd been subjected to. His uncle had submitted meekly enough, and in private Marsilio had been given a lesson in politics. Il Grande told him to admire their conqueror; noted that Cangrande was everything a prince ought to be. Marsilio's bile rose at the thought.

He'd sat, digging his nails into his palms, as these two and that damned Alaghieri were knighted before his very eyes for deeds done against his homeland. Unable to resist, Marsilio urged his courser between the impromptu juggling act. Plucking one of the knives from the air, he called out, "Catch me if you can, children!" He listened to their curses behind him as he tucked the silver dagger into his boot.

They banked left with the curve of the walls. These fortifications were new, built in Cangrande's plan to expand Verona's defenses. The addition of these walls had increased the size of the city proper by nearly one-fifth, enclosing the farms that fed the city.

From one of the farm's trees hung another crimson flag. The crowd of farmers and their families cheered deafeningly as the lead riders turned east, back toward the heart of the city.

✦　◇　✦

Trailing after the leading horses, Pietro was jeered by the farmers, though a few shouted encouragement. Turning at the dirty corner of the Via Santa Trinita, Pietro was only two lengths behind the small clump of leaders. He hoped he hadn't pressed his horse too hard doing so. There was still a second lap to go.

On the Via Cappucini they passed under another ancient arch, left again, and the Arena loomed before them. They rode toward it, careful on the cobblestones lest a horse slip and break a leg. Their slower pace brought them all neck and neck as they burst forth into the Plaza Bra.

The seven of them thundered past the Arena in a line like something out of a painting or a plate in a German *fechtbuch*—a perfect row of horsemen galloping toward some unseen enemy. Above, men were perched across the Arena top and in the arched alcoves. Several were knocked over the edge into space as their fellows pushed for a better view.

Pietro headed toward the Gavi Arch, old and crumbling. They had already passed under the plain white marble pillars once, and now they did so again, turning to briefly traverse the Corso Mastino once more. Confused citizens stood in their way, almost getting trampled for their trouble. Their confusion stemmed from witnessing a whole stampede of horsemen racing the other way just two minutes before.

One man threw himself to the ground, covering his head with his hands. "Watch out!" Pietro cried as his horse jumped over him. The palfrey landed well, never breaking stride as he pressed on toward the river. They were tracing the same path they had already taken along the river's edge. This time there was less joking rivalry and more aggression as they jostled and butted for position. Since they all now knew the course, each thought he could measure his mount's endurance for it. By now they'd all realized that they seven were alone. Only Pietro knew it was Marsilio's cleverness that had caused an erroneous detour for the others.

Chance placed Pietro and Marsilio side by side at the back of the pack. "Neat trick with the flag!" Pietro called. Carrara heard but didn't reply.

It wasn't Marsilio but a Veronese rider who raised the next obstacle. This cavaliere was by far the oldest of the racers still in contention, closer to forty than thirty. On the last pass he'd seen the stack of barrels by the waterfront. Lashing out with his foot, he dislodged one of the lower wooden containers, creating an avalanche of malmsey casks.

The other riders were too far along to be incommoded. It was only Marsilio and Pietro who had to contend with the barrels. They'd have to slow to navigate their way. Or else . . .

Marsilio's tall, beautiful, hot-blooded horse made the leap with ease.

Damn his eyes! Pietro's little palfrey was too short. It was sure to catch a hoof and send him toppling end over end. But he was going too fast to turn or halt! His breath caught, and he recalled the sound at Vicenza as the horses had toppled over each other. Under him the beast's hindquarters tensed. With a mighty heave they were airborne. Pietro's eyes clamped shut. The next thing he'd hear would be the crack of a rear hoof catching a barrel. Then there would be pavement and mud and the horrible crunch of his bones shattering.

The jolt sent a chill through him. The front hooves connected with the mud. And then nothing but the rhythm of the running horse. He heard the cheer from the crowd before he realized that his palfrey had made the leap. Opening his eyes, he patted the horse vigorously. "Good boy, Cunnus! Good boy!"

He was hardly out of step with Marsilio. Looking back in disbelief, the Paduan gave Pietro a mocking salute.

Pietro wanted to give the palfrey the praise it deserved, but the race wasn't over. Out of gratitude, he didn't use his spurs. Instead, he squeezed his thighs inward. The noble beast understood. Ducking its head low, the lathered mount chased after the figures hurtling toward San Zeno.

It was as they were coming up the slopes towards the church that Pietro hissed out a breath of awe. There was no flag! The flag had gone! All the riders checked, cursing. There was no flutter of crimson anywhere. Could it have fallen?

Pietro's eyes automatically sought out Marsilio. The Paduan was looking in as much confusion as the others.

"Do you see anything?" called Mariotto.

"Nothing!" Pietro called back, scanning the skyline. They'd ridden directly across the front of the church last time. There had been a series of flags, marking each turn in the piazza. But if not there, then where . . .

"There!" A wind was stirring a flag on the opposite corner, leading left down a narrow winding street.

Pietro remembered the Scaliger's grin as he'd mentioned surprises. The route for the second leg of the race was different from the first. The Capitano's servants were in the crowd around them. They had waited for the participants to race by, then moved the flags.

It was a whole new race.

All seven men hesitated as this sank in. It was another new knight in the purple and silver who turned his horse and whipped it forward. The others instantly followed, riding two abreast down this narrow lane.

"Wonderful!" Mari yelled.

"I love that man!" Antony called into the air.

"Move your podex!" Pietro used his elbow in as friendly a way as he could.

"Move yours!" Antony's gloved fist flew at his shoulder, but Pietro was gone, moving up the line to second place. Behind him he could hear Mariotto and Antony slapping at each other. To their rear was Marsilio da Carrara in his white farsetto—the pride of Padua, fifth in line among the remaining seven knights.

Pietro could see the next flag far ahead. Instead of turning right onto the Strade di San Bernardino, as they had before, the flag's position called for them to make a left on the Strade di Porta Palio. Pietro doubted that they would travel far before turning right again. Otherwise they would ride the way the misled horsemen had and find themselves down the Corso Mastino, in the marketplace by the Scaligeri palace.

For the first time Pietro thought he could win. If a sharp right turn was coming directly after the next left, it made sense for him to be on the right-hand side. He would lose a little ground on the left turn, but if he hung in, he could be the first to make the right turn he expected would follow. He might even be able to block the others from making the same turn until they were past, forcing them to stop and retrace their steps. If that happened, his lead would be almost impossible to beat.

He edged the palfrey right. The crowd was running alongside to watch the final lap and cheer for anyone who looked handsome on horseback. Pietro hoped he cut a dashing figure, though he rather doubted it. Mud from the riverbank jump had spattered his breeches, his fur was gone, and he was unable to stand in the stirrups the way other knights did.

Behind him Mariotto said something that sounded like thunder. "Hear that?"

Excitement made Pietro ignore him. "Come on, Cunnus. Get ready, boy!"

Pietro had an instant of warning. As he neared the intersection of the two streets he saw heads turn in the crowd. People moved away, looking east and pointing. One man started to wave his hands at the riders to stop. He was pulled aside by friends, yanking him back in time to save his life.

The thunder. Pietro realized what it was. The horsemen duped by Carrara had finally realized their mistake and reversed their direction up the Corso Mastino where it became the Strade di Porta Palio. Chance brought them to this intersection at the same moment the leaders were trying to cross it.

The knight in front of Pietro was about to break the plane of the building and cross the street. Pietro tried to shout a warning, but it was too late. The instant the knight burst out on the street he was struck broadside by another horse. The horse began to fall sideways, steam from its last breath escaping from its nostrils.

If that had been all, the knight might have lived. But two more sets of riders rode over him, unintentionally mauling him with punishing blows. Then five more horsemen, pulling back frantically on their reins, reached the wreckage and became a part of it. The new knight fell under his horse as it was pitched onto its side and then trampled. Crimson darker than the flag above speckled his Tyrian purple.

Horses kept streaming past the mouth of the alley, and Pietro was still racing for them. He yanked frantically on his reins as a sound rose between the four- and five-story buildings that ringed the intersection. It was a horrible noise, thick and wet, a cacophony of limbs twisting, shattering, disintegrating. In the chill air the noise had a bizarre resonance. Horses screamed. Men yelled. Forty-one riders collided, brought from full gallop to dead stop by the living barrier across their path.

Pietro's horse wasn't checking fast enough. He was about to be thrown into that swirling mass of flailing hooves.

Only a length behind the lead rider, he'd been along the right-hand side of the street. Desperately he steered left, still heaving on the reins. As momentum carried him out of the sheltering alley Pietro changed direction again, steering right to join the flowing river of men and beasts. He jostled hard in self-defence to avoid being rammed into a wall. The horses around him were frightened. They had heard the screams of their kindred. It was all the remaining riders could do to keep them from rearing.

One of the onrushing knights leapt from his saddle and landed sideways across the tail of Pietro's palfrey. Pietro shot out a hand and hauled him up. It was Pietro's friend from the tunnel. "Thanks," he murmured, clinging to Pietro's shoulder as he looked back at the carnage.

"You hurt?" shouted Pietro.

"Dear God!" cried the man, unhearing.

All around there were screams under the clatter of hooves. Pietro gagged as the smell of blood assaulted his nose. On a battlefield it was one thing to taste the metallic tang in the air. It was quite another on a holy day, surrounded by friends and allies. But he was being swept along, his horse instinctively pushing to get clear from the horror. In a moment he was out of the press, the rescued man hanging on behind the saddle.

Pietro lifted his head to the open sky above, his whole body trembling. *I'm alive. Jesu Cristo, I'm alive.*

His next thought was the race. Could it still go on? He glanced back. The horses were steadying. There was the gap in the alley, crowded by horsemen trying to clear themselves off the corpses of the fallen men and beasts. Suddenly he saw Carrara trying to thread his horse through the carnage. After causing this, the bastard was trying to win! Pietro couldn't allow that.

He tried to turn his horse but was too far away to reach the alley. Then he saw Mari and Antony just behind Carrara and said a quick prayer for their victory. "See that cunnus loses, boys," he added as Marsilio's white doublet disappeared into the alley.

Pietro's horse lifted its head. "Not talking to you," soothed Pietro, rubbing the palfrey's neck. "We're done."

✦ ✦ ✦

Pietro had missed the scene in the alley moments before when Marsilio had kicked his way past Antony and Mari, who had pulled up short at the mouth of the alley. "Move, dullards!"

"Bastard," growled Mariotto. "After all this, he's still thinking about winning."

Antony had smiled, his hands open. "Well, are we going to let him?"

Mari had shot his friend a searching look, then smiled back. Together they had edged their mounts away from the pulped carcasses and into the street.

Now, carefully navigating the bloody street, Antony caught sight of his brother in the milling masses. Luigi called out to him to stop. Antony hunched his shoulders. Though not far apart in age, they'd never been close. Perhaps it was because of young Antony's ambitions. By rights, the second son should have been studying for the priesthood or law, as Pietro had done before becoming Dante's heir. Instead, Antony trained for war as an elder boy would and took great interest in the family *commenda*—legal and illegal both. To achieve this, he'd created a strong bond with their father. They laughed and drank together, much to old Capecelatro's doctor's dismay. It helped when Antony could make himself stand out through some event or other. It was why he'd agreed to marry the Carrara brat. The knighthood was a blessing to him in a way it could never be to Mariotto or Pietro. For he was determined not to let the order of his birth deny him his place.

Luigi was aware of all this, and hated Antony for it. Now he called out, "Antonio! Come here!"

Luigi didn't look hurt, so Antony turned a deaf ear and entered the far alley that led to victory. Because of the vagaries of the crowd he was the first to reach it, followed directly by Mariotto. Behind them was another young noble, not clad in the purple of the day. The older knight who had released the barrels was fourth. Last, because of the hard jostling in the street, was a furious Marsilio da Carrara.

These last remaining racers thundered down the open alley. The Via Scalzi was at an odd angle to the street they'd entered from, slanting southwest. It then curved east. The five horsemen chased each other around the curve fairly uneventfully. The tremendous speed of Marsilio's courser was countered by the greater weight of the other horses as they jostled against each other. He passed the fortyish Veronese, whose horse was close to exhausted. Nothing could urge it on. He'd run a good race, but for him it was over. He dropped back a length, letting those in close contention fight for the last few strides.

The curve led them back toward the Arena. Antonio and Mariotto were joint leaders and had it in mind to block out the others behind them. One of them was going to win, just a question of which.

Carrara had other ideas. He shot past the rider in third place, whose horse was blown and lagging. The street finished its curve—only two more blocks and they would emerge into the Plaza Bra. Far ahead flew the flag signaling the turn that would take them into the Arena itself.

Mariotto and Antony were breathless, faces radiating excitement. In only a minute more, one of them would be victorious. Neither noticed Carrara until he pressed his courser between their two horses just as they emerged into the Plaza.

"Give up, boys!" called Carrara.

As one Mari and Antony pulled their leather reins inward, cutting off the Paduan before his courser's nose reached the level of their saddles. Carrara let the Capuan butt into him. This sent him bouncing into Mariotto's left flank. He let himself rock a little in the saddle, leaning far right. Something in his hand flicked to the underbelly of Mariotto's horse. Montecchio saw the silver glimmer just before he started slipping sideways. The Paduan had slit the straps of his saddle. "Antony!" he cried.

Antony saw his friend's arms flail even as Marsilio plunged between them into the lead. Mari's horse, confused at the shift of weight, had begun to veer off. Mari threw his weight right to counterbalance the slipping saddle, but he was about to lose the struggle and fall.

Antony stretched out a hand. Mari grasped it and fairly leapt onto the back of Antony's horse. Even before he was settled he cried out, "Catch that bastard!"

Too late. It had only taken four seconds for Mari to transfer himself from his horse to Antony's, but already Carrara's lead was too great. They rode into the Arena just behind him and saw the crowd leap to its feet and fill the air with petals of winter flowers.

A length of red silk floated to the ground, released from the Capitano's fingers. Marsilio dismounted and lifted the red cloth to his shoulder so all could see. Then he knelt, bowing his head very slightly. Raising his head he met the Scaliger's eyes. His lips moved, the pride of a city and a people summed up in a single word.

"*Patavinitas.*"

EIGHTEEN

In a darkened passage under the Arena a stout man strode with purpose. His name was Massimiliano da Villafranca, his office constable of Verona. He was pushing his way past barrels and servants with determination. The moment the Palio had begun, Cangrande had pulled his constable aside and ordered him to bring the oracle to the Tribunale for questioning. Massimiliano thought he knew why. That unusual prophecy. Someone had delivered a message to the Greyhound via a unique medium. Villafranca was a soldier and not skilled at palace intrigue, so he had no idea which of the Greyhound's enemies had arranged this, or why. But he was eager to find out.

Ducking past the men running to view the horse Palio, bobbing around the torches hung on brackets in the walls, the constable approached a curtained doorway. He noticed the torches had been recently extinguished. Still smoking, having been doused in water. A distinct metallic smell assaulted his nose.

Smell and taste are closely related. It was the recollected taste that told him what it was.

"Hello?" he called softly in Occitan thick with German. No answer. Lifting a dead torch from its bracket, he marched back down the hall and relit it from one of the active flames. It took time, but the constable was in no hurry. When he returned, the torch's illumination reflected on a pool outside the curtained doorway. Thicker than water, and darker.

The constable pushed the curtain aside and stood in the doorway staring down at the oracle. She sat upright against the wall of the small chamber. Her dark hair, so long and lustrous, was matted to the body, soaked in her own blood. Mercifully, her face was hidden in those long tresses—or so Villafranca at first thought. Upon examining closer, however, he found that her head had been twisted back to front, so now her eyes gazed behind her.

The Scaliger would have no more answers from the oracle.

✦   ◇   ✦

A fistfight on the floor of the Arena was unseemly. Yet in spite of the presence of both Carrara's uncle and their own fathers—not to mention the Veronese lord—this was exactly what Mariotto and Antony had in mind. They dropped from the back of the sweating horse and strode towards the kneeling Paduan, fists clenched.

Cangrande was no fool. Though it might prove amusing, it could become a political nightmare. The peace with Padua was fragile enough, and though he wanted it broken, this was not the way. So he swung his legs over the edge of the balcony and dropped. His knees barely buckled as he touched down. In a moment the Capitano was upright and moving forward. "A well run race!" By rights he should have been approaching Marsilio to congratulate him. Practicality dictated he intercept Mariotto and Antony instead. "It is your first winter with us, Antonio. How does your Capuan blood like our cold air?"

"The air's fine, my lord!" spat Antony. "It's my blood that's hot! I want this bastard's head! I'm calling—"

"No!" said Mariotto abruptly. "I'm calling him—"

Both were attempting to issue a challenge. Cangrande beat them to it. "I'm calling him the victor."

"But, my lord!"

"That son of a—"

It was rare for the Scaliger to deliberately use his height to impress others. He did so now, stopping both them both in their tracks. "I'm also calling on him to dine with me this evening." He noticed two more riders entering the Arena. "It seems that this is one of those years where there are few victors."

"There was an accident." Marsilio managed to sound pained by the event.

If the duo had known what Pietro knew about the "accident," they might have persuaded the Capitano that their challenge was necessary. As it was, they had only the deliberate cutting of Mariotto's saddle strap, which they began to describe with overlapping rage. Marsilio interrupted them, tone airy.

"If you have a problem, cavalieres, I will gladly face you in the Court of

Swords. One or both, I care not at all. As the accused, I choose my weapon to be the longsword."

"Why not a crossbow?" Antonio growled.

The smug look grew even more satisfied. "It is not my best weapon. If it were . . ." His right hand moved casually toward Mariotto.

The Scaliger cut off any retort. "There will be no challenges today. It is Sunday, and a day of Lent as well. You've run a good race and are here to speak of it. Others are not." He spied Carrara's uncle walking toward them, having taken the long way down. He strode over to face the young Veronese cavalieres, gripping his nephew's elbow as he bowed. His knuckles went white as his nephew's doublet, as did Marsilio's face. Il Grande and the Scaliger exchanged a few pleasant words, wherein the latter invited his Paduan guests to dine close to him at the table of honor. "But now your nephew must mount the victory horse in preparation for his ride around the city."

A groom was standing by with a pure white stallion that was to carry the winner of the first Palio. Beside the magnificent snow-colored animal stood a nag, his traditional companion. The nag was truly a sad beast, an ancient limping, farting animal with a sagging spine, sprained shoulder, swelled limbs, loose teeth, and a sticky nose. That animal had no designated rider yet.

The crowd booed when the handsome winner in white started to leave. No fools, they had read the body language of the three knights who had finished the race. That the Capitano had interceded was a disappointment. They hadn't seen much of the race, and there was no better sport than watching one of the knightly caste engage another in a duel for God, Truth, and Justice. So they jeered.

Over the boos and catcalls Mariotto and Antonio again tried to explain their wrongs. The Scaliger listened, then shrugged. "These things happen in the Palio each year. If I allowed personal retributions for anything less than a knife in the back I would be adjudicating duels all year round." He put an arm around each shoulder. "Be of good cheer, lads. In your first outing you tied for second. There will be many more in years to come—including the more important race this evening. Now go. Greet your fathers."

More riders were emerging from the tunnel. Some waved halfheartedly to the audience. Most rode dejectedly toward the Scaliger to dismount and kneel, throwing angry glances at the winner as they did.

At the very rear of the pack rode Pietro Alaghieri. Having seen that all the wounded were being looked after, he'd ridden straight back to the Arena. He was the last to kneel, struggling to make the gesture smooth. Exhausted, his bad leg shook beneath him. Looking up he saw his brother and father watching him from the balcony. Mercurio barked.

The Capitano looked at him, an odd expression on his face, encompassing compassion, amusement, and sorrow. "You live, Pietro? My sister will be gratified. Now, straighten your doublet. You've another ride to make."

"I—what? A ride?" At this moment he never wanted to be on horseback again.

Cangrande indicated the empty tunnel. "You are the last one in, I'm afraid. New knight or no, you appear to be the loser. There's a horse waiting for you." The Capitano pointed at the nag that stood beside Marsilio's beautiful white stallion. A huge leg of salt pork hung from the nag's neck.

Aided by several stewards, Ser Pietro Alaghieri found himself settled in the nag's saddle. A young groom took possession of Pietro's palfrey, patting it in a friendly way. "Hello, Canis. There's a good lad."

Pietro leaned down from the nag's saddle. "What did you call him?"

"Canis, sir. He's named for the Capitano's own horse, who was his father."

"Canis?" asked Pietro. "As in 'Dog'?"

"Yes. Why?" The poor stable boy stood amazed as Pietro laughed and laughed.

At the Capitano's signal, both the boy leading Marsilio's fine beast and the old crone tugging on Pietro's ugly one started moving. They led the two mounts in a slow circle around the Arena as flowers were strewn across their path. Pietro saw blurred faces as the spectators leapt up and down in their seats. He heard wry cheers for Carrara. He also distinctly heard jibes aimed at him. His face burned crimson. He wondered what Donna Katerina would think and reddened further. Catching sight of Mariotto and Antony, restored to the balcony, he thought they looked rather downcast. *What do they have to be upset about?* But at least they seemed not to take pleasure in his humiliation. Pietro watched Antony argue with his brother Luigi and saw Mariotto sit sullenly by his father's side. Then the nag turned and he lost sight of them.

They repeated this circular parade three times, Marsilio waving and shaking his clenched hands above his head. At the end of the third lap the boy and the crone led them out of the Arena and into the city streets. The crowd inside groaned its disappointment as the mob outside roared its approval.

"Quite a reception," observed Marsilio over his shoulder.

"Did you mean for it to happen?" blurted Pietro. He hadn't meant to ask. He hadn't wanted to speak at all.

"What? You mean the accident?" In answer, the Paduan shrugged elaborately. He glanced at Pietro's steed. "Nice horse." Marsilio turned back to the adulation of the crowd. Pietro gave him the fig.

"Don't you pay him no mind," said the old woman holding the nag's lead. "This here's a noble's horse! Yessir, a noble's! The Capitano borrowed it from Ser Bonaventura himself, he who's as noble as a noble, and mad to boot. Just ask his wife!"

For the next hour Pietro rode the nag through Verona. Carrara was marked as the pride of Mercury by the red ribbon across his chest, Pietro as the slowest knight in Verona by the leg of pork at his nag's neck. But slowly the humiliation wore off. There was a celebratory feeling in the air, and even the loser could not help basking a little in its glow. None of the jeers were personal, nor were they heartfelt. He soon found it in him to call back insults and raise his fist and play the part he had been assigned—by the stars, or just by luck.

There was a part of the ceremony no one had warned him of. Citizens brandishing knives rushed forward to carve a slice of the pork from its bone. Dogs chased after his horse, requiring several hands to fend them off. Every now and then the hacked pork leg was replaced by a fresh one by the crone. No one but the dogs seemed to be eating the salted flesh (it was Lent, after all), but everyone wanted their piece. Perhaps it was meant to be lucky.

They passed through several large city squares. In each one there were caged or tethered animals that had appeared like magic at dawn's first light. The more inebriated of the crowd took their sliver of salted pork and taunted the animals with them. These men were sometimes bodily lifted by Cangrande's men and thrown toward the animals they were offending. Only when they had been frightened sober were they rescued.

The terrific cold caused Pietro to miss his fur shoulder-cloak. Up on horseback he was more exposed to the bitter winds whipping around the corners. In the past hour, snow had started to fall lightly, dancing through the air around the vast crowds. Little mists breathed in and out over the crowd. Pietro wished he were among them just for the warmth. But not for their smell. The nag smelled bad enough.

He was so focused on keeping warm he hadn't noticed his way was

blocked. Two youths in heavy cloaks brandished a single knife between them.
"I'll hold the horse!" called one. "You get it!" They grabbed at the nag's bit
and bridle and neatly sliced large portions of the pig's flesh. The dagger they
used was silver.

Pietro snorted. "Take what you like, Mari, I'm too tired."

Mari threw back his hood to reveal his grin. Antony got the sliver of pork
off the bone and ripped a bite out of it, forgetting it was a time for fasting.
"Pleh!" he said, spitting it out. "Too much salt!"

"Most people don't actually eat it," Mariotto told him. "They hang it from
their door to ward off evil spirits."

"Does it work?"

"Mainly it collects dogs."

They fell in on foot on either side of Pietro's steed. "Glad to see you," he
said.

"We're glad to see *you*," said Antonio gruffly. "You weren't hurt?"

"No." The nag wasn't tall, and Pietro was barely a head higher than the
bulky form of his friend. "You got through all right?"

"Yeah, we did," scowled the Capuan.

"Until that son of a bitch sliced my saddle to ribbons," said Mariotto,
voice matching Antony's expression. Marsilio was busy waving, laconic smirk
in place.

They related their near victory. Pietro was outraged. In turn he told them
of the Paduan's trick.

"That bastard!" cried Antony. "I'd like to carve a piece of him, rather
than the pork."

Mariotto slapped his hands together. "Let's trip his horse and strangle him
with that silk ribbon."

Carrara glanced back, a look of delight on his face. "Boys, I think this belongs to you!" Mariotto caught the knife while Antony gave Carrara the fig.
The Paduan simply waved in return.

They were moving among expensive mansions and palaces nestled into
the top of the Adige's curve. Just to their north was the roof of the Duomo.
Adjoining it was San Giovanni in Fonte, in whose cloister stood a massive library, rich in precious manuscripts.

Between these churches and the parade were several streets of private
dwellings. These were recent constructions, the rise of the merchant class
having created a new center of wealth inside the city. Those common citizens

who had lived and worked near the Adige were now shuffled off to ever-expanding suburbs as the city center grew into a collection of homes for the prosperous. Pietro had seen the same phenomenon in Florence. Every prominent signore owned an estate in the country, but in recent years no one could do without a home in the city itself. In Verona this northern bend of the river had become the fashionable place to settle. Small private homes had been leveled to make way for grand three- or four-story mansions with balconies, window gardens, and grand carved statuary. The Montecchi family owned a fine house near here.

A man burst out onto one of the balconies above. He was in his twenties, muscular and broad-shouldered. Pietro recognized him at once—it was the man who had bemoaned his chances of a wife back in September. Bonaventura, friend to Cecchino della Scala. The handsome beard he had sported then was now bushy and ill-kempt. Holiday ribbons hung extravagantly from his open doublet, over which he wore a long houserobe of the finest brocaded heavy red linen. But the linens were covered in meat and malmsey stains. His hat was askew. Under his hat a mass of dark curly hair was matted to his neck as if it were high summer. In spite of the cold, the shirt under his doublet was open almost to the navel. Indeed, sweat was pouring past his eyes. The interior of the house must have had a hundred fires burning.

In his hands he clutched what looked like the remains of a lady's gown. It had been lovely once—lavender in color, with a silver underdress and a delicate lace pattern woven into it. But as it dangled in his grip one could see that an arm had been torn from it, and a huge rent was visible in the bodice.

Running to the edge of the balcony, he pitched the gown over the rail to the crowd below. "Not good enough!"

Just as the ruined gown left his fingers a woman came shrieking out though the doors behind him, grasping at it as it fell. She was dressed in another fine gown, probably her Sunday best. This cream-colored garment, though, had seen worse wear than the one now floating amidst the snowflakes. Spattered with mud past the waist, the brocade had begun to unstitch itself, hanging limply at her breast and waist. The woman's hair was in as bad a shape, falling out of a roughly pinned bun. There were small orange blossoms scattered willy-nilly through her auburn hair. She flung herself out after the flying gown with no thought to her safety. The man caught her about the waist to save her from diving into the sea of people below, who now stopped to watch this extraordinary scene.

"Let go!" she cried, using her elbows and her heels to strike at the man behind her.

"As you wish," he replied happily. He released his grip and she slammed into the stone railing of the short balcony. The crowd flinched.

Slowly the lady rose and turned to face her tormentor. "I liked it, *husband*," she growled.

"It was beastly thing, *wife!* I'll have no wife of mine parading around on a holy day in such a mockery of decency." He belched when he finished, wiping his lips with his sleeve.

"It was beautiful. And modest. And. I. Liked. It."

"And I say, my sweet dearest one—It. Wasn't. Fit. For. You. If you want to go out, we'll have to find you something worthy of you."

He'd taken a slight step to look over the rail after the gown and, like a well-trained soldier, she had countered his move. Now she faced him from her corner of the railing, a sly look crossing her face.

"Fine," she said. Her hands flew to the laces of her gown, ripping the seams apart where the laces were too caked with mud to be removed. Stockings and slippers flew down into the crowd, followed by the cream undergarment she had been wearing. A hand went up to her hair and removing the pins that held it in place. As she tossed the pins aside a cascade of red hair fell about her shoulders. To the amazement and overwhelming approval of those below, she stood brazenly naked, hands on hips like her husband, making no concession to cold or modesty, though her pale body showed the cold in the most obvious way. "Well? Is this better?"

The crowd was in a frenzy to get a better look at this mad young noblewoman. She ignored them as thoroughly as she ignored the weather. Her focus was her mate. He had laid down a challenge. She had responded with one of her own. She seemed interested in, even eager for, his response.

The bearded man had stood bemused through her disrobing. Any second now he would throw his robe over her shoulders and hustle her out of sight— the only decent thing to do! Yet he was just standing there, looking her right in the face without moving a muscle. She stared back at him. When he did nothing, her chin rose in triumph.

It might have been this that sparked her husband to action. Looking her up and down, he clapped his hands in approval. "An excellent solution, my love!" He leapt up onto the thin stone railing. "Let one and all bear witness!" His grin widened. "Bare witness—ha! I have tried tailors up and down this land of ours, and I have found them to be knaves! My wife has hit upon a home truth. From this day forward, no clothes are good enough to adorn her!"

His wife looked up at him in shock. For the first time she seemed embarrassed. She folded her arms across her chest. Or perhaps she was really feeling the cold.

He turned to the open doors. "Cousin Ferdinando, call forth my men! Grumio, call the horses! My bride and I will journey to the Scaliger's feast together—I mean, in the all-together!" A cheer from below, accompanied by offers of horses for the bride to straddle. Her husband pivoted on his precarious perch to face her. "Come, Kate. Let's to dinner!"

"Husband," she said levelly, "where you are going, I cannot follow." With a tremendous heave she pushed with both hands. For a moment he was suspended above the street, his arms flapping wildly, his boots barely touching the stone railing. Then he toppled backward down two stories into the thronged masses below. He roared the whole way down.

Without waiting to see if he landed safely she turned and walked back into the house. A frantic-looking servant nervously closed the double doors behind her.

"What the hell was that about?" Pietro exclaimed. Eyes streaming, Antony gasped for air. Any response Mariotto might have made was cut short by the arrival of Bonaventura. He had been caught by the crowd and was now being passed from hand to hand over everyone's heads. The man himself was crying with laughter. Upon passing the neck of Pietro's nag, he reached out with his right hand and grabbed at the pork. He missed, but immediately a dozen knives were back to cutting the poor shank of pig. People beseeched him to take some, and he did. "I'll give it all to my Kate—she hasn't eaten in some time! My servants are terrible cooks!" He grinned again. Then he was passed off to other hands, and so rode the human tide through the snow away from his own house.

Probably for the best, thought Pietro. *If that lunatic has a brain in his head, he'll never go home again. Not to a shrew like that.*

✦ ✧ ✦

Massimiliano da Villafranca found the Capitano in the Scalageri palace halls late that afternoon. The Scaliger had been to the site of the crash, only the first of several deaths today. There had been two brawls ending in murder,

and several men had been injured in a goose-pull with one particularly ferocious goose who did not fancy being the object of sport. A full eighteen people had been fished out of the Adige, having been toppled in as the losers in
quarterstaff matches. Cangrande kept himself apprised of all these events
through his stewards. The constable found him giving orders to Tullio d'Isola
for compensation for the dead and prizes for the living.

"Signor della Scala," said Villafranca softly. They had known each other a
very long time, these two men. The form of address indicated the level of the
privacy the discussion required.

The Scaliger turned and sent his Grand Butler off with instructions, then
said, "We only have a moment. If I disappear from the festivities for too long,
someone will come looking."

Nodding sharply, Massimiliano began. "She's dead."

If the Scaliger was surprised he didn't show it. "Not suicide, I take it?"

"A wound in her chest, and—I don't quite know why, but her head . . ."

"Was it removed?"

"No. It was back to front."

"Ah." That Cangrande reacted to. "So we'll never know who paid her."

"There was no money except what you gave her on or about the body. I
looked. You're certain that prophecy was bought?"

"All her prophecies are bought. Only this one wasn't bought by me. What
did you do about the body?"

"I paid some actors to move her. I gave them enough to ensure their silence, but someone is bound to notice anyway."

Cangrande shrugged. "It'll only give her prophecy more credence if she
disappears mysteriously. I'll post a reward for her murderer tomorrow."

"Do you have any idea—"

"No." The Scaliger gestured for Massimiliano to walk with him. "Whoever he is, he's clever. Suborning an oracle—that's something I would do."

"You know that damn Moor's back."

"Are you changing the subject, or are they connected in your mind?"

"It's bad enough there's a Jew in the palace. But that Moor! They're heathen sorcerers, both of them . . ."

"I don't believe I've ever seen Manuel drink a child's blood. When he
does, I'll hand him over to you. Until then, leave the heathens to me. Especially the Moor. Anything else?"

Villafranca almost turned to go, but a question weighed on his mind. "Would you have killed her?"

"Of course. It leaves us grasping at air."

"You're not worried?"

Cangrande yawned. "Frantic. Now, if you'll excuse me, I have to see and be seen."

He strode off with casual disregard. It took some getting used to, but Massimiliano da Villafranca had known the boy since he was born. Though to call Cangrande della Scala a boy was deceptive. He might still be young, but he'd never been a boy. A wolf in sheep's skin, he was an emperor waiting to unleash himself on the world. The constable was certain of it. He just hoped he'd live to see it.

"Excuse me, Massimiliano," came a feminine voice. The constable turned to find the Scaliger's wife approaching him, flanked by two grooms, with a maid scuttling along in attendance. He bowed as she addressed him. "Did I hear you say the oracle had been murdered?" The constable hesitated, then confirmed the report. "By whom?"

"We have no idea, my lady. Your husband feels she was used to send him a message."

"Again, I ask by whom?"

"If we knew that, lady, we would be closer to finding her killer. Probably Paduan, or even a threat from Venice."

Giovanna da Svevia nodded, her brow furrowed. She said, "Find out."

For a moment the constable was reminded that she was descended from Frederick II. "He's in no danger, lady," he said.

As she started to walk away she said, "Obviously you didn't listen to the oracle."

NINETEEN

The snow outside the palace had begun to fall in earnest, and Pietro was glad to step into the warm feasting hall. The beginning of the month-long depriva-tion had not dampened the spirits of the men within. There were dozens of men in cheerful conversation, a few in a corner singing. Apparently the women were dining elsewhere. Pietro was surprised, but grateful. He had no wish for the Scaliger's sister to see him at this moment. He hadn't embraced his role as butt that thoroughly.

Being Lent, there were no decorations, but the dozen torches reflecting off mirrors threw a festive light around that not even the most pious bishop could object to. The light danced and shimmered along the plaster walls.

Carrara walked into the hall as if he owned it, with the trio close behind. At the far end of the hall Cangrande spied the four young men entering. He stood and raised his goblet. Taking the cue, the assembled *signoria* raised their cups to the winner and the loser of the day's first Palio. They also drank to the duo that had tied for runner-up. Pietro left his friends to join his father and brother at a low trestle across from the Scaliger's seat. The moment he sat, Mercurio leapt up and licked his face, the Roman coin at his collar slap-ping against Pietro's chin. "Hey, boy! I'm fine, I'm fine!"

"He's almost as glad to see you still walking about as I am," someone said cheerfully. Pietro pushed the dog away and turned to see Dottore Morsicato. "Always a good testimonial to one's skills, having a patient live." He greeted Pietro's father, then told Pietro to find him later. "I want to know how it's healing. And you can tell me all about the Palio!" The doctor's forked beard bristled as he walked off.

Morsicato wasn't the only person who asked for the tale of the Palio. Pietro resumed his place beside his father, Mercurio curling up at his feet.

Dante was in the midst of a conversation with Bishop Francis, but paused to reintroduce his son. Pietro was congratulated on surviving the race, then was left standing next to the handsome young monk he'd noticed that morning. The two began chatting amiably. The monk's name was Brother Lorenzo, and he worked in the Bishop's herb garden when he was between the hours of office.

Suddenly Dante turned with gleaming eyes upon Brother Lorenzo. "Sebartés!"

The young brother lost all his color. "P—pardon, my lord?"

"Your accent!" said the poet. "You're from the Sebartés region, are you not?"

"My—my mother was born thereabouts, I believe. I have never been." Brother Lorenzo looked like a cornered rabbit. "My lord Bishop, the Scaliger is waiting."

With an indulgent smile Bishop Francis allowed the young monk to lead him away, nodding to Dante as he left.

"Curious fellow," observed Dante. "There's deep water in Brother Lorenzo."

Pietro looked at his father closely. "Where is Sebartés?"

"In lower France, north of Spain, about two hundred miles from Avignon."

Pietro chuckled. "Maybe he's afraid they'll make him pope."

Dante said, "You didn't tell me you intended to ride in the race."

Pietro's throat closed. "I didn't know myself."

"Well. I'm pleased you're unhurt," said the poet, sipping at his wine.

"Thank you," said Pietro, discarding any intention of describing the race. "What has your day been like?"

As Dante launched into an account of his hours with the Scaliger, the servants rushed to bring forth the first course—stuffed anchovies and sardines and another strange-looking fish. After a lengthy prayer in which the Scaliger bid everyone pray to the Virgin for the souls lost this day, they began to eat.

In the second place of honor, Giacomo da Carrara masticated the odd-looking fish carefully. Looking past his nephew, he addressed the Scaliger. "These are delicious. How does one prepare them?"

Cangrande's head snapped around. "Where's Cardarelli? Damn, probably in the kitchens." He thought, then snapped his fingers. "I know. We have a gourmand in our midst." Cangrande craned his neck until he spied Morsicato.

"Giuseppe! O, Doctor? Take your head out of your cups and answer something for us!" Seated far down with the Scaliger's personal physician, Morsicato looked up. "Il Grande wants to know about the preparation of fish!"

Morsicato's great barrel of a chest swelled. "I asked Cardarelli that myself. You put the fish in hot water after making them *rovesciata*—which means removing the bones and head without piercing the belly skin, spreading the skin with a stuffing, and closing the fish so that the flesh is on the outside. You begin by grinding marjoram, saffron, rosemary, sage, and the flesh of a few fish. Fill the anchovies or sardines with this stuffing so that the skin is next to the stuffing and the outside in. Then fry them up."

Across from Pietro, Bailardino Nogarola was smacking his lips. "Never in my wildest culinary dreams would I imagine opening a fish from the back. What's the benefit of that?"

Morsicato's left hand stroked his beard sagely. "Well, certain fatty fish— and this inside-out technique is used only for suckling pig and fatty fish—will render some of its fat when exposed to direct heat. And the results are excellent from the standpoint of flavor."

From down the table Nico da Lozzo called, "Does it bother anyone that the doctor is an expert in cooking flesh?"

"It amazing he's an expert in anything, the way he lives in his cups."

"I happen to have an exquisite taste in wine," replied Morsicato tartly.

"No wine is better than Verona wine!" said Bailardino, thumping the table.

"Personally," said Dante, "I agree with Diogenes the Cynic. I like best the wine drunk at the cost of others." There were several choruses of "Hear, hear," around the hall.

" 'No poem was ever written by a drinker of water,' " observed Il Grande. He raised a cup to salute the poet.

"Monsignore knows his Horace," observed Dante, returning the gesture. "It is a shame he does not also know his nephew's tailor, that he might have him flogged."

Pietro choked on his drink. Others hid their guffaws with coughing. Il Grande smiled indulgently, resting a hand on Marsilio's arm as the youth made to rise. "What has become of Masurius Athenaeus—'Wine seems to have the power of attracting friendship, warming and fusing hearts together.' "

Dante shrugged. "*In vino veritas.*"

Cangrande snapped the fingers of both hands in front of him. "This is the way it should be! I am surrounded by the best and the brightest! It has been too long since I had so many distinguished visitors. Monsignore Alaghieri, when was it that we two last dined in this hall?"

Pietro sensed his father being reined in a little. Dante, never mindful of the social niceties, gazed upon his patron in thin-lipped amusement. "You abandoned us at your nephew's wedding, so let me see—not since your brother Bartolomeo, God rest his soul, occupied the place you now hold."

Men crossed themselves in fond memory of the man who had been Dante's first patron in exile. Bailardino lowered his head and spoke soundless words of blessings.

Cangrande leaned back to allow a servant to place a platter before him, his eyes taking on a wicked glow. "God rest his soul, indeed. But I think you are mistaken, dear poet," said the Scaliger. "I remember when my brother died, you spoke quite eloquently at his funeral. You were here some months after Alboino took his place. Surely you dined here before you left us."

"Ah, yes. The bones."

Cangrande's *allegria* widened. "Quite so. The bones." He raised his voice so that all around could hear. "You may not believe this, but once upon a time I was given to practical jokes."

"*Ma, no!*" chorused several voices.

Cangrande waved a hand in acknowledgment. "I know, I know, it's hard to imagine. But when Monsignore Alaghieri was first with us here, I tried his patience. Alboino was giving a feast. I made sure that the servants took all the bones they cleared from the dishes and placed them under Dante's seat. As a consequence, when the table was cleared there was a mountain of bones beneath him, with the dogs circling eagerly." Cangrande shrugged. "I was very pleased with myself. I had found the poet somewhat insulting the day before."

"I can't imagine," murmured Pietro. Poco sniggered into his sleeve, and Dante's spine stiffened.

Cangrande hadn't heard. "But our infernal friend here had the last word. What was it you said, monsignore?"

The poet succumbed to his love of an audience. "I said, '*Cani* chew their bones, but I, who am no one's bitch, leave mine behind.'" Having never heard that particular story, Pietro chuckled along with the rest.

"Ah, the fabled Alaghieri wit," said Bailardino.

"Even today that wit was in evidence," said Mariotto's father from a nearby table.

"Yes," snorted Bailardino, "and about Verona's latest distinguished citizens. What was it he called you, Ludo? The baby Capuan?"

Across the table Ludovico Capecelatro colored slightly. Before he could reply, however, the poet filled the gap. "Capulletto," said Dante. "I called him Monsignore Capulletto."

"That's it!" Bailardino slapped his knee. "The Little Capuan! I love it."

Dante rarely softened any witty statement, yet he softened this one. "It means something more than that, really."

"Of course it does," said Cangrande, nudging his mentor-turned-friend. "You don't remember the Capelletti family?"

"I surely do!" snorted Bailardino. "They were a sore on my ass a decade before you were even born, rascal. But they all died out or were killed—when was that? Barto was still alive, I remember."

"The last three died the year I first came to Verona," said Dante.

"Right! They were part of that stupid feud with the—oh, sorry, Montecchio. It was your father, wasn't it, who put the last of them to the sword in a duel?"

"No," replied Gargano Montecchio grimly. "It was me."

There was an awkward silence, broken by Mariotto saying, "Those bastards deserved to die."

Gargano sighed. "They weren't bastards, son. They were men from a noble line, who gave this city many consuls and podestàs in their time. It's important that we remember that."

"Why?" demanded Mariotto.

"Because they are no longer with us. The worst thing you can do is destroy a man's name." He turned to address the room at large. "Names have power. Ask the Capitano, he knows. Men live and die, their sons live and die. Deeds are forgotten—wars, romances, all of it. The only legacy we have is our names. I took that from the Capelletti. There are none of them left, no one to carry on a once noble house."

From his seat far down the table Antony said, "I've never heard of this feud. What was it all about?"

Gargano furrowed his brow. "No one seems to remember the exact cause. About a hundred fifty years ago, there was some minor squabble over something—land, a woman, who knows? Whatever it was, it set the two families at odds. It wasn't until the Guelph and the Ghibelline strife really started that we came to blows."

"That's no surprise!" cried Marsilio da Carrara. "The Capelletti were dedicated Guelphs!"

Carrara's uncle, unable to deny the truth of the statement, deflected it. "They were a fine and noble house—though if I recall rightly, they were fiercely Veronese. They fought against our city alongside the Montecchi."

Gargano bowed his head. "Monsignore is correct. It was quite a duality. They loved their city and hated its politics. But my young lord might have forgotten that Verona has only been tied to the imperial cause for eighty years. Before that, the Montecchi were as firmly Guelph as you yourself."

"What about the duel?" Antony clearly wanted to get to the good part.

But Lord Montecchio had his own reasons for starting at the beginning. "It began to get violent a century ago. At the time the Capelletti were strongly tied to the counts of San Bonifacio." There was a stirring around the table at the mention of the name. "My ancestors opposed the policies that those two families were introducing into government. In the fall of 1207, with the aid of the second Ezzelino da Romano and a Ferrarese noble named Salinguerra Torelli, my family took over the city."

"Not for long," said Cangrande.

"No. The San Bonifaci were powerful allies for the Capelletti. A month later Ezzelino and the Montecchi were exiled from the city. With them in exile was young Ezzelino da Romano the Third, the man who would grow into the Tyrant of Verona. Because the Montecchi had shared his exile, we were his natural allies when he eventually rose to power. When he changed sides from Guelph to Ghibelline, my family went with him, but the Capelletti remained staunchly in favor of the pope."

"That was around the time my great-uncle Ongarello della Scala was a consul," the Scaliger put in "1230 or so."

Montecchio nodded. "Then there was the sack of Vicenza. As a Paduan possession, Ezzelino the Tyrant treated it brutally. The Capelletti were outspoken in their opposition. Ezzelino exiled them as traitors, but when Ezzelino was slaughtered, they were recalled."

"By my uncle, Mastino." said Cangrande.

Bail said, "Yes. Verona was in turmoil, and Mastino della Scala stepped in to calm matters. He recalled the San Bonifaci, too, but they refused to enter while Mastino lived. Mastino granted the Capelletti reparations for their losses and promised to keep the Montecchi in line." He threw Mari's father a sorrowful look. "I don't mean to make it sound like your family was out for blood."

Gargano shrugged. "Both sides were full of hate. It was mindless. I know. I was born maybe five years after the Capelletti were recalled. The loathing for that family pervaded every fibre of our house here in the city. Out in the country, far from them, it wasn't nearly as bad. But I remember seeing a boy my own age once when I was out walking though the city with my family. My father pointed to the boy and told me that I should be wary of him, he was a Capelletti. I remember actually spitting at him. His name was Stefano." Gargano shook his head in disbelief. "It was absolutely without reason, mindless," he repeated. "What had that boy ever done to me? How had he hurt me or mine?"

"He did, though," said Cangrande softly, "eventually."

The long-faced noble said sadly, "I provoked it. By everything I ever said or did with regard to that family, I helped cause it to happen."

"What happened?" It was hard to tell who actually said it first, so many voices had chimed in. This was better than a poem or a ballad or an ode. That Montecchio was reluctant was fascinating to them all, even his son. This was what men longed for—tales of duels, feuds, honor.

Hearing their eagerness, Lord Montecchio looked to the Scaliger with an appeal. In answer, the Capitano took up the tale for him. "After the Mastiff died, the feud slowly began to burn hot again. My father was a great man, but he lacked the fearful presence of my uncle. He wasn't able to scare the two families into obedience. Nor did fining them do any good. They fought and they fought—in the streets, in homes, in workshops, in markets, afield—wherever they encountered each other. They could hardly leave their homes without a duel beginning. For a time my father actually repealed the right to trial by combat. And when he died, the feud exploded. The men of the latest generation began dueling in the streets wherever they met." He looked at Mariotto. "Your father must have been an excellent swordsman to have lived through that period."

Mariotto blinked. He had never seen his father lift a sword in practice, only when leaving to take his place in Verona's armies.

"In any case," Cangrande continued, "the citizens were up in arms. No one was safe. My brother Bartolomeo was Capitano then. I remember him considering exiling both families. Then, one night in early summer, a fire broke out in the country estate of the Montecchi."

Antony was at the edge of his seat. "What fire?"

Mariotto turned his head. "My mother burned to death that night."

"My son was a toddler when she died, and his sister was an infant. Excuse me. It's just—I doubt you remember her, how beautiful she was."

There was an awkward pause as Lord Montecchio wept. There was no shame in it, he made not a sound as the tears streamed down his face.

"So. There was some evidence that it had been started by Stefano and his brothers, the only Capelletti men still living. But it wasn't enough to take to the Giurisconsulti. So I spoke to Cangrande's brother, who was Capitano then. I had not only lost my wife, Mariotto's mother, in the fire, but my father as well. Somehow I convinced Cangrande's brother to restore the right to trial by combat. Then we arranged matters. My two uncles and I called the three remaining Capelletti to the Arena at dawn. There was no fanfare, and no crowd. A handful of nobles, like our distinguished poet here, were invited to act as witnesses. Of the Montecchi, I was the only youthful one. All three Capelletti men were in their prime. Both my uncles fell bravely, fighting well to the end and slaying one Capelletti before they died. It was up to me to avenge the deaths of my father, my uncles, and the mother of my children." Montecchio looked up, and for a moment there was something other than remorse and regret in his eyes. There was a fire that echoed the fire of that day, the last embers of a rage that would never fully leave him. "I did."

Lord Montecchio gazed around at the assembled nobles, some of whom remembered the story, some who had never heard it. His eyes stopped on Dante. "You remember."

"I do," said the poet. "It was my first time in the Arena."

Pietro suddenly recalled a remark his father had made months before: "that unfortunate business with the Capelletti and Montecchi."

Bailardino was saying, "I remember hearing about it in Vicenza. It should have been a song. Why was that ballad never written?"

"I didn't hire the minstrels," said Montecchio, not hiding the tears that fell down his face. "I didn't want it written. There are more important things in this world than fame."

"Indeed," came a rumbling voice. "Honor is one."

Ludovico Capecelatro stood. Gargano Montecchio looked at the father of his son's friend. "Yes. Honor. I upheld my honor, and the honor of my family. I would do it again in a moment. I have no regrets for my actions. That is not the source of my shame. Do you understand that?"

"I think I do," said Capecelatro. "My family had a similar feud with the Arcole family in Capua. It died out on its own, over time. But I do understand. Hate's a poor reason for men to lose their lives." It was strange to hear the large man in the sumptuous furs speak with such gentleness.

Montecchio walked to stand close to the newest Veronese nobleman and addressed the assembled *signoria.* "I know that Alaghieri meant his comment as a joke. But it started me to thinking. I want you, all of you, to remember the nobility in the name Capelletti. Theirs was a proud line. Their deeds were no better or worse than mine. If I had died, my sons could have carried on my family name. The Capelletti had no sons, no heirs. They are lost to history—unless we can resurrect them." He looked first at the Capitano, then at Ludovico.

Capecelatro seemed to understand. He stood and gripped Gargano Montecchio by the arm. "I have brothers in Capua," he said, "and cousins in Rome. My family name is in no risk of being lost to history. If the Capitano is willing, and if it would please you, I would gladly take up the name of an old Veronese family that is in disuse."

"It would please me greatly."

Cangrande rose. "A noble Veronese family has been resurrected! Let it be known from this holy festival day onward that the noble family of Capecelatro has taken up the fallen mantle of the Capelletti! Raise your cups and drink to Ludovico, Luigi, and our own Antonio! Long live the Capulletti!"

There was a roar of approval, redoubled when Gargano Montecchio fell on the neck of the newly dubbed Capulletto. They embraced and kissed as friends. The only one who looked aghast was Antony's brother Luigi. Antony himself brimmed over with delight. He fairly leapt over the table to take Mariotto in his arms, lifting him up and dancing him around in a bear hug.

"At least we can be sure there will never be a feud between our sons," said the new Capulletto.

Montecchio eyed his son with pride. "I expect not. Ludovico, I appreciate what you have done. It has removed a blight from my honor."

"I had heard of the sad business once or twice before," Ludovico said. His chins unfolded as his head bobbed up and down. "Besides, it all works out rather well. The house I have in town is in the Via Capello! Now it's named for me!"

Listening close by, Pietro Alaghieri had an unworthy thought. *There's the real cause of his ready acceptance of the new name. By becoming a Capulletti,*

Ludovico Capecelatro has ennobled himself and his heirs. He'll let his distant relatives cling to the Capecelatro name. Suddenly he can cloak himself with the rights and power of an ancient family. He's got the money. Now he has the name.

But there had been a slight difference in the pronunciation between Capelletti and Capulletti. The Greyhound was clever to make such a distinction, one Ludovico had probably missed. This new line of the ancient clan would always be marked as tenants, not owners, of the title, their name always denoting their point of origin.

Mari was rubbing his ribs where the rechristened Antonio Capulletto had hugged him. "Perhaps with a new name your marriage contract is void!"

"Aw, did you have to go and spoil it?" groused Antony, his face transforming in an instant. "I had forgotten about the stupid woman."

"That's right!" said Giacomo da Carrara, not taking any offense. "We have a betrothal to affirm." He turned to Ludovico. "This act of honor makes me doubly glad to send my niece's daughter to join your family. She's here, dining with the women. My lord, may I send for her?"

"Of course," said Cangrande, waving his hand. "What better moment than this? Marsilio, here, taste this wine."

Il Grande sent a page scuttling off through the huge double doors. Antony plopped down beside Mariotto with a deep sigh that let all and sundry know of his exasperation. "I bet she's cross-eyed."

"Maybe a harelip?" speculated Mariotto, amused eyes twinkling.

"Who knows? She can't be much. Her uncle's pretty eager to rid himself of her. Dear God, what could be worse? Married at eighteen!"

His dismay was understandable. Though eighteen was an acceptable age for marriage, it was customary to let young men grow into their twenties and even their thirties before burdening them with a wife. For women it was quite different. The trend was moving toward earlier and earlier wedding beds for girls, to the point of betrothing daughters at ten and marrying them off at fourteen or fifteen. It was fashionable among older men to marry young girls, barely initiated in the women's mysteries. Pietro knew it was a fad his father deplored. It was why Pietro's sister was still unwed—too many new mothers died in childbed because they were brought to bear too young. But marrying young assured virginity, that prized possession.

As he contemplated his doom, Antony eyed his friend. "You will be my best man?"

"Your second, you mean? Of course! If only to make sure you go through with it. Otherwise I might have to rid the world of another Capul-letto."

Antony's frown became more intense. "Does it bother you? Me having the name of the family that murdered your mother?"

Mariotto took in a sharp breath. He wasn't quite ready for Antony's insight and bluntness. The combination of plain speaking and shrewdness appeared to be a family trait.

Mariotto slowly released the air in his lungs. "No. You're my friend, whatever you call yourself. The Capelletti were dishonored by their actions. You will restore the title to a place of honor."

"With you beside me." They drank to their friendship.

Pietro leaned close to his father as he scruffed Mercurio's ear. "What do you think of all this, *Pater?*"

The heavy beard turned, the eyes above it blinking. "I'm not sure. It is a wonderful gesture. But it was God's will that the Capelletti be destroyed. Is it His will that they be reborn? I can't help thinking of Eteocles and Polynices."

"Who?"

Dante frowned, severe disappointment etched into his long face. "The children of Oedipus and Jocasta. I swear, how can you appreciate poetry if you have no sense of the players?"

"Sorry. What about them?"

Dante huffed for a moment, then continued with his point. "After they learned the truth about their father's incest, the two brothers forced him to abdicate. In return, Oedipus cursed them to be enemies forever. Such curses have strength. They alter the course of nature, they challenge God, who is alone in meting out justice." The poet glanced over at Pietro's two friends. "I think they should consult a good astrologer before embarking on such a venture. Or, better still, a good numerologist. For Lord Montecchio is quite correct. Names have power. And through their history the names Capelletto and Montecchio have made themselves synonymous with *enemy.*"

Pietro made a face as he swallowed a scoff. Mari and Antony were the best of friends, closer than brothers. Nothing could change that.

He was about to say as much when he felt a gust of chill air against his neck. Until now the doors to the great hall had been closed due to the weather. Now they opened to admit a delicate figure swathed from neck to toe in fur.

Heads turned. The doors were closed behind her as a servant approached her and removed her robe. The removal of the fur revealed a brocaded gown of deep blue. Her head was covered behind the hairline, allowing just a glimpse of dark hair before it was swallowed in a gauzy haze. The pins holding the veil in place were in the shape of rosebuds, simple and finely wrought.

Conversation ceased throughout the firelit hall. Men sat as if turned to stone just by gazing at her. But she was certainly no gorgon. Her hair was raven-black and long, if the length of the mantle was anything to guess by. Her skin was fair. Her nose was thin and delicate. Under the full lips her teeth were straight and white. In spite of her smile there was something sorrowful in her expression. She had a fragile elegance, as if she might shatter with a breath. A man could hardly help wishing to be the one who rescued her from that state, protect her from the cruel world outside. She was a damsel in distress, Guinevere waiting for her Lancelot.

Above her high cheekbones the eyes were luminous. They were eyes to sink into, die for, kill for.

This was Gianozza, great-niece of Il Grande, cousin to Marsilio, and more lovely than Helen on the night Ilium burned.

III

THE DUEL

TWENTY

"Ah, Gianozza," said Giacomo da Carrara, breaking the room's sudden silence. "Barely do we decide to call you, and you are here. Were you listening outside the door?"

For a moment everyone hoped she wouldn't speak and spoil the illusion. When she answered, her mouth barely moved. "No, uncle. Should I have been?" Her voice was demure, not at all foolish.

Il Grande studied his niece. "Perhaps you should have eavesdropped, since the details of your engagement have changed."

She didn't frown. Her lip didn't curl. She merely smiled like an obedient child. "Oh?"

"You were to marry the second son of Ludovico Capecelatro. That young man no longer exists."

The dark eyes went wide. Her hands, until now folded enticingly just under the curve of her breasts, rose to her face. "No. Was he injured during the race, or in one of the games?"

The elder Carrara glanced at Antony staring openly at his prospective bride. The Paduan noted the lad's awestruck look with a smile. Women were so useful in the world of politics. Carrara would gain a strong alliance with a family he thought was worth cultivating. New to the area, with loads of money—exactly how much no one seemed to know, but it was estimated that the fat Capuan could buy and sell half the men in the room. He might even give the Scaliger a run for his wealth.

The first son was a sour dud, and Giacomo was glad he was already married, though the pregnancy of his wife was not pleasing. It was this magnificent second son who would make something of himself. Had already caught the Scaliger's attention. In Gianozza and Antonio's children, Paduan and Veronese blood would mix, giving the Carrarese a solid foothold in this city. This boy was going places.

Tonight's name change reaffirmed Giacomo's desire to see the marriage consummated. He decided to push forward the date of the wedding— perhaps to Easter. That wasn't indecent haste.

The girl was still standing, awaiting her uncle's next words. As she should. The flower of Paduan womanhood, just fifteen years old at Christmas, it was her duty to marry where he directed. She had worried him the whole trip to Verona. The girl certainly was a beauty, but she was also educated, which had led to a disappointing independence. Worse, she was a romantic! She actually believed this nonsense of courtly love! Carrara had little use for the fad himself. It ran counter to the idea of chivalry, the way a knight should behave. But in recent years the two had become intertwined.

He'd made it clear to her that the fortunes of her family, his poor cousins, depended entirely on how she played her role today. Now to put the girl to the test. Giacomo waved a hand toward where the prospective bridegroom sat.

Because he was staring at the girl, Antony missed his cue. Mariotto saw it, though. Instead of prompting his friend, Mariotto Montecchio rose deliberately from the bench. Until now, Gianozza's smile had been fixed, polite but wary. Now it softened as they gazed at each other.

"No, no." Il Grande pointed to Antony and said, "Gianozza, this is the young man who, until this night, bore the name of your betrothed. Tonight his father has taken up an ancient name, until now sadly lost. You are now engaged to marry Antonio Capulletto of Verona." There was applause from the envious knights and nobles in the hall.

Antony stood up and bowed awkwardly as he was introduced. The girl took a moment more to gaze at Mariotto, then turned her eyes to her betrothed. She didn't understand the significance of the name change, but she was quick enough to note that it was something to be celebrated. She walked over to Antony and curtsied. She held out a hand to the young man who loomed over her. Taking hold of her fingers as if they might break, his lips didn't quite touch the skin, as the custom was, but he held them longer than decency dictated.

If she minded, she didn't show it. Antony released her fingers and straightened. "Lady, I—hope to make you happy. It is my only wish."

She smiled. It would have taken an effort on the part of anyone in the hall to see the slight hesitation in that smile. Three men did notice it. The first narrowed his eyes, waiting for her to commit the indiscretion he feared. The other, standing beside her, wondered if he'd only seen what he wanted to see. The third was Pietro, who felt a growing sense of unease.

Antony tripped as he made space for her on the bench. There was amused chatter in the hall. Mariotto graciously stepped aside to give her his place. She slipped into the space he made, and Antony sat down beside her. "Would you like some malmsey?" he asked.

"Yes, I would," said the girl simply.

Antonio managed to pour her a cup—heavily watered—without spilling any on the table. He handed it to her and didn't know what to do with his hands afterward. He reached out for his own cup and, without waiting for her, took a deep drink.

Giacomo was relieved. If there was hesitation, she had reconciled herself to the man. He was nice enough, and Il Grande had no doubt that she would rule him easily. Even though he was assured of her hand, Capulletto was attempting to win her heart.

✦ ✧ ✦

Now that the meal had ended, men were sitting on the tables, or standing in small clumps telling ribald stories, or kneeling down to play a surreptitious game of dice. Pietro heard whispers nearby him. "Who's that lucky bastard that bagged that game?"

"Clear out your ears, fool! Young Capecelatro—Capulletto, I mean."

"Oh yes. He looks smitten. I'll wager he hadn't met her yet."

"Are you sure she's his? Young Montecchio looks like a hound with scent on the wind."

"Well, they share everything else . . . !" The guffaws rippled around the hall as the same conversation was had among all the tables.

Pietro looked over at Mari, standing forgotten as Antony marshaled all his imagination to win another smile from Gianozza. He was quoting half-remembered poetry and talking at length of his home. After a few minutes of being entirely excluded from the conversation, Mariotto crossed to the bench where Pietro sat with his father and Poco.

But Mari didn't sit down. Pietro, excusing himself, lifted his crutch and stood to join his friend. To Mari he said, "What do you think of her?"

Mariotto was staring at the back of her head. "She's a Julia."

Pietro glanced over at the girl again. "You mean a Helen, don't you? Julia was definitely a blond."

"No, she's a Julia. Look at her. She has the power to make men happy." He pulled a face. "Antony's certainly changed his tune about marriage, hasn't he?"

"He does look smitten," said Pietro, grinning. He tried to catch Antony's eye, but the big cavaliere was wholly focused on the girl who was listening politely, acting in every way as the adoring bride-to-be.

"Such a waste."

For a moment Pietro didn't recognize Mariotto's voice. "What is?"

"Her, marrying that great lummox. Like Caesar's daughter being married off to Pompey. She's another Julia. She's wasted on him. He's nowhere near her equal in birth."

"I thought he was your friend!"

"Of course he is! I know better than anyone. He'd be happy with a milkmaid—someone to do his sewing and bear him huge sons. That lady will wither and die with him."

This was more than simple ribbing. Mari's eyes were locked on Gianozza. *He isn't serious, is he?* "That lady" was sipping her gingered malmsey and listening to a story Antony was relating. That Antony finally remembered Mariotto was evident a moment later when he looked up to beckon his friend over. Mariotto was gazing down into the bottom of his wine cup just then. Antony shrugged and continued to speak.

The look on Mariotto's face made the hair on the back of Pietro's neck rise. "Mari? What's wrong?"

If Montecchio planned a reply, it was lost in what followed. The other women were arriving, the Scaliger's wife playing the hostess, teasing the men she knew, complimenting the ones she did not, all the time aware of the level of wine in the pitchers and the height of the torches on the walls. It was she who ordered a fresh round of mead for those who drank the stuff, and she who had the servants carry those too drunk to move to the upstairs palisade, where the cold would wake them in time for the second Palio. She arrived at Pietro's side, and he made the clever bow he'd worked out using his crutch for balance. "Madonna," he said.

"Ser Alaghieri," said Giovanna della Scala. "You know you are the most desired man here. All the ladies were asking after your prospects."

Pietro flushed. "Lady, jokes like that aren't kind."

"You think I'm joking? There are a half-dozen girls longing to know you better. And since you won't be running the foot Palio, you'll have them all to yourself for the better part of two hours while your fellows are freezing themselves to death. I plan to make it my business to introduce you to all of them. No, no protests. I am the hostess, it is your duty to honor me." She smiled at him and moved on to talk to another guest. Pietro turned back to find Mariotto was gone.

Other wives were entering, though not Katerina, Pietro saw anxiously. Bailardino seemed in no way put out by his wife's absence. When there were enough women in the room that Pietro thought he could ask the question without undue suspicion, he addressed Bailardino. "I don't see Donna Nogarola."

"Oh, no, she's a little uncomfortable these days," grinned the bearish man. "But she's happy enough to have a bun in the oven, so her bouts of sickness don't get her spirits down."

Pietro's blood froze. Nico da Lozzo's voice saved him from an embarrassing silence. "It's about time, you brute! What, don't you pay her enough attention?"

"I try, but she locks me out of the bedroom more nights than not!"

"So you take an axe and knock the hatch down!" cried Nico.

"And she takes the axe from me and buries it in my head for ruining her beautiful carved doors! No, I think we have her brother to thank for it." More hoots and hollers. Glancing up from the drinking game he was teaching Marsilio da Carrara, Cangrande raised a curious eyebrow. Bailardino spread his hands and said, "Well, it's that little brat of yours. I think he caused her womb to sit up and notice it was being supplanted by one of your bastards. So it got busy, and I got lucky. Crack, boom! She's pregnant!"

Not a few heads turned to see what Giovanna's reaction to this would be, but Cangrande's wife was engaged and paying no attention.

Pietro retreated to where his father pretended to doze. Poco had disappeared to watch the older men play at dice. Pietro looked for Mariotto but didn't see him. His eyes traveled to where Antony sat with Gianozza. Seeing her, Pietro let out a breath he was unaware he was holding.

Antony pointed a stubby finger toward Pietro and his father. Gianozza looked over and rose to her feet. Antony followed as she glided over the rushes to halt in front of Dante. Thinking the poet was asleep, she addressed Pietro. "Ser Alaghieri, it is a pleasure. Signore Capulletto—"

"Antony," her betrothed hastened to correct her.

She smiled. "Antony tells me that your father is the poet Dante."

"Yes," was all Pietro could think to say. She was even lovelier up close. Her eyes were so blue they put her dress to shame.

"I quite enjoyed *La Vita Nuova*," she said.

"Have you read *L'Inferno*?"

"No." She shook her head sadly. "I haven't been able to find a copy."

"I'll get you one!" said Antony quickly. "As a wedding gift." To Pietro: "Do you think your father will sign it for us?"

"My father loves signing his name to things." Pietro saw his father's face squeeze tighter. But since the old man was pretending to be asleep, he had to endure without interrupting. "I'll arrange a time for you both to meet with him and tell him just what you want written. Perhaps he'll even do a reading for you." His father's expression was a gift from God.

Pietro was startled to find himself being kissed gently on each cheek. "Thank you," said Gianozza. "I simply adore the new style of poetry—*il dolce stil nuovo*." She closed her eyes and began to recite softly:

> *In the season when the world's in leaf and flower*
> *the joy of all true lovers waxes strong:*
> *in pairs they go to gardens at the hour*
> *when little birds are singing their sweet song;*
>
> *All gentle folk now come beneath love's power,*
> *and the service of his love is each man's care,*
> *while every maid in gladness spends her hours . . .*

She blushed suddenly and opened her eyes as if caught doing something villainous. "I can't recall the rest."

"It's beautiful, though," said Antony. "Who wrote it?"

"I don't know. No one does. It's anonymous."

Pietro glanced at his father, half-intending to ruin his father's charade and ask who the author was. A curious expression on Dante's features stopped him. When he looked back up, Gianozza was smiling over Pietro's shoulder. She said, "Excuse me, Signore Alaghieri, Antonio, but my uncle wishes me to meet someone." Sure enough, a glance revealed Il Grande beckoning to the girl. She moved away, her skirts tickling the rushes at her feet.

Antony sighed. "She's beautiful, isn't she? Hey, where the devil did Mari get to? She wants to meet him. I've been telling her all about us—the trio!"

"I don't know where he's gone," said Pietro, glancing toward the door.

"He does like her, doesn't he?"

"He called her a Julia."

"What? A Giulia?"

"It's a reference to Julius Caesar's family. It was said that each Julia had the gift of making her man happy."

"Good! Then he does like her. I was worried when he wandered off like that. But he's right," he sighed contentedly, "she certainly is a Giulia. I don't mind telling you now, I was a little worried."

"A little? You were afraid she'd be cross-eyed, buck-toothed, and drooling!"

"Shhhh!" chuckled Antony. "She might hear you!" He looked up to find Lord Carrara beckoning him over as well. "Excuse me," he said, dashing off to his betrothed's side.

Pietro turned back to his father's reclined form. "Next time you see them you'd best have your quills ready."

Sotto voce, Dante said, "I should have drowned you at birth."

✦   ✧   ✦

Outside the palace, the crowd waited for the feast's end, which would mark the start of the foot Palio. They clustered in little clumps facing fires, sharing warmth. Among them but apart from one another, two cowled figures watched and waited.

The festivities indoors had reached an irreligious pitch. Yet everyone was sober enough that when Cangrande's Grand Butler entered, all eyes trailed his wending path up to the top table. Tullio d'Isola whispered in the Scaliger's ear. Cangrande della Scala stood up at once. "Would all the ladies please re-tire to my loggia, along with all of us too old or too inebriated to run." He glanced sideways to the prone figure of young Carrara. The winner of the first race was in no shape to enter the second.

Clever Cangrande, thought Pietro. *There'll be no accidental slips, no revenge from an overeager Veronese.*

"How come all the women go to your room?" shouted Nico da Lozzo from down the boards.

Cangrande ignored him. "On the other hand, those men who think they are still able to stand, please move to the square outside! It is time for the foot Palio to begin!"

Rising, Antony carefully took Gianozza's hand in his. Again the proper bow. This time, though, Pietro thought he saw the lips actually brush the tiny wrist. He couldn't hear what was said, but the cadence indicated more poetry. The young lady smiled, wished him a good race, then quickly joined her hostess as the women were driven from the hall by the sight of the men beginning to strip.

Strip they did, down to the raiment God made for them. That the Palio was happening this early in the year made no difference. The runners would have to endure the cold and the four inches of snow that had fallen since midday. Not rain, nor snow, nor flood could stop the foot Palio from being run.

Antony was red with anger that his fiancée had been exposed to so many disrobing males all at once. As soon as she passed out of sight, though, he began to tear at his own clothes. "Where the hell is Mari?"

Pietro shrugged, leaning over to shake his father's shoulder. The poet pretended to wake up. "Is it time?" he asked innocently. Then the shrewd marble eyes glanced about. "Where's Jacopo?"

Pietro's brother was indeed nowhere in sight. "He's probably set on entering. Should I stop him?"

Dante paused, thoughtful. "No," he said at last. "He's in a desperate rush to grow up. All we can do is let him go and hope he doesn't get himself killed." Dante grimaced. "Your mother would flay me alive."

Pietro's eyes settled on Carrara's unconscious form. "He'll be fine. Do you want to watch the start of the race or go straight to the Scaliger's loggia?"

"Doesn't matter," the poet said, focused on not being knocked aside by one of the many young men stretching their muscles around the hall. He sensed his son's inclination. "Let's watch the start, then go inside where it's warm."

In the naked throng pressing through the doors, Pietro finally caught sight of Mariotto. He was outside, waiting in complete undress. Pietro waved. Mariotto nodded brusquely. When Antony appeared, Mari turned immediately to walk ahead out the main doors. Antony raced to catch up to him. "Where did you go?" he asked as they fell in step.

"I wanted to get ready for the race," said Mari plainly.

"I could have used your help. I'm really bad about poetry."

"Maybe you should try reading some."

Antony's grimace was amused. "She wants a copy of Pietro's pap's pap!" Antonio paused, quite pleased, then continued. "I promised I'd get her one—do you have one? I'll pay you back! She's really not all bad, is she? I mean, I know she's a Carrara, but they can't all be Marsilios, can they?" Antony continued in this vein as they passed out through the doors into the Piazza della Signoria. As he talked, Mariotto's eyes set in a determined squint that would have made a stone griffin proud. Pietro watched them go.

"Did you like her poem?" a keen voice said in his ear.

Pietro dragged his attention back to his father. "What?"

"The girl," said Dante. "Did you like her poem?" The poet reached up to adjust his long cap, jostled in the crush. "I enjoyed her recitation. She has a fine sense of the dramatic."

"I was going to ask you about it," said Pietro. "I didn't recognize it."

"Ah, but I did. Isn't it strange that she quoted it so perfectly, then all at once forgot the words?"

"Who wrote it?"

"Oh, it was anonymous, but that's because it was written by a woman. I happen to know which woman, in fact." His twinkling eyes told Pietro that the poetess's identity was going to remain a secret. "But it's the lines she left out that fascinate me."

They emerged last out into the square. Pietro was getting used to being at the back of the crowd. Beneath their feet the snow crunched. It was falling harder than ever, yet the crowd outside was as large as any that day.

"The animals are gone," observed Dante, mischievously changing topics.

"Probably to make room for the racers."

"Look," said the poet, pointing. "I was mistaken. One leopard remains."

It was true. A single leopard was visible on the steps to the Giurisconsulti. "I wonder why," said Pietro.

"Oh, I think keeping it there day and night from here to eternity is a brilliant notion. Only a just lawyer will risk being mauled just to pursue a case. And we both know such a thing doesn't exist."

Pietro laughed. "He looks to be in a foul temper."

"Wouldn't you be, kept out in the cold all day? Look at him pace to keep warm. Ha! Some of the runners are doing the same."

"They'd better keep away from him." There was a pause, then Pietro sighed. "So what were the missing lines?"

Grinning, Dante opened his mouth to speak, only to be interrupted by the Capitano's voice. "I don't want to keep you standing still for long!" He was a dark shape in the falling snow, lit from behind by the stewards holding torches. "Follow the torches, and try not to frighten the womenfolk."

Amid the laughter, all eyes scanned for the first torch. It hung on a corner of the walls of Santa Maria Antica.

"The finishing line is my loggia, so keep your hands nimble enough to climb! When I give the signal, start running!"

Pietro had difficulty seeing in the falling snow. He thought he spied Antony and Mariotto taking their places in the line. There were noticeably fewer knights participating in this trial, though if it were modesty, drunkenness, or weather that prevented those missing, he didn't know. The numbers were swelled by the common citizens. Excluded from the first Palio because they owned no horses, they could still rely upon their legs to carry them through the second. Several of the watchers in the crowd, on impulse, tore off their clothes and joined in. This event was open to all comers. Pietro's brother was probably among the three hundred men in the crowd. Pietro wished he could be, too. But a man had to know his limitations. Pietro could not run. *Hell, after the horse Palio I can hardly walk!* Instead, he stood beside his father, leaning on the crutch that was now a part of him. His other hand held Mercurio's leash. Otherwise the dog might run the race for him.

Cangrande dropped a flaming torch into the snow. With a gust of excited breath that smoked the air around them the runners started, slipping and falling in the initial steps. There were shouts of encouragement and curses, hands grappling at ankles as the fallen tried to trip the upright. One fellow was thrown toward the angry leopard. He barely rolled away as a huge paw slashed at his head.

The racers disappeared in the curtains of snow, and Pietro gestured toward the open doors. "Let's go get warm." Beard frosted with snow, Dante nodded vigorously. They climbed the slippery steps back to where braziers burned and hot spiced wine flowed. "Come on, Mercurio," said Pietro, urging the dog inside.

As Pietro waited in the doorway for the hound to pass, he glanced back. Alone in the center of the square stood the Capitano, head back. Snow fell on his face, into his mouth. His eyes were open, looking into the sky that was obliterated in a sea of white on the darkness. Tonight there were a million-million stars, all falling earthward to melt and disappear into every living thing they touched.

A rough elbow in Pietro's side abruptly ended study of the lord of Verona. A huge man in hooded robes cut across his path. "Excuse me," came a voice from within the folds of the cloak. It was painful to hear, rasping as if it had to scrape its way out of the man's throat. The words were strangely accented. He wore what looked to be a thin cottony material that wrapped Eastern-style around his midsection. His hood was up, but above the wide scarf wrapped around his face the skin was dark as soot, eyes black as night. It was the face of a Moor.

The creature moved off into the crowd, leaving Pietro wondering. Moors were not uncommon here in Verona, but they were mostly servants or slaves; few were free men.

Dante was inside already, halfway up the wide stairs leading to the rear loggia. Dismissing the startling figure, Pietro gritted his teeth and started the long ascent.

✦ ✧ ✦

Moments later a panel slid shut on the noise of the street and a hooded figure dusted the snow from his shoulders before beginning his own climb. He left the secret door slightly open for his escape, but after the first few steps all light vanished. He had to use his left hand to feel his way up the spiraling staircase. His right was filled with steel.

TWENTY-ONE

The noise was deafening even before Pietro reached the top of the stairs. Two hundred men and women were pressed into a space that was meant to comfortably accommodate half that. A dozen braziers were scattered about, taking up space even as they warmed the air. Pietro could see that shutters had been affixed to the tall windows to eliminate the chill wind. In the center of the east wall of the palace, two lone arches were free of shutters. Pietro counted from the edge of the loggia and decided that those were the very arches that the Scaliger had leapt through five months before. Now they were the finish line for the race. Pietro grinned.

Tonight none of the guests were made to doff their shoes in favor of soft slippers. With all the people packed in here, there probably weren't enough to go around. Or else the Grand Butler had acknowledged it a lost cause.

Before he entered the hall, Pietro was stopped again by Giotto's fresco of the five Scaliger lords. This time, though, it was the first knight who drew his attention. This man was noticeably lacking a regal bird atop his *scala,* and his visage was odd as well. His face was not as clear as the others, his features obscured in the shadow of his simple helmet.

"Leonardino della Scala, *detto* Mastino," said his father in his ear. "The first of the Scaligeri lords."

Pietro continued to study Mastino's face. "He seems different from the rest. He looks—I don't know . . ."

Dante cocked his head to one side. "No one knows much about him."

"I saw his tomb this morning. It bore the title *Civis Veronae.*"

"A common citizen," observed the poet. "He's remembered more for his humility than his deeds. It is known he organized a rewriting of the city statutes. And though he is generally acknowledged to be the first great Scaligeri, he was never lord of the city. Not officially. He never held the two major offices that the rest of the family have."

Pietro changed his gaze from the painted wall to his father. "Which are?"

Dante looked grave, as though it were Pietro's duty to have already ferreted out this information. "Capitano del Populo and Podestà of the Merchants. The two are technically separate. They combine command of the military with the merchants' financial power, creating the most secure power base of any family in Italy. Better than being king."

Pietro returned his gaze to Mastino's fresco. It wasn't the shadowy face that bothered him. It was something else. All the Scaligeri shown were surrounded by armed men. In the other four portraits, those men's spears and swords and halberds pointed out at unseen enemies. In Mastino's portrait, though, those arms were turned in toward their lord. "Why are the swords pointed inward?"

Dante's eyes narrowed as he examined the painting more closely. "I hadn't noticed that. It is disturbing, isn't it? Perhaps it is because of the way he died. Mastino was murdered not far from here. He and Bailardino's father were riding through the Volto Barboro on their way back to the palace when they were ambushed and slain. In fact, the story goes that their bodies were thrown down into the well that stands outside our current residence."

Behind them a man coughed, and Pietro decided he'd blocked the hallway long enough. As he enter the loggia people made way, recognizing him by the fine clothes that marked the new knight. Men he did not know called congratulations to him. He waved in return, speaking vague words of thanks.

"Hey! Alaghieri!"

Pietro found his arm held in a steely clasp and a moment later he was embraced. He tried to identify the man, who did look familiar . . .

"We met today—though I'm afraid I was something of a cad. Sorry about the tunnel."

Oh! "I was a little evil myself. Don't worry about it."

The man let out a breath of relief. "Good. I was afraid you'd want to duel or something. My name's Ugo de Serego!" Again Pietro's arm was encased in that strong grip. "Some friends of mine are over in the corner—we've had enough racing for one day. Come and join us! I want to introduce them to the man who saved my life."

"Don't say that. We were both lucky."

"Come over anyway. I want to hear what it's like to be descended from a great poet."

Pietro saw someone he'd longed to see all evening. "Can I catch up with you? There's someone I need to talk to."

Serego was roughly scruffing Mercurio's neck. "Of course! We'll be over here when you want to celebrate." Serego strode back to his friends while Pietro and Mercurio made for another corner of the loggia.

Katerina della Scala in Nogarola was seated away from the crush of men and women. Pietro had expected her to hold court in the style of her brother and sister-in-law, surrounded by the best and the brightest, making use of her wit and her grace. But, with the exception of a serving girl, there was nary a soul by her, a feat on this crowded loggia.

Cradled in her arms was the reason why. Pietro was amazed that she would bring the boy to Verona, let alone here in public. It was tantamount to a slap in Giovanna della Scala's face. *Here is the son you could not give him,* Cangrande's sister was saying, *and I will raise him. We cannot even trust you to do that.*

Cangrande's wife was holding a boisterous court across the loggia. Men and women kept their eyes deliberately averted from the stately woman and the child she held—a child that bore such a strong resemblance to their lord.

Katerina passed the time by chatting with her girl, who must have been the child's nurse. Pietro looked around. Bailardino was nowhere in sight, which was unfortunate. Pietro required a chaperone, otherwise it would be improper—even if only he knew it.

He was rescued from his dilemma by his father. The poet arrived with a fresh goblet of steaming wine. The vessels here were finer than those in the feasting hall, these made of ornate rock crystal. Cangrande's famous disdain of ornaments evidently had no effect on his wife's tastes. Or his Butler's.

"Would you like to sit, Father?" The reply was a raised eyebrow, indicating that idiot questions would not be answered. Crutch in hand, Pietro led his father to the corner occupied by Donna Katerina.

The lady smiled at his approach. "Ah, Pietro, you mean to join me in my exile?"

Pietro bowed as best he could. He remembered trying to bow to her directly following Vicenza. Then she had briskly dismissed his attempt, more concerned with his wound. He wondered if she would pity him now. Instead she pretended offense at his gallant obeisance. "Pietro Alaghieri! Do you dare to mock me by bowing when I cannot rise to curtsey in the proper way?" She indicated the child twisting restlessly in her lap. "I decided that, since I was banned from partaking in polite society, I might as well carry the cross with me. He is the cause of my plight. The least he can do is share it. And it gives the other guests a topic of conversation."

Pietro said, "You know my father."

"Who doesn't? I'm pleased I can say I knew him before he went to Hell. And who is this?" she asked of the hound staring at the child in her arms.

"His name is Mercurio." Nudged, the dog obediently curled up at Pietro's right foot.

"You seem to be weathering exile well," observed Dante. He settled himself onto a bench and added, "An active child."

"Too active for his own good. His nurse was about to throw him from the window. He's small for his age, and I'm convinced it's because he uses up all his energy staying awake. Pietro, please don't stand on ceremony." She freed a hand from the child's clutches to wave to a seat near her. Immediately the boy tried to wriggle himself onto the floor.

"He is a trial, then?" asked the poet, leaning forward to study the baby. A tiny hand darted out to grasp his beard. Dante chuckled. The child heaved up with his tiny muscles as if he viewed the poet's face as a mountain to be scaled hand over hand. As the next handhold was Dante's protruding lower lip, the poet let out a yelp.

"Cesco! Monsignore, please. Allow me." Katerina removed the poet's fumbling hands then wrapped her own slender fingers around each of the infant's wrists. Pietro saw her knuckles go white. The child's eyes opened wide. When she released her grip, the baby's hands opened instinctively, allowing Dante to pull back. The child looked up as though entertained by the rebuke. She spared him hardly a glance in return.

The nurse came forward. "Should I take him?"

"Thank you, Nina, no. I will deal with him. As you see, Monsignore Alaghieri, he has recently taken to climbing. He's scaling everything in sight. I positively dread the day he takes his first step."

Her knee began to bounce, providing the child with a new stimulus to distract him. But little Cesco's eyes remained fixed on the poet's beard. In return, Dante was eyeing the child with a wary respect, massaging his chin with the back of his hand. "Pietro, if that laugh escapes I'll disown you. It is quite a grip, madam. I assume he gets it from his father?"

"I wouldn't know. Really, monsignore, I have been the intended victim of a hundred such traps, and I have yet to stumble."

Dante was grinning like a child caught filching sweets. "I am so sorry. My son can tell you, I am an inveterate gossip. Though I think it says enough that your brother asked you to raise the boy. If I recall, your relationship was not one of requests and favors done lightly."

"You're thinking of someone else, surely. There is nothing but warm amity between my brother and myself."

"Indeed? I seem to remember an incident—"

"Pater," interrupted Pietro, "weren't you going to tell me the last lines of a poem?"

Dante looked momentarily put out, but the new topic held enough entertainment value for him to endure the clumsy deflection. "Ah, yes. As I said, I know the poet. She is Florentine, and was known in our little circle of friends as La Compiuta Donzella. She was not particularly prolific, but her poems were such that I cannot help but admire the young lady for referencing her verse."

Pietro turned to Katerina. "You've met Antonio's betrothed, the girl Gianozza?"

"Pretty, but a little too tragic for my tastes," judged Katerina.

"Well, she quoted a poem to us this evening, but suddenly stopped. My father thinks there's some import in that."

Instead of replying directly, Dante began to recite:

> *In the season when the world's in leaf and flower*
> *the joy of all true lovers waxes strong:*
> *in pairs they go to gardens at the hour*
> *when little birds are singing their sweet song;*
>
> *All gentle folk now come beneath love's power,*
> *and the service of his love is each man's care,*
> *while every maid in gladness spends her hours;*
> *but I am filled with weeping and despair.*
>
> *For my father has treated me most ill*
> *and keeps me often in the sorest anguish:*
> *he would give me to a lord against my will.*

And this I neither do desire or wish,
and every hour I pass in sharpest grief;
and so receive no joy from flower or leaf.

"It goes on to claim she wants nothing more than the convent. I doubt, however, if this girl shares that particular sentiment. I fear," concluded Dante, "your friend Antonio does not have her wholehearted affection."

Pietro spied the lady in question across the long hall, listening to the excited prattle of several young men. Lively and bright, smiling at everything, she was what Mariotto had called her—a Julia.

"You recite beautifully," said Katerina. Dante made an immodest murmur of agreement.

Pietro noticed that little Cesco had ceased to fidget. He stared at the elder Alaghieri, drinking in the man with his eyes. Those eyes were wide and green. Deep green. In that, the child was unlike the Scaliger. In everything else you saw the lines of the fine bones, though in the child they were rough, less refined, somehow purer. Katerina's face was cut of similar stone, by the same artist. It was difficult to remember that Donna Katerina was not, in fact, the boy's mother.

The lady noticed Cesco's fascination. "Perhaps I should hire you as a nurse, monsignore. This is the longest he has been still all day."

"He has a poet's soul," said Dante, smiling ruefully as he stroked his beard. "In spite of his warlike tendencies."

"I often wonder if he has a soul at all."

"His eyes are very green," said Pietro.

"Today. Tomorrow they will be blue. He is a traitor to his core, he changes his colors daily."

"Then he should be fostered out to Nico da Lozzo when he is of age," observed Dante.

"Or perhaps your friend Uguccione della Faggiuola?" asked the lady innocently.

"I fear he will not be able to take any under his wing for some time," the poet replied. "He is planning a venture into Florence later this year."

"Yes, he even asked Francesco's advice on the venture."

"And what did your brother say?"

"He said only a fool would attack Florence now. It did not seem to have the desired effect."

"Well, I, for one, wish him luck. Then perhaps, by the time Cangrande's son is grown, Florence will be a city worthy of respect."

"It is strangely warm in this loggia, is it not?" replied Katerina, waving a hand before her face. "In spite of the chill winds outside. I believe we could have survived without quite so many braziers. But of course, I cannot say so to our hostess."

"I doubt the racers will mind," said Pietro. "I don't see your husband. Is he taking part?"

Her nod possessed a rueful quality. "He did not finish the horse Palio and is determined, in spite of his great age, to make a good showing tonight." Her voice warmed as she spoke of her husband.

"I understand congratulations are in order," said Dante, further depressing his son.

"Yes," said the expectant mother with tranquil ease. "I am finally to make my husband a proud father. He has been considerate, waiting all these years, not putting me aside for some young thing. Perhaps it is because I do not quote poetry at him." Dante chuckled appreciatively.

"Are you faring well?" asked Pietro. Pregnancy at her age was rarely uncomplicated.

"I am surviving. I am sorry I could not watch you race this morning, Pietro. I understand that you rode with great skill."

Pietro colored, remembering legs of pork and a hundred knives. His father spoke for him. "He did. The fact that he can ride at all is due in part to you. I would like to thank you again for all your ministrations to his injuries."

"Send me a copy of your next epic when it is complete. That will be payment enough."

"I have had a similar request from your brother. But you might have more use for it—you could read it aloud to the boy. Poetry, like music, has soothing charms." He glanced down. "You appear to need something of the kind."

At it again, young Cesco had managed to turn himself about in the lady's arms and was pushing against her with both feet, trying to propel himself away from her. "I was thinking of letting go, just to allow him to get into trouble."

"What prevents you?" asked Dante.

"I do not wish to aggravate my sister-in-law more than necessary. If the boy begins to cry, he will go on for hours. Once he gets into a vein, he is loath to leave it. If left to myself, at home, I would let him topple end over end, damn the consequences. I prefer him noisy—then at least I know where he is. When he's quiet, he's plotting." She twisted the child around and he suddenly found himself upside-down. He giggled and swung his arms in front of him, twisting in space.

Dante poked a cautious finger at the boy. "Does he sleep?"

"He does, but does not like to. I begin to wonder if he has nightmares."

"Dreaming so young?"

"Oh, I know he dreams. Sometimes when he's dreaming it is impossible to awaken him. But I wonder if they are pleasant dreams . . ." Her arms began to tremble with the strain, and she righted the child. He clapped his hands together and grinned around. Was that not the most wonderful thing ever?

Suddenly the lady's eyes narrowed. Her voice sharpened, rising in volume. "Don't skulk in shadows, child. It shows poor breeding to spy."

Both Dante and Pietro were startled. They tried to follow her gaze, but the lady's face was solidly immobile. "I said come out here. Or would you like me to summon Tullio?"

From behind a tapestry at her shoulder little Mastino della Scala emerged. His face was sullen. "I wasn't spying . . ."

"Of course you were," said Katerina. "Now run along. I'm quite sure you aren't supposed to be here."

Mastino started to argue but something in his aunt's icy glare forestalled him. He crossed in front of her, heading for the exit. As he did, his fingers snaked out and tugged at the baby's small crop of curly blond hair. The infant yelped and began to whimper. Pietro reached out a hand to grab Mastino but the boy had broken into a run, disappearing among the legs of the revelers.

"Let him go, Pietro," said Katerina in a singsong voice, calming the child before he broke into a full-out wail. "Shhhh. The aggravation would not be worth the result. Shh."

"He reminds me of his father," said Dante. "I never liked Alboino."

"You were not alone." The child was struggling furiously to be free. "Monsignore, would you mind reciting another line of verse? It might avert a scene. Mastino has inflamed Cesco's desire to be rid of me."

Pietro held out his arms. "May I hold him?"

Donna Katerina did not hesitate. "Be on your guard, he'll have your fine farsetto in ruins."

Finding himself transferred from one adult to another, Cesco glanced briefly at his new captor, then reached for the silver dagger hanging on Pietro's belt. Pietro gently interposed his own hand between the child and the knife. The boy's nimble little fingers reached around, grazing the pommel of the dagger. The child's other hand shot out and grasped the weapon's hilt, and Pietro had to pry the little fingers free. Holding the wriggling, giggling child in one hand, he removed the dagger bearing his name from his belt and placed it on the floor beside Mercurio.

Cesco twisted suddenly, his feet brushing the tiled floor, dangling by one arm. The child could have easily dislocated a shoulder, but Mercurio jumped up and slid underneath the boy, holding him up until Pietro got a firmer grip across his middle.

Cesco giggled at the dog, then noticed the feather on the top of Pietro's hat. Suddenly he changed directions, tiny fingers questing desperately up. Pietro quickly removed his cap and set it on the floor atop the dagger. The child's expression was pure disdain.

"He seems to have your measure," chuckled Dante. Mercurio snuffed and settled back down.

"I'd like to see you hold him," retorted Pietro, struggling.

"No, thank you. One encounter is enough." Dante turned to Katerina. "Is he very like his father as a child?"

"I wouldn't know."

The poet shrugged. "I shall give up my attempts to snare you and instead woo you with verse. Would you like something old or something new?"

"Something fresh, please. Nothing I might have heard."

Dante began with the final lines of *L'Inferno*:

> *Into that hidden passage my guide and I*
> *Entered, to find again the world of light,*
> *and, without taking a moment's rest,*
> *we climbed up, he first and I behind him,*
> *far enough to see, through a round opening,*
> *a few of those fair things the heavens bear.*
> *Then we came forth, to see again the stars.*

He carried straight into the opening of the sequel he was calling *Purgatorio*. It never ceased to amaze Pietro that his father could render verse one day and recite it the next. He was very particular about his words and fought for hours about each one. Once satisfied, though, it became engraved in his mind as if in stone. If the poet's notes were ever lost, he could recite the whole of his *Commedia* from memory.

Cesco's frantic quest for the feather ended. He listened, rapt, to Dante's encounter with Cato, Virgil by his side. Freed from the struggle, Pietro was able to glance around. The Scaliger had arrived, striding into the loggia with a laugh and a wink. His wife drifted over to take her place at his side. He wrapped an arm about her as he listened to a lighthearted argument between Giacomo da Carrara and Passerino Bonaccolsi. He laughed, and with that grand laugh the crowd finally felt that the festivities were truly under way.

The race had been afoot for over half an hour. Signore Montecchio was reclined on a daybed close to the new Signore Capulletto. Pietro thought that he had never seen Mariotto's father looking quite as relaxed as he did at this moment. Usually abstemious to a fault, he was imbibing his share and more in the wake of the long confession at dinner. Perhaps this evening's events would make him a more joyful man. All he had to do was to wed his son and daughter off, the way Capulletto was doing. Give him grandchildren, an assured continuation of the name, and Montecchio would be a satisfied man.

Thinking along these lines, Pietro eyed Antony's bride-to-be. Gianozza had withdrawn from her admirers to the gap in the shutters that formed the race's finishing line. When she noticed Pietro staring, he blushed. She waved, and a huddle of young women by her noticed him and waved as well. Pietro turned quickly back to Katerina, who was listening to the poetry with her eyes closed. She owned the Scaligeri love of language. Cesco had fallen asleep. Pietro decided he could depart for a little while without offense. "If you'll excuse me," he whispered to Katerina.

Her eyes opened. "I will, if you promise to return after the race and keep me company."

He promised, passing the sleeping bundle off to the nurse. As Pietro stood, his greyhound rose to follow. "Mercurio, stay." The dog obeyed happily, curling up beneath Cesco's dangling feet.

Pietro crutched through the crowd. Gianozza watched him approach and curtsied when he drew near. "Cavaliere." The ladies around her giggled.

"Ladies." Pietro nodded to them, then addressed Gianozza. "I'm sorry, I didn't mean to stare. My mind was elsewhere."

Some of the girls nearby tittered and made sly comments. Realizing they were looking at him, Pietro blushed. Taking his arm, Gianozza moved him closer to the open window. "Is there no woman in your life, Ser Alaghieri?"

"No, not that I could marry."

The girl cocked her head to the left. A little breathlessly she asked, "Does that mean there is someone whom you cannot marry?"

Pietro could have cut out his treacherous tongue. "No, lady, that's not what I meant. Simply, I know few women of marriageable age."

"Mmm. It's a shame I don't have a little sister at home." She turned toward the dark night outside. Torches were burning atop a building off to the left, the grand domicile of Cangrande's cousin Federigo. A party was going on there as well, the guests no doubt enjoying their excellent view of the finishing line. A similar torch burned at Pietro's elbow, perched just on the exterior of the Scaliger palace to mark the finish line.

Gianozza gestured at the snow. "Do you think it is too cold for them?"

"Not at all, lady. In the race this afternoon I was surprised at how quickly I forgot the cold." He told her of the fur-lined cloak that was now trampled into the mud of the river.

"Perhaps a duck will make a nest of it?" she suggested.

"Cold comfort, lady. It was a very nice cloak."

"I'm sure it still is," she replied.

"I'm sorry. It's foolish, but I was brought up to—well, to be frugal."

"As was I. I expect that being married to Ser Capulletto will be a shocking change for a girl used to thrice-mended gowns. But your donation of the cloak was a fine Christian act. At this very moment you are being praised by the duck family for your generosity." She laughed, then said, "Are you sad not be racing with them?"

The girl was forthright! That wasn't something you got from looking at her. "Yes, I'm afraid I am a little jealous of Antony and Mari."

"You're honest," she noted with approval. "Signore Capulletto said you were very brave at Vicenza. You and Cavaliere Montecchio. Tell me—was he in some way displeased with me? He left shortly after I entered the hall downstairs. Is it anything that I did?"

Pietro didn't want to answer. He certainly didn't want to tell her Montecchio's opinion of her match. "No, lady. He had a great deal on his mind. Just before you arrived his father had recounted the tale of his mother's death."

Gianozza's brow knit in concern. "May I ask you to tell me the story?"

"It is not my story to tell. You should ask him yourself." He asked a personal question of his own. "Are you and your uncle close?"

"Great-uncle. I suppose. He's the lord of the family, but I rarely saw him until I came of age."

Until you became useful. Peasants could marry for love but not the nobility. To them, marriage was a contract between families, an effort to produce children and further familial designs. Love was for extramarital affairs. Even the Church, which had proclaimed marriage a sacrament only sixty years before, winked at this custom. Courtly love, the love that yearns, pines, and burns—this was reserved for the world outside of marriage. *Isn't that backward?*

For a long time now Pietro had felt his hackles rise whenever the subject was broached. Perhaps it was because of his mother, and the sad look on her face whenever she read her husband's works. Their families had arranged Dante's marriage to Gemma, but the poet's heart belonged to another— Beatrice, the Bringer of Blessings. Dante had dedicated his life's work to her, all the while sharing his days and his bed with a woman who was merely his wife. Perhaps peasants had the better bargain.

Still, the girl before him was in no danger of being marginalized. Antony had clearly set his cap on winning her heart. Even if she could not return his love, she would always be adored.

The girl was gazing out into the snow that rose and fell in the short gusts of wind that blew between the buildings. "My family comes from a small hamlet to the southeast of Padua—Bovolento. My father was Signore Jacopino della Bella. I doubt you've heard of him. He died last year."

"Of what?"

"The gout." She said this last sadly, her eyes welling with tears.

"I'm so sorry," said Pietro, hoping to forestall any crying. "So you're not properly a Carrara?"

The girl sniffed and blinked. "My mother is Il Grande's niece."

"Oh."

The conversation ground to a halt. Pietro didn't know what to make of the girl. There was something about her that made him uncomfortable.

The wind outside picked up, throwing snowflakes into their eyes like tiny daggers of ice. To escape it, they faced in toward the festive throng. Music played. Deeming the hour right, Manuel, Congrande's fool, had produced his lute and pipe. He managed to play both at once, a lively tune that men and women clapped along with. Among them, capering on his thick legs, was ruddy-faced Ludovico Capulletto. The middle-aged man hopped to and fro in opposition to the notes. Lord Montecchio was laughing in spite of himself, and many others leapt up to join the sportive Capuan.

"I'm afraid he's got it, too," said Gianozza.

"What's that?"

Nodding at Capulletto, she said, "You see how he's favoring his right foot? Each step is painful. That's the beginning of the gout. No wonder he's trying to marry all his family off so young."

"Who else is there for him to betroth? Antony is his only unmarried son."

"There is a grandson."

"Really? I didn't know he had a grandson."

"Well, there's no reason you should," said Gianozza. "He hasn't been born yet."

"You mean Luigi's baby?" His voice was louder than he'd intended. "He's engaged his unborn grandson? To whom?"

"A daughter of the Guarini family. She's about one now, I think. So they'll be of an age."

"That's ludicrous!"

"It's—unusual. As I understand it, part of the reason Signore Capulletto chose Verona was his strong ties to the Guarini. They've been partners in many business deals. Not," she added hastily, "that he's in trade any longer. He employs others to run those parts of his affairs these days." The girl's hands balled up into little fists. "Oh, I'm making a terrible fool of myself!"

Pietro ignored the distressed damsel in her tone. "How do they know the child will even be a boy?"

"All the midwives have said so. It's low, they tell the mother. That means it will be a boy. They've even named it."

"What name?"

"Theobaldo, I believe."

Pietro tried to imagine being betrothed from the womb. "Poor Theobaldo."

"Well, the alliance keeps his family on strong terms with theirs. It's better than the alternative."

"Which is?"

"Breaking Cavaliere Capulletto's engagement to me and betrothing him to the Guarani child instead."

The image of Antonio carrying his infant bride toward the altar made Pietro laugh sharply. He had to turn into the biting snow to hide his face. Each time his breathing came close to normal, he pictured Antony slipping a wedding band on the baby's tiny little finger. Beside Pietro the girl was giggling, and the other young girls moved closer to find out what was so funny.

Just then a cheer rose up from outside. In the snow, it was impossible to see beyond a few feet, but occasionally a gust of wind would open a patch of clear air before them. The crowd at his back jostled Pietro toward the open air. Gianozza was pressed up close to him. She smelled of orange blossom. The torch that marked the finish line lit her features as she scanned the street below them, looking from one end to the other. *She is lovely,* he thought.

Before he could say something, Gianozza pointed down into the snow-laden alley and said, "Look! Here they come!"

TWENTY-TWO

At the end of the alley blurry figures hurtled into view, shoving and pushing and tripping each other. A few in the back were limping heavily, and no one was running as quickly as he had at the race's start. Foot by dogged foot, they pressed on toward the Scaligeri palace.

On the balcony of Federigo della Scala's home there was cheering and the waving of torches. "Stop waving those torches, you idiots!" shouted a man at Pietro's shoulder, but either they didn't hear or didn't care. Attracted by the cheers and the waving firebrands, several racers began to climb the wrong balcony in their blind desperation to finish. They were halfway up when they realized their mistake. Some dropped back to the earth to try again. Some found themselves bodily lifted up onto the open-air balcony and feted by a congenial host determined to ply them with drink and pry a story or two out of them.

Two figures in the snow approached the correct wall. They knew which was the loggia of the Scaliger palace because they had leapt from there five months before. Mariotto's dark hair was damp with melted snow and bore a crown of icy white around the fringe. By his side ran the newly christened Antonio Capulletto, whose hair was shorter, making the snow invisible. In the torchlight both their bodies glistened with snowmelt and sweat.

Pietro said, "Perhaps you should retire until the race is finished. It won't be long."

"I can endure the sight of a naked man," said the girl, her face turning red as she said it.

"I'm sure. But I doubt they can take being seen."

"Oh! Of course!" She stepped back to the far end of the loggia, where most of the women had gathered.

Pietro turned back to the railing and called out, "C'mon, you two! Get up here and have a drink!" He doubted they could hear him. In the street, on the loggia, on the balcony opposite, men shouted. Behind him on the loggia, Manuel was piping away like a madman. His tune was high-pitched and frantic, an apt counterpoint to the action below. Nevertheless, Pietro continued to call encouragement to his friends.

Antony and Mari were struggling to find a handhold on the icy walls below. Antony got a firm grip on a post extending outward from the stable. A moment later Mariotto leapt into the air and clutched at a sconce above his head. Both got their feet under them and started the climb. Other men were beneath them now, trying to either mimic their actions or else dislodge them and bring them crashing back to earth.

Mariotto and Antony ascended, their fingers probing the wall for the next handhold. Finding one, Antony pulled himself higher, only to slip. He found himself dangling one-handed, his feet swinging free while he scrabbled at the wall for another grip.

Less than four feet away Mariotto found a place for some toes to grip, enabling him to stand as his hands quested. He looked to his right and saw Capulletto almost level with him. From above, Pietro glimpsed Antony's grin as he twisted around to face Mariotto. The Capuan kicked out at someone beneath him, knocking the fellow sideways off the wall and into the crowd. At the same time he stretched out a hand to Mari.

Pietro saw a momentary hesitation in Montecchio. Then Mariotto extended his own hand. The duo's fingers met and closed about each other, and Mari pulled Antony up to the next handhold.

They climbed together, racing for the top. One of them was certain to win it. A bare twenty feet below the window, Antony's joyous voice rang loud enough to hear over the cacophony. He had found a place to set his feet, leaving both hands free. This was even more dangerous. Leaning in toward the wall, without anything for his hands to grip, he could topple backward into the struggling mass of naked men beneath him.

Mariotto was higher on the wall, poised to clamber over the rail of the balcony and emerge victorious. If Antony was going to win he had to make a tremendous final effort. He balled himself up, tucking his knees under his chin, and launched himself up toward the balcony's railing.

Pietro caught his eyes as he leapt. Reaching up, Antony's face showed elation. That expression was instantly replaced by a sickening look of fear as Antony's angle of ascent changed. His chin banged against the railing of the loggia and his hands slipped off it. Pietro lunged forward to grasp Antony's wrists but the cold wet hands fell away from his fingers.

Mari's hands appeared that very second. He was standing on the outer lip of the balcony, having heaved up from firmer footing.

"Mari!" yelled Antony, real fear in his voice, arms grasping at air.

Mariotto didn't turn.

Pietro watched Antony fall, limbs flailing. There was a sickening crunch as Antony bounced off the men below him, then a great thud as he landed among the breathless runners on the ground. Some had the sense to try to catch him. Others who hadn't seen him tumbling toward them were unwitting cushions. Then he was on the ground, holding his leg and shouting words it was best his fiancée not hear.

Pietro grinned at Mariotto. "He's hurt, but he'll live."

Leaning over to look down, Mariotto was ashen. A blanket materialized around him and he was led swiftly away as more runners began to emerge. Pietro remained to help up the others who successfully completed the climb. Servants brought forward cloaks and socks. Bricks were already warm on the fires. The smell of mulled wine grew as vast tubs were brought out. Everything was ready to remedy the ills of the racers cheerfully huddling under blankets and gulping down drink so hot it scalded their tongues.

A steward came in with a length of green silk, and also the rooster and the pair of gloves for whoever lost. Cangrande decided not to wait for the loser. Pietro watched as the green ribbon was bestowed on young Montecchio, then pushed his way through to congratulate his friend. "How are you feeling?"

"F-f-frozen," said Mariotto, teeth chattering. "F-feels like a thousand n-n-needles in my feet. Ant-tony's n-nn-not hurt b-bad?"

"I don't know how bad it is," said Pietro. "Do you want to go find him?"

"We s-s-should, shouldn't we?"

"I think you should get warm, champion. I'll find Capecelatro."

"C-C-Capulletto."

"Right, I forgot." Crutch in hand, Pietro exited the loggia and plucked the sleeve of a servant. "Do you know where they took the injured runners?"

"I believe they're in the salon, sir."

"My thanks." Downstairs, Pietro opened several doors until he found the

salon. Here the rushes were pungent, soaked by snow-covered boots tramping in and out. Candles lit, torches lined the walls. The men here were not
particularly ill-tempered, just annoyed by their injuries. The Scaliger's personal doctor, Aventino Fracastoro, was here, as well as the ever-faithful warrior of wounds, Giuseppe Morsicato. The latter nodded to Pietro even as he
massaged life back into someone's foot.

A cheerful Antony was stretched out on a long bench, wrapped in heavy
blankets. His left leg stuck straight out in front of him, wooden splints em-
bracing it. "P-P-Pietro! How is Gian-n-nozza? Is ss-she worried?"

Pietro felt guilty for not even imaging she might be. "I'm sure she is. Mariotto and I were. How bad is it?"

Antony groaned. "Broken! Badly, they say. Fracastoro put the splint on to
keep me from moving it, but they still have to get everything back in place. I
won't be riding for months!" He made a disgusted face. "And I was so
close!"

"I saw you jump. What happened?"

"I hit my shin on something and lost my balance. I fell on Bailardino!" he
added sheepishly.

Good, thought Pietro, chiding himself as he thought it.

Antony looked imploringly at his friend. "I don't want Gianozza to see me
like this. Could you and Mari entertain her tonight in my stead?"

Pietro ignored the pricking sensation in his left thumb. *It is not premonition,* he told himself. *It's just the cold.* "I've promised Donna Katerina I would
visit her, but perhaps Signorina della Bella will join us."

"Make sure Mari's there, too. I want them to be friends!"

"I will," said Pietro. "I promise."

✦　◇　✦

Outside the palace, a group of inebriates leaned against a frescoed section of
wall. Suddenly one jerked himself upright. "Jesus!"

"What's the matter with you?"

"I swear to God—the wall moved!"

"He's drunk!"

"So? It doesn't make me a liar!"

"Oh! Look at this one, who can move the walls of the palace!"

"No, really it gave a little . . ."

"He's fat enough to make it fall over!"

"Who said that? Which of you drunks said it?"

"We may be drunk, doesn't make us liars!"

"Damn your hides! I'm the very image of fitness! Watch this!"

"Go to it, Hercules!" He was cheered on as he performed a disastrous handstand. Roaring and egging him on, no one gave the moving wall another thought.

✦ ◇ ✦

It took half an hour for Mari to return to the loggia, resplendent in fresh clothes. Pietro was waiting by the door when he arrived. "Pietro! How do I look?"

Gone was the new knight's garb, replaced by his own colors of blue and white, a touch of pink in the lining, green ribbon across his shoulder marking him victorious. Mariotto smelled of orange peel and mint, his dark hair was groomed, and his face was freshly shaven. Pietro, having neither bathed nor changed, felt shabby in comparison.

"Fine. Better than Antony, he's—"

"Thanks!" Mariotto was already breezing past him into the crowd of guests. Pietro followed, looking around. Dante had retired, but Jacopo was there. He hobbled over to Pietro, walking on the outsides of feet that were clearly split and bleeding into their bandages. "Did you see me? Did you see me climb over the rail? I made it! And I was right there in the middle of the pack, not last like you!"

"Oh, thank you very much!" Pietro's determination to stay with Mariotto overpowered the impulse to throttle his brother.

The young Montecchio's eyes sparkled as he seized hand after congratulatory hand. He refused several offers of malmsey and cheese pressed on him by admirers. He moved quickly through the throng, looking for someone.

Then he found her. All the air seemed to suspend itself within Mari's lungs. He paused, rapt, then walked directly at her. "Signorina, we've not been properly introduced," he said, kissing Gianozza's hand. "I am Mariotto Montecchio, eldest son of—"

Gianozza cut him off. "I know who you are. Oh, Ser Alaghieri! Hello!" She gestured to another girl beside her. "This is Lucia."

"Charmed." Pietro bowed as much as the crowd and the crutch allowed.

Lucia hid her face and tittered. Uneasy, Pietro said to Gianozza, "Lady, your betrothed is well. His leg is broken, but apart from that he's fine. He asked Mariotto and me to entertain you in his place."

Mariotto made a little flourish with his hat. "May we join you?"

She patted the cushion of the box upon which she sat. "Of course. I'm honored to be in the presence of the winner of the Palio. Please, tell us all about it." The other girls were looking at Mariotto coyly. Lucia had forgotten Pietro entirely. But Mari couldn't be bothered with any of them as he told Gianozza about the race, turn by turn, each slip momentous. Nowhere in the narrative did he mention Antony.

When he finished, Gianozza clapped her hands. "How exciting! But, Ser Montecchio—I heard something this evening . . . but perhaps you won't wish to speak of it."

"No," said Mariotto eagerly. "Please, tell me."

"Signore Alaghieri said that there was talk this evening . . . something to do with your family."

"Of course—the feud." In a hushed tone he spoke of his mother's death and the ancient feud with the Capelletti. Gianozza listened, eyes wide, head to the side.

Does she give that look to everyone? thought Pietro, watching from the outskirts of the group. *No wonder Antony fell under her spell so fast.* Watching now, it was obvious she was working hard to weave that same spell over Mariotto. *Almost as hard as he's trying to fall under it.*

Pietro was trying to figure out a way to politely drag Mari away when a voice whispered in his ear, "For shame, Pietro. Forsaking me for younger girls." Katerina received the curtsies of the young ladies, saying, "No, don't rise. You wouldn't mind if I stole Ser Alaghieri away for a few moments, do you?" She didn't wait but took Pietro by the arm. The moment they moved away, the girls burst into close whispers.

Katerina glanced back at Mariotto. "All hail the conquering hero."

"Yes, he's the man of the hour."

"So I see. Quite the Lancelot, isn't he?"

This rang a bell in Pietro's memory. "I suppose so."

"I didn't want to interrupt. I just wanted to say goodnight. And return these." She extended his knife and his hat to him.

Pietro blushed as he tucked the blade into its sheath. "I'm sorry, lady. I was going to find you. I just—"

She laughed. "I am not pining, Ser Alaghieri. Today is a great day for you, I should not be monopolizing your time. I'm grateful for the attentions you've shown me. I am leaving because I must put Cesco to bed."

"Is he tired out?"

"I am. He has the energy of the men in my family, he rarely sleeps." She stopped, her mouth twisting wryly. "If your father were here, he would tout that gaffe to the skies."

"It's not much of a secret," confided Pietro. "Is he with his father?"

"No, little Cesco is with the nurse." She gestured to the corner she had occupied. Sure enough, there was the nurse, back turned to them. The Moor Pietro had noticed earlier was passing across his line of sight in a great hurry.

There was a great deal of noise on the balcony, including several animals. But Pietro swore he heard Mercurio's growl from the nurse's side. Squinting, Pietro thought that there was something wrong with the way the nurse was sitting. She was slouched forward, one arm hanging loose.

"Donna," he said with an edge of urgency. Katerina turned and immediately spied what disturbed him. With Pietro in her wake she walked back to the nearly deserted corner of the loggia. "Nina?" Each step was quicker than the last. "Nina? Cesco?"

Reaching the nurse's side, Pietro laid his hand on her shoulder. Instantly the body fell from the stool and lay awkwardly on the tiled floor. Pietro knelt and turned her face to the light. Her skin was white, her body limp and lifeless. Glancing down, Pietro saw a crimson stain spreading outward from a knife in her chest.

Breathless, Pietro confirmed his worst fear. The nurse's arms were empty.

TWENTY-THREE

"Francesco!" Standing at Pietro's shoulder, Katerina called not her foster son but her brother. Across the loggia the Capitano turned and saw the expression on his sister's face. At once he barreled across the crowded hall, leaving his wife behind. Reaching Pietro's side, he took in the scene at a glance. "Where is he?"

"Gone. I stepped away for a moment." Katerina's voice was firm, though she was shaking.

Cangrande snapped his fingers and men appeared—Passerino Bonaccolsi, Nico da Lozzo, Bailardino, Tullio, and Ziliberto del Angelo, his Master of the Hunt. "Little Cesco has disappeared. Tullio, find Villafranca, tell him to seal the bridges. Nico and Passo, get your men and make a house-to-house search, starting with the nearest. Nico, go north; Passo, south. Bailardino—go dunk your head, get sober, then take my men west. Ziliberto, get across the San Pietro bridge. It's closest. All of you, go."

As they dispersed, Katerina laid a hand on Cangrande's sleeve. "He can't have got far. This just happened."

Pietro opened the shutters beside them. A huge crowd milled about in the alley below—an alley that led in one direction toward the stables and in the other toward the Piazza della Signoria. Pietro's eyes searched all the faces desperately. He said, "I saw a Moor."

"I know about the Moor," said Cangrande.

"I think it was him," insisted Pietro.

Katerina said, "He might have his reasons."

Cangrande frowned uncertainly. "True. I'll search the palace. You'll organize things here."

"Let Tullio," said Katerina. "I'm coming."

"Pietro, I'm taking your dog." Slipping his hand into Mercurio's leash, Cangrande made for the exit, only to find his path blocked by his wife. "Husband?"

"No time." Cangrande pushed past her without a glance.

More gawkers pressed in, fascinated by the dagger protruding from the nurse's breast. Half the men on the balcony had military backgrounds. One by one they offered their services to Cangrande, who was struggling toward the far door.

Pietro remained behind, feeling utterly helpless.

✦   ✧   ✦

When the panel swung open to disgorge a man with a bundle, the drunks gave an ironic cheer. Nursing a broken head, one exclaimed, "I told you! The wall moves!"

"Let me pass," said the man. He had been delayed by the darkness of the stairwell and the wriggling of the bundle's contents.

"What's that door?" asked one of the sots, looking inside.

The man with the burden said, "They're giving away free drinks up there. But it's a secret."

Already men were staggering for the sliding panel. The man tried to push past them, and as he fought, a blond head emerged from the blanket in his arms.

"Cute kid," said one drunk as he passed.

✦   ✧   ✦

Pietro stared down upon the milling crowd in the Piazza della Signoria. It was hopeless, he knew that, but he couldn't stand around waiting. He was looking for one face, a single face in the throng.

An elderly voice at his elbow snapped, "What's happening?" Pietro saw Constable Villafranca examining the body.

"Cesco's been kidnapped."

The constable visibly started. "When?"

"Just now, dammit!" Turning back to the window, Pietro peered through the falling snow at the crowd below. To one side a noteworthy figure emerged from the palace doors, struggling through the sea of staggering drunkards. It was the man Pietro had been looking for. The Moor.

Something wasn't right. In spite of the bulky cloak, Pietro could tell the Moor's arms were empty. But he was certainly moving fast. In fact, he seemed focused on another figure ahead of him, a figure making better progress through the throng. The Moor was trying to intercept him. The man in the lead was passing almost directly beneath Pietro's balcony, which meant he couldn't have come through the main doors. A tall man in a knee-length tunic and a long trailing hood with awkwardly distended limbs, he looked like a *spaventapasseri*, the creatures farmers created to scare off scavenger birds.

In the scarecrow's arms was a bundle, something wrapped in a blanket—

"There. There!" shouted Pietro, pointing. "Stop that man!"

The fugitive gave a panicked glance back. In that moment Pietro got a good look at the man's face. Beneath the short beard it was grotesque, with long sallow cheeks under the shadows of the hood, conjuring up Pietro's every childhood nightmare. "There he goes! That's the man!"

Cangrande had barely reached the doors to the loggia. Now he whirled about and saw Pietro pointing down, out the window. The Scaliger cursed and cried, "The back stairs!"

Mercurio was ahead of him, his nose leading him to a door hidden in a recess just around the corner from the loggia. Cangrande reached it moments after the hound and pulled on the latch. It didn't move. "Why in the name of the Virgin is this door locked?!" He battered uselessly at it with one hand, then spun on his heel for the crowded front stairs.

At the window Villafranca stood beside Pietro. "Show me!"

"There!" Down among the populace the scarecrow was not able to run, but he was pushing steadily on, hugging the walls of the Giurisconsulti where the crowds were thinner because of the leopard on the steps. No one was moving to intercept him or the Moor. They were going to lose the child.

Pietro's leg was over the railing before he knew what he was doing. He beat away Villafranca's grasping hand with his crutch and, using his left leg to propel himself, dropped off the balcony onto the crowd below. Some saw him coming and threw up hands to protect themselves. Some were taken by surprise. Pietro's hip cracked on someone's head, but his outstretched arms grasped enough men to keep him off the ground.

There was a good deal of cursing until someone noticed his clothes. "It's a knight!" Thinking him drunk, they held him aloft and passed him from hand to hand. On a sea of men reeking of drink and sweat, he was being carried away from the kidnapper and the Moor. "No! Stop, dammit!" His frantic shouts were lost, so he started lashing out with kicks, swinging his crutch. One man ducked and let go of Pietro, which sent the young knight rolling over face-first toward the earth. He caught himself, though his left knee struck hard on the cobblestones. He forced himself to stand, thinking he was lucky it had been his left knee, not his right.

Ducking this way and that, he tried to see through the crowd. The slouched figure of the kidnapper was still jostling people near the leopard, trying to get by. Pietro stumbled in that direction, shoving bodies out of his path.

A great cry from behind him made him glance over his shoulder. The huge Moor in the hooded cloak was brandishing a falchion, scything the air above his head as he threw men out of his path, heading directly for Pietro, protecting the scarecrow's escape. Pietro's hand went instinctively to his belt, but he was armed only with the knife Mariotto had given him that morning, the one with his own name on it. The thin miseracordia was useless against the falchion's blade, which could remove head from neck in a single stroke.

The crowd parted for the Moor, who began moving faster. Pietro stumbled but kept on in the direction of the scarecrow, casting frantic glances behind him at the approaching falchion. Then, farther back, he saw a sign of hope. Cangrande was emerging from the palace doors, a firebrand held high in one hand, Mercurio's leash in the other. Pietro's dog was straining toward the chase, and Pietro prayed Cangrande would let the hound free to aid his master.

Forcing himself to forget the Moor, Pietro trained his eyes on Cesco, squirming this way and that in the scarecrow's arms. The boy was crying now, shrieking for all he was worth. The kidnapper was obviously having trouble holding him. Pietro cupped a hand to his mouth and shouted, "Cesco! Francesco! Cesco!"

The little head turned and frowning eyes found Pietro, a known face. A hand broke free from the blanket and reached for Pietro, who was gaining now that the crowd was scattering. Ignoring the pain in the leg that threatened to give out entirely under him, Pietro broke into a full run. *Damn me and damn this leg and where the hell are Cangrande and Bailardino and the rest of them? And how close is the Moor?* In desperation, he threw his crutch over his shoulder, a weak missile. Maybe it would trip the Moor up.

Now all Pietro had was the silver dagger. Suddenly an idea struck him. He held the weapon up high and cried out, "Cesco, look!"

Cesco saw the dagger glinting in the torchlight. The child started to struggle, pulling both hands free and straining for the pretty weapon. The kidnapper cried, "God bless it, child! Be still, in the name of God!" The bastard shook Cesco, who cried out and grabbed onto a thin chain around the scarecrow's neck.

Mere feet away, Pietro saw the villain cast about in desperation. The crowd had backed off, but it wouldn't be long before they understood who was in the wrong. His path would be blocked, his life ended. The scarecrow had no hope of escape. Pietro drew a shallow breath and said, "Give up, man! It's over!"

"The devil it is!" The scarecrow whirled around. There was a knife in his hand, resting on the back of Cesco's neck.

Pietro checked his run. "Don't!"

A fierce growl cut him off. Nearby the leopard was straining its leash. The scarecrow glanced at the animal. Pietro saw the thought forming. A smile curled the edge of the fiend's mouth. *No. He can't!*

The kidnapper heaved Cesco sideways at the leopard. The child was still clutching the man's necklace, but it broke and the child sailed through the air.

Pietro's heard Katerina's scream from far behind him. It drowned out all the gasps and cries from the drunken crowd. Wrapped in the blanket, Cesco bounced off the leopard's shoulder and fell. Landing roughly on the top stone step, the small bundle rolled down two more stairs. Cesco ended facing upward, looking at the snow falling from the sky. His mouth was open in a scream but there was no sound coming out.

The startled leopard crouched back on its hindquarters, looking at the boy and growling. Pietro forgot all about the scarecrow and the Moor. Willing the leopard to be still, he darted forward, reaching out for the boy. The leopard lifted a forepaw big as the child's whole body.

Pietro ducked low over Cesco's body and threw up a fist to ward off the leopard's blow. The weight that struck his fist was crushing. The leopard bellowed as something was torn from Pietro's grip. A second swipe hit him like a furry brick to the head. Damp stones buffeted his shoulders as he was flipped in the air and landed flat on his back.

Dazed, Pietro rolled onto his side, blinking hard. Something dark was blurring his sight, but he could hear the leopard howling. Pietro cuffed his eyes and looked up.

Cesco lay nearby across the stones. The leopard was perched on the top step of the Giurisconsulti. Something was amiss with its right forepaw because it limped, trailing blood behind it. Pietro's dagger, forgotten when he'd jumped, had pierced the leopard's paw. Pietro gazed for a horrible moment at the beast's strange mouth and the row of teeth just within.

But the leopard wasn't looking at Pietro. It snarled at the Scaliger, who leapt to protect the child, flaming torch in hand. To Pietro's eyes Cangrande looked a thousand times fiercer than the animal.

Cesco dragged in a huge breath, and this time his scream was audible. Pietro blinked again and tried to focus his eyes. A huge shape close to Cangrande resolved itself. The Moor! Standing behind Cangrande, that evil blade hovering over the child!

"No no no," mumbled Pietro. He stretched out a futile hand to ward off the blow.

Cangrande didn't see the danger to Cesco. He was busy swinging the torch, forcing the leopard to hunch back. But fear of fire did not diminish the creature's rage. A snarl, a clamping of jaws, and it leapt into the air.

Cangrande lunged forward, one arm protecting his head, the other still holding the brand. The Moor stepped over Cesco and drove in behind the Scaliger, arms crossed, bashing the animal under its chin with the flat of his blade. The crushing weight of the beast landed on the Capitano's shoulders and the Moor's forearms. Together they staggered, both throwing their legs wide for support. If they gave ground at all, the leopard would land squarely on the child.

Cangrande used the brand to fend off the claws of the uninjured paw, then pressed the flames upward, scorching the beast's underbelly. The massive cat screeched and flailed. The Moor took a step forward and twisted himself so his back was pressed against the animal's wounded belly. Cangrande dropped the brand, twisted around the Moor and away from the animal. In two steps he swept up the shrieking Cesco and dashed to the edge of the crowd, handing the bundle to his sister, just arrived.

"Could someone help me, please?" Voice low and rasping, the Moor's Italian was hardly accented. The calm tone disguised his enormous strain as the held the leopard at bay.

Someone in the crowd cried, "Let them kill each other!" The sentiment was echoed. Quick bets were made, the leopard was cheered on.

Cangrande was about to aid the Moor when Ziliberto del Angelo appeared, a long stick with a leather noose on its end in his hand. With a flick of the wrist the Master of the Hunt collared the beast and hauled upward. Immediately the Moor stepped away, to the jeers and hisses of the crowd.

"You're not a light love, are you?" demanded Ziliberto. The leopard was angry, hurt and frightened. Landing on the steps it limped away from the crowd. Ziliberto followed it, cooing, making strange animal noises.

Pietro felt hands hooking into his armpits, but his eyes were on Cangrande. The Scaliger was breathing hard, and blood flowed from his shoulder and back. But he seemed steady. As he was settled on his feet once more, Pietro looked for Cesco. "Is he hurt?"

"The Capitano's fine," someone told him.

"No—the boy! Is he hurt?"

"He's fine," rasped a low voice. A dusky hand touched Pietro's head, feeling for damage. "Someone needs to look at those cuts."

Pietro looked into the Moor's face. "How—who are you?"

The man might have answered if a rock hadn't come hurtling from back of the crowd, anonymous and vicious. The blow struck the Moor on his back. He grunted and hunched down. A second projectile, this one a patch of ice, struck the back of his head. This was followed by snowballs with rocks inside them. Pietro threw his arms up about his ears and ducked under the volley of missiles aimed at the man beside him.

"How dare you!" cried Cangrande, leaping forward into the crowd. His doublet was gone, his shirt in tatters and his body streaked with blood. "That man just risked his life while the rest of you stood by watching! You dare attack him? Want to show how brave you are? Find the one who started this! The tall thin man in the patched cloak! I promise riches to the man that finds him, and death for the next stone thrown!"

As he spoke men in Scaligeri livery hustled the Moor away down a side street. The crowd departed quickly, though if to hunt the fugitive or to escape the Scaliger's wrath Pietro couldn't tell.

Pietro's head was ringing, and he forced himself to sit down again on the Giurisconsulti steps. He stayed there for hours, if the pulsing in his head was any measure. He was roused by the constable gently shaking his shoulder. "You need to go in, boy. The doctors will want a look at you."

Pietro accepted the man's help to stand. "Thanks."

"You're a damn fool, boy," said Villafranca, shaking his head. "Then again, never seen a brave man that wasn't."

Pietro squinted against the pain. "Where did he go?"

"Don't worry, we'll find the bastard."

"No, the other one—the Moor."

"Oh, him! Fearsome devil, ain't he? I swear, he may be a heathen, but I've rarely seen a feat like that. I'd forgotten—well, we hadn't seen him in years."

"Who is he?" persisted Pietro.

"I suppose you couldn't know, could you? They call him the *Arūs,* whatever that is. He's the property of Lady Katerina's personal astrologer. Damn sorcerous bastard. I half wish they'd put an end to him just now. Him and his master both."

Katerina's man? Pietro glanced at the constable. "How did you get here?"

"The same way you did. You managed it better than I did." Villafranca nodded toward his left ankle, which was visibly swelling. "Broken, I think. Shall we go in to see the good doctor together? Mind you, first thing Fracastoro will do is squeeze the piss out of you. Then he'll smell it, taste it. If he's really upset he'll set it out for the flies, and if they like it, well, that's when you're in real trouble."

Pietro squinted at the square. "Cangrande?"

"Searching for the kidnapper with all my men. My orders are to look after you. Don't worry. I fancy he'll find us when he's through. Let's get you to the doctor." Pietro started to protest. "Young man, neither of us is in any condition to give chase to a snail, let alone that creature. Come inside like a sane man and get drunk."

✦　✧　✦

In the confused aftermath of the foiled kidnapping, young Mariotto left the Scaliger palace. He returned twenty minutes later, armed with a book. Making his way through the buzzing crowds in the Piazza della Signoria, he slipped into the church of Santa Maria Antica through the small western door. Had his thoughts not been elsewhere, it might have occurred to him to wonder at the state of his soul for bringing a book called *L'Inferno* onto holy ground.

Closing the door on the excited revelers in the square, he looked around.

In the darkness of the quiet church he couldn't see anyone. He shook the snow off his cloak and crept forward, his boots leaving damp patches in his wake. Ahead there was a dim light where a single candle flickered. His hands on the book were shaking. He rounded the pillars, then stopped.

"Gianozza."

The girl was kneeling. She crossed herself before turning to him. "I thought if I was found, it better be in prayer. Then I'd just say I'd come for confession."

"What could you have to confess?"

The girl blushed and came to take his hand. "I came here to meet you."

"I know. I'm glad you did." Her body was close, their faces inches apart. His breath felt very warm.

"I'm glad, too," she whispered, looking up into his eyes. "You poor man," she said, observing the snow that clung to his hair. "You must be frozen stiff."

"I don't think I'll ever be cold again."

"That's pretty of you to say."

He felt her breath on his cheek. "So, this is courtly love," he observed.

"What?"

"Loving an unobtainable woman."

"Am I unobtainable? I thought I was brazen." For an instant her cheek was against his face. He felt the flicker of her eyelash against his skin. Then, with an inhalation like the trickling water of a stream, she stepped back and pulled him by the hand toward the confessional.

"What are you . . . ?"

"I want you to read to me, Cavaliere. If I'm going to listen, I can't be looking at you. I'll never hear a word you say." She nodded him through the door reserved for the priest.

Mariotto's heart was so full he didn't even protest as she closed it behind him. She had already lit a candle and placed it in the cell. Another door slid shut, and the girl was in the penitent's chamber. "Forgive me, Father, for I have sinned."

Mariotto bit back his first three demands for repentance. "Say three Hail Marys and come kiss me."

"Oh, Father !" she cried. "If you can't come up with anything better than that, you'd better start reading."

Dutifully Mariotto unlocked the book and opened the binding. The frontispiece was signed. Turning the page, he began to recite. *"Nel mezzo del cammin di nostra vita . . ."*

✦ ◇ ✦

The constable's prediction was correct. The Scaliger returned to the palace after an hour. By now the salon-cum-infirmary was nearly empty. When Cangrande erupted into the room he found Antony, Pietro, and Villafranca, each lying on backless couches pushed close together to ease the sharing of a bottle. The bloodied cushions under them declared that the couches would never again be fit for guests. Doctors Fracastoro and Morsicato had tended their wounds and were waiting to see if more came in. Off in a corner lay Marsilio da Carrara, drunkenly spread-eagled on a daybed.

"I hope there's some wine left," said Cangrande. He was still shirtless, but the blood had been washed off by the snow that had melted as it touched him.

The men lying prone shifted to face him, and the two doctors took him by the arms and sat him down. The Scaliger looked at Antony and Villafranca and said, "You two are a matched set. With those splints, you should be bookends."

"I'd do a better job at that than I did as constable tonight," groused Villafranca.

"Stop fretting, I'm not going to sack you."

Pietro sat up. "Did you catch him?"

Cangrande was thoroughly disgusted. "Disappeared! Completely gone. Vanished. I'm beginning to think he's a ghost."

Pietro voiced the speculations that they had been sharing. "He might have had an accomplice or a rented room."

"There's a door-to-door search going on in the entire Roman quarter. But why do I have the feeling it's not going to turn this man up? He's a magician!"

"Necromancy isn't the only explanation," observed Morsicato, poking at a slash in the Scaliger's shoulder. Fracastoro slapped Morsicato's hand. The Vicentine doctor withdrew, giving his friend the fig as he did.

Villafranca said, "Many people do dislike you, lord."

"Hmph! Don't see why." At his doctor's urging, the Scaliger lay down on a free couch. Fracastoro then began to prod at him in earnest, medical tools ready at hand. The Capitano closed his eyes but didn't wince. Only when the doctor paused did he repeat his demand. "Damn you, Aventino! Aren't you going to offer me any of that foul stuff?"

"Of course, lord," said Fracastoro. "I just wanted you to ask for it." Fracastoro lifted a wineskin and handed it across.

"Hey," protested Antony. "That's not what you offered us!"

"You don't pay my keep," smiled the Scaliger's personal doctor.

Pietro said, "How's Cesco?"

The Scaliger took a deep draught from the skin. "I hope he's sleeping. He didn't seem to be badly hurt."

"A few bruises from where the bastard gripped him," said Morsicato. "Nothing more."

"And where is your shadow?" asked Villafranca of Cangrande.

"The Moor is guarding Katerina's house. He'll be there all night."

Villafranca looked angry. "I can have men placed there—men who won't let them get within a mile of the boy."

"Do what you like. It will make no difference to him."

"Feh," grunted Morsicato dismissively. "The Moor. He once told me that I would travel to far-off places and make a name for myself abroad."

Cangrande glanced at the visiting doctor. "What's wrong with that?"

"I hate traveling," confided Morsicato. "I get seasick."

The constable, nursing his pride as well as his ankle, drained the closest bottle. "Speaking as we are of prophecies, does this business have to do with the oracle, you think?"

Cangrande shrugged, wincing as he did.

Morsicato said, "I heard she was murdered. What did you do with the body?"

Villafranca said, "I hired some actors. They saw her burned."

"You should have called us," said Morsicato, gesturing toward himself and Fracastoro.

The constable shook his head. "She was beyond saving."

"What he's saying," interjected Fracastoro reprovingly, "is that we might have been able to tell you something about her death. Lord knows between us, we've seen enough battlefield wounds. It might have given you a clue to her murderer."

"Oh. I'll remember in the future," said Villafranca with a belch.

"I think we know who the murderer is, in any case," said Cangrande. He made a face as Fracastoro started sewing up a wound. Morsicato opened his mouth to suggest something, but a withering glance from the other doctor reduced him to watching. No one would tend Cangrande's wounds but his personal surgeon.

"The *spaventapasseri*," said Pietro.

"The scarecrow? That's a good name for him," agreed Cangrande. "And I believe the oracle's death was his message to us."

Pietro said, "How so?"

Villafranca told them about the oracle's head. Cangrande snorted. "An excellent *contrapasso*. Someone's an admirer of your father's," he said to Pietro.

"What?" asked Antony.

"The twisted head," said Pietro, "making her face backward. That's one of my father's tortures in Hell—it's the price seers and diviners get for trying to see the future."

"So whoever killed her was making a statement about her prophecy," deduced Morsicato.

"Or has a sick sense of humor," supplied Cangrande.

"Who is this scarecrow anyway?" demanded Antony. "What did he want?"

"Who he is will take some tracking, but we have a clue. The child ripped something from around his neck. A medallion I have never seen before. As to what he wants, we'll ask him when we find him."

The constable ventured an opinion. "Perhaps he thought to kidnap him for extortion purposes."

If he'd expected Cangrande to rise to the bait, he was disappointed.

"Should I go join the searching parties?" asked Pietro, rising. "I got the best look at him."

"God forbid," said Cangrande before either physician did. "Go to bed. Rest. That was a nasty clout you took. When you awaken tomorrow, come see me. Don't rush, though. I have a feeling I'll be busy." The Scaliger closed his eyes.

"What happened to the leopard?" asked Morsicato.

"Del Angelo thinks it should be destroyed. I think the animal was defending itself in a frightening circumstance and should therefore be allowed to live. We'll have it out tomorrow."

"What I don't understand," fretted Pietro, "is how he got down to the street so quickly."

"We'll look into it." The Scaliger's tired eyes half-opened. "So much has happened tonight, Pietro, that my manners have slipped. Tomorrow, remind me to thank you. Again."

Pietro flushed slightly. Antony winked at him. The Scaliger's eyes closed as Fracastoro dug his needle into the scarred and bloody back.

Morsicato had a few quiet words of advice for Pietro regarding the cuts on his forehead, which he listened to. Saying goodnight to everyone, he balanced on his crutch, preparing to go.

A pluck at his sleeve pulled him down so Antony could ask, "Where was Mari? Why didn't he help you?"

"He was talking to . . ." Pietro hesitated. "He was talking to your fiancée. They were across the loggia. He probably didn't realize what was happening until it was over."

Antony grunted. "Well, at least they get along. That's good news. Could you imagine it if they didn't?" He settled back, elevating his broken leg, waiting for a litter to transport him to his father's house.

Pietro exited the makeshift sickroom and crossed the hall toward the front door. Bailardino Nogarola was there, stomping the snow off his boots. Seeing Pietro, he smiled tiredly. "The very man. I swear, I'm moving to Rhodes, become a Hospitaller. Glad to see you up and about, boy."

"Glad to be here, my lord," replied Pietro.

"Word is a leopard cracked your skull."

"Yes, my lord."

"Damn stupid of you to let him."

"I guess I'm just not that bright." Pietro gestured to the bandaged claw marks just over his right eye.

"God's wounds! An inch lower and you'd be blind!"

"He just swatted at me. No sign of the kidnapper?"

Bailardino shook his head. "None. At least, not in the houses west of here. My men are still searching, but I promised Kat that I'd check on you. Yes, you! You've got to stop risking your neck for our family. It's giving her grey hairs." He laid a beefy hand on Pietro's shoulders. "She's taken a liking to you, you see. She'd hate to see anything happen to you. As would I."

A nearby tapestry shuddered. There was no wind in the hall to make it do so. Pietro and Bail both looked at it, their tension rising. A tiny lump in the tapestry was half hidden by shadows.

Bailardino raised his eyebrows at Pietro, who lifted his crutch. "Yes," said Bail loudly, easing his sword from its scabbard. "We've all taken a real liking to you, Pietro."

Pietro moved closer and, leaning his shoulder against the stone wall beside the tapestry, he struck the lump hard.

"Ouch!" yelped the lump. From underneath the tapestry bolted little Mastino della Scala, rubbing his shoulder and looking mutinous. "Uncle Bail, put your sword away!"

Pietro lowered his crutch and shook a fist. "You've already been told—don't spy."

Mastino glared daggers at him. "I'll fix you!" he cried, then ran through a door under the staircase.

Bailardino sheathed his weapon. "Fut. Little puke. Needs to be walloped more often." He shivered. "Damn, it's cold!"

"It must be hard, going out after the race."

"That reminds me," Bailardino said, "tell your friend Montecchio that that was the slickest move I've ever seen. And I've seen them all."

Pietro frowned. "What move?"

"What he did in the Palio. Slicker than goose shit."

"What did he do?"

"Heh. The little Capuan was going to win. Your boy knew it. So he kicks out at just the right moment and barks the little Capuan right on the shins. Took him down, and left the field clear to win." Bailardino chuckled.

Pietro's blood was in his boots. "How do you know?"

"Damn if it wasn't me the Capuan fell on! Mind you, if I could have done it myself, I would have. Those two are just too young for me—but I put up a good race for an old coot. You have to admit that!"

"Yes," agreed Pietro absently.

"Is Cangrande in the salon? I'll go in and tell the peacock that we're still holding our dicks, then I'll go over to our house and tell Kat you're unhurt. She wants to see you, by the way. Come by tomorrow, but not before noon. She's not at her best in the morning." Pietro agreed, they bid each other goodnight, and Bail went off in the direction Pietro had come.

It had been Pietro's intention to cross the Piazza della Signoria, climb the stairs to his father's room in the *Domus Bladorum,* and crawl into bed. Instead, tired as he was, Pietro stayed to search the Scaligeri palace. There was no sign of Mariotto, and he drew the line at knocking on the door of the Paduans' suite of rooms to ask if Gianozza was in.

An hour later, Pietro staggered into his father's suite. Poco was still out reveling, but Dante was writing by lantern light when Pietro opened the door. "Will the light bother you? The muse is upon me."

Apparently the poet had missed all the excitement—not surprising, if he was in the midst of penning new verses. He'd even failed to notice the new bandage that graced his son's forehead. Pietro grunted and simply fell into bed without removing his clothes. Within moments he was asleep.

Dante stood from his littered papers and ink and, crossing to his son's bedside, he pulled a coverlet over Pietro to keep him warm. He waited a moment, watching his son's sleeping form, then returned to his Purgatory.

✦　✧　✦

Had Pietro's search extended to the chapel across from the Scaligeri palace, he would have found his quarry. The candle had lowered but was still burning bright as Mariotto reached the second circle of Hell.

> *I began: "Poet, gladly would I speak*
> *with these two that move together*
> *and seem to be so light upon the wind."*
>
> *And he: "Once they are nearer, you will see:*
> *if you entreat them by the love*
> *that leads them, they will come."*

Gianozza was an excellent audience. Every now and then she made small noises of delight that encouraged her reader to continue. The rest of the time she kept her breathing audible but not rhythmic so he could be certain she was not asleep.

Now she leaned forward in delight. "Who are they? The lovers, which? He's already mentioned Cleopatra and Paris and Tristan. Is it Lancelot and Guinevere?"

"Be patient," chided Mari. "All will be revealed." He read Dante's entreaty to the lovers floating on the wind, and their pitiable reply. When asked to tell their tale, the man groaned as the woman spoke:

> *"Love, quick to kindle in the gentle heart,*
> *seized this man with the fair form*
> *taken from me. The way of it afflicts me still.*

"Love, which absolves no one beloved from loving,
seized me so strongly with his charm
that, as you see, it has not left me yet.

"Love brought us to one death.
Caïna waits for him who quenched our lives."
These words were borne from them to us.

Mariotto paused when he heard a snuffle from the connecting chamber. "Gianozza?" He pressed his faced against the carved grille that separated them. The door to the penitent's cell opened and he heard the girl flee from it at a run.

Oh no, he thought. *No no no! I've upset her! Was it my reading? Did I do something? Did I not do something? Should I go after her?*

She's Antony's bride. How can I chase her?

God, how can I not?

The door to his cell opened. The gust of air made the candle gutter then die. Quickly the girl stepped inside and closed it behind her, engulfing them both in pitch darkness. She collapsed weeping into Mariotto's arms.

"What?" asked Mariotto frantically. "What is it? What's wrong?"

"It's so beautiful!" She buried her face into his doublet, fingers clutching him in desperation.

Mariotto sat rocking her in his arms and pressing the top of her head with his cheek. That he did not kiss her then was probably the single greatest act of self-denial Mari had ever performed. He desperately wanted to shift in his seat, lest the girl notice exactly how excited she had made him. But he could not deny himself the pleasure of her weight in his lap. And part of him wanted her to know how excited he was. Their hands roamed, they breathed the same close air. As long as she wept he daren't caress her as he wished to, but he could stroke her hair, her neck, her shoulders. After a time the girl's tears ceased to flow. She pressed her face into his. "I'm so sorry, Ser Montecchio. You must think me a foolish girl."

"Mariotto," he said. "Please call me by my name. And no, not foolish, never that."

"Do you mind if I stay here?" she asked in a small voice. Mariotto found himself unable to answer. She settled in against him and he smelled once more the sweet orange blossoms. He drank it in as the gods of old drank nectar.

His hands began to stroke her back again, this time more insistently. In the tense, excited silence, the girl asked suddenly, "Who are they?"

"What? Oh! Her name is Francesca. Her lover is named Paolo. They were both murdered by her husband."

"Tell me their story," she said. He tried to relight the candle but she forestalled him. "You tell me. I'd much rather listen to you than Dante."

Trembling, he started to tell Francesca's story. "Francesca da Polenta of Ravenna was married to Gianciotto Malatesta da Verrucchio of Rimini."

"Gianciotto?" The name meant, literally, John the Lame. "Was he?"

Mariotto nodded as if he'd been in Florence thirty years before. "Yes. His body was twisted while his brother Paolo's limbs were straight. Both of them were brave and virtuous, and together fought in many battles. Around the year 1280, Gianciotto sent his little brother to Francesca's father to offer a marriage contract. When Paolo arrived in Ravenna, Francesca mistook him for her future husband and agreed to the match. When she arrived in Rimini, she was presented with Paolo's older brother with the twisted limbs. They married, of course, but his business kept him away from home and he always left Francesca in the care of his younger brother."

"And they . . . they had a liaison?"

At this precise moment Mariotto saw the beauty Pietro's father had given the story of the two lovers. "They were sitting, reading a French romance— the story of Lancelot and Guinevere." In the darkness, her face close to his, Mari was having difficulty finding words. "They—I can't say it as well as the poem, but they were so excited by the story, so moved in emotion and spirit, that when they looked at each other they couldn't help . . ."

Her mouth found his, or perhaps his found hers. The kiss was tentative at first. Mari was afraid almost to breathe. She pressed harder. He responded, and their hands clutched at each other in the darkness. Breathing in the smell of her, his lips moved from her mouth to her neck. She gave a wonderful little moan. Encouraged, his fingers traced a line from the base of her neck to her shoulder, from there to her breast. She shivered and said, "Oh Mariotto, Mariotto, be my Paolo . . ."

"My Francesca, my Julia . . ."

A thudding against the doors of the church made them both start. Gianozza wrenched herself away and out the door of the confessional before Mari could speak. He heard the side door of the church open and slam shut. The drunks at the main doors carried on past the church, not knowing the moment they had ruined. Shaking, Mariotto sat lamely in the priest's seat and wondered what in God's name he was supposed to do now.

✦　◇　✦

Gianozza pressed her way through the revelers to the palace door, where she was admitted at once. She ran up the stairs and didn't stop until she reached the small chamber adjoining her uncle's rooms. She bolted through the door into the lit room, expecting and deserving a scolding from her unfeeling chambermaid.

The room was indeed occupied, but not by a woman. Reclined deep in a chair, head in hands, legs splayed out before him, was a comely knight holding his face as if he thought it might fall off. As she closed the door his head came up.

The hungover Marsilio da Carrara gazed blearily at his breathless cousin. "So—where the devil have you been?"

TWENTY-FOUR

It had been a long fortnight for Antonia Alaghieri, who had never traveled long distances before. The jostling of the carriage often made her ill. The time of year made roads less reliable. New snow crunched beneath the horses' hooves. Her anxiousness to join her father had her peering out of the little windows every few minutes, staring at the landscape until her cheeks froze.

The driver of the hired gig despaired of a decent tip and was eager to rid himself of this troublesome child. Had he not been promised a huge sum when he delivered her unmolested to Verona, he would have left her and her two servants in one of the inns they had passed. Or simply by the side of the road. Anything to ditch the little harpy.

The sun was perhaps two hours away from its zenith when Verona's famous forty-eight towers came into view. Discarding comfort, Antonia leaned frantically out of the window to see it. If she had come from the north, she would have been able to look down on the city. Coming from the south, she was blind to all but the vaguest impression as they passed through the gates.

That Verona was similar to Florence somehow surprised her. Like the city of her birth, it was cleft by a river. The roof tiles were of a slightly different hue. Many of the buildings seemed new, but enough aged ones were intermingled to give a sense of gravitas.

It was certainly as busy as Florence. There were crowds of people *every-*

where. Her driver called around for directions to the palace of the Scaligeri. Twice they were turned the wrong way before someone gave them proper instructions. They ended up crossing a bridge that must have been more than a thousand years old yet was solid as ever.

Antonia was studying the cityscape when a young couple riding in the other direction drew her attention. The girl was about Antonia's age, but beautiful. Raven hair and pale skin, full lips set in a bewitching smile. The boy beside the girl was handsome, too. Just a touch older, it made them look perfect for each other—girls always looked more mature than boys their age. His dark hair was longish, but overall he was well-groomed. His clothes under the riding cloak were quite fine.

Following them were two more young men. Something in the line of the chin of one proclaimed a relation to the girl—distant, but evident. The other wore the grey robes of a Franciscan.

The party seemed in a hurry. Both the lay young men looked around furtively. The girl tried to hide inside her hood. Noticing Antonia staring, she pulled the hood tighter about her face. In moments they had crossed over the bridge and out of sight.

It was an hour before noon when the carriage pulled up to the stables of the Scaliger's palace. A groom ran to fetch a steward. In moments, servants arrived to remove her three small boxes of luggage.

Antonia paid the driver herself. He looked curiously angry when he realized she had been carrying the money with her all along, thus confirming her suspicions that, had he known, he would have robbed and murdered her. With that idea fixed firmly in her head, she in turn confirmed his suspicions about the tip. He remounted his gig and cantered off, grumbling.

The palace servants led her and her followers across a beautiful square and into a grand building—not the main palace, she was informed, but the original Scaliger domicile, the *Domus Bladorum*. As they entered her father's rooms, she was nearly frantic at the prospect of meeting her father for the first time. All through the journey, excitement had fought the fear within her. She recognized that her coming here would forever alter her relationship with her father. Until now she was the beloved confidante, far away, faceless—safe. At a distance he could impose on her features the visage of his lost love. Meeting might destroy his illusion, ruin the bond she had struggled to form from the time she was seven.

Nevertheless, disappointment set in when she discovered the rooms empty. Dante's steward said, "Your father has gone to view the Basilica of San Zeno. Ser Alaghieri—"

"Who?"

"Your brother Pietro, miss," said the steward. "You won't have heard, but he was knighted yesterday. Your brother accompanied Master Dante, but said he would be calling on Lord Nogarola this afternoon. Master Jacopo did not return last night." Years of reading between the lines allowed Antonia to guess what the steward was implying, but neither commented on it. "I shall settle your possessions in the chamber we have set aside and instruct your servants to their new duties here while they inform me of your requirements. Would you like a refreshment?"

She would not. The steward offered to guide her, but she declined that offer as well. She set off back the way she had come and promptly got lost. She turned one corner then another, trying to retrace her steps in the unfamiliar city. Finally she admitted to herself that she had no idea where she was. Turning about, she collided with a man on crutches who was coming the other way. "Oh, I'm so sorry!" She reached out to steady him. Despite the wooden splints encasing one of his legs he was a full two heads taller than Antonia. "Please forgive me," she said. "I was careless."

"Don't worry about it," he said easily. "I'm still getting used to these things."

There was an awkward pause. His eyes were narrowed, examining her as closely. Moving his head to the right to get a look at her in profile, he ventured, "Beatrice, right?"

She took in a little breath. "I am the daughter of Dante Alaghieri," she said. For the past week she had used the other pronunciation without receiving a smack on the back of the head.

The man nodded. "You look a little like him," he said. At that moment the sandy-haired brute became her favorite person in the world. Other than her father, of course. "I'm a friend of Pietro's. My name is Antony—Antonio Capulletto."

Her brow furrowed. "I've heard of Pietro's friend Antony," she said cautiously, "but I thought that the surname was different."

He laughed. "Until yesterday, it was. We took it up last night. It's an old name, but all the Capelletti died out years ago."

"Oh." He had a bald way of talking that was difficult to deal with. "Do you know where my father is or where my brothers are?"

Her heart sank when he shook his head. "I'm surprised Pietro's out," he said. "What with his wounds and all."

Antonia's eyes opened wide. "I thought his leg had healed."

"Oh, his leg's fine. I mean the cuts he got from the leopard." Antonia looked at him in shock. "Oh! You don't know! Oh, shit—I mean . . . oh hell! Look—it's like this . . ." He quickly outlined the previous night's adventures. He concluded, saying, "He was fine when he went up to bed. He probably just wanted to get out. Hey, I'm looking for someone, too. We can search the palace together—if you don't mind walking about with a cripple."

Antonia fell into step beside him, grateful to have a guide. Socially, Capulletto was not particularly graceful, but he was definitely charming in a rough way. She could understand why her brother liked him.

Something was slung in a small case over his back. In shape it looked like a book. "What have you got there?"

"Oh, yes! If we find your father, he can sign it for me. It's a copy of his book. I bought it this morning for Gianozza."

Capulletto instantly went up in Antonia's estimation. He was clearly smitten with this Gianozza—her name peppered their conversation. She learned that Antony's leg had been broken the night before, in a footrace that his friend Mariotto had won. "Though if I hadn't hit my shin on something, I would have won easily. Bad luck, that's all." He obviously bore Mariotto no grudge for winning. But the same couldn't be said of the winner of the horse race—Antonio couldn't disguise his dislike for the Paduan named Carrara.

Gianozza, Mariotto, Marsilio—those three names were the cornerstones in young Capulletto's conversation as they strolled. Mostly the names meant nothing to her. She made no connection with the three fine riders on the Roman bridge.

Eventually they came across a man Antony knew, and the Capnan arranged for her to be taken to San Zeno's. To her father.

✦ ◇ ✦

Being a sensible fellow, Pietro had intended to spend the better part of the day in bed. But Dante had been up early with the discovery that his younger son hadn't been home all night. Out whoring, the poet was sure. Pietro suggested that they walk over and look at San Zeno, the church he'd passed during the race. It was intended as a distraction, and Pietro's father accepted it as such. Tullio d'Isola arranged a guide for them, and they set off.

"I hear you're a hero again," said Dante as they walked.

"With the scars to prove it," said Pietro.

"Serves you right," said the poet. "Besides, nothing should come easy." He paused, then said, "Still, I'm glad you saved the boy."

"Me too," said Pietro. He suddenly recalled his appointment with Donna Katerina and informed his father that he had to leave their jaunt a little early. Dante was sanguine. "San Zeno sits next to the river. I can watch the water and write." He patted the satchel at his hip. "I came prepared, you see. In case the hero was needed to slay another giant."

Not knowing how to reply, Pietro walked on, Mercurio pulling hard on his leash. Pietro wore a heavy cloak to disguise himself, but the crutch and the dog gave him away, and people waved or cheered him as he passed. Dante made several noises of impatience, but was smiling nonetheless.

Their guide pointed out a synagogue, and they paused several minutes to examine it. Verona owned a large Jewish population, but, with the exception of Manuel, Pietro had rarely seen any outside the marketplace. In other cities, of course, Jews were easily recognized by the yellow stars they were, by law, forced to wear. Here there were no such signs, just the odd caps they wore of their own volition marking them as Hebrews. With so many other types of men in much stranger dress, Verona's Jews did not stand out.

Dante and his son spent two chilly but instructive hours inside the basilica of Verona's patron saint, looking at tombs, frescos, windows, and the famous doors. Then Pietro limped back toward the Piazza della Signoria in plenty of time for his meeting with Donna Katerina.

Aching, stiff, cold, wishing he'd ridden Canis and cursing the dog that strained forward, Pietro knocked on the door to the Nogarola house. It was across the street from Santa Maria Antica, at the back of the main Scaligeri palace. He was greeted warmly by Katerina's servants, and after they took his cloak they admitted him into an upstairs sitting-room with fires blazing. The doors to the balcony were open to provide ventilation for the smoking braziers.

The room was well ordered for one that housed so rambunctious a child. Perhaps it was because he wasn't walking yet. The staff had to be dreading the day that tiny Cesco became ambulatory.

The child himself was in evidence, sitting with a new nurse on the far side of the chamber. The girl was trying her best to entertain him with colored puppets with wooden heads. They were carved in the style of classical allegorical figures. The boy seemed particularly fascinated with the crimson head of Malice, banging it against a tiny tiger. *Well,* thought Pietro, blinking, *it looks a little like a leopard.*

Mercurio bolted from Pietro's side to press his nose into Cesco's face. The boy giggled as the young hound snuffed him, then began licking his face. Cesco's tiny fingers grasped the coin at the hound's neck.

"Mercurio! Heel!" Pietro called to no avail.

"Let them play." Close to the child sat Katerina holding a small loom. In a long patch of sunlight that streamed in from the open balcony doors, two chairs were set out facing her. One was occupied, with a servant hovering over the high back. Pietro blinked. It was the Moor standing before him.

The occupant of the chair rose. He was in his middle years, told only by the touch of grey at his temples. Well dressed and well made, he might have been handsome but for the fact that he was all chin. The cleft in it was the size of Pietro's knuckle, and Pietro had an absurd desire to see if it fit. It was a moment before Pietro registered the outstretched hand. "Ser Alaghieri, congratulations. You had quite a day—but then, I could have told you that!" One eye above the monstrous chin dropped in a wink.

"And you are?"

"Who am I?" The man turned to Katerina. "You haven't . . . ? I mean, madam, when you called upon me, I thought you would trumpet it from the—"

"Pietro, may I introduce you to Ignazzio da Palermo, astrologer and diviner to kings and princes. Theodoro of Cadiz you have already met."

"Yes." Pietro crossed to take the Moor's hand. "You saved my life. Thank you." As the Moor inclined his head, it was as difficult not to stare at the scarred neck as at his master's chin. An odd pair.

Katerina gestured to the open chair. As Pietro sat, he noticed three scrolls lying out on a table. Each was made from long, thick parchment sealed with yellow wax, the color that best revealed signs of tampering. It looked as if the seals had been covered again with a light layer of honey. What were these papers that they required such precautions?

Katerina turned her head. "Marianna, put Cesco in his crib. Luciana, please stoke the fires a little. Then you may both leave us. We shan't need you. If the fires require tending I shall prevail upon my guests."

With a wary glance at the dark-skinned guest, the nurse carried the child to a wooden crib with high barred walls. Little Cesco was up on his feet in a moment, holding onto the bars of his cage for support, reaching though the bars for Mercurio, who had followed him. *He'll be walking soon,* thought Pietro. *Look at him. He isn't even wobbling.*

Both girls bowed their way out of the chamber, closing the doors firmly. Pietro heard them whispering to each other as they walked down the corridor.

"They're still upset about Nina," said Katerina. "Are you well?"

"Quite well, lady. Thank you."

"No. Thank you." She set her loom aside. "Ser Alaghieri, you have taken several wounds for a cause that you don't understand. We are about to remedy that. It is time to bring you into our little circle. What we discuss now, only five people in the world are aware of. My brother is one. The boy's mother is another. Ignazzio and Theo here. I myself. No one else—not my husband, no one—knows what we are going to tell you today."

"I—I'm honored."

"There is a price. By hearing this, you will be obligated to help us shape future events. I don't put you under this obligation lightly, for an obligation it is. If you wish to decline hearing—"

"Madonna," interrupted Ignazzio. "This is unfair. He will be incapable of saying no. He will also be unable to retreat before you, for fear of losing your respect. The stars have chosen him. Having been chosen, it is foolish to offer him escape. He will not take it, and the offer can do nothing but act as a salve for our consciences."

"You are right, of course. Shall we begin?" She lifted a scroll and handed it to Ignazzio. Placing a board across his lap, his fingers broke the honey-covered seal. It was hard work, because honey was prone to crumbling. At last Ignazzio unfurled the wide parchment on the makeshift desk.

Pietro looked and saw multicolored lines, various signs of the zodiac, and several small notations in Greek and Latin. A star chart.

"This was made many years ago," said Ignazzio da Palermo, "for a newborn son, the third son of Alberto della Scala by his wife."

Pietro remembered Cangrande mentioning a star chart and what that chart said. To Katerina he began, "Your brother said that he'd consulted Benentendi—"

"Benentendi!" scoffed Ignazzio. "A charlatan! Why, he wouldn't—"

Katerina cut him off by asking Pietro, "How much do you know of astrology?"

"Some. My father insisted I have some formal training in it when I was younger."

The astrologer gestured to the parchment before him. "This chart is plain and clear. Francesco della Scala—Cangrande to you—is destined for great things. Probably the most important of his aspects is the fact that Mars is in the house of Aries, which creates both his great skill as a leader and his recklessness, his need to prove himself in personal valor. Interesting, too, is the position of Saturn. It is also in Aries, one of the few contradictions in the Capitano's chart. In that placement, Saturn usually leads to a serious self-doubt in leaders. In the Scaliger it seems to have had an opposite effect, probably because it shares the house with Mars. It has led the Scaliger to reject fear in its entirety." Pietro noted that, unlike his master, the Moor was not looking at the chart. Instead, he watched Pietro. Unsettling.

"That is the thing I worry about most," observed Katerina. "He's never acknowledged fear."

Ignazzio pointed to some lines for Pietro's benefit. "There are few sextiles, trines, and squares in his chart. Do you know what those are?"

"It's geometry, isn't it? The angles of one planet to another at the time of birth?"

"Correct. Different angles create different relationships between the planets. There were ten such relationships formed at the time of Cangrande's birth—fewer than normal. Most of them are minor—three trines, two conjunctions, three squares, one sextile, and one pure opposition. It's the last two that are the most interesting. In Cangrande's chart, Mercury forms a sextile with Mars, giving him his sharp, strategic mind. But Mercury also forms an opposition with Uranus. He is aware of his talents and must fight to retain his humility. It is interesting that Uranus, the creator of self-doubt, should have pushed this man so far in the other direction."

Pietro detected an unvoiced laugh from Katerina. Himself, he was feeling uncomfortable, as if he were spying on Cangrande just by looking at this chart.

The astrologer continued. "The Scaliger's sun sign is Pisces, the last sign of the Zodiac. It has created in him a strong sense of his stature. Not that he wishes to aggrandize himself, of course. More that—how to say—he wishes to receive his due."

"That's only fair," said Pietro.

Ignazzio rolled up the chart. "All in all, it is the chart of a capable, intelligent man with finite potential. Being finite, that potential will be achieved.

My man here was present at the hour of his birth, he took the signs personally. Cangrande will succeed martially and politically."

"But no more," said Katerina, retrieving the scroll.

"Then what he told me is true," murmured Pietro. "He's not the Greyhound."

Katerina said sharply, "He told you that? When?"

"The night at the church, just before—" He paused, trying not to look at
the Moor and the astrologer.

Katerina said, "You may speak freely."

"Just before Cesco's mother arrived."

Katerina clucked her tongue. "That night must have been harder on him
than I supposed. Because it's true, Pietro. My brother is not *Il Veltro*."

As understanding dawned, Pietro glanced over at the child standing in his
crib, holding on to the bars to keep himself upright. Mercurio was curled up
next to the bars of the crib. *I know what you are, now,* thought Pietro. Aloud
he said, "Cesco is *Il Veltro*."

"Yes," said Katerina.

"And no," said the Moor.

✦ ◇ ✦

Antonia entered the Basilica of San Zeno shaking from head to toe. Not from
cold. The sanctuary was empty save for some monks. She retreated into the
attached garden beside the river. Here on a bench was a man with a dark
beard, hunched up against the biting wind.

The long, almost beakish nose made her heart stop beating. Years of
studying portraits had made her familiar with all her father's features. But
that beard! Pietro had written of it, but she hadn't really expected something
so huge and black, with small veins of grey, that reached almost down to his
breastbone.

She nearly cried out and ran to him, but checked herself sharply. *Compose
yourself! He won't appreciate a little girl.* Forcing a measured walk, she
crossed to his side—not in front of him, which would have demanded
attention—and stood quietly waiting for him to look up. He was writing.
How wonderful! He was writing!

For Dante's part, he was in the midst of penning the sixth canto of the new
poem. Part of his mind registered the presence of a mortal being at his side,

but she shared the space with Virgil and Sordello and the bulk of his attention was engaged in their meeting. After a time he glanced at her in annoyance. "I don't sign manuscripts," he said brusquely. "No matter what you may have been told."

"I know, *Pater*," said Antonia, smiling.

He continued to write, trying to banish the girl from his mind. *Ella non ci dicëa alcuna cosa* (she's still there) *ma lasciavane gir* (what was it she said?), *solo sguardando a guisa di leon* (she said *Pater*—does she think I'm a priest?) *quando si posa . . .*

His head came up. He looked at the girl, squinting hard. Slowly he laid his quill aside. Standing, he looked down into a face that was rather like his own.

"Beatrice," he said, nodding.

From that moment on, had he given her the back of his boot or berated her in the foulest terms imaginable, it would not have mattered. He had set the seal on the happiest day of Antonia's life.

✦ ◇ ✦

"What do you mean, yes and no?"

Katerina said, "I believe he is."

Pietro looked at the Moor. "You're not sure?"

The large black man's expression did not change. Ignazzio answered for him. "It may be in his stars. It may not. Sadly, I was not present for his birth. None of us were." He took a newer scroll from Katerina and began the work of breaking the seal.

Pietro pointed out an objection. "So why—I mean, why did we go to get him before a chart was even made?"

Ignazzio gestured to Katerina. "I also created a chart for the lady when she was young. It was unequivocal. A child given into her care, a child that was not her own, would grow up to be *Il Veltro*."

Pietro studied Katerina's composed face. "You thought it was your brother."

"I hoped so."

"So you raised him as if he were going to be the Greyhound."

"Yes."

"But you had his chart."

Katerina's eyes grew flinty. "Is that an accusation?"

"No—no, lady, I just . . . I'm just confused."

The Moor spoke, his voice rasping painfully out of the scarred throat. "The chart said he would be a great man within Italy."

"No," said Katerina, "don't soften it. I never told my brother he was the Greyhound. I never told him he wasn't. Because of his name, because of his extraordinary skill, people began to talk. If he listened, it is no fault of mine. I raised him, Pietro, as I saw fit. I believe I was successful. He reached his potential and more. If he assumed he was the mythic hero, it did no harm."

No harm? A man raised to believe himself a creature of destiny, only to discover his destiny belonged to another. It was a miracle he hadn't turned out to be a monster.

Katerina's lips turned down. "You will be gratified to learn the noble astrologer and his major domo here disagreed with me. When Francesco turned fifteen he was shown this chart, against my express wishes. After that, my relationship with my brother became somewhat—strained." She crossed to a brazier and prodded it with a poker. "But if that is the price I must pay, I will. It has always been my opinion that we must take an active hand in our fates. I intend to raise Cesco in the same manner I raised my brother—as if he were the Greyhound. If it proves not to be true, as it did with Cangrande, again there is no harm done." She used the poker to point at the parchment now spread over Ignazzio's lap. "But look at it, Pietro. Look."

Pietro did. Immediately he could tell there was something wrong about it. Painted lines crossed each other, as in Cangrande's chart, but double thick, and double in number. This was because so many of the planets shared the same positions. The Sun, Mercury, and Venus were all in the first house, clustered together. The latter two formed strong relationships with the Moon, which was in Aries, while the Sun formed a sextile with Leo. Other lines crisscrossed the chart, forming odd geometrical patterns. He suddenly wished he knew more about the subject.

Ignazzio said, "Odd, is it not? Such clustering is rare."

"What does it mean?"

"It means that this person's character is full of contradictory impulses. The child's sun is in Gemini, ruled by Mercury, which is also in his first house. His personality, therefore, resonates with the traits of that planet. He will be restless, and will dabble in all manner of trades and experiences. He will be free, swift as quicksilver. He will prize his wit above all else.

"Then there is the Moon—the first contradiction. It is in his eleventh house, in Aries, and also forms a strong relationship with Mercury. He will not be ruled by reason, but by his dreams. It will cause unbalance in his emotions. He will be detached from them, as if in conflict between his mind and his heart. But because of the Moon's similar relationship with Jupiter, he will suffer from an excess of emotion. Among the many ill-effects that may cause, the worst is that it may—*may*—dampen his ambition."

Pietro again glanced at the child in the crib who was no longer paying any attention to the adults. He was fiddling with the bars on the far side of the crib, pulling at them and swinging himself backward and forward, teasing the hound who jumped about with delight.

Ignazzio drew Pietro's attraction back to the chart by tracing a finger along a single line, much interwoven with those about it. "Let us look at his own planet, Mercury. It was in Cancer at the hour of his birth, and in his first house. The sign will cause him to be extremely susceptible to outside influences. The house will make him adapt quickly to any situation . . ." Sign by sign, house by house, they went through the child's chart. Pietro was amazed at the number of times the words *willful, inventive, intuitive, witty, quick,* and *aggressive* came up. But always were the warnings that pitfalls lay in the realm of emotion. *Temperamental. Anxious. High-strung. Fickle.* He would suffer from periods of extreme apathy. He would have difficulty choosing any single path. Prolonged relationships with anyone were problematic, especially his relations with women. There were three deep loves, but only one marriage. Venus was especially dangerous to the child as he grew to manhood. As with them all, he had to use his strong will to dominate these faults within him or else fall victim to their influences.

Behind them all was Mercury.

"Here you are," said the astrologer, pointing at a symbol.

Pietro straightened. "Me?"

"At least, I believe this is you. You have saved his life. If I am correct, you have a lasting influence on him. You are destined to be a major part of his life." Ignazzio sat back, with a quick glance to the Moor. "That concludes the basics. There is nothing," he emphasized, "to indicate he will not overcome these faults. But there are many pitfalls before the child. More by far than the Capitano ever owned." A finger unfurled to trace a spot on the chart as yet untouched. "Now we move on to portents of the day itself. As you may have heard, there were many favorable omens when the Scaliger was born. My man here was present to observe them himself. As I said, though, no one here was present for the birth of this child. Nor have we been able to find a reliable witness to the events of that night."

"When was he born?" asked Pietro.

Katerina had taken up her loom again. Working it, she said, "He was born in the middle of the night, in Padua, on the Ides of June."

The astrologer continued. "I arrived in Venice at the start of the Roman year. I first made my way to Vicenza to interview the lady and meet the child. I then set out for Padua, where I interviewed several men in my own profession. I have been unable to create a clear picture in my mind as to the movements of the lesser stars that night. Several observers have said that a star fell from right to left—that is, east to west—at about the hour of the boy's birth. That would be a great omen, one of the finest the boy could have. This chart is based on that observation. It creates stability for all these contradictions and amplifies his traits. He will thrive. He will attain a greatness unknown in this land since the Caesars. I have no doubt that if that was the omen, the child will find nothing but success."

Katerina said, "Based on that chart, he will certainly be the Greyhound."

Pietro heard the unspoken omission. "I take it that isn't all there is to say."

"No," said Katerina, lowering her loom and handing across the last roll of parchment. "There is another side to the coin."

Ignazzio's nails scrabbled at the last seal. "That last chart was based on the reports that the star had fallen from east to west. I have one man whose opinion I trust more than the others. He insists that a star did cross the sky that night, at that hour. But he swears that it passed from west to east." He unfurled the final scroll. "This is the chart based on that report."

The houses and planets were all the same as in the last chart, but the relationships were subtly changed. Lines crossed at strange angles. All the green and blue lines of the last chart had become red and yellow.

"How is that possible?" asked Pietro. "The planets didn't move." He'd never been so interested in astrology in all his life.

"They didn't have to move. This falling star changed their meaning. Take Aries in the twelfth house. On the former chart it would cause him to be placid, slow to anger. That was based on the movement of the star coming from the east. But here," he pointed to the symbol of Aries on the chart, "his anger grows irrational. The house does not move, nor do the stars. But their influence is altered dramatically." He went through and showed a dozen places where the change of direction created differing interpretations. In each instance, where in the last chart the darker impulses were overcome, here they were dominant. "The core elements remain the same," the astrologer concluded. "He will be a leader of men, a warrior of surpassing excellence, a thinker. But who he will lead, whom he will fight for, and what he will think are uncertain."

"All because we can't determine the direction of the star that crossed the sky that night?"

"Yes."

"Is there any way to tell which it was?"

The Moor said, "We wait and see."

As the scrolls were furled, wanting resealing, Katerina gazed intently at Pietro. "I want to see this child's future be the brighter of the two laid out here. Do you agree?"

"Yes," said Pietro. "Of course. But what can I do?"

"Just know, Pietro. You are in his chart. You are a part of his life. You have to know what is at stake. Cangrande is not the Greyhound. Cesco is—or may be."

Pietro had to ask. "Does the Capitano know I'm here?"

The lady frowned. "My brother and I disagree about how destiny is created. He wants the boy to find his own way, and for us to simply allow this to happen. I disagree. I think we should act in every way as if the first of those charts is the correct one. We should foster all the good traits in him, and sharply curtail the lesser ones. It is what your father says—we must actively interpret the stars." Pietro opened his mouth, and Katerina said, "The answer is no, Pietro. He does not know we have told you."

Pietro thought for a few moments. "Is there any way the kidnapper could know? Is this connected to the murder of the oracle?"

"You heard her prophecy," said Katerina. "A tortured youth who will cause Verona's destruction? She was paid to say it, so I have no fear about it coming to pass. But her allusion to a child indicates that someone knows how important Cesco will be. The question is who."

"And why," said Pietro. "I mean, what would someone gain by kidnapping the boy? Why not just kill him? Ransom?"

"More like to have a hand in the destiny of Italy," said Katerina.

"To thwart the stars," said the Moor.

"Or just for revenge on Cangrande," said Ignazzio.

Pietro was struggling with another question, this one for the astrologer. "This might sound foolish."

"There are no foolish questions," said Ignazzio, patting Pietro's shoulder.

"Uh, right. I was just wondering—what if there were two stars?"

Ignazzio da Palermo blinked several times. "What?"

I knew it was a stupid question, thought Pietro. "Never mind."

The Moor darted out from behind Ignazzio's chair, crushing Pietro's shoulder with his grip. "Speak."

"Well—that night, the night Cesco was born—if there were two stars, what would that mean?"

Ignazzio was leaning around the Moor to listen. "Two. One from the east *and* one from the west."

Stupido, stupido, stupido. "That crossed in the sky, yes. Would that change anything?"

A stunned expression hung on the astrologer's face. The Moor released Pietro's shoulder and crossed to stare into the brazier. Katerina and Pietro watched Ignazzio, whose eyes seemed unfocused.

The Moor said, "From the mouth of babes."

Ignazzio roused himself. "Donna, forgive me. Ser Pietro has seen in a single hour a possibility I have not seen in weeks. I should be flogged."

"Never mind," said Katerina hungrily. "What would it mean"

Ignazzio leaned forward, pressing his hands together. His smooth demeanor had vanished. He seemed more like a student puzzling through an unexpected test. "We have no way of knowing."

The Moor said, "My master means it would depend on which star was closer, and which farther away. The angles of descent, while relatively unimportant singly, would be vastly important if two were involved."

Katerina arched an eyebrow. "I want that chart made."

"Charts. Two at least. More, with variations." It was the Moor, playing the role of haggler for his master.

"I don't care how long it takes or the cost, get it done."

"As you wish." Ignazzio stood and bowed to Pietro, his façade back in place. "You have my respect, sir."

"I—it wasn't . . ." Flustered, Pietro didn't believe he'd done anything wonderful. Thankfully a noise rose outside, some commotion in the street. He looked away from the astrologer, listening to the shouts that came burbling up from beyond the shutters.

"What the devil . . . ?" Katerina walked to the balcony, Ignazzio and Pietro trailing her. In the street below people were huddling in clumps, whispering, some scuttling back and forth between the islands of men. Some looked shocked, others tittered with glee. The overwhelming majority seemed to be amused, if rather darkly. For perhaps a hundred fifty men and a fair number of women something was deliciously exciting.

The doors to the suite opened and Bailardino came striding in, looking no worse for his long night drinking. "Well, here's a coil! It'll cause some joy in Padua, I guarantee it!"

"What's happened?" asked his wife.

"You haven't heard? It's all the rage. Young Montecchio has eloped!"

"With whom?" asked Katerina. Pietro leaned heavily against the wall. He didn't have to ask. *Mari, what have you done?*

Bailardino was mirthful. "With Capecelatro's little bride—the little Carrara girl! She scampered away this morning with her cousin to meet Montecchio and a priest!"

That opened up Pietro's eyes in a hurry. "Marsilio was there?"

"He acted as witness! Gave the bride away—so the rumors say, anyway."

"Where did this story originate?" asked Katerina. She obviously doubted its authenticity. Pietro didn't, but he was interested in the answer.

"The Carrara boy sent a note to his uncle immediately following and ordered his page to read it out in front of Cangrande and the court!" He chuckled. "He's got balls, does that Paduan. His uncle was furious! Giacomo can't rebuke him too strongly in public, though I imagine there will be hoarse voices in their suite tonight."

"Does Antony know?" asked Pietro, voicing the only question that really mattered.

"How can he not? The whole city is buzzing with it. Old man Capecelatro must be pulling out his hair. He was telling me last night how delighted he was with the match, that he wanted to bring Padua and Verona closer together though this alliance."

"Well, this will do that as well," said Katerina evenly. "There are few families more at the heart of Veronese politics than the Montecchi."

"Capecelatro won't take this sitting down, you can bet on it," Bailardino said with a grin.

"Not Capecelatro," said Pietro, shaking his head. "Not anymore."

Bailardino snapped his fingers. "You're right! Now that's irony for you." Frowning, Bailardino noticed the astrologer for the first time. "Oh, you're here, are you? You probably think it was inevitable? Your precious planets were spinning at the right moment, and Montecchio got an itch in his pants?"

"I'm not sure it had anything to do with the stars," said Ignazzio.

"Oh, you're not?" Bailardino's dislike was palpable.

"Numerology. Names have power. When a man takes upon himself a new name, he changes. So too does his fate."

"Horseshit," growled Bailardino.

"This is an old argument," said Katerina. "It does nothing about the problem at hand. What has my brother done to quell this potential disaster?"

Bailardino turned his back on the astrologer. "He sent a messenger to Montecchio's castle with a summons for Mariotto to appear at the court. Until then, there's nothing he can do. It's up to the Capulletti now. How they respond will determine everything."

While the older occupants of the room stood discussing events, Pietro returned to his seat. A foul lump was growing in his belly. *I saw it coming and I did nothing. How can I face Antonio?*

Something lapped Pietro's hand. Mercurio was pressing his muzzle into Pietro's palm. So, the hound had finally left little Cesco. Pietro's eyes flickered left to the crib, and he blinked. The crib was empty.

Oh God! Cesco's gone again!

Before he could even voice an alarm something tugged at his sleeve. Pietro saw Cesco looking up at him. Little Cesco, aged less than one, standing upright without aid. In his hand he held one of the puppets he had been playing with.

Pietro's eyes returned to the crib. All the bars were in place. *How did he get out?*

The wooden puppet head banged against Pietro's shoulder. The boy's face brightened as Pietro took it from him. Task done, Cesco turned and walked to the balcony. He didn't toddle. He didn't wobble. He walked. It was an easy movement, well-practiced. As if—

As if he's been doing it for weeks.

Pietro ran his fingers over the puppet in his hand. The tiger puppet. Near enough to a leopard. How astute was this child? How had he gotten out of the crib? And how long had he been hiding the fact that he could walk? For he had been hiding it, Pietro was certain.

The conversation stopped as the other adults noticed the little boy walking over to the balcony rail. Bailardino shouted, "The little imp! Kat! You never told me he could walk!"

Katerina stared at her foster son. "I didn't know."

Near the balcony Cesco turned and grinned. Ignoring the three men, he looked to Katerina. The lady met his eyes, then deliberately sat down and lifted her loom to continue weaving.

The child's face fell. Turning again, Cesco's small hands gripped the carved stone railing of the balcony. The slats between the rungs were just wide enough for his body to pass though . . .

Mercurio barked sharply. Pietro saw the child's intent and leapt forward, but stumbled on his bad leg. The Moor was faster and got a handful of the child's shirt between the fingers of his right hand. Pietro was there moments later, reaching around and over the railing to grasp Cesco, twisting in the Moor's grip. Angry, intent on being free, the child kicked and hit. To the mingled relief and disappointment of the crowd below, they brought the child over the railing and back into the room.

Holding Cesco hard against himself, Pietro turned to Katerina. Standing, she said, "Thank you. Obviously we should keep rooms on the ground floor from now on. And I'll ask the carpenters to construct a new crib."

Cesco began to wail. He shook his tiny fists and wriggled violently. The lady lifted him out of Pietro's arms. The child's fighting became more frantic. Ignoring him, Katerina said, "Pietro, would you be kind enough to carry a message to my brother? Tell him, please, to reconsider calling Ser Montecchio to court just yet. Though I agree the young man must account for his actions, I believe that doing so now would only add fuel to the flames."

Pietro bowed formally, his eyes not on the lady but on the furious child who beat at her breast and chin as best he could. But he never kicked her pregnant belly. Bailardino made to take the child up, but the lady sat in her chair, the child a tempest in her arms. "No, Bail. He is my cross to bear."

The Moor scooped up the scrolls. "With your permission, Donna, I shall remove these and have them resealed."

Katerina nodded, hands pinioning the wrestling child. Pietro lifted his crutch from the floor and began walking toward the exit. At a loss, Bailardino walked over to a carafe and poured himself a drink. He downed the goblet's contents at a gulp. "Would you like a glass, Kat?"

"Yes, if you please. Oh, Pietro? Remember, as before . . ."

Pietro nodded. *"Herkos odonton,"* he said.

The lady smiled thinly. "Just so."

Preparing to leave, Pietro had to pull hard on Mercurio's collar. Ignazzio and the Moor followed him out, the little man bowing several times to Katerina.

When the door was closed behind them, both Ignazzio and Pietro released a shared breath. "I've never seen anything like that," said Pietro.

"I'm not a subscriber to possession," said Ignazzio. "But still . . ."

Pietro said, "Was it like that with Cangrande?"

It was Theodoro who shook his head. "No."

They began to descend the stairs, and Ignazzio said, "You may regret being drawn into this little circle, young sir."

"Maybe," said Pietro. "But now I have to go and find out how much damage my friend has done."

"How will the spurned groom take his loss, do you think?"

"Badly," said Pietro with certainty. "Very, very badly."

"So there will be war, at least between these two young men, if not their families. How will you fare, caught between such animosity?"

Pietro shrugged. "If I'm closer to one, it's Mariotto. But Antony is completely in the right. Mari has behaved atrociously. Honor dictates that I side with the Capulletti family."

"But that is not where your heart lies."

Pietro shook his head. "How can I say?"

The Moor said, "You should get away—travel, make a name for yourself."

"What about all this?" Pietro gestured at the room they had just exited.

Ignazzio said, "Theo's quite correct. Who knows when they will need your services, or in what capacity. You can do nothing better than build a thriving career for yourself. It would also remove you from this current difficulty with your friends."

It was sound advice, honestly given. Pietro decided that perhaps the Moor was not to be feared. Respected, definitely, but not feared. Still, he shook his head. "It would be cowardly."

"I saw you last night, and again just now. Cowardice is not a trait you own."

Pietro glanced at the Moor. "If you don't mind my asking—someone called you the *Arūs*. What does it mean?"

The rasping voice replied, "Merely a name given me long ago. Excuse me, I must dispose of these scrolls and help my master dress."

Ignazzio said, "You'll wait for us, won't you, Pietro? Then we can go to wait upon the Capitano together."

In the hallway outside Ignazzio's chamber, Pietro recalled the Scaliger's words in that rain-soaked church.

"How can a man live life as a myth?"

"If I thought that I was truly the chosen champion of the heavens, I would fight it."

"Just to see her—to see them fail, I would fight it with all my might."

At the time, Pietro had thought Cangrande had been talking of himself. Now he knew better.

TWENTY-FIVE

Antonia was so swept up in her father that she hardly noticed the return to the *Domus Bladorum,* the removal of capes and scarves, the many people moving about. Poco came running up with some confused news about Pietro's friends. Then he spied his sister. "Imperia!" he cried with such obvious joy Dante couldn't help smiling.

"But we're summoned," said Poco, returning to his news. "Well, you are. To the court! Montecchio has gone and married Capulletto's Paduan bride! It could mean the truce is off, and we're at war again! Isn't that fantastic?"

Together they made their way next door to the great Scaliger court in the *Domus Nova.* The chamber was replete with rich tapestries and ornaments. Though her father always praised Cangrande's disdain of open displays of wealth, here the wealth and prosperity of Verona was ostentatiously visible. If Cangrande had been king, this would have been his throne room.

She was still looking adoringly at Dante when he pointed. "That, my dear, is the Scaliger."

Tearing her eyes away from her father, Antonia had to stifle a gasp when she saw her father's patron. The ballads and poems were one thing, beholding the living man was quite another. He was a tower of might and self-assurance. His crop of hair was longer than she had expected, making him look young. The fact that he *was* young didn't register in her mind. He was powerful—everything else flowed from that.

From the Capitano Antonia's eyes moved on to Antonio Capulletto. The nice fellow who'd shown her around the palace was now a pitiable sight. He looked wounded. Defeated. Shattered.

Antonia couldn't help thinking, *What a drama! Things like this never happen in Florence!* Not being in love with love as many girls her age were, she nevertheless understood the concept. After years of her mother's rule, she also grasped the desire for freedom, the impulse to disobedience. This girl, Gianozza, had taken hold of her own fate, however stupidly. Antonia tried not to admire the courage that must have taken.

A wide man with sandy hair, not particularly tall, stood shaking his fists at the center of the hall. Unlike Antonia's distinguished father, his ornate clothes were at war with the opulence of the hall. He was shouting, but he'd been shouting since the Alaghieri clan had arrived.

". . . an outrage that the girl's own cousin was a party to this! It was an arranged match! A match that, as you all remember, bore my lord's seal of approval, and that of our esteemed visitor from Padua! What right did her cousin Marsilio have to grant the girl's hand in marriage when his uncle, the lord of his family, had already granted that right to my son?!"

Antonia tried to listen as Capulletto railed on, but her eyes kept returning to her father—entirely still, placidly watching events unfold. He glanced over and winked at her. Embarrassed, she shifted her gaze to the tapestry at their backs. It bore an amusing image of rabbits doing battle with mounted knights. Antonia giggled, a sound she quickly stifled for fear of disgracing herself before her father.

But Dante was bored with the Little Capuan's oration, into a fourth repetition. Hearing his daughter's smothered laugh he glanced at the tapestry. "Absurd, isn't it? Look closer at the vines in the back," he said, nodding at the background, thick with the green of a forest. There were tiny demons there, causing the rabbits to behave as they were. "As you know, my Beatrice, even the most innocent things can be the tools of the underworld."

Antonia nodded, then listened as he explained the politics of the moment to her in whispers. "The girl who has eloped is Paduan, the niece of Giacomo da Carrara. Though our host is on friendly terms with Carrara, it is generally acknowledged that the struggle between them is only beginning. At the moment, Verona is at peace with Padua. Cangrande wants to keep it that way for a while longer."

"So," murmured Antonia, "whatever way Padua blows, that will direct the Scaliger's sails?"

"Just so."

Jacopo touched the hem of Dante's sleeve and nodded across the hall. "Pietro's here."

Antonia looked up. A knight was entering the hall, accompanied by a little man and an enormous Moor with scars on his face and neck. The knight was clothed in a long doublet and breeches that, contrary to fashion, hid his thighs. The crutch he used did not bow his shoulders at all, just canted his body slightly right. At his heels padded a lean greyhound. For a moment Antonia fancied they should have been the subject of the tapestry, not the demon bunnies. She tried to see around them to view her brother.

Then she remembered. Pietro had been injured in his leg. At once she recognized the color of the hair almost hidden by a hat and a bandage. She saw the familiar cant of the head. She saw her father's lean face, her mother's nose. Somewhere in that well-shaped youth was the boy that had pulled her hair when she'd been small.

Poco started to wave but Dante caught him by the wrist and held him still. Antonia watched as Pietro edged through the crowd, eyes fixed on young Capulletto. His face seemed full of empathy for his friend, but his expression was calm, like her father's.

She stole another glance at Dante, and couldn't help giving his arm a little squeeze. He patted her hand as he listened to Capulletto rant. Antonia knew dire events were transpiring in front of her, but she couldn't help smiling as she watched.

✦ ✧ ✦

Pietro didn't feel at all like smiling. Under his calm expression his thoughts would have shocked his sister. *Damn Mari, damn him straight to Hell! Come on, Antony! Stand up, roar! That's the only way to get past this. Get angry, then get on with your life!*

But Antony sat still, head down. Pietro was sure he wasn't hearing a word his father said. Old Ludovico didn't falter, his voice filling the hall as he cried, "And as for the cupidity of the Montecchi clan, we see now how old money can buy its way into any privilege. No doubt there was heavy bribery of young Carrara to give the girl away to the puffed-up stripling . . ."

Pietro halted close to the Capitano's dais, the crowd moving aside for the combined presence of a war hero, an astrologer, and his demonlike servant.

Servants placed Mercurio with other hounds, including his father, Jupiter. They sniffed, then ignored each other.

Pietro had been in the *Domus Nova* only twice before—it was rare that Cangrande used the chamber for anything but business of state. For internal communal business he favored his loggia or the offices he kept in the Giurisconsulti. Today, though, the gathering was not to greet the head of another land, or a dignitary from a neighboring city-state. Today people had gravitated to the center of power to watch Cangrande deal out justice.

"What of our rights?" cried Capulletto. "Are we not as worthy of the protection of the law as the lowest citizen of this nation? Does an ancient line have more rights than one new to the state? Have we not proved our worth here? If there is any who deserves favor in the eyes of Verona's fathers, it is my son. Antonio rode to Verona's defense before he was even a citizen. He earned his citizenship with his blood—blood spilled beneath the walls of Vicenza!" He was speaking well, and had obviously spent time in the courts. *As advocate or client?* Pietro wondered.

As the Little Capuan (*Apt, Father!*) railed on, Pietro turned his gaze to Cangrande. If the Capitano was angry, he didn't show it. Every few moments he would lean over to discuss something with Passerino Bonaccolsi, and once he conversed with Il Grande, seated on the Scaliger's left.

One august personage Cangrande did not consult was Gargano Montecchio. The father of the "bride-thief" sat rigidly on a bench with the other nobles of the city. No one spoke to him, nor would they until the Capitano made his ruling on the affair. *Last night he was full of joy,* Pietro thought. *Now he's aged a thousand years.*

Pietro's eyes moved to the cluster of Capulletti. Ludovico was spitting mad. Standing behind him, Antony's brother looked unperturbed, perhaps even a little satisfied. As for Antony himself, his face was blank, eyes glazed, a slight crease across his forehead as if he couldn't get his mind around it. Until he did, there was no room for anger. Just shock and confusion.

Ludovico had enough outrage for them both. "Was not my son knighted by the Scaliger's own hand just yesterday? Did he not race valiantly in the horse Palio? And was he not inches away from winning the foot Palio when the bride-thief got in his way? Did not the Scaliger himself confer upon our family the right to an ancient and respected title? Is this the show of favoritism Verona grants its citizens? To have wives and daughters stolen away, married off to foppish youths who bathe in perfume?!" He was no longer speaking to the Scaliger. He was playing to the crowd, trying to swing opinion his family's way.

Since it did not appear that Capulletto would run himself out any time soon, when he stopped to hack his phlegm into a napkin the Scaliger spoke. "We are, as you have pointed out, aware of all this, Monsignore Capulletto. I assure you, I am not staying my hand in this matter. I only wait for the parties involved to arrive. In the meantime," he said, raising his eyes to the crowd, "I have a decree. As in the days when my honored father served this state as Capitano del Populo and Podestà of the Merchants, from this time forward private dueling is forbidden." There was excited murmuring in the crowd. "The settling of quarrels may not be determined by the sword, but must be litigated through the courts! This is not just true within the city walls, but in all the lands under Veronese stewardship!"

Pietro saw the purpose at once. Cangrande wanted no fresh outbreaks of feuding between families in his territories. The law his brother Bartolomeo had repealed a dozen years before to allow the final duel in the Capelletti-Montecchi feud was once more enacted. Those sharing family names could not exact revenge for wrongs to their kin. This struck Pietro as a cruel twist of fate. *Father was right. Ignazzio said it too. And even Mari's father. Names have power.*

But Cangrande's new law went further, entirely ruling out trial by combat as a legal remedy. Several lawyers piped up to ask questions. Not that they were angry. Quite the contrary, it was a boon for their practices. If trial by combat was illegal, citizens would have no recourse but to hire lawyers to settle their differences.

Shouting down the lawyers, Ludovico raised an objection. "You're doing this to stop my son from regaining his honor!"

Cangrande shook his head. "No, I am making sure of my citizens' safety. I am also protecting the honor of your son and your family. You were not here, Monsignor Capulletto, when there was a feud inside Verona's walls. The participants put public safety aside in order to redeem what they mistakenly believed to be their honor. Their honor suffered far greater stains from the public hazards they caused than any slights, real or otherwise, from another family. This law will protect all our citizens in a number of ways."

Ludovico wasn't done objecting, but a clamor outside forestalled him. All eyes came up as six Veronese soldiers entered clad in their best armor. Between them strode Marsilio da Carrara. Chin high, he ignored the collected

Veronese nobles. His gaze locked on the Scaliger and though his face was composed, the smirk did not vanish from his eyes.

Before addressing Marsilio, Cangrande turned to Il Grande. "Giacomo da Carrara. This young man is your nephew and not a citizen of Verona. Do you consent to his being questioned in this matter here and now, or would you rather he be questioned in a Paduan court?"

Giacomo leaned forward. "As his actions have implications for the honor of my family, he must be questioned as soon as possible. I trust both in your wisdom, lord Capitano, and in that of your noble Veronese councilors. Let him be questioned in Verona!" As the crowd's murmur of approval died away, he added, "I might put a question or two to him myself."

"As you wish." Cangrande turned the full weight of his gaze on Marsilio. "Ser Carrara, there is a story circulating that you witnessed a marriage between your cousin, the lady Gianozza della Bella, and Mariotto Montecchio."

"I did more than witness it," said Marsilio. "I gave the bride away."

The Capitano ignored the hushed mutterings of the crowd and the not so hushed voice of Ludovico Capulletto. "I see. You did this knowing that both your uncle and the girl's father had arranged another match for her?"

"I did."

"Where did this marriage take place?"

"At the private chapel of the Montecchi, in their grand estates east of Illasi."

"Who officiated?"

"Some Franciscan monk. I heard Montecchio call him Brother Lorenzo."

Pietro recalled the good-looking young friar he had met yesterday, the one who was embarrassed about being French. Cangrande glanced at the Franciscan bishop, who looked grave. "To clarify, Ser Carrara—when you say Montecchio, you mean Cavaliere, not Monsignore."

"Correct. I don't think Monsignore knew anything about it," said Marsilio, smiling at the ashen figure of Mariotto's father.

That's damned gracious of him, thought Pietro bitterly, *admitting what's clear to anyone with eyes!*

Cangrande continued. "What do you know about this couple?"

"I know that before last night neither of them had laid eyes on one another."

"Do you know what happened last night?"

"She told me they—talked." Carrara's tone implied more than his words.

The mob shifted. Pietro wondered why the Scaliger didn't dismiss them.

He could get to the bottom of this much more quickly without their interruptions. Then Pietro realized that if this were to be defused, it would have to be in public. Rumors had to be put to rest.

"We have no use for innuendo. Define your terms, please."

"Forgive me. Montecchio read to the girl from the latest work of your resident poet, Monsignore Dante Alaghieri."

Oh Christ. Without thinking Pietro joined the crowd in looking toward his father, who was standing between Poco and a short, stern-looking girl. Dante had the good sense not to react in any way. Pietro couldn't help thinking, *Well, it will probably help sales.*

Cangrande brought the crowd's attention back by asking, "Then what happened?"

"They fell in love," said Marsilio simply.

"And how did you become a party to their affections?"

"She told me early this morning."

"What did you say in response?"

The crowd pressed forward to listen to Carrara's answer. "I said that if she truly loved this young man, she should marry him."

Ludovico made some burbling sounds of indignation. The Scaliger paused, then he said, "So marriage between them was your idea."

"Love is a rare commodity these days. It should not go unnourished."

"You felt it was your responsibility to nourish this couple's affection."

"Exactly. I felt it my knightly duty."

"I may be a little rusty," said Cangrande without a trace of humor, "but I do not recall fostering love as one of a cavaliere's duties."

"Does the great Capitano wish me to refresh his memory?"

"I pray you, do."

Marsilio's back was spear-straight. "The rules of Courtly Love are explicit—'No one should be deprived of love without the very best of reasons.' Rule Eight."

"And a contract of marriage between your family and the noble Capulletti household is not reason enough?"

"No formal betrothal ever took place. I felt—and still feel—that a love as rare and pure as that between my cousin and Ser Montecchio is worth a dozen such alliances."

Ludovico snarled. Cangrande said, "You spoke with the young man, assured yourself of his honest intentions?"

"I visited him early this morning. I found him to be of good character. Rule Eighteen. 'Good character alone—"

"'Makes any man worthy of love,'" Cangrande finished for him. His eyes were narrowed.

"I also found him to be jealous of her betrothal. He had not eaten since laying eyes on her, nor had he slept."

"I trust he was not vexed by too much passion," said Cangrande with an ironic tone.

"No, my lord."

"Did you consult the girl's betrothed? Perhaps the same could have been said of him."

"He was not the object of the girl's affection, my lord Capitano," said Marsilio, bowing his head in mock obeisance.

Pietro saw Antony sag slightly. *So he is listening.*

"Ser Capulletto's feelings on the matter did not weigh in your mind?"

Marsilio shook his head. "They did, my noble lord. But then I recalled the last rule of Courtly Love—'Nothing forbids one woman from being loved by two men.'"

Cangrande pursed his lips. "I suppose the real question, Marsilio da Carrara, is why did you not consult your uncle? He is the paterfamilias, the head of your line. He had made the arrangements for the girl's wedding. Should he not have been consulted?"

"He was closeted with your lordship this morning, discussing matters of state," said Marsilio. "I did not feel it appropriate to disturb you both for a private family matter. As for needing my uncle's approbation, my uncle has repeatedly told me that I should be more interested in family affairs. I was trying to solve this problem in a way that would best honor my ancestors."

"I see. Why such haste?"

"The girl was going to be betrothed at supper this evening. I wanted to resolve this unfortunate conflict before it went any further. Once the formal betrothal had taken place, it would have been more difficult for the girl to extricate herself from an unwanted arrangement."

Pietro saw Antony flinch.

Cangrande said, "So you moved to forestall that event by marrying her off."

"To the man she loves," confirmed Marsilio. *"Amor ordinem nescit."*

Giacomo da Carrara said, "My lord, may I?" Cangrande nodded, and Il

Grande turned to his nephew. "What makes you believe this young man was worthy?"

Marsilio blinked. "I thought that would be obvious, uncle. He is from an ancient house, full of honor. His ancestors have been consuls and podestàs, a few of them even emissaries and citizens of Padua. His family estates are almost at the border between Padua and Verona, just south of Vicenza. I thought it a good symbol for our two cities to be united through such an alliance. As for the man himself, I have seen him on the field of war. He is brave and noble. During the race yesterday he was every ounce what a knight should be."

Pietro was unable to contain himself. "You tried to kill him!" The ugly smirk Marsilio turned on him goaded Pietro on. "Both at Vicenza and during the Palio!"

Marsilio's answer was humble. "At Vicenza we were at war. I assume he would have killed me had the chance arisen. As for yesterday, we rode as we should have—in competition. Many knights lost their lives. It is to his credit that he didn't."

"They lost their lives thanks to you!" cried Pietro.

Carrara shook his head sadly and looked at Cangrande. "I don't know what he's talking about."

Pietro was about to shout again but Cangrande interrupted. "Ser Alaghieri, you are not on the city council. Your rights as a knight allow you to proclaim a formal hearing, if you so choose."

Marsilio spoke before Pietro could reply. "My lord, young Alaghieri is obviously unwell, to make such accusations. The collision that caused so many noble Veronese to lose their lives was an accident. You said so yourself."

"Are you calling me a liar?" asked Pietro hotly.

"I say you are mistaken," replied Marsilio. "You've taken one too many knocks to the head. No doubt your leg keeps you from ducking in time."

Pietro twisted, facing the Scaliger. "To prove the truth of my words, I challenge him to—"

"No!" Cangrande leaned forward and fixed Pietro with a hard look. "Perhaps you didn't hear my earlier dictate, Cavaliere. There is no more recourse to the Court of Swords." His eyes swept the whole crowd. "Let me make this clear. Dueling is illegal. Anyone caught dueling will be exiled from Verona's walls, denied food and fire in all of my lands. That is one choice. I also reserve the right to declare summary execution for the offense of dueling. In this war-like time I will not see the future nobles of my lands cut down in the haste of youth!"

His eyes scanned for any possible dissent. Seeing none, Cangrande returned to the Paduan. "Marsilio da Carrara—both times you saw young Montecchio in action he was in the company of this young man," he indicated Antony. "Is he not as qualified as his friend?"

"Antonio Capulletto is brave, no doubt, my lord," said Marsilio. "But I felt he lacked a certain—well, a certain quality that only the nobility can recognize. He lacks the true spirit of chivalry. That is only my opinion, of course."

Pietro groaned inwardly. Here in this chamber the assemblage was made up of men of noble descent. Exclusivity was their passion. Newly made nobles like the Capulletti were necessary evils at best. There was no argument Carrara could have used that would score him more points. He was winning the crowd by preying on their prejudices.

Cangrande was clearly thinking along the same lines as Pietro, for he dismissed Marsilio to one side, which effectively silenced the Paduan. The Scaliger called forward the Franciscan bishop and asked after the credentials of this Friar Lorenzo.

"The fault is mine," said Bishop Francis. "This young Paduan knight called upon our order this morning, and I told Brother Lorenzo to provide any service Ser Carrara might require. Lorenzo was only following my instructions." Francis looked stern. "It goes without saying, I knew nothing of any marriage. But if anyone is to be punished for the Church's role in this, let it be me."

"That won't be necessary," said Cangrande. "Still, we must speak to Friar Lorenzo and discover if there were any irregularities in the—"

He was interrupted by a flurry of movement at the back of the crowd. Whispers became muffled exclamations of "They're here!" and "Look at her!" The rows of nobles parted to make way for Mariotto Montecchio and his bride, Gianozza.

They were a stunning couple. Though they must have known they were walking into a lion's den, nothing could penetrate the armor of their delight. The girl positively glowed. Walking to her right, Mariotto was straight and sure of his step, dignified. What Marsilio's exclusivity argument had begun, their appearance clinched. No one in that crowd could deny that, as a couple, they were perfection.

Pietro saw Marsilio da Carrara grin broadly. Nothing at that moment would have given Pietro greater pleasure than making the Paduan eat that smirk. Pietro knew Mari's mettle. Mari would never have gone so far as running off with the girl without the active connivance of Carrara. Mari was a lovesick fool. The real villain of the piece was Carrara, trying to sow discord among the Scaliger's knights.

But had he succeeded? What would Antony do now that the couple was here, right in front of him? Holding his breath with the rest of the crowd, Pietro watched as Mariotto knelt before the Scaliger, careful to keep his hand in his beloved's, curtsying beside him. To Mariotto's right sat the friend he had wronged so severely. To the left, the father whose honor he had soiled. He didn't look at them, keeping his gaze on the impassive face of the Scaliger.

The invitation to speak wasn't long in coming. "Ser Montecchio, Verona thanks you for your swift response to our summons. I imagine you know why we sent for you."

"I do, my lord," said Mariotto. "I have married this young woman against the will of her family and without the knowledge of my own. I will never be made to regret this decision. But I do understand that I have caused injury to many people, most notably my best friend in the world. I—" He faltered, unable to look at Antony. "I will make whatever reparations I can to the Capulletti family, and bend under the weight of whatever punishment you decree—even death."

Pietro imagined he saw the Capitano sigh. "I don't think you will be called upon to die for your love." He then explained for the third time his decree regarding dueling. Antony sat hangdog as ever, broken leg sticking out in front him. His eyes had come up briefly as the couple passed, then returned to gazing blankly at the floor.

"I do not know if punishment is within my purview," concluded the Capitano. "You have not committed a crime against the state. You have transgressed against two families."

"Three," Mariotto corrected. "I have broken faith with my father. I am certain that, had I spoken to him, my father would have been adamantly against this union. Which is why I did not consult him."

The crowd stirred again, and to Pietro's ears these murmurs were approving. Mariotto was not shirking his responsibility. He was the perfect model of a chivalrous young knight in love.

"Three families, then," said Cangrande. "Your punishment lies with those families, as does your forgiveness. First, we must ask the girl's guardian if he wishes to press charges." He turned to Giacomo da Carrara.

Giacomo was stroking his trim beard. Technically the girl was his property. Il Grande could try the boy for theft if he wished, though Marsilio's connivance made that matter less clear. "I am of two minds in this affair," he said slowly. "My quandary lies not in the behavior of this young Veronese, but that of my nephew. He overstepped his authority in the family, usurping my right to choose the girl's husband. However, it is possible that he was correct. The amity between this young couple is clear. It is possible, then, that she might not have been right for the match with Capulletto. If that is true, then my nephew acted correctly."

Il Grande took a pondering breath. "Whichever is true, this young man is cleared from blame as far as the Carrarese are concerned. He acted with the implied consent of the girl's family. Knowing his father and hearing the lad himself speak, I am satisfied that he is a worthy youth. The Carrara family accepts the match."

The assemblage let out something akin to a collective sigh.

Ludovico Capulletto leapt back up to his feet. "The Capulletti do not! Do you hear me? We do not! The Capulletti—a name we only undertook to oblige the father of this bride-thief—we do not accept this match! We demand justice!"

"I understand what *you* demand, Ludovico," said Cangrande with hard patience. "But I have not yet heard from the member of your family most wounded in this affair." His voice became gentle. "Antonio—what do you have to say?"

The moment dragged out. Pietro could see on Antony's face that he didn't want to speak. He looked at Gianozza, then at Mariotto. His head shook slightly, his lips were parted, but there were no words coming out.

Mariotto released his bride's hand and crossed to his friend. Ludovico moved to intercept him, but a sharp look from Cangrande froze the aggrieved father in his tracks. Reaching the place where Antony sat, broken leg extended, Mariotto halted. Bowing his head, he knelt before his best friend.

Antony's head raised slightly, and it seemed for a moment he might actually speak. But his head sagged again, eyes falling away from Mariotto.

This was too much for Ludovico Capulletto. Grasping one of his son's crutches, Ludovico swung it at Mariotto's head. The blow caught Mari across the temple, the crack splitting the silence in the hall.

Mariotto hit the floor, poleaxed. Gianozza cried out and knelt by Mariotto. Gargano Montecchio stirred, then kept resolutely to his seat. The Scaliger leapt to the elder Capulletto's side, gripping the brandished crutch with white knuckles. "Ludovico! Stand down! Stand down, or I'll have you arrested!"

Purple-faced, sweat streaming, Antony's father released his grip on the crutch and stepped back from the Capitano. "See what this has done to my son! He is unable even to speak! I demand justice! It is unfair to deny us recourse to the Court of Swords. If the law was fit enough to mete out justice yesterday, let it be today. Enforce your new rules tomorrow, Capitano, but for this one day allow us to avenge our honor in the best way we know how!"

Ludovico's voice was joined by a score of the gathered nobles as he clamored for a duel. The nobility wanted this duel carried out, even if Cangrande did not. Searching for an objection, the Capitano observed, "Antonio is not well enough to stand, let alone fight a duel. And I will not permit you, Ludovico, to face a man a third your age in this ridiculous matter."

There came a choked sound from Antony. The Scaliger held up a hand for silence. "What was that, Ser Capulletto?"

With great deliberation, Antony rose from his seat. Blinking back tears, he spoke. "I am fit."

Ludovico crowed his delight. Cangrande shook his head. "I won't allow it."

"My lord—" Ludovico began.

Again the Scaliger cut him off. "No!"

"My lord," said a voice from the bench of the *Anziani,* "may I speak?"

Cangrande sighed in relief. Ascending the dais, he resumed his seat. "My lord Montecchio, please. The floor is yours."

Dark robes swirling about him, the patriarch of the Montecchi clan rose and strode into the center of the room. Ludovico glowered. Cangrande sat in patient attendance. Pietro thought that here, at least, was a staunch ally for Cangrande's ban on dueling. If there was one man who could attest to the terrible damage it could effect, it was Gargano Montecchio, who had lost father, brothers, uncles, and wife to the terrible strife of a feud.

In a strained version of his usual measured tones, Gargano said, "Dueling is a practice traced back to biblical times. Cain and Abel, unable to settle their claim in any other way, agreed to stand the test of a duel. The ancient pagans settled matters in much the same way. The Umbrians of old held that trial by combat was just as fair as trial by jury. Homer tells of the duel between Paris and Menelaus to prove who held the right to Helen.

"All these could be the acts of barbarians, using their physical might to overpower the law. Through the tale of David and Goliath, though, we see clearly how divine will leads to a just conclusion in a legally constituted duel. Charlemagne urged trial by combat for his men, saying it was preferable to the shameless oaths his knights gave with such ease. What is war, if not dueling writ large? In battle, God chooses the side of right and lends his strength to the sword of justice. So it is in a duel. Not in a brawl or ambush, but a legal duel, with rules and witnesses."

Cangrande was frowning as Montecchio turned to face the injured Mariotto. "I had planned, after today's events, to disown my son. His actions have betrayed every trust placed in him. The trust of his lord, his friends, his father. I have no other son, but I have a daughter whose loyalty and fidelity lie in quantities unknown by her brother." Gargano's head came up to sweep the crowd. "But I have changed my mind. The honorable Lord Capulletto demands a duel. It is my opinion that his demands be honored. Better this duel takes place now, with the due weight of law behind it, than on some future day in a back alley or sewer. Let justice be done! Instead of spouting meaningless oaths and apologies, let my son defend with his body the deed that has set him apart from us. He claims that his cause is love, the noblest banner to raise. Let him prove it. If he dares to face this challenge, he may still bear the name he has shamed this day."

Pietro glanced at Cangrande, who looked understandably grim. The walls were closing in upon him. "And if Antonio cannot fight for himself, who will represent the Capulletti in this matter?"

"Let him choose a champion," replied Gargano. "Perhaps his brother—"

"I'll be that champion!"

Heads turned as Pietro pushed past the crowd to stand in the open. Antony looked up and gave Pietro the barest nod. Mariotto, unable to stand unaided, stared at Pietro in disbelief.

Among those visibly startled was Cangrande. "Pietro—Ser Alaghieri. You would fight in Antonio's place?"

"I would, and I will," said Pietro.

"Why?"

"Because, my lord, I knew something of the attraction between these two last night, and I did nothing to stop it."

"Pietro, it's not your—" began Mariotto, only to have his father cut him off sharply. "Mariotto! Be silent, you cur!"

The Scaliger continued. "As I recall, Ser Alaghieri, you had other things on your mind last night," he said, reminding the crowd of the attempted kidnapping and the leopard.

"It is no excuse, my lord. You knighted me yesterday." Closing his eyes, Pietro quoted: *"To become a knight is to take upon you the responsibility of being God's sword of Justice here on earth. A knight rights wrongs. A knight protects the innocent. A knight listens to the words of the Lord."* He opened his eyes again to gaze at Cangrande. "I let this happen, my lord. It is a stain on my honor."

By quoting the Capitano's own words, Pietro was sure he had won, but Cangrande said, "Isn't Mariotto your friend as well?"

Pietro looked at the pained, bewildered expression on Mari's face. "He is, my lord."

"But you're willing to fight him?"

Pietro made certain he was looking directly forward as he said, "He just took a powerful blow, my lord. I do not think he is fit to duel at this time. I would suggest another champion take his place."

The look Cangrande gave Pietro was disgusted. He had caught on. "You have someone in mind? The accused's aged father, perhaps?"

"No, my lord, though I am sure Lord Montecchio is as able as he ever was." The blood pumping through him was making him rush his speech. Forcing himself to make each word clear, he said, "In all this, no one has mentioned the role of the lady. She, too, had a choice in this affair."

"You wish to fight the bride?" Cangrande's amusement stopped just shy of his eyes. He was attempting to shame Pietro, belittle him into retracting his challenge.

In response, Pietro removed a glove and clutched it tightly in his bare hand. "No, my lord. I propose the one person who has tied these two together. Ser Carrara is intimately tied to this union. He is related to one, he chose the other. If he believes in this marriage, let him defend it with his life!" That said, Pietro hurled down his gage.

Over the shocked gasps of the crowd, Marsilio shouted, "I accept! I accept!" He tried to push his way over to take up the gauntlet.

"You do not!" cried Il Grande, leaping forward to slap his nephew across the face.

"The Capulletti do not—!"

"The Montecchi will not allow another to wear our sins!"

"Quiet! Quiet! Be still!" The Scaliger shouted them all into silence. "Ser Alaghieri. My gratitude to you runs deep. But I cannot allow this to proceed. My decree on this matter is law."

"Actually, lord, that isn't true," said Gugliermo del Castelbarco, rising from his prominent place on the front bench. The senior member of the Anziani, he carried with him the weight of both money and valor. "You have followed the tradition started by your noble uncle, the great Mastiff, in that only when your decrees are written and properly noted are they law."

"Then write it down," said Cangrande. "I will not have my city endure the strife of a feud!"

Another voice, that of Passerino Bonaccolsi, joined in. Studying the ceiling, he said, "I don't know how it is in Verona, but in Mantua all such decrees have to be witnessed by the *Anziani,* in a duly commissioned session."

Growing testy, Cangrande glanced about at the assembled nobility. "I declare the Council of City Elders is in emergency session. I call for a voice count of those present to form a quorum." He began calling off names, the first being Guglielmo da Castelbarco. Castelbarco remained silent. By the time Cangrande had gone through the entire list of the nobles present, not one had raised his voice.

"I see," said the Scaliger in a dangerous tone. "Lacking a quorum, we cannot proceed." He strode down off the dais, past Pietro, to stand in the center of the hall. In freezing tones he addressed the city elders. "You want this duel to take place. Do you realize what a duel means? I will leave aside the fact that one of those challenged is from a neighboring commune, with whom we are newly at peace. Instead I say, think back! Remember the days when the feud between these clans rampaged through our streets! Remember the innocents caught in its midst! Recall the dead and dying in the back alleys—for it was outlawed then! It was illegal because it was immoral! That dueling is still permitted is an oversight on the part of my brother Bartolomeo. Do you remember why he reinstated dueling? To finish what had started in blood with the only thing that could end it—blood! The last blood of the Capelletti! Until yesterday we had none to bear the name, for they were all dead! Buried! Lost, not to lawful wars or foreign devils, but to our own—idiocy!"

He turned to face Mariotto's father. "My lord Montecchio, look past your anger. You, of all people, know what such a feud can cost!" The Scaliger turned again toward the crowd. "Think well on this—if we allow another feud to stain our city's honor, it will swallow us whole! Count on it! Hate begets hate! One duel will not satisfy honor, especially in matters of the heart. When it is money stolen, men can be repaid. When it is land lost, men can be recompensed. But once blood is spilled, it can never be recovered! It can only be satisfied by more of its own! Blood will have blood! Think well before you unleash yet another blight on our fair city! I speak now, not as your Prince, but as your fellow citizen! Think of us, think of how you want Verona to be remembered!"

He turned in a slow circle, scanning their faces. They had heard, but were not prepared to listen.

"Very well. I could call out my men-at-arms and force an end to this foolishness. But I will not be that kind of tyrant. As you insist, I will allow this one night of madness—if you will swear to me that, at sunrise tomorrow, you will all sign into law my decree against dueling. If I do not get that oath from you, elders, I swear by all I hold dear that I will call up my troops this very minute."

The Council of Elders were magnanimous in victory. Each assured their Capitano that they would sign his decree into law the next day and defend it ever after with their lives.

"I require another oath, this from the fathers. Ludovico, Gargano—you must swear on all that you hold dear, on your fortunes and your very lives, that as long as you both shall live there will be no reprisals. Whatever the outcome, this duel must be the end of the matter."

Gargano said he would gladly swear, since he held no grievance with the noble house of Capulletti. Ludovico grudgingly nodded his head and signaled his consent. Cangrande considered them both briefly, then closed his eyes. "Marsilio—take up his gage."

Carrara pushed past his uncle to take up Pietro's gauntlet. He lifted it above his head and crushed it in his closed fist. "I accept the challenge!"

"Then let's get this over with." Cangrande stalked from the chamber. "One hour, in the Arena!" he shouted.

The crowd erupted into excited noise. Mercurio left the pack of dogs to pad over to his master, who was breathing hard. The hound licked his hand, and Pietro patted him absentmindedly as he wondered if he'd live through the night. He heard a myriad of voices calling out to him, most wishing him luck. Pietro ignored them, eyes fixed on Marsilio da Carrara arguing furiously with his uncle across the hall. In the midst of the old man's speech, young Carrara turned on his heel and stalked away. His path took him away from Pietro, but the bastard remembered to turn before leaving to send a mocking salute Pietro's way.

A heavy hand landed on Pietro's shoulder. On edge, he turned about, bringing up his hands.

"What, precisely, are you thinking?" demanded Dante, sotto voce. "Christ, boy . . ."

Beside Pietro's father appeared a bright-eyed Poco and a glowering girl who looked familiar. He blinked, recognizing a disapproval he'd often seen in his mother. "Antonia!"

He made to embrace her, but she brushed his arms aside. "Answer our father! What are you thinking? Are you trying to ruin his relationship with a patron? How dare you oppose the will of our father's host?"

"A valid, if erroneous, assumption, my Beatrice," murmured Dante, patting her gently on the arm. "I was referring to the idiocy of issuing a challenge to one of the best-trained knights in the Feltro while he can barely hold himself upright without the aid of that crutch."

"I'll manage," said Pietro. "I can run a little, I proved that last night."

"If you are bent on self-immolation, I cannot stop you. But why demand to fight Carrara?"

"Mari's being a fool, but Carrara created the situation."

"You can't win, though," opined Jacopo.

Pietro took a deep breath. "I can if I'm right."

"Are you?" asked his father.

"Yes, he is!" Ludovico Capulletto came up to repeatedly shake Pietro's hand. "Thank you, boy, thank you! It's no small thing to have such a noble young man stand up to take your side in a quarrel. No one can sneer at our claim now, much as the Capitano might try."

"I'm not doing this to spite Cangrande," said Pietro carefully. "Antony was wronged. And I believe it was Carrara who wronged him. This is my way to prove it. Where is Antony?"

"Right here." The corpulent Capulletti patriarch stepped aside to let his son hobble past. Antony's voice was surprisingly soft. "Anything you want, Pietro. I'll give you anything I have."

"I don't want anything from you, Antony," said Pietro. "I'm doing what I think is right."

Antony ducked his head. "Hell," he said, "I'm sorry. I'm an idiot. It's just—" Tears came to his eyes as he lifted one of his crutches. "I can't—and why—why did he—Why?"

This last tortured cry hit the awful truth of it. It wasn't Gianozza's betrayal that wounded him the most. It was Mari's.

Pietro's sister stepped into the awkward moment, suggesting Antony move along to the Arena since it would take him some time to get there. Pietro, she added, had to arm himself. Antony nodded and let his grumbling father and brother lead him out.

"She's right," said Pietro. "I have to go arm myself."

"You didn't answer my question," said Dante.

"Which is?"

"Are you in the right? Think back to last night. Yesterday, these two families were as thick as thieves. Today, they are at each other's throats. Why? The girl is just an agent of the stars, Pietro. The fault may lie in taking up a name better left dead. The Montecchi and the Capulletti may be destined to war forever."

Pietro shook his head. "I can't fight an eternal war, only this fight, this minute."

"Between you and this Carrara boy," said the poet shrewdly. "Your own private feud. He already took your ability to run. Tell me, boy, is he worth dying for?"

Before Pietro could answer another voice intruded. "Your son is in the right. He has to know that."

The whole Alaghieri clan turned to find Gargano Montecchio still seated on his bench. He looked very tired. "What you point out, Monsignore Alaghieri, is not lost on me. Nor did I miss that this ancient feud is being resurrected on the very spot where I laid it to rest—the Arena. It is ironic, is it not, that you are here to once again chronicle the perfidious follies of the Capulletti and the Montecchi?" Mariotto's father rose to his feet. "But your son is correct. The stars influence us, but we do have free will to interpret them— I believe you said so yourself. My son has chosen his path. He must tread it now. I am just sorry—" Not knowing what more to say, he laid a hand on Pietro's sword arm. "God be with you." With that, Lord Montecchio departed the chamber.

There passed several moments in which no one knew what to say. A steward entered, bowing to Pietro. He said he'd been sent by the Scaliger to help in the process of arming. Pietro looked to his father. "I have to go. Look after Mercurio for me."

Dante told Jacopo to go help his brother. As the two young men followed the steward, Antonia gripped her father's arm. "Is that all? What else can we do?"

"We can pray, my Beatrice. We can pray, and leave it to God."

They exited, and the hall was now empty save for two men. Ignazzio da Palermo and Theodoro of Cadiz remained to reflect on the poet's words.

"We must make a chart for this remarkable young man whose life is now at risk."

"That will take time. It will be no help to him tonight."

"But you agree?"

"I do. Yet some things are best left to the unfolding of time. All we can do for him tonight is be spectators."

Together they made their way to the Arena.

TWENTY-SIX

A half an hour before sunset, Pietro Alaghieri rode toward his first duel. Possibly his last.

The Arena was even more packed than for the horse Palio. Somehow in a single hour word had gotten around to the whole city. Everyone came for the entertainment. This one had it all—sex, politics, personal and family quarrels. Better, these were the two from the Palio the day before. The Paduan had even been Alaghieri's prisoner after Vicenza.

Pietro emerged through the main gate on the west side. His breath smoked the chill air. He wore the newly made armor presented to him for his knighthood. He'd also taken a page from Carrara's book and dressed lightly in anticipation of the heavy work to come. Over all he wore a thick cloak he would doff before the fighting started.

He rode his monstrous new destrier. The Scaliger's groom hadn't known the warhorse's name and Pietro hadn't yet thought to give him one. At this point it hardly mattered. It would take weeks of training for the beast to respond to a name. His life was in hazard now.

Leading his nameless horse, as the rules of chivalry dictated, was a woman, whose token he would bear into battle. The young woman was his sister, Antonia, drafted quite against her will.

"This is not the reunion I had in mind," she said.

"I wanted it to be memorable," murmured Pietro in reply.

"If you lose, I won't cry."

"Just promise me you won't poke fun if I make an ass of myself."

"You realize there's a place in Hell for those with excessive pride?"

"You know, I think I read that somewhere."

Antonia couldn't help herself—she chuckled. She took a scarf from around her neck and handed it up to him. A knight must always carry a lady's token into battle. Pietro wished instead he could have a glove from a certain married lady in the crowd. Doubtless Carrara had one from Gianozza.

Poco rode Canis, and he preened with excitement. Pietro had wanted an experienced page, and Jacopo was still walking gingerly on his cut feet. But when his brother offered to be his second, Pietro found he hadn't the heart to say no. Seeing Antonia's scarf, Jacopo protested, "Imperia, I gave you that!"

"Yes you did," replied Antonia tartly, "and it's awful and ugly and I hope it gets covered in Carrara's blood because then I'll never have to wear it again." Poco made a face at her, which she returned. Pietro made a visible appeal to the heavens.

Held high over Poco's head was the banner of the new Capulletti, commissioned this morning by Ludovico's steward. The Alaghieri party was followed by a pair of servants bearing between them Pietro's coffin, as the law dictated. It was perverse that most of the last hour had been spent finding a carpenter to sell him one. More perverse was the fact that he'd had to pay for it out of his own purse—Antony's father hadn't wanted to spring for it.

Don't think about it. Focus on the fight.

The act of arming hadn't stopped him from receiving a series of visitors. Bailardino had come, and Nico da Lozzo. The handsome monk, Brother Lorenzo, had come at the instruction of his bishop to make certain that Pietro's soul was prepared in case the worst should happen. He had also come to apologize. "I'm so sorry, I didn't know! It was so romantic, and they were obviously in love! What could go wrong? But I shouldn't have married them . . ."

"It's all right," said Pietro, wondering who was confessing to whom.

"I saw a duel once, back in . . . back home. It was terrible, and I vowed never to be party to such a thing again. Now I am the cause of one!"

"You're not the cause."

"But it isn't my fault, not really. My bishop said to be serviceable to the Paduans . . ."

"I don't have that much time," said Pietro pointedly.

"Then I'll be brief," said Lorenzo. Pietro made confession, and the young brother fretfully told Pietro he'd be praying for him.

The one person Pietro had flatly refused to see was Mariotto. Claiming the impropriety of an interview at this time, he asked the steward to send Mariotto away. The steward had returned while Pietro was strapping on his leg greaves. "Ser Montecchio says he regrets the position he has placed you in, and that he understands why you feel the need to act as you are."

"Big of him." It occurred to him that Mari thought Pietro didn't care about the wedding, only the duel with Carrara. *What if my petition had been denied and I'd been forced to fight Mariotto? Could I have done it? Probably not,* he admitted.

Pietro had allowed Poco to bard him fully, against his own better judgment. It would protect him while on horseback, but if Pietro fell, the weight would drag him to the Arena floor. *I'll just have to try not to be unhorsed.* It was amusing, though—just yesterday he'd doubted if he'd ever wear the Scaliger's gift. *"Unused, unbloodied, hanging on the wall"—*sure, if I'd been lucky!

Carrara was already in the Arena on a destrier borrowed from Cangrande's stables, a massive grey beast that looked like a wall in motion. *At least we're both riding unfamiliar animals. No advantage there.*

Standing beside Marsilio's horse in a fine dress meant for one wedding and worn for another, Gianozza della Bella looked a vision of youthful femininity: ivory breasts hardly swelling below the bodice, her ebony hair fallen just loose enough to give her a slightly untamed look. Who in that crowd could honestly blame Montecchio?

Pietro watched as Carrara said something flippant to his cousin before cantering forward. To add insult to injury, Carrara wore the red ribbon that marked him the victor of the horse Palio. Seeing Carrara coming, Pietro whispered to his sister. "Time to go. Find Father. He's in the balcony up there." He gestured with his chin.

Antonia debated for a moment the proper blessing. Finally she settled on, "God give you strength." Then she followed Gianozza up to the balcony where Dante could be seen in the front row. *At least I was able to improve his seating arrangement,* thought Pietro wryly.

He gave a spur and the destrier picked up the pace, cutting across the Paduan's path. With a deft flick of his reins Carrara pulled his mount alongside. "Touchy. At least you look like a proper knight. Brand-new armor, eh? Never been used, not a scrape on it. For show, I suppose. You could keep it that way. Are you truly ready to have me hand you your head over a trifle?"

Pietro wasn't even aware of opening his mouth. "I'm ready to drive my sword through your skull."

"Good luck with that. Thank you, by the way."

"For what?"

"Ever since Vicenza my soul has longed for a chance to even up with you. With the help of the girl, I took my vengeance on your two friends today. But you're the real prize."

Pietro felt as though his teeth would shatter, he was grinding them so hard. "Happy to oblige."

"Yes, Pierazzo, when I kill you, I'll only have one more. I'll make it my life's work to kill the Greyhound of Verona."

Pietro knew he meant Cangrande, but in his mind's eye he saw Carrara's boot on Cesco's little neck. The image made Pietro's hands shake. Carrara saw it and, misunderstanding, laughed. "Oh yes! And his *putanna* of a sister—the *donna di strade* you moon after! I'll bet she ruts like an icy cunt. But that's fine—I'll warm her up."

Reaching a position before the Scaliger's balcony, the combatants brought their horses to a halt. Scanning faces in the dying light, Pietro saw Katerina sitting beside Bailardino, Cesco in her arms. *Good. At least here, under the eyes of the citizenry, he's safe from another kidnapping attempt.*

Antonia was slipping in beside Pietro's father. Mariotto and Gianozza gazed at each other, separated by Mari's sister Aurelia. The lovers knew the outcome of the duel would represent God's sanction or condemnation of their union, and that rested on the victory of a man they might otherwise root against.

Far from Mari and Gianozza, Antony was propped up on pillows close to the edge of the balcony so he could witness the duel. With him sat his brother and father, who looked to be arguing.

Leaning over the edge of the balcony in eager anticipation were Cangrande's two nephews, Mastino and Alberto. No need to wonder who little Mastino was rooting for. Guglielmo da Castelbarco and Passerino Bonaccolsi sat behind them. Close by, Nico da Lozzo gave Pietro a high sign of victory, ignoring the angry glare of the Capitano. "Give him what for, Pietro!" cried Nico. Others joined in with him, cheering not his cause but Pietro himself.

The Scaliger spoke, but Pietro couldn't hear him. His own heartbeat filled his ears. Yet he recited the ritual oath and gave the forced handshake, quick and humiliating. Then Ziliberto del Angelo gave the signal to begin. For a mad moment Pietro wondered what bizarre pecking order had placed the Master of the Hunt in charge of judicial duels. Shaking away the thought, he placed his helmet on his head and rode to the Arena's far end where Jacopo waited with lances and other weapons.

"Are you ready for this, big brother?" asked Poco, as he handed up a lance.

"Just stay back where it's safe," instructed Pietro. "Father'll kill me if I let anything happen to you." Even under the circumstances the threat of Dante's wrath seemed both real and terrible.

Poco nodded, swallowing several times. Pietro watched him and thought, *He's more excited than I am and just as scared. Terrific. All I need is a squirrelly page.*

On the balcony, Antonia could hardly watch. Her brother looked so small atop that beast, dwarfed by his own armor. Carrara's armor was molded to his shape, creating the appearance of grace and poise where Pietro looked clumsy and brutish.

Yet her brother lifted his lance with ease. As the challenged party, Marsilio had been offered choice of weapons. His squire held up his first tool of destruction and the crowd gasped. He'd chosen the halberd.

Gripping her father's sleeve, Antonia asked, "What does that mean?"

"Carrara's chosen a polearm rather than a lance. It's also a two-handed weapon, so he can't carry a shield." That Pietro had stuck to the traditional lance was probably wise, Dante informed her. Her brother hadn't ever fought with a halberd, and it was a tricky weapon to wield, having a spike, an axe, and a hook, all at the end of a long pole. "They'll have an equal reach," Dante explained over the crowd. "But Pietro has a shield, one with a good spike for goring if he gets in close. Carrara's weapon is for killing, Pietro's is for unseating. If he can get Carrara to the ground without losing his own seat he'll have the choice of finishing it there and then. All he has to do is avoid the halberd's head."

Was that all? It sounded like a lot to Antonia. For the first time she understood why young men devoted so much of their time to learning about different types of weapons and combat. But Pietro had spent more time with his head in books than actually on the turf.

On the Arena floor, Pietro was thinking much the same thing. His one lesson in swordplay hadn't covered fighting from horseback, let alone polearms. But he'd seen enough jousts to know the rules and a little strategy. Don't hit the horse, knock the other fellow out of his seat. *Easy. I'll have this wrapped up by dinnertime.* He laughed at himself, and it sounded a little hysterical to his ears. Across the Arena floor Carrara looked deadly peaceful. Pietro had the insane urge to make faces inside his helmet. Maybe he should wave. Or give Carrara the fig. But, no. That was unchivalrous.

Cangrande gave the nod, Tullio d'Isola dropped the flag, and Pietro spurred at Carrara, who was kicking his own mount into motion. The crowd surged to life as the two combatants raced at each other.

Pietro fought the instinct to lean forward. His armor was heavy enough to unseat him if he got unbalanced, and that would be a stupid way to lose. Instead he held his lance crooked in his arm and tried to breathe as the monster beneath him thundered across the pitch. Everything seemed to be happening too fast. He and Carrara were surely both going to die. That halberd was a wicked-looking thing. It was angled right for Pietro's heart, and only a heartbeat away.

There was the clatter and scrape of metal on metal. Pietro beat away the halberd's spike with his shield and Carrara's horse sidestepped the lance. A thousand voices seemed to sigh.

Up on the balcony, Antonia was covering her eyes. "What happened?"

Dante was terse. "They missed. They're circling around again."

Antonia peeked. Yes, Pietro was almost directly beneath her, turning his warhorse about for the next charge. His round shield bore a scar just below its center. With a shout she could feel, he urged his mount on to another charge. This time Antonia kept her eyes open almost to the moment of impact, then saw what Carrara was doing and screamed.

Pietro was riding full tilt for Carrara when the other suddenly checked his horse, trying to get the halberd's axehead sweeping upward. Too late to stop, Pietro swerved and brought his shield across. He missed with the shield but, dumb luck, got his lance across the halberd's path. There was an awkward *clack* and the axehead was deflected.

The line of both their charges broken, the two horses moved away from each other. Pietro was desperately trying to disengage, pull his horse back to a safe distance to begin a new charge. In these close quarters his lance was all but useless, while the halberd bore hook, spike, and axehead. Carrara now brought both into play.

Above, Antonia watched in horror as she saw her brother's horse step the wrong way, opening up his back to a blow from the axehead—a blow that descended, aiming for the center of Pietro's spine. No matter how strong the steel of his back-plate or how much of the impact the pourpoint absorbed, he would be stunned, leaving him open for a killing blow. Antonia screamed.

Pietro heard the scream even as he realized how exposed he was. How he got his shield up and over his head he never knew. He felt the halberd's axe-head strike, and the impact twisted the muscles in his left arm. He turned his head in time to see the silver hook at the halberd's back catch the edge of the shield and rip it downward. Pietro involuntarily released his grip on the shield, but the strap across his upper arm held it in place. His eyes were on the axehead. Carrara was swinging it around to complete the disarm by taking Pietro's arm clean off. The lance in his right hand was useless, so he raised his left arm, shield dangling, hoping to somehow ward off the strike.

The stars favored Pietro again. His shield's spike caught the halberd between the axe and the shaft and deflected the blow. Pietro had been kicking with his spurs, and finally the destrier under him responded, tearing away along Carrara's left side. With a flick of his own spurs, Marsilio twisted about to pursue.

Pietro cursed. In close-quarter fighting he was at a disadvantage. Raising the lance, he pitched it backward. With any luck, Marsilio's horse would trip on it, and that would end the fight. That wouldn't happen, of course, but it was pretty to think so.

Pietro's hand scrabbled to draw his sword from the saddle's scabbard. It was a longsword, more than twice the length of Pietro's forearm. He had tried it out before the duel. It was slightly point-heavy, the better to bring a blow down onto an opponent's head or neck. Brandishing it in his gloved right hand, he shifted in his saddle. Carrara was behind him, spurring hard to close the gap and bring the halberd to bear. Swinging the weapon from the very end of the shaft, the Paduan had a long reach but poor leverage.

As long as Pietro allowed himself to be chased in circles around the Arena, Carrara had the upper hand. But the moment he stopped, he would be eviscerated by the spike or axehead.

A sudden image appeared in Pietro's mind. It was of the Scaliger facing a spear on one side, a sword on the other, and a morning star behind. He remembered the Capitano's leg snaking out to grasp the spear. Pietro couldn't do that with the halberd. But he could remove the halberd from play, if he was willing to sacrifice . . . Yes. But first, he had to build Carrara's confidence.

Pietro recalled Cangrande's lesson as they looked at the walls of Vicenza. He had to show his enemy what he expected to see. So he yanked his reins inward, cutting across the Arena floor in a close facsimile of panic. He twisted the reins again, cutting south instead of west.

"What is he *doing?*" demanded Antonia.

"I'm not sure," her father breathed.

From across the balcony Ludovico Capulletto roared in outrage. "He's running away!" His two sons were silent, for different reasons. Antony was rigidly watching the duel unfold. Luigi, silently rooting against his brother's champion, hoped Carrara's weapon would find its mark. Mari and Gianozza were unable to turn away, their feelings horribly conflicted.

"He's a coward," sneered young Mastino della Scala, inviting a clout from Guglielmo da Castelbarco.

"Kill him, Carrara!" cried someone. Antonia twisted around to see a short fellow seated beside Ser Bonaventura. They looked related. She gave the ass a frosty glare, then returned to covering her eyes.

Down in the Arena something drifted across the slit in Pietro's helmet. A snowflake. Calm and quiet, snow had begun to fall. If it got any heavier, it could be an aid, obscuring his actions from view. But he couldn't wait for the weather. Pietro touched his mount's left flank, turning it north. He'd lost all sense of where Marsilio was. Hopefully he'd gained a few steps. If not, his next move would see him killed.

Turning his horse left once more, he yanked back on the reins. His horse was now almost broadside to the approaching Carrara, with Pietro's round shield protecting his body. Behind it, Pietro raised his blade and hacked down. To the crowd, it looked as if he were cutting off his own arm.

"What's he doing?" shrieked Antonia again.

Eyes fixed on the battle, Dante just shook his head.

Pietro peered over the top of his shield. His opponent was approaching fast, and Pietro could almost hear the options register in Marsilio's brain. Pierce the shield with the spike, drag the axehead across it, or hook it again in the hope of stripping away Pietro's best defense. Carrara veered his horse to the right. He'd chosen the hook. It made sense. If Carrara dragged the shield away as he rode past, the strap on Pietro's shield would yank him out of the saddle, cutting him at the same time with the spike. A *mollinello* over Marsilio's head would bring the axehead around into Pietro's chest, finishing him.

Carrara choked up on the halberd's shaft, gaining a finer measure of control. A thousand voices shouted warnings at the boy cowering behind his shield, awaiting the blow that would eviscerate him.

Flexing his grip on his sword, Pietro was praying he was dexterous enough to pull off the move he'd imagined, conjured from his own pure brain. He heard the hooves and saw the snow rise in a gust of air created by the legs of Carrara's horse. There was a flash of steel as the hook swept in.

Here it comes. Oh, God, please don't let me fail.

The halberd's hook caught the edge of the shield. Riding from right to left Carrara used his mount's momentum to heave, expecting Pietro to be dragged uncontrollably forward with his shield, opening him up for the spike and axe.

But Pietro didn't jerk forward. The shield came away from his arm easily. Severed by Pietro's own sword, the loose ends of the strap fluttered in the chill air.

Pietro already had his blade in motion, beating away the halberd's spike with a clanging parry. The Paduan felt his trailing halberd head leap upward of its own volition. His right arm was dragged up with it. That exposed his side . . .

"Look! Look!" cried Antonia.

The stroke started on Pietro's left side and rounded his head in an arc that ended in a smashing blow to the Paduan's ribs.

Marsilio was almost past his adversary when the sword impacted. The armor prevented Alaghieri's blow from severing flesh, but it almost didn't matter. The force of it cracked several of Carrara's ribs. Marsilio retched, and the crowd cheered as he spat blood and howled in rage.

"Clever," breathed Guglielmo da Castelbarco in admiration.

Nico da Lozzo slapped Dante on the shoulder. "Quite a son you've got there!" At the center of the balcony Bailardino and Morsicato were cheering loudly. The doctor roared, "Never seen anything like it!" The short fellow next to Bonaventura was booing loudly. Cangrande watched with a carefully imposed air of impartiality.

Down on the pitch, Marsilio's left hand involuntarily went to clutch his dented armor as his horse pulled him away from Pietro's next stroke. In his right hand Carrara kept hold of the halberd, dragging it along behind him. If Pietro had hoped to end the fight with that surprise move, he had failed. Now he faced a halberd with only a sword to defend him. His shield lay uselessly on the ground, far out of reach.

Pietro cursed. He'd thought only so far and no further. His second stroke, a *roversi* at Marsilio's helmeted head, had sliced only air. No clever moves left, he would have to rely on straightforward fighting.

But Carrara hadn't turned his horse yet, was just now gripping his weapon with his second hand to brandish it anew. Spurring forward, Pietro took up position behind Marsilio, hoping to give chase as he himself had been chased just seconds before.

This time it was Pietro who was lured into position. He was too close for Marsilio to turn his horse about and face him with the halberd. But Marsilio was a practiced rider, well used to tricks of the saddle. As his horse trotted away from the point of last impact, seemingly without direction, Carrara glanced back and cried, "Poor fool! One lucky blow and you think you actually stand a chance? Time for a lesson in reality."

Pietro couldn't make out the words, but he knew they were a taunt. He spurred harder, drawing closer, though not yet within his sword's reach.

Suddenly Carrara slipped his right boot out of its stirrup. With a skill that bespoke years of riding, he stood upright in his single stirrup. At the same time he lifted his right leg, dragging the spur across his horse's flank. The horse turned into the cut, angling right. Suddenly, instead of being pursued, Carrara's horse was at right angles with Pietro's. Hitching his right ankle on the wooden *arcione* at the back of his saddle, Carrara brought the halberd around, the axehead driving in for Pietro's breastplate.

Pietro's sword was high, ready to release a vicious downward stroke. In desperation he drove the point down to catch the axehead whistling toward him, but nothing could parry the blow's force. The curved point of the axehead cracked against Pietro's shoulder, trapping his sword between the halberd and his chest. Pietro's forward momentum was stopped. His stirrups snapped. His horse rode on while he toppled through the air, heels toward the sky. He landed on the dirt with a crash that drove the air from his lungs.

Dante was on his feet, screaming. Antonia heard her father's voice but was too breathless to echo it. Blessedly the nature of Marsilio's move made it impossible for him to turn his horse quickly, preventing him from delivering the killing stroke. He was halfway across the Arena floor before he was settled in his saddle once more. Antonia watched him heft his halberd and start back to where Pietro lay unmoving.

Though Dante did not, several people turned to the Capitano to plead him to halt the combat now. Marsilio had unseated Pietro. He could be declared the victor.

Cangrande said nothing. All eyes returned to the fray.

On the Arena floor Pietro was gasping for air, head ringing inside his helmet. His left shoulder ached, but he was able to lift his arm above his head and wrench himself free from the metal bucket. He swallowed at the cold air that burned his bruised lungs. Blinking the dancing lights out of his eyes, he focused on breathing. A calm, resigned voice said, *Lie still. The end will be quick.*

He agreed with the voice. There was nothing he wanted to do less than move. Yet he found himself turning his head. He saw the horse pounding across the dirt floor. Its path would trample him, even if Carrara's halberd didn't spear him to the ground.

Don't move. Just relax. It will be quick.

Pietro rolled onto his right shoulder and tried to stand, but his weak knee buckled under the weight of his armor. He fell forward, his left hand barely stopping him from crashing face-first into the dirt.

See? You're just prolonging the inevitable. Don't move. It will only hurt for a moment, then you can rest.

Over last night's bandage Pietro's hair was damp with sweat and new snow, making it cling to his eyes and obscure his sight. *I should have shaved my head.* Through the haze Pietro could just discern Carrara's horse tossing up chunks of snowy earth a dozen yards away.

His fingers found the helmet and suddenly the voice in his head changed. *Do it! Don't think! Do it now!* Discarding pain, Pietro pitched the helmet. Carrara easily ducked the missile, but he took his eyes off of Pietro for a split second. Pietro rolled across his good shoulder, propelled by his good leg. His blade rose in the *montante sotto mano,* a rising backhanded slash. He'd never done it, only seen the pictures. He had no hope of damaging the armored horse. Instead he wanted to invoke the horse's training to leap upward and drive its hooves into an attacker. This the horse did. Pietro checked his blow and rolled again, clearing himself to the right of the deadly nailed hooves. Carrara's horse landed on empty ground.

Pietro staggered to his feet. He had succeeded in slowing Carrara's horse and confusing the Paduan, who now saw Pietro standing with brandished sword at the ready. Carrara brought his horse around again for another pass. The crowd booed him for remaining mounted against an unseated foe.

At the far end of the Arena, Jacopo called frantically to his brother. He held a second shield in his hands, unscarred and ready. This shield was meant to be used on the ground, two-handed for defense and offense both. It was as tall as a man, with a long pole running north to south, a spearhead at either end. Jacopo was furiously debating whether or not to rush out into the center of the Arena and pass it to Pietro. He saw Pietro glance over at him. That was all the encouragement he needed. He dashed forward, into the fray.

Pietro's glance backward was to be sure that Poco wasn't doing something foolish. Pietro felt he was in pretty decent shape, all things considered. His breath was coming back and he was armed. Carrara was still on his horse, but Pietro had an idea about that. The halberd wasn't too much of a worry, as long as Pietro didn't lower his guard.

But here came his little brother like a good little squire. Only there wasn't time! Carrara was beginning his next charge. There was no way Jacopo could get out onto the field, pass off the shield, and get clear in time.

"Pietro! Pietro!" shouted Poco, though in greeting or in warning Pietro couldn't know.

Carrara was closing in. With his free left hand Pietro waved Jacopo off. "Down! Down! Get back!"

Jacopo ran faster. Pietro mentally cursed his little brother. They were both going to die. Carrara could trample them and claim it was a terrible mistake, the boy shouldn't have been out there.

The savvy crowd redoubled its jeers for Carrara. Swearing aloud, Pietro did the single thing he knew he shouldn't—he turned his back on his attacker and ran to meet his brother. He heard Marsilio's sour laugh behind him as the Paduan spurred in pursuit.

Pietro and Poco had a single chance, one that hinged on Pietro reaching his brother before Carrara removed his head from his shoulders. Pietro's right leg was trembling and weak, ready to collapse at every step. *Come on, damn you! You can hold up a little longer!* Why couldn't Poco run faster? Pietro remembered the split skin at the soles of his brother's feet, remnants of the foot Palio last night. *I should have asked Antonia to be my squire,* he thought savagely.

Antonia was watching the scene on the Arena floor in absolute terror, no longer able to turn away. The crowd made more noise than ever, most calling foul on Marsilio. Bonaventura's friend was mocking the idiot squire that was running into a duel at the wrong time. She sent another withering glance his way, then silently urged Pietro on. *Don't die, big brother! Do something!*

Pietro reached Jacopo barely five yards ahead of the charging horse. He was screaming something to Jacopo and waving his hand in the air. Apparently Jacopo understood, for he lifted the shield in both hands and flung it forward. In one move Pietro dropped his sword, caught the shield, and pivoted. Driving the spearhead at the bottom of the tall shield into the earth, he dropped to his knees. Jacopo slid across the dirt to shelter himself with his brother behind the shield's protection.

The nobles on the balcony went hoarse crying their praise. Even Mariotto stood to cheer as Carrara's horse balked at the obstacle, veering to the side instead. Pietro caught the spike of Carrara's halberd on the shield and deflected it easily.

"Oh thank God," breathed Antonia. The bastard behind her was booing again. She whipped around, unable to contain her annoyance any longer. "What *is* wrong with you?"

The short fellow looked surprised. "What?"

"Why are you rooting for a Paduan?"

"Why shouldn't I?" he demanded hotly. "A Paduan fighting a Florentine? Neither one is Veronese." He gestured to Bonaventura, hooting and cheering beside him. "My cousin married a Paduan, so I'm supporting the family. Besides, Florence is a cesspit. Have you read what Dante said in his *Inferno*?"

Antonia stared at him in disbelief. All she could think to say was, "That's my brother."

"Then *you* cheer for him," said Bonaventura's cousin, dismissing her.

Petruchio Bonaventura smacked his cousin across the back of his head. "Ferdinando, show some manners!"

"What, to her?"

Resisting the impulse to hit the oaf, Antonia turned away. She heard Nico da Lozzo proclaim, "This is the best fight I've seen in years!"

Guglielmo da Castelbarco cried out, "After this, I'll back Alaghieri in any tournament he chooses!"

Not far away, Bailardino turned to address Giacomo da Carrara. "Your nephew likes his advantage."

"He always had an eye for the easiest course," agreed the elder Carrara. "To my shame, if not his." He looked back toward the field of battle, adding, "Not that it seems to be doing him good now."

Under the deafening cheers, Pietro panted behind the shield's protective cover. "How am I doing?"

"Getting your ass kicked," Jacopo grinned back.

Pietro took a swipe at Poco's head, then gestured toward the far wall. "Get out of here!" He peered over his shield to where Carrara was pulling around again. "Now!" Jacopo ran while Pietro looked around for where his sword had gone. It lay to his left, between himself and Carrara.

The Paduan saw it too. He was slightly slumped after that last charge. Hopefully his ribs were hurting him. Seeing Pietro's discarded sword he jerked his reins, urging his horse forward. Pietro took a step, then saw it was hopeless. Carrara hadn't overshot him by much on that last charge, and he'd easily reach Pietro's lost weapon first.

That might not be a bad thing, though. Pietro had the shield to defend himself, but more, this shield was designed to be a weapon as well. Gripping the haft in both hands, he held it longways across his body. If Carrara wanted to charge again, he would have to leave the sword. If he wanted to grasp the weapon, he'd have to dismount and face Pietro on foot. Either was better than the current circumstance. Pietro had one weapon left on his body, his eight-inch-long silver dagger at his right hip—if he could close distance enough to use it.

Somewhat surprisingly, Carrara chose to dismount. Holding the halberd in his left hand, he dropped to the ground directly over Pietro's lost sword. Reaching up, he drew his own sword from his saddle scabbard and fitted it into his gloved right hand. He swung it at the halberd's haft once, twice. The shaft splintered in two. Now the head of the halberd was a hand weapon. Sending his horse off to his waiting squire, Carrara advanced toward Pietro, brandishing both sword and halberd head. The helmet hid all Marsilio's features except the flash of teeth that emerged in the darkening glow of the winter evening. Puffs of white breath escaped the steel helmet like a dragon's breath.

Pietro planted his feet, the right ahead of the left. That put his wounded shoulder at the back of the driving force, but that couldn't be helped. Besides, he'd always been told the power lay in the hips, not the arms.

Carrara's first blow was, predictably, with the sword. The halberd head was awkward to use this way, unbalanced without the haft. Pietro caught the downward stroke easily, then beat the shield's right side forward to block the halberd's hook. But the clumsy hook was a feint. Pietro saw the sword driving down, trying to slip over Pietro's guard. Twisting hand-over-hand, Pietro spun the shield around and sent the thrust into the dirt. There was the hook again, coming up under the shield this time. Pietro understood Marsilio's plan—attack with the sword and use the halberd to strip the shield away.

Pietro would never have the opportunity to lift the shield to drive the bottom spearhead forward.

Beating the hook away a second time, he was already moving to block the sword stroke. He knew where it would fall and he caught it easily. *If I can't use the spearhead I can still use the shield to attack.* He glanced right. Yes, there was the hook again. Pietro caught the hook with a spearhead and flicked it upward. Before the next sword stroke he pushed off his back foot and rammed forward with the shield, slamming into Carrara's body with all the force he could muster.

Carrara didn't lose his feet, though he did trip over Pietro's sword. Before he could recover Pietro was driving forward again, this time with the spearpoint at the bottom end of his shield. Marsilio sidestepped, bringing his sword around and forward to beat the point away. But the force of his own blow brought the other end of the shield around. The side of the tall oval struck Marsilio in the shoulder above his wounded ribs. He staggered, dropping the halberd to clutch at his metal-sheathed side.

Expecting a counterattack, Pietro had stepped back, bending down to pick up his sword. When he looked up he knew he'd missed a chance to win the duel outright. But he hadn't expected Carrara to be so thrown by a single hit. Pietro thought about the sword in his hand and the tall, ungainly shield that would be impossible to manage singlehanded. He tossed it aside. He and Marsilio would face off sword to sword, point to point.

To the crowd, Pietro's gesture of discarding his shield seemed the perfect act of chivalry. To the soldiers in the crowd, it was the practical action of a smart soldier. But Antonia was confused. "Why did he drop his shield? The spear on it has a longer reach!"

"Too heavy," grunted Guglielmo del Castelbarco, eyes on the fray.

"Good, *mi filio,*" whispered Dante.

Down in the pit Marsilio and Pietro were circling each other. Each panted for breath, glad of the brief respite. Carrara reached up to tear his helmet off as Pietro had done. "Are you—ready to finish this—boy?" he gasped, keeping his right shoulder low to ease the pressure on his ribs.

"Yes," hissed Pietro through gritted teeth. His right leg was shaking, and he'd just noticed the blood seeping from the dent in his shoulder plate. "But—you won't like—how I end it."

"What do I care, as long as you die!" Marsilio's sword rose high, slashing forward in the "thrust of wrath." Pietro parried the blow with an upward stroke, the force of it resounding through his body. His blade came immediately down, cutting the space occupied a moment earlier by Carrara. Side-stepping, Marsilio was already bringing his sword around for a second blow. Pietro caught this too, beating the strike away. Marsilio was focusing on Pietro's wounded shoulder, directing his attacks at Alaghieri's left side. Pietro returned the favor, parrying Carrara's next blow and immediately riding his blade in a glissade back toward the Paduan's wounded ribs. Pietro's hours of horseplay with his friends was paying its dividends. In a fight they had not caused.

Broadsword fighting was not a matter of finesse, more a question of bashing your opponent enough to crush a bone or drive the wind from them. Alaghieri and Carrara hacked and slashed at each other, trading blow for blow. Their attacks brought them closer to the Scaliger balcony in movement that resembled a crescent. Pietro would block a strike to his left that would stagger him sideways. He'd then deliver a blow to Marsilio's right, that would have the same effect, returning them to even footing.

After seven minutes with no decision, both men pulled back, desperate for air. The battle had to end soon. Both felt it. They were past the first rush of battle, the excitement and fear that made the humors flow and wounds easy to ignore. Fatigue was setting in, and fear was causing little hesitations. The falling snow had thickened, the sun was setting. Soon it would be too dark to see. Cangrande had refrained from sending torchbearers into the Arena, probably to force an early end to the duel.

Both men, however, were determined to finish it. Carrara was the first to return to the attack. Drawing a long breath he ran forward, his broadsword spinning in his grip, flicking this way and that.

Pietro watched the arcing slashes of Carrara's blade, unsure where it would fall. His hands shook, his vision blurred, his stomach tightened. He might faint soon. He had to end this. For a deadly moment his mind froze. He couldn't think what to do.

An image came to Pietro's mind. Cangrande, mace in hand, using the handle to block while he spun and struck. The murder stroke. Gripping his sword near the point with his gloved hand, he used his guard to beat aside Carrara's downward blow and spun around. With a hand at either end of his weapon, he intended to put all his weight behind the naked tip above his left hand and drive the tip straight through Carrara's breast.

Carrara blanched, instinctively bringing his blade down to parry. But too late. There was the tip of Alaghieri's sword, inches from his chest.

Then the traitor in Pietro's body made itself known. His weakened leg buckled, and Pietro's sword merely scraped across Carrara's breastplate, sending sparks flying into the snowy air. It was Marsilio's luck that it didn't pierce the metal, but that was all the luck he had. Sheer chance had trapped his sword's cross in Pietro's own guard. The force of Alaghieri's strike sent the Paduan's sword flying.

Pietro's vision was so blurred he didn't see it. He'd wagered everything he had on this thrust. When it had failed to drive home he thought he was finished. Then, blinking, he saw his opponent was disarmed before him. It was as if the Virgin herself had descend to kiss his hands. He extended his sword arm, aiming the point at Carrara's throat. He barely had the breath to say, "Yield."

"Never!" Carrara turned. Ducking low, he threw out a hand to balance himself on the cold dirt of the Arena floor. His armored leg shot out, driving into the fold of Alaghieri's right leg, just above the knee.

The pain seemed to start from the ground, rising through Pietro like water through a geyser. From the elation of victory, Pietro's world became one of agony. As he fell he thought the snowflakes were holding still in the air, as if time had ceased to flow. Each flake drifted into his sight, unique creations of a benevolent God who would surely now call Pietro to his bosom.

Then the ground hit him, face first, slamming his forehead with a stunning blow.

As one the crowd was on its feet. To strike a man's wound received in the duel was an accepted practice. To strike a cripple's bad leg was decidedly unchivalrous.

Pietro struggled to rise, but his body wasn't answering. But he was moving. He felt himself being rolled onto his side. Above him Carrara lovingly produced a miseracordia. It was thin, meant for driving into the chinks of a wounded man's armor. Marsilio lifted Pietro's wounded shoulder to drive the needlelike blade through his armpit, into his heart.

On the very edge of consciousness, Pietro's breathing was labored. His left arm was growing numb. He knew Carrara was about to murder him and was helpless to stop it. He saw the arm draw back, ready to drive in the killing stroke. Pietro's right hand fumbled towards his own dagger, strapped to his right hip. The Paduan slapped the hand away with scorn.

This is it, thought Pietro. *I'll die in battle. A battle over love, one jilted amour. How stupid.*

A whistling pierced the air above him and something thudded into the ground. The hand gripping Pietro's arm faltered. Carrara was looking away from his victim, up toward the Scaliger balcony. Pietro was more interested in the little snowflakes that fell across his face, the feel of them as they melted into his skin.

Carrara shook his head angrily, pulled back his knife again. A second whistling sound followed by a thud at Pietro's feet. Carrara cursed and stumbled backward. He didn't seem to have any more energy than Pietro did. Now that he was denied his chance to finish the fight, the Paduan collapsed in a heap, eyes closed. Carrara's breath had a strange rattle to it as he breathed in and out.

Pietro lay still, feeling his own breathing grow easier. Rolling slightly he could make out two fletched arrows sticking out of the ground at his feet. From this angle, the Scaliger's balcony looked very tall. One leg perched on the edge of that balcony, Cangrande was lowering a bow.

The duel was over.

And, though with questionable honor, Carrara had won.

TWENTY-SEVEN

Flat on his back on the Arena floor, Pietro considered passing out. Suddenly he was gripped under his armpits and lifted up. Sighing, he decided he didn't care where they took him. Eyes closed, he was aware of the journey back towards the Piazza della Signoria and the palace, but it was as though he traveled through a fog. The most urgent thing that pressed on his mind was the need to urinate. He did this the moment he was lowered from the shoulders of the Capitano's servants, even before they removed his armor. He stood beside the wall of the palace and relieved his bladder, knees trembling. Wonderfully, the servants did not protest or mock him. When he was finished he allowed them to strip off his armor and carry him to Morsicato, who dressed his shoulder wound. Morsicato talked, but the words didn't make any sense. Since the tone was reassuring, not worried, Pietro didn't bother fighting the haze to listen more closely.

He came back to himself when he was dressed and seated once more in the great hall in the *Domus Nova*. A hand touched his shoulder. Dizzily, he turned to see his father and sister. They were seated on the bench on either side of him. Dante was talking, but again it was hard to focus. "What?"

"You fought well and honorably," repeated Dante. "I'm proud."

"What happened?" Eyes on his father's lips, he was confused when Antonia answered. "The Greyhound stopped the fight. He said he would adjudicate the matter now, based on your actions."

"What?" For the life of him, it didn't make sense. How could little Cesco have broken up the fight? Or maybe she meant Mercurio. She couldn't mean Cangrande, he wasn't the Greyhound. Pietro's head came around to his sister, but her eyes were fixed on the next bench over. Following her gaze Pietro saw the bandaged Marsilio staring at him through half-lidded eyes. Pietro's focus sharpened instantly. *You honorless son of a bitch. Damn you, and damn this leg. Damn it all.*

The haze had lifted, and Pietro saw the crowd was back, this time hushed in anticipation. Antony was seated on one side, father and brother beside him. Opposite them stood Mariotto and Gianozza, with Monsignore Montecchio and Mari's sister at a slight distance.

A hush fell as Cangrande entered. He did not take his seat, taking instead a firm stance upon the dais. "The duel is finished. Both men fought bravely. I declare the decision to be inconclusive."

Marsilio's energy returned in an instant. "No! I won! If you hadn't interfered—"

"Marsilio da Carrara," interrupted the Scaliger, "you proclaimed that your great motivator this day was chivalry. It was your insistence that Antonio Capulletto's lack of chivalric qualities made your actions permissible. It is decidedly unchivalrous, Cavaliere, to use an opponent's infirmity against him when you are at a disadvantage yourself. I assume you were caught up in the heat of battle—these things happen, even to the best of us. Based on your earlier words, I felt sure when your head cooled you wouldn't want to have won the contest in so despicable a way. So I stopped the match. I declare the decision inconclusive."

Skewered by his own cleverness, the wind went out of Marsilio's sails. Had he not been so tired, had his side not throbbed in agony, perhaps he could have countered the Scaliger's decision. He turned to Il Grande for help. "Uncle . . . ?"

"I have talked this over with our host," said Il Grande. "I concur with him on all points."

Eyes blazing murder, Marsilio sank back in sullen resignation.

Cangrande nodded his thanks to the elder Carrara. "As Vicar of the Trevisian Mark, as well as Capitano del Populo and Podestà of the Merchants, I have the ultimate authority in judicial matters in this region. I have made my decision regarding the duel. But before I proclaim that decision, I will hear once more from the parties involved."

He turned to Antony, whose eyes were fixed on Gianozza. She gazed back at him. Tears started at the corners of his eyes. The moment the first fell across his cheek, the girl strode across the hall to his side, leaving her new husband standing full of fear and confusion. She leaned over her spurned suitor and kissed a tear away. In a voice so soft that none but Antony could hear, she began to speak. He shook his head. Kissing his cheek again, she leaned back. He looked at her, not bothering to wipe away the tears that were flowing freely down his face. Then he turned to Mariotto, who had taken a single step forward.

"Mariotto," said Antony, voice croaking in his throat. "I cannot forgive you for what you've done." There was a long pause. "But neither can I blame you." Again the crowd emitted that sigh. Ludo began to speak but was cut off by his son. "No, Father. I can understand why he did this—though I can tell him I wouldn't have done this to him."

This scored a hit. Mariotto opened his mouth to protest, only to clamp it shut again.

Antony continued. "I love her, Mari. I love her more than you ever will, ever could. She is my Giulia. But I only want her happiness. If you're the one she wants—" He took her hand from off his own and held it up for Mariotto to take. "I give her to you."

Pietro heard his sister's furious whisper, "She isn't his to give!"

But Pietro himself was breathing easier. It was the solution to a bad situation. The girl had said something to salve Antony's pride. He was able now to walk away from this horrible mess the bigger of the two men. His reputation would be immeasurably enhanced, all the more for his obvious fondness of the girl. It was chivalry at its height. All it required was one broken heart.

This was probably what the Scaliger intended all along. Had Pietro not issued his challenge, had Marsilio not accepted, Cangrande would have brought about this same peaceful resolution. The whole duel was pointless, a futile gesture to perceived slights. The Capitano had seen past such things, and angled towards a better, more stable, resolution. But hotter heads had prevailed, and blood had been shed. *My blood,* thought Pietro.

Now the ruler of Verona watched Mariotto and Gianozza as they removed themselves from Antony's side to stand before him. Their ordeal was not over yet. "I cannot express," he said, "how pleased I am with this young man's words. Through his courage we have avoided a feud. It is obvious to me that Marsilio da Carrara was mistaken. Ser Antonio Capulletto is the very essence of chivalry. We are fortunate to have such a man in our lands."

"I agree!" It was a grave voice. Gargano Montecchio stepped forward. "I commend his Christian clemency. I, however, am not at all satisfied. Mariotto

Montecchio has shown none of his fellow's foresight or nobility of spirit. Nor has he shown the courage evidenced by his friend, Ser Pietro Alaghieri! I insist that my son be forced to pay for his transgression." He visibly steeled himself. "I move that Mariotto Montecchio be exiled from Verona."

Ashen-faced, Mariotto stared at Gargano. Never in his wildest dreams did he expect his father's outrage to be so extreme.

This time there was no stirring in the great hall. In the silence the Capitano slowly shook his head. "I cannot see exile as a reasonable punishment. He has not committed a treasonable offense. Besides, there is still the matter of the duel to contend with." The Capitano looked from Pietro to Marsilio. "With no definitive victor, it must be God's will that there be no final decision in this matter. I shall adhere to the will of the Lord. I fine Mariotto Montecchio a thousand silver soldari for breaking the girl's engagement. Half will go to the Carrara family, half to the Capulletti." He focused his eyes on Mariotto. "I have one more stipulation. You have not, in your haste, consummated this marriage, have you?"

Gianozza flushed. Mari said, "No, my lord."

"Good. Then I have reached my judgment. Marsilio da Carrara has said that he arranged for this marriage because he judged it a love too strong to deny. I mean to test that claim. Mariotto Montecchio—I appoint you my envoy to the papal court at Avignon. There you will emulate the Venetian Dandolo and act as my representative in the choosing of the next pope." Cangrande leaned forward. "You may not bring your wife. She is to remain in Verona, a guest of your father's house."

Mari's face burned brighter. "For how long, my lord?"

"For as long as I see fit," said the Scaliger coldly. "This marriage was enacted with indecent haste. I want to see if it will last when the passion cools. You will not consummate your marriage until I relieve you of this duty. If at that time your love is as strong as it is today, you will live out your lives together unmolested. If, however, your ardor has lessened, there will be grounds for an annulment." He looked to all the parties involved. "Is that acceptable?"

"Quite," replied Giacomo da Carrara.

Ludovico was primed and ready to protest. Before he could, however, Antony's head moved once to the left, once to the right. Silently the elder capulletto nodded his consent.

Gargano nodded gravely. "It is wise and well considered, my lord. Let us see if my son can maintain his passion while in your service. I want to further stipulate that my lord della Scala not be out of pocket for this embassage. My son must pay for this trip out of his own monies." Which meant, of course, that Gargano himself would be paying for it. He was determined to flog every ounce of penance out of this.

"So ordered. If that is all, I thank the city fathers for their time and dismiss this assemblage." Cangrande turned to face Pietro. "Ser Alaghieri. If you are sufficiently recovered, I would speak with you in private."

Oh damn, thought Pietro, quailing. He watched as Cangrande exited, followed by most of his retainers.

The Capulletti were already moving, anxious to be gone. Antony looked like he wanted to say something more to Mari, but he was hurried out.

Mariotto turned to his bride, meaning to take her in his arms. At once Gargano interposed himself, forcibly removing the girl's hand from his son's grip. Mariotto's face was a ragged sea of emotion. Removing Gianozza to one side, Gargano fixed his eyes on his son. With lightning speed his open hand came up to slap Mari's face. It returned, backhanded, across the other cheek. Mariotto was so startled he couldn't move. His eyes began to water, his breath began to stutter. "Father—"

"I do not disown you," said Gargano. "Your shame is mine." He departed, daughter-in-law in tow. Frozen with shock, Mari had to be led out by his sister.

Pietro had watched all this in silence. Now he cast about for something to say to his father, something to hide the mounting fear in him. "Where's Jacopo?"

"He's seeing to your weapons and horses," said Dante. The poet meant his expression to convey sympathy, but it came across as stern. "You'd best go see the Capitano."

Pietro nodded. As he departed, Mercurio by his side, he heard Antonia say to their father, "Is it always like this?"

The poet couldn't help laughing.

✦ ✧ ✦

Tullio d'Isola was waiting at the door to the Scaliger's private office. "The Capitano will see you now." He stepped aside to allow Pietro and Mercurio to pass and then closed the door.

The walls inside were of dark wood hung with tapestries. It was a warm and intimate workspace. The Scaliger's marble-topped oak desk took up the whole of one wall. Opposite it were two maps, one of Lombardy, one of the Holy Roman Empire.

Cangrande stood at a marble basin beside his desk, washing his hands. The Scaliger did not wave him to a seat, so Pietro remained standing. Cangrande splashed some water on his face and lifted a towel.

From one side of the room came a rasping voice. "You should be proud, Ser Alaghieri," observed the Moor. Beside him his master was seated, holding some kind of gold disc, a medallion with an oddly twisting cross surrounded by small pearls. Some pearls were missing. "You fought well."

Cangrande's head came up from the towel. "That he did," he said flatly. Setting his towel aside he gazed at Pietro.

"I hear you've been talking to my sister."

✦　◇　✦

In the rooms that belonged to her father and brothers, Antonia was busily bestowing her luggage. The bulk of it would go in the room next door, currently occupied by Dante. Upon returning from the *Domus Nova* next door, Dante had announced his intention to write. "My dear, I am overwhelmed to see you, but the muse is upon me. If you can wait, we shall do all our talking once your brother returns."

"Of course, Father. Nothing is more important than writing." Then, because she couldn't not, she asked, "Is it *Purgatorio*?"

Dante nodded gravely. "I am one-third of the way through the sixth canto—the move and my duties to my new host have kept me from my quills."

"But, Father," interjected Jacopo, who had been waiting for them, "shouldn't we be doing something? I mean, Pietro just fought a duel!"

"And what, little Jacopo, do you think we should be doing?" asked the poet.

"Maybe I could go out and hire some bodyguards—or some thugs," he added eagerly, "to beat up Marsilio!"

Dante's face became flinty. "Though your sense of injustice does you some small credit, you can't possibly imagine that I want our family entangled in a feud. There is quite enough of that idiocy rampaging through the world. Even Cangrande cannot halt it. Pfah!" The poet threw up his hands in disgust. "It will be our ruin! O, Italy, enslaved to a brothel of reasonless passions!"

Antonia rushed into her father's study and started lighting lamps. "Father, sit down. Put this to good use. Jacopo, if you're determined to do something, be useful and have some water heated for Pietro—he'll want to wash when he gets back." Taking her father by the hand she led him to the table littered with his scratchings. Not knowing what his habits were, she simply placed the quill in his hand and headed for the door.

"But, Father," protested Poco from just inside the study door, "Carrara's had it out for Pietro since Vicenza!"

"Jacopo, Father's busy!"

"Don't tell me what to do, little sister."

"Then don't get in my way, Poco!"

"Oh, I can't write at all!" shouted Dante.

Antonia rounded on her brother. "You see?"

"Shut up, Imperia!"

Antonia slammed the door on him. "I'm sorry, Father. I'll make sure he's quiet."

From the table Dante waved his left hand in the air in frustration. "No, it isn't just Jacopo, it's the whole situation! I almost watched my only—I almost said my only remaining son, and that's not true. But Pietro is my heir and I almost watched him die tonight, and for what? I am as angry as I am proud. He is developing a strong need to see justice done, and I'm afraid of what that will do to him in this unjust world! Cangrande understands—oh, why could he not be emperor? Meanwhile the Church consents—consents!—to trial by combat! How the Lord can approve such an infamy, I'll never understand!" He shook his head. "I cannot continue in this frame of mind. Virgil just met Sordello, and they are supposed to speak of poetry, then go to the Valley of the Princes. No, I'm too angry to write!" He threw his quill onto the table.

"Nonsense," soothed his daughter, lifting the quill and tucking it back into his fingers. "You've written me often saying the work you're proudest of was never planned, but extempore. If the wind is blowing you toward invective, use it. You can always remove it later on, but if you are moved, it would be a shame to lose what your muse gives you."

Dante nodded slowly, then with more determination. "Quite. I'll make ears ring from coast to coast—and I'll let these feuders know how they spoil our fine land!" He lifted the quill, dipped it in ink, and began to write in that cramped hand that Antonia knew so well. *Ahi serva Italia, di dolore ostello . . .*

She watched for a few seconds, then slipped out of the study and took a deep breath. *It's good I came. He does need me.* Another daughter might have been hurt that her long-removed father had not sat down with her to effect a proper reunion. But not Antonia, who had the rare experience of a dream come true being better than the dream itself.

Poco was gone, though probably not to have a bath warmed. Antonia spoke to a servant and ordered it done. Unable to start unpacking until her father was finished writing, she sat on the edge of a bed and reflected upon the day. Almost at once she found herself thinking of the short loud fellow, Bonaventura's cousin—Ferdinando? What kind of name was that?—and began to think over the retorts she should have used during the duel.

She was still reimagining the verbal conflict when she heard the outer door open. Dante's manservant greeted someone, and a moment later Pietro emerged from the passageway and into the main chamber, his fine greyhound by his side. Pietro gave her a tired smile. "Welcome to Verona."

Not knowing what to answer, she stood. "Are you all right? Is the Capitano very angry?"

A strange expression passed over Pietro's face. There was sadness around his eyes, but also a strange excitement. "Come here, let me look at you. Good God, you're all grown up."

She studied him in return. He was more than the bookish boy who'd left Gemma's house three years before. He was wearing his hair shorter, there was stubble—though brown, not black like their father's. But his eyes—bright, yet concerned, as if the weight of the world was on his shoulders.

Suddenly moved, she rushed over and hugged him close. Gasping a bit, he hugged her tight for a moment, then patted her on the back. "I'm fine— really. Or I was."

"We're all so proud of you," she said, stepping back. Then added, "But Father also says he's—well . . ."

"Angry? I don't doubt it. Where is he? And where's Poco? I expected them to be waiting to pounce."

"Father's writing, and Jacopo's off somewhere."

"Looking to avenge my honor, right? Just what we need."

"I think he's feeling the need to step out of his big brother's shadow."

Pietro appeared surprised. "I've never had a big shadow. Father's is much more impressive."

"That depends on who you talk to. I imagine all the girls of the city think you walk on water tonight."

"That's Jacopo's area of expertise." Pietro sat down on a bed. "Well, he won't have to worry about my shadow for much longer. I'm going away."

Antonia blinked as if he'd just grown a second head. "What?"

"I'm going away."

"But I just got here—*you* just got here!"

Pietro patted the bed beside him and she sat down. "It's something I have to do. The Scaliger is like Father—proud and angry both."

"For fighting the Paduan?"

"Yes. He could have had the same end result without my risking my life. And I also made him look foolish in front of the *signoria*. Oh, he didn't say so, but I know it. I didn't intend to, but I chipped away at his power a little tonight. This is a story with legs. Having me at his court will be an embarrassment. Besides, I'm going to be persona non grata with the Paduans for a while. With the peace newly established, I can't stay here."

The reasons all made sense, but Pietro made it sound rehearsed. "There's something you're not saying."

Pietro frowned, which crinkled the corners of his eyes. "No," he said slowly. "That's everything."

"But he's not exiling you— your knighthood isn't revoked?"

"No, nothing like that. It will just be better for him if I go away for a while. And better for Father! With my embarrassing Cangrande in front of the Paduans and the *signoria,* I could create a problem for the family."

That Antonia grasped immediately. It made sense to her in the way nothing else could. "I'll be sorry to see you go."

"I'll be sorry to leave. I love it here—and I'll miss my chance to see you deal with publishers. I hear you scare the living daylights out of them."

Antonia started giggling and quickly stopped, embarrassed. It wasn't a grown-up sound, and she had to be an adult, especially now. "I don't suppose you'll take Jacopo with you?"

"God above! I already have one lame appendage to drag along. Don't wish another on me."

Antonia looked down at his right leg. "Does it hurt?"

Pietro shifted so that the limb stretched out full length in front of him. "Like the devil himself was sticking it with hot needles. But, I have to tell you, if this is the price I pay for the life I have now, I wouldn't have it any other way."

"You were able to run tonight."

"Amazing what fear can motivate," he laughed.

She studied him. "You really are very brave. No offense, but I wouldn't have thought it."

He grinned at her. "Me either. Things just—happen. No one wants to look less than what we want to be. I think there's a real truth there. Bravery is not wanting other people to think you're a coward. I know I push myself to do lots of things that I'd never do in my right mind."

"Father says you have a strong sense of justice."

"Father talks too much," said Pietro, but very softly. "What about you? How was the trip? And how is everyone back home?"

Antonia told the tale of her journey, then went on to relate all the Florentine news she could remember. Most of her time was spent describing the wrangling over the new duomo. Twenty years of work, and it was still hardly more than a frame. There was talk of having Giotto do some painting for it, but the joke was that he'd have to draw his grandchildren a sketch to work from.

She spoke of old friends of his. Several of them were getting married or already had. "Do you ever think of getting married?"

Pietro shook his head. "Not in the foreseeable future."

"Tell me. This desire to go—does it have to do with your friends?"

He sighed. "Yes and no. I'm really angry at Mari, but—"

"But?"

"But it's easier to talk to him than to Antony. I mean, when we're all together, it just feels right. The trio. If I'm mad at Mari for anything, it's for breaking that up."

"Poor Ser Capulletto. I met him this morning. He showed me around."

"Well, if it makes things any better, word is he's leaving tomorrow to visit his uncle, who's in Padua conducting some business. In fact, he's been invited to a wedding there. Antony and Mari were both supposed to go, but now it will just be Antony."

"Maybe he'll find another girl and settle the whole mess with a marriage."

"The way he acts, Giulia was the only girl for him."

"I thought her name was Gianozza."

"Oh, no! Not to him. She'll always be Giulia, the perfect woman. Though how she could be perfect and break his heart I'll never understand."

"So you don't believe in true love?"

Pietro studied her. "Do you?"

"I think Father's right . . ."

"Shocking!"

"Love has to lead to something greater than earthly passion."

There was a knock at the door. The steward answered it and admitted a tiny man with unmistakably Semitic features. "Manuel," said Pietro, standing to embrace the visitor like an old friend. "May I introduce my sister, Antonia. Antonia, this is Emanuele di Salamone dei Sifoni, Cangrande's Master of Revels."

Antonia took the hand with little grace. She was a good Church girl and believed much of what was said about Christ's killers. The stories of baby-eating were probably exaggerated, and she'd never seen one with actual horns on his head. But the rest made her want to count the fingers on her hand as she quickly withdrew it.

Her reaction made the man chuckle. *All the more sinister,* she thought. But then he turned to Pietro, saying, "Cangrande has asked me to pass on the name of my cousin who lives in Venice—he'll be able to help you with whatever you need. Just tell him you're coming from me. No, I mean it. Use my name. He likes to play games with new people, and he has a real chip on his shoulder. An ass, but a man of his word."

"I'll be careful," her brother assured the Jew. "What's his name?"

"Shalakh."

Pietro tried to work his tongue around the strange sound. "Shy. . . . ?"

"Gentiles! Here, I've written it down, along with the street he lives on. He should be in a good mood—his wife's just given him a daughter. Give them all my best will you?"

"I will," said Pietro, taking the little slip of paper and tucking it away in his shirt.

The jester's eyes were full of mirth. "Do you remember the song? I've composed some new verses." To Antonia's amazement, he began to sing a cappella:

> *Here you have feasts*
> *With many blond heads*
> *Here you have tempests*
> *Of love and to love.*

They find maids
Always fresh
To prepare trysts
To amble and go about,

One says "So,"
And the other "Also So,"
And the other "Stay Here"
That soon I'll be back.

"Very funny," said Pietro dryly.

There was a crash as something was thrown against the inner door. Manuel said, "Oh, is the old man scribbling again?"

That was it. Antonia said, "I'm afraid I have to ask you to leave."

The little man grinned. "God forbid I should disturb his devoted muse. Pietro, take care of yourself. Like the song said, you'll be back, I have no doubt." Manuel turned to Antonia and bowed, twirling his hat at the end of his fingertips. "*Enchante, mademoiselle.* I'm sure I'll see you soon. Your father and I often like to play a game of chess in the evenings. Feel free to join us." With another farewell to Pietro, he departed.

Seeing the face Antonia was making, Pietro made one of his own. "He's fine! A good man. And, yes, he's one of Father's closest friends here. So it's no harm for you to like him."

Antonia colored. To divert the conversation, she seized upon something she had heard. "Venice?"

Pietro shrugged. "To start. Then I'm off to the University of Bologna, I think."

A brief jealousy flared in her. "To study what?"

"I'm not sure. Medicine, perhaps. Or law."

"When are you leaving?"

"Not for a couple of days," he told her. "I have to hire a groom to come with me and look after my horses, and maybe a page. I don't know. Wednesday, maybe, or Thursday at the latest." He must have seen the tears welling up in her eyes, despite her every effort to keep them back. "There's still time. Now, sit down. I have to tell you all about Father's routine."

✦ ◇ ✦

Pietro did not in fact depart Verona until sunup on Friday, the preparations having taken much more time than he'd imagined. On a kind recommendation of Cangrande's wife—who seemed to take pity on him—he'd hired a twelve-year-old boy named Fazio, the child of one of her servants, to act as combination groom and page.

Of course the rumors flew. Pietro had been in residence in Verona less than a month and already it was bruited about that he was being exiled, that Cangrande had thrown a tantrum and sent the boy packing. It damaged the Scaliger's reputation and only made Pietro appear more the tragic hero. Though it was also noted that Pietro spent a good deal of time during that week closeted with the astrologer and the Moor. Cangrande was said to be as displeased with them as with Pietro. The cause for this was unknown, though many remembered the murder of the oracle and wondered.

Dante was more prolific that week than he had been in months. Three whole canti were completed, including both the angry invective against Italy and a telling section in the Valley of the Princes having to do with father-and-son duos— good and bad.

On Friday morning Pietro was preparing his bags when Tullio d'Isola knocked on the door. In his arms he carried a neat bundle of letters, all signed and sealed. "The Scaliger wishes you to take these to the Ambassador Dandolo of Venice, with his compliments."

Pietro tucked the letters in the leather satchel slung on his shoulder. "Thank you, Tullio."

"I was also asked to deliver these to you, sir." The Grand Butler handed over two letters sealed with wax.

The first was from Antony, thanking him for sticking up for him with the Scaliger. In his plain style, mirroring the way he spoke, he wrote, *You're my one true friend. If you ever need anything from me—even my life—I'll give it in a heartbeat.*

"Poor Menelaus," said Pietro. Two days after the duel, Dante had quoted Homer at court, calling the girl Helen and young Montecchio Paris. The Verona wags had found this particularly apt, since Mariotto was himself banished to France (though not Paris). So Antony was suddenly saddled with the nickname Menelaus.

The second letter was from Mariotto, in which he expressed his deep regrets that his actions had affected Pietro. It ended, *I hope someday you'll understand, and we can be friends again.*

Pietro tucked both notes in with his belongings.

"There is also a letter," said the Grand Butler, "from Donna Nogarola. She left instructions to give it to you in person."

Katerina had left with Cesco for Vicenza the day after the duel. Pietro's breath shuddered a bit and he coughed to cover it. Opening the folded note, he read the brief message written in her fine hand:

> *Dear Pietro,*
>
> *I know why you and my brother quarreled and over what. I regret that I have placed you in a bad position. This exile will not last. You have my word on it.*

> *Katerina*

The paper held the faintest hint of lavender. Pietro tucked it in his shirt. "Say farewell to the staff for me," he told Tullio. "They've made my stay more than welcoming—brief though it was."

"No man can control fate," replied Tullio, and departed.

Curious, thought Pietro as he returned to his packing. *Did he mean fate, or Fate?*

An hour later he mounted Canis and joined a small band departing the city. He and Fazio were not alone. Exiting the city with him were Ignazzio da Palermo and the Moorish servant. Their destination was also Venice, and they had offered to accompany Pietro that far.

Ignazzio and Theodoro led the way toward the Ponte Pietro, the eastern bridge out of the city. Pietro's destrier was tied to a lead that rested on Fazio's saddle. Atop Canis, Pietro lagged behind to allow Mercurio a last snuff at Dante. Father, brother, and sister were all there to see him off. Jacopo made a joke about the world ending if they were ever all in one place too long. Antonia and Poco both waved, but it was Dante's gaze that Pietro felt. The old scoundrel had a good nose, he could sniff out a lie. The poet knew something was going on, just not what. He was not pleased.

No doubt Katerina would have told him that Pietro was leaving because of the boy. That was true. But not in the way she thought.

Pietro hated lying to them all—but he couldn't very well tell them the truth, could he?

That he, the astrologer, and the Moor were off to hunt a scarecrow.

IV

THE EXILES

TWENTY-EIGHT

Calvatone

27 OCTOBER 1315

Exhausted, the soldiers of Verona took their ease in one of the camps that surrounded the blackened walls of Calvatone. The fifth town to fall to Cangrande this month, it had been the hardest nut to crack. But this morning the town had surrendered, and the Scaliger had granted a single night for celebration before his forces moved on to the final goal—Cremona.

October was hardly prime campaigning season, but it had been a nasty summer. First a scorching heat, then heavy rains that had ruined crops all across the north. Meat and eggs began to run out, capons and other fowl died of pest, swine could not be fed because of the excessive price of fodder. Even bread wouldn't bake unless the grain was first put in a vessel to dry.

Up until the rains began, the ruler of Cremona, a staunch Guelph by the name of Cavalcabo, had been a worried man. He had heard the rumors that, with the Paduan wars suspended, Cangrande would be looking to expand west. The Scaliger's excuse would be an old claim that Mantua had rights in Cremonese territory. But without food, it would be madness to march.

In the first days of October Cangrande showed signs of madness. Staging his forces out of friendly Mantua, he swiftly took Ponte di Dossolo, Viadana, and Sabbionetta. This last was a huge blow, for it was where Cavalcabo had sent his money and women for safekeeping. Cangrande sent Cavalcabo an offer—food in exchange for his family. Cavalcabo cursed and, stalling Cangrande's messenger, secretly prepared Cremona for a siege.

Meanwhile Cangrande's soldiers survived on the supplies captured from each town, though the Capitano promised that any surrendering town would be allowed enough food to survive. Towns that held out, like Viadana, were left without means to last out the winter.

Even with the confiscated food, Cangrande knew he couldn't remain in the field long. To his good friend Passerino Bonaccolsi he said, "We have to strike like lighting. If we stall, we're through."

The lord of Mantua was Cangrande's partner in this enterprise, and had the promise of ruling over all the captured towns. Thus he was eager to keep the campaign moving. A week after taking Sabbionetta he led the attack that opened up Piadena, a bare fifteen miles down the road from Cremona itself.

The next city on that road was Calvatone. By now the combined armies of Verona and Mantua with their many mercenary condottieri were well accustomed to siege work. But the hardy Calvatonesi resisted mightily. Three times Cangrande himself led the assault, and each time he was repulsed just as he was on the verge of scaling the walls.

This morning Cangrande had pulled Passerino aside. "We're stalled. Another day and we'll lose our momentum."

"Do we want to make an all-out attack?" suggested Passerino. "Split our forces, hammer them on two fronts?"

"I'd rather not have a slaughter on our hands. I'm going to make them an offer."

"What kind of offer?"

"If they surrender, they can keep their provisions. I know, the men need food. But it's why they're holding out so fiercely. They don't love Cremona or Cavalcabo—it's not pride, it's fear. We'll remove their fear, promise not to hurt a hair on their heads, just let us garrison the city and move on."

Passerino saw the sense in that. "Who should we send?"

Cangrande grinned. "Who's the most practical man we know?"

✦ ◇ ✦

The offer was made by Nico da Lozza. Standing before the town gates under a flag of truce, the Paduan turncoat proposed the Scaliger's terms. "In return for your submission, the honorable Cangrande della Scala, Capitano of Verona and Vicar of the Trevisan Mark, promises to spare the lives of every Calvatonesi, be he old or young, Guelph or Ghibelline! Moreover, he promises that the food and water that is currently yours will remain yours! There will be no looting, no rapine! Every man within Calvatone will remain unharmed, every woman virtuous, all property in the hands of its current owner."

The spokesman for the town called down from the wall, "We must be assured! There must be no reprisals!"

"There will be none! On that, you have the Scaliger's own word. And he is, as you all know, an honorable man! He has never broken a bond! And know this—if Calvatone refuses this generous offer, he pledges to remove your town from the face of the earth. No one will ever know you existed. The land will be salted, nothing will ever grow here again."

"He would lose the war with Cremona!" protested the spokesman. "We are not worth such vengeance!"

"His honor is! His honor could not bear to let you defy him. If you refuse his generosity, it will soil that perfect honor! He would not eat, not sleep, until that stain was removed! Citizens of Calvatone, why risk the wrath of the Greyhound of Verona? Why try his patience, when he wants nothing more than to garrison your city for as long as it takes him to smash Cremona? What do you owe the Cremonese? Is Cavalcabo a close ally, or a tyrant who taxes you and leaves you defenseless before his foes? Use your sense! Hate the Greyhound if you must, but do not stir him to anger! For, I assure you, this hound has the both the teeth and the will to bite!"

The spokesman withdrew. Nico turned to the page behind him and grinned. "How did that sound? Too strident? Did I give myself away? If they say no, he'll probably leave. He's never been one for slaughtering innocents, bless his soft little heart. Here, pass me that wine."

Jacopo Alaghieri shifted the flag of truce to one hand and passed his commander the wineskin. Dante had begged Cangrande to take his younger son on this campaign. "Make a man of him," the poet had said. "The way you did with Pietro."

"Pietro was already his own man," Cangrande had replied. "But as you will."

Assigned Nico's service, Poco knew his commander wasn't well pleased with his performance so far. It was just that Poco couldn't see the sense in polishing something that was going to tarnish again within an hour, or in oiling the joints of some armor that wasn't even going to be worn today. His brother hadn't had to play the page. No, one madcap ride and Pietro was a knight. Poco longed for that kind of action, the moment when he could prove his mettle. Today might be the day. Consequently, seated atop a horse, riding with his master to an enemy gate, he behaved perfectly.

Now he pointed over Nico's shoulder. "My lord, look! They're opening the gates!"

"Of course they are. They're not fools." Nico passed the wineskin back to his page, who was so eager-eyed Nico couldn't help laughing. "Yes, yes, you did well! If by this afternoon my horse is properly rubbed down and my helmet so shiny I can see my reflection, you may join me in the command tent for the inevitable celebratory dinner. Now come, and remember to look grave and respectful. These poor bastards may have done the wise thing, but it's hard for some men not to feel like cowards." Nico chuckled. "Not clever fellows like myself, you understand. I mean men with less imagination."

Poco went along to present the Calvatonesi leaders to Cangrande, then rode in the perfunctory tour of the town that was more about showing the Scaliger off to the people than to look over the battlements. An hour later they were all back in camp, with only some of Cangrande's German mercenaries garrisoning the town.

In Nico's tent, Poco rubbed, scrubbed, polished, and shined everything he could see. He accidentally ruined a finely engraved leg-greave by scrubbing with the wrong wire bristles, but he hid that at the bottom of a trunk. When Nico came to dress for dinner he was suitably impressed. "This is more like it. Go on, wash yourself up and change your shirt."

Soon he was standing behind Nico's place at the table in the command tent, watching as Cangrande and his four generals took their seats. Castelbarco sat across from Nico, and Bailardino Nogarola beside him. Cangrande took the head of the table, and Passerino Bonaccolsi the foot.

Cangrande lifted his goblet. "To the wise Calvatonesi. I am so very pleased I was not forced to emulate Otho. Passerino, if I killed myself in despair, would you do as his captains did and throw yourself on my funeral pyre?"

"I would throw Nico on it," said Passerino.

Cangrande nodded. "That will do."

Nico sneered. "Oh oh! Nice talk, considering it was my silver tongue that opened Calvatone like a woman's flower."

"If Calvatone is a woman, she's a cheap whore to open up like that," said Bailardino.

"An ugly cheap whore," opined Passerino. "Did you see the state of their town hall?"

"Poverty is not a sin," said Castelbarco.

"No, but lack of civic pride is."

"I blame Cavalcabo," said Cangrande. "A skinflint and zealot. And his heir apparent, Correggio, is ten times worse. Say what you will about the other Guelphs, they aren't stingy. You'd never see Florence's smaller cities in such a state."

"Oh, Correggio's not a bad fellow," protested Bailardino. "His niece is going to marry my brother."

"Oh, well, that makes him the salt of the earth," scoffed Nico.

"Speaking of Florence," interjected Castelbarco before Bailardino could rise to Nico's bait, "Jacopo, what's this I hear about a pardon for your father?"

Cangrande started laughing. "Yes, yes! Tell them!"

Grinning, Poco took a step forward and said, "My father got a letter in July—"

"Addressed to 'Durante Alighieri, of the Guild of Apothecaries,'" interjected Cangrande. "No mention of poetry. Sorry, Jacopo. Go on."

"Well, the letter offered Father amnesty. He is free to return to Florence whenever he likes."

"Big of them," said Passerino.

"No, no, wait! It gets better," said Cangrande. "There are conditions."

"Conditions?"

Poco rolled his eyes. "The conditions are, one, that he pay a huge fine, and two, he submit himself to an oblation."

"What kind of oblation?" asked Passerino.

Before Poco could answer, Cangrande burst in. "He has to enter a city jail on his knees and from there walk clothed in sackcloth and a fool's cap with a candle in his hand through the city streets to the baptistery of San Giovanni—the saint that shares a name with Dante's dead eldest son, whose burial the city fathers refused, by the way. At the baptistery he has to declare his guilt and his repentance and beg the city fathers for forgiveness."

Passerino said, "I take it he refused."

"Astonishingly, yes." Everyone grinned. Annoyed that the Scaliger had taken away the best part of the story, Poco was about to step back to his place behind Nico when Bailardino asked, "What about your brother? How is he doing?"

"Is that you asking," said Cangrande, "or my sister?"

"I do have the occasional independent thought," said Bail. "Jacopo, how is Pietro doing?"

"He's settled into the University at Bologna," said Poco. "From what I hear he's doing well."

"I've arranged an income for him, not far away from his studies," added Cangrande placidly. "A little benefice in Ravenna."

"You know, you could just recall him," said Castelbarco.

"Or I could banish you. That would end the conversation even more easily."

An awkward silence ensued. Nico broke it by saying, "I'm glad we're moving on. If we take Cremona, it will eclipse all the talk about Montecatini."

"Be fair, Nico," said Passerino. "Uguccione della Faggiuola is a friend and an ally. We can't begrudge him his victories. Besides, he needed one much more than we do."

"Ten thousand dead and seven thousand prisoners," said Bailardino, whistling. "Not too shabby."

"He couldn't have done it without Castricani's men," said Castelbarco. To Cangrande he added, "Does it ever occur to you, my lord, that these floating condottieri may be leading us to trouble? Each season they are free to hire on to whatever war suits their fancy. Some are making a habit of fighting for one side this year, and the opposing side the next, thus keeping the war from ending. We're spending vast sums on these hired swords, but gold does not purchase loyalty."

"True," said Cangrande. "Nico, what buys loyalty?"

"Land," replied Nico at once. "Land, land, and land. Some men will fight a battle or even a war for a prince or for God. But if you want a man to fight for you the rest of his life, you have to give him land. Look at Capulletto. You could have filled his purse to overflowing, heaped him with titles, but nothing could have bound him to you more than the land you gave him near Bardolino. He's now bound to you more than if you were his father."

Cangrande appeared dubious. "Hmm. We'll see. Certainly he was generous enough in return. The feast he threw in honor of San Bonaventura was magnificent. I haven't danced like that in years."

Castelbarco passed across a tray of food, saying, "The whole affair was definitely a triumph. Ludovico confided to me that he's planning on making it an annual event."

"The only shame was that Gargano wasn't there," said Bail.

"He was invited," said Cangrande. "I made sure of that. But he chose not to come. Said it might mar the occasion. As you say, a shame."

Swallowing, Nico pointed his knife aimlessly and said, "You know who I liked that night? Bonaventura and his wife. I'd heard she was mad, but I don't think I've ever heard sparring the like of theirs."

"Well, they were on display, weren't they?" said Bailardino, reaching over to fill Nico's bowl of wine. "As a Bonaventura, young Petruchio shares the name of the feast's saint. That mad wife's a Paduan, no?"

Cangrande said, "Yes, we seem to be stealing all the Paduan brides."

"I hear she's pregnant," said Poco, earning him a sour glance from Nico. None of the other pages had spoken without an invitation. But his news was enough of a pleasant surprise that the others overlooked the poor protocol.

Bailardino clapped his hands. "Excellent! A year of children! Where did you hear that?"

"Yes, where?" asked Cangrande in a droll tone. "Your spies must be better than mine."

Trying to disguise his pride, Poco said, "There's a girl in Ser Bonaventura's house. I've gotten to know her . . ."

He was answered by laughs and sly looks. Bailardino in particular was gleeful. "Well done, lad! Are there any other pregnancies we should know about—what the devil?"

The tent flap had been thrown wide by one of Cangrande's soldiers, who burst in. "My lord, trouble!"

The five generals were on their feet in an instant. Throwing aside the benches they followed the soldier outside, Poco and the other pages at their heels. "There, my lord," said the veteran, pointing.

Tracing the line he indicated, all heads turned towards the town walls. They were glowing red.

"Treachery?" asked Passerino.

"I'm afraid so," said Cangrande in a grim tone. "But I don't think the kind you mean."

"What is it, then?" demanded Castelbarco. "Is Cremona attacking?"

"No. Someone has taken it upon themselves to break my word. Horses! Arms! Let's see if there's any way to salvage this!"

Nico rounded on Poco, who stared with horror at the growing flames. "Move it, boy! Don't bother with the fancy stuff, just a gambeson, a helmet, and a sword. Move!" With a shove Nico sent him running.

Fifteen minutes later Cangrande led his personal guard as they galloped into chaos. Men on fire, women screaming under the weight of armored men, mercilessly having their way. Not all the women screamed—some had had their throats cut before they were violated. A lone child wandered into the street to be trampled by a mad horse running wild. Blood pooled in the streets, sprayed the pitted stone walls, bubbled in the mouths of blackened corpses.

Poco felt a shiver run from his forehead to his fingertips as he stared wide-eyed at the carnage. But it was the sudden smell of burning human flesh that made him turn his head and vomit down his horse's side. His stomach heaved, then heaved again. He looked around, embarrassed, his eyes watering in the smoke. He saw Nico kill a rapist as Cangrande used his sword to bring final peace to a burning man. Drawing his sword, Poco followed the leaders up and down the street, helping those they could.

Entering one bloody and smoking piazza they heard a voice cry out, "Havoc!" The shout was echoed from mouth to mouth among the garrison of German mercenaries Cangrande had left within the town walls. The havoc cry was famous, a foreign idea that had quickly translated into a simple rule— there were no rules. For the duration of one day, theft, rape, even murder would go unanswered at law. It was the free pass that allowed soldiers to vent their basest desires, enriching themselves or taking out their revenge against the world. Generals sometimes allowed their men to wreak havoc on a town as a reward for their efforts. Sometimes soldiers raised the call themselves.

"Round them up!" shouted Cangrande to his men. "Kill anyone who doesn't instantly fall in!"

His men responded with vigor, turning their blades on their allies with a feral fury that matched their commander's eyes. They worked to secure one piazza at a time, leaving soldiers behind to guard the few survivors. It took almost an hour to gain control of the situation, that being achieved mostly because by then there was no one left to save. During that time Poco watched Cangrande, who never seemed to rest. He was a whirlwind of tightly controlled violence. Terrified, Poco trailed along, barely swinging his sword as he watched each grisly scene open up before him. The worst was when they came across a square where the mercenaries were playing some sort of game, using burning poles to hit balls into overturned baskets. A closer look revealed the balls to be human heads. Some were very small. Poco wept and, in that square, he killed his first man. In that square, none of the mercenaries survived.

The Capitano recognized early on that the town couldn't be saved and so abandoned the idea of fire brigades in favor of rescue parties. Only when the smoke threatened his men as much as the fire did he call for the withdrawal of his troops.

As the sun set its burning eye, the town of Calvatone was a smoldering ruin. Lined up before the collapsing gates were the remaining mercenaries, forcibly dismounted and down on their knees. None had escaped some kind of injury. They looked up at Cangrande, sitting atop his magnificent horse and watching the last timbers fall inward, sending up a spray of sparks and ash. He remained there a good deal longer, his eyes unfocused. Then he turned and murmured an order to Castelbarco, who whipped his horse back towards the camp.

From his knees, the German leader called out to the Scaliger. *"Der Hund!* Why do you persecute us? We were only following your orders!"

Cangrande leapt from the saddle and ran over to the man, striking him across the face with the back of his hand, then the front. "My orders? To murder, to despoil, to ruin my own honor? I vowed that I wouldn't have them harmed! Who gave you these orders?" The leader of the condottiere swayed and shook his head, mumbling something. Cangrande struck him again. "Who!"

"There were written orders," protested the man around his cracked and bleeding mouth.

"Show me these orders!"

"I cannot, *Der Hund!* The last command on the paper was to burn it!"

"Convenient! Who brought these mythical orders?"

"A man I never before had met! But in your colors! And the orders bore your seal!"

Cangrande paused, then struck the man again, a mailed fist full in the German's face that broke teeth. The Scaliger wheeled about and remounted. There were tears in his eyes not caused by smoke. To no one he said, "Now I know how Ponzino felt. Passerino, Bail, bring these curs back to camp. Do not molest them further until I decide their punishment. Nico, take charge of the Calvatonesi, see to their needs. Protect your men, though, in case they try to take vengeance for this. As well they should!"

Cangrande rode off in the direction of the camp. Nico had his men open a path for the disgraced mercenaries, then issued orders for the housing and tending of the few survivors of the massacre.

Poco disobeyed those orders though. Rather than tend to the blackened, the bleeding, the weeping, or the dazed, he found himself a fat tree to hide behind. He wasn't seen again until after the moon had passed halfway across the sky, and when at last he stumbled into his tent he was dead drunk.

✦ ◇ ✦

At dawn the construction was finished. The remaining Calvatonesi were invited to watch. Nico, furious with his page, had ordered him to be present also.

In groups of twenty, the members of the condottiere were led up the wooden steps, hands bound behind them. The nooses in place, they were shoved off the low platform without even the benefit of a priest. The first to go was the German commander.

A knot of horsemen watched the suspended bodies rocking in the air, ropes creaking with each kick and twitch. In the middle of the generals and their men, Passerino watched the mercenary leader choke and said, "Well, he did us a favor."

The look Cangrande turned on him was dangerous. "How do you mean?"

Passerino remained brash and confident under his friend's glare. "Well, however this happened, it will make the Cavalcabo and his Cremonese minions quail in their boots. They'll be shitting themselves to give up."

Cangrande eyed the Mantuan. "Or else make them more determined than ever to hold out. We're stretched thin on food as it is." He shook his head and resumed watching the condemned as they fought for breath, eyes bulging and faces changing colors.

Poco couldn't stand it. "Couldn't we at least help them die? Pull on their legs?"

"No," said Cangrande firmly. "They have to suffer, and more importantly be seen to suffer. We must treat them like common thieves and murderers. I will not be disobeyed. Even if this campaign is over."

His generals turned, all uttering a verbal protest. He responded angrily. "Oh, it would look good, wouldn't it! Even if we take Cremona without starving first, which we won't, this will be what gets the credit! Not honor, brutality!"

"What about the note?" asked Castelbarco. "Did you discover who sent it?"

"If it even existed," said Nico.

"Oh, he insisted he'd gotten the order," said Cangrande, who had spent the night in his tent with the mercenary leader. "Though I am loath to believe him, it remains a possibility that one of us did this."

"Someone with access to your seal," Castelbarco pointed out.

"Or a decent copy," said Bail. "You'll have to have a new one made." Cangrande nodded.

"I think he was lying," opined Passerino, spitting at the dying man twenty feet away.

"Possibly," said Cangrande. "If not, heaven help the man who did this. My martial honor has been marred. I will not rest until the stain is expunged."

"This is a good start," said Bail. The first man had ceased to kick and was cut down, his replacement already being marched into position.

"No, Bail," said the Scaliger. "A poor one, since it shouldn't be necessary. How we win is as important as the victory itself."

They watched to the end without further comment. When the others turned to go, Nico grasped his page's arm. "Pack your bags. You're going back to your father. There's no room for cowards in this army. Or for drunkards who care more for drink than for orders and looking to the injured. In a day of dishonor, you added more shame to the tale."

It sounded strange, coming from the easygoing Nico. Another man might have shown more compassion for a youth facing his first real taste of warfare. Certainly, if applied to, the Capitano would overrule the dismissal.

But Jacopo didn't care. He had already decided that his life as a soldier was over.

Milazzo, Sicily
7 MARCH 1316

"Signore Ignazzio? The wine stands by you."

The astrologer's mind was elsewhere as he fingered the medallion's twisting cross, touching upon each remaining pearl. Hearing himself addressed, he roused himself and passed the fine glass carafe to the regent of Sicily. It never did to keep a king waiting, even a vassal king. Frederick III was king outright of the island of Sicily and ruled its surrounding lands for his brother, King James II of Aragon. That Frederick was only the second of that name to rule Sicily was a touch confusing to Ignazzio, but he didn't bother asking. He had other business on his mind.

Yesterday the king had ordered the arrest of certain bankers, despite what it had done to the local financial markets. Ignazzio and the Moor had been allowed the night and morning to question them. In return, Ignazzio had spent the better part of the day going over the king-regent's chart, reinterpreting it in light of recent world events. Frederick was a practical man, and such men often disdained astrology. But this king seemed to feel that any information gained was worth something.

The sky was darkening by the time the reading was through, and the king was pleased enough to invite Ignazzio to join him in a cup of wine. The cup had become a bottle, the bottle two. Now, as the king-regent refilled his glass he said, "I begin to think you have spies in Palermo. You have described me down to the last wisp of hair on my head. But it seems you spent more time telling me about myself than what awaits me."

"Your majesty, astrology is as much the art of seeing who we are as of where we are going." It was a favorite phrase of Ignazzio's, learned at the foot of his master.

"Mmmm," said Frederick. He was a lean man, with angular features and dark skin—not Moorish dark, but indicative of a life spent outdoors. His hair was indeed thinning, but he retained a youthful vigor. It showed when he spoke, waving his arms before him to saw the air. "It seems a cheat. But still, it must open many doors at court. I mean, here you are, alone with a king."

Of course, they weren't truly alone. Servants hovered somewhere behind them. The Moor was among them. It was awkward, but there was nothing to be done about it. At least here the Moor did not stand out in any way.

Frederick resumed gesticulating. "I'm fascinated by your travels. You must visit many far-off lands. What other princes have you shared wine with?"

Understanding dawned. It was not the reading of the charts but the passing on of news that would repay Frederick's hospitality. Well, Ignazzio wasn't averse to spending the evening singing for his supper. He only wished they could have gotten to this point sooner and spared him the afternoon hunched over parchment.

"As you know, recently I called upon your brother the King of Aragon in Zaragoza."

"Lovely city."

"Before that, Theodoro and I were in England. Before that, France. A year ago we were in Venice, I believe."

"Well traveled. It is something I sometimes miss. I got around more in my younger days. So tell me, what—"

Just then Frederick's eleven-year-old son, Pedro, tousle-haired and smiling, came in to be presented and to kiss his father goodnight. With him came a darker child, younger and just as handsome, if a bit leaner. He was introduced only as Juan.

"I'm raising them together," said the king regent to Ignazzio. "Heir and bastard. That way, there will never be a hint of enmity between them."

"Wise. But then, I already knew it. My spies."

The king laughed and sent his children off to bed. In truth, Ignazzio wasn't sure of the wisdom in pairing these boys. Seeing them together made his fingers itch, and he had to force himself not to ask their respective dates of birth.

The regent clapped his hands together. "Now, where were we?"

"I was about to tell you of my travels." Taking a modest sip of wine, Ignazzio tried to separate news and gossip. "Beginning at the far corner of the earth, some Scottish barbarian named Edward the Bruce has just accepted the Irish crown from Ireland's nobles, so he is now able to add *king* to his title. His brother Robert has already declared himself King of Scotland."

"So there is a Scottish king?" laughed Frederick. "That must have the English beside themselves!"

"Actually, most men seemed more concerned with the trouble closer to home. When I was in London most everyone was talking about Edward II's continuing troubles with some earl—"

"Lancaster," supplied the king.

"Yes, and the rest of the Lords Ordainers."

"Well, they're the ones who truly rule," said Frederick, opening his hands expansively. "That has been going on and will continue. But what of France? Is the new king dead yet? Has the curse struck him down?"

Ignazzio didn't laugh at curses, but he managed a feeble smile for the king. "Not yet. But already there are riots and fighting in the streets. Examinations of the treasury found it bare, and inquests into the state of the finances led to the hanging of many of his father's advisors. To alleviate his finances, Louis has married the daughter of the King of Hungary. I hear they are expecting a son."

From there he expanded upon the news from Norway about a new kind of forge, from Bruges about the wool trade.

"Fascinating," said Frederick flatly. "What about Spain?"

Of course, the regent already knew about the Spanish king's nephew assembling an army, ostensibly to attack Granada. At the last moment, however, the army had changed course in favor of an unauthorized attack on the frontier stronghold of Tiscar. "But," added Ignazzio, "the king is said to be much more disturbed by news from Egypt."

Frederick looked suddenly serious. "Which is?"

"Sultan Muhammad al-Nasir has finally completed his mad canal, dug between Alexandria and the Nile."

"Good God!" The king-regent stroked his chin for several thoughtful second. "So he must really be serious about trading in the Mediterranean!"

"Yes. At least, your brother and the King of Spain think so. The canal reportedly took one hundred thousand men five years to dig."

This last snippet of news was clearly of real value to Frederick. The king relaxed, and the next flurry of questions was less urgent. Ignazzio assumed that he had sung enough for his supper.

The king wasn't so rude, though, as to dismiss him at once. They discussed trends in art, like a new painter in Sienna everyone was raving over. He was called Simone Martini, and he had just finished a work entitled *La Maesta,* an image of the Madonna and child. Already Martini was being compared to Giotto.

"From what I hear," ventured Ignazzio, "that comparison makes Maestro Giotto laugh in despair."

"Truly? I have never seen Giotto's work. Have you visited the Scrovegni Chapel in Padua?"

"No, but I have seen some of his brilliance displayed in Verona. In fact," Ignazzio added, "I heard recently that the maestro has returned to paint an exterior fresco depicting the poet Dante and his patron, the Scaliger."

"That's too bad!" said the king, shaking his head and throwing up his hands in lighthearted dismay. "Exterior frescoes never last. But at least it will erode a little of this Cangrande. There has already been too much talk of this man, this so-called Greyhound. Ever since he humbled the Paduans we hear of little else. That business in Calvatone—disgraceful! Besides, we Sicilians feel a kinship for the Paduans. It was their man Antonio who came here to become a saint. You must visit his sanctuary before you leave us."

"I shall," vowed Ignazzio. He always made a point of visiting holy sites and churches. Too many men looked upon his art as witchcraft, devilry, and he worked hard to counteract such impressions.

Already Frederick was hinting at an end to their talk, aided by the empty carafe of wine. The regent soon brought the evening to a close by saying, "I hope you learned all you needed from those pesky bankers."

"All they had to give," said Ignazzio, feigning sadness. "Alas, it was no aid."

"I am sorry to hear it. Do you think they were holding back? Shall I put them to the torture?"

Ignazzio thought of the Moor hovering over his shoulders as he put his questions to the little staff of clerks and couriers. "No, I think they honestly knew nothing of interest."

"Sad, sad," said Frederick. "But just as well. It never does to torture men today you may be borrowing money from tomorrow. Well, there are always the Jews. Thank you for sharing your learning with me. You may go."

Ignazzio bowed his way out of the royal presence, accompanied by the Moor.

In another half an hour they were riding out of the castle of Milazzo, their saddlebags full and their faces grim. But Ignazzio didn't angle his horse toward the town gates. Instead he headed down a slope toward the seashore. "Just a quick stop at the cave of San Antonio," he said. "I'll bend a knee, remount, and we can still reach Messina by morning."

"It's well we hurry," said the Moor in his rasping voice. Most emotions were lost in the effort to scrape sound from the injured throat, but the clip of the words indicated urgency.

"I know, I know. But you heard me promise the king."

"A promise he had no intention of holding you to."

"But a promise before God nonetheless. Do you disapprove?"

The Moor was silent for a time. "Of course not. I am envious. I have not practiced my devotion in a long, long time."

That gave Ignazzio pause. He knew that the Moor was adept at the Christian style of prayer, but that it was not the faith he had been born into. "After Messina we could—"

The Moor was curt. "After Messina we shall be voyaging to Padua. You saw the symbol."

"Symbols," corrected Ignazzio. The arrested bankers had drawn them copies of the seals on their orders for gold. One was strange to Ignazzio, though not to Theodoro. The other was the Scaliger's own. "Once again someone is using Cangrande's seal to work against him."

"True. But that is not for us to investigate. We must watch the man the other seal belongs to."

Which meant there was no time to waste indulging the Moor's envy. Ignazzio was certain his companion gleaned more danger in the information at hand than he himself could see. What did they know so far? In Venice they had learned that a man fitting the scarecrow's description had received a handsome sum, drawn on a famous bank with offices in Bruges and Sicily. With that information, they decided to head north and see if they could trace the Scarecrow via the bank's branch in Bruges.

During the journey north, luck had blown a small favor their way. Ignazzio had made it his habit to show the medallion that little Cesco had snatched from around the kidnapper's neck to every jeweler and smith he could find. Perhaps someone could at least identify the kind of pearl. But in Antwerp a silversmith said he thought the workmanship looked English. So after a fruitless interview in Bruges, they had pressed on to London. There they had the misfortune of being taken for Scottish sympathizers, which at least told them the medallion was Scottish, not English. They had been forced to flee back across the Channel to France, leaving them with the choice of sneaking up into Scotland by ship and risking capture, or journeying south to Sicily to the other branch of the bank. Ignazzio had been for the former, but Theodoro hadn't wished to chance their fate to the whims of the seas. Which brought them to today, and the image of two seals. One was unmistakably the Scaliger's. The other? The Moor certainly knew. Had Ignazzio ever seen it before? He was sure he hadn't. So then, whose was it? Dying to ask, he fought to restrain himself.

But then he realized Theodoro had already given him a clue. They were heading for Padua, which meant the seal's owner was a Paduan. Or resided there.

Glancing over at the Moor, lit now by the stars and the occasional torches in the street, Ignazzio said, "When can you tell me his name?"

"When we are gone from this place."

Ignazzio nodded. "All the more reason to pray to San Antonio for a safe journey." With that the astrologer kicked his heels, urging his mount down the cobbled decline.

Milazzo was not so much a town as a seaside getaway for the wealthy. Situated on a bluff just north of the road between Palermo and the city of Messina, its only true claim of notoriety was in being the place where San Antonio was shipwrecked a hundred years before. The Patron of Lost Things, the Poor, and Travelers, Antonio held the distinction of receiving the second quickest ordination as saint in church history, a mere 352 days. The holy man who held the record, ironically, was a Veronese. Rivals in everything.

San Antonio's cave was at the bottom of the bay, far below the castle. The bluff the town was built upon was known as the Head of Milazzo. If that were literally true, the cave would have been the nose, with the mouth opening out onto the rich blue water. The cave could only be reached on foot, however, by a panoramic stair cut into the stone facing. Ignazzio dismounted at the plateau leading to the stairs and began tying the lead of his mount to a spindly tree.

The Moor was gazing at the starlit water and the small vessels bobbing along the quay. "It may be prudent, this time of day, to sell our mounts and hire a fisherman's boat for the night."

Ignazzio was pleased by the notion—he'd had no desire to risk the lonely ride to Messina. He took his horse's reins and handed them up to the Moor. "Excellent. I shall meet you here."

With that, the astrologer lifted the hem of his robe and began the descent.

✦ ◇ ✦

Having at last found a willing fisherman—pleasantly also a Moor—Theodoro returned to the appointed spot later than he had expected. He was surprised, therefore, when he did not find Ignazzio waiting for him. He looked about the plateau for a place to sit, sure that the young astrologer was taking his ease. There was an impression in the cliff face just opposite the carved stairway. The top jutted at such an angle that no light penetrated its depth.

Something about the shadow made him draw his blade. Stepping closer, he heard a sound until now drowned by the slap of the surf below. It was a gibbering whimper, made by a voice he knew.

Placing the blade near at hand, the Moor knelt down without speaking and sent his hands questing into the shadow. At once he encountered flesh. It recoiled from his touch. "No-o-o!" cried a ghostly version of Ignazzio's tenor.

"It's me," said the Moor.

"Oh Master!" Ignazzio grasped the Moor's hands and dragged himself gasping into the starlight. "I'm sorry—so sorry . . . !"

"Who did this?"

Ignazzio doubled over in pain. He was covered in blood, which seemed to be coming from his midsection. "S-scarecrow! He was here—waiting! For months, he said! He knew we'd—we'd come here—bankers—"

"Hush," said the Moor. Most of Ignazzio's clothes had been ripped away by some kind of blade, revealing the small, pudgy body. "You need not speak."

The astrologer shook his head. "No—you have to—he, he said I—I had something of his! He searched me—I'm sorry, tell them I'm so—" Ignazzio's scream became a long whimper. "He took it, he took it!"

"I know." The Moor had already seen the absence of the medallion with its twisted cross. He was busy examining the wound while he listened. A curved knife or sickle of some kind. Stabbed in the groin and torn upward almost to the breastbone. It was a marvel Ignazzio had lived so long.

The dying man moaned, twisted. In a voice that was more complaining than grieving, he cried, "I never saw this in my stars!"

The Moor sat and cradled Ignazzio's head in his arms. "The stars show the path, but not each step."

"Oh dear God, dear Christ! It hurts so . . . !"

"Shhh. Through this pain there is peace."

Ignazzio shook his head violently, then stared up with pleading eyes. "Master, I have served my purpose. Have I your goodwill?"

The Moor nodded. "You have. That, and my thanks."

"Then spare me, master! Spare me this—indignity!"

Theodoro of Cadiz, which was one of many names the Moor used, leaned forward and kissed his pupil's forehead. Then he put one hand on each side of Ignazzio's head and, taking a shallow breath, he pulled up and to the left. There was a sound like splintering brush, a rattling exhale, then the shivers and convulsions that follow such a death.

So. The medallion was worth more than they had thought. It was worth murdering for. Not only that, worth the effort of tracking them here. Or had he been waiting? Was he crouched nearby, listening still?

The Moor wasted no more time. He laid his pupil's corpse across the mouth of San Antonio's cave with enough gold to pay for a decent funeral. Then he returned to the fisherman and boarded the rickety boat. Halfway to Messina he changed their destination. He disembarked in a small village and immediately disappeared into the Moorish community there. It was time to blend in, to resume an old identity. Perhaps even his real one.

But first he must write to Pietro. The boy needed warning. Their enemy was on the move again.

Vicenza

17 AUGUST 1316

In June Cremona's Cavalcabo had stepped aside as ruler to be replaced by Giberto da Correggio, a rabid Scaliger foe despite the fact that his niece was married to Bailardino's brother. Annoyed by this appointment, the Scaliger and Passerino Bonaccolsi returned to their western war and laid siege to Cremona by land and water. Jacopo was not sorry to be among those left behind.

There were those who were sorrowful, though. One was Bailardino, who refused to war against a relation. Another was Giuseppe Morsicato, barber, surgeon, and knight. He had not been at Calvatone, which he lamented, for they had certainly needed his skills. This year his master was not taking the Vicentine army out on campaign, and so Morsicato was forced to sit around, wasting his days nursing cases of heatstroke and overindulgence.

This particular evening found him at the Nogarola palace looking after an ailing squire. The youth was stricken with a summer fever, and there was little to be done other than make him sleep. Morsicato's favored mixture of poppy seed juice and crushed hemp seeds would make the boy rest until his fever either broke or killed him.

It promised to be a long night, and he was hungry. Morsicato's wife had been asleep when he'd gotten the call and so hadn't ordered the maid to send food with him. Typical of Morsicato himself, he simply forgot. That was the way it always was—the urgencies of his profession overrode all practicality. Now, having seen the boy and tended him as best he could for the moment, the balding doctor with the forked beard made his way down to the kitchens of the Nogarola palace.

He spent twenty minutes scrounging food from the cupboards, ending with a cold pheasant leg and a hunk of hard, crusty bread. He tried to find something other than wine to sop the bread in and was rewarded with some broth, which he spooned into a large wooden bowl. Having been a soldier, this was a meal he could appreciate. It was similar to a campaign meal, which was appropriate—most of the doctoring he'd done in his life had been on one battlefield or another.

It had been after his first battle (dear God, decades ago) that he'd learned how to set a broken arm, bind a broken head, and saw off a limb that would otherwise grow gangrenous. His amateur skill and steady stomach had been noticed and he'd been trundled off to Padua to learn medicine. It was note-worthy that even during the flare-ups of the interminable war with Padua, any Veronese wishing to study medicine could go and learn. There were never enough doctors—especially ones skilled in battlefield treatment. It was his luck that he was good at all aspects of war.

I ought to be with my patient. He gathered what was left of his meal and climbed the stairs, chiding himself for his thoughts of war. His first knight-hood had had nothing to do with battle. He'd been doctoring on loan to the late emperor's army when he'd restored the adopted son of one of Heinrich's men. As everyone knew, though, the rescued boy had been Heinrich's own bastard. The Emperor had been grateful enough to create Giuseppe Morsi-cato a knight of the Order of the Knights of Santa Katerina at Mount Sinai. Morsicato's twin knighthoods by Cangrande and the *Anziani* of Vicenza had followed shortly thereafter, given out of a kind of piqued pride, so now Mor-sicato carried three Orders of Knighthood on his shoulders. All for saving a bastard son of a bastard ruler.

Thinking of that, his mind came inexorably around to progeny. Heirs. One in particular, under this very roof.

Thinking of the boy, he decided to check on the little scoundrel. Passing his patient's door, he continued on down the hall until he reached Cesco's door. Something was odd, but it took him a moment to realize what was miss-ing. There should have been a guard here. Instead, there was a closed door lit only by the moon shining in the casement at the end of the hall.

Something glistened on the tiled floor. Not even a pool. A few drops, nothing more.

Morsicato laid his meal aside and glanced about. No weapons hung on the walls because the little imp had proven too successful at prying them down. Morsicato only had the thin knife he used for probing wounds. It would have to do.

Advancing toward the door he leaned his ear against it and heard a rustling, then a whisper. "Where are you, my little puppy? Come out and play."

The voice inside the room was playful. The drops on the floor were not. Morsicato wondered how many there were and where they had hidden the body of the guard.

He could try the door. But if he made noise they'd be warned, and he'd have to break it down anyway. And noise was his friend, not theirs. Stepping back, he lowered his left shoulder and ran.

The door burst open with a great rending of wood. Knife ready, Morsicato stumbled into the chamber, looking about quickly.

They had a covered lantern. It was the first thing he saw, and almost the last. A blade came at him and he threw himself aside. The Scaliger would have rolled, or blocked it, or done some dazzling feat of physical prowess. Morsicato barely avoided being gutted. Stumbling into a table, he dropped to his rump and ducked under it as the second blow came. "*Aiuto! Aiuto!*" he hollered, kicking at his attacker's shins. He had to hold out long enough to raise the alarum.

There was a shuddering vibration over his head, then the table lifted into the air. Morsicato was struck in the head as the table was tossed aside by a second man. Morsicato threw himself forward and lunged out blindly with his knife. He felt a jolt as his blade met flesh. A kick from the second man jerked his arm, twisting the knife. A man yelped and fell on him. They struggled while the other man kicked them both.

Morsicato heard the sound of footsteps in the distance, many of them, pounding their way toward Cesco's room. He'd awakened the household and, in answer to his cries, they were coming. Morsicato's foes extricated themselves and ran to an open window. Morsicato tried to follow, but one of the villains knocked the lantern off its resting place, spilling oil and fire across the floor. Morsicato cringed back from the burst of heat. Grabbing a tapestry off the wall he threw himself down to smother the flames. At once he was engulfed in pitch blackness.

The darkness was brief. Torches from the hallway created flickering shapes on the wall in the room. Then the chamber was filled with armed men—two knights with swords, some servants with chamber pots poised for throwing, a page with a sword much too big for him to wield usefully.

Bailardino appeared, shoving his way to the front. His expression was one of disgust. "What the hell is it? What's he done now?"

"Two men—" gasped Morsicato. "No guard—I tried to . . ."

Instantly Bailardino changed his tune. "Get a light in here!" The torchlight showed that the room had been thoroughly ransacked. "Bloody hell." He issued orders to search the courtyard and the surrounding streets at once. The knights and the page ran out, encountering more men in the hall and recruiting them for the chase. More lamps were lit, and Morsicato tried to assess the damage.

The room was a shambles, but not from the brief fight. Quiet but determined, the two men had been tearing the room apart, looking for something. Someone.

Trembling, Morsicato reached the child's bed. He was unaware of holding his breath until the air hissed out of him. He glanced over at Bailardino. "Look at this."

"What is it?"

The bedding and mattress of straw were hacked to shreds. No blood. No flesh. No sign of the child.

"Where is he?!" The question came from the door. In her robe, her long tresses released from their coil for the night, Katerina della Scala was a lovely sight. Until one noticed that her face was the color of day-old ashes. At a run she crossed the room to gaze down upon the ruined bed. Her hands twitched slightly. "Where is he?"

"This wasn't a kidnapping," her husband said, touching a loose feather floating in the air. "They mistook the pillow for him at first."

His wife had already come to the same conclusion. "Then he was hiding."

Morsicato looked around at the ransacked room. "If that's true, they hadn't found him by the time I interrupted them. He must still be here."

Their adult eyes scanned the room in the same arc, left to right and back again. They saw no place for a child to hide that had not been ransacked.

"Where could he have gone?" asked Morsicato.

From above, there came a stifled giggle.

As one their eyes traveled up to the rafters. Setting his right foot on the ruined bed, Morsicato gripped the wooden struts of the crossbeam above. With an awkward hop he pulled himself up. Bail's hands made a cup for the doctor to stand on, lifting the doctor until the forked beard jutted over the massive wooden brace.

Twinkling green eyes flecked with gold gazed back at him. "H'lo."

"Hello, Cesco," replied the doctor with a sigh. He sent a look of triumph down to the others, then found himself being used as a ladder by the child. Stepping first on Morsicato's head, then his shoulders, the child dropped lightly onto the bed.

How he got up there they could never afterward discover. But clearly when he'd heard the scuffle outside the door he'd climbed to a place of safety and waited in complete silence while the intruders searched for him. The timber was wider than his small body and entirely hid him from view.

From the remains of his bed, two-year-old Cesco grinned up at his foster mother. But for the tear-streaks down his face, he might have been unaffected by the events of the night. "Here I am, 'donna."

She made no move to embrace him. Her gaze was level, her voice calm. All sign of emotion vanished in the blink of an eye. She said, "I've been wondering where you hid when I looked for you. I shall remember to look where only monkeys, not men, may go." The child was momentarily downcast. Katerina held out a hand. "Come. Since you've made a mess of your room, you are being demoted. You shall spend tonight in the nursery."

Cesco's entire face lit up. The nursery was the room where his foster brother slept. The only time one could count on Cesco to be well behaved was when he was with Katerina's young son. Which meant they were often kept together.

At the door Katerina turned to her husband. "I'll write to Francesco."

"I'm Cesco," said the boy.

"Hush." Katerina led him away, leaving Bailardino and Morsicato looking around the disorderly chamber.

The doctor said, "She realizes what this means?"

"Not much slips by her. I'd better go find where they hid the guards. I hope they're hurt, not dead."

Morsicato followed Bailardino out of the child's room. "They had accents," he said, just remembering. "I don't know what kind—it wasn't familiar to me."

"Splendid. Now the enemy is hiring mercenaries."

But the doctor's mind had already moved on to imagine what Katerina's note to Cangrande would say.

He might have been surprised at the tone of the letter. She used a code known only to her father's children, of whom only three remained. After describing the evening's events, she added a coda that proved she had come to the same conclusion as the doctor:

The stakes of your game have changed. This time they did not seem intent on taking Cesco. They appear bent on murdering him. The time for your precious secrets may be past. Next year he will be three, and you know what the astrologer's charts say. If you know who is threatening the Greyhound's future, you must take whatever steps you deem necessary to stop them.

Her brother's reply arrived three days later and was characteristically brief:

I have no proof, and I will make no accusations without proof. If you want to see the boy live, you'd best protect him better. Or else trust the stars. Isn't that what you always told me?

Reading this, Katerina balled up the note and threw it in the fire.

TWENTY-NINE

Ravenna

15 MAY 1317

The May sun above reflected off the waters of the Rubico River. Pietro reached into Canis's saddlebag and lifted out a hunk of cheese, made locally. Today was an idyll. The weather was glorious. Returning from a lecture in nearby Rimini he pondered the topic, the need for good judges in this lawless world. "There's a real need," the professor had pronounced in the open-air theater, "for justice in the world today. And if the world needs knights to enforce laws, doesn't it also need judges and advocates to decide what those laws are and what they mean? Judges are more important than knights because, in the end, it's the judges who have to decide what justice is."

Atop Canis Pietro now wondered, *Isn't the man who enforces the justice as important as the man who decides what justice is?*

Pietro was coming to love the law. Before going to university he could never have imagined loving a concept. Oh, he knew his father loved poetry. But now he understood. What poetry was to Dante, law was to his son.

It was a passion two years in the making. After the brief stay in Venice, where Ignazzio and Theodoro had picked up the scarecrow's trail, Pietro had gone to Bologna. It was supposed to be a pretense, Pietro pretending to study while waiting for news of their quarry. But the weeks had turned into months, and for Pietro the end was lost in the means.

Growing up in Florence, Pietro had been trained in the basics of learning: grammar, logic, music, arithmetic, geometry, astronomy, rhetoric. But a hundred miles north of Florence, young men were striving daily to know more. Eschewing the common precepts of learning, they came to La Cittia Grossa, where the learning was as impure as the sausage invented here. Mortadella—bones, gristle and hooves, the deadest part of the pig, turned into a delicious meal. So the faculty explored the darker sides of life to find the unsavory but longed-for truth.

Bologna was second only to Paris as a repository for written knowledge. But unlike Paris, where the students ran around creating unchecked chaos, students at the Studium of Bologna made the rules and hired the faculty. Many of the students were already practicing doctors and lawyers. The motto here was *Bononia Docet*—Bologna Teaches.

Pietro had found it fascinating, and had been greeted as a kind of celebrity—he was, after all, the son of the great poet Dante. Through Cangrande's subtle influence Pietro had started by taking classes in law, but soon he couldn't resist dabbling in other topics. He had found himself thrust headlong into new ideas, scandalous thoughts having to do with the body as the root of truth, or Truth. The new art of opening up the dead for knowledge of anatomy and alchemy was as horrifying as it was enlightening. The latest argument in the new field of theology was that sex was the path to God.

Then, just after Calvatone, Pietro had received a coded letter from Cangrande. It was quite usual for letters to be coded, having to pass through so many hands. Typical of the Scaliger, the letter didn't mention the stain on his honor. Instead, he had been entirely solicitous of Pietro's situation:

> *It seems the hunt is going to last longer than we expected. I want you to stay where you are. As you reside between Padua and Florence now, you are in a perfect position to hear things of interest to me. Especially since it is generally thought we quarreled. On top of which, I have directed Ignazzio and a few other of my spies to write any news they have to you. Calvatone is further proof that someone close to me is acting against my interests. As long as that person is at liberty, I cannot have sensitive information coming here to the palace. I am relying on you to coordinate any information that comes to me. I will make arrangements for those to be brought to me by a hand I trust.*
>
> *In the light of this change in your assignment, I have a suggestion to make. A rented room is impermanent, it suggests mobility. I want your name to be linked to Bologna—or rather, unlinked from Verona. To fur-*

ther this, I have arranged with your father's friend Guido Novello of Po-
lenta for you to be appointed keeper of the Benefice of Ravenna. It is a
secular post for the Church, and your only duty will be to collect tithes
and settle minor disagreements. It also comes with a casa. You will move
in at once, and hire a couple of local servants. You will be close enough to
Bologna to continue your studies, and it will be more secure if you have
visitors.

The job also requires you to train a few men-at-arms. Make certain
you do. Contact Manuel's cousin in Venice if you require more funds.

Cg.

For more than a year now Pietro had made Ravenna his home, leaving for
weeks at a time to study in Bologna, then returning to collect tithes and arbi-
trate disputes between the laity and the Church. It was good training, he
thought, for the career that now lay spread before him. Though he was wary
of being a lawyer. That was worse than being an actor.

Wading his horse through the water by Pietro's side, his groom, Fazio,
said, "Hot enough."

Pietro felt the glare of the cloudless sky. Beneath him, Canis finished pushing his way through the waters. The ankles of Pietro's boots were wet, but no
higher. A slight breeze passed pleasantly by. "Let's stay here a moment, let the
horses cool off."

Fazio obediently dismounted and led his horse back to the water's edge.
Pietro did the same with Canis. They both stood looking down the length of
the divide. Pietro said, "Nearly fourteen hundred years ago the greatest soldier in history picnicked over here."

"Who do you mean?" asked Fazio.

Pietro laughed. "Caesar!"

"Oh, him," said Fazio dismissively. From a smallish boy he had grown into
a wiry fourteen-year-old. He rarely had much to do and, to Pietro's dismay,
had taken to throwing dice in his spare hours.

"What, you're not impressed?"

"He's got nothing on Cangrande."

Pietro chuckled, shaking his head. But the act of crossing the Rubicon was
a legal question that fascinated Pietro. *It was almost this exact spot that Caesar*
left legality behind to claim his due. That act brought about an empire—the

rule of one over the rule of many, the way God intended. But how can a man who puts himself above the law then claim to defend it?

On the far side of the river Mercurio darted out of some bushes and made for his master. In a moment both Pietro and Fazio were sprayed with water as the hound shook himself dry.

Fazio shouted, "Dammit, Mercurio!"

The hound was already stalking a woodchuck in the bushes. Ravenna had agreed with Mercurio. The dog had grown into a fine-looking hunter, also becoming a father last winter with some neighborhood bitch. Pietro had adopted the whole litter, though being mixed they wouldn't have the promise of Cangrande's purebreds.

Ravenna had agreed with Pietro, too. A fine coastal town close to both Polenta and Bologna, too near to Venice to be a great sea power, it was a quiet city. Sleepy. Pietro liked it. And he'd become a welcome member of the community. His duties didn't demand much time, consisting mostly of riding from farm to farm, knocking on doors, sharing a glass of wine, and taking the tribute due the Church. He'd been given command of twenty men in case of local strife or trouble collecting dues, but so far he'd never needed to call them up. But, based on Cangrande's hint, he had kept them training even when he was away in Bologna. As a result they were in better fighting shape than he was.

His readiness for war was always near the forefront of his thoughts. He worried that Cangrande meant to call him up for the war in Cremona. Cangrande and Passerino Bonaccolsi were currently besieging Brescia on the far side of the Laga da Garda. Verona itself was being guarded by Dante's former patron, Uguccione della Faggiuola. The former Pisan lord was one of Pietro's many correspondents.

As was Donna Katerina. She kept Pietro informed on a variety of subjects, but her main topic was always the boy. Cesco was just past his third birthday now, and his volatile nature was keeping the entire palace staff on their toes. Each day she could see the wheels of his mind turning on some new project or plot or quest. Brilliant, but dangerous, was the general consensus. Katerina's pride shone in every inked word.

Smiling up into the warming sun, Pietro whistled Mercurio back. Remounting Canis, he tapped him with a booted toe. It was a lovely day, and Pietro was in no hurry. In three or four hours he would arrive at his house on the outskirts of the city. He could spend the afternoon in the shade of his loggia reading scraps of parchment, looking down on his neighbor's vineyard. The local wine wasn't bad. Pietro could open a bottle when he got home, perhaps even read the new pages his father had sent him. *Purgatorio* was reaching a conclusion.

Yes, he knew he *could* do these things, but that he probably wouldn't. Instead he would heft his sword and spend the latter part of the day imitating a real soldier, working the muscles of his shoulders, arms, and hips. Fazio would happily partner him and waste no time in showing how fast he could move.

Pietro's eyes had taken in the mounted figure in the road before his mind had registered it. It took Fazio's saying, "There's someone in the road," to make Pietro straighten in his saddle.

"Stay close, and keep an eye behind us," he told his page. "But don't be obvious about it." The fear wasn't so much the man in the road as the possibility of a dozen men behind them. A man who took in taxes for the Church was a ripe plum for highwaymen, and there were a lot of unemployed soldiers in the world who had to make a living somehow.

The figure was remarkably still, and remarkably odd. Tall, he was dressed in loose robes and had what looked like a cloth helmet on his head. Then Pietro took in the man's skin color and the shape of the sword at his side and kicked his horse into a faster trot. He pulled up in front of the Moor and shook his hand. "Where the devil have you been?" he demanded, a grin stretching his face.

"In hiding," said the Moor baldly. "You got my warning?"

"I did," said Pietro. "Ignazzio's dead?"

"He is." The Moor turned his horse around to the direction Pietro had been traveling. "I have news, and orders. Come, we can talk as we ride."

"You'll come home with me," said Pietro, half question, half offer.

"No," rasped the Moor. "It would be best for us not to be seen together." He looked at the page and saluted. "Hello, young master Fazio. You have grown." Fazio didn't know how to respond, so he gave a hesitant half-bow. "Your master and I must speak in private. Will you ride ahead and keep watch?"

Fazio looked to Pietro, who nodded. Resentfully Fazio remounted and started his horse walking, trying to remain within earshot.

Pietro pulled his horse level with Theodoro's. "You said orders. You've talked to him?"

"Yes. I have spent the last several months in Padua."

"Isn't that dangerous? You're fairly memorable."

"As long as you play into men's expectations, you can become invisible. I was in the guise of a lion tamer's assistant." Pietro could not keep a laugh from escaping, and the Moor flashed him a brief smile in return. "Yes. There is an Egyptian who owed me a kindness. He is a rather famous animal-master. At my urging he brought his menagerie to Padua. I went with him, wearing a covering on my face and throat. The story was that I had been careless one night and gotten mauled by the lion."

Pietro's smile had a different quality, an admiring one. "So everyone pitied you, and thought you were a fool."

"Yes. I often sat in the street, drinking to soothe the pain of my injuries. As it happened, the house I lounged in front of belonged to the Count of San Bonifacio."

Pietro's smile vanished. "He's the one who paid the scarecrow."

"Yes. We learned that in Sicily. He's working with whoever is plotting against the Capitano. I watched his house for weeks, noting everyone who entered. Last month he received a visit from an acquaintance of yours— Marsilio da Carrara."

Pietro's eyes narrowed. "That can't be good. Do you have any idea . . . ?"

"I had already determined the best way to break into the Count's lodging, and I thought that this meeting was the moment for it. The Count proposed a plan to your friend, and the other man accepted. Warily, I might add. Carrara doesn't trust the Count."

Pietro said, "It makes me like the Count a little more. What's the plan?"

"They mean to take Vicenza."

"Oh-ho."

"Yes. He's got the support of maybe fifty dissatisfied Vicentine citizens and all the exiles. He's convinced the Paduans that they can't lose. Vinciguerra's plan was to bribe one of the city garrison to admit his men and the Paduan army. They'll storm the gates and have the city within an hour."

"You told Cangrande, of course."

"Yes. Under the pretence of being sent to buy a unicorn, I met the Scaliger and informed him of their plans."

"So he's going to bolster the guards in Vicenza, make sure no one can be bribed?"

"He could do that," replied the Moor, "but he'd rather let the attack go ahead."

Pietro recalled a conversation years ago in a lonely church. "Because they'll be breaking the truce."

"Yes. If he waits seven days, he'll have a just war to fight."

Pietro wasn't sure if it was truly a just war if you chose not to avoid it. "Seven days?"

"Cangrande has arranged for a young Vicentine guard to accept a generous amount of gold from the Count."

"Who?"

"A squire named Muzio. The young man seems to think our mutual master walks on water."

"What's Carrara's part of the plot?"

"Once Bonifacio has got the gates open with a smaller force, Carrara will lead the full Paduan force in and sack the city."

Pietro protested. "But his uncle—"

"His uncle will have nothing to do with it. He is to be kept entirely ignorant until the venture is complete."

Pietro thought about that for a moment, then posed the real question. "And what does the master of Verona want me to do?"

The Moor lowered his voice, forcing Pietro to slow his mount and lean closer. "On the day of the attack Uguccione della Faggiuola will hide a small armed force outside Vicenza. He'll be outnumbered, but that's the only way to keep the secret. Cangrande's troops have two years of constant warfare under their belts while the Paduans have been sitting on their laurels. But Verona's side needs an edge. You are to enter Vicenza a day or two before with a hand-picked group of soldiers. Those men can't know what is happening, and the group must raise no suspicion."

Pietro frowned thoughtfully. "I see. I go to visit Donna Katerina. It's known that I'm friendly with her, just as everyone knows I'm out of favor with her brother. But why will I have soldiers with me?"

"The pope has requested an accounting of your time here in Ravenna. You'll be transporting money for the papal coffers at Avignon. Of course, you'll bring along a squadron of soldiers for protection."

Clearly this plan had been worked out well ahead of time. "And Cangrande wants me to do this? What about the fiction that we're quarreling?"

"You're there by accident, and defending his sister's city. It will only enhance your reputation. But do you have your own men? The plan hinges on them."

"I have twenty-three men in the militia—is that enough?"

"Make it thirty."

"Well, my neighbor has a son who's been itching to carry a sword. But what am I supposed to do when the attack starts?"

"For Cangrande to have his legal pretext for war, the gates of Vicenza must be breached. The Paduans must get inside the walls. That's when Uguccione will attack."

"If I'm letting them in," asked Pietro, "what's to stop them from slaughtering me where I stand?"

"Ah," said the Moor. "That's the best part." He related his reason for smiling.

Pietro couldn't resist returning the grin even as sweat started to run down his back. "But where will Cangrande be?"

"He needs to be seen far away, otherwise the Paduans won't attack. He's leaving this to Uguccione."

Though it worried him, Pietro saw the wisdom of this. "When should I leave?"

The rest of the planning followed. Pietro's band would depart two days hence, giving their destination as France. Long before they passed Padua, Pietro would loudly declare his intention to visit his friends, Monsignore and Signora Nogarola. The party would shift its track and head for Vicenza. As long as they were within the walls by sunset on the twenty-first, all would be well.

"You may see a familiar face in Vicenza," added the Moor. "Another of Verona's exiles is returning. The Capitano has recalled Montecchio."

"Really? Well, it makes sense. Mari's sister is getting married, and I know Mari was planning to ask permission to attend."

"The Capitano said he's done well in Avignon. He kept the Scaliger from being excommunicated through charm alone. But even charm runs out. Cangrande needs a man with more influence, probably with a title. He means to ask Bailardino."

"I don't think Bailardino would want to go," said Pietro. "Rumor is he's enjoying fatherhood too much." *Besides,* he didn't add, *Donna Katerina is pregnant again.*

The Moor kept Pietro's thoughts on topic by asking, "Are you and Mariotto friends?"

Pietro sighed. "Yes, I think we are. We write, at least. His first letters pleaded for my forgiveness. I don't know . . . I gave it, but without my blessing. And pretty soon everything was back to normal."

"And his feelings toward Capulletto?"

"Hmm! Two years, and every letter he writes still laments that Antony refuses to answer his letters. I can recite you the form his letter will take. A greeting, a vow of friendship, a curse on Antony's stubbornness, then a page or two praising Gianozza to the stars. Then there will be a little court news that he thinks will interest me. Like some young Italian fellow he's met in Avignon who shows promise as a poet. The boy's father is a tyrant, but the boy writes in secret. Petrarca, the family is called. As if I care. He'd be better off writing to my sister. She knows far more about poetry than I ever will." Pietro gave the Moor an amused glance. "Have you heard? Antonia has made the unlikeliest of friends—Mari's wife, Gianozza. They both share a love of poetry, and it brought them together. So I get yet another letter talking about the bitch—excuse me, about Gianozza. My sister, Mari, and Antony."

"Capulletto writes of her?"

"Of her and little else! His letters follow the same form as Mari's—praise, oath of loyalty, a rant against Mariotto, and page after page about Gianozza. He saw her in the street, he heard about her from someone, do I think she regrets her action. I hope Mari's return will end this one way or another."

A sparrow crossed the road in front of them, and the dog ran ahead to bark at it. Pietro said, "What about the Scaligeri seal? Have you discovered who . . . ?"

"No. I have been focused on the Count."

"Oh." Pietro watched the bird torment the hound by swooping low, then up out of reach. "I haven't either. Cangrande wrote and said there were only two men who had access to the seal, as far as he knew. He was one. His butler was the other. He sent the butler away, gave him to Uguccione to serve. But I don't think he really believes it was him."

"No. If he did, the butler would be dead."

"I imagine you're right."

The Moor frowned a little. "I have traced the medallion, though."

"What?"

"The scarecrow's medallion, the one that was stolen back from Ignazzio the night he was murdered. That trinket, or one very like it, was sent nearly twenty years ago by a Scotsman called Wallace to an Italian as a token of thanks. The Italian had sent this Wallace arms and a few knights to help train his men."

"And the Italian was . . . ?"

"Alberto della Scala. Cangrande's father."

Pietro's head reared back as if he'd been struck in the face. "What? But . . . what the hell does that . . . ?"

"I don't know what it means. Cangrande claims he has never seen the medallion in his lifetime. But the object obviously has a great deal of meaning for its owner. While we were tracing him he was hunting for us, waiting for a chance to steal it back."

"So it's more important than we thought."

"Evidently so."

They rode along together for a while, each with his own thoughts. Mercurio padded along nearby, and Fazio rode ahead, happy to do his job now that the two men weren't sharing secrets. Suddenly Pietro said, "What did the Egyptian lion tamer owe you?"

"I made a star chart for his son. It allowed the family to make certain provisions for the future."

Pietro nodded, looking the Moor over from head to foot. "Ignazzio wasn't the astrologer. It was you."

"He was born with a certain skill at the pendulum and came to me as an apprentice."

"And also a walking target."

"That, too, was part of his duties."

That's cold of him, thought Pietro with discomfort. *Clever, but cold.* "Is there a way I can reach you?"

"The menagerie is leaving Padua, and I shall rejoin it on the road."

"Let me guess—they're heading for Vicenza next."

"Yes."

"Are you still Theodoro, or . . . ?"

"They call me the *Arūs.* But my true name is Tharwat al-Dhaamin."

"I can't even say that. But I'll remember it."

"Do. And be alert in Vicenza. The stars tell of a coming change in the boy's life."

"What kind of change?"

"I am unsure, but it is drastic. All the charts agree. During his fourth year the boy comes under a new influence that will help to shape him. You are involved."

"Me? How?"

"Again, I cannot say. The stars show danger for you during this change."

Pietro looked accusingly at the Moor. "You've made a chart for me."

The Moor shook his head. "No. I have been to Florence to study the chart your father commissioned when you were born. It has the value of more precise omens."

Pietro blinked. "My father had a chart made?"

"He did. It shows what I suspected all along—you are important in the Greyhound's life."

"If he even is the Greyhound. Did you ever . . . ?"

"I made several more charts, taking into account your idea of two falling stars, crossing in the sky. Some were wonderful, some horrifying, but until events unfold there is no way to tell which is the true chart." The Moor reined in his steed. "I will part from you here. If things go awry, or if you ever need me, send a message to the cobbler in the town of Alhambra, in the Spanish province of Grenada. It will eventually reach me."

Pietro was aware of the honor being done him and bowed his head to acknowledge it. They saluted, and the Moor rode off. Theodoro of Cadiz, the *Arūs*, Tharwat al-Dhaamin. How could a man live with so many names? But then, reflected Pietro, Cangrande had just as many. Francesco della Scala, the Scaliger, the Capitano. But not the Greyhound.

That's what this is really about, reflected Pietro. *The Count wants the boy, and his agents have failed. The only way he can think of now is to take the whole city.*

But what does he want with Cangrande's heir? What value is he? Ransom? Revenge? What is the goal?

"So," said Fazio, falling back to ride beside his master, "what was all that? Are we going somewhere? Is there news?"

Pietro fell in with Fazio but continued to ride in silence, thinking. In a week he'd be back in Verona with his friends and family. And Cangrande would show the world how he valued his errant knight. Ser Pietro Alaghieri, knight of Verona, dispenser of justice. He would then become a lawyer, and maybe someday a judge. And before that, one more battle, one more chance to blacken Carrara's eye. More than that, it was a chance to expose the

Count's partner. Capture the Count of San Bonifacio and force him to give up the name of his spy in the Scaliger's court. It was all about to happen. The waiting was over.

Capulletto Estate

Closer to Verona, on the land southeast of the Lago da Garda, there was a beautifully built mansion some two centuries old surrounded by the best arable land. This respectably sized estate held no castle, but the mansion was as fine as anything to be found. Until the turn of the century it had been inhabited by that staunchly Guelph family, the Capelletti. Then, after the line had died out, the lands had been under the stewardship of the lords of Verona. Every few years a new tenant would come and lease the lands until he was evicted by a new court favorite. Cangrande and his brothers had been sure not to let any one man grow too attached to the land.

Until two years ago, when the mansion suddenly became a beehive of activity. A new family was in residence. Or rather, a new old family. The Capulletti.

It was a week before the attack on Vicenza, and rumors were flying. None of them mentioned Padua, but all of them revolved around the massing of troops for some new offensive Cangrande was planning. Luigi Capulletto had heard the rumors, and now he stalked through the halls of his father's mansion in a foul temper. Slamming doors and careless of those in his way, he pushed his way into Ludovico's bedroom, which doubled as an office. Each day found the old man less able to walk on his gouty leg, and the summer heat wasn't helping.

Now, seeing his heir hurtling toward him, the elder Capulletto grunted. "What are you so hot about?"

With an effort of pure will Luigi stilled himself, though his fingers itched to wrap themselves around the fat man's throat. "Uguccione della Faggiuola is gathering a force of men. Something's happening, and you know what it is, don't you?"

"I may," said the old man.

"And you're sending Antonio to go to war with Uguccione!"

"Yes," rumbled Ludovico.

"No!" Luigi slammed his fist against the wall. "No, Father, no! As much as you may want him to be, Antonio isn't your heir! I am! Remember me, your wife's first son? Just because Antonio makes you laugh doesn't mean he can run your affairs. Hell, *you* can't run your affairs! Maybe Cangrande would be interested in why we really left Capua. If that story got about, you'd sure feel the pinch, wouldn't you?"

Ludovico had started sputtering long before Luigi reached the peak of his tirade. As the son continued to shout curses and epithets, the old man leapt out of bed and hopped two steps forward on his good foot. Luigi saw the blow coming but for once didn't feel like taking it. He grasped the swinging arm and threw his father backward to land in a heap on the floor. Half disbelieving what he'd done, Luigi stood shaking.

Ludovico lifted himself onto the bed, there being nothing wrong with his arms. "Young fool! You think you'll get my money after that?"

"Hang the money! This isn't about money! Is that all you care about? Why, Father? Why Antonio?"

"He does make me laugh," snarled old Capulletto. He coughed up a ball of phlegm that he spit into a canister two feet away. "That's all you give me."

"I gave you a grandson!"

"Yes, I am aware," said Capulletto. "He looks like his mother. At least he'll be pretty—he'll make the Guarini girl happy."

"That's all we are to you, isn't it? Cogs in the machine! Me, my son, that stupid business between Antonio and the Carrara girl—all of it grist for your mill. Well, you're there, Papa! Land, money, respect! Isn't that enough? What comes after?"

Ludo snapped his fingers at Luigi. "*That's* why Antonio. He never has to ask what comes after—he knows! He sees the possibilities, the openings, the way to greater heights. Example: if you'd put your wife forward a little more, you could have had that new water forge the Scaliger's building. But instead Rienzi gets it, all for the price of his wife's virtue. The Great Hound. Heh. That man certainly deserves his name." The old man dissolved into laughter that quickly turned to coughing.

Luigi didn't even wait for the spasm to subside. "You want me to sell my wife to the Scaliger?"

Through watery eyes Ludo sneered at his son. "Small enough sacrifice for such a reward."

Luigi's jaw was locked shut. He felt like tearing apart the ancient heap that was his father with his bare hands. Instead he said, "I demand you send me to Uguccione to represent the family."

"You demand, eh? Very well. I shall send you—to serve under your brother. No, don't gainsay me! It's this, or you don't go! You shall serve your brother. After all, he's a knight. What are you? A country squire, little more. You'll serve him, and I'll be there to see it. I think I can rouse this old corpse one more time—though not for the fighting! No, I'll just be along to watch how you honor the family name."

It was insulting, it was humiliating, but Luigi had what he wanted—an opportunity to prove himself. He turned on his heel and walked straight-backed out into the hall.

Antony was leaning against a wood-paneled wall outside. "Jesus, I told you—"

"Go to the devil!" Then Luigi remembered his best weapon. "How is young Menelaus lately? Heard from Paris?"

Face ashen, Antony gave his brother the fig and stormed off. Luigi went to find his son.

Theobaldo was napping. Letting the anger flow out of him, Luigi stood beside his son's crib and stroked his thin icy hair. His son, wholly his. Two years old, and still Luigi was loath to let even the nurses near the boy. He would have kept his wife away from the child too if he could. The bitch. Another one of his father's great schemes. But at least she had given him his son. Theobaldo. It was a family name—the old family, their true family, Capecelatro, before his father had leapt at borrowed nobility. *Look how well that turned out, Papa. You bought your way into a feud!*

That problem, at least, looked to be dying out. Old Montecchio had been more than gracious to Luigi's father, and the bride-thief was in France for who knew how long. Particularly pleasing, Antonio had gotten a well-deserved kick in the pants, and the fat old man had used his son's humiliation for everything he could get. Rights and lands that would pass to Luigi's son someday.

The toddler snored lightly. Luigi chuckled, something he only did with his boy. Theobaldo, the name of Luigi's great-uncle. An Italian name, though the boy's mother preferred the Dutch version—Thibault. Strange, yet Luigi liked it. Thibault.

"We'll show them all, won't we, Thibault, my son?"

THIRTY

Under the early summer sun, Antonia Alaghieri let her bare feet brush the dewy grass. The moisture crept up between her toes. The log she sat on was slightly damp, but through her many layers of clothing she couldn't feel it. Only her bare hands and feet could sense the dawn condensation.

A rustling in the bushes off to the right startled her, but it was only a hare. "Look," she whispered, pointing.

Gianozza della Bella (*in* Montecchio) had lifted her skirts higher, showing a fine thin calf to the morning sun. Looking at the hare she said, "Better run, little one! Or else Rolando will catch you up!"

Rolando was an old stiff-legged mastiff held on a tight leash. Frustrated, he barked at the hare. It scampered away into the brush. Satisfied, the dog settled onto his haunches and allowed himself to be congratulated by the two young women.

As Antonia stroked the dog's muzzle she said, "So, precisely where is Aurelia today?"

"Being fitted for her wedding dress. Her seamstress is a phenomenon. Maybe when your time comes . . ."

"A shame Aurelia couldn't be here," said Antonia tartly. "It's a lovely day. And what pretty landscape."

"Oh, mainly they use this as grazing land. No, the real pretty land is over that way. It belongs to Ser Bonaventura, though his cousin—"

"Gianozza! Enough!"

Gianozza threw her head back and laughed, a sound not unlike water trickling between tiny stones. Antonia imagined Gianozza staying up each night after her prayers and practicing it.

As she finished her laugh, Gianozza said, "I'm so glad you finally came."

"I'm not." But it was a lie. Antonia had resisted coming, not because she didn't want to, but because she felt it her duty to stay with her father until his latest work was ready for publication.

Two years had established Antonia's dominion over all things to do with her father. When the poet was writing, she became an immutable force to any who desired to steal his time. After twice being firmly refused an audience, even the Scaliger had to respect the iron in the sixteen-year-old girl. No one was allowed to interfere with Dante's muse.

In the field of publishing she was no less firm. She'd recreated in Verona the copying houses of Florence. When the great poet was satisfied with a canto, Antonia would take the complete work and disperse it among the scribes. No house had consecutive pages, so there was no fear of it leaking early, yet the moment *Purgatorio* was finished it would be available to the public. Demand was enormous. *L'Inferno* was already more popular than the legends of Arthur, better known than the *Song of Roland*. Dante was being compared to Homer and Ovid. Princes, blacksmiths, bishops, and tailors were reciting his verses. At the University of Paris, a new chair had been added to lecture on the meaning of the great epic *Commedia*.

But Antonia was secretly frightened. Her father wasn't looking well. In her two years with him the poet had visibly withered. Doctors were useless. It had been Pietro who had diagnosed the true cause. In one of his letters he had observed it was not age or illness, but the act of creation itself. Their father was pouring his life force into the pages he produced. Dante's work was his life. It was a race to see which ended first, the poet or the poem.

Which made it worse when her father ordered her to take a holiday. "My dear Beatrice," Dante had said, "You've been flogging yourself for weeks. *Purgatorio* is almost done, there is nothing more you can do to ease the publishing. Go visit friends or even your mother. Take some time for yourself, I insist!"

Reluctantly, she had agreed. A twenty-mile journey outside Verona brought her to Castello Montecchio and her only female friend, Gianozza.

Those that knew them thought their friendship odd. Gianozza was seen as a tiny gadfly who would, given time, cause her husband as much misery as she had her betrothed. Antonia, on the other hand, was believed to be made of granite. The merchants hated the girl in plain clothes with the basilisk stare. How these two young women had become intimates baffled the court.

To know the answer, one had to hear them talk. They brought out qualities in each other otherwise hidden. Beneath their public facades were two girls who were fiercely independent, but in different ways, and who enjoyed poetry, but in different ways.

Of course, staying at Castello Montecchio meant being caught up in the midst of the wedding preparations. Mariotto's sister, Aurelia, was marrying a local knight who was famous for jousting. So the castle was a mixture of anxiousness and excitement. Aurelia sometimes came running into a room breathless with fear, and it was up to Gianozza to console her. With Antonia's arrival, there were now two girls for the bride to turn to.

To aid in distracting her, the two always recited poetry. Most of the preceding week had been spent reading aloud and debating meaning. This morning, for a change, and a break from Aurelia, Gianozza, and Antonia were undertaking a hike. For protection they'd brought Rolando, a massive hound who had grown up in these hills. Gianozza had also brought a small satchel whose contents were secret. All she would say is, "I have a surprise."

Antonia was in no hurry. Here in this dell the rest of the world seemed quite distant. She was reminded of stories of Eden or Avalon. Looking at the sun filtering through the canopy of leaves she said, "When you agreed to marry Mariotto, did you know that you would be getting this wonderful home in the bargain?"

"No," sighed Gianozza happily. "He told me, of course. But I thought he was exaggerating—everyone loves their home. It took me weeks after I arrived here to even leave the castle. I so wanted to please Monsignore Montecchio. For Mariotto's sake."

Antonia indicated the keys that hung at Gianozza's belt. "Clearly, you've made an impression."

She'd done that and more, succeeding in winning over Mariotto's father in spite of himself. Aurelia, too, after a standoffish start, had come to like her sister-in-law, though more like a puppy than a person. Still, it went a long way toward Mariotto's redemption.

"Yes, now that Aurelia is leaving, father Gargano has made me lady of the house." Gianozza stood, brushing flower petals from her dress. "Come with me. There's something we need to see." She tugged Rolando's leash and started off.

They walked for a ways, until Rolando stopped. Gianozza tried to tug him along, but he refused to budge. He was happy to walk to the side, but not forward. Antonia crept forward and he barked at her.

"What's bothering him?" asked Gianozza.

Antonia had an idea. Taking an old stick from the ground, she prodded at the grassy earth in front of them. Solid at the first poke and the second, then suddenly the stick sank into the ground as far as she could push it. "It's a trap for game," she said. "Or something like it."

Gianozza bent down and rubbed Rolando's ears with both hands. "That's a good puppy!" She stood and allowed Rolando to guide them around the hole with the ingenious turf covering.

At last they reached an old oak, huge and gnarled. There was a rude kind of symbol cut into it. Antonia recognized a crude version of the Montecchio crest. It seemed that this was what Gianozza had been looking for, because from here she paced off almost a hundred steps north, then twenty west.

Following, Antonia said, "Where are we going?"

"Shhh," replied Gianozza. "I have to count, or we'll miss it. Twenty-three . . . twenty-four . . ."

They walked another ninety paces before turning north again. The terrain changed from grassy to rocky as they climbed up a rise. In the dirt Antonia could make out wolf tracks. Rolando sniffed at them but didn't seem concerned.

They approached a sizeable boulder, flat on one side. It was pitted all over with little shelves upon which green patches grew. "Here," said Gianozza with satisfaction.

Antonia looked around but saw nothing of interest. "Where?"

"This is a secret of the Montecchi family," whispered Gianozza. "Go around the boulder."

With a scornful look Antonia said, "If something jumps out at me, I'll kill you." Clambering awkwardly over some fallen stones, Antonia came to a turn in the path. She wiped a faint dappling of sweat from her forehead, hoping that when she got around the big stone she could rest in the shade of the hill behind it.

But there was no other side to the stone. Instead, it split in two. The gap was hidden from any angle but this and was wide enough for two men to pass through, shoulder-to-shoulder. But what puzzled her was the darkness on the other side of the gap. The ground sloped down to a pitch-black infinity.

It was a cave! A cave hidden in the hillside. Hearing Gianozza's footfall behind her, Antonia asked, "What is this place?"

Gianozza's excitement was luminous. "Mariotto wrote out the directions for me in his last letter. This is the cave where the ancient Montecchi hid the horses when bandits came looking for them."

What she means, thought Antonia with amusement, *is that this is where the ancient Montecchi hid the horses they stole when they were bandits. That was also probably their trap back there.* But Dante's daughter was far too well-bred to say so aloud. Instead, she peered into the dark. "Have you gone in? How far does it go?"

"I only went in a few paces. I didn't have a light with me then." She opened the satchel she'd brought and produced a candle and flint. "This time I thought ahead."

"Does Lord Montecchi know you've been here?"

"No, Mari asked me not to tell anyone. But I didn't want to go in alone."

Antonia rubbed her hands briskly. "Well then, get that candle lit!"

In the still air between the split rock halves, lighting the candle wasn't difficult. Getting Rolando to enter the cave was harder. Antonia bore the light while Gianozza half-dragged the reluctant mastiff into the damp, dark cave under the hill.

"Do you think there are more traps?" asked Antonia.

"Mari said all the old traps had been taken down. I don't think my husband would have sent me here if there was any danger."

The passage was not too tall, barely high enough to accommodate riderless mounts. But it was wide enough, after the opening, to take three horses abreast. The path turned and after a few paces in daylight disappeared.

Rolando was unhappy but stayed silent, sniffing at shadows. Slowly the ground leveled off. The earthen roof rose, then suddenly vanished high above. Gianozza let out a gasp. The cavern was enormous, large as a castle courtyard. There were fire pits, and along the earthen walls there were bunk beds, hitching posts for horses, and two long water troughs. Above, roots of trees and plants hung down. Yet the ceiling was so high that had the girls jumped they would have been unable to reach them.

"Why did your husband tell you about this place?" asked Antonia, wondering why she was whispering. But Gianozza answered in the same hushed tones.

"He said this was to be our secret place, and that if he knew I was here he could always find me in his dreams."

Porcheria, thought Antonia tartly. Romantic, yes, and sweet. But also crafty. If Mariotto was at all concerned about his bride having eyes for other men—one man in particular—he'd created a ritual that would put him in her mind for a good hour or two every day.

Antonia thought with satisfaction that Ferdinando would never be so manipulative or foolish. She suddenly reddened, as she did whenever she thought pleasing things about Ferdinando. She turned her head, wishing the candle would go out to hide her embarrassment.

Her wish came true. A surprising movement of air extinguished the flame. Rolando began to growl. Antonia thought she heard something moving in the cave. "An animal," she whispered.

"Or a demon," said Gianozza.

Antonia dragged her friend back toward the tunnel. "An animal, like a rabbit or a squirrel." From Rolando's continued growl she wondered if it might not be a bear. This was a fine home for a bear. Or a wolf. She whispered, "It's probably more scared of us."

Climbing out without light was a disaster. They fell several times, making far too much noise. But by the time they had reached the sunlight their fears were subsiding.

Antonia was the first to start laughing. "You ought to see yourself!"

Gianozza brushed at the front of her skirts. "You don't look any better!"

The danger of the cave now passed, Rolando was bored by the girls. He yawned, and licked his chops. Suddenly his ears pricked up. Seconds later he was barking wildly. Tearing the leash from Gianozza's hand he leapt forward and dashed around the path out of sight. "Rolando! Rolando!" They called and started to chase after him.

They were stopped by a voice. Someone was talking to the hound. Who? How many? In an instant a much more real fear replaced the nameless one of the cave.

"Back up!" hissed Antonia, pulling Gianozza towards the cave's mouth. Why had the dog stopped barking?

A cracking twig. Someone was coming closer. Antonia stooped, feeling around her feet. There was dirt, but no fistsize rocks. With nothing else, she took a handful of soil and hoped she could hit the intruder in the eyes. Gianozza did the same.

A figure emerged around the bend, and they let their missiles fly. "Hey!" cried the young man, throwing up his hands to cover his face. The dog was leaning against his leg, tail wagging furiously.

For a moment Gianozza stared. Then she ran to him, calling out, "Paolo! Paolo!"

Antonia had to look again. The man's name wasn't Paolo. She had only seen him once before, but she could never forget his handsome features. It was Mariotto Montecchio, finally returned. Paolo must have been some kind of pet name Gianozza had for him.

He cried out, "Oh, my love!" Husband met wife, his arms encircling her and lifting her off her feet. Their mouths met in near desperation.

Antonia looked away, but after a long moment she continued to study Montecchio out of the corner of her eye. He was even more handsome now that age had taken away some of his prettiness. But what clothes! He was dressed almost entirely in the latest French fashion. Leather doublet cut short, the better to show off the line of his upper thigh. Sleeves slashed to show off the fancy scalloped sleeves with bright rainbow-colored lining. His hat was a curled liripipe. His practical riding boots, the only Italian feature to his attire, were sorely out of place.

Mariotto breathed in the scent of his wife's hair. "Oh, Francesca, I've missed you!"

Paolo? Francesca? Realization struck Antonia. *Francesca da Rimini and her lover? That's the basis for their great romance? The idiots! The fools! They didn't understand* The Inferno *at all!*

Gianozza pulled back from his embrace. "You beast! You knew you were coming home!"

Mariotto ducked his head sheepishly. "The Capitano released me three weeks ago. I wanted to surprise you." He frowned. "Who's with you?"

"Oh, this is Antonia Alaghieri."

"Pietro's sister?"

"Yes. I didn't want to come in here alone."

One arm still around Gianozza's waist, Mariotto crossed to Antonia and held out his hand. Hers was filthy, she realized. Yet he still bent low over it as he bowed in greeting. *"Mademoiselle. C'est une plaisure, vraiment."*

"Signore," she replied in Italian as she curtsied. Now that he was closer she saw the design on the tunic under the doublet. There was a finely embroidered rendering of the Montecchi family crest. Just beneath that, directly over his liver, were three initials—*G.d.B.* That, at least, was sweet.

They exchanged a few perfunctory pleasantries, Antonia feeling awkward as could be. The fact that the marriage had never been consummated was written in flaming words above their heads. Mariotto intended an assignation with his wife. Their first.

Mariotto smiled at Antonia. She returned the smile weakly. Gianozza was gazing at Antonia too, surely thinking of nothing but how to get rid of her.

Glancing down at her clothes, Antonia made a choking sound in her throat. "Oh! I must look frightful! Is there a stream or something nearby where I can clean up before I return to the castle?"

"Just head back the way we came," said Gianozza quickly, "and off to the south about a half a mile is a stream." Mariotto beamed, but Gianozza frowned in genuine concern. "Are you sure you can find your way back?"

"I'll take Rolando with me," Antonia said, reaching down and taking the dog's leash. "He can guide me."

"Of course he can!" cried Mariotto cheerfully. "This old mutt knows these lands better than I do!"

"Well, goodbye, then!" Antonia tugged on the leash, hard. Her cheeks burned. As she turned down the path she wondered, *Would it be too indecorous to run?* There was a cooing sigh from behind her. *Oh, wait until I'm out of earshot please!*

The dog resisted, straining back toward his master.

"Come on, Rolando," whispered Antonia. "They don't want you there either."

✦   ◇   ✦

Pietro rode with Fazio and a band of thirty men. They were passing Ferrara when he was hailed by a large man ridiculously perched on the back of a mule.

"*Hola!*" Waving, the man almost fell off his mule. "*Señores! Por favor*—I need, ah, I need some *ayudo.*" A wide floppy hat shadowed his dark skin, black hair, and beard. There were crimson stains on his shirt. "I am riding to Treviso, and—well, I am, how you say, lost. May I ride with you?"

Pietro said, "We're not going that far."

"As far as you do go, then." His accent was definitely Spanish, but his Italian wasn't half bad. It was the drink that was giving him trouble.

"We're in a bit of a hurry . . ."

"So am I! It will work out so well for me to come with you!"

It was common practice for a band of soldiers to take charge of any lone travelers. There were already three women and their grooms in Pietro's party, so he couldn't very well say they weren't taking on extra people. Still, this Spaniard could be a thief. "What do you do for a living?"

"I am a world-class notary, señor! Perhaps you could use a notary on your travels?"

"No, thanks. What's your name?"

"Oh, I am a lout! My name is Persiguieron La Mordedura. But if you allow me passage, you may call me whatever name you wish! Just do not call me early!" He laughed at his own joke.

Pietro sighed. "Very well. Ride up front, where I can keep an eye on you. And don't bother the ladies."

"Señor! What do you take me for? A cad?" He raised his hands in mortification and fell out of his saddle entirely. While he righted himself Pietro signaled Fazio to start the small band moving again.

✦ ◇ ✦

Antonia took her time at the river. When she looked respectable again, she woke Rolando from his nap and set off for the castle. She was in no hurry to get there. Arriving alone would cause a stir, and Gargano shouldn't learn of his son's return from a slip of a girl he barely knew. That was up to Mariotto and Gianozza.

Paolo and Francesca, she thought wryly. She had laughed at the Paris-Helen-Menelaus triad her father had coined just after Gianozza's marriage. After that there had been Arthur, Guinevere, and Lancelot jokes. But Paolo and Francesca? Well, Gianozza had always said it was Dante's poetry that brought Mariotto to her. *People just don't understand that story.*

Antonia and Rolando strolled along the stream, looking at the green mosses and listening to the birds. When the mastiff sniffed some prey out, Antonia released him, then settled herself on a rock beneath a shady tree to wait. They were near Ser Bonaventura's land, Gianozza had said. Maybe she would see Ferdinando. She had thought up some particularly demeaning taunts since their last encounter.

It bothered her that her feelings were so obvious that Gianozza could tease her about them. She hadn't really admitted to herself that she had grown to rather like Petruchio's awkward cousin. That they were consistently mean to each other was their defense, the unspoken agreement between them, each keeping the other at bay.

She forced herself to think of her father's work, determined not to think about *that person*. Eventually the great hunter would return, lap her hand to let her know he was ready, and they would begin their walk anew.

It was growing late when she finally angled back toward the castle. In another hour the sky would begin to redden. *If they aren't done by now . . .* Antonia primly refused to finish the thought.

Castello Montecchio stood at a hilltop some five miles southwest of Vicenza. Built on the ruins of a similar fortress constructed some centuries before, the new castle was well fortified. The horse stables for which the Montecchi were famous weren't within the castle, but had a separate walled compound north of the castle.

As Antonia drew close to the castle, she began to wonder. There seemed to be more men-at-arms on the ramparts of the castle walls than when she'd set out this morning. It was a little unnerving, seeing the lines of spears and helmets. Squinting up, she saw that all the soldiers were turned inward, looking down from the high walls into the main yard.

She managed to keep the mastiff restrained as she walked through the main gate. A hundred mounted men-at-arms occupied the yard in front of her with their squires, pages, and extra mounts. Among them their pages dashed, unstrapping a buckle here, replacing a thrown shoe there. The soldiers sat on their horse's backs, waiting for orders. Several had dismounted and now strolled through the compound to stretch their legs.

Then Antonia saw a face she knew. It was not the face she was looking for. *God, what is he doing here, today of all days?* Approaching him she said, "Ser Capulletto?"

Antony turned at once, hoping she was someone else. Seeing who it was, he still smiled and greeted her. She asked what brought him here. "We've just been told that Padua's breaking its treaty," he told her. "My guess is that we've come to ram it down their throats. Uguccione is leading us, and he says we're to wait in these parts until we're needed." He glanced down at her. "You look like you've been rolling in the mud."

"Gianozza and I were out for a walk . . ."

"Yes, Gianozza. Where is she?" He tried to make it sound casual.

Hedging, Antonia said, "I came back without her."

"You mean she's in the forest alone? Antonia, there're Paduans about, spies and mercenaries, not to mention wild animals!"

"She's not alone," said Antonia quickly. "She—ran into an acquaintance and they fell to—talking."

"I'm going out there," said Antony, turning to his groom. "Andriolo, my horse!"

Oh God, isn't this a disaster in the making? She opened her mouth to say something, anything. But a louder voice called, "Capulletto! I need you!"

It was on the tip of Capulletto's tongue to snarl that he was busy, but he caught himself and walked to where Uguccione della Faggiuola waited in the company of Lord Montecchio and several other leading Veronese. Antonia followed, jostling though the crowd of soldiers and servants. Here were the familiar faces of Nico da Lozzo and Ser Petruchio Bonaventura, whose grin shone from under his beard. "Got my orders," he rumbled delightedly. "A leader of men at last. Won't that amuse my Kate."

"Take her mind off that bun in her oven," remarked Nico.

"The way she gets around while preggers, I doubt she's noticed it yet."

"How long have you been married, now?" asked Nico da Lozzo.

"Two and a half years," the proud husband declared.

"Two years, and four children," said Nico, clucking his tongue derisively. "Blessed with fertility! A girl, then twin boys."

"This next child will be another girl if the wisdom of nurses means anything."

"That might be a record. Unless you had a head start?"

Petruchio roared with laughter. "A late one! Ask cousin Ferdinando, or any of my servants. My wife took some particular wooing before she yielded to my charms."

At the sound of his name, Petruchio's cousin turned. His eyes fixed at once upon Antonia. She stared defiantly back, daring him to mention the state of her clothes. But instead he answered his cousin. "They fought like cats in a sack. Maybe passionate love requires a little bite back."

Some men had traced his gaze to Antonia and were chuckling. Antonia drew herself up and said, "I always suspected you were a backbiter, signore."

Ferdinando opened his mouth, stopped, then bowed. "I cannot spare the time to spar with you, lady. There'll be nothing left for the Paduans." He was booed.

"But you're a Paduan sympathizer, I thought."

"Still with that?" Ferdinando cocked his head. "I think every man here would cheer Padua on against Florence or Venice. It's a shame for you, but you can't help where you're born."

"Any more than you can help being a—" But Petruchio cut her off with a tut-tut. She curtsied to him, made a face to Ferdinando, then turned back to Capulletto, who was receiving orders from the general. "... with the drought, there's not enough food here. I want you and Bonaventura to take some of the men and hole up at Illasi tomorrow. Nico will do the same, heading for Badia."

Capulletto was anxious to begin his hunt for Gianozza. "Is that all?"

Uguccione frowned. "Shame no one taught you manners, whelp. No, that isn't all. Take some hounds and some squires with you. Make it seem innocuous, like you're a hunting party."

"A very well-armed hunting party," quipped Nico da Lozzo.

"One hell of a doe," Bonaventura grinned.

Ferdinando was trying to catch Antonia's eye. He must have come up with a new retort. Normally she would have liked nothing better than to make mincemeat of him. But Capulletto was preparing to ride out. She hurried to Lord Montecchio's side and tugged at his sleeve. The Lord of Montecchio looked down at her. "Antonia, my dear? What is it?"

It took remarkably few words to convey the problem. The lord of the castle's eyes opened in comprehension just as Capulletto said, "I'd be delighted to lead a troop. Now, if you'll pardon me, I've got an urgent errand." He yanked on his reins and mounted.

"Just a moment!" cried Gargano. Too late. Capulletto was touching his spurs to the horse's flanks. He shouted, "Clear a path!"

Antonia waved her hands. "Wait! Antonio, wait!"

Capulletto suddenly checked. For a moment Antonia thought he'd heard her and she rushed to catch up.

But his eyes were fixed on the main gateway. Emerging from its shadow were Gianozza and Mariotto. Both on one horse, she was seated across his lap as they trotted forward into the courtyard. His doublet was unlaced. Her head was uncovered, hair was loose about her shoulders. She clung to him like a nymph to the prow of a ship.

Then the lovers saw him. Montecchio's horse came to a halt as its rider gazed at his former best friend. "Antony."

Capulletto was entirely still. "Mari."

Come on, Antonia's mind cried out. *Put it behind you. Mari, say something, make it easier on him!*

"Mari!" cried Aurelia from a window. "Mariotto, is that you? You look like a Frenchman!" She bolted from the window and came tearing out, the rest of the household following. Amid the greetings Mariotto allowed his gaze to drop to where his father stood, waiting. Ignoring Antony, Mari set his wife gently on the ground, dismounted, and pushed past the servants to kneel at his father's feet.

Gargano spoke stiffly. "The Scaliger has spoken highly of your service abroad."

"I regret that I was unable to do more," was Mari's neutral reply.

A moment passed, then Gargano reached out a hand. "Welcome home. We have all missed you." After their embrace, Gargano took his son by the shoulders and turned him to face Capulletto. "Now, greet your friend."

Capulletto had not dismounted, so Mariotto walked over to stand next to his horse. "Antony. It's good to see you."

Through a rigid jaw Antony said, "Montecchio."

Mariotto's back stiffened but he pressed on. "Please accept the welcome of this house, old friend." He reached up a hand. Antony looked at it then deliberately dismounted without the offered aid. They shook hands stiffly, then Antony stepped back, hands clasped tightly behind his back.

Antonia heard a snort from nearby. Looking over her shoulder she saw Antony's brother Luigi, a wide grin plastered across his face. He was enjoying his little brother's misery.

In the center of the crowd Mariotto masked his disappointment by saying brightly, "So, what brings you all here?"

"A little vacation, a little war!" Uguccione della Faggiuola thumped him on the back. "Well, you're more solid than I remember. And your timing is perfect. We need strong men for the coming action!"

"Action?" Mari's eyes gleamed with excitement. "After two years surrounded by conniving priests and backstabbing courtiers, I could use a good fight."

"Come inside," said the general, "and I'll tell you all about it! Perhaps your father can spare a few men for you to lead."

"Of course," said Gargano. "Come inside, everyone! My servants have malmsey prepared."

Mariotto slipped his hand into Gianozza's as the crowd of knights and soldiers streamed into the hall.

Quite forgotten in the dispersing throng, Antonia walked across the courtyard toward the guesthouse. She would change into fresh garments before returning to the hall.

At the steps to the guesthouse she turned. Capulletto remained alone in the mouth of the castle gate. Reaching for his horse's saddle, he removed a long silver dagger. He studied it for a long time before slipping it into his belt. With a deep breath to steel himself, he strode into the hall after his lost love and the man that had been his friend. It brought tears to her eyes.

"Well, that was awkward," said Ferdinando. He had returned to find her.

She turned away, wiping a tear brusquely away. "I'll be in soon. You can taunt me then."

Antonia was surprised to find a gentle hand on her arm. "Lady, you don't think much of me. But I would be the lowest man to taunt a friend in distress."

She turned to look up at him, wiping her eye. "By what right do you call yourself my friend?"

He shrugged. "I make no claim. Not to sound dramatic, but in a few days I'm riding into a fight. I just wanted things to be, ah, clear. Right. Between us." Uneasily, he took her hand. "I would like to be your friend, Antonia."

He was an awkward-looking fellow, short with a long neck and sloping shoulders. But handsome wasn't the world. Let Gianozza have her Mari. There were better things. Like a mind. Like a friend.

"You are my friend, Signore Backbiter."

He laughed and sighed at once, his smile mirroring her own.

THIRTY-ONE

Vicenza

21 MAY 1317

Pietro's small company of soldiers rode up to the gates of Vicenza. In the midday heat the guards who policed the gates watched them come. This condottiere wasn't girded for battle; most of the soldiers gazed at the sights of a new city.

One of them rode up to discuss entry. He wore no armor and in the hot day his shirt under the red leather doublet was open. At his side stalked a sleek and panting greyhound. The fellow introduced himself to the guards, who formally asked the party's destination. "France, eh? Be sure to bring your own wine."

"Hell, I'm bringing my own cook." The guards chuckled and Pietro asked, "Are the Nogarolese in residence?"

"Yes, sir. Lord Bailardino and his family."

"Who's the giant?" asked another of the garrison. His eyes were fixed on the massive form astride an uneasy mule. The big man was slapping his knees at some remark from his neighbor, almost falling from the mule's back. He was clearly drunk.

Pietro scowled. "A Spanish notary who asked for protection on the journey. He's caused me a great deal of trouble." Last night he'd slipped into bed with a woman who'd also begged Pietro's protection for the trip. Not that she'd minded, but her husband wouldn't have been amused.

"He's a right monster," muttered a guard. He was watching Pietro's men as they steadied the Spaniard. A gust of wind took the hat off the Spaniard's head. Reaching for it he fell out of his saddle again. His hair and beard were black as the night sky and his skin was deeply tanned.

Pietro shrugged. "He speaks seven languages, he tells me."

As the guards admitted Ser Alaghieri's band, they laughed at the swaying Spaniard. He didn't seem to notice that he was entering a city, so intent he was on his wineskin. His fellow travelers ignored him. For them it had clearly been a long ride. As they passed through San Pietro, the Spaniard called out to women passing by, his flow of vulgar language both wretched and constant, punctuated only with belches and nose-blowing. The way his mule staggered, it was clear the Spaniard had been debauching his steed as well as himself.

Fazio trotted up to Pietro. "Let's be rid of him, eh, master? We've gotten him here safely. Let's just dump him and be done."

Pietro nodded. "Good idea. Persig—Per—Hey, notary! Yes, you! You're here. Understand. No, look at me! This is Vicenza. Vi-cen-za! You're here!" The notary looked blankly at him from under the brim of his frayed straw hat. "Do you understand? You can go now?"

"But, señor, I can—mmm, heh, 'scuse please—I can serve. You need a fine notary, no?"

"No," said Pietro firmly. He'd been afraid of this. "We don't need a scribe."

"Truly?"

"Truly, no."

The Spaniard shrugged elaborately. "If you say, señor. Farewell."

"Adios." Pietro watched the drunken mule stumble off, its rider in search of another patsy to support his drinking.

By the time Pietro reached the Nogarola palace, the other followers had all broken off, finding their lodgings or going about their business. Pietro brought Fazio and his thirty men to the huge double doors of Katerina and Bailardino's home. They were welcomed by servants, and Pietro asked that his men be fed. He then gave instructions to his band of soldiers to be asleep by nightfall. Since they were unaware that a battle loomed, they thought him a killjoy, but swore they would obey. Pietro entered the palace and was shown to a guest suite, Mercurio padding by his side.

He was unaware he had been observed.

✦ ✧ ✦

Four hours later, refreshed from a bath and a nap, Pietro followed a maid into a wide reception hall on the first floor. It was just how he remembered it—the fresco of a colorful pastoral scene, the gauzy curtains framing the arched doors that led to the peristyle garden. Beyond the billowing curtains, a fountain burbled up a clear stream of water. Pietro remembered sitting on the balcony above, trying to identify the sculpted figures. Now, after two years of university study, it was obvious. Holding the vessel for the water were three muses—Calliope, Clio, and Melpomene. He reflected that, given the amount of power astrology held in this household, Urania should have been present instead.

Mercurio watched the flowing curtains warily, as if a hare might suddenly emerge. Pietro felt the same prickling sensation at the base of his neck. He saw nothing, but felt sure he was being watched.

His eye caught a reflected twinkle in the garden. A soft, moist pair of eyes peeking out from behind a bush. He smiled and said, "Hello, Cesco."

The youth stood. He was barely the height of Pietro's knee.

"I I'llo," the boy said. His clothes were clean but had seen much darning, especially about the elbows and knees. His hair was more curled than Cangrande's and of a lighter hue, bright and blond. The ringlets had been allowed to grow long, covering the eyes that now flickered from man to hound. "Wha's his name?"

"This is Mercurio."

"M'curo!" The boy clapped his hands together in a demanding way. Amazingly, the dog trotted over and fell at the child's feet.

Watching the boy scrub happily at the dog's neck, Pietro said, "You're lucky. He generally doesn't do that for anyone but me." He advanced a few paces into the garden. "You don't know it, Cesco, but we've met before. My name is Pietro. I'm looking for your mother."

"La Donna's not here," the child said, still stroking the dog. He played for a moment with the Roman coin dangling from Mercurio's collar, then glanced up at Pietro's head. "You don' have hat."

It was an odd statement. "No. No, I don't." Then it struck Pietro. "*Do you remember me?*"

"You don' have a hat," the child repeated.

"You tried to play with my hat once," said Pietro, "when you were a baby. Remember?"

"I have a toy," replied the child, holding forth a tangle of metal. One twisted piece hung from another.

"Did your father give you that?" asked Pietro.

"God is the father."

Pietro blinked, then tried again. "Who gave you this?"

"Cesco."

"You're Cesco."

The child made a face. "The other Cesco."

"Oh," said Pietro, smiling.

The boy offered the puzzle. "Do it." As Pietro walked closer, the child fixed his gaze on Pietro's limp and cane. "You're hurt."

Pietro patted his thigh. "A long time ago. It's nothing."

"Don't show it," advised the child. "No one will help." Cesco's light green eyes met Pietro's brown ones, and the boy pressed the puzzle into Pietro's hands.

Pietro was far more interested in the child than the tangle of molded metal bits, but Cesco was expectant. Examining the two pieces, Pietro gave it an experimental tug. They clinked together fruitlessly. Cesco did a little dance as Pietro struggled to decipher the twists and turns necessary to free one piece from the other.

Finally Pietro shrugged and handed the pieces back. "Can you show me?"

Cesco grinned. Taking the pieces with both hands, the boy twisted. It was awkward, for the curves of metal were too large and unwieldy for the hands that manipulated them. Once, twice, three times the boy pulled. And suddenly the two parts were free of each other, one in each hand. He looked up at Pietro.

"How did you do it?" asked Pietro, bending low.

Before the smiling child could respond, another voice echoed across the walled garden. "Cesco, don't bore Pietro. He's had a long journey."

At Katerina's words the sun vanished from the boy's face. What remained was light reflected from some inner source, carefully hidden. Cesco dropped the puzzle and walked straight-backed to Donna Katerina's side. He did not take her hand, but waited close to her, gazing at Pietro. The dog Mercurio followed, standing by his side.

Katerina was as beautiful as ever. If her hair was pulled in a more austere fashion than of yore, it only served to outline her fine cheeks and mouth. Her latest pregnancy was just beginning to show in the folds of her dress. A faint dappling of gray was appearing around her temples, neatly disappearing into the blond streaks in her chestnut hair.

Pietro greeted her by sweeping into a full bow. "Domina."

"Cavaliere." She matched his formality by reaching out a hand for him to kiss. His lips brushed her wrist. "You are more handsome than ever. You will be joining Bailardino and me for supper? I am looking forward to adult conversation." Cesco's head came around at those words. Katerina took no note. "We have a guest staying here, but he sent a maid to inform us that he is unwell. And you remember Morsicato? He has asked to examine your leg, but I suspect it was just to hear the gossip from Bologna. I've invited him to dinner, which should spare you a prodding."

"I don't mind the prodding. He was the one who saved my leg. He probably wants to hear about the latest in the science of autopsy. But who is your ailing guest?"

Katerina scowled. "No one of consequence—though he would disagree. A very rich banker called Pathino, from Treviso. He wants to set up some sort of business here and is wooing Bail."

"He'd do better to woo you," said Pietro.

"How gallant!" Katerina extended an arm. "Shall we retire to the sitting room until supper? You must tell me all about Ravenna, and then we must plot to get you back in my brother's good graces." She leaned forward to whisper in his ear. "I'm pleased he chose you to defend the city. Surely this means your exile must be nearly over."

Together they exited the garden. The moment they were gone, Cesco and Mercurio began chasing each other around the fountain. Suddenly Mercurio growled. Cesco looked down to see what was the problem, then followed the dog's gaze up and up to a little ledge high above. There, luxuriously stretching out its paws, rested an orange and white cat.

Cesco shivered. Lifting a small stone he pitched it at the cat. Usually his aim was perfect, but he'd thrown in a hurry and so missed the feline's head by a couple inches. The creature leapt to its feet. Just as a second missile was launched, the cat sprang up through a high window and disappeared, the dog barking after it.

"Cesco?" came Donna's voice from behind him.

He froze. He knew he wasn't supposed to fight the cats. But he still said, "Cat."

"Leave them alone. They're survivors." She withdrew back behind the curtain, where the knight with the hurt leg asked, "He doesn't like cats?"

"He loathes them. Nothing gets him angry like a cat. We try to keep them out of the palace, but they like it here. He thinks they taunt him."

Cesco remained behind, this time watching until they were well out of sight behind the curtains. There was a rumble of deep, raspy words, and Cesco knew that the dark man was greeting the adults. Cesco didn't know why but the dark man scared him a little. He tried to spend a lot of time with the dark man to find out why.

Making sure the cat was really gone, Cesco retrieved the pieces of his puzzle. After brushing the garden dirt from their metal limbs, he went to the fountain. Last month he'd found a spot under the lip of this sculpture, a crevice that made a tiny invisible shelf. His stubby fingers fitted the puzzle inside, wedging it tightly so there was no way it would come loose. Other prized possessions rested in this secret chamber as well. He wanted to keep them safe until his brother Detto was old enough to share them.

The hound began to bark. Cesco glanced around the garden. No one had seen him hide the toy. But the dog was insistent. Cesco followed Mercurio to a small bush. Lying under the shrubbery was a wax tablet with some numbers inscribed upon it. Frowning all over his little face, Cesco gazed at it.

"It's a puzzle," he whispered to the hound. The dog snuffed once. "For me, not you, silly." Cesco played with the numbers in his head. A puzzle! He decided to hide it until after supper. Then, when he solved the puzzle, he'd show it to Detto. It was never too early to teach Detto the fun of puzzles.

✦ ◆ ✦

Morsicato looked healthy, though his face bore more lines and his beard was dappled with white. He greeted Pietro warmly, and the first words out of his mouth were, "I hear you've got a woman professor! Tell me everything!"

Pietro laughed aloud. "I should have known! Yes, the mysterious Novella d'Andrea. She teaches from behind a curtain, lest we poor students lose our focus."

"So no one's ever seen her?"

"Not as far as I know. I haven't, anyway. But there are scads who claim they have."

"Excellent! Oh, why oh why didn't they have female professors when I went to school?" He linked his arm into Pietro's. "Come, let's in to dinner, and you can tell me everything that's happening in the scandalous world of higher knowledge!"

On the way in to dinner Pietro met little Bailardetto, just being put to bed. Less than two years old, walking well and talking a little, Detto was certainly his father's son—the same black hair, the same strong face. He was a regular baby, no less wonderful for the lack of Cesco's brilliance. Pietro was surprised to realize he liked children. He'd never really thought about it before.

Dinner was pleasant. Pietro was surprised that Cesco was allowed to eat at their table. The boy was quiet, though, eating and staring off into space. He did perk up a bit as Pietro described for Morsicato an autopsy he'd attended. But then the talk turned to politics and he vanished behind his eyes again.

Pietro began the subject change by asking, "Do you think Frederick will be declared emperor?"

Bailardino shrugged. "No one knows."

This was the great event that had occurred in Verona during their absence. Just two months ago the Scaliger had come to a momentous decision, finally choosing which imperial rival to back, Ludwig or Frederick. The Scaliger deemed Frederick the Handsome of Bavaria to have the better claim, so on the sixteenth of March, Cangrande della Scala had formally pledged his allegiance—and his armies—to Frederick.

"There's a candidate no one has mentioned as yet," said Morsicato slyly.

"Not Cangrande?" asked Pietro.

Bailardino laughed. "No no no. He means the Duke of Vienna, the reluctant Vincentio."

"Oh."

Katerina said, "I didn't get the sense that he is reluctant. From what I hear he's a shrewd administrator, and rather manipulative, for one so young. He just doesn't like the pomp of office."

Her husband shrugged. "In spite of his Italian nickname, he's a good German candidate, with a distant relation to the throne. He could pursue it."

The talk shifted to the war Cangrande was waging, to news from France, and came around to the return of Mariotto. Pietro said, "I know Aurelia's getting married, but to whom?"

Bailardino frowned. "I'm not sure, to tell the truth."

Katerina said, "His name is Ser Benvenito Lenoti, and he is as handsome as he is brave."

"That doesn't mean much, unless he's uncommonly daring. Wait—Lenoti. Isn't he the tilter? Well, he's assured himself of a lifetime of good horses."

"M'I be 'cused?" asked Cesco, pushing his platter of half-eaten fruit away.

Katerina considered. "Finish the apples and you may." Cesco shoved a handful of apple slices into his mouth, hopped down from his seat, and ran from the room. "Finish them," called Katerina after him. "Don't let me find spewed apple bits in the halls!"

The men were all laughing. "Oh, yes!" cried Katerina. "It's all funny until the roof falls in. He's up to something," she added, motioning for a maid to follow him.

"Let him alone, Kat!" sighed Bailardino.

"You'll be sorry when the palace burns down around your ears."

Pietro said, "And how is Cangrande's namesake?"

Katerina pursed her lips. "If I say he's brilliant, it will only be a mother's opinion. The same if I call him a trial. Perhaps the doctor has a more objective assessment."

A bemused look crossed Morsicato's face, making his forked beard jut out at an odd angle. "Well, he's active. I'm always bandaging up his scrapes, setting a sprain. Loves to whack me with his little wooden sword."

"Me too," said Bail, mournfully rubbing his backside.

"He took to riding like he was born to it—swimming as well. And I think he's reading now. But he seems to best enjoy fiddling with machines and things, seeing how they work. Donna Katerina has this horizontal loom with foot pedals. Cesco took the thing apart when no one was looking, then watched as it was reassembled—thought it a tremendous joke."

"He's not the only one," said Katerina with a sour look at her husband.

"Well, it was damned clever!" he protested. "Anyway, since then Cangrande's been sending the imp puzzles—interlocked rings, that sort of thing. We're all thankful. They keep him occupied for hours at a time."

"I saw one puzzle," said Pietro. "I'd think he'd finish them quickly."

"He does," replied Bail. "He has an uncanny knack for them. But when he's done with one, he studies it. He's fascinated at how pieces fit together. And he likes showing them to his little brother."

"Is he sleeping more?"

Katerina sighed. "I'm afraid not. I don't know if it's nightmares or if he simply believes that the moment he falls asleep is when we bring in the dancing elephants. Sometimes I have to ask the doctor for a draught to help him sleep, though always as a last resort. But even with the potion he only rests four hours a night."

Bail put his hand over his wife's. "What she's not telling you, Pietro, is that he wakes up shaking every night. He won't tell us what his dreams are about, but it must be dreadful."

Dinner ended and Bail dismissed the servants. Then he began to discuss their plans for the next day. Unsurprisingly, Katerina stayed to voice her opinions.

Pietro's main concern was the signal to Uguccione's troops. Bailardino told him, "Cangrande said we should ring the bells of the duomo. It's close to where the fighting will be, and the Paduans will think it's an alarum, not a signal."

"But if it's that close to the fighting," Pietro pointed out, "won't we be in danger of being cut off from it? If that happens, how do we give the signal?"

"It won't happen," insisted Nogarola. "I'll station ten men inside and a dozen more to move in once the fighting starts. That bell tower will be the best-guarded building in the city."

"How will they know when to give the signal?"

"I'll ride over and tell them myself."

Pietro glanced at Katerina. "Are you sure the people at the palace will be safe? Wouldn't you rather get Donna Nogarola and the children out of the city for the day?"

"Of course he would," said Katerina before her husband could respond. "But I would not leave without shackles, a gag, and a blindfold." She ignored Bail's ribald response and said, "This is my home. No one will force me to leave it. Besides, the Paduans doubtless have spies in the city. Any move would give us away. No, our preparations seem adequate."

Katerina departed soon thereafter. Pietro, Morsicato, and Bail stayed up for a while playing at dice. Morsicato lost badly, and promised to pay up if he survived the next day.

Sometime before midnight Pietro returned to his room. Fazio was asleep on his pallet by the door, though he woke hazily to ask if Pietro needed anything. "No, go back to sleep."

Pietro stripped and climbed beneath the covers of his own fine bed. The combination of wine and fatigue washed away the fears of what tomorrow might bring. It was a hot night, and he decided to sleep without coverlet. After a quick but devout prayer, he fell almost instantly asleep and soon began to dream.

He dreamt he was scrambling down a rocky slope toward a river. It was like the shores of the Adige, but past landslides had left giant stones lining the water's edge. There was a ferocious black hound by Pietro's legs. Together they ran from something terrible that bellowed behind them, hurling stones at their heads. Only if they crossed the river would they be safe.

A battle was being fought by the river's far edge. Centaurs lined up two at a time. They did not fight with bow and arrow, as centaurs should. They were using strange curved swords that flashed and danced through the air in unceasing arcs. Drops of blood showered the air. As soon as one centaur was slain, another would step forward to take his place in an unending procession. Beyond the centaurs naked men writhed and danced in the river, some up to their ankles, others only visible by the tops of their heads.

This was not the Adige. It was blood red and on fire. A burning river of blood.

The scene altered, the way dreams shift of a sudden. They were still above the fray, the battle raging on below them, the river flowing on. But Pietro no longer stood on the detritus of the earthslides. He was on the Scaliger's balcony in the Arena.

The dog beside him had turned into a young man. Without turning to his companion Pietro said, "We're safe now."

Speaking had been a mistake. The centaurs paused in midstroke, their heads turning to look up. One cried out, *"A qual martiro venite voi che scendete la costa? Ditel costinci!"* Another pointed to Pietro and shouted, *"Siete voi accorti che quel di retro move ciò ch'el tocca? Così non soglion far li piè d'i morti!"* There was an ugly growl from the centaurs. Even the bloody corpses on the Arena floor turned their heads.

Pietro's companion held up his hands to forestall the impending violence. "It is true," came the voice. "He is not dead! I am his guide here, at the request of la Donna Katerina."

Pietro suddenly knew he was dreaming because he knew this scene. It was from his father's poem. He relaxed, knowing how this scene was supposed to play out. He would climb onto the back of one of the centaurs and ride across the river.

But his companion was not Virgil. Turning, he saw Cesco gazing back at him disdainfully. The boy's hair was no longer blond but brown, worn so long it hung well past his neck. He was also taller, thinner, more muscled. But the eyes were the same unearthly green. "Who were you expecting?"

Pietro gazed at the face that was level with his own. "A god. Or a poet."

"Granted in both!" Cesco grinned, showing long canine teeth that were very unlike those of Cangrande. A ring dangled on a chain from his neck. Pietro watched as Cesco faced the centaurs and, with a shrill cry, leapt off the balcony. Snatching up a fallen sword, Cesco laid about him right and left. All the idle centaurs leapt forward, determined to kill the youth who ran like lighting though their ranks. Fighting with strokes Pietro had never seen, Cesco cut a swath to the river. At its edge he turned and called, "Are you coming?"

"Mercurio!" called Pietro. "Mercurio!"

" 'Twill serve!" shouted the warrior-child, laughing aloud as he killed one centaur after another. *"Si Dieu ne me veut ayder, le Diable ne me peut manquer!"*

Pietro noticed that the boy was fighting one-handed. His left hand clutched a white cloth to his chest. The white cloth was turning red.

Pietro jerked awake. He was bathed in sweat, could smell the fear on his body.

"Master," said Fazio from across the dark room, "are you hurt? I heard a cry."

"It was n-nothing," said Pietro, hands fumbling for a blanket. His teeth were chattering in spite of the heat. "Ah, a b-bad dream, nothing more. Don't—don't worry. Go back to sleep."

Pietro heard Fazio slowly lie back, and he waited until he heard the boy's breath ease once more. Then Pietro swung his feet to the tiled floor and sat, his head in his hands.

Nerves, that's all. I'm afraid for the battle tomorrow—today, probably. I'm not an oracle or a prophet, my dreams don't come true.

But the truth was he'd had a dream like this one before. Three years before, the very day he was wounded, he'd lain in a room in this very palace and dreamt almost the same dream. It was only now that it came back to him, and before it had been Cangrande in the role of the lunatic swordsman.

It's a sign, all right. It's a sign I've read father's poem too many times. The Inferno *has eaten into my brain. This has nothing to do with tomorrow.*

Still, as he laid his head to rest once more he recalled the dream Cesco's final words. *If God won't help me, the devil won't fail me.* An apt phrase for the coming dawn.

THIRTY-TWO

Vicenza

22 MAY 1317

Pietro awoke to a light tapping on the door to his suite. Fazio was up quicker, though, and answered it. It was Morsicato and Bailardino, with a few servants behind them. The doctor was wearing armor. Pietro stood and shook his head clear. Pulling on his breeches he said, "What time is it?"

"About two hours before dawn," said Bailardino. "Time to armor up and gather your men."

Fazio made for the chest that contained Pietro's armor, but Pietro stopped him. "Not today." He pointed to the servants bringing in another chest. As they lit the tapers about the room, Bail threw back the lid of the trunk, revealing another set of armor, much more worn than Pietro's. The helmet sat on top, a peaked dome with gilded metal rings providing the protection for ears and neck. Underneath it lay the breastplate. This was both gilded and plated in sliver, the two shimmering colors acid-etched into fantastic flowery swirls.

Bail grinned at Pietro's expression. "Gaudy, isn't it? I'm sorry, but you're going to have to swallow your pride and wear the awful thing—at least for a few hours."

Pietro slipped a shirt over his head. "It's not that—how am I going to fit it? He must be built like a wall!"

Bail snapped his fingers and the servants began strapping padding to Pietro's midsection. "Oh, this is good," he groaned.

"Don't knock it," said Morsicato from the door. "Many knights would kill for extra protection."

"Most knights would get killed in extra protection," retorted Pietro.

The breastplate was put in place, then the codpiece, followed by the arm and leg greaves. As he helped Pietro fit on the gloves, Fazio asked, "Whose armor is this?"

Bailardino smiled. "It's the armor abandoned by Count Vinciguerra da San Bonifacio when he fled Vicenza three years ago. The Scaliger's been saving it. When the invaders get to the gates they'll see a friendly face beckoning them in. Everything will be as inviting as possible."

Fazio nodded thoughtfully. He had heard and seen enough to guess what was really happening, and the news of invaders was no shock. Instead he asked Pietro, "But why give it to you, sir?"

Pietro patted his leg. "Because the Count and I share a limp. We both list a little in the saddle. It will make the disguise that much more effective."

Fazio looked into the empty trunk. "Is there armor for me?"

"No," said Pietro. "No, don't argue. You're staying at the palace. I don't want to have to explain your death to the Scaliger's wife. Now help me get down the stairs."

Bail wished him good luck. It had been decided the night before that Morsicato would join Pietro's band of soldiers. Bail wished to as well, but Katerina had pointed out that the Paduans were sure to have spies in and around the palace. If he were to disappear moments before a "surprise" attack, the whole thing might fall apart.

The hardest part of leaving the palace was convincing Mercurio to stay behind. The hound sensed something was afoot, but he was a hunter, not a war dog. Eventually they were forced to lock him in a side chamber without windows.

When Pietro, Morsicato, and Fazio emerged from a side entrance to the palace, the sky was still dark. So when a shadow beside the door moved, every man drew his sword. "Who's there?" demanded Pietro in a whisper.

He was answered by a rasping voice scraped from a friendly throat. "The *Arūs*."

Pietro lowered his blade and the Moor stepped close. He was dressed in some kind of eastern battle gear, lighter and quieter than theirs. Pietro sheathed his sword and took the hand the Moor offered him. "I hope you brought that blade of yours."

"Don't be nervous, Ser Alaghieri. You will not die today."

Pietro let out a short laugh, half hope and half disbelief. "My stars said that?"

"They did."

"What about me?" demanded Morsicato.

The Moor looked at the face under the nondescript armor. "Is that the doctor's beard I see? My apologies, Doctor, but I did not consult the heavens for you."

"Marvelous," muttered the medical man.

"Thanks for that. I'm a little jumpy today. I had this dream last night . . ."

Theodoro's brow furrowed. "Tell me."

"Oh, it was nonsense." Pietro quickly described it.

The Moor was quiet for a moment, then said, "That's from your father's poem. The descent among the violent."

Pietro didn't pause to appreciate the Moor's grasp of Dante's work. He was feeling foolish. "It was nothing."

"You recall the proverb regarding early morning dreams?"

Pietro did. They were the ones that most often came true.

The Moor was pensive. "Perhaps I should not go with you."

Morsicato said, "Afraid? Do your stars say you won't die today?"

The Moor looked at the doctor with a level gaze. "The dream indicates danger to the boy."

Fazio piped up. "You should stay with Ser Alaghieri. What if he needs you?"

"I'll be fine," said Pietro. He wondered if his voice carried any conviction. The truth was that he liked the idea of that wicked falchion covering his back.

The Moor said, "Someone needs to look after Cesco. Just to be certain he's safe."

Fazio said, "Why not me? You won't let me fight, but I'm fourteen. I'll be a man next year. I can watch him."

"That might answer," allowed the Moor.

Pietro considered. "Very well. Take Mercurio, Cesco likes him."

Fazio saluted. "I won't let the boy out of my sight!" He rapped on the door and was readmitted by a Nogarola servant.

"A good solution," said the doctor. "Keeps him busy."

"I hope so." Pietro led the way to the stables that housed his soldiers, all soundly asleep. As Pietro woke his men, someone groaned, "What time is it?"

"What's the matter?" asked a veteran, snapping awake at the sight of Pietro in full armor.

Pietro cleared his throat. "Today, we have—that is to say—ah . . ."

Morsicato stepped forward into the light of the single taper. "There's a plot to take the city. Word has reached the Podestà this morning that the Paduans are planning an attack." He glanced at Pietro, who added, "I've offered our services to defend the city. So, ah, arm yourselves. Quickly."

They were already moving, throwing open their packs. Even the inexperienced worked with a minimum of fuss, helping each other with chain mail and gauntlets, swords and pikes.

Pietro spent a few moments stroking his palfrey's long head. "Sorry, but today's work is for Pompey." He used a small stool to clamber onto his destrier's back. "Is everyone ready?"

"Yes!" The son of Pietro's neighbor was anxious for his first battle.

The Moor stepped into the light. "Don't be too eager."

"Who the devil is that?"

"A heathen!"

All the men wheeled about to draw weapons. Pietro put his horse between them and the Moor. "He's with us!"

One veteran looked horrified. "You want us to fight side by side with a backstabbing Moor?"

"As long as he's beside you, he can't stab you in the back, can he?" countered Pietro. "Look, there's no time. You trusted me with your lives. I trust him with mine. That should be enough. Now let's get moving."

✦   ◆   ✦

Even now the enemy was scaling Vicenza's walls. In a replica of his family's armor, Vinciguerra, Count of San Bonifacio, led his small army of mercenaries and exiles up the battlements of San Pietro, repeating the action he had taken three years earlier. Reaching the top, the Count's men quickly secured the turrets and made their way to the guardhouse. The guards put up no resistance, moving aside to allow the invaders access to the gates. The Count looked about him in delight. *Whatever today brings, within a month the Scaliger will be no more.*

As promised, his sympathizers within the walls cheered the returning exiles. The Count saw a large man with dark skin and a floppy hat leading the citizens in their repeated brays for the invading force. Other citizens, seeing which way the wind was blowing, began slipping north or east, away from where a battle loomed. It was old hat now—they would wait, and the Scaliger would come to the city's rescue.

The Count, too, was hoping for Cangrande to come. He had a special treat in store for the wily Lord of Verona.

In the meantime, he had a job to do. He had his men lash ladders to the battlements, making it a chore for the Vicentines to dislodge the invaders. As he beat the lax with the flat of his blade, he glanced down. Down in the crowd the Count saw the man in the floppy hat disappearing around a corner. *Excellent. He's off to spread the word. We're coming.*

✦ ◇ ✦

At the base of a hill just south of the city, Marsilio da Carrara waited for the Count's signal. Carrara was uneasy. It wasn't the impending battle. It was the Count's manner. The old bastard had seemed positively overjoyed to have Marsilio with him. Why?

That the Paduan *Anziani* had come to Marsilio and not his uncle was a measure of how his stature had grown—Vicenza, Verona, the Arena, the brokered marriage, a few skirmishes with Treviso last year—all of it marked him as the first in the new generation of Paduan nobles. When they'd presented this plot to him, Carrara had approved every measure except the involvement of the exiled Vinciguerra. But the plan relied on the Count. To counterbalance this, Marsilio insisted on picking his men, his place of hiding, and his own time to attack; on being present for every war council; and on reading over Vinciguerra's every order before it went out. Like a beaten man, Vinciguerra had agreed.

"Marsilio," the Count had said, "I'm an old man. I've given up the hope of ever seeing Verona again—unless I'm in chains, and I'll die before I let that happen. But I can live to see Vicenza stripped from the Pup. For that, I need your help." He'd stood there, humble, begging for Marsilio's help. Knowing his uncle would never have approved, Carrara had decided it was worth the risk.

Still, he'd been suspicious. The Count had gained a new shadow, one that trailed him to secret meetings around Padua. Thinking the Count meant to betray Padua, Carrara had laughed aloud when he'd discovered the Count was just keeping a mistress as well as his childless wife. Randy old goat. If that was the extent of Bonifacio's deceiving, a broken man's solace, then the attack could go forward.

But this morning it had been a different Count saluting him and riding off to scale the walls. Cheerful and energetic, almost giddy with delight. And that raised Marsilio's hackles. Yet the Count couldn't be planning a betrayal—he was spearheading the attack! If he chose to, Carrara could hold his reinforcements just long enough for Vinciguerra to be cut to ribbons. The Count had to know that.

Marsilio thrust the question aside and gestured Asdente over to again discuss the order of riding. "Scorigiani, you're leading the second wave of men, mostly foot. Wait until I'm well into the city to start your charge. I'll flush out the *figli di puttana,* and you can come in and decimate them."

"Gladly," replied Asdente, his broken mouth looking old and evil.

Carrara grunted, remembering what Asdente had said upon being offered the junior command. "Of course I'm damn well coming. After the last Vicentine adventure, my reputation is covered in mud. They won't let me lead a band of eunuchs to a brothel. I'm in for anything that will restore my reputation."

Marsilio turned to his Captain of the Horse. "You ride with me—though I want a few hundred foot soldiers with us, too."

The captain nodded. The Paduan troops were happy to have Carrara at their head. They might not have been so serene to follow him had they known his uncle would have opposed this venture. Marsilio hadn't told them. He had more important things on his mind now than his uncle's approval. He had a city to win, a treacherous Count to watch.

✦   ◇   ✦

In a low dale two miles to the west of the Paduan forces, Uguccione della Faggiuola was also reviewing his own dispositions with Nico da Lozzo. Mariotto Montecchio was nearby, clad in new French armor. Also present was Benvenito Lenoti, soon to be Mariotto's brother-in-law.

"Where the hell is Bonaventura?" growled Uguccione. "The Illasi group was supposed to be here an hour ago."

"They'll be here," said Nico.

"They better get here soon. Twenty men could make the difference."

Mariotto was silent. He too wanted Bonaventura's men to get here soon. He had something to say to Antony.

Life was nearly perfect for Mariotto. United with his wife, reconciled with his father, he felt he stood at the precipice of a whole new life. The only blight was his shattered relationship with Antony. Mari wanted a chance to set things right before the battle, in case something happened.

"Any word on Bonifacio?" Benvenito was nervous and eager to talk.

Uguccione chuckled nastily. "A farmer told us that a group of soldiers and horsemen tramped across his field under cover of darkness. Had to be him, moving into position. I haven't sent out scouts, in case he caught them. We know where he's supposed to be and when."

"How many men-at-arms do the Paduans have?"

"About a thousand in all," said Uguccione. "They'll outnumber us, but just barely. Bailardino's whole garrison is hidden away inside the city. And there's another force waiting for the Paduans. Cangrande commissioned someone to wear Bonifacio's armor to amuse the enemy. They'll engage first."

Mari laughed. "Clever. And where is the Scaliger?"

"Off whoring in Cremona," replied Uguccione disdainfully. "Actually, he's probably on his way by now. He and Passerino were raising holy hell with the Cremonese a week ago, just to put the Paduans at ease. But however fast he rides, he'll miss today's fun."

At the sound of hoofbeats they turned. Bonaventura's force arrived, late but fresh and ready to fight. Capulletto rode in among these men and moved to a place in the front line, as his rank dictated. His brother Luigi was in the row behind him, looking sourly eager.

Mariotto had hoped for a little more privacy, but now was the time to try. He cantered over. "Morning, Antony."

"Montecchio."

Mari tried to remember that he deserved the cold greeting. "I wanted to talk to you."

"Good. I want to talk to you, too." He reached to belt and drew a silver dagger. "Remember this? I've had this since the Palio. You might not have noticed, but we switched daggers that day." He rotated the blade until the name showed, the acid-etching looking quite dark against the light color of the blade. "After we're done here today, I'll give it back to you."

Mariotto's blood drained to his boots. "Antony—what are you saying?"

Antony slipped the dagger into his tall boot. "I'm saying if we live through this battle, I have a blade with your name on it."

Mari stared, then nodded. With nothing more for either to say, Mariotto returned to his station in the right-hand files of knights and men-at-arms, his mind far from the impending battle.

✦ ◇ ✦

Pietro's soldiers raced into position. Word was filtering back from the south of exiles scaling the suburb walls and approaching the gate to the city proper. Citizens followed a well-ordered plan to evacuate this part of the city.

Pietro turned a corner and saw the gate across a wide expanse of a court-yard. He halted his men. This was the same gate that had stopped the Paduans three years before. Today the gate would open like magic, the bribed Muzio pretending to follow the Paduan plan. It would be up to Pietro's band to hold the gate until Uguccione and Bailardino's hidden troops arrived. He wondered how many the Paduans had brought. He wondered how long he could hold.

He could hear the cheering exiles and mercenaries. The time was close. A guard—Pietro assumed it was Muzio—started pulling the ropes that con-trolled the massive gates. One of Pietro's men looked at him anxiously. "What's he doing? Surely the gate should stay closed!"

"Abandon hope, all ye who enter here." Pietro drew his sword and held his breath.

✦ ◇ ✦

On the walls of San Pietro, Vinciguerra's face was red with excitement. So far his plan was going perfectly—better than perfectly. He nodded to his three archers, lined up along the outer wall. As one they lit their arrows and shot them high into the breaking dawn.

✦ ◇ ✦

"There's the signal!" called Asdente.

After all the worries about the Count's possible treachery, Carrara's reac-tion was immediate. He turned to the troops. "Men! Now we reclaim what is rightfully ours!" The quick speech was the retelling of a history so well known it was taken for granted—the noble Guelphs, supporters of the pope; the wretched Ghibellines, tools of the empire, the worst tool being the bastard of Verona. Marsilio ended by invoking the motto that defined Padua: "*Muson, Mons, Athes, Mare Certos Dant Michi Fines!*"

His men cheering him, he spurred his horse and cried, "Ride! For Padua! For *Patavinitas!*"

Mounted or on foot, his troops raced toward Vicenza. As they ran they cheered, hoping to frighten the city into submission with noise alone.

✦   ✧   ✦

The Count watched them come, Carrara at the front as a brave leader should be. *Brave but foolish.* More experienced, Asdente held his troops back a little, allowing Carrara to enter first. Only when the battle was desperate should a commander fight in the thick of it. The Count planned to hold himself in reserve. He'd done what he promised for the Paduans. He'd gotten them in.

A young fellow came running by. His armor was poor and his boots were falling apart. But his sword was well cared for. "You there," shouted the Count. "Your name!"

"Benedick, sir!"

"Signore Benedick, I charge you to come back once we've reached the inner walls and tell me."

"I will, my lord." On foot, he raced to catch the mounted Paduans who thundered across the bridge and under the archway, the site of the massacre when Cangrande had dressed common citizens as archers and broken a whole army with only eighty men.

Let the Pup come, thought Bonifacio with a savage joy. *I hope he does. I hope he's got some miracle at hand to salvage this. Let him feel the taste of sweet victory before I dash the cup from his lips.*

Vinciguerra's voice joined the other exiles on the wall as they cheered the three thousand Paduans racing towards victory.

Three thousand. More than Verona's generals had anticipated. Far, far more. The *Anziani* of Padua had decided that this first thrust of the renewed war would also be the last.

Three thousand, faced by thirty rustic men-at-arms under the command of Pietro Alaghieri.

THIRTY-THREE

"I hope you're a decent actor," whispered Morsicato. At the far end of the courtyard Muzio almost had the gate fully open.

"Do you want to play the part?" hissed Pietro. "I could stab you in the thigh."

Morsicato chuckled nervously. "You should have thought of that earlier."

"I did." Another worry popped into Pietro's mind. "What if the Count's with them?"

"He won't be." Morsicato didn't sound too sure.

"But what if he is?"

The doctor shrugged. "If he is, I won't have to pay you my losses from last night."

"Wonderful," muttered Pietro. He glanced behind him. The Moor had moved his horse to the back of the group, hoping to go unseen. He was rather distinctive looking in his light, Eastern-style armor and conical helmet, and it was doubtful that the Count would travel with such a man.

Pietro addressed his men. "All right, listen. The city has been betrayed. The Paduans are about to come through that gate. They won't know who we are, though, and that works to our advantage. Just follow my lead, and don't attack until I give the signal."

Then pray that Bailardino and Uguccione get here in time.

Reading Pietro's thoughts, Morsicato said, "They'll be here."

"I'm sure," said Pietro. "Christ, are they racing cattle ahead of them? There can't be that many horses in the Feltro." Muzio finally heaved the tall oak doors wide. "Here we go."

The first rider through the gate was in full armor and wore the colors of Padua. Behind him came the captain, bearing the standard that proclaimed their origins for all the world to see. There followed a hundred more soldiers, spreading themselves out behind their leader.

Pietro knew the leader's crest all too well. "Shit! It's Carrara!"

"You don't have to fool him long. Go!" The doctor kicked his heel and nicked Pompey's leg. The massive horse jolted forward, Pietro with it. The charade had begun, whether Pietro liked it or not.

"Hell and damn," he murmured as he raised his hand in greeting. *Why couldn't Carrara have been sensible and commanded from the rear?*

Carrara spied Pietro at once. A look of rage swept over the Paduan's face inside his open visor. Giving his horse the spur he came straight toward Pietro.

"No, no, you *pezzo di merda,*" whispered Pietro, "don't come here. Talk to your men, look around, sharpen your sword. Just don't—"

Carrara reined in beside him. "Count," he said in cold greeting. Pietro grunted once in return. "I thought you were supposed to remain up on the walls. I thank you for getting that gate open. Now get out of my way. My men can take the city."

Pietro said nothing.

"If you think that you're going to take the credit for this—this is my day, Bonifacio! Remember that!" Carrara turned away contemptuously and rode back to his men.

Pietro sagged in his saddle. *Oh, God, thank you. How did I escape that one?* In his anger Carrara hadn't noticed that the armor fitted poorly, nor that the wearer was half a foot shorter than the Count. Certainly Pietro had none of the Count's bulk. But somehow, impossibly, the disguise had worked.

Morsicato rode forth to join him. "Well, you pulled that off."

"He's too concerned with his own dignitas," said Pietro softly. "He thinks the Count will steal the glory of the moment."

"He's in for a shock."

"Maybe not," said Pietro. Paduan soldiers were still streaming through the open gate. The yard was filling up rapidly, and there seemed to be no end of them in sight. "The moment Marsilio has enough men through that gate, he'll massacre the city. If Bailardino doesn't move now—"

"*Buenas dias!*" A voice echoed around the cobblestoned yard, reverberating off the many houses and apartments that enclosed it. All eyes looked up to the roof of a nearby tavern where a tanned man in a floppy hat was standing, wineskin in hand. It was the notary who had hitched a ride to Vicenza with Pietro's men. He was dressed in the same clothes, though he might have had a shave—it was hard to tell under the shadowy hat. "Señores!" he called drunkenly down to the Paduan knights. "I welcome you all! I hear Padua is very nice this time of year! I'll have to come and visit! You have fine women, yes?" He dropped his boodle bag and watched it spatter all over the road in front of the tavern. "Ah, now there's a sorry sight! I don't suppose any of you have a little ale to spare? Or better yet, wine?"

Clearly the Spaniard was no threat. Carrara started giving orders, yet still the man persisted. "Can any one of you give me a drink? I can pay!"

A Paduan captain shouted, "We don't need your money."

A sly look entered the notary's face. "If I had money I would not be begging. No, my, how you say, currency, my currency is information. I can tell you where Señor Nogarola is right now. And his men."

A lump formed in Pietro's throat. He tried to swallow it as Carrara rode nearer the Spaniard's perch. "Tell me," the Paduan called up to him.

The Spaniard countered with a demand of his own. "Where's my drink?"

Carrara ordered ten of his men to break down the door to the tavern. "There! You can drink yourself dead on what's inside. Now tell me where they are!"

The notary belched in a satisfied way as he heard the final crash of the door coming down. "Why, they're right here!"

Immediately four of the Paduans flew backward from the tavern, crossbow bolts piercing their chests. Vicentine men-at-arms sprang up from hiding places in all the surrounding buildings. Pietro was staring up at the man on the roof, who now tore the hat from his head. The soot of yesterday washed away, the sun-bleached hair gleamed in the dawn light.

Cangrande della Scala. The Great Hound had come.

Rows of crossbowmen appeared from all corners of the yard. In windows, behind barrels, from rooftops, as one they fired. Two dozen Paduans jerked from their horses. The Paduan standard fell. Two Paduans lifted it again only to be dropped in the next wave.

Pietro gasped in delighted outrage. "That son of a bitch!"

"Attack!" cried Carrara. There was no way to retreat even had he wished to, but he still had the advantage of numbers. "Attack!" he cried again, spurring his horse directly at the tavern.

Crossbows are devilishly slow to load. Already hundreds of Paduans as yet unscathed moved towards their ambushers. The Vicentines on the ground level dropped their crossbows and drew their swords, while those above reloaded and took aim.

Carrara stood in his saddle and swung at the Scaliger, who skipped backward up the tiled roof. Bending, he ripped up a clay tile and threw it backhanded to shatter against Carrara's helmet, rocking him back in his saddle. Another tile struck the Paduan's shoulder, a third crashed against his head. Marsilio peeled away, racing his horse out of reach of the projectiles. Immediately Cangrande shifted targets, aiming for the Paduan men-at-arms who were swarming up the sides of the tavern to reach him.

Pietro was watching all this in awe. Morsicato said, "Time to jump in, I think!"

"Right!" Pietro led his men into the center of eight hundred Paduans who had formed a ring of shields to defend against the crossbows. The Paduans believed Pietro's force to be friendly and opened the ring to them. His men guessed his thoughts, and so pretended until the last instant that they were coming in to reenforce the Paduan center. At the center Pietro wheeled about and, using his sword's pommel, started clubbing at the backs of the Paduan knights, knocking them from their horses. Bearing in mind what the Code said about attacking from behind, he didn't aim to kill, but focused on unseating as many as he could.

For a moment shock confounded the Paduans. Then from the roof Cangrande cried, "Betrayal! We are betrayed!" The Paduans picked up the chorus. Suddenly all was chaos.

Beset on all sides, the gates blocked by more of their fellows, the besieged Paduans had nowhere to go but farther into the city. Where they ran into the waiting jaws of the Nogarola brothers. Bailardino resembling a huge bear and Antonio looking like a stocky one-armed ferret, they had brought their horsemen up at the first sound of real fighting. The Paduans came running headlong into a wall of Vicentine spears. Still more crossbowmen on the roofs took down the second row of knights, so that the third row was facing a wall of their own dead.

Carrara screamed at Pietro, "Damn your eyes, you traitor! I'll see you dead for this!"

"Come and try it!" called Pietro, not bothering to disguise his voice. But Carrara was no longer paying attention. Pietro traced his gaze to the gate the

Paduans had come through. The hidden Vicentines had rushed forward to heave it shut, cutting Carrara off from his reinforcements.

The Paduan leader spurred hard in the direction of the gate. Pietro knew what was going through Carrara's mind. If Padua was going to win, that gate had to stay open. Pietro called, "Stop him!" But none of his men were near enough. Carrara ducked low as a half-dozen bolts hissed overhead.

Dozens of Paduan soldiers were huddled behind wounded or dead horses, every one waiting for the moment to charge and take their revenge. Carrara called out for them to follow and pressed his horse toward the gate. Recognizing the dire need for reinforcements, they obeyed, hacking furiously.

Pietro saw a youth working hard to close the gate against the tide of invaders. Pietro had seen him three years before in Cangrande's palace. Muzio, the fellow who had pretended to betray Vicenza today. Now that the charade was done, he was straining along with the Vicentines that had leaped from nearby buildings, assigned to this single vital chore. They all pulled the ropes that swung the doors, hauling against the press of Paduan bodies on the far side.

Pietro kicked and kicked, but there was no room for his horse to maneuver out of the struggle. He watched as Carrara carved a path toward the rope. Muzio's back was to the fray, so he never saw the blow that separated his head from his shoulders. His hands continued to pull for a long moment. Then the body crumpled. The Vicentines scattered under the fury of Carrara's attack. He then turned his rage on the thick rope controlling the door. One cut, two, three, four. The thick braid parted. With no more resistance, the vanguard of Asdente's fifteen hundred troops began to swing the gate open again.

Pietro felt the change in the momentum. The yard was thick with struggling bodies pressed against each other, fighting for room to maneuver. But more Paduans were appearing every second. Soon sheer numbers would force the Vicentines out of the yard, leaving his thirty men in the middle of the fray to be unhorsed and run through.

The sun now broke the horizon, glinting off the bloody armor of the Paduans and Vicentines who battled for possession of the city's heart. Pietro could hear Carrara urging on Asdente's reinforcements pouring through the widening gap, and then the Paduan turned his mind to the bowmen. He was pointing at torches in brackets along the city wall, still lit from the night just ending. "Burn them! Burn them out!" Pietro saw Carrara lift a hanging torch from its bracket and ride to the side of a building holding snipers. He tossed the firebrand into a window on the first floor. Carrara's men immediately caught on and aided him by grabbing anything flammable and holding it against the structure. With the unseasonable dryness that had plagued the Feltro this year, the flames were quick to spread. In minutes the ambushers on the second and third floors would find themselves shooting through smoke.

Other Paduans quickly applied the idea to other buildings. Smoke filled the courtyard, ending the effectiveness of the crossbows. They could shoot, but the Vicentines had no idea if they were aiming at friend or foe.

Pietro's destrier slipped on cobblestones made slick with blood. Pietro lurched in the saddle, just avoiding the pike that drove upward for his head. Morsicato speared the pike's owner and called to Pietro. "We're in trouble!"

"We'll hold!" cried Pietro. He glanced around. There were about twenty of his thirty men left in their saddles—not bad for being so horribly outnumbered. The element of surprise had worked for them, and the bowmen had kept most knights too busy to fight back. But now, with smoke blocking their covering fire, Pietro was sure that the Paduans would rip apart the "traitors" in their midst.

A blow on his shield rocked him back in his saddle. He returned the blow with all the strength he owned. The attacker reeled back, then lunged again. Pietro dodged, swallowing smoke that had drifted into his helmet. His eyes were tearing up, his lungs were choked. He swung his shield, felt it connect, and used the respite to tear off the borrowed helmet. Already his adversary was back, but Pietro got there first, throwing the hereditary helmet of the Bonifaci at the man's head. As the Paduan ducked, Pietro got his sword around to bash in his skull. The Paduan sagged sideways in his saddle, then his face disappeared as Pietro's well-trained horse opened his mouth and clamped down on a target. The Paduan screamed in his throat as he died.

Pietro was already on to his next opponent. "Where's Cangrande?" he shouted, blocking a mace aiming to remove his head from his shoulders.

"Don't! Know!" said the doctor, hacking with each word. Pietro let Pompey bite another horse's neck, then pulled the reins. In the melee the destrier managed to turn enough to let Pietro face the tavern. It was obscured in smoke, having been quick to burn because of the barrels of alcohol within.

Pietro's men moved to cover his back, several chanting a fighting song as they beat at the Paduans around them. Some of those Paduans began singing as well, and both sides of the struggle set up their cuts and parries to the sound of their mixed voices united in song.

A gust of wind cleared the smoke, inviting a hail of crossbow bolts from above. The archers had decided to risk the flames in order to snipe away when an opportunity presented itself. Fifty Paduans dropped away in a hail of blurred streaks. Suddenly unopposed, Pietro looked up to wave his thanks.

Suddenly he spied Cangrande, still atop the tavern. The Scaliger was hopping away from spears and pikes that thrust up at him from below. He'd run out of missiles to throw, and the untiled patches in the rooftop now blazed with fire. Any moment now the roof would collapse under him. The Paduans saw this and penned the Capitano in, jeering darkly.

Far from looking concerned, Cangrande called back lighthearted insults to his assailants below. A few Paduans ignored the flames and climbed the roof to confront him, hoping to claim the honor of having killed the great Scaliger lord. Unencumbered by armor, he danced around their slow and clumsy attacks, kicking them from the flaming roof. One, more determined than the rest, rushed at him with sword low, ready to eviscerate the Scaliger from groin to chin. Cangrande skipped backward across a piece of roof that was already showing some sparks flying up through a hole. It held—barely. When his attacker reached it moments later, the weight of his armor sent him crashing through the timbers and into the inferno below.

The Capitano picked up the tune the soldiers sang and blared it loudly, defying the smoke that billowed around him. The fire was burning so hot now that the Paduans had to cease their harassment and back away from the blazing tavern. Cangrande could only have moments before the timbers collapsed under him.

Pietro turned to Morsicato. "Pull the men back to the Nogarola line! We'll be slaughtered if we stay here!"

Morsicato was putting down a pesky Paduan. By the time he turned Pietro was driving though the Paduan soldiers toward the tavern. "Pietro! Where are you going?"

Pietro didn't bother with his sword and shield. He dodged between the Paduans, calling out as he did so. "Francesco! Francesco!" By using the Scaliger's baptismal name he hoped the Paduans wouldn't realize whom he was trying to rescue.

A thunderous crash came from the tavern. Clouds of sparks and great billows of smoke rose from the building. The Paduans let out a massive cheer. Still Pietro called. "Francesco! Francesco!"

Another gust of wind revealed the Scaliger. He was standing on the lip of the roof, covered in soot and smoke that made his dyed skin even darker. He coughed, staggering and half blind.

Pietro cried, "Francesco!"

The Scaliger's head came around. Seeing the friendly face, Cangrande's eyes flickered about him. One Paduan was edging closer to jab upward with his spear. Ducking low, Cangrande grabbed the spear with both hands and kicked the shaft. The Paduan's grip slipped, allowing Cangrande to yank the spear free. Reversing the spear in his hands, Cangrande leapt.

How he saw where to place the spear's tip through the smoke Pietro couldn't tell, but the spear landed in a space between two cobblestones. Cangrande swung his body around the spear and landed like an acrobat three feet from Pietro. "Ride!"

Pietro was already giving Pompey the spur. Cangrande ran alongside, his hands clutching at the second arcione of the saddle. With a heave the Scaliger leapt up across Pompey's rump. "Go go go!"

Shock held the Paduan men-at-arms in place for a few seconds. Then as one they howled their pursuit. A sword edge came flying at Pietro's head. He took the blow on his shield even as his armored horse drove on through the furious Paduans.

In his ear, Pietro heard a muttered, *"Gracias, señor."* He was too busy to reply, weaving in and out of the clusters of Paduan soldiers. He felt some movement in the saddle behind him as Cangrande dragged a weapon free and busied himself parrying blows from behind. There were too many, though—blows were coming faster and faster. Pietro could feel them glance off his armor. It was worse for Cangrande, who wore no armor and had to twist to avoid every hit.

Seeing a gap in the Paduan lines, Pietro urged his mount on. *Faster!* But destriers were bred for endurance, not speed. Only the smoke and Cangrande's quick hands kept them from mortal harm. Pietro saw more horses, closing in on them from the front. He caught a spear tip on his shield, but saw a longsword descending for his skull. *Father, forgive me . . .*

A falchion intercepted the weapon. Pietro slashed his attacker's face, not seeing but feeling the Moor riding beside him. There was a rumbled noise from deep within the black man's chest as his wicked point found an exposed throat.

Suddenly Cangrande shouted, "Pietro! Veer right!"

The command turned them directly into a new line of oncoming knights, but Pietro's trust in Cangrande was unhesitating. He braced himself, but felt only a rush of air as the mounted knights raced past them. Suddenly Pietro found himself riding in the clear. He looked back. Morsicato had led a charge of Pietro's men, protecting his retreat before wheeling around and sprinting back for safety themselves.

The Paduans decided not to give chase, choosing rather to reform their lines for the next attack. For the moment Pietro's party was safe. They were between the Paduans pressing Nogarola's men and Marsilio's force by the gate. It gave Cangrande a moment to assess the condition of the battle. "Pietro, Tharwat, get your men into the mouth of that alley!"

Pietro obediently steered for the alley the Scaliger was indicating, the Moor protecting his flank. Morsicato and the men who had survived this latest ride followed them. There were only a dozen of them, a third of his original force. Pietro was glad to see the face of his neighbor's son. "Glad you're still alive!"

"Wouldn't have missed it for the world," the boy replied. He was just Pietro's age, yet he seemed to think Pietro some sort of hero and not just a lucky fool. His eyes traveled to Cangrande and opened even wider. "You—you're the Spaniard!"

"At times like this, I wish I were." It was a lie. The Scaliger never looked so alive as he did during a battle. Now he addressed Pietro's men, the same men he'd fooled for three days with his accent and his drunken manners. "My name is Cangrande della Scala. This is my city you're protecting. If we live through this day, I promise you all women, honors, and riches. Until then, obey Alaghieri like you would obey God and, for the love of the Virgin, enjoy yourselves!"

They cheered. Cangrande turned to Pietro, beckoning Morsicato and the Moor also. "The Paduans brought more men than we anticipated. A lot more. We'll still win this, but we have to hold. You understand. We must hold! Uguccione is coming, but he'll have to cut his way through the Paduans on the other side of that gate and break through to us."

Pietro asked, "Where do you want us?"

Cangrande nodded to the alley. "Right here. Pretty soon Marsilio is going to think of Thermopylae—he's going to use these alleys and side streets to cut around and bash Bailardino and Antonio from the sides. They'll be massacred unless we can hold these alleys for them."

"We'll hold them," said Pietro grimly.

Cangrande nodded. "It's good to see you."

Pietro laughed. "I've seen you for three days but I was too blind to know it. What did you dye your skin with?"

"Nutmegs." Cangrande flashed his perfect teeth. "You realize, if we live through this battle, my sister is going to have me eviscerated for letting you risk yourself to save me. Again."

"I won't tell her if you won't."

"A deal!" Cangrande lifted his stolen sword and glanced out into the main fray. "I'll send reinforcements when I can. But first I have to make sure the signal is given. That dimwit Bailardino let himself get cut off from the bells."

"No hurry," said Pietro, raising his voice to add, "We can hold the gates of the inferno!"

His men cheered again. Cangrande clapped the doctor on the shoulder, bowed to the Moor, then dashed out into the blood-slick streets. Grasping the mane of a passing riderless horse, he swung himself into the saddle. His blackened face looked like something from the netherworld. Cangrande saluted with his sword, then spurred toward Nogarola's men, slicing through the threefold lines of Paduans to get there.

Pietro ordered his men to hurry up and find something to barricade the alley. The battle was far from over, and they had work to do.

✦　◇　✦

At the other end of the yard Marsilio was greeting Asdente in the center of the formation just spilling through the gate. "What in all-fired hell is going on?" cried the Toothless Master, looking at the smoking carnage.

"They were waiting! Bonifacio betrayed us!" Carrara slammed his mailed fist into his palm. "I knew it!"

"The Count?" Vanni clearly found it hard to believe that the old fox would set them up this way.

"I saw him," confirmed Marsilio. "He was here—even saved Cangrande's life, from what my sergeant said."

Asdente brushed that aside. "What's to do?"

Marsilio looked around. The bolts from the crossbows had ceased as all the fires took hold and the archers leapt from windows to try and escape.

Some managed to get away; most were rounded up and pressed back into the burning structures to face their deaths.

"Bring your men in here—all of them. If we take the Nogarola palace, we can press outward and take the whole city."

"What about prisoners?" Asdente had ruined his reputation by slaughtering innocents without orders last time they had come this way. This time he wanted explicit instructions.

Marsilio paused. What would his uncle do? Take prisoners, ransom them, show them all the mercy and generosity that Cangrande had shown three years before. "No prisoners. Havoc. Kill them all."

Asdente loosed his twisted grin. "As you command." He returned to his men crying, "Havoc! Havoc!"

We were betrayed, thought Carrara for the hundredth time. Of one thing he was sure. The Count of San Bonifacio would not leave this field alive.

+ ◇ +

Cangrande slashed right and left, trying to get through the soldiers barring his path to the church. His deadly smile was unchanged, but his thoughts were grim. If Uguccione didn't get the signal soon, the city would fall.

He heard, as he often did, his sister's voice in his head, scolding him. *You always leave it too late, Francesco. You never think things through. You play your little games, have your theatrics, and forget what needs to be done!*

Well, dear sister, his mind retorted in a parody of conversation, *if you think I am too tardy, why don't you take care of it yourself?*

His head came up as he heard bells. For an instant Cangrande was stunned. His eyes opened wide, then he began to laugh, for he knew— *knew*—who was ringing the bells, giving the signal to the reserve army.

He turned his horse about and spurred back to the line being held by the Nogarolese. There was nothing more for him to do now but fight.

+ ◇ +

"It's got to be time," said Benvenito. "It's got to be! They've been in there for half an hour!"

"Fifteen minutes, more like," replied Mariotto, looking at the rising sun.

"I'm getting fed up with waiting," announced Bonaventura, not renowned for his patience.

"He'll give us a signal," said Uguccione softly. "He said he'd give us a signal."

As if in answer came the pealing of bells. Uguccione clapped his helm on his head and shouted, "On! On! Kill the bastards!!"

Bonaventura was already off. Mari kicked his heels as, down the line, Antony did the same, his brother Luigi right behind him. Nico whooped as he dug his heels into his horse's flanks. They led their forces toward Vicenza, toward the unguarded rear of the Paduan army.

✦　◇　✦

The Count saw them come. Just moments before, he'd been waiting impatiently, his horse moving from foot to foot in reflection of his rider's mood. The young soldier he'd sent had come running back with the news that Carrara's men had entered the inner walls. Now they stood together on the wall of San Pietro, watching the army of Verona ride to the rescue.

"Dear God," breathed the redheaded soldier. "What do we do?"

"We can either warn Carrara or save our skins," replied the Count calmly. "Make your choice, son, and stick to it."

Benedick looked down at the Paduans still outside the walls. "I have to fight."

"Eager for victory?"

The lean young man looked the Count in the eye. "I don't have a title, or land, or prospects. If I'm going to make a name for myself, I have to fight, and be seen fighting."

"I admire your honesty, Signore Benedick. But let me point out that we are about to be routed. Fight a little, be seen by a commander or two, then melt away into the city. In a week, return to Padua with a dramatic wound or two. You'll be a hero."

Benedick looked at the Count with distaste, then ran off to join the battle. "Poor fool," muttered the Count. Despite the danger he was in, he began to laugh. Everything was going according to plan. The Scaliger had indeed gotten word and set a trap for the Paduans. Vinciguerra was actually glad. If Cangrande came through this battle alive, he would find it a most bitter victory.

✦   ◇   ✦

Katerina released the bell rope and stepped back, nodding to her servants to do the same. "That's enough." She was dressed in men's riding breeches and a shirt and doublet, her long hair hidden under a cap. She was no stranger to male garb, having adopted it often enough in her youth. Today it assured she would not be singled out while running through the streets. A woman in such a crush could easily become a hostage, or worse.

Knowing the plan as well as any of the commanders, she'd recognized when things went awry. The fighting had sounded too desperate. It seemed her husband was too busy fighting to spare even the ten men it took to ring the alarum bell. So, leaving Cesco and little Bailardetto in the care of their nurse and Pietro's groom, she had run to give the signal to the waiting army. It took all her servants' strength to pull the bells, with her own weight added to it. Now she looked at the cuts the rope had burned into her hands and cursed her brother.

Francesco, where are you? Why are you not here, protecting your city, your heir?

Like a wraith, she imagined his reply. *If I wanted him safe, why leave him with you? You, who have left him alone.*

Katerina was filled with an indescribable premonition. Her hands began to shake. "Quickly," she commanded, "back to the palace."

THIRTY-FOUR

Pietro's men had barely finished overturning a wagon across the mouth of the alley when the Paduans launched an assault. As Cangrande had predicted, they were focusing not on driving Bailardino's forces back but on circumventing them entirely. Just as the Persians had found the goat trails above the cliffs of Thermopylae, so too did the Paduans discover the alleys, all blocked by small forces like Pietro's, all under heavy attack.

Filled with straw and nightsoil, the upturned wagon wasn't enough to hold back the soldiers who pressed forward, hoping to capture the glory of victory by beating down these paltry few defenders. Pietro ignored the growing ache in his bad leg as he stood in the gap between the wagon and the wall beating aside blade after blade. His horse was at the far end of the alley for a hasty retreat, but he didn't wish to use it.

Behind him the Moor swung a captured halberd like a demon's axe. On the wagon's far end Morsicato was swearing like the devil. The rest of Pietro's men were singing again, much feebler now that their numbers were reduced. The attacking Paduans trampled their wounded and their dead in their desire to break free from the yard and wreak havoc on the city at large.

Half-blind from the smoke, Pietro swung and blocked and beat weapons aside. Someone pitched a torch into their midst. It bounced off Pietro's armor, sending a flutter of sparks up to singe his face. He winced, then saw an opportunity. As he pulled back from a stab he kicked the stick of burning pitch into the overturned wagon. At once he tasted the gratifying stench of burning straw. In another minute the wagon in the alley's mouth was ablaze, and Pietro's men could step back and recover their breath. A few mounted

Paduans tried to jump the flaming hurdle only to be skewered on spears or the Moor's halberd. Their bodies became additional barriers in the blaze.

A skin of wine appeared from somewhere. Pietro sloshed the liquid around in his mouth, spitting away the distasteful remains, then swallowed a few gulps before handing the bag off to the next man. One of Pietro's men was wiping some blood from the Moor's face. Pietro turned to Morsicato. "How are we?"

"We're holding, but they're going to break through somewhere. They have to."

"I heard the bells," said Pietro hopefully. The exhausted doctor just nodded.

The Moor was staring at the sky. "It's going to rain—that's good."

The doctor stared at him in horror. "That's good?"

"Of course." The Moor grinned. "It will help the drought."

Morsicato goggled. Pietro's men started hooting. Apparently the black man had earned their trust. Pietro murmured, "Tharwat. Not Theodoro. Yes?"

The Moor nodded. "You will become used to it."

"Tharwat al-Dhaamin, secret astrologer to princes and kings. I just thought I'd like to call you by your right name . . ." Pietro's voice trailed away and he looked in the direction of the battle.

"Before you die? You won't die today, Ser Alaghieri."

Pietro laughed. "I take that as a binding promise. So, tell me, what does *Arūs* mean?"

The Moor grinned at him. "The Bridegroom. If we live through this, I may tell you the story."

"Now there's a reason to survive."

Suddenly their overturned flaming wagon jerked toward them. It stopped, then skidded another five feet up the alley, away from the yard. Something was bashing at it with tremendous force, pushing it forward.

Pietro swore. "A battering ram! Pull back! We can't stop them here!"

Already his men were retreating. The Paduans had torn doors off the few intact buildings and were using them to bash the wagon up the alley. Pietro's cleverness with the fire didn't seem so clever now that it prevented his men from stopping the moving barricade.

Running to the alley's end, he remounted his horse. It was oddly peaceful the next street over, with nothing but the smoke to show where the battle raged. That and the tremendous noise. He turned to Morsicato. "Go find Cangrande, let him know they're coming! We'll hold this street as long as we can!"

"You can't hold this street yourself!"

"Don't worry about us! I've got a plan! Go!"

Morsicato wheeled his horse about and galloped north on the empty street. At the corner he turned right, circling around to the back of the Vicentine forces.

Pietro looked around at the expectant faces of his men—*my men,* he thought. There were only seven of them left. Nine, counting the Moor and himself. Pietro grinned at them all. "Nine is my father's lucky number."

"Let's hope it runs in the family," said one. "What's your plan?"

Pietro had no plan. He'd said that to get rid of the doctor. Now he looked around at the empty street and no masterstroke of military strategy popped into his head. He shrugged. "We kill every *figlio di buona donna* that shows his face in our street."

Pietro was gratified to see his men's grim nods and determined smiles. They would die, but it was a glorious death, a death their fathers and children could be proud of.

To Tharwat he said, "How are those stars looking now?"

"Too much smoke. Can't see the sky."

"I suppose it's up to us then." The crashing in the alley was close now. "Pull back, down the street! They'll be blind and stumbling when they come out. They'll be expecting us to run! And they'll be looking north! We'll ride from the south and take the fight to them!" They rode to the end of the block and turned their horses about. "It's been an honor knowing you all."

The flames of the cart licked at the corners of the alley. The next bash of the Paduan ram would send it out into the open street.

"Ready," roared Pietro in a choked voice.

The flaming cart shattered as it tumbled into the street before them.

"Now!" Pietro gave his horse his spurs, driving the massive beast forward. He saw the edge of the makeshift battering ram pull back and bash forward again. The wreckage of the cart cleared from their path, the Paduan foot soldiers ran out into the street, turning north to loop around and catch the Vicentine forces from behind. Only a few noticed the nine men on horseback racing toward them from the south. These men tried to warn their fellows, but for the first wave of Paduans through the mouth of the alley there was nothing to do but dive for cover. The nine horses trampled anything in their path, the swords above them slicing through the air around their ears, battering them to pulp.

The charge carried them past, and Pietro's men were in the open again. The Moor looked to Pietro. "Stay or run?"

It was their last chance. They could escape to one of the north or west gates. Pietro said, "We have to hold them as long as we can." They wheeled around.

Scenting victory, more Paduans poured through the unstoppered gap in the defenses. This time Pietro let them come to him. Pietro's men shouted curses and jibes, taunts and insults, as their swords met.

One of Pietro's men fell to a spear in the chin. Pietro killed the spear's owner, shouting, "Come on! *Avanti! Avanti!*"

The astrologer fought like the demon he appeared to be, dark skin covered in blood, scars on his neck and face pulsing white. Pietro blocked a blow to Tharwat's side and together they hacked into the sea of men who hungered for their deaths.

Hands pulled at Theodoro's reins. He fought desperately but was struck a blow that dented his conical helmet. Pietro tried to grasp the Moor's toppling figure, but something bashed into his weak leg. He was wincing but still swinging when a heavy blow to his back unseated him. He felt himself sliding through the air, bouncing off the bodies of Paduan foot soldiers. He struck the ground heavily, but struggled up to keep swinging.

His horse took a step and pulled him with it. His right leg was still in its stirrup, dragging him behind his steed. He sliced the strap with his sword, freeing himself just as a spearpoint angled in for his head. He rolled and the spear struck the road, sending up sparks and chips of stone. He tried to stand but his poor leg sent him to his knees. He looked the spearman in the face and was surprised recognize the mounted knight. They'd had dinner once, talking about plays and stars. The man was missing most of his teeth. "Asdente."

Recognition showed on Vanni Scorigiani's face, too. He laughed as he saw Pietro's naked head coming out of San Bonifacio's huge armor. "Alaghieri! Good ploy! Carrara will hate you even more!" The Toothless Master pressed his lips together. "No prisoners!"

Pietro nodded. "Tell my father I died well."

"I will," said Asdente, not without kindness, even as he drew back the spear.

The ground began shaking and thunder rumbled in Pietro's ears. Vanni's eyes flicked up, fixing on something far down the street at Pietro's back. The spearpoint lingered for a moment, hovering in the air.

Instinct roaring at him to roll away and live, Pietro instead turned to see what had frightened the Paduan warrior.

A charge of Verona's knights was coming at them. In the front ranks were familiar faces—Uguccione della Faggiuola, age vanished in the joy of battle; Nico da Lozzo, grinning all over his face; Morsicato, grim and ruddy-faced, his beard soaked in blood; a bearded knight Pietro recognized as the man with the mad wife—the knight was currently looking a little mad himself. And something Pietro thought he'd never see again. Mari and Antony, side by side. They rode fiercely, swords poised to scissor the air.

In front was Cangrande, black from top to toe, his mouth set in a rictus of perilous delight. "On! On!"

The power of movement returned. Pietro rolled, pulling himself out of the reach of Scorigiani's spear. He found himself looking down at his neighbor's son, who was bleeding from his chest. "No!" Wrapping his arms about the boy, Pietro pulled him back from the stampede. For it was a stampede. The Paduan forces broke, turning to fly in full retreat.

With one exception. Vanni Scorigiani, the Toothless Master who had bragged for years that he ate steel for breakfast, held his ground. He positioned himself directly in the Scaliger's path, spear braced on the stones at his horse's feet.

Cangrande did him honor. Even as his horse dodged the spear, Cangrande stood in the stirrups and gave the Paduan knight his most powerful blow. The sword severed Vanni's head from his body, which lingered in the saddle for an instant before being battered to the ground by the galloping horses that followed. What happened to the head, Pietro couldn't see. His eyes were filled with tears of joy and sorrow as horse after horse passed him by.

✦ ◇ ✦

The change was as indefinable as it was palpable. The Paduan army shook, panicked, and fled.

In their midst, the Count of San Bonifacio was riding among the leading elements of the fleeing exiles. They had owned the best place for a retreat, being stationed on the outer walls. Though everyone around him shouted with terror, he was smiling. His plan had worked—probably. Certainly the Pup's forces were distracted. The battle had lasted far longer, been far more devastating, than the Count could have dared hope. All he had to do now was slip away from the army—

"Bonifacio!"

The naked rage in the voice made Vinciguerra grab at his sword. He turned, seeing the upraised sword, helpless to prevent it falling. The blow scraped off his helmet, struck his armored shoulder. Before he could bring his own weapon to bear, a second blow ripped open the flesh on his left leg. Blood pumped up toward the sky, almost as high as the Count's head.

"Traitor!" The contempt in Carrara's voice was unmistakable. The young Paduan drove the tip of his sword into Vinciguerra's armpit, hoping to pierce his heart. The armor prevented a fatal blow, but he did manage to unseat the Count, toppling him into the dirt.

The flow of men swept Marsilio on, but he was satisfied. Honor had been served. The Count was finished.

On the ground, Vinciguerra lifted his head. His helmet was heavy upon him. *He called me a traitor. I suppose I am, to Padua. But not to Verona—never to Verona. I am a patriot. And I was so close . . .*

He saw the red-headed soldier called Benedick arrive over him. Sparing the Count a single glance, the man said not a word. He sheathed his sword, jumped into the Count's saddle, and rode for his life. Groaning as the first real wave of pain swept over him, the Count still managed a nod of approval. "Not a fool after all."

✦ ◇ ✦

The battle had swept on into other streets, leaving the wounded and dying in its wake. His neighbor's son died in Pietro's arms without a last word for his father. Pietro wept as he stood and tore the boiling armor from his torso, relieving his legs of the awful weight. He looked at the *petta,* and the crest of San Bonifacio on it—the image was now bruised and covered in blood. He let the breastplate fall from his fingertips and wandered among the dead and the wounded, looking for friends. Amazingly, five of his men had survived relatively unscathed, with more possibly still alive in the yard where this bloody business had started.

He found Tharwat under three Paduan corpses. The Moor was breathing, though shallowly. Pietro ripped some cloth from a dead man and bound the head gash as best he could. Tharwat's left arm hung at a strange angle, but Pietro knew nothing about mending broken limbs. He decided to wait for Morsicato's advice to do more. He propped the Moor's head against a wall and moved to look for other wounded men.

Just then he heard more horses approaching. These were not the hoofbeats of warhorses. Coming out of the smoke, a young man on a light riding horse almost trampled Pietro before he checked. His two attendants did the same.

"Pietro!"

It was a familiar voice that cried his name. Pietro looked up to see a thin fellow in riding clothes who looked oddly familiar. Then he saw the delicate features and the sky-blue eyes and realized, impossibly, who it was. "Donna Katerina?"

"Pietro, thank God!" The lady's voice was full of panic as she leapt down from the saddle.

He rose and held her by the arms, steadying himself against her. "I'm fine, lady."

"He's gone, Pietro! They've taken him! The chart was right! He's going to die! They both are!"

Hot and tired, he couldn't follow what she was saying. Had someone taken Cangrande somewhere? "What? Lady, calm yourself. What's happened?"

"The guest, the man who was staying in the palace—the exiled banker who bought his return! He called himself Pathino."

Pietro shook his head. "What about him?"

"He came yesterday—said he's trying to rebuild his old business—but he's taken them both, both of them!"

Pietro felt his flesh begin to crawl. "Who, Donna? Who did he take?"

Tears were flowing freely now. "Cesco! He's gone! And he took my son with him! Cesco and Detto are gone!"

V

THE FEUD

THIRTY-FIVE

Cangrande halted his pursuit of the Paduans at Montegalda, refusing to let his men cross the Paduan frontier lest he be accused of violating the peace himself. Now that he had the just war he'd been hungering for, he had no wish to spoil things.

The armorless Scaliger rode along the line of his soldiers as they cheered him, crying "Sca-la! Sca-la! Sca-la!" Uguccione was grinning through a face smeared with blood. Nico sported an arm that hung limply at his side, yet he hopped lightly in the saddle as he mocked the fleeing knights. Morsicato looked tired as he wrung blood from his beard. Luigi Capulletto looked annoyed that the battle was over, and his brother, Antony, shared his expression.

But Antony wasn't looking at the backs of the fleeing Paduans. The Scaliger traced Antony's scowl to a figure in a blue cloak. His armor bore the Montecchio crest, the clasp on the cloak carrying the same device. But he was too short to be Gargano. That left only one answer. "Ser Montecchio, welcome back! I trust you've been home to see your father."

"*Oui, mon Capitan,*" replied Mariotto, much to the Scaliger's amusement.

"You provided me good service. I trust all your affairs are settled?"

Cangrande saw Mari's eyes flicker toward Capulletto. "I expect they soon will be."

A frown formed on Cangrande's brow. "Where's your father?"

"He's on our lands, coordinating the net for fleeing Paduans."

"Go join him." Cangrande raised his voice. "I want all Paduan prisoners back in Verona the day after tomorrow. Every one, even the lowliest, is to be treated royally. The nobles may be ransomed to their families, but this time

Padua itself will have to pay to get its soldiers back. I'll ransom them as a group."

Nico da Lozzo studied the sky, all innocence. "I don't suppose it's occurred to you—"

"It has. The answer is no. They live." The Scaliger was about to instruct Capulletto to stay with Uguccione, thus keeping the two idiots away from each other, when something pricked at his ears. Light horses and voices calling. He turned and saw his sister—her cross-dressing never fooled him. She was probably angry with him for sneaking into town. She'd always loathed his playacting. "Thank you, my dear, for ringing the bell. I felt certain it was—" His expression changed as she came close enough to reveal her face.

Katerina told her tale in a very few words. She concluded by saying, "Ser Alaghieri has already started the hunt."

Cangrande issued crisp orders. "Uguccione, trace Pietro. Morsicato, find the Moor, make sure he's well, then follow. Nico, get your arm looked at then find me, wherever I am. Capulletto, you and your brother take fifty men and throw up a cordon west of here. Once that's done, ride to the old Bonifacio estates and see if there's any activity there. If not, find me for more orders. Mariotto, find your father and use his men to throw up a dragnet. Go with him, Benvenito. Bonaventura, you and your cousin comb your lands. Forget the Paduans. I want people searching every castle, hamlet, farmhouse, outhouse, cave, ravine, and riverbed between Illasi and here. Bailardino, do the same thing to the east. Take as many men as you want. Antonio," he said, addressing the elder Nogarola, "take the north. Everybody, throw the net wide and then draw it tight. Take your time, be thorough. They could be anywhere. Whoever finds Pietro Alaghieri first sends word immediately! He's got nearly thirty minutes on us."

Cangrande looked up. The daylight was two hours' old but the sky was darkening. *Always rain, when it comes to Cesco.* "Use what light we have. Move!"

Bailardino called out loudly. "Remember, this bastard has children! Do what you can to pin him, but don't make him desperate!" Everyone was reminded that one of the children was Bailardino's own. The grim soldiers all hurried off to gather their men. Bailardino cantered to his wife's side, touched her face. She shook her head, saying, "No. Go. Find them!" Bailardino nodded and rode for his men. He didn't misread her anger, which was reserved for herself.

And for her brother. "You're a clever one," she said. "He was waiting for you, you know."

"What?"

"Cesco. He thought he was going to meet you."

"Me?"

She handed over a wax tablet with numbers on it. "I got this from under Cesco's bed. Pathino must have left it for him. Read it." She watched as his mind worked the code. When he tossed the tablet aside, Katerina saw no change in his expression. "You and your games!"

"You, of course, never indulge in them."

"They used his love of puzzles against us. He slipped away from his nurse, thinking you'd be there, and took Detto with him."

"So it's my fault, not yours. That must be comforting." A page came running up, and he bent down in the saddle to listen. Katerina waited for Cangrande's attention to return to her, then said, "I heard your orders. While your men are out looking, what will you be doing?"

"I think I'll go see an old friend."

The blow was swift, cracking across his cheek. "No games! Who is it you mean?"

He didn't rub his crimson cheek. But neither did he smile. "I mean Vinciguerra, Count of San Bonifacio, who, I have just been told, has been found, badly wounded."

"What are you going to do?"

Cangrande met her eyes. "I'm going to beat the life out of him until he tells me where the boys are. Care to watch?"

✦ ◇ ✦

Stupido, stupido, stupido.

Pietro repeated the imprecation over and over as he rode though Vicenza's western gates. He'd traced the kidnapper this far with relative ease, but now the search grew more difficult.

How could we have been so blind? Even the Scaliger had been fooled. They knew the Count of San Bonifacio was behind it all, and still they hadn't seen that the whole attack this morning was a feint, a costly, bloody feint that disguised the real target.

Still, Pietro couldn't fathom the reason—unless Bonifacio wanted to remove the Scaliger's only heir. But then why not kill him outright? What could the Count gain by taking him?

Of cold consolation was the fact that they now had a name for the kidnapper. Gregorio Pathino, he called himself. Katerina's description had matched the newly restored exile, Nogarola's guest, to Pietro's scarecrow of two years before. No wonder he'd avoided supper last night. Of all people, only Pietro could identify him.

A kidnapper thrice over. Not only had he snatched young Cesco, he had grabbed up little Bailardetto and Pietro's groom as well. Bailardetto's disappearance had the lady just as panicked as Cesco, if not more so. Cesco had the protection of destiny—if he truly was *Il Veltro*. But Katerina had revealed a horrifying fact—Tharwat, the true astrologer, had made a chart for Katerina's real son as well as her adopted one. This chart said Detto was in danger of an early death, well before he reached his prime. Katerina hadn't told anyone, not even her husband, but in her fear she'd blurted the truth to Pietro.

The moment she'd finished, Pietro had ridden back to the palace. He'd exchanged his warhorse for Canis, collected Mercurio and one of Cesco's shirts, then headed for the northwestern gates out of the city. He'd questioned everyone he saw, a task made more difficult since everyone wanted information from him as badly as he wanted it from them. Quickly he gave up until he reached the gates—the same gates he had come through three years before, the first time he'd ever laid eyes on Vicenza. Here he asked the guards if they'd seen anyone pass out. They'd said yes, twenty minutes before a tall man had ridden out with two children perched on his saddle, a youth trailing behind. Ignoring their questions about the battle, he'd set out at once. He knew then that Pathino had taken Fazio as well.

Pathino. It was good to have a name. Probably not his real name, but useful all the same. Pietro could focus all his loathing on that one name. Pathino. Gregorio Pathino. The man who had murdered Cesco's nurse in Verona, probably murdered the oracle as well. The man who, failing to steal little Cesco, had thrown him to the leopard. Gregorio Pathino. It was a name to hate.

Pietro couldn't help remembering the Moor's words last night. A new influence—a danger to Pietro and the child. Could that new influence be Pathino? Would the kidnapper succeed, and then—what, give the child to the Count? Sell him into slavery? The possibilities were terrifyingly endless.

Once he reached an open space, Pietro dismounted. He knelt next to

Mercurio, holding the scrap of Cesco's clothing up to the greyhound's nose. Within seconds the greyhound lifted his snout to the air, then dropped it to the ground. Remounting, Pietro followed the dog south. South and west. The direction surprised Pietro, who had expected to be led toward Padua. If they headed far enough in this direction they would reach Verona in a few hours. Could that be? Was Pathino taking the boys to Verona? Or was he just making a wide loop to avoid the two armies? That made more sense. So where was he going?

Pietro hoped he was traveling more swiftly than the ex-banker, encumbered as he was with the children and Fazio. But what if Pathino decided he needed to move faster?

"Come on, Mercurio! Fly! Let's see those winged feet!"

✦ ◇ ✦

The sounds of battle are unmistakable, even from far off. Eight miles to the southwest of Vicenza, at the Montecchio estate, the distant clashing was clearly audible in the still summer air. Forewarned, the residents of the castle were forearmed, but that didn't stop them from worrying. Lord Montecchio, dressed in full armor, fretted over his son, while his daughter kept plaiting and unplaiting her sister-in-law's hair as they waited for news.

Antonia Alaghieri hadn't intended to stay on at Castello Montecchio once the young master had returned. She believed her presence would be awkward as the two lovers settled down to a true married life. But a few kind words from Gargano and Aurelia as well as the pleas from Gianozza convinced her to stay. If Mariotto was heading directly out to war, the girls needed a friend to help ease the waiting. So Antonia found herself in the tallest furnished tower of the castle watching the three Montecchi fret over the outcome of the ambush just a few miles away. She was fretting too, concerned for Ferdinando, her—friend.

Distraction was the key. The girls had already admired all the fine clothes and gifts Mariotto had brought back from France, unpacked from the baggage that had arrived this morning. They had pored through the illustrated pages of the many books he'd purchased at the papal court. They had discussed the furniture and the wine and all the little trinkets. Now they were experimenting with braiding pearls and jeweled combs into Gianozza's hair as a template for Aurelia's wedding day.

"I smell smoke," said Gargano. The girls, whose sense of smell was better, had detected the acrid scent long before. "There," he added, pointing, "there's a haze on the horizon."

"I'm sure they're in no danger," said Antonia reassuringly. "The Paduans will break and run, and they'll all be fine."

Gargano shook his head. "I should have gone with them."

"Lord Faggiuola wanted you here," she reminded him. Gargano's responsibility was to lead the hunt for Paduan fugitives once the battle was finished. Yet he was impatient. Barely forty in years, he was as fit as any man his age, a tried warrior anxious to take up a sword in the Scaliger's defense.

They heard hoofbeats. All four moved to the window to see a horseman ride through the gates. But the angle from the tower was poor, and the cluster of men surrounding him made it impossible to see. Someone shouted, and all Gargano's soldiers took up the cry.

"The devil take this," cried Montecchio. He crossed to where his cloak lay, and Aurelia moved quickly to fit it over his shoulders. It was an exact duplicate of the one Gianozza had draped over her husband's shoulders that morning, a heavy blue knit that didn't flap up while riding. Gargano placed his helmet on his head. It was new, a gift from his son, a fierce French mantle that resembled the one given Mariotto by the pope. "I'll send word," said Gargano already racing down the steps.

Aurelia looked at the other two girls. "Do we follow?"

"I don't know," said Gianozza.

"Of course we follow," declared Antonia. She snuffed the candles, Aurelia picked up their cloaks, and Gianozza opened the door only to find the passage blocked by her father-in-law running back up. Only the cloak was spattered in blood and reeked of smoke.

Suddenly she was enveloped in a swooping embrace, quite unfatherly in nature. "Francesca!"

"Paolo!" Husband and wife murmured a few endearments to each other. To Aurelia Mariotto said, "Benvenito is downstairs, gathering up more men. He's fine. Not a scratch." She hugged him and fled the room to find her betrothed.

Gianozza asked the question Antonia could not. "And Ser Bonaventura's cousin?"

"Ferdinando?" asked Mariotto. Not having been at court these last years, he was surprised by the question. Still he said, "Fine. Whole and hearty, obnoxious as ever."

Antonia didn't sigh, didn't smile. She merely nodded and said, "What's happening?"

"We can't stay," he began. "Cangrande's bas—his, ah, natural son, Francesco, has been kidnapped, along with Bailardino's son. Pietro's out looking for them now."

Antonia started. "Pietro who?"

"Your brother! By the Virgin, I was shocked. I didn't even know he was in the area, much less hidden in the city. I thought he and the Scaliger weren't on speaking terms. Goes to show you can't—"

"Wait a moment," said Antonia sharply, her hand slicing the air before Mariotto's face. "Start from the beginning."

Mariotto related the course of the battle and the bizarre aftermath of kidnapping and treachery. "Pietro's out there now, on the trail. We're to spread out through the countryside and find them."

"Then go!" shouted Antonia, pushing on his chest. "Pietro may need you this second!"

"He can take care of himself," Mariotto assured her. "He held that street longer than anyone thought he could." He glanced at his wife. "There's one thing. Antony threatened me this morning, before the battle. He wants a duel. Today, or as soon as we're done carrying out the Capitano's orders."

Gianozza gasped. "You won't fight him, will you? It's against the law!"

He stroked her cheek. "Law or no, I can't let a challenge like that pass. It would stain my reputation. It's too bad, too. Today, fighting side-by-side—it was almost like old times." He ran his fingers through his neatly trimmed hair. "Francesca, I have to go." He kissed her, nodded to Antonia, scooped up his helmet, and ran.

At once Gianozza crumpled to the floor. Antonia rushed to her side, thinking, *The poor thing never seems to have trouble producing tears.* She wept now, ruining the bodice of her lovely new French dress as she whimpered and wailed, while Antonia talked her up to her knees and convinced her to pray. They prayed to the Virgin, and San Pietro, San Giuseppe, and San Zeno. They heard Gargano's auxiliary forces ride away, and Gianozza started to go to the window, but Antonia dragged her back down to the hard stone floor to finish their prayers.

By the time they finished, Gianozza's tears were dry. Hiccoughing, she asked her maidservant to bring a bowl of water to wash in. She said, "I'm a baby. Antonia, please don't tell Paolo that I wept this way. It might embarrass him."

Feelings of anxiety mingled with annoyance made Antonia snappish. She couldn't help demanding, "Why do you call him that?"

"It's a pet name. I call him Paolo and he calls me—"

"Francesca, I know."

Gianozza heard the disdain. "What is it?"

Antonia gave a little sigh. "It's nothing, really."

"You don't approve of Francesca da Rimini?"

She couldn't hold back her snort. "Hardly!"

"Why not?"

"Gianozza, if you've read my father's poem, then you know that Francesca and Paolo are in Hell!"

"Yes, but she has an excuse for that—it wasn't their fault, it was—"

"It was what? The poetry made them do it? The weather? The stars?"

"Antonia, your father felt such pity for them when he talked to them that he fainted."

Perhaps her father was correct when he said a little learning was a dangerous thing. "Gianozza, do you understand allegory? In the poem, my father isn't Dante the poet, he's a character. He represents every man. Of course he feels pity for them—what Christian soul wouldn't? But it's God, not man, who put them there, and God is infallible. The Lord knows Francesca's excuses are meaningless—the fault is hers. She's the one who committed the sin, and no matter what she says, she's the one who will suffer for it."

"But—but it's romantic, it's—"

"It's tripe! And Paolo knows it! He weeps even as she speaks because he understands, you see? He knows why they're made to suffer. But Francesca convinces herself that it's anyone's fault but hers—even God's. Francesca is one of the worst people my father comes across in Hell. Technically, she's even guilty of incest! She's everything that's bad in women—from Eve all the way down to today!"

Gianozza walked suddenly to the window, where the smoke rising from Vicenza was now visible. She was silent for a long time. A very long time.

After several minutes Antonia began to feel guilty. She got to her feet and sighed. "Gianozza, I'm sorry. I'm worried about my brother. Here I am fretting about Ferdinando and I didn't even know Pietro was here, I thought he was safe at the university, and now he's out there again, and I probably spoke too harshly. I'm sure I did."

"No. You're right. I'm a fool."

"What?"

Gianozza turned back to face her. She had a wild look. "I'm a fool. I just saw the romance of it. I should have married Antony. I mean, he's not so bad. But I thought that—it was the poem that Mari read to me that night. He read to me from *L'Inferno,* and I heard their story and I thought it was a sign, a sign we were meant to be together. But now I see that it was a sign, a sign that I would go to Hell! And Mari, poor Mari! He will, too. For my sin! It's my fault that Mariotto will be killed! He'll die dueling Antony, and he'll go to Hell, and it will be my fault!"

Antonia realized there and then that Gianozza didn't love poetry—she loved romance. Poetry was just the vehicle. The girl had to be set straight. There was poetic love and there was real life. "Gianozza, I didn't mean—"

"No! You're right! It will all be my fault! If I'd only given Antony what he wanted!" Gianozza turned back to stare vacantly out the window.

She's living a French romance, thought Antonia with amazement. But she didn't know what else to say, and now that Gianozza had stopped crying Antonia had another duty. Opening a small box that contained her writing things, she took out a sheet of paper, her inkwell, and a hardy quill.

Gianozza turned from the window, clutching herself tight. "What are you doing?"

"Father needs to know," said Antonia, writing swiftly. "Do you think you could find a servant willing to ride to Verona?"

"Yes." Gianozza walked over to a wardrobe and pulled out a riding gown and coat.

"What are *you* doing?"

"We can't stay here and do nothing. I'm going to see your letter is delivered, then I'm going to find Antony and stop this feud nonsense, however I can!"

✦   ◇   ✦

Mercurio hadn't slackened his pace. So far they had mainly stayed on the road, veering off only twice. Both those times the trail had led to a clump of trees, and Pietro imagined that Pathino had heard some noise on the road that had frightened him into taking cover. Each time he'd returned to the road a few yards ahead of where he'd left it and continued on his way.

If Pietro remembered rightly, this road led past Mariotto's lands at Montecchio, past Montebello and Soave, and directly towards San Bonifacio. So when Mercurio turned off a third time, Pietro thought it was another dodge. He was surprised, therefore, when the hound failed to return to the road. Determined as ever, Mercurio now headed south among bushes and trees.

Perversely, Pietro wished he hadn't fought so hard in the battle. Pathino could be lying in wait behind one of these trees, and Pietro's sword arm was weary, his right leg weak. He slowed Canis's pace, which earned a withering look from the eager dog, pressing the hunt before him. But Pietro didn't want to risk falling to a hasty ambush. The closest aid was a half-hour behind. If Pietro let himself be killed, Cesco, Detto, and Fazio would disappear like breath into the wind.

Pietro's most valuable sense in this environment was his hearing, and he strained to listen for the slight hints of breathing or metal clanging or a horse shifting. He heard water running—a brook or a stream. Birdsong, and all around him an angry wind rustling the leaves.

And something else. It came from somewhere ahead of him. Pietro's instinct was to kick his spurs and race forward, but he forced himself to dismount and advance slowly, drawing his sword. The hound crept along close to his side. Poking through the brush with his sword, he saw a riverbank. And the source of the noise.

A toddler sat on the bank, whimpering in fright. Pietro dismounted and hurried forward, looking about warily. At the sight of Pietro the toddler shied away, protecting his right arm. The hound sniffed at Detto, then walked directly to the water's edge and strained to cross.

"Bailardetto," said Pietro, watching the opposite bank. The sky was darkening under storm clouds, and it was hard to see through the first rank of trees. He tried to keep his voice friendly. "Do you remember me? We met last night. I'm a friend of your mother."

Barely two years old, Detto was too scared to speak in any coherent way. But in the midst of his tears the boy called for his mama. Pietro knelt and reached out a hand. In response the child held up his good arm to be picked up.

"May I see it?" asked Pietro, indicating Detto's other arm. "It's all right," he said reassuringly when the boy shied, "I won't touch it." There was a livid bruise growing, and scraped skin all around the elbow. Pietro ruffled Detto's hair. "It hurts, but you'll be all right." In response the boy buried his face into Pietro's neck. Pietro put an arm around him and patted his back lightly. At once Detto's breathing relaxed and his mouth found his thumb.

Pietro hugged him even closer, still keeping his sword arm free. It was while he was holding the sniffling toddler that he saw Fazio. The teenager was facedown, half-floating in the shallows of the opposite bank. The water around him showed wisps of blood. Too much blood.

What to do? Pathino had crossed here to hide his tracks, leaving Detto and Fazio behind to delay his pursuers. Pietro released Detto, rammed his sword into the sandy earth, and used his fingers to lift Detto's chin. "Hey there, little man. Which way did your brother go?" The child looked at him without comprehension. "Cesco. Which way?"

"Da' wey." Bailardetto pointed downstream.

Pathino wants me to turn back, so I won't. But what do I do with Detto? If the boy had been older he would have set him in Canis's saddle and sent the horse back. As it was . . . "Detto—I need you to be brave. Brave, like your father. We've got to go help Cesco. Is that all right?"

The child looked up at Pietro with huge watery eyes. How much did he understand? Then Detto nodded. "Help Cesco," he parroted.

Retracing his steps to the trees, Pietro led Canis back toward the water. He retrieved his sword. Then, with the boy in his arms, he somehow managed to mount. Placing Detto on the front of the saddle, Pietro started off across the river. Mercurio dove in after, paddling to pick up the trail on the other side.

They passed Fazio's body. Pietro tried to shield the child's eyes from the sight of the dead groom. *Fazio, I'll make Pathino pay, I swear it.*

✦   ✧   ✦

The Count of San Bonifacio lay under guard on the bloody field. He was dying, and he wondered how long it would take. He was lightheaded, and his vision swam in and out of focus.

Then, blinking, he saw Cangrande. The Pup. They had never met, these two. Never passed a conversation in private. But there was a look to the family that the count knew too well. Now he was coming closer, accompanied by a woman garbed as a man. She, too, had the family look. His sister, no doubt. Vinciguerra pulled himself as upright as his wounds allowed. Settling his back against a tree stump he steeled himself.

"My dear Count." Cangrande's tone was neither cold nor angry but warm, almost affectionate.

"Puppy."

Cangrande dismissed the guards, then knelt to examine the Count's bandaging. He clucked his tongue. "This is bad. We have to get it clean. It doesn't hurt too much?"

"It's numb, now." The Count wondered what this solicitude was for. He was a dying man, and dying men are immune to charm.

"I imagine you bandaged it yourself? It's not a bad job, but perhaps a doctor should see it."

"Don't bother."

"I'll try to find one, nevertheless. As my guest, now, you are to be treated as the lost brother you have always been." Vinciguerra blinked while Cangrande looked around. "Damn. Morsicato was here just moments ago. You know, Count, he treated a wound almost exactly like this three years ago. If not for him, my friend Pietro Alaghieri would have lost his leg, if not his very life." He looked down at the leg again. "This does seem a little worse than Pietro's. I wonder where Morsicato got himself to."

"You sent him on an errand," supplied Katerina.

Cangrande frowned in puzzlement. "Did I? Oh yes, he's looking after some knights in the city. Well, there are other doctors. We'll get you to one, Count, never you fear. You'll be up and making trouble for us again in no time." Cangrande patted Vinciguerra's shoulder as one might pet a troublesome child injured by his own folly. The Scaliger stood and turned, clearly planning to move on. His sister looked as if she had swallowed something distasteful, but said nothing as Cangrande made to go.

"Wait," the Count said sharply. "What about the boy?"

"What boy? Pietro? He recovered from that injury. A touch of a limp, but today he was able to don armor and lead his men in a glorious battle inside the city. Not often a man gets to see such valor in action. Pietro was the very picture of knighthood—as he should be, since I invested him. Now, if you'll excuse me, Count, I am a trifle busy."

The blood-loss was affecting the Count again. "No—not Alaghieri. The boy—her boy—your son—Francesco." He took a breath. "Send some men back to the palace, O mighty Scaliger. You'll find your little prize has vanished from under your nose."

Cangrande looked amused. "You mean Pathino? My dear Count, do you really think us so foolish as that? Didn't you hear me? I said Pietro was here. He was the one that foiled Pathino's attempt two years ago, and his memory is excellent. He recognized your agent and informed my sister at once. Your man has had a score of eyes on him all night. Really, Count—such a fellow as Pathino to carry out your bold plan?"

"One does one's best with the tools at hand," said the Count, his mind racing. Clearly they hadn't discovered who Pathino really was . . .

"True enough," said Cangrande brightly. "I am fortunate, then, in my tools. Pietro apprehended Pathino as he tried to abscond with my sister's charge."

"So you don't claim him as yours?"

Cangrande let ring a full-throated roar. Wiping an eye, he said, "You know, Count, you're the only one to ask! The only one! No one else has dared. Perhaps I'll even tell you someday. Then again, a man who entrusts such as task to someone like Pathino cannot be worth confiding in. Really, Count—Pathino? What a pathetic plan it must have been. Where on earth was he going to go?"

Vinciguerra actually opened his mouth to reply before catching himself. He laughed. "You don't have him, do you?" He saw Katerina stiffen and knew he was right. "Oh, very good! Very nicely done! My lord Scaliger, I take my hat off to you!" Vinciguerra gave a mock salute.

An instant later his dry chuckling turned to a scream of agony as the lady ground her heel into his wounded leg, not so numb after all. "Your tool took not only your prize, but also my only son. I want them back, Count, and I warn you, there is nothing I will not dare to regain them." Her voice was everything her brother's hadn't been, yet beneath it all was that same eerie calm. The lady did not make idle threats.

The foot lifted, the weight disappeared, and the Count gasped for breath. "Dear madam, your threats are of little value. My life's blood is slipping with each breath I take. It will take a day, perhaps more, but soon I will be finished. It is only a matter now of how I expire. What do I care if I die in a comfortable palace or in your dungeon, with thumbscrews loosing more of that same blood?" He transferred his eyes to his nemesis. "Your heir is gone forever, my lord Scaliger."

"Even if that is so, it does you no good, in your present state." Cangrande's words were not a threat, merely a statement of fact.

"For myself, that is true," agreed Bonifacio. "Soon the eternal night shall pass over me, and I will have no cares. But I hear you believe in prophecies. Then listen to this one—your line shall never be free of my hate."

Cangrande knelt down. "Vinciguerra, friend, loyal son of Verona, do you want to appear before God with this sin on your hands? The death of this child alone is enough to blacken your soul before the Almighty."

The Count shrugged slightly. "My sins be on my head and there an end. Come what may, I am reconciled. Perhaps I will end up among the eternally violent. You may join me there."

Cangrande rested on his haunches for several moments more, then lifted his head to the darkening sky. The clouds had not yet entirely obscured the sun, but soon they would make an artificial night. "If the boy dies, Count, your soul will twist in the land of the treacherous. The pit of Antenora, where those souls who have betrayed their country and their cause lie frozen forever." He gestured for the guards who bore a litter between them.

The Count was feeling faint, but he was determined to have the last word of the interview. "My cause has never wavered, my little lord of the ladder. I have longed only for a Verona free of you and your ilk. You'll ruin the homeland of my fathers. Better the city should fall altogether."

The guards transferred Vinciguerra's bulk from the ground to the litter. Before they carried him into the city, Katerina leaned over to speak in the Count's ear. "Tell me where they are, or I shall make certain you live to enjoy all the pain your wound can give."

"You are welcome to take what vengeance you can, dear lady, I've already had mine. Pathino has gone to ground where you cannot find him, and your son with him. Your son too, my lord!"

Cangrande was in the process of mounting a fresh horse. He looked to the guards. "See he's well treated, and given something to make him sleep. He needs rest."

As he was carried off, the Count tried to look over his shoulder, but dizziness made the corners of his vision turn black. Lying back on the stretcher, he could see only the darkening sky above him. Then suddenly he passed under a huge stone lintel. He was entering Vicenza for the last time. Smoke drifted past his face and he closed his eyes, trying to remember every word of the exchange. It was all the victory likely to be given him.

✦ ◇ ✦

At that moment Antonia was pleading with Gianozza, begging her to see reason. A broken army on the loose, no men left in the castle to escort her—this was no time to go riding through the woods. "Mariotto and Antony are surrounded by soldiers and have many more important concerns than some foolish duel. If you were to venture out, you'd probably wander all night without finding either one! And what could you do if you did? You might make matters worse. Come, write a letter to Antony if you must. But stay here!"

Gianozza was busy ordering her horse saddled. Seeing her companion was implacable, Antonia threw her hands in the air. "Fine. Fine! If you must go, I'll go with you, even if it means risking my life in the most ridiculous cause I've ever heard of. But if I die it will be entirely your fault!"

She had hoped that this would make Gianozza think twice. Instead the foolish creature rushed forward and embraced Antonia fervently. "Thank you, thank you! You're such a friend! Whatever would I do without you?"

Predictable. I can't make her see reason, and so I become a part of her romance.

They took the dog Rolando with them, but no men-at-arms. There were none to be had. Antonia brought a kitchen knife for comfort, certain that if they met with any danger it would do her no good.

✦   ◇   ✦

Back at the tree that had sheltered the wounded Count, Cangrande sat in his saddle looking down upon Katerina, who was glaring up at him in return. She said, "That was quite a beating."

Cangrande shrugged. "He's a soldier. You saw how your threats gave him strength. I hoped he was weak enough that the ploy would work. It didn't. After that, I hoped he might try to twist the knife, and in so doing give us something to go on. Again, nothing. Try again in a bit, by all means—you are, after all, the expert in killing with small cuts. News of Alaghieri?" This was asked of a messenger, running toward them. The boy said no, but that the doctor sent word that the Moorish astrologer would live. Cangrande grunted, then turned back to his sister, who said, "What about your plea for his soul? That was real."

"It was. Coming or staying?"

"I will be of little use in the hunt. I will return to our friend Bonifacio and we will talk more freely. Perhaps I can employ tactics other than threats."

"Offer him sweetmeats," said Cangrande, kicking his heels. "It always worked on me."

She watched him ride off. "Nothing worked on you," she murmured.

Her own horse was close by. She mounted and returned to a city still reeling from the battle, trying desperately to put out the fire that raged along its inner wall. As she felt the first pindrops of water, she cursed. The rain would aid in the extinguishing of the fire, but it would make the hunt for the children all the more difficult.

✦   ◇   ✦

Katerina was not alone in cursing the cloudburst when it came. Pietro had followed Mercurio back and forth across the river three times now. Pathino had evidently doubled back on his trail in an effort to throw off pursuers. Now they had left the river only to be drenched by the clouds. But the wonderful hound pressed on, nose low to the ground, oblivious to the rain.

The rain did bother little Detto, however, making him huddle against Pietro's chest. Pietro covered him as best he could, letting the boy burrow beneath his cape. Detto was too tired to cry anymore, he just shivered and whimpered.

Pietro had lost all sense of direction, though he thought the west bank of the river was behind them. If that was true, they were headed back toward Castello Montecchio. Perhaps they would come across some of Montecchio's men and enlist them in the chase.

Mercurio slowed to a prowl. Pietro knew the sign. The dog's quarry was just ahead of him. That meant Cesco was nearby.

Pietro slid from the saddle and led the horse into a tight group of trees, hiding it from view. He tied Canis's reins to a branch and lifted Detto silently down. Putting the child down under the horse, he unfolded a blanket from his saddle and covered Detto with it. Wet and cold, the child whimpered some more. Pietro whispered, "Wait here," hoping the boy understood. He wished he could order the dog to stay with the toddler, but Mercurio was a hunting dog, not a guard dog.

Besides, Pietro needed him. They had to flush out the game.

His leg was ready to give out, so against his will he lifted his crutch from the saddle. It was made of mahogany, pitted and scarred where he'd fended off some cutthroats last year. Using it was better than slipping and being unable to stand again. The noise of the rain would cover the occasional breaking of twigs.

Sword drawn, he crept forward.

✦ ◇ ✦

Antony and Luigi Capulletto reached the Castello San Bonifacio to find it still manned by the Scaliger's loyal troops. They had seen neither hide nor hair of an assault on their walls and knew nothing of the attack on Vicenza. Learning of the Capitano's kidnapped son, the captain of the guard formed a search party to cover the ground east of the castle.

Mission accomplished, the brothers left their men to spread out while they turned back towards Vicenza. Stopping at an inn along the way, Antony exchanged his helmet for a wide-brimmed hat, the better to keep the rain off his face. Buying three skins full of wine, they continued on.

The two men encountered a small patrol of men belonging to old Montecchio. It was led by Benvenito, the fellow who was marrying Mari's sister. Luigi wanted to join up with them, but Antony said no. So they simply exchanged news and went their separate ways.

"Why the hell not join up with them?" demanded Luigi.

"Because we're going to be the ones to find the boy," said Antony. "And we're not sharing the glory with anyone."

"You mean we're not sharing it with Montecchio."

"With anyone," said Antony. "Look, if you want to go off on your own, do it. It'll make us both happier. I grant you leave."

Luigi bristled at the implication that his brother was his master. "Fine!" He spurred his horse hard up the dirt road, leaving Antony behind.

Antony was glad to be rid of Luigi—always watching, always ready to leap in with a jibe or cutting remark. It was partly Luigi's presence that had made Antony issue that idiot challenge to Mariotto. It was a move he was already regretting. It was true that a large part of him wanted Mari dead as a salve for his pride, yet he now understood it wouldn't win Giulia's heart back. Giulia, his perfect woman.

Yet, if he'd been able to be honest with himself, it was less about the girl than Mari. His best friend. Among all the drinking companions, panderers, and revelers he'd associated with for the past two years, nowhere had Antony found a friend to equal the one he'd lost in Mari. That betrayal had cut deep. He'd thought their friendship, forged in a day, would last forever. It hadn't. If there was a reason to kill, that was it.

Then this morning in the close fighting he'd twice been at risk. The sword that saved him both times had been Mari's. Antony had repaid him in kind, protecting Mari's flank as he battled away at some Paduan spearmen. For a heartbeat the enmity fell away and things were as they had been.

But the challenge had been issued, he couldn't retrieve it. Not without shaming himself in front of his friends and father. And that bastard Luigi. Antony gave his mount a vicious rake with his spurs and pressed on.

✦ ✧ ✦

Gargano Montecchio led a band of soldiers through the woods. They came across another party of his men, led by Benvenito.

"We saw the Capulletto brothers, they said that the road between here and San Bonifacio is now being watched.

Gargano nodded. "Then take four men and scour the other side of that hill. Look for Mariotto's party. He knows these parts. There are lots of places a fugitive can go to ground." His daughter's fiancée turned to go, but Gargano laid a hand on his arm. "Son? Watch your back. Having successfully negotiated the battle, it would be a tragedy to lose you before we welcome you to the family."

Benvenito saluted his prospective father-in-law, then called for a few men to follow him. The men looked to their lord, who nodded. Gargano, reassured of the safety of his own family, returned to searching for the heirs of Cangrande and Bailardino.

✦ ✧ ✦

It was a nerve-racking quarter hour as Pietro followed Mercurio through the heavy brush. Each moment he expected the muted twang and thunk of a bolt being fired and sliding home between his ribs. Soaked to the skin, Pietro wanted to lie down and sleep for a year. The gauntlets he wore were stiff around his sword and crutch. His right leg had hardened into a rigid, brittle limb that hampered each step.

The dog skirted a patch of earth, and Pietro saw it was an old game trap of some kind. No, too big for game. It was a pit loosely covered. He had to be doubly careful.

The trees around them were not of a kind. Some were tall and towered over him, providing a canopy. Some were barely twice Pietro's height, with thin needles that brushed his face and made him wince. Often these were surrounded by shoulder-high bushes that worried Pietro more than anything, for they could hide a man with ease.

Still Mercurio pressed on. Ahead stood a series of large rocks embedded in the side of a hill. On top of the hill, above the largest rock, a tree stood tall and glistening in the rain. Passing it, Pietro noticed a twig broken and hanging by the barest thread of bark. Pathino had passed by here. How recently? The rain had turned any footprints to mud. But when he looked at the interior of the twig where it had been snapped, he saw that it was still dry inside. It couldn't have been long.

Mercurio seemed lost, and Pietro wondered if the hound was having difficulty holding onto the scent. Which brought another thought in its wake—if Cangrande used his hounds to trace Pietro, would they be able to follow that tortuous path by the river after a few hours of rain?

Now he was conflicted. He thought of poor Detto. If anything happened to Pietro, Detto might never be found. One voice kept telling him to turn about, cut his losses, and take Detto to safety. He could lead Cangrande's men back here and trap the bastard.

But if Pathino left, taking Cesco with him, Pietro would never forgive himself. He glanced up at the top of the hill. A hard climb for him. The grass would be slick, the rocks treacherous. Pietro took a deep breath and carefully placed his crutch.

He'd taken a few steps up the slope before realizing the dog wasn't with him. Looking back, he saw the dog snuffling around the large stone. Then Pietro saw a pair of hoofprints in the dry earth sheltered from the rain by the rock. Moving from right to left, he noticed a gap in the center of the rock that was wide enough for a horse to ride through.

A cave. This had to be one of the hiding places Mari's ancestors had used when they absconded with their neighbors' horses. *Clever bastard.* Pathino intended to hide the Scaliger's son right under his nose, on the lands of the Montecchi.

Pietro was trying to make up his mind when he heard a blessed sound. Hoofbeats. Not Pathino, he was sure of it. He debated making noise and settled for showing himself in the open.

The rider wore the Bonaventura crest. When he saw Pietro he shouted, but Pietro waved him to silence and beckoned him forward.

"Alaghieri?" asked the man.

It wasn't Petruchio, didn't look anything like him. But Pietro thought he remembered the face and took a chance on the name. "Ferdinando? Quiet. He's around here somewhere."

Ferdinando nodded and made to dismount. Pietro gestured him to stay where he was and quickly related the news. "Here's what I want you to do— go that way and find Detto. Get him to safety and bring back Cangrande or anyone else you can find. I'll keep the bastard trapped here as long as I can."

Ferdinando cast a dubious eye over him. "Are you sure? Together we would have a better chance."

"We have to keep Detto safe. And we'll have a better chance if someone knows where I am."

Still Ferdinando hesitated. "If you get yourself killed, your sister will never forgive me."

Why does he care what my sister thinks? "If you know my sister, you know she'd tell you the same thing. Don't waste time, get Detto to safety. I'm count-ing on you."

Ferdinando muttered something about Florentines. He didn't look happy, but he trotted off in the direction Pietro indicated.

Pietro turned back to the cave. The dog was looking up at him. Detto was safe. That left Cesco. Raising his sword, Pietro ventured silently into the darkness.

THIRTY-SIX

Having recovered as much composure as a dying man may, the Count of San Bonifacio greeted his guest with a smile. "My dear, forgive me for not rising. Would you like to start with thumbscrews? Have you any salt? Or would you prefer to unleash one of your brother's menagerie upon me? If I may choose, I think I'd take the baboon. I have never seen one."

"The jackal is more appropriate. Or the leopard. That was what Pathino tried to feed Cesco to—a leopard. He told you?"

"Some. I try not to rely too heavily upon his word. Is that wine?"

"It is."

He sniffed it warily. "Poppies?"

"Not much. My doctor's own brew. When the pain leaves you, I will give you nothing but water. We must talk."

The Count lifted the sweet-smelling mixture of wine and drug to his lips and drank deeply. Wiping his lips he said, "Certainly, we shall speak. Let me tell you about my father."

"Fine. Then I will tell you of my son."

✦ ◇ ✦

The cave's depth was surprising. The path was steep, and the twisting descent masked the distance down to the main chamber. Pietro was surprised to hear drips of water hitting a pool. Was there a spring down here, or was the roof so saturated with the rain that water was seeping down into the secret stable below?

He smelled the fire before he saw the glow on the curved tunnel wall. How best to handle this? His sleeveless leather doublet was stiff and cold, his shirt clung to his skin, hampering his movement. He stripped these off. He knew he ought to remove his breeches, but if he was running to his death he was going decently covered.

The water-filled boots were a problem. They sloshed as he walked. If he took them off, his bare feet would be at the mercy of whatever ground was down there. He couldn't do with noise, though, so he removed them as well. Barefoot, Pietro laid his crutch carefully across the path. Then, gripping his sword in his good hand, he moved ahead, placing each foot with care.

Mercurio was tense, long curved teeth bared. Pietro edged around the corner, then quickly pulled back. The cavern opened up into a wide chamber. Tree roots hung down from the earthen roof. The ground dipped at the center of the chamber. It was full of water, creating a natural barrier to crossing to the far side. The water came from above, the soaking rain falling just like the Old Man of Crete's tears fell to form the rivers of Hell.

The fire pit lay beyond the water, at the far end where the earth rose again. By the fire's light Pietro thought he'd seen a horse and a couple of figures camped close to the flames.

How to cross the water unseen? More importantly, unheard? Even if Pietro could sneak across the water, how quiet would the dog be? Mercurio was amazingly well-trained—even now he held back, waiting for Pietro to make a move. *Best get a second look.* Pietro leaned out again.

Something had changed. There were no longer two figures by the fire. There was only one. The man. Where was the child?

Pietro pulled back, assessing his options. *I could go slowly into the chamber, or—*

The hell with it. He turned the corner and ran, the balls of his feet the only things to touch the ground as he lumbered straight for the pool of water and the man beyond. Reaching the water he plunged in, creating great splashes in the murky liquid. His progress was slowed almost to a walk. Pathino was seated upright but unmoving, his back to his approaching attacker. Pietro's eyes scanned right and left. No sign of the child. Where was he?

Something was wrong. Pietro was making enough noise to wake the dead in their graves, but the man still didn't move. Pathino's horse was shying away, yet the kidnapper was rigidly still. Why?

Something's wrong. That isn't—

His legs caught on something just beneath the water's surface. He fell onto his face just steps away from the shore, throwing him onto the bank a scant three feet from the man by the fire.

Pietro's eyes rose to look at the shape, sitting within grasping distance. It was a dummy of straw and mud, covered with a cloak and hat. A lure to bring any would be rescuer across, prey to the tripwire stretched just under the surface of the dark waters. A trick used by the Montecchi horse thieves in their day, Pathino had discovered it and made it work for him.

And you fell for it. But then where—?

A grotesque creature rose from a cleft in the earth hidden from the fire-light. Pietro rolled back into the water as a long broadsword flew at his head. The first blow missed Pietro's neck by three inches. The creature shrieked, already pulling the blade free of the damp earth. Tangled in the tripwire, Pietro lifted his sword in a frantic defense. Pathino's sword scraped along Pietro's hanging parry, sending brief sparks into the shadow between them. Pathino's teeth were bared in a vicious grimace as he dragged his blade back for a thrust that would pierce Pietro's chest. Swallowing water and struggling, Pietro couldn't move fast enough.

Pathino let out a cry of triumph that turned into a scream as Mercurio leapt up to close his teeth on Pathino's wrist. The kidnapper pummeled the dog with his other fist. Mercurio took the blow and landed gamely, ready for a second pounce.

By now Pietro had gotten his legs under him. He felt his feet sinking into the soft muck under the water. Pathino let fly a third strike and Pietro ducked, thrusting with his own sword. But now Mercurio got in the way, leaping up to stagger Pathino back. Pietro's killing blow instead glanced off Pathino's thigh.

The pommel of Pathino's sword came up and down, shattering the dog's skull. Mercurio crumpled to the ground, blood pouring from his head. The dog tried to right himself, stumbling helplessly toward the fire.

Pietro screamed and Pathino barely turned in time to parry his vengeful blow. The scarecrow leapt back and pitched a handful of dirt into Pietro's eyes. Pietro turned his head and only caught a few specks in his left eye. Already he had his sword moving up to block the descending skull-strike. He half felt, half saw Pathino's blade bite into his own. Pietro surged upward, knocking his opponent's weapon aside as he swung for his belly.

The scarecrow jumped back a second time, watching Pietro's stroke hiss past his middle. He kept dodging backward until he reached into the cleft neatly hidden by the fire pit. From it he dragged Cesco, bound hand and foot with a rag stoppering his mouth. Tossing his sword aside, Pathino drew his *miseracordia* and held it to Cesco's throat.

Alaghieri halted immediately but didn't lower the point of his blade. His eyes flickered down to the child in Pathino's grip. Arms and legs bound, the boy looked dazed.

Both men panted for breath. Pathino said, "Drop your sword."

Pietro said, "You can't escape. Give him to me and I'll let you walk out of here."

"I said drop your sword." Pietro hesitated, and Pathino pressed the flat of the thin dagger into the child's flesh. It drew no blood, but that could change with an ounce of pressure and a flick of the wrist.

"You can't hurt him," said Pietro. "The Count would never forgive you."

"You have no idea what the Count wants with the boy. Drop your sword."

Reversing his blade so that it pointed down, Pietro rammed it into the soft earth.

"Now step away from it."

Pietro obeyed, easing sideways, putting the firepit between them. Pathino remained where he was, holding Cesco upright in his grasp. "Sit down." The knife left Cesco's throat as the kidnapper gestured to an old crumbling log close to the fire's edge. Pietro sat, trying to hide his shivers. His bare arms and chest dripped with cold water, and though he warmed himself by the blaze, his eyes remained on the scarecrow.

Pathino lowered himself onto a rock on his side of the fire. He roughly shoved Cesco down to his knees, then pulled the boy's head up. His knife remained ready. Cesco's wide eyes were looking curiously at Pietro.

"Everything will be fine," Pietro told him.

Pathino's expression was smug. "For him, perhaps. I wouldn't take a wager on your own life, though. Who are you?"

"Someone who's wanted to meet you for a long time." He was imagining how Cangrande would handle this situation. "How did you know I was here, by the way?"

"Answer for an answer, boy. Like eye for an eye."

"Pietro Alaghieri."

"Ah. Ser Alaghieri. I should have known. To answer your question, I saw your sword reflecting the firelight."

Pietro nodded, too tired to feel foolish. "This is one of the old Montec-chio caves, isn't it?"

"Yes. I grew up near here. I found this cave as a boy and always remem-bered where it was. Though I had a scare last week as I was setting up. Two girls came in to explore."

"Did you murder them, too?"

"Hardly. I merely pretended to be an animal and scared them off."

"You weren't pretending. So, what's the plan?"

"You'll sit there until we're joined by my patron."

"You mean the Count of San Bonifacio." When Pathino didn't respond, he said, "Then what?"

"Then, I imagine, you will die."

An idea occurred to Pietro. "The Count's dead. Killed at Vicenza."

Was that a shadow of fear? "You lie."

"Sadly, no," said Pietro, sounding much calmer than he felt. "I took his ar-mor for myself to wear and impersonated him before his men."

Pathino's voice carried nothing but scorn. "Then where is it?"

"I shed it when I started after you."

Clearly disbelieving Pietro's words, Pathino said, "I guess we'll just have to sit here to find out. By midnight the Count should be with us."

"A long wait."

"If you wish to save some time and open your wrists, I won't stop you. I may even bury you, though not on holy ground of course."

"And lose the pleasure of speaking with you?" The bravado rang hollowly in his own ears. He directed his gaze to the boy. "Cesco? Detto's fine."

Pietro saw the child visibly relax in spite of the knife resting on his col-larbone.

"So, Ser Pietro Alaghieri, cavaliere of Verona," hissed Pathino, "tell me—what do you want to spend your last hours speaking of?"

Pietro shivered. He said, "I want to know what brought you here."

✦ ◇ ✦

The rain beat down on the tiled roof of the Nogarola palace but didn't drown out the captive's words. ". . . and he died a broken man, longing for nothing more than to return to his childhood home. Your uncle and your father took control of Verona, destroying the natural order of things. We have no kings here, no Caesars. No one man can be allowed to rule over his fellows."

"Yes, I can see how the Bonifaci suffered all those centuries as unelected rulers of the Feltro."

The Count sneered. "My family rose to the top because of ability."

"I'm sure the hoarded wealth of generations had nothing to do with your prosperity."

"Ability shines in my family."

"As it does in mine. Not just in my brother. There's Cesco."

"Indeed there is, indeed there is. Or there was."

"So, to avenge your father, you'll murder Cangrande's heir?"

The Count made a face. "Nothing so simple as that. When I heard about the boy I saw new possibilities. Nothing else could have moved Pathino to my side."

"Pathino, yes. Why would you want him? He made a hash of that first kidnapping attempt."

"True. I heard he barely escaped with his life. To be fair, though—" Vinciguerra had to break off for a bout of coughing blood into a napkin. "To be fair, none of the others I sent were successful, either. They couldn't even get close."

"I would say the two who tried to kill him got fairly close."

The Count looked puzzled. "I never tried to have him killed. That would have spoiled my plans."

"Then your minions were confused—they hacked his bed to pieces."

"When was this?" demanded Vinciguerra.

"August of last year. Tell me that, at least, was a mistake."

An odd expression spread over the old man's face. "I sent no one in August—or July or September, for that matter." His face became quite earnest.

Katerina believed him. That meant there was someone else's hand at work—someone subtle enough to hide his intent to kill the boy under the guise of yet another kidnapping attempt. From the Count's expression, he'd reached the same conclusion. "You know who it is," observed Katerina.

"I might," confirmed Vinciguerra. "But believe me, lady—I wanted no harm to befall that boy. In fact, I swore an oath to Pathino that he would not be hurt."

"Why? What is he to Pathino?"

The Count grinned. "Can't you tell? Didn't you see it when you met the man? I mean, he's thin and has lived a hard life. He's quite a devoted man of faith, wears a hair shirt. All that adds years to a man's face. But still . . ."

"What are you talking about?"

"You asked what Pathino was to the boy. I'll do one better. I'll tell you what he is to all you Scaligeri.

"He's kin."

✦ ◇ ✦

"I never knew my father well, but my mother took great pride in him. The great Lord of Verona. Just like your beloved Cangrande, my father ran about the Feltro sowing his filthy seed in every wench that caught his eye. My mother was a local girl destined for a good marriage before he took her and used her for his lust. Then he tossed her aside for another whore, leaving her pregnant and alone. Oh, there was gold, of course. Devil's payment, the Devil's due for the Devil's deed. But did he ever confess it as a sin? The pious man, so pious that he burned the Paterene heretics in Verona's Arena— the same place you fought that ridiculous duel—did that pious man of faith ever confess the act that brought nameless me into the world, a shame to my mother?"

Pietro was trying to piece this story together. "You're talking about Cangrande's father."

Pathino gave him a tainted smile. "Alberto della Scala, yes. Five children in wedlock, dozens out. I have prayed all my life to forgive the stain of my blood, the soil of my progenitor, a man who appointed one of his own bastards to the holy office of abbot. That he is remembered for his piety is an abomination against God."

Pietro was still grappling with the concept. But looking at Pathino now in the flickering flames, there were signs. The cheeks, the chin. The eyes. "Cangrande is . . ."

"My brother, yes. Or rather, my half brother. We had different mothers, thanks be to God."

"But . . . if he's your brother, tell him so and he'll see to you."

"I'm sure."

"No, I mean, he'll welcome you. Nothing is as important to him as family. I've seen . . ." Pietro stopped speaking.

"Yes?"

There could be no harm in saying it. "I saw him give up victory over Padua to take in that boy there. That's how much his family matters to him."

Pathino remained silent. The dancing light played over a face that might have just as well been made of marble. Finally he spoke. "So, to claim his bastard he gave up a great victory. A noble deed, almost atoning for the sin of siring the bastard in the first place. Yet it kept him from greatness. It proves that he cannot be the Greyhound."

Pietro blinked, leaning forward. "The—what do you mean?"

"You know the prophecy? Good, good. God has ordained that the Greyhound will bring about another age of man. Everyone believes that your precious Cangrande is that man. But there is a hint in the name itself. *Veltro.* Greyhound. The bastard. Think about it. It has to be a bastard. Only a bastard, born in sin, can transcend that sin and win Christ's approval to help bring mankind to its senses, recreate the Church in his image, and do away with the heathens once and for all. A world ruled for God by God's faithful. That is the new age of man, Ser Alaghieri. That is the secret behind the prophecy."

"So you kidnapped the boy to help make the prophecy come true, turn the Greyhound into the man you want him to be?"

"What? No. No! I kidnapped the boy to give him to the Count, or sell him into slavery, or anything." Pathino began to swell, to tower. In that moment he truly looked like Cangrande's kindred, but mottled, as if reflected in dark water. "When the Count told me that Cangrande had adopted his own bastard I knew it was a sign from God. The prophecy was threatened. Divine influence was split between the two candidates for His plan."

"Two?"

Pathino shook Cesco slightly. "Him, and me. I will be *Il Veltro.* I am the Greyhound."

✦ ✧ ✦

When Antonia's message arrived at the Scaliger palace in Verona, the lovely Giovanna da Svevia was being entertained in her husband's parlor by the poet Dante. Feeling sour, he was reading aloud to the female members of Cangrande's court. Not that most of them listened, which was only to be expected. Bubbleheaded ninnies, wives of minor nobles. Only Giovanna, great-granddaughter of the Emperor Frederick II, paid him any heed. Related by blood or by marriage to half the rulers of Italy, Germany, and Sicily, she had a fine respect for the written word.

Jacopo was present as a courtesy to his father and was presently making moon-eyes at one of Giovanna's attendants. The ones he'd already bedded and discarded were full of barely concealed malice. Dante was ashamed and slightly awed by his younger son's prowess with the ladies.

Their hostess was lively today, cheerful and active for such a gloomy day, dark with storm clouds. Dante himself was weary of court and looking for an excuse to escape. So the messenger bearing a note for Monsignore Dante was a welcome interruption.

Seeing his daughter's hand, Dante imagined this had something to do with copyists fees or foreign translations. And she was supposed to be on holiday. The girl was as hard a worker as her father. Pity her brother Jacopo was such a . . .

Reading the first paragraph Dante gasped, straightening in his seat. Jacopo saw the blood drain from his father's face. Forgetting the girl, he darted forward. "What? What's the matter?"

"Wait." Scanning the brief single sheet again, Dante spoke to his hostess. "My son is in Vicenza."

"Your other son? The noble Ser Alaghieri? How wonderful!"

"Yes. But it seems he's joined my Lord della Scala, your husband, on another of his idiotic—I mean, wild flights of martial endeavor."

"May I?" Giovanna took the paper and read over the few well-shaped lines. "So, that's where my husband is. He forgets to tell me these things."

"But surely, lady," said Dante, "this is good news."

"Indeed." Aware of the anxious looks from the women around her she said, "The Paduans have broken the treaty. They have tried to take Vicenza. If we are to understand our esteemed poet's daughter, the attack has been beaten back and Verona is victorious."

The women clapped their hands in relief. A couple of them wept. Alone among them Dante knew the second part of the message and was pondering what, if anything, there was to be done about it as he said, "A great happiness, lady."

"Yes," said Giovanna. "Francesco does love his surprises. But what a joy that your son has returned to Verona! He seems determined to regain his lost glory. He's out searching for a missing child as we speak."

Dante blinked. He hardly thought that the lady would make that part of the message public. It was followed by the inevitable voices, all asking the same question. "What child?"

"It hardly matters," Dante told them. But Giovanna surprised him when she said, "In the confusion of battle, Donna Katerina's son has been kidnapped. Bailardetto. And her foster son as well. I believe his name is Francesco."

There were many knowing looks, wide eyes. Jacopo leapt to his feet. "Cesco! And Pietro is looking for him? Father, we have to go help!"

Dante knew full well the social perils of leaving this lady to join in the search for her husband's bastard son. But again the lady herself solved his dilemma. "We will all go. Send for my grooms, have them arrange a carriage and gather an escort. We ride to Vicenza. Immediately."

✦　◇　✦

"This was a terrible idea."

Antonia's horse trotted beside Gianozza's, the rain falling steadily over them both. Their whole beings were focused on not falling from the sidesaddles. In the dark afternoon Gianozza's horse did not see the rabbit hole in its path. Gianozza shrieked as the horse stumbled and she fell skidding across the ground.

Antonio slid out of her wet saddle and landed running on the sodden earth. "Gianozza!" She reached her companion's side. "What's the matter?"

"My leg! My leg is broken!" cried Gianozza. Rolando whined in empathy.

It didn't look broken to Antonia, who was admittedly no great judge. She looked up to see Gianozza's horse limp away, whinnying pitifully. "I guess you're both lame." It was perfect. Trust the girl to end up a crippled and helpless heroine. "Can you ride on the back of mine?"

"No, no. It hurts!"

"I could walk," offered Antonia. Again Gianozza shook her head. "Do you want me to get help?" The girl nodded. Antonia took the knife from off her belt and placed it in Gianozza's lap. "Just in case you need it. And keep Rolando close!" She started toward her horse. "I'll find someone!" Climbing back into the saddle, Antonia spurred off in the direction she'd come.

✦　◇　✦

Pietro had silently digested Pathino's claim, wondering if it could be true. "If you're related, prove it."

Pathino reached into his shirt and withdrew the medallion. "This was a gift from a great Scottish warlord to my father. He passed it on to me. If I ever needed to prove whose son I was, this would do it."

"So that's why you had to have it back. But why didn't you ever . . . ?"

Pathino was amused. "Why would I throw myself into a nest of vipers? No, it was far better to bide my time and let my siblings die off, one after another. Bartolomeo and Alboino are dead. Cangrande cannot last much longer, he has too many enemies. Then I would have stepped forward to claim my father's legacy to make up for his sinful ways."

Pietro tried a new tack. "You hate your father for being sinful. But what about you? You've committed murder. Not on the battlefield. You murdered the nurse in Verona—the one you stabbed in the chest."

"A tragedy. I prayed for her."

"Decent of you. What about Fazio? Have you already prayed for him?"

Pathino shook his head in honest sadness. "Poor fool. He made a scene by begging. He didn't understand why he had to die."

Pietro trembled again, but not with cold. "What a fine figure you'll cut before God, the slayer of women and boys. Did you kill the oracle, as well?"

"No, I had nothing to do with that. I wish I had, the heathen bitch. The nurse, yes, I confessed to that sin and was forgiven. But the whoring soothsayer was killed by the Count's partner."

Pietro squinted at him across the flames. "Partner?"

A laugh. "You know so little. Yes, the Count's partner had the oracle killed. The message sent, the messenger had to die."

It was worth a try. "I'm going to die anyway, so tell me—who's this partner?"

Pathino smiled, a horrid version of Cangrande's famous grin. "That would be telling."

But another odd suspicion was forming in Pietro's mind. "You're willing to kill women and children. So why didn't you murder Detto? Why haven't you killed him yet?" He pointed to Cesco, on his knees under Pathino's blade.

Pathino was silent for a very long time. Suddenly he spat into the fire. "My father was a clever man. He told all his whores of a curse on his bloodline. I don't know who began the curse or how. Perhaps it was Alberto himself. It may be he feared one of his sons doing him ill. Perhaps it was a guilty conscience or simple foresight. But whatever the curse's origin, we are not allowed to take the life of anyone who shares our blood. *Sanguis meus,* the old bastard said. Blood of my blood. Anyone who does will suffer death untimely and eternal damnation." Pathino shivered. "I will not be damned to fulfill my destiny. God would not ask it of me. That is why I did not kill Nogarola's boy—he is my nephew, through Cangrande's bitch of a sister. And that is why I will not kill this one."

"But you will be damned, Gregorio. Is that even your real name? You've committed murder today, and you will not have a chance to confess or even pray before Cangrande comes here to kill you." Pathino just laughed. Pietro said, "Think on this. One hour. That's the head start you had. Four hours. That's how long it took me to catch up to you, even though I had to trace you back and forth across the river. One minute. That's how long it will take for Cangrande and his merry men to notice the signs I left for them—a broken twig, a sword slash in the base of a tree. I figure it'll take them about three hours to trace us here. How long have we been sitting here? Any minute you'll hear the hoofbeats of a thousand knights—and I mean real soldiers, not cowardly backstabbing, woman-murdering scum like you.

"I'll make a deal with you—if you give up now, I'll let you pray before they hang you. You can ask forgiveness. That way you won't be damned. Your soul will fly to heaven. Now, give me the boy."

It almost worked. But Pietro made to stand too soon. Pathino's dagger pressed against Cesco's face just below the eye. "Don't you move! I may not be able to kill him, but I'll take out his eyes. I mean it."

Cesco was still, not even blinking. He made sounds that the gag muffled, but his eyes were on the blade that threatened his skin. Pathino shook him. "How would you like that, nephew? I hope you're not afraid of the dark—because you'll live in blackness forever. How does that sound?" Pathino's head snapped up again to snarl at Pietro. "The Count wants him alive—fine. But he'll be blind. Is that what you want? *Is it?*"

Almost a whisper: "No."

"Then sit down. Sit!"

"Listen—"

"No! No more talking. We'll sit and we'll wait for the Count to get here. And you better hope that your master missed the trail you left. If not, my beloved brother will get his son back, mutilated and scarred. Even dear sister Katerina won't be able to look at him without vomiting."

Pietro opened his mouth to let an insult fly, but Pathino drew the knife lightly over Cesco's skin, making a small cut just under the eyebrow, off to the side. Blood trickled down the small face.

Cesco didn't move, but made a sound almost like a growl. Pietro saw the child staring past Pietro at the ground nearby. Again the boy growled. Pathino shook him once, with real violence. "Shut up, you."

Cesco looked straight at Pietro, green eyes direct and imploring.

What's he trying to tell me?

THIRTY-SEVEN

Surrounded by an armed escort of twenty men, the coach from Verona moved swiftly. At Soave they encountered Vicentines guarding the road. Giovanna and Dante were informed that the battle was indeed won, but there was no word yet of the missing children. Jacopo, all excitement, asked to borrow a horse and ride at the front of the small party. This was arranged and, thanking the Vicentines for their news, the lady ordered her men to press on without delay.

Dante was now alone with Cangrande's wife in the carriage. The downpour beating down on the roof effectively drowned out polite conversation. When the lady said something Dante was forced to ask her to repeat it.

"I said, do you find that great men are incapable of fidelity?"

This was definitely not a path the poet desired to travel. But he couldn't not reply. "There is much to be said for the powers that lead a man to greatness—strength, will, grace, intelligence, the ability to persevere against all odds, ambition—a great man must embody all these in great quantities to survive the pitfalls of this world." A flash of lightning outside. Dante waited for the roll of thunder to pass. "An excess of these lead to other excesses."

"If these great men are so intelligent, why do they not understand . . . ?"

"I never said they were wise, my lady, only intelligent. Wisdom is not innate in greatness. It can only be gained through the trials of a man's life."

"Is infidelity admirable?"

"Certainly not."

"But you were not cruel to the promiscuous in your great poem," observed Giovanna of Antioch.

"God punishes, not me," said Dante. "To the matter of fidelity—think of Odysseus. He took lovers all his life. Yet there is not a couple more revered for their fidelity than the King of Ithaca and his Penelope."

After a moment she said, "I have no children."

Dante nodded. "And it is a mark of his affection for you that he has not set you aside."

"Yet." Her voice was harsh. "Not yet set me aside. I suppose I should be grateful." She drew a curtain aside to stare out at the storm. It was Dante's impression that she was weeping, but he did not choose to look.

✦ ◇ ✦

Vinciguerra was dozing when Cangrande entered the smoke-filled room, his sister in his wake. "I understand I have another sibling. I rejoice. You must now tell me where I may effect a touching family reunion. I have no more time for these games."

"Ah. In that, too, you are quite like all your charming siblings. No, no games. But I will not tell you where they are." Vinciguerra was determined to enjoy this, their last confrontation. "I have spent some time thinking about what my lady Nogarola has told me of star charts and prophecies. She clearly believes such nonsense. But I wonder—do you?"

"We are men of the world, Vinciguerra. This world, no other."

"That is hardly an answer. But I think you do. I think you believe in the story of the mythical beast who will transform the world. Certainly it consumes your brother. You both long to be that beast. So why not kill this child to begin with? He is nothing but a threat to you."

"If he is the Greyhound," said Cangrande with a sour look at his sister. "There is some debate on that point."

"But why take the risk?" demanded the Count. "Why let him live?"

Cangrande smiled, but it was a cold smile. "For the same reason your Pathino has not, and will not, kill him. *Sanguis meus.* He is blood of my father's blood. Now tell me where they are."

The Count swelled in his triumph. "No. They are as well hidden as if the earth had swallowed them. You will never see them again."

"What did you say?"

The Count froze mid laugh. Blood loss and spite had made him say too much. Now Cangrande's smile was warmer, friendlier. "What was that you said out on the battlefield, Count? Pathino had 'gone to ground?' And just now—'as if the earth had swallowed them.' For a man of few words that is a remarkable metaphor. Come, Kat. Perhaps we'll have that family reunion after all."

✦   ◇   ✦

Where the devil is Ferdinando? The question nagged at Pietro's brain, as did the fear that Ferdinando had gotten lost on the return trip.

Pietro decided he had to try something. If he didn't move soon, he'd be no use at all. After a morning of battle and riding followed by hours of sitting in this damp cave, Pietro's limbs were stiff. In spite of the fire that blazed before him he was cold.

The real question was, what was there to do? Bare-chested, barefoot, weaponless, and tired, he was in no position to do much of anything. Pathino still sat with Cesco in front of him, the long miseracordia held loosely in his right hand. Even if Pietro could move, get a weapon, act somehow—as long as the other man held the child, there was nothing to be done.

Pathino was gnawing on some smoked bacon. He'd removed Cesco's gag so he could feed the boy too.

Surprisingly, Cesco found his voice. He asked Pietro, "Why d'you like funny hats?"

Pietro blinked. "Sorry?"

"You like funny hats."

Pietro had to grin. "How on earth do you remember that?"

"Shut up," muttered Pathino, tearing into a bite of bacon.

Pietro shivered again. He asked, "Mind if I stoke the fire?"

After considering, Pathino lifted the dagger to Cesco's face. "No tricks."

Pietro lifted a half-burnt branch, stirring up the fire and sending sparks up to vanish against the earthen ceiling. As he prodded the flames he watched Cesco. "How are you?"

"Dog tired," said the boy.

Dog tired? What did that mean? Where had he even learned the phrase? Besides, he didn't look tired. His eyes blazed as bright as the fire. What was he trying to say?

Pathino noticed Pietro's hesitation. The dagger became actively menacing. "Sit down. Now."

Pietro retreated slowly, lowering the piece of wood he'd used as a poker so that it was unthreatening. He left half of it out of the fire, the end protruding toward him. Cesco's gaze, even with a blade against his cheek, held the same scorn as yesterday when Pietro had been unable to solve the puzzle. Slowly the boy's eyes moved down to the body of the dog. Blood was still seeping from its skull . . .

Pietro saw Mercurio's chest move. Pathino's blow hadn't killed him.

That was it. He looked across at Cesco, who grinned at him.

Now it was a matter of when.

✦   ◇   ✦

Gianozza was huddled in a ball, raindrops pounding on her head and back. She was wet despite her hood, and she was cold. Her ankle kept her from doing anything more than rocking back and forth.

Slowly she realized where she was. It was not far from here to the cave she had shown Antonia, in front of which she and Mariotto had become properly married.

She considered limping there. It would be dry. She might be able to make a fire. But then she recalled the creature that had scared them from the cave. It was probably still there. Besides, if she went now, Antonia would return to find her missing. And there was her ankle.

In an unaccustomed moment of practicality she chose to stay where she was, patting the dog Rolando who burrowed against her for warmth. This was no pleasant summer rain. This was what it must have been like during the Great Flood, when God wiped the face of the earth clean of evil. She closed her eyes. *Perhaps the rain will wash away my sins as well.*

When she opened her eyes again, she saw a figure across the clearing. A man on horseback. He was massively built, with a large farmer's chest and arms. He was also wearing a farmer's straw hat, wide and drooping under the heavy fall of rain.

Dismounting, the man began walking toward her. Ankle protesting fiercely, Gianozza struggled to her feet, drawing Antonia's knife. "Stay back!" she called, waving the weapon in front of her. "I have a knife!" Beside her the dog growled.

The man said, "Giulia, I could never hurt you."

Gianozza's hand slowly lowered. "Antony?"

"What are you doing out here, in this weather?" Capulletto was indignant on her behalf.

She slipped the knife into its sheath and leaned her back against the tree. "I—Antony, I heard about your challenge to Mariotto." He stiffened, then nodded. "I rode out to find you, stop you. But my horse tripped. Antonia went to find help."

He removed his cloak and added it to her coverings. "You came looking for me?"

She could smell him, a raw musk, purely male. She wrinkled her nose, then looked into his eyes and said, "It must stop, Antony. I'll do anything you ask, but it has to end. He's your friend."

"Friends don't do what he did."

"No. People do what he did. Friends forgive."

"You don't understand."

Gianozza laid a hand on his arm. "I do. I truly do. It's my fault."

His voice choked. "I never felt anything—never felt things so much, so strong, before you. Just that one night, that one happy night—I was the best I could remember being. I was the man I always wanted to be." He turned his head upward, allowing the rain to beat on his face.

"Will you be that man if you kill Mariotto? My husband? Is that the act of a man who wants my happiness?" Antony shrugged. She took hold of his face. "Ser Capulletto, I didn't reject you for you. I fell in love with your friend."

His voice was bitter. "Of course you love him. He has everything—looks, a name, friends, a kind father. He's the oldest; he won't have to scrape a living together of his brother's leavings. So of course you married him! He's got everything. And now he wants to be friends again. Friends! Well, he won't have that! He won't get me, too!"

Gianozza stepped back, only to cry out. "Oh! My ankle!" This utterly unmanned him, and he helped her to sit again on the earth. When he was kneeling beside her she said, "Antony, how much of this is really about me?"

His breathing was coming in ragged bursts. "You don't understand."

Gianozza's breathing was shallow, compared to the bellows his lungs had become. They were very close now. When the kiss happened, it was as tender and soft as anything she'd ever experienced. It was almost reverential, as if he feared offending her.

"I want you," he whispered in her ear. "I love you, Giulia."

She pulled back from him. "Giulia?" It was a name she had never heard herself called.

"You're my Giulia. The perfect woman." He leaned in to kiss her again. This second kiss was more passionate, and Gianozza felt herself kissing him back. Oh, what bliss! What joy! She was—

Francesca. Francesca and Paolo, the illicit lovers. The damned lovers.

Wrenching herself away, she stared at him in horror. "This isn't the—no! No, Antony! Listen to me! We can—we're supposed to be friends now, that's all—"

"How now?" said Antony, frowning sharply. "What is this to you, a game? I'm serious, girl! You are all that I want in this life! You are my everything!"

She pulled away from him. For a long moment he stared at her. Then he cried, "Damn it! Does he get everything? Then give him this!"

Drawing out a silver knife he approached her, tears running down his face.

What he was about to do, she never afterward could guess. She was certain he would never have harmed her, or told herself she was certain. Would he have given her the knife? Hurt himself with it?

Whatever Antony intended, she was saved from it by the sound of horses approaching. Antonia had found a group of five men, led by Benvenito.

Gianozza gazed at Antony, who stood still in the rain looking back at her. Then he turned away.

"Gianozza," called Antonia. "Are you all right?"

Antony stayed long enough to ensure she was safe. Then he clambered up into the saddle and rode away. Gianozza watched him go. Just before he passed out of sight she saw his gloved fingers open, releasing the silver dagger. It fell, landing point first in the muddy earth.

Antonia was kneeling beside Gianozza. "What happened?"

"I made it worse! I made it worse! I told him not to—he's supposed to listen, to love me enough to listen—"

She heard Antonia sigh. "What did you think would happen, Gianozza? That if you played the scene right, all would be forgiven? This isn't a play, a poem."

Gianozza wept. They persuaded her to mount a horse. All the long ride back toward Castello Montecchio, she repeated one thought over and over. "This isn't how it was supposed to happen."

+ ◇ +

In the cave they heard distant hoofbeats. At first Pathino grinned. "I'm sorry, Ser Alaghieri, but I'm afraid the Count won't let you walk alive from this place. Perhaps if you beg."

But then the sound multiplied. Four or more horses trampled the earth not far away.

"Was he bringing friends?" asked Pietro.

"He could have brought some Paduans with him," protested Pathino feebly.

"And have them kill him when they learned this whole enterprise was a feint for him to kidnap a Veronese child? I doubt it."

It was time. Pietro stood up. Immediately Pathino leapt to his feet, dragging the child up with him. "Don't!"

"You know what I think? I think the Count has been captured, and in exchange for his life he's given them you." Pietro reached out an open hand. "Give up now, and I won't let them hang you." Subtly he edged his left foot closer to the protruding half-burnt stick. Mercurio's eyes were open now, though his whimpers were too soft for Pathino to hear.

Pathino glanced wildly about, then smiled again as the hoofbeats rode back the way they had come. Pathino's relief brought back his awful version of Cangrande's smile. Across the fire pit he said, "You won't let them hang me? How generous. But I think it's time I do something about you, Count or no." He brandished the knife.

Now. Pietro made a show of sagging. His next move would have to be bootless, and he'd pay for it later—if he survived.

Pietro stepped into the fire. With the flat of his foot he kicked the half-burnt stick through the air toward the *spaventapasseri.* Pathino's hands flew up to ward off the flaming embers.

Cesco dropped to the ground and rolled away. Cursing, Pathino grabbed, but his fingers clutched only air. Dagger in hand he turned on Pietro, still across the flames.

Seeing his only chance, Pietro shouted, "Mercurio! *Avanti!*"

The great greyhound rose from the pool of its own blood and threw itself through the flames. The long mouth clamped down hard on Pathino's left hand in a spray of blood. The bastard Scaligeri screamed as the weight of the dog yanked his arm down. The hound pulled, driving his teeth in with a savage growl.

Pathino plunged his long thin dagger into the hound, piercing its eye. Mercurio's jaw went slack and the greyhound fell to the earth without a rattling whisper.

From somewhere in the darkness a young voice screamed, "M'cur-o!"

Pietro had scooped up his sword and was running around the fire pit. Pathino freed his blade from the dead dog and lashed out at Pietro's face. Taking the slash across the back of his hand, Pietro heard the next cut whistle past his ear. He rolled, putting distance between himself and Pathino. Leaping to his feet, he twisted around to lunge at his enemy.

Only Pathino wasn't there. The bastard was running to his horse, tethered just a few feet away. He slashed the leather ties and clambered into the saddle. Sword raised, bellowing like the devil himself, Pietro limped toward the horse. But he was too slow. Pathino kicked and the beast jumped. His scalp brushed the ceiling of the cave where it dipped low, pushing through the dangling roots of the giant tree above. Then he was around the fire, angling toward the cave's exit.

Pathino had forgotten the tripwire. The horse's forelegs caught it, sending both Pathino and his mount headlong into the muck. Pathino struggled to free himself of the flailing horse. The firelight exaggerated his scarecrow figure into a grotesque form in the shadows on the cave walls.

Pietro jumped the tripwire and splashed after him. Out of the corner of his eye he saw Cesco, free of his bonds, running toward the dead dog.

A flash of reflected firelight brought his attention back to Pathino. He still held the miseracordia and he swung it wildly. Pietro's sword had a better reach, though. He thrust with it and Pathino had to leap backward in the knee-high water, scrabbling to keep his feet.

"Damn you!" cried Pathino, turning and racing for the mouth of the tunnel. Pietro slogged after as best he could, knowing that it was hopeless. He was too slow. Pathino would be free in moments.

Behind him came a splashing sound. Pietro threw a glance over his shoulder. Cesco was in the water, chasing Pathino too. Turning back, Pietro saw that Pathino had stopped in the tunnel.

Cangrande's bastard brother gave his pursuers a look of wild delight. His left hand came up, grasping something, then yanked down hard.

Pietro paused as he heard a horrible sound from above. Wooden beams hidden in the roof just above the doorway shifted. They creaked and groaned for a moment, the noise they made sounding like earthen screams of agony. Then the beams fell.

It was an old trick designed by the ancient horse thieves to seal off the cave in times of trouble. In desperation, they could leave their stolen mounts and hide all evidence. But now it worked too well. The heavy rainfall had softened the earthen roof above. Almost half of the cave shifted, then came crashing down.

Down upon Pietro and Cesco.

✦   ◇   ✦

Pathino reached the open air, looked about him, and cursed. He'd hoped that Alaghieri had left his horse hobbled right outside the cave, but there was no sign of it. "Of all the damned . . ."

Damned. Yes, that was the right word. He was damned. He had hoped that only the entrance to the cave would fall. But now he had broken the one rule of his family. He'd killed his father's blood kin. He would certainly burn in Hell.

He stumbled down the path, away from the collapsed cave and into the forest. He tried to orient himself so that he was traveling north, but without the sun it was difficult.

After ten minutes of walking, he heard hoofbeats. Ducking behind a tree and clambering up into the low branches, Pathino held his thin knife white-knuckled in his grip as he waited for the rider.

A lone horseman approached. Obviously a noble, with a fine beast and delicate tabard. Pathino recognized the Montecchio crest, for he had grown up in these parts. He climbed higher in the branches just as the knight turned toward the cave. The mounted man's face under the open cheek pieces was hidden by rain. That worked for Pathino, as did the rain. With the water hitting the metal shell, the rider didn't hear the snapping twigs above him.

Pathino dropped, landing hard on the rump of the horse. The rider cried out and began to turn. Wrapping his left arm over the rider's neck, Pathino slid the knife's point into the man's right armpit, just where the front and back plates gapped. The rider's life ended with a gasp.

Pathino struggled to free his dagger, then tossed the corpse from the saddle, fighting to remove the feet from upturned stirrups that dragged the body along with the cantering horse. Done, he turned north and rode for Schio. In an hour he would turn east for Treviso. It was only twenty miles from Treviso to Venice. From the great port he could take ship for anywhere in the world. For now that he was damned, what did it matter where he went?

Yet—yet he wasn't through. He was the Greyhound, he felt it in his bones. With or without the boy, he would carry out the plans he and the Count had made. He would redeem the blood that flowed through his veins, and in so doing, he would redeem himself before God.

The boy's death, though regrettable, meant nothing in the end.

THIRTY-EIGHT

It was an hour before sunset and Mariotto's men were riding yet again along the riverbank looking for a sign, any sign. They were all tired, and they huddled under their capes and hoods for protection from the rain that was obliterating any traces that Pietro may have left.

Mariotto was doing his best to hide his fatigue as he pushed his men further. He shared the fear that their quest was hopeless, but he refused to be the first to turn back. His thoughts were so focused on home and hearth that when he heard the noise he didn't register it as important. Then slowly he became conscious of a sound different from rain and river and horses and trees in the wind. They were voices. A man's and a woman's, to be precise, issuing orders loudly. Gesturing to his men, Mariotto set out to find the sound's source.

As they rode, the voices grew in number and in volume. Mariotto's troop arrived at a clearing high on a hill. There were several Scaligeri soldiers about, their armor discarded and their arms tossed aside as they knelt around the base of a toppled tree. The tree didn't so much look fallen as sunken, held aloft by branches stuck on other trees.

In the midst of the digging men knelt the Capitano, using his breastplate to scoop up and toss aside clods of damp soil. The other men were doing the same. Standing at one side was the Scaliger's sister, still clad in male attire. By the way her weight shifted back and forth it was clear she wanted to dig, but was withholding herself in favor of her physical superiors.

Mari dismounted and made his way carefully along the slippery slope to the lady's side. "Donna, what news?"

Cheeks flushed and lips tight, she said, "Mariotto! Thank God! This is the cave, isn't it? Your brother-in-law gave directions. Bonifacio hinted that Cesco and Detto were under the earth." She gestured to the base of the hill. "We arrived to find the cave collapsed. They're buried in there. We're trying to dig them out!"

It took Mariotto only a moment of thinking before he cried, "What a fool I am! It's perfect! But do we know that this is what Bonifacio's hint . . . ?"

"There are traces in the part of the tunnel uncollapsed. Hoofprints. Pietro's shirt, boots, and crutch. They were here—and they were buried. The position of the tree—look at it. It fell in the last couple of hours, the side leaning away from the rain is still soaked."

Mariotto couldn't argue with her reasoning, so he volunteered to help. As he stripped off his armor he asked, "Where can we best be of service?"

Katerina looked at her brother, already knee-deep in a hole he and twenty knights had made. "Start in the tunnel. We began here to provide us with more room—there's nowhere to throw the excess dirt down there. But if your men set up a relay, tossing the rubble outside, you might have better luck."

Mariotto touched his hand to his forehead and ran skidding down the mud-strewn hill. He kept a hand on the felled tree to balance him. Behind him the tree's roots angled toward the black and grey sky, twisting like fingers reaching for God.

His quick orders were instantly obeyed. Even if there was little likelihood that anyone lived, they would do nothing less than their utmost.

They plunged into the dark tunnel. A torch was lit, and by its light Mari and two others used breastplates to stab, then cup the fallen earth, passing them back through a line of men to be tossed aside at the tunnel's mouth. Soon they had a rhythm going, and they could sing, grunt, and chant in time to their labors.

After a considerable time Mariotto emerged to let someone take his place at the head of the chain. Rubbing his aching arms, he let the rain fall over his hands to cleanse them. He wished the storm would abate. By now the cellars of Castello Montecchio would be flooded, and the chicken coops, and the kennels. He would listen again to his father's declaration that this was the year they'd dig the drainage ditch, as he had each time the summer rains came. Mari hadn't realized how much he'd missed his home and his family.

He kept stretching out his arms, working the life back into them, and as he did he walked, looking over his father's land. His land. He was almost out of earshot of the digging when he decided to turn back.

The wind changed direction just then, and the rain's force eased just a fraction. In that moment a noise came to Mariotto's ears, a gentle mewing like that of a cat crying. Picking up a tree limb, Mariotto followed the sound, straining his ears over the cries of men and the fall of rain. Was that something shifting behind that tree? Was it. . . . ?

A horse. It was Pietro's palfrey, well hidden and tied to a tree. Huddled under a cloak beneath the horse was a tiny figure.

Mariotto ran over and lifted the cloak's edge. A terrified toddler, too small to be Cangrande's bastard, looked out at him with red-rimmed eyes. Mariotto crouched down. "Hello there. You must be Detto. We haven't met yet. My name's Mari."

✦ ✧ ✦

Luigi Capulletto stood looking at the chance fate had granted him. Dared he take it?

When he had spurred away from his brother, he had then concealed himself in the trees and watched his brother pass him in turn. Luigi had been convinced that Antony had an idea of where the children were—he'd been too quiet, too remote, not his usual gregarious self. It was just like Antony to bait Luigi into leaving so that he could have the honor of saving Cangrande's son all to himself. So Luigi had followed his hated brother.

But the fool hadn't found the child. He'd found the girl instead. To Luigi's intense pleasure, he saw his brother's rejection at her hands. After everyone had left, Luigi had retrieved the silver dagger with Mari's name etched into it. At the time he hadn't known why he did it. Now it was clear. He would ruin his brother once and for all.

Bending down, he began to work the dagger into place.

✦ ✧ ✦

Filthy, weary, Cangrande stood flexing his arms, his eyes on the pool of water that was filling the pit his men were frantically digging. There were torches and covered lanterns all about, and more men arriving every minute, bringing with them pickaxes, spades, and dogs. Beside him was his sister. Their combined attention was so intent on the earth being shifted, the buckets of water being removed from the crater, the incredible slowness of it all, that they didn't notice a young man slip up beside them. "Madonna Nogarola? I think this young fellow belongs to you."

"Mama!" The toddler threw himself toward her, careless of his injured arm. Exhausted with fear, he collapsed against his mother's chest.

Heads came up from the pit. In a ringing voice Mari quickly explained. All the joyful mother could manage was, "Thank you, Mariotto. Thank you!"

This fresh success gave them all heart to continue at breakneck pace. Cangrande embraced Mariotto, just as covered in muck as himself. "Good God, Mari, you look like you just climbed out of your own grave. Good work. Perhaps in our haste we have overlooked some other clues out in the brush. Could you take a few of the more tired men and search the woods hereabouts? We can keep at the digging." The Capitano gestured to the fresh reserves just arriving.

Detto's father was among the latest arrivals. Bailardino saw his son and bellowed for joy. Katerina passed Detto, already asleep, to the weak-kneed father, who refused to let his son out of his grasp for the rest of the night.

As ordered, Mariotto took some tired workers and led them down the slopes with torches and dogs. Cangrande followed him but turned away at the base, angling instead for the mouth of the tunnel. Beside the opening of the cave there was a growing mound of excavated earth. The Scaliger announced the discovery of one child, giving them even more incentive to find the other.

He was just turning away when he heard a shout. "My lord!"

He whirled about. "Have you found something?"

"No, my lord! There's a carriage on the path!"

"Damn you and damn the carriage! Keep digging!" But Cangrande was not so far gone that he missed whose carriage it was. Bare-chested, covered in mud, he crossed to where the carriage was reining in. The door opened and his wife emerged into the rain. One of the two burly foreign grooms Giovanna of Antioch employed aided her descent to the sodden ground. The other groom attempted to hold a cloth over her head to keep the wet off. Ignoring him, she walked through the squelching earth and faced her husband. Cangrande, covered in filth, stepped in to buss his wife on the cheek. She leaned away from him, saying, "Have you found the boy?"

"No. Lady, you shouldn't have come."

"I could say the same about you," said Giovanna. There were times when you could see the faint traces of Frederick II's iron will in her face.

Cangrande flashed his perfect teeth in return. "I had little choice." His consternation turned to surprise when he saw his client poet emerge from the carriage's high wooden door. "Maestro Alaghieri—you've heard?"

Coming close, Dante said, "I heard that my son was hereabouts, my lord, and something about a battle and lost children. Can you enlighten me further?"

"Please, Francesco," said Giovanna in her golden tone, "enlighten us all. We understand you're at war with Padua once more."

"Yes, but that's for tomorrow," said Cangrande. "Of the lost children, one has been found—Bailardino's son. The other is lost, we think, in that mound—with Ser Alaghieri," he added darkly.

Dante's other son was atop a nearby horse. He leapt from the saddle and started to run to the mound of earth. "Somebody get me a shovel!"

The poet's face was rigidly controlled. "Is—is there any chance they're alive?"

Cangrande's answer was interrupted by a shout. "We've got something!"

Dante actually outpaced the Scaliger on the run to the tunnel. Shoving past the men crowding into the tunnel, they both struggled deep into the muck crying out, "What? What is it?"

Face glowing in the torchlight, the lead digger waved the Capitano forward. "We heard something. A voice. It seemed to be singing."

"Singing?" Dante could hear nothing over the noise in the tunnel. Cangrande snarled, "Quiet, you bastards!"

The men quieted, listening. All digging stopped. When they heard it, so faint it was barely distinguishable, they hardly believed their ears.

> *Hear the tramp, tramp*
> *Foot soldiers stamp.*
> *Tramp tramp tramp tramp tramp!*
> *Hear how they go!*

More than a voice. Two voices, both weak. Grasping a shovel, Cangrande began shifting earth with all his might. Dante and Jacopo joined him and the others as they pulled and rent the earth wide.

A hand appeared before their eyes. They heaved on it, but they dislodged the roof, and the arm disappeared again in a fresh fall of earth. They worked to brace the top of the tunnel so that nothing more fell. The hand clawed free again. They made a hole, all the time shouting the names Pietro and Cesco.

"We're here!" came the faint reply. They dug harder. Suddenly a hole opened and Pietro Alaghieri lunged sideways out of it. It was not pure air he emerged into, but enough like it to be a breath of spring. He blinked, obviously unable to make out shapes after the endless dark.

Dante and Cangrande stared back at him. "Pietro? Are you all right? How are you, boy?"

Pietro laughed, but it came out as a cough. Someone handed a wineskin forward, but he shook his head. He retreated into the alcove of space and air under the fallen support beams that had saved his life. Dante reached after him, but Cangrande restrained the poet, lest he collapse the makeshift supports they had wedged above them.

Another shape began to emerge from the little gap, but it was not a man. It was a child as black as night, with eyes as wide as the new moon. He looked around the way Pietro had, unseeing at first. Something cued him, though, to the presence of his favorite playmate, for he cried out, "Cesco!"

"Cesco!" Cangrande echoed. He hauled the child through the opening, pulling him past the throng of cheering men and out into the rain.

Katerina stood there, awaiting news. The lady actually fell to her knees when she saw her foster son.

Cesco looked up at his namesake, coughed twice, then asked, "Wha's the matter with Donna?"

"She's just tired," replied Cangrande. He lifted the boy high above his head and shrieked a single word. "Scala!"

From all around him, above and to the sides, ranged about like a pack of wild animals, like the inhabitants of some ancient, primal civilization, the soldiers and nobles and common workers echoed his cry to a man. "Sca-la! Sca-la! Sca-la! Sca-la!"

This morning they had cried out for the man. Tonight, they cheered his heir.

Watching from the shelter of the carriage, Giovanna turned away to confer with her grooms.

Back in the tunnel, other men helped a weeping, cursing father pull his sore and breathless son out of the shelter. No one understood the nonsense the youth kept muttering over and over. Someone whispered that the ordeal had driven him mad.

"Giach giach giach," Pietro croaked, laughing through his tears and not caring who saw.

✦　◇　✦

Soon the mood on the hill became something of a festival. The rain lessening to merely a drizzle, it was possible to build a real fire, and there was enough wine about. A few ingenious men got a spit started in the mouth of the tunnel, where they roasted some hares. There was horseplay all around. A game of tag had begun between some of the half-naked men and one of the rescued boys. Cangrande played right along, pretending that he couldn't outpace the child. Then the child spied one of Cangrande's hounds and began to weep.

Pietro and Dante were seated by one of the fires. While Katerina talked with the mourning Cesco, Cangrande joined them and listened to Pietro's story.

"The look on Pathino's face gave me a warning," croaked Pietro, sipping water. "I dropped my sword, threw my arms around Cesco. I kept a hand over his mouth so he wouldn't swallow the muck. There was an awful sound. I was sure we were going to die. But then the noise ended. In the darkness I felt around. The wooden slats in the trap fell at an angle, making a shelter from the falling earth. As long as we didn't move, we could survive."

"As long as the air lasted," said Cangrande.

"Yes," said Pietro with a shiver. "I thought of that."

"How did Cesco behave?"

Pietro shook his head. "He was a hero. In the dark, in the wet, everything waiting to fall on us, he let me teach him that song."

"You're a fool," said Dante. "You should have built a fire outside the cave—something to send up a signal."

Suddenly remembering, Pietro opened his mouth, croaked, swallowed, and tried again. "Ferdinando. I met Ferdinando—sent him back for help."

Cangrande frowned. "Petruchio's cousin? Then where is he?" Pietro shrugged and explained entrusting Detto to Ferdinando's care.

Cangrande shook his head. "Mariotto found Detto with your horse. Which means we have another person to look for. I'll see to it." He called Nico over and gave him the order. Then he turned back to Pietro, his face showing real sadness. "I'm sorry about Mercurio."

Pietro bowed his head. "Thank you. He was a good fellow. But he will live on in his children." He swallowed again and said, "I'm sorry I let him get away."

Dante sputtered. "A choice! Let him escape or let the child die! I think God applauds the valiant more than the vengeful."

"Live a life that is worthy of respect and honor. Protect the innocent," recited the Scaliger.

Pietro's tired grin stretched from ear to ear. "You remembered. How am I doing?"

"Damn well, I'd say."

From the confines of her carriage Giovanna emerged and approached her husband. "My lord, your young friend here is both wounded and tired. You should send him back to Verona."

"I'm fine," protested Pietro. It was feeble in comparison to the exhaustion that was printed on his face.

Cangrande said, "You're right, my love. Pietro, you've done enough for one day. Vicenza is closer. I'll send you there —" He began looking around for horses.

"Might I suggest another conveyance?" She gestured to the carriage that had brought her here. "It seats four comfortably. If you're determined to send it to Vicenza, it could carry the child and your sister, with the knight's father as well. I shall ride with you, if you'll allow it."

After a long moment of consideration, Cangrande leaned forward and kissed his wife. "You are my angel." He leaned back, his mind grappling with something. With an air of decision, he declared, "Amen. Let it be."

Pietro told Jacopo to take Canis and help Nico find Ferdinando. Around them the revels were becoming extreme. Women had arrived from a nearby village, and the men were attempting to impress them with tales of the day and contests of stamina and strength. Pietro soon found himself seated in the carriage beside his father, who clucked over him like an old hen. Seated across from him were Cesco and Katerina.

Cangrande saw them all settled into the cushioned seats, then firmly closed the door and nodded to the groom. The man grinned in return, gave a loose salute with his hand, then snapped his whip. The horses trotted off toward the road.

Morsicato arrived at the mound just as the carriage was pulling out. He dismounted next to Cangrande, who was mildly surprised to see him. Cangrande said, "Things under control in the city?"

"As much as they could be," said the doctor, staring after the carriage. "I thought I might be needed here."

"I'm glad to say you're not. I've just sent Pietro off in a carriage. He has a few scratches that bear looking at, but otherwise no doctoring for you. You might as well enjoy a flagon of wine before heading back. It seems that our victory celebration has spontaneously erupted here."

Morsicato accepted the flagon and drank deeply. "That carriage—I thought I recognized the grooms."

"They belong to my wife," the Scaliger said, pointing to where Giovanna was standing with Nico da Lozzo, laughing more brightly than she had in a long time. "She volunteered her carriage to transport child and hero back to the city."

Bailardino approached with little Detto. Nogarola's huge bear paws cradled his son against his chest while Detto sucked his thumb in blissful sleep. Smiling brightly, Cangrande clapped his brother-in-law on the shoulder. "I thought you'd left."

"I keep getting waylaid. Was that my wife you sent off in the carriage?"

"It was."

"Why weren't there any guards riding along?"

Cangrande blinked. "I ordered twenty men on horseback to accompany them. I thought that was enough."

"Well, they didn't go. I just talked to the commander. They were told they weren't needed."

Cangrande's voice grew icy. "By whom?"

"They thought the order came from you."

"Really?"

Bailardino seemed angry. "I'd think you'd be a little more concerned. Kat told me about the Count's secret partner. He's still out there, you know."

"Bail, don't worry. I'll send twenty men off right now. They should catch the carriage in no time."

"All right, peacock. I'm going to stay here and let Detto nap for a while before heading home." Bailardino lumbered away, his sleeping son in his arms.

Cangrande turned to Morsicato. "Join me, Doctor? Or perhaps you'd like to ride back with them?"

"There are other doctors in the city. If you say Pietro's wounds aren't serious, I think I'll join you for another drink."

The Scaliger nodded. "Speaking of wounds, how is Theodoro?"

"The Moor? He's up and moving. In fact, I wanted to speak to you about him. He's been divining. Hardly was he awake when he had the pendulum out and swinging. Then he kept trying to get up, saying he had to leave. I had him tied to his bed."

"What did he divine?"

"A danger to Pietro and Cesco."

Cangrande laughed. "A little late! But when we return, we can put his fears to rest."

The doctor persisted. "What's this about a secret partner?"

"Some spy in my palace was working with him. He's the one who—"

The doctor stopped in his tracks and grabbed Cangrande's arm. "That's it! That's where I've seen those grooms!"

"What grooms?"

"Your wife's! They were the ones in Vicenza last year, in the palace! The men with the accents!"

"What are you talking about?"

"They're the ones who tried to kill Cesco!"

Morsicato watched Cangrande assimilate that information. "You're certain they're the men you saw?"

"Yes. Dead certain."

Morsicato expected the Scaliger to leap onto a horse and cry for all and sundry to follow him as he raced to the rescue of his son once again. Yet this one time the Capitano stood frozen. The doctor's voice was urgent. "Cangrande! Those men have Cesco! He's in danger! We must go!"

Eyes unfocused, Cangrande nodded. "Quietly, just us. No soldiers. Not a word to anyone."

In moments they had mounted their horses and were off.

THIRTY-NINE

Dante observed, "This is taking a long time."

Cesco was playing with something. In the light from the covered lamp Pietro saw it was a coin. "Cesco, where did you get that?" Cesco clutched it to him and didn't answer. Pietro thought he knew what it was. "You can keep it. I'm sure Mercurio would want you to." Cesco didn't smile, but he relaxed and returned to fingering the old Roman coin.

They bounced hard and everyone had to hold onto the walls. "The road must be muddy," replied Katerina. "Why are they going so fast?"

"We are going at a good clip, aren't we?" Pietro was trying to keep his bruised and aching body from jostling overmuch.

"It's because the bad men are driving," said Cesco with a yawn.

Pietro looked at the boy. "What bad men?"

"Th' men who tried t' cut me last year. They tore my pillow," he added confidentially to Dante.

"What do you mean, Cesco?" asked Pietro.

The child looked out the window.

Katerina said, "Cesco, Pietro asked you a question. You didn't answer him."

"I said! Th' men on top're the men who cut my bed."

Katerina's arms tightened protectively around Cesco's shoulders as she gazed at the others.

Dante said, "Is he imagining it?"

The child made a face and returned to his coin.

"How would they . . . ?" began Pietro, only to see Katerina turn ashen. "What?"

"Giovanna!" she cried. "Giovanna is the Count's partner!"

It was like ice water flowing into his veins. "Cangrande's wife?"

Dante said, "No, you must be mistaken."

"I'm not. It all fits. She had the keys to let Pathino out of the loggia. When Pathino failed, she got tired of waiting and sent her own men."

"But why?" Pietro thought he knew, but it was too awful. Cangrande's wife trying to murder his only son?

"Obviously to protect her future heirs. Francesco is a fool." The child looked up. "Not you, Cesco. Though why you didn't tell us this before we got into the carriage I can't say."

"I tho't you knew," the three-year-old replied. He closed his eyes again. "Besides Pietro's here." The child shrugged as if that were all that mattered.

They were moving much too fast to leap from the carriage, even if they weren't a wounded knight with a game leg, an old bent poet, a pregnant woman, and an exhausted child.

"Quite right," said Dante. "Pietro's here. He'll think of something."

✦ ◇ ✦

Nico da Lozzo was not drunk. He wanted to be, but his orders kept him sober. "I don't believe this! Pathino's still out there! He can't have more than a couple hours' head start. We could catch him!"

Bonaventura was far less sober, but just as adamant. "I agree. Hurting children! I'd like to take him home and let my brood at him."

Nearby, Uguccione shook the water out of his long hair. "But instead of that, all our men are hunting for your idiot cousin."

Bonaventura belched. "He'll turn up. He always does."

"I delegated and put Montecchio in charge of finding him," said Nico. "He's had the luck today."

At that very moment a grizzled old soldier stepped forward. "My lords— you'd best come see this."

"You find Ferdinando?" demanded Bonaventura.

"Yes, lord. But there's something else."

Something in the man's tone made several other men follow behind Nico,

Bonaventura and Uguccione. After a winding walk through the wood, they came to a body. Young Montecchio was kneeling beside it. The figure was draped in a cloak the mirror of Mariotto's own, but this cloak was stained with blood.

Nico bolted forward. "Oh God. Mari—is it . . . ?"

Mariotto gingerly turned the shoulders of the dead man, tenderly shielding the face from the rain as he removed the gilded helmet. Everyone stood for a long time without speaking.

Another blue-cloaked figure came riding over in haste. Benvenito reined in close by and dropped lightly from his saddle. "Mariotto! Somebody said . . ."

Mariotto remained kneeling in the mud, looking down at the face that had always, but for one night, looked severe and reserved. Now the features were relaxed, peaceful. So should every man look, the assembled men thought, as he found himself at his Creator's knee.

"Ambushed, looks like," said Bonaventura.

Benvenito glanced up sharply. "By whom? A Paduan?"

"No. Not a Paduan." Tenderly Mariotto laid his father's head to the ground. He then removed a silver dagger from his father's armpit. He had to work hard to slide it out, showing how forceful a blow the killing stroke had been. He wiped the blood from it on his own cloak. There, etched on the blade, was his own name.

There was a murmur of voices from the hillside, then a pair of figures came into the clearing under the tree. Luigi and Antony Capulletto walked forward into the light of the torches. Antony said, "We saw the lights on the hill. What's happened? Are they found?"

"Capulletto," said Nico softly, "you don't want to be here right now."

"Why?" Antony looked at the dead body. "Who is it?"

Mariotto's head rose. Uguccione saw his muscles tense. So did Nico. As Mariotto sprang forward, they were there, wrapping their arms about Montecchio to restrain him. Mariotto struggled hard against them as he shouted, "Bastard! Coward! Can't even come at me face to face! You have to stab in the back! Only you missed! You *missed!*"

Antony turned red. "If I wanted you dead, Mari, you'd be dead!"

"Christ, Capulletto," murmured Bonaventura, "shut up, can you?"

"I will when you tell me who the hell is that dead man?"

Benvenito answered. "Aurelia's father. His father." He jerked his thumb at Mariotto.

Antony went from red to ashen in an instant. "No!"

Mariotto's face streamed tears. "You jumped-up nobody! She'd never have you! Kill me and she still wouldn't come to you!"

Antony realized everyone's eyes were upon him. "No! I didn't—the old man was kind to me—stood with me against his son! Why would I want him dead?"

Mariotto raised the silver dagger in his hand. "Because you thought it was me! Me!"

"Where did you get that?" asked Antony, a horrified look on his face.

"From my father's corpse! Can't tell a young man from an old, but you can tell back to front! You lily-livered coward!"

"Mariotto," said Uguccione in his ear, "calm yourself. I'll arrest him for this . . ."

"No! Let me loose, damn you!" Mari strained against the men holding him. "You want a fight, Capulletto? You want a duel? Fine! Here, now. Daggers only. You can use the one you stabbed my father with!"

Antony held out his hands. "I swear, I threw it away! I dropped that thing this afternoon!" Looking at the faces around him, it was clear that no one believed him.

"Everyone heard you, Antony!" Mari turned savagely to face Bonaventura. "You heard him, didn't you?"

"Well, I—"

Capulletto interrupted. "I was going to—"

"What? What? Embrace me, then stab me in the back *like you did my father*!" Mariotto broke loose of the arms that held him fast and took up a fighting stance. "Come on! Come on!"

Crimson crept back into Antonio's face. "Listen, you little shit! I didn't kill him!"

"But you'd kill me, or someone who looked like me!"

"No!"

"Then prove it! Prove it! Win your life before God, and walk away with my blood on your dagger too. For if you don't, I swear, Capulletto, by all I hold dear, I swear on my marriage, on my wife's life, that I will never rest until your whole line are as dead as my father!"

Antony's rage broke at last. "Then come on, boy, and try your accusations with a weapon sharper than your tongue!"

Uguccione shouted, "Arrest them! Both of them! They're breaking the law and are subject to punishment. By the Capitano's own orders, there will be no dueling in his lands. Beat down their weapons! Bind them if you must, but get them out of here!"

As they were dragged away, Antony was spitting curses and epithets that Mari hurled back in equal number. Uguccione sighed. "Bonaventura, go find Bailardino and tell him about this mess. Someone find Montecchio's wife. And, Benvenito, make sure his sister is safe. She needs to be told, and Montecchio is in no fit state." He turned to Luigi. "I don't suppose you can tell me if your brother did this?"

"I can't tell you he didn't," said Luigi, with a sad look. "We parted on the road, and I only found him a few minutes ago."

"Very well. I would appreciate it if you would go tell your father that we've arrested your brother, and things look bad for him. That knife is pretty damning."

Luigi said, "It certainly is. I'll leave right now."

"Thank you," said Uguccione. He was disturbed by the whisper of a smile on Luigi's face as he departed.

Uguccione arranged for the body to be moved to Castello Montecchio. Mariotto would be released in a couple of hours to make the arrangements for the funeral. For he was now Lord of Montecchio.

If ghosts haunt the places where they have work yet unfinished, the spirit of Gargano Montecchio remained, watching the rebirth of a feud, an ancient grudge broken to new mutiny.

✦　◇　✦

Just when Pietro believed they had no choice but to jump, the carriage slowed. They were stopping. He was weaponless but for his crutch, returned to him by the Capitano's men. He gripped it tightly.

Cesco had fallen asleep. He woke now with a rush. "Are we there yet?"

"We're stopping," replied Pietro. "Cesco, I hear you're good at hiding. Do you see anyplace you can hide in here?"

Cesco looked up at Donna Katerina. She asked him, "Where would you hide, Francesco?" He shook his head. "Of course you can. You always know where to hide." Cesco grinned and shook his head again.

Dante interrupted. "Madonna, if I may. Child, do you know a place to hide?"

The child nodded.

"Then why didn't you . . ." began Katerina.

Dante smiled in spite of their predicament. "I think he doesn't want you to see it."

"Oh, for heaven's sake!"

"Madonna, we have little time. If you wouldn't mind . . . ?"

With an exasperated sigh, Katerina della Scala covered her eyes with her hands.

Immediately the child jumped up and pushed Pietro out of his seat. Lifting the cushion Pietro had been sitting on, he opened a wooden lid that led to a small compartment. In it were riding clothes, an empty chamber pot, and the various necessities of a lady who travels a great deal. Cesco hopped inside and began to close the lid. Pietro stopped him, his eyes having caught something in the gloomy light. Reaching in, he pulled a dagger out of the compartment, then rubbed Cesco's head. "It'll be better than the cave. Nothing will fall on you." With one last look to make certain that Donna Katerina's eyes were well and truly covered Cesco ducked into the compartment and closed the lid. Pietro replaced the cushion and resumed his seat.

"May I open my eyes?" Receiving assent, Katerina glanced about the carriage interior. Pietro pointed to the seat he was on and she raised an eyebrow, wondering how the child had noted the compartment's existence. The telltale hinges were well concealed in the woodwork.

The carriage reached a complete stop. The occupants heard the drivers leap off and approach them from either side. Pietro fingered the hilt of the dagger and called out, "What's happening?"

"The way is blocked! A tree fell across the road ahead! We'll have to send for help!"

"We'll wait in here, then," called Pietro. "We're all pretty tired! Why don't you unhitch the horses and ride back to Cangrande!"

"We need to talk to you!" the speaker responded. This one seemed to be doing all the talking. *Where's the other one?*

After a pause in which Pietro failed to emerge, the speaker continued. "We have orders not to leave the boy alone."

"We'll be here with him! Leave us a sword, and we'll be fine!"

"Why don't you come out and we'll discuss it!"

This was getting bad. Pietro decided to try a different tack. "I can't walk! My bad leg, it's seized up!"

"Then open the door and we'll help you out!"

Seeing Pietro at a loss, his father piped up. "He's got to rest it, and the boy is asleep. Just go!"

There was no answer. Pietro motioned for Katerina to move to the center of her bench, away from the doors, then changed his mind and ushered her into his own seat. He placed himself in the center of the empty bench. He needed freedom of movement. There was no telling which side the attack, when it came, would begin. If the grooms were planning to assault the carriage, they'd open both at once. He leaned against the wall by the left-hand door. His right arm would have better range of motion. If someone came in through that door, he would receive a blade in the eye. Then Pietro could wrench the weapon free and attack the other.

He waited, but no attack came.

✦ ✧ ✦

Cangrande and Morsicato galloped up the muddy road in the darkness. The Scaliger carried a torch overhead, using it to make out the carriage tracks that were devilish hard to see.

The doctor called out, "We have to overtake them soon."

Cangrande slowed a bit to let Morsicato catch up to him, turning in the saddle to examine the trees about them. Just as the doctor pulled level, the Capitano shouted, "Archers!" He pointed with the torch.

Morsicato twisted to follow the Capitano's indication but was struck a blow on the head. As he toppled from the saddle, the last conscious sensation he could make out was the smell of burning hair.

✦ ✧ ✦

There was a rustling sound under Pietro's seat. Katerina whispered harshly, "Cesco! Stop fidgeting!" The rustling stopped. They waited in more silence. The curtains over the windows were drawn, but they knew their attackers were outside. Every now and then a torch moved in the darkness, shifting the light hitting the curtain.

Pietro smelled the smoke before he heard the crackle. "Oh no."

"What?" asked Dante. Katerina was looking for where the smoke would come from.

"The bastards have set the coach on fire." Smoke poured in through the floor. The fire was catching faster than he could imagine. Pietro's breath choked. "Must have been covering the thing with pitch," he gasped. "That's what they were—" He was unable to say more through the coughs that racked his lungs.

There was nothing for it. They had to risk the door. Pietro handed his father the crutch, pointed at the right door, then kicked open the left. As Dante worked the handle on his side, Pietro stabbed into the smoky darkness opposite with his dagger, hoping to feint the murderers out of position. But if these men had sense they'd be well back from the carriage, waiting for their prey to run into their waiting arms.

Which is what we're about to do.

As Dante bolted out the right-hand door, Katerina lifted the lid of the bench under her. "Cesco!"

There was no answer.

Pietro ducked out the right-hand door after his father. He limped heavily down to the ground. His father was just outside, the crutch raised high over his head, ready to fell any attacker. Pietro took position on the other side of the door, every muscle tight, his lungs burning. His watering eyes were blinking furiously, and he didn't see the figure approaching in the smoke. He bent to cough, and the sword stroke missed his head by a fraction. He gasped and lunged, burying the dagger all the way to the hilt in the man's thigh. Pietro's momentum continued carrying him forward, toppling both him and his assailant to the earth. Dante was over them a second later, using the crutch to club the villainous groom senseless.

Inside the burning carriage Katerina's left hand searched the compartment. She reared back with a shriek, her flesh smoking. The compartment was already burning. Choked, faint, she was unable to call for Cesco. Yet she couldn't leave. She reached down again, willing herself to ignore the pain. Her fingers encountered burning straw, and for a moment she believed it was hair. She clutched and pulled at it, scalding her hands on a sizzling chamber pot that she tossed aside. She smelled her own flesh burning, yet she didn't stop digging, throwing the burning thatch this way and that, until her hands felt the floor of the compartment.

Empty.

She heard the hoofbeats. A horse approached. Friend or foe, she couldn't be bothered—where was Cesco? Where where where?

In the smoke outside, Pietro watched his father continue to beat at the groom's head with a fury that was surprising. Then he saw a glint of light from the fire reflecting a few feet away. A sword, an axe, something deadly. The hand that gripped it aiming for the great poet's back. Pietro was too choked to cry out. He was weaponless. He tried to stand, but his body failed him at last. There were no more reserves. There was nothing he could do to save his father's life. He watched as the weapon's blade began its descent.

There was an ugly clang, metal on metal. The weapon fell away as the attacker turned to his right. A gust of wind showed a surprised expression cross his face. "But my lord!" Then his face split apart as a sword hacked down with an incredible force.

It was a sword Pietro recognized. *Thank God!* Cangrande had come.

Pietro collapsed to the ground with another fit of coughing and felt himself get dragged a few feet away from the blaze. It was easier to breathe over here. Pietro twisted around onto his back and saw Dante point toward the carriage, gasping out some words in Cangrande's ear. The Scaliger dashed into the blazing conveyance. A moment later Katerina reeled from the carriage, wrapped in her brother's arms. She screamed and fought, kicking and clawing to return to the flames. Her sleeve was on fire, her left hand and arm and shoulder burnt and blistered, her hair singed and black. Cangrande threw her to the earth and rolled her back and forth to extinguish the flames. She coughed and screamed and tried to return to the carriage that was nothing but a shell of raging fire.

Her brother gripped her right wrist as she struggled. "Kat—your baby! Stop fighting, damn it! The baby!" She moaned once as she fell to the earth, her hands on her belly but her eyes on the fire.

Cangrande paced over to the man Dante had beaten and checked to see if he was breathing. He must not have been, for Cangrande lifted the lifeless body over his shoulders and pitched it headfirst into the blaze. He did the same for the man he had killed. He then joined Dante and Pietro, kneeling by Katerina's side as they watched the fire. After several minutes Katerina spoke.

"He wasn't there." It took her several breaths to speak again, and when she was able, all she could do was repeat this single fact. "He wasn't there!"

Dante shook his head. "He must have been stuck, or curled up in a corner."

Pietro wiped his eyes and face. "How could he be in there and not make a sound?"

"He was a remarkable child." The poet's voice trembled. "My lord, I am so sorry."

Dante was behind the Scaliger, as was Katerina. Only Pietro, prostrate on the ground, had a view of Cangrande's face. Pietro blinked in disbelief. Engraved on Cangrande's every feature was an expression of pure, boundless—

Joy. Ecstasy, raw delight, the face an angel might bear doing the bidding of the Lord. Only this face was delighting in the death of a child. Blood of his blood.

There was a giggle from behind them and they all whirled about. Stepping into the road from by the treeline was Cesco. With nothing worse than muddy knees and hands he stood in the light of the fire, smiling happily.

Dante goggled, Katerina let out a sighing sob, Pietro stared between the flames and the child. Then he looked to Cangrande. The Scaliger's face was back to its old self. With a twinkle in his eye he bowed to the boy, who made a fine bow in return. Then Cesco ran forward to embrace his foster mother, who was too tired to deny him the affection he so clearly deserved. She wrapped her right arm about him and wept.

Later they would reconstruct his miraculous escape as something quite simple. The compartment under the seat also had a door leading to the rear exterior of the carriage, allowing the disposal of waste or stowing of luggage without disturbing the passengers within. Cesco must have forced the catch just as they halted, then dashed for the trees. That rear door also explained why the carriage went up in flames so swiftly—the two grooms had taken damp straw from a nearby hut and stuffed it into the compartment. What Katerina thought was Cesco moving about under her was really the murderers, planning their demise.

"It's a shame they didn't live," observed Cangrande. "We might have discovered who hired them."

"But we know, my lord," said Dante, blinking. Then he realized what he was about to say would be quite a blow to his patron. "I have a heavy tale to tell, my lord," he began, then quickly outlined their deductions regarding Cangrande's wife, Donna Giovanna da Svevia.

When he was finished, the Scaliger turned away. "I see. That reminds me—Morsicato. He's nearby, unconscious. Rogue Paduan soldiers attacked us on the way here. He was knocked out, and I had to tie him to his horse to bring him along. If he's up to it, perhaps he can examine your wounds, Kat." The Scaliger vanished up the road.

With the two carriage horses, removed before the fire, and the two horses that bore Cangrande and the senseless doctor, they were able to slowly make their way back to Vicenza. Pietro rode one horse, Katerina another, Morsicato lay over Dante's lap, and Cesco sat in Cangrande's.

No one spoke overmuch on that ride. For Pietro it was a ride filled with one thought, one image that returned over and over to his mind— Cangrande's expression when he thought that Cesco was dead. That horrible delight tormented Pietro's imagination the whole weary ride back to Vicenza.

FORTY

Perched atop the roof of the Nogarola palace, his back to a turret, Pietro stared down at the sleeping city. The wet rooftops of Vicenza glistened under the light of the moon and the stars.

He heard bells. *Barely midnight.* So much had happened since the dawn. He'd lived a whole life in the span of the rising and falling of one sun. Yet, while his inner eye ran over all the events, in his ears he heard only a child's voice singing through tears of fright. They'd been dropped into complete oblivion, he and Cesco. Without each other neither would have survived. Never out of reach, always conversing or singing, they had kept away the korai—the gods the Greeks believed called men to madness. It had seemed eternal, though he now knew it was less than an hour. He also knew how close they had come to running out of air altogether. He wondered if he'd ever be comfortable in enclosed spaces again. Hence the rooftop.

Cangrande had insisted that they creep into town unseen. Until it was clear that there were no more threats to them, Cangrande deemed it best to keep their arrival a complete secret. Once Morsicato, hair singed and head bandaged, had seen to Katerina's arm, he had sewn up Pietro as well. The doctor hadn't bled him, deciding Pietro had already bled enough to release any foul elements in his system. Pietro had refused to add any contents to the doctor's *jordan,* rightly saying he was too parched to produce a drop. But Morsicato had insisted on bringing forth the maggots once more, this time wrapping them into the gash across Pietro's left hand. Recalling how close that cut had come to his face, he tried not to imagine the maggots embedded in his cheek. And failed.

Dante had been granted a set of rooms, and Morsicato had given the poet a sleeping draught. Jacopo was still at the revels by the hillside. Antonia was off with Gianozza somewhere. Bailardino, one of the few who knew of their return to the city, had stopped by briefly to pay his respects, but spent the rest of the time divided between his frightened son and his pregnant, injured wife. Left alone, Pietro had wandered up here, leaning heavily on his crutch.

He'd heard the news of Lord Montecchio's death with real anguish. By now it was also common knowledge that the girl had been out during the day, had spoken to Antony. She said she had seen him drop the silver dagger before leaving her. Pietro's sister had confirmed this. So the damning piece of evidence against Antony was now gone. There would be no trial, no execution. Everyone now believed that a stray Paduan had found the knife and used it to steal lord Montecchio's horse.

Everyone except Mari, of course.

Bailardino had brought that news back with him. He also brought word that they had found Ferdinando's body. Bonaventura's cousin had never reached Detto's hiding place, but had fallen into the covered pit, the same trap that Mercurio had saved Pietro from entering just minutes earlier. It seemed Ferdinando had survived the fall only to be kicked to death by his thrashing horse. A horrible death.

It's my fault. Why didn't I warn him about it? I saw it and didn't even think to warn him. It's my fault . . .

Behind him a trapdoor opened and someone climbed the stairs to the roof. Listening to the fall of footsteps he knew precisely who it was. In the shadow of the turret Pietro was invisible, and he decided to stay that way.

"A lovely night," remarked Cangrande. "How are you feeling?"

At first Pietro thought the Scaliger was addressing him. Then he heard Katerina's voice. "Tired. My hand will look somewhat like al-Dhaamin's neck."

Shifting in his shadow, Pietro saw both brother and sister. Even after such a terrible day, even with her hand wrapped in salve and bandages, the lady was as perfect as the very first time Pietro had seen her. She had resumed her usual attire, her gown's hem barely brushing the rooftop. Cangrande too was immaculate in fresh clothes, though his skin was still unnaturally dark.

"And Bailardino's next son?"

"The baby should be fine."

"Regardless, you should be in bed."

"Morsicato has prescribed complete rest, but that is difficult to achieve with the Count raving like a lunatic in my own chambers."

"So you came hunting for me."

"Tharwat kindly offered to sit with the Count and transcribe all his visions, in case there are some portents in the man's dying imagination. Is there any news of Pathino?"

"Yes, in fact. We traced him to Schio, where he traded Montecchio's horse for another. Another vindication for Capulletto. Pathino seems to be headed for Venice. From there he can take ship to anywhere in the world. We'll try to head him off."

Pietro wondered if he was going to be sent to hunt Pathino again. It would be easier this time, knowing the man's name. In fact, it could be a good excuse to escape the quarrel between his two friends. That, and the other thing preying on his mind.

Because he was thinking it, he was startled to hear Cangrande say, "There's something troubling Pietro."

Katerina replied, "I expect he wants to know the same thing I do. Though I doubt he has realized all your perfidies. Shall we begin?"

Cangrande drew his sword, the sword of his father, and began stroking the edge with a small honing stone. "It isn't fair. You're wounded."

"My soul, however, has never been more at ease."

"And if mine is not, that sets us on equal footing?"

"Your wounds don't show, is all. The time has come for us to have it out."

Cangrande threw back his head. "A duel! Excellent. As the challenged party, I have the honor of choosing the weapons. I choose truth."

"Really? Perhaps I should go fetch Pietro. No doubt he would love to hear something so rare from you."

"Ah, we might as well begin there. What do you know of spies and what not?"

The lady's eyebrows arched. "I know you employ informants. These past few months, you are better informed than you used to be."

Cangrande raised a finger, wagging it in the air. "Ah, but did you ever wonder how I was receiving the information? Through whom?"

Light dawned. "Pietro." Her voice was grave, and in his shadowy perch Pietro felt a flush of guilt.

"Pietro," confirmed Cangrande. "You thought we were estranged, and you thought you knew why. But really I'd given him a task, a quest. With Tharwat acting as his eyes, Pietro was to track down the kidnapper."

"I see. A shame he didn't have all the necessary information. But today you were seen fighting side by side. How will that affect your fictional feud?"

"We'll say he and I fought together grudgingly, for the sake of your child. It is no secret how fond he is of you. Rather like a puppy." Hearing this, Pietro reddened. "I will rebuke him publicly, and he will return to Ravenna, smarting."

Pietro sat up straight. He'd thought that, after today, he'd be returning to Verona with all honor restored!

Katerina said, "I see I shall have to divorce him from you. I had no idea he was so much your creature."

"As much yours as mine, but that's not to the point. How do you intend the divorce?"

"What were your orders at Calvatone?"

Cangrande scowled slightly, laying his sword against the parapet. The lady pointed out, "You made the rules. You chose the weapons. You cannot complain of them now."

"True, true." Cangrande looked up at the night sky and sighed. "I ordered the town sacked. I ordered every woman and child raped, the men tortured, then all put to the sword. Havoc. That really was my seal."

"Why?" asked Katerina, echoing Pietro's horrified thought.

"Oh, it's obvious enough. A reputation for savagery is almost as useful as one of clemency. Ask Caesar. Or better, Sulla."

"And yet you had your German commanders executed for disobeying you."

"Yes, well, I couldn't have that sort of thing stain my honor. It's a pity, they were loyal men. Is that all you have, my dear? Perhaps you do require bed rest."

"Oh, surely you recognize an opening gambit."

"Testing my walls, looking for a breach? Then you'll set your siege weapons to work?"

"If necessary. I rather think I'll be able to find a tunnel through. Leaving the siege, let's move on to the Moor. You recall that, directly after Cesco came into my care, I summoned al-Dhaamin to produce one of his miraculous charts for us. Upon arriving in Venice, he and Ignazzio were assaulted. Was the Count was responsible for that?"

"Of course not. Until today the good Bonifacio had no notion of your passion for astrology."

"Then whom do you suppose set the murderers at the heels of the astrologers?"

Cangrande shrugged. "There are really only two choices."

"I doubt your wife knew enough about al-Dhaamin at the time to guess at his coming."

Cangrande clapped his hands. "Very good! Oh, Kat, I didn't know you had it in you. I will confess. I tried to have them killed."

Katerina clucked her tongue. "And after Tharwat was so good as to reveal your star chart to you when you came of age."

"A true ingrate I am."

"Yet he continues to live. No doubt you've had plenty of opportunities since then."

"Yes, but once he completed the boy's chart, he could do no more damage. In fact, he proved useful at times."

"I'm sure. I move on now to a matter more pressing."

"Giovanna?"

"No, not yet. I want to ask about Morsicato. I want to know what really happened on the road between the cave and our carriage."

Cangrande released a dark chuckle. For the first time he seemed unwilling to speak. "You have talent." He took a breath. "I distracted him, then struck him. He thinks I was saving his life."

"So there were no rogue Paduans?"

"Don't be absurd. I had to protect Giovanna. At that time I thought he was the only one who knew her trespasses."

Pietro felt a shiver pass over him. *He tried to kill both Theodoro and Morsicato? I don't believe it!*

"And when you discovered that the rest of us suspected her as well, you decided to spare him. I suppose there was little point in his death if we all knew. Though I'm surprised you left him alive in the first place."

A shrug. "It pays to look ahead."

"True, foresight has rewards. Like tucking loyal young Pietro in Ravenna and keeping him for when you needed him. I wonder how many other little surprises you have in store."

The Scaliger's eyes were bright, almost glowing. "She is my wife."

"And I am your sister," said Katerina. "Which is why the doctor lives. You cannot allow Giovanna to be maligned, but neither may you remove me. There was no point in killing Morsicato when all of us knew. But tell me— would you have killed Pietro if he had been the one to discover it?"

Pietro leaned forward, exhaustion banished. Cangrande shook his head as if dismissing a fly. But he did not answer.

"Come, brother! Cane Grande, O Great Hound," mocked Katerina. "It is time to reveal yourself. You play regret and humanity well, but on this night of truth please admit you have neither."

Cangrande turned away, his shoulders hunched. Pietro heard a voice quite unlike the Scaliger's usual measured tones. "Have I none? I suppose you should know. Yes, let the demons out. It is close enough to midsummer." He stared over the rooftops, head cocked to one side. "Of course I would have killed him. His father, too, even if it meant his great epic was never completed. She is my wife. I would kill a hundred of my dearest friends to protect her reputation."

"To protect her reputation?" asked Katerina. "Not for love."

"Caesar's wife must be above suspicion."

"But *you* suspected her."

Cangrande laughed. "More than suspected—I knew. I've known for two years. It was clear that someone had opened doors of my loggia to allow Pathino to escape. Pietro wondered at the time how Pathino got into the square so quickly."

He knew, even then. He made me think it was the Grand Butler, the man with the keys and access to Cangrande's seal. But there was also a woman from whose belt dangled all the keys of the household. Cangrande's wife.

Katerina gazed at her brother. "And you say that you sent Pietro away to hunt down the kidnapper."

"Yes."

"There wasn't another reason?"

Cangrande's smile grew. "We really must play more often. This is more fun than I could have dreamed."

"Answer the question."

"It's true. He posed the one question I could not have asked. Having a decent grasp of the obvious, he would have eventually reached the inevitable conclusion. To throw Giovanna off, I laid the blame on the butler." Cangrande clucked his tongue. "Poor Tullio may never forgive me for his ongoing exile. But I have suffered for my folly. One can never truly replace a really competent steward. At least I salted him away where I can recall him, instead of having him killed—which was my original intention."

Pietro was shaking. *Dear God, what is he saying?*

"Frederick's descendant is well matched in you," agreed Katerina. "So, some time before the Palio, your wife and the Count reached an understanding—but she had to let you know who it was you were really playing against. Is that why she suborned the oracle?"

"I imagine so. Those were certainly my wife's words the weird woman uttered—or some of them. I remember Giovanna's face during the oration. She seemed genuinely surprised by a few statements. Perhaps the old girl was really divining." Cangrande shrugged as if it was of little consequence to him. "We'll never know. Giovanna's grooms—the same two grooms, by the way, who were so inconsiderate as to die tonight—they took care of the oracle."

"Turning her head back to front, the price she paid for divining. Poetic irony."

"Dante would say *contrapasso*. I recall he'd read that part to the court just the day before."

"As you said, it's a shame the grooms are no longer with us. But then, Caesar's wife . . ."

"Exactly. No witnesses. Another good motto. I was slightly worried the one might wake up before the fire killed him—you see, I didn't realize our war was reaching its zenith tonight."

"And where is your charming wife now? Can Cesco sleep soundly in Detto's room, or will he receive a dagger in the night?"

"At my request she's at Castello Montecchio, counseling the aggrieved Gianozza. She has no idea we suspect anything. No doubt there is a banker's draft somewhere for her grooms, signed by the Count. She is very thorough and must have covered herself in case of exposure."

"She can't be let live. Not after tonight."

"She is family."

"But not blood."

"Perhaps not. Whatever I decide, it will take some time to arrange." Katerina made a very slight curtsy. Cangrande said, "In the spirit of full disclosure, there is something else you should know. There was a reason Pietro never found out too much about Pathino. There was a spy in Pietro's camp."

Pietro had a terrible sickness in the pit of his stomach. *No, not . . .*

Katerina said, "His groom?"

"None other. The late Fazio. Recommended by my charming, considerate wife. Alaghieri really can be a fool. But then, that's why I like him. He's so trusting."

"So Pathino killed him to—"

"To protect my wife, yes. It was certainly one of Bonifacio's orders. Pathino didn't know who the Count's partner was, but the groom did, so he had to go. Then, if Pathino killed the boy and was caught, only the Count would be implicated. If Pathino got away, the child would be gone with him. Either way, Giovanna wins."

"Her motive, of course, was to clear the path for any heir she might have with you. It is a foolish hope. She's too old."

"How old are you, dear?"

Katerina gestured with her good hand at her pregnant belly. "Did I expect this? Or Detto? No. I am blessed by God, but I had given up hope."

"They say some women grow fertile in the presence of children. Perhaps . . ."

"Don't even say it when you know you don't mean it. Cesco wouldn't survive a week."

"Well, one of them wouldn't. But you're quite right, my wife is too old. At least I am no longer half her age, but a mere score younger, give or take. I was so young when we married, but I think she was lying about her age even then. Still, I believe it is as you say. My aged wife still holds out hope for an heir."

Katerina took in a satisfied breath. "Well, with that out of the way, we may move on. I notice that, so far, you have refrained from taking the initiative."

"I was waiting for my moment to break out of my citadel and drive you back."

"I just didn't want you to think it had gone unremarked." Katerina walked to one side, putting the moon over her shoulder. Thus she could see his face. "We come now to the centerpiece of your board, dear brother. Cesco."

"Ah, *Il Veltro.* The star-crossed child. Again Pietro is able to see the painfully obvious. Two fallen stars, not one. So many possibilities. Is he the Greyhound, is he not? Cesco's future is written, but in a language no one knows. Are we clever enough to read it?"

"Why even try, when you want him dead?"

"I would never raise a hand to hurt him."

"No, of course not," mocked Katerina. "Your family is your weakness. You said it yourself. Our father's so-called curse."

"Yes." Cangrande took in a short breath. "*Sanguis meus.*"

"Precisely. He is blood of your blood. So you play the coward and let others spill it for you. The Count, your wife. As long as the blood is not on your hands."

Cangrande shook his head doggedly. "It isn't that simple, as you're well aware."

"You knew of the threat. You did nothing."

"Untrue. I left him with you."

"Effectively washing your hands."

"Effectively giving him even odds. But that's what I've never understood about you, Kat. If you believe the prophecy, why be concerned? The true Greyhound will survive, regardless of his situation."

"You still doubt that he is who he is?"

"I doubt everything I hear. It's a failing of mine. As for the boy, time will tell."

"Yet you allowed the attacks to continue."

"Yes. Thanks to Pietro, we learned that it was Vinciguerra's purse behind the plot. Pathino was the missing piece. I didn't want to move until I knew who he was. Little did I realize we would discover a long-lost brother."

"So you let him into my house."

"No," said Cangrande pointedly, "you let him into your house. It was your duty to protect the child. You failed. It took Pietro to rescue him."

"I wonder—are you pleased, because I failed, or are you enraged, because Pietro succeeded?"

The Capitano returned to where his sword lay. Retrieving the honing stone, he leaned against a turret as he again began working the blade's edge. "Neither. Both. Why would the boy's death please me?"

Katerina's lips were tight. "You cannot spill blood of your blood, but you can hardly stand to see him, however well you hide it."

The Capitano said, "Any poor skill I have at dissembling I owe to you. But tell me why. You obviously own the key to my soul, so tell me—why do I detest the child so?"

"Because you are like Pathino. Because you've always hoped, secretly, in your heart of hearts, that the Moor lied. Until Cesco was born, you could cling to the hope that you were the Greyhound."

Cangrande shook his head. "True or false, it means nothing. I do not want him dead."

"I saw your face, lord." Legs shaking, Pietro stood and moved out of the shadows. His voice sounded oddly hollow. "When you thought he was dead. I saw your face, my lord."

Katerina started. "Pietro? How long. . . . ?"

Cangrande was thoroughly unruffled. "Ah, our judge has arrived. Just in time. My sister brings up an interesting point. She says that, due to jealousy, I hate the boy, loathe him, want him dead. But I cannot do the deed myself or even order it. By her estimation, I wear both green and yellow in equal measure. Fine. I will confess. I confess that, in my weaker moments, I wish to be what I once thought I was. Of course I want to be *Il Veltro*—I was brought up to walk in his shadow! How much do I hate the boy for being what I should have been? There is no measure in human invention—if he truly is the Greyhound. He may be another me, and then my compassion for him is limitless. But Pietro, either way, I do not want him dead. I said this is a night for truth, so I tell you that is the one part of my sister's theory I will utterly refute. Let me say it again. I do not want Cesco dead."

"I saw your face," repeated Pietro.

Cangrande's head bent, he examined the edge of his father's sword. "I see I have much to explain. But first, let us examine Katerina's own feelings for Cesco, and by extension, for me. How much does it rankle her, I wonder, to be told that her only part in the raising of this legendary figure will be as *mother?*"

He paused, the moon's light on his face. "Mother. The giver of life. That was her role. Not the birth mother, but the true mother. Was that good enough? Not for Katerina." The scorn crept through his voice into the air. "She's a woman. The stars she so reveres gave her that form. You know better than most, Pietro, what it is to be held back due to a physical liability. But your leg is not nearly as damning as her gender. Imagine her frustration! Just as my stars withheld true greatness from me, they denied it to her at birth!"

Katerina said, "All that is irrelevant."

Her brother smiled and replied, "Then, pray, tell us what is relevant."

"Cesco's future. Even if we are to believe that you don't want him dead, your wife does. Pathino, too—or at least removed from the field of play. He'll probably sell him into slavery or something. Until they are dealt with, they are each a threat."

"True," agreed the Scaliger.

"Then Cesco cannot stay here."

"I concur."

Katerina showed genuine surprise. "You'd let him go? So you'd let me take him off, someplace you cannot reach?"

"Not so fast, my dear. One part of al-Dhaamin's prophecy will come true. Little Cesco will be passed into new hands to thrive. I'll make certain he's well taken care of. But you, my sweet—you will have no part of it."

Katerina's chin rose defiantly. "You cannot do that."

"Oh yes I can. And here's why—Pietro, did you ever wonder why Cesco's mother gave him up?"

Pietro recalled the conversation over his sickbed. "Someone was trying to kill him."

"Quite right. Now, my wife didn't know of his existence then, nor did the Count. Nor did I. In fact, there was only one person other than Cesco's mother who knew he'd been born."

Disbelief raced across Pietro's face. Cangrande winked at him. It had to be a lie. But no, there was no other explanation. A horrible emptiness opening within him, Pietro turned to Katerina, who held his eyes with a steady gaze.

Cangrande laughed. "Yes. She wanted—needed—Cesco's mother to give him up. Katerina hired the killer to force the lady's hand, and mine. The threat of her child's death sent the poor woman running into Katerina's arms, seeking protection for her son."

Katerina said, "He was in no danger. I knew the prophecy would protect him."

"If he was truly the Greyhound. If not, what better way to find out, eh? One less mouth to feed. Though it was a dangerous game. If he had died, she would have incurred the wrath of our father's curse. Blood of our blood extends to her. But it did work, and she got to raise the boy. Her dream has come true. Such a shame it has to end."

Ignoring Pietro's horrified stare, Katerina said, "You can't take him in yourself, Francesco. He will only become more of a target."

Cangrande nodded. "Which is why he's going to Ravenna. With Pietro."

That rocked her back on her heels for a moment. "To Ravenna? With Pietro?"

"Is there an echo? Yes, my sweet parrot. Ravenna is the answer to all our troubles. I will sign a document certifying him as my heir if I have no legitimate issue. But hereabouts we will say he died from shock. There was plenty to shock him today, so it will be believed. We will bury an empty coffin here—perhaps build a church in his memory. In the meantime, Ser Alaghieri has proven himself capable of meeting any challenge with a rudimentary grasp of subterfuge. He will raise the boy as his own kin. Cesco will live safe in Ravenna surrounded by great minds and decent people. There he'll be safe from everyone—including us."

"Us? Oh!" The lady opened her arms in appeal to the clear skies above. "Oh, are we to do this once more? I wish you would give me one of your birds, that I could teach it to recite my part. I wounded you, I withheld your destiny. Do I have it properly memorized?"

"Something like that. The boy must go."

"To protect him from me? From my evil designs? I didn't realize we were in the theatre! From what are you protecting him?"

Cangrande didn't look up from his sword's edge. "From the weight of your expectations."

The lady began to circle him, an eagle homing on its prey. "Stop posturing," she snapped. Katerina's unbandaged hand shot out to encompass his wrist, stopping the stone's repetitive motion. "Put away your props, Francesco. The best actors don't need a crutch."

Cangrande slid his father's sword into its scabbard. Touching the hilt with two fingers, he said, "I wonder, how much does it gall you that you will never wield this?"

Katerina hand fell to her side. "Do you hate me so much?"

"To this day you remain the single most important person in my life. I am what I am because of you." All unexpected, tears came to the lady's eyes. Cangrande's voice became relentlessly harsh. "Unfair, Donna Katerina. Tears are unbecoming."

"They are a woman's weapon," she said, trying to quell them. "And as you pointed out, I am a woman. I use what I have. Francesco, everything I did was for you."

The Scaliger coughed, or sputtered, or cried. He bent over, clutching his stomach as if struck. Then he flung his head back and stumbled to a turret for support. Only when the light of the moon reflected on his perfect teeth was his expression recognizable as a smile. "Kat, you're priceless! If you'd take the job, I'd fire Manuel in a heartbeat. All for me? For yourself!"

"You admitted it. You want to be the Greyhound."

A stabbing finger. "Not half as much as you wanted me to be."

"I wanted the best for you," protested Katerina.

The Scaliger slowly slid down the stone wall, ending flat on the rooftop with his legs splayed out before him. "The best would have been to let me grow unmolested! If love was too much to ask, then at least indifference!" He calmed himself, returning his voice to one that would not distress the guards far below. "There is a tale, Pietro, of a thane of Scotland—Donwald, a loyal servant to the true king. He was told by some mystic hags that he would someday be king himself. That very night he and his wife murdered honest King Duff while he slept. Here's my question—would he have done it had he not heard the prophecy? Would it not have happened in any case? Why not sit back and allow Fate to run its course?" Cangrande winked at Pietro with dark humor. "A man may control his actions, but not his stars. It has become my motto, I will blazon it through the sky." His gaze shifted to study Katerina coldly. "You would slay the king in his bed to bring the future to you. I would serve the king as best I could and wait to see fate unfold itself."

"More fool you, then."

Cangrande extended an accusing finger. "That! It is that which ultimately convinces me that, in your heart of hearts, you don't believe in the prophecy. You work too hard to make it come true."

"If I believe too little, then you believe too much."

"Perhaps." The Scaliger stood and began pacing the length of the roof. "Pietro, you wondered at my expression tonight? You thought I was over-joyed to see Cesco dead. It wasn't that at all! It was because Fate had failed. Destiny was wrong. Cesco was not the Greyhound. The stars were fallible. Everything that Katerina pins her hopes on was less than dust in the wind. That's what you saw: for a single moment, I felt free—free to finally step up and claim the destiny I've wanted, tasted, since I could think or hear or walk." He stretched his arms toward the sky. Pietro looked at the power in those limbs as they quested to pluck at the stars themselves. "I was told it was mine. From the time I was born until I became a man, I was told I was des-tined to be something great. I wasn't rejoicing in the death of the boy—I was seeing my future open up again."

"But he's still alive," said Pietro harshly.

The arms fell. "And so the walls reappear to hem me in once more. I am not the Greyhound. I never will be. But I want it, Pietro, I can taste it. That's what she did. My loving sister was so afraid of not fulfilling her destiny, her part in a myth, that she tried to make me into something I'm not. She let *me* live a lie to soothe *her* own need for power."

Tears were streaking down her face, but there was no hitch in the lady's breath. "It was not I who took the dream from you."

"True. But I blame you for giving it to me in the first place."

"I had no choice! It was my destiny! My fate is to raise *Il Veltro*! I am supposed to be the—"

Cangrande's voice filled with contempt. "You are! You have what you wanted! If Cesco is the Greyhound, you've shaped him, his mind, his thinking! He'll bear your brand forever! Do you think he will ever forget you? Do you think he could? Or is it recognition you crave, when he is grown and a figure of international fame? Is that the part you see yourself in? Caesar's mother? Christ's? Well, Madonna Aurelia Maria, you've done your part. Now it is time for Cesco to go to people who will love him."

Katerina gasped. "I love him!"

"Yes, you do." Cangrande touched the hilt as his hip. "As I love my sword. It is a tool. But, unlike you, without it I am my own person. I do not define myself by my sword alone. You love all your tools, Katerina, but only as much as they are of use to you. No tool can transform you into that which you are not. Believe me, if you discovered this minute that Cesco was not the mythic savior, you would forget him as easily as you forgot me."

Katerina's voice was small. "I never forgot you."

"Well, you can now. From this time on, I want nothing more to do with you."

He had delivered the killing stroke. Yet in doing it he'd exposed the chink in his own armor. Katerina was too tired, too spent by the fortunes of the day and the violence of Cangrande's feelings, to notice. She did not recognize as Pietro did that Cangrande was inviting her to protest, to plead, to beg, to yell, to clamor to be a part of his life still. It was her opportunity to refute everything he'd said.

She said, "May I visit him? May I have that, at least?"

In that moment, she lost. Pietro watched the closing of a door that would never be opened again. The Scaliger was victorious once more. Yet how bitter, to win by losing all.

"Yes," said Cangrande. "You may cling to your precious destiny. But never in the open, and never for long. We cannot let you be traced there. No one can know where he has gone. We must rumor it that he is dead, or driven mad, or spirited away by demons. Or all three."

The lady had regained some of her composure. "I understand."

"Don't fret, dear sweet sister. It is not too late to be a mother yet. There are your own children, who will not trouble you, for they are merely mortal. As are we all. You can instill in them a deep and abiding belief in the Church, or the stars, or the pagan gods, if you like. And if you're worried that little Cesco will take after me, you can be sure that with Pietro, the Greyhound shall grow to be all you wish him to be, without either of us ruining him."

"No."

Brother and sister turned to face Pietro, who had retreated to the roof's edge. Face half in shadow and half in light, he stared at these two people he had respected, loved, for so long. Now he told them, "No."

Cangrande bowed his head. "Ah, Pietro. You're quite right. We've forgotten our judge. So, we submit to your wisdom. Who is the victor? Who is at fault? What should be done with the boy? It is for you to say."

One after another Pietro's illusions were falling away, and he stood here more naked and alone than he had been in the cave. "Listen to you—both of you! This can't be about your personal war, or your place in history! Neither of you is interested in the boy!"

Katerina stepped nearer. "Pietro, think about what you've heard tonight. If you refuse, Francesco will only find someone else, someone nowhere near as brave and honest as you."

Pietro kept shaking his head. "No."

Cangrande picked up where his sister left off. "You're correct—our feelings about the boy are colored by our own demons. You're the selfless one. You've risked your life to save him how many times? With never a thought to yourself. He must go with you."

"Demons is right," said Pietro coldly. "No one would believe me if I told them what lies under the della Scala skin. No. I won't be a part of your games anymore. You tried to—you would have killed my father? Morsicato, Tharwat? Cesco? You can't pass a child off to me and declare a victory. I refuse."

He turned, and without another word, he limped to the stairs. In moments he was gone.

Brother and sister watched him go and the Scaliger let out a long sigh. "It worked."

Katerina's eyes opened a fraction. "You knew he was there?"

"Yes."

"You also knew that I'd come after you, so you staged the scene?"

"*Alterius non sit, qui suus esse potest.* He's quite correct. We're monsters, you and I."

"We are what the stars make us."

"We are what we will be."

"He'll hate you, you know."

Cangrande shrugged. "Any birth takes pain."

Katerina strode to her brother. Her hand in bandages, she couldn't embrace him. Instead, she kissed his cheek. "Does this end our war?"

Cangrande put his hands on her shoulders. "Are you dead? Am I?"

Stepping back, Katerina nodded her understanding. "You know, you still surprise me from time to time. With all your calculating and your infinite rage, I often forget your nobility."

"Darling, let's not get carried away. Do you think he'll accept?"

"I don't see what choice you've left him. I wonder if he sees that."

"Pietro's eyes are open now. To many things."

"If I may ask—when did you choose him?"

Cangrande blinked. "That first day, here in the palace. Before you came in he was talking in his sleep. Something in his dreams, I think. It wasn't very clear. But when you told me the boy had been born, I knew he would need a champion."

Katerina cocked her head to the side. "He spoke in his dreams? Has he inherited his father's magic?"

The Capitano opened his hands in a helpless gesture. "I don't know about magic powers, but I've seen Dante when he writes—he's in another world. And there is more to his writing than the choice of words. I think God brings about certain times in history, certain energies that merge in men—I don't know. Pietro has dreams. That is something he and Cesco share."

"And you."

"And you." The Scaliger started for the stairs. "Come. We both need rest."

"I'll sit up here for a bit. The sky is so lovely after a storm."

Cangrande glanced upward. "Really? I find it oppressive. But as you will."

Katerina remained on the roof for some time, unable to move. The conflict had been far more draining than she'd ever imagined. Her heart was broken, but she was proud. Her brother was learning. Someday he might actually become a great man.

But not *Il Veltro*. That destiny belonged to another.

EPILOGUE

Pietro turned a corner and was addressed by a rasping voice. "So. Now you know."

It was a long time before Pietro answered. "Now I know."

Al-Dhaamin's head was thickly bandaged. "I owe you my life."

Pietro remembered the curved sword that had protected his head and shoulders as he had ridden to rescue Cangrande. "Consider all debts paid."

"I am only sorry I could not be there when you truly needed."

"Oh? When was that? The cave? The coach? Or just now? For I'll tell you, nothing today compares with what I just heard. Oh, but I'm forgetting— you know everything already." Pietro laughed sourly. "They want me to take Cesco to Ravenna. But if Cesco is the Greyhound, nothing I do matters. If I don't take him, it'll all turn out the same. Right?"

"You know that is not so. Your faith denies predestination. I am inclined to agree. There is much talk of the stars' influence on men. No one ever speaks of man's influence on the stars. There is no relationship in the Almighty's creation that does not extend both ways. The boy may or may not be the Greyhound—that we cannot control. But what kind of man the Greyhound will be, that is open to our influence."

They stood gazing at each other. Pietro said, "You're a part of this, too. You let them play their little games, you encourage them. You play them off each other. What is it you want out of all this, Tharwat al-Dhaamin? What are you after?"

The tall, scarred man gazed down at Pietro. "I fear that by watching the battle between brother and sister, you have lost sight of the war. The struggle between siblings, the feud with Padua, the designs of Venice, the rancors of Florence, the hopes of the pope, the dreams of those who would be emperor—all those are as nothing to the fate of this boy. If he is the Greyhound he can reshape the world as we know it. Who would not wish to be a part of such an epic? It is a slim hope, I know, the promise of a promise. But who would hesitate to give up his life to bring such a new age to pass?"

"That's not an answer. What is it you want?"

Al-Dhaamin lips pressed together. "Ask yourself this—if I have made charts for the child, and for Katerina and Cangrande, is it not possible that someone once made a chart of my own poor life? That I, too, find a destiny that revolves around this child? That I have even found the end of my life intersecting at a place along his chart."

"You've seen your own death?"

"Possibly, yes. You played a part in that discovery. Had you not suggested that there were twin stars, I could not have made the chart that showed the intersection of my death and his life."

That was a chilling thought. But Pietro was sick to death of prophecies and star charts. "Do you think you can postpone your death?"

The Moor's chuckle was an eerie rumble. "Nothing can do that, my young friend. We die whenever the stars will it. It is futile to strive against them. The stars are powerful enemies." Pietro was quiet, so Tharwat said, "The Scaliger has no plans now to control the child's life. He's taken his revenge on his sister and placed the child where he is most likely to thrive while not growing to be a threat to himself. It is a remarkable act of self-abnegation, not to be confused with altruism. He has, for a brief moment, transcended himself. At the same time, he has bestowed his greatest gift upon you."

"Gift? What gift?"

The astrologer laid a hand on Pietro's trembling shoulder. "He has shown himself to be something less than what you've always imagined him to be. He has revealed a darker side, peeled back the layers of his persona to show you the person underneath. He has freed you from the thrall of worship."

Pietro glared at the Moor. "If that's true, why don't I feel grateful? And how do you know all this? Did you divine it?"

"Sometimes a well-tuned ear is far superior to the pendulum. Pietro Alaghieri, the master of Verona has given you a choice. Will you step up to the task the stars have lain at your feet and grasp your destiny, as I have mine?

Are you going to deny the child his brightest future out of your own need for independence?"

"I don't know. I'm a puppet noticing his strings for the first time. Perhaps that's a gift, but how much happier was the puppet when he was unaware of the tugging?"

"Pietro. You are old enough now to discard the notion that life is about happiness. This is your destiny. It is a worthy one. I am only helping you to embrace it." The Moor bowed his head and laid his hand on his heart. "I will go with you, if you like."

Pietro blinked. "You would?"

"I have nothing more to bind me here. My place is with the boy. If you will have me."

Lifting his crutch, Pietro started to walk away. "I'll think about it."

The astrologer watched him go. Then he went to pack his few belongings. The stars had already given him Pietro's answer.

✦ ◇ ✦

Dante lay in bed, trying to breathe easy after his adventures. He was not the young man who had fought at the Battle of Campaldino. His wars were now waged with words, not swords. The sudden excitement had tired him to the point of turning his lips blue. Morsicato had ordered a draught to help him sleep, but Dante hadn't felt like taking it. He didn't want to be insensible just yet. There were things going on around him. He wished to be aware of the outcome.

Antonia rushed into the room. Seeing his still form she whispered in a frightened voice, "Father?"

Dante raised a hand. "I'm fine. Just resting."

"I was at Castello Montecchio when word came that you'd been attacked. There are rumors flying everywhere—you're dead, Pietro's dead, Cangrande's son . . ."

"All fine. There was some trouble, and the Scaliger has much to contend with. But I am well, the child is unhurt, and your brother—your brother is braver than I ever dreamed. But dear, in all the excitement, perhaps you haven't heard about poor Ferdinando." Drawing her down to sit beside him, Dante related the news that she most needed to hear.

She took Ferdinando's death soberly, at least outwardly. Dante tried to peer beneath her controlled expression, but he failed. They had not been be-trothed, not even courting. She said only, "I will pray for him. He was a good friend."

What Antonia did not know—and what Dante would never tell her—was that recently Ferdinando had come to Dante and baldly asked the poet's per-mission to court her. Since Ferdinando was not his ideal notion of a son-in-law, Dante had asked for time to consider. But now he was ruing his delay. His children should be allowed whatever happiness they could snatch in this turbulent world.

She was looking particularly distant at the moment. Convinced that all good parenting rose from the art of distraction, the poet changed topics. "My dear, I am considering taking up Guido Novello's kind offer and domiciling myself in Ravenna. Jacopo will consent, if with little grace. We shall be near Pietro again, and the University at Bologna would enjoy my lectures. When you are able, I want to hear your thoughts on the matter."

"Oh Father," she cried, wrapping her arms about his neck. She wept, but only from her eyes. Her voice remained almost steady as she related the hor-rible state of affairs at Castello Montecchio. "Mariotto is swearing vengeance, Gianozza's weeping inconsolably, and Aurelia is just wandering around like a ghost. Capulletto has evidently fled back to his father. It's dreadful. I was wishing all night for nothing more than to escape them all and return to you!" *And now this,* she didn't add. She didn't have to.

Dante sighed. "It's settled, then. When all the wounds are healed, all the affairs settled, we shall accompany your brother back to Ravenna. I will have my family together at last." With unaccustomed feeling he hugged his daugh-ter to him. "Verona is no place to be, now. I think there are dark times ahead. Especially for the Capitano. Tomorrow I shall inform him of our intent."

✦ ◇ ✦

What drew him to the room Pietro could never later guess. He entered the sa-lon that was once again a converted sickroom. The scents from the brazier were sweetly familiar. Before him was a man he had glimpsed once, three years before, on a battlefield just south of the city. He lay white-faced and bloodless now, yet he still retained an air of authority.

"Who's there?" asked the Count of San Bonifacio.

"Alaghieri. Pietro Alaghieri."

"Ah. My shadow. The wounds I bear, I understand, were delivered for actions on your behalf—half behalf. Do you have any oysters, child?"

"What?"

"My armor!" The old man clutched the scarred bloody breastplate that Pietro had discarded in the streets that morning. "The Pup brought it me. Thank heaven—Father, I have it back! I'll bring it. It won't pass to my heir— my heir . . ." He was raving. Pietro took a step backward but the Count caught him by the wrist. "I hear you rescued the child. The little bitch-pup. Did you kill Pathino?"

"He escaped," said Pietro.

"Good, good. She'll be pleased. Once I'm dead—dead, down, but never forgotten! Never, you hear me! Never forgotten! Of course—of course, the irony is lost on you."

"Tell me."

The deep-set eyes were momentarily lucid. The fog lifted. "The irony is, I have spent all my life trying to bring down the Scaligeri when all I had to do was let them alone. They are perfectly capable of destroying themselves." Sweat poured down the Count's face. There was spittle flecked at the corner of his mouth.

Morsicato appeared, followed by a priest. The doctor frowned and told Pietro that he shouldn't be up here. The Count had to receive extremunction. The last rites.

Bonifacio said, "Come back and see me, boy, when I'm dead. I have stories to tell. I have a secret. It's one secret no one else knows. Not even your master! It's only mine. All mine. Two secrets, twins, entwined snakes! The *caduceus*! When I'm gone, someone has to know. I want to tell someone— someone who will suffer in the knowledge—someone who will, can, when the time is right, tell Cangrande the truth of it—"

"Then tell me now."

"No, no, no! You'll tell him too soon! Too soon! I have to have my secrets! Their lies killed me, so my lies have to live to kill their lies! And you, too, boy! You wore my armor! They told me! From beyond the grave I'll haunt you! Down, down down!"

Morsicato pushed Pietro aside. "Go. He won't be lucid again."

Pietro exited and made his way down the stairs to the open loggia he knew so well. He dropped down onto a stool, tired beyond all reckoning. In the garden a firefly blazed to life, momentarily visible in the dark night. Pietro tried to predict where it next would be when it glowed again. He was wrong, so he guessed again. He was wrong a second time and it became a game, a silly, stupid, mindless game that Pietro enjoyed because it kept him from thinking.

Somehow he knew that the Scaliger had taken up a position over his shoulder. He felt no need to turn his head. "Tharwat has made a strong case. The Count as well, though he didn't know it. Was that part of the plan, too?"

"The decision is yours."

"Is it?"

"Grow up, boy." Cangrande's voice was flat. Affectless. Unmusical. A scroll tube was dropped beside Pietro's stool. "Here. I just finished writing this." Pietro knew what was in it—a formal acknowledgement of Cesco as the heir to Verona. A stroke of the pen more dangerous than any of steel. Pietro didn't pick it up.

Cangrande said, "Your father and sister are upstairs. Tell them what you like, but you need to take them with you. The doctor as well. Whatever your decision." Pietro heard the crunch of the booted heel. Cangrande was gone. Pietro was alone.

Or so he thought.

Unseen, the boy had been creeping through the grass for minutes, stalking the firefly. All at once he sprang up and clapped his hands gently around the segmented insect. It glowed in his grasp, making two of his knuckles shine. The hands lifted. When next the firefly glowed, it cast light upon the delighted face of a child.

Watching, Pietro thought of his dream of yesterday morning. He thought of prophecies, star charts, all the accumulated weight that lay upon those tiny shoulders. Unbidden, words came back to Pietro. *Live a life that is worthy of respect and honor. Protect the innocent.* Pietro's choice was already made.

Grinning at his glowing hands, Cesco opened them. The firefly circled into the darkness, winking like a star. A second glowing ember flew across its path. They hung in the air like lovers before disappearing into the night.

AFTERWORD

Historical Apologies and Literary Addendums

Now that the story has been launched, a few notes.

My sources were many and varied. The major ones were Barbara Tuchman's *A Distant Mirror*, Alison Cornish's *Reading Dante's Stars*, Asimov's *Guide to Shakespeare*, by Isaac Asimov, and a collection of differing versions of *Romeo and Juliet* (ironically published by the Dante University Press). This last includes works by Masuccio, Luigi da Porto, Bandello, and, of course, the Bard of Stratford. Then there was the first volume of *Narrative and Dramatic Sources for Shakespeare*, which reprints Arthur Brooke's (long, awful, boring) *Tragicall Historye of Romeus and Juliet*.

Most important for historical data was A. M. Allen's century-old *A History of Verona*. Though Allen takes much legend as pure fact, her analysis of events and her insights into the people and the politics are fascinating. She also has several lovely turns of phrase, making her book an enjoyable as well as informative read. I am indebted to the Newberry Library in Chicago and the University of Michigan Graduate Library in Ann Arbor, both for their copies of this book and the several other diamonds of data in the historical rough. For hunting down a copy of my own, I have to thank Barnes and Noble Online for their used and out-of-print book search.

I also quite enjoyed *Padua under the Carrara* by Benjamin G. Kohl, again thanks to the University of Michigan.

For details of Dante's family history, I relied greatly upon *Dante e Gli Allighieri a Verona*, by Emanuele Carli. For more personal information, I was honored with an interview with Count Serego-Alighieri, the direct descendant of Pietro. Visiting him on the vineyard bought by Pietro in 1353, my wife and I found him gracious and generous with his time and his knowledge of his family's history. And the wine grown on the estate is superb.

Though I've read the Longfellow, the Oxford, and the Penguin translations of *The Inferno,* the new one by Robert and Jean Hollander flows better than any other, and their commentary is magnificent (though not for the faint of heart).

For the duel in the book, I went to the fifteenth-century fight master Hans Talhoffer, whose illustrated manual of swordfighting and close combat has been used for centuries. This was where I discovered the oval shield-spear I put in Pietro's hand.

At the eleventh hour I discovered a tome that is to be treasured—the *Dante Encyclopedia.* In spite of the occasional error (the Lucius Junius Brutus that killed the Tarquin was decidedly not the son of the Marcus Junius Brutus who murdered Caesar!), the vast effort of compiling so much knowledge regarding the Infernal Poet and his scribblings is to be commended and savored.

Harriet Rubin's *Dante in Love* came in during the final edits to give me a little period flavor—which side of the hat Guelphs wore their feathers on, etc.

Many of my other source texts were in Italian, German, or Latin. When this is the case, it behooves one to read these languages with something that resembles fluency. Though my Italian has improved greatly, I was still often forced to rely on translators. For their work in this capacity, I must thank Sylvia Giorgini (Italian), University of Michigan professor Martin Walsh (German), and my old high school chum, Professor John Lober, for his help with a bit of Latin.

Then there are the living Veronese. Antonella Leonardo at the Ministry of Culture was unbelievably kind and helpful, answering questions and arranging for my wife and me to meet a half-dozen fascinating people while we stayed. It was due to Antonella that we were invited to visit the vineyard and estate owned by Dante's descendant, Count Serego-Alighieri. The count was the soul of graciousness, giving us the details of his family's history and showing us around the home they have occupied since 1353.

Antonella also connected me with Professor Rita Severi. Rita teaches at the University of Verona. She, her husband Paulo, and their lovely daughter Giulia took us out for the single most enjoyable evening in a three-month tour of Europe. I learned more about Verona in that night than in two years of reading. Rita led me to the city library, where I was inundated with books as a gift from the head librarian. She also translated Manoello Guido's verses for me. I am very much in her debt.

Two days later we were taken on another tour by Daniela Zumiani, who showed us the Roman ruins under the city, available through shop basements and restaurant wine cellars. She was as enthused as could be by our little project. In her honor, let me plug her book, *Shakespeare and Verona— Palaces and Courtyards of Medieval Verona,* available in both English and Italian.

In spite of all this research, there will be errors. They are entirely my own.

Of course, none of this would be possible without the words, wit, and wisdom of William Shakespeare.

✦　✧　✦

I expect to get mugged by Shakespeare and Dante scholars alike. The Dante folk will take issue with several of my choices. His movements prior to his arrival in Verona are much debated, and I've chosen one of the more contentious routes, having him go to Paris to teach at the university. It was merely an excuse to have Pietro witness the final humiliation of the Knights Templar, but it is still plausible, if not probable. I also have Dante growing a long beard, something his contemporaries say he had, but some modern scholars deny vehemently (who cares?). And I spell his name wrong. Alighieri is the Florentine spelling of the name. But after he was exiled from Florence, why would he use their spelling? I have him returning to an earlier variation of the name, and Pietro, ever the obedient son, does likewise. I am always one for flouting expectations, and I find I'm in good company. Dante himself uses this spelling in his Epistle to Cangrande—specifically, "Dantes Alagherii." Of course, there is debate whether Dante himself wrote it. And on and on . . .

The historical Pietro is something of an enigma. There are a few facts, but none of them deal with his early years. So I gave him a life that will be seen as ludicrous by the Dante set. All I can say in my own defense is, Dante would have done it. So would Shakespeare. They both loved a good story.

For all that I'm going to piss off the Dante brethren, my treatment of Shakespeare may well be worse. I'm not messing with the man, they're used to that. I'm screwing around with his work. To the lovers of the Bard, I say this—all my initial ideas came from Shakespeare's text, including the origin of the feud. I never work to correct him, as other authors have done (quite well, in some cases). Unlike the historical Macbeth and Richard III, Romeo and Juliet were not real people in need of defense.

Besides, Shakespeare was something of a thief himself. He stole plots right and left—including the story of Romeo and Juliet. His talent was in taking old stories and breathing new life into them. In a way, I feel I am honoring the Bard by following in his thieving footsteps.

For the various inspirations, as well as cut scenes and editorial debates, please visit the book's Web site, www.themasterofverona.com.

✦ ✧ ✦

A bit about names. Mariotto and Gianozza are both taken from Masuccio Salernitano's thirty-third novel from *Il Novellino*—an early version of the R&J story involving secret marriages, deaths of kinsmen, and a young groom fleeing to Alexandria. The bride is then forced to marry against her will, but is given a draught by the Friar that makes her appear dead. Unfortunately, the Friar's message detailing the plan is waylaid by pirates (shades of *Shakespeare in Love!*). The story plays out the same as *R&J*, except Gianozza flees to a convent in Sienna, where she dies. Pregnant, if I recall correctly.

The love scene between Mari and Gianozza in the church is my homage to Luigi da Porto's version, in which the lovers court each other in secret in Friar Lorenzo's church all through a long winter until they can resist their passion no longer.

The name Antonio I also borrowed from da Porto, a native Vicentine. In his version of the story (the first to name the lovers Romeo and Giulietta), he mentions the young girl's father is called Antonio. Juliet's mom in that story was named Giovanna, but that was the name of Cangrande's wife. Besides, it's way too close to Gianozza, so we won't be running with that.

Most other characters I borrowed from Shakespeare or from history, or else extrapolated from family histories.

About Kate and Petruchio—a lark, but putting them in this tale was actually a textual choice based on two sets of lines in the party scene from R&J. A lovely in-joke for anyone who's seen *Shrew,* and thus we have our time frame between the two plays.

✦ ◇ ✦

One historical caveat. I have, with a few exceptions, stayed true to chronological history, something Shakespeare himself would never have bothered with. That said, records indicate that Katerina della Scala was replaced by her husband with a new wife in 1306, by whom he had two sons. I assume Katerina was dead when he did this, though one can never be sure with these medieval Italians. But I chose instead to breathe life into her for a good while longer, giving Bailardino's second wife to his brother, Antonio Nogarola. In a moment of pure practicality, I have kept the two children of Bailardino and made them Katerina's own, conceived late in life.

There is another problem, this one having to do with what building was called what when. The current layout of the Piazza della Signoria is almost exactly what it was, except there have been so many façades added; so many rebuilds, that it is almost certainly nothing like what it was. I have blended the then with the now in my mind and, though it may be wrong, the square is at least clear in my head. I hope it is as clear to you.

As for the Scaliger himself, I wish to point out that all the great feats I have attributed to him are true. I've played with numbers of the enemies he faced, downsizing them from the tales that have grown over the centuries. But he did break the Paduan army in 1314 with less than a hundred men, he did appear in disguise in 1317, cheering the invading Paduan army on, only to fight them back minutes later. In short, Cangrande is one of those figures whose life is greater than fiction.

For an idea of what Cangrande's sword looks like, find Del Tin Armories online. Among the Italian swordmaker's exquisite reproductions is the sword that was unearthed when Cangrande was exhumed in the 1920s.

In a fit of silliness, I hid two Shakespeare-related anagrams in the text. Go drive yourself mad.

Those who have studied Shakespeare's sources will be critical of my choice of years. As stated above, Luigi da Porto, whose version of the story was penned in the early sixteenth century, firmly places the events of the play between 1301 and 1304, during the reign of Bartolomeo della Scala, Cangrande's older brother. Working backward from there, the events of this book would have taken place about 1276. While this is a fascinating period in Veronese history, with such notable characters as Mastino della Scala (the first) and Ezzelino da Romano (the third), for me it lacked the drama of the fall of Verona. Verona reaches its greatest heights under Cangrande. That gives it so much farther to fall.

I claim da Porto was misinformed. The original feud between the Montecchi and the Capelletti was indeed buried in 1302, when Gargano Montecchio and his uncles slaughtered the last of the Capelletti in the Arena in Verona. But it flared up again in 1315, and did not die for another twenty-five years, when Verona lost everything it held dear. The tragedy of Shakespeare's play is not just the demise of the young lovers, but the death of every young knight in the city. The flower of Verona's youth is blighted in a single week. For Mari and Antony, it is indeed a plague on both their houses, but the scourge takes other lives as well. From the height that Cangrande lifts it to, Verona falls, never to rise again.

✦ ◇ ✦

To my editor, Michael Denneny, I owe more than I can say. His initial words had a profound impact on me, the kind of thing that you carry with you the rest of your career. He told me that I had confused "what a writer needs to know to write the book with what a reader needs to know to read the book—which is much less." Setting aside his professional skills, his enthusiasm for the story spurred me just when I had stalled. Thanks, Michael.

To my other professional editor, Keith Kahla at St. Martin's, I can give only thanks, and thanks. Eighteen months after passing on it he contacted my agent and said, "Hey, is that Shakespeare book still available? I can't get it out of my head." Ever cheerful, he guided me through the process of getting the thing sold and published with honesty and style. He then forced me to write new chapters, focus on being focused, and through two rounds of edits shaped the novel into what you're holding. I realize how lucky I am. There is nothing in the world like an editor who believes in you, and I've had two.

Early readers were vital. The gifted playwright and heartbreaking actress Kristine Thatcher was the second to read the book, and her excitement carried me through the end of the first year. That year I also had the joy of sharing a stage with Mike Nussbaum, popcorn fiend and actor par excellence. He kept pestering me backstage to finish the second draft, and thank God he did. Also big thanks to Jeremy Anderson, actor and writer, who trod the boards in the production of R&J where all this was dreamed up. He swore he "couldn't put the damn thing down."

For their support, I have so many friends to thank. The Michigan contingent, where all this started, includes Jeff, Nona, Jason, Dennis, Gabe, Pat, and Paulie. In Chicago, where the bulk of the writing and all the waiting was done, I found Tara, Gwen, Ben, Breon, and Page, among others.

I must express gratitude to every cast of R&J I've ever worked with—among them, Greenhills High School, the Shadow Theatre Company, the Ann Arbor Civic Theatre, the Michigan Shakespeare Festival, Arts Lane, the First Folio Shakespeare Festival, Chicago Shakespeare Theatre, and A Crew of Patches.

Big thanks to Dave "Pops" Doersch for introducing me to the wild world of stage combat, not to mention the production of R&J he directed. For him, of course, this book was "so simple a monkey could do it."

My parents, Al and Jill, are inspiring role models as well as tireless supporters of the arts. They gave me a unique gift in raising me as they did, and I am ever grateful. My brother Andrew has taught me how to be open to the whole world.

My son Dashiell came onto the scene in April 2006, as the edits for this book were under way. In fact, we had just found out about him when the novel sold. As Mike Nussbaum says, babies bring good things. Thanks, Dash.

Saving the very best for last, we arrive at my best friend: my love, my wife, Janice. The unofficial coauthor of this book, she set aside her own efforts to listen to me read whole chapters at a time. I don't know how many times she's read it—more than I have, I'll bet. Armed with red, green, and black pens, she settled in and, like a surgeon with a scalpel, excised sections I was too lily-livered to cut myself, and she kept me from doing dumb things like starting at the ending just because I was bored.

Jan, cara mia, you are my friend, partner, coconspirator, and love. I breathe you.